Forever Yours, Always Mine

TARA CONRAD

HIS ONE HER ONLY PUBLISHING

Contents

PART THREE
THEIR FOREVER

PART ONE
Her Surrender

To my Sir,

i've loved You for more than half my life. i hope to love You for many more years—there will never be enough. You are the heart and soul of this book. It's Your love that gave me the courage to write this story. You are my moon and stars. The breath I breathe. My world. i love You.

Natalie

HE'S GOING TO PROPOSE TO ME. I'LL FINALLY BE ONE STEP CLOSER TO becoming Mrs. Thomas Moore. Since Thanksgiving break is so short, I was able to talk my professors into letting me take my mid-terms a few days early, and I was able to change my flight to Missouri. Between classes and working, I've never been able to visit Tommy on campus. But that's all going to change with this trip home. He's not expecting me until Wednesday evening, so I can't wait to see his face when I show up at his dorm tomorrow morning.

Tommy's mom took off after he was born. He never knew who his father was. It was his Aunt Delia who raised him. Right after we graduated high school, she had a major heart attack and needed surgery. Although Tommy had a full-ride football scholarship to The University of Missouri, he didn't want to leave her until she'd recovered. Thankfully, the school was willing to hold his scholarship for him. While I'm in my first year of graduate school, Tommy's still an undergrad. He plans to spend five years at Mizzou to maximize his football eligibility. When I graduate, he will, too. Then, we can have our happily ever after.

My parents didn't want me to leave Northmeadow to live in New York City. They felt the distance would put too much of a strain on Tommy and me. Even though we talk almost every night and see each other on school breaks, the past five years haven't been easy, but they will be worth it.

It was a bit of a last-minute scramble, but I was able to make it to the airport with just enough time to clear security and board the plane. Before I left, I downloaded enough bridal magazines to keep me busy for the entire flight. I've been so busy scrolling through them that I don't realize how much of the flight has passed until the fasten seatbelt light turns on. An announcement plays through the plane's overhead speakers, alerting the passengers that we'll be landing shortly. I stuff the E-reader into my bag and look out my window. My heart beats wildly, knowing this trip home will change my life.

An hour later, I'm heading to Mizzou's campus in my rental car. Thankfully, it's not a long ride, and before I know it, I'm pulling up in front of the Rotunda building.

The campus is beautiful, but it's enormous. Although I know the name of Tommy's dorm, I have no idea where it is, and I don't want to waste time driving around. So I'm thankful when I spot a group of what appears to be students walking down the sidewalk. I hit the button to lower the window.

"Excuse me?"

"Do you need something?" a girl in a Mizzou hoodie asks.

"Can you tell me where Center Hall is?"

"Take the main road through campus. It's the big, red brick building in the middle." She points me in the right direction. "You can't miss it."

I find the dorm easily and park in a visitor spot. My hands shake as I drop the keys in my purse and make my way to the building.

When I get to the door, I try to open it, but it's locked. Putting my hand up to the glass to see inside, I notice a few guys sitting in a lounge area watching a football game on a large flat-screen TV. I knock on the door, hoping to get their attention. It only takes a second for one of the guys to come over.

"You looking for someone?"

He towers over me, and I have to lift my head to see his face. "I'm looking for Tommy Moore."

"You're in the right place." He steps aside and lets me in.

"Is he here?"

"What's your name?" he asks.

"Natalie." My voice is quiet, and I feel a bit intimidated being the only girl here with a group of guys.

"I'm Mike." He reaches out to shake my hand. "We're on the team together. Are you his sister or something?"

"No, I'm his girlfriend."

The room goes silent.

I know it's not a coed dorm, but I'm sure I'm not the first girl who's come by.

"I have his room number. If you can point me in the right direction."

"Is he expecting you?" Mike asks.

"No." I smile. "I flew in early to surprise him."

He glances back to the group, who are now whispering to one another, before shrugging and turning back to me.

"Come on. I'll bring you up."

Mike leads me down a hallway and opens the door to the stairwell. We begin the climb up when I hear a shuffle of feet and voices behind us. When I look over my shoulder, I see several of the guys in the lounge area are now following us up the stairs.

"Why are they coming?"

"Guess they want to see the big surprise, too."

I hoped this would be a private moment, but the best-laid plans and all. It doesn't matter. I'm so excited to see Tommy that I don't care who's following me.

We arrive on the third floor and walk down a long hallway. Doors line both sides, and bulletin boards hang on the walls announcing all the latest campus happenings. People are coming and going, reminding me why I'm thankful I don't live on campus anymore.

Finally, we stop outside Tommy's room. I find it odd that there's a tie draped over the doorknob.

"You sure about this?" Mike asks. "It's not too late to turn back."

The vibe I'm getting from these guys is off. Why do they care that I'm here to see my boyfriend?

"I'm sure."

"Hey Scott, you have your key?"

"I don't think this is a good idea, Mike," a tall blond guy behind me says.

"Key." Mike puts out his hand.

Scott pushes his way through the group. "Move. I'll do it." He grabs the tie off the knob before unlocking the door and pushing it open.

When I look into the room, the sight in front of me nearly brings me to my knees.

A blonde woman is on top of Tommy. "Yes. Just like that, babe. Harder."

Scott clears his throat.

Tommy pops his head up. "What the fuck?" he yells and pushes the girl off him.

She turns around, seeming not to care that she's naked in front of a group of men. When she sees me, she offers a smug smile.

"Ash?" She and I just talked yesterday. She knew I was coming—knew I'd find them. "How could you?"

I spin around and see Mike and a few guys laughing and elbowing each other. Scott's standing in the doorway, clearly unamused by his roommate's behavior.

"I need to get out of here."

"You're an asshole, Moore." Scott throws the tie on the floor. "Come on."

I rush down to the main floor, needing to get as far away from Tommy as possible.

"I'm sorry you had to see that."

The realization of what I just witnessed hits me, and tears fill my eyes. I squeeze them shut. I can't cry. Not here.

"How long have you two been dating?"

"Eight years."

"Damn."

"Has she—" Do I really want to hear the answer? Deciding I need to. I continue, "Has she been here before?"

Scott looks as if he's asking if I really want him to answer.

I nod.

"Yeah, she's been coming to see him since he started here. He introduced her as—"

"Stop, please." It's too much. "I have to go." I push the door open and run to my car.

"You're in no shape to drive," Scott calls after me.

"I'll be fine." I look up and see Tommy rushing out the door.

I fumble through my purse, trying to find the keys.

"Natalie, wait," he yells.

Without waiting or looking back, I head straight to the airport and secure a seat on the next available flight to New York City.

The flight back feels like a blur. It's not until the jet's wheels screech down on the runway that the image of Tommy and Ashlynn together finally fades, and I'm brought back to the present.

I feel lost as I stand in the center of the bustling terminal, surrounded by noise and chaos. I watch the hurried travelers grumbling as they maneuver around me. Some rush to catch their flights, while others embrace each other as if celebrating a homecoming. But I am alone, left behind by my best friend and the man I was supposed to marry, feeling betrayed.

When I step outside, I'm hit with the cold night air. It helps snap me out of the haze I'm walking around in. There's a line of yellow taxis waiting for a passenger, or I can use the ridesharing app, but then I'll have to wait for a car to get here. Even though it'll cost a small fortune, I decide to take a cab. I'm desperate to get back to my apartment.

I open the door to the nearest taxi and slide onto the leather seat that's cracked and worn from use. Immediately, I'm hit with the strong scent of incense. The driver, an older Asian man, turns slightly in his seat. "Where do I take you, miss?"

I give him my address in the Village, and he types it into his GPS. Then, we begin the slow process of driving out of the airport.

"You've been crying," he says. His voice is soft and kind. "Are you okay?"

"Not really." I sniffle.

Opening the glove compartment, he grabs a small pack of tissues and hands them to me. I guess I'm not the first passenger he's picked up in this state.

"My name's Shusuke," he says as he glances in the rear-view mirror. "I listen if you want talk."

"Thank you, but not really."

I stare out the window, watching the cars pass by. Maybe I should call Lana and let her know I'm on my way home? I pull my cell phone out of my purse and turn it on. There's a barrage of alerts from missed calls and texts. Almost immediately, my phone starts ringing. Tommy's picture flashes on my screen. I send the call to voice-mail, but he doesn't leave a message. The phone rings again. This time, I answer.

"What do you want?"

"Please let me explain," Tommy says.

"How can you explain me finding you in bed with my best friend?"

"It was a mistake. It won't happen again."

"I know it won't happen again." I let out a sarcastic laugh. "Because we're over."

"Natalie, wait—"

I disconnect the call.

The phone rings, but I'm not playing this game all night. Instead, I power off the phone and throw it back into my purse.

"That's who makes you cry?" Shusuke asks.

"Yes," I say softly. "It's my boyfriend—was my boyfriend." I try to take a deep breath, but grief weighs heavy on my chest. "I flew home early to surprise him, but instead, the surprise was on me." The fissure in my heart grows when I say the words out loud.

"You loved him."

"We've been together for eight years. I was supposed to marry him."

Shusuke takes the Queensboro Bridge, which is not the typical way a cabbie usually goes, but I'm glad. This is my favorite way to enter the city. The view of the skyline from the bridge, especially at night, is breathtaking. Once we cross and enter the city, I feel a weight lift. I'm back in my comfort zone—a place untainted by Tommy.

Fortunately, Shusuke knows all the side streets to avoid the traffic. I want to get home, crawl into bed, and pretend this night never happened. Finally, the taxi pulls in front of my apartment. I gather my things to get out when Shusuke turns in his seat.

"Your heart is broken now. It is blessing when wrong person leaves your life. Don't let hurt turn to anger. Tonight is start of new journey. Now right person comes." He offers a kind smile.

His words play in my mind as the elevator carries me to my apartment. I'm sure he meant well, but I'm not taking a chance with my heart again.

Natalie

I DON'T EVEN KNOW WHAT TIME IT IS WHEN I FINALLY WALK INTO THE apartment I share with Svetlana. We met two years ago when we shared a dorm room on campus and became fast friends. Over the summer, right before we started graduate school, her dad rented us an apartment in the Village.

The lights are off, so I try to be quiet. I don't want to wake Lana and end up explaining why I'm home early. Right now, I just want to sleep. Tomorrow will come soon enough.

Using the flashlight on my phone, I tiptoe down the hallway to my bedroom. That's when I hear it. Lana's whimpering, begging someone to stop. A male voice yells at her to shut up.

Without a moment of hesitation, I dial 911.

"What's your emergency?" the dispatcher asks.

"There's someone in my apartment. My roommate's being attacked," I whisper into the phone and give them our address.

Although they tell me to wait on the line, I disconnect the call, intending to stop the attack. I grasp the doorknob and take a deep breath before I throw the door open.

Shining the light toward Lana's bed, I yell, "Stop! The police are on their way."

Lana's head flies up. "Natalie?" she shrieks. "What are you doing here?"

My cell phone isn't bright enough, so I flip on the overhead light. When I look over at Lana, I scream. She's naked and tied to the bed. A man I've never seen before is holding what looks like some sort of a gag in his hand. "You. Don't move," I yell.

He drops the object. It lands with a thud as he puts his hands up in surrender.

"Nat, this isn't what it looks like. Can you untie me?" she asks the man.

He looks between us before quickly untying her.

Svetlana climbs out of bed. "I thought you were in Missouri," she says as she slips her robe on and hurries over to me. "What are you doing home?"

"Are you okay? Did he hurt you?" I examine Lana for injuries before glaring over her shoulder at the man who's busy putting his shirt on.

We're interrupted by banging on the door. "NYPD, open up."

"Oh my God, you really called the police." Lana's voice is panicked.

"Of course, I called them."

They pound on the door again. "NYPD, open the door."

"Come with me." Lana grabs my arm. "We need to fix this."

Lana drags me out of her bedroom and into the living room. She makes quick work of the locks before opening the door.

"Good evening, officers. Please come in."

"We received a call of an assault in progress." The officer looks past me. "You, put your hands up and don't move."

I spin around and get a good look at the man. He's tall with creamy brown skin. His dark curls are pulled back into a neat ponytail. It's obvious he works out, as evidenced by the T-shirt stretching tight across his chest. But it's the color of his eyes that strikes me the most. They're a deep gray like clouds before a storm, and right now, they're fixed on me.

I collapse onto the couch from a mix of exhaustion and confusion.

Lana and the officers are talking by the door. I hear their voices but can't make out what they're saying. She turns and motions to the man, who cautiously walks across the room. Their conversation continues for a few minutes longer.

"Thank you, and sorry for the confusion," Lana says, shaking the officers' hands before they turn and leave the apartment.

"Do you want me to stay?" the man asks Lana quietly. "I can help you explain."

"I don't think that's a good idea. I'll call you in the morning."

"Okay, talk to you tomorrow," he says, kissing her forehead before leaving.

Lana locks up and then sits next to me on the couch. "I don't know where to start." She turns to face me, and the expression on her face changes. "You've been crying."

I'm overwhelmed. Thoughts and emotions run through my mind so quickly that I can't make sense of them. All I manage is a nod.

"What's wrong?" she asks. "Why are you home?"

"Tommy," I say, trying to change the subject. "What was going on back there?"

She glances down the hall before answering. "It wasn't what it looked like."

"Did he hurt you?"

"No. Well, not any more than I asked for." Lana giggles.

"What?" Why is she laughing after nearly being assaulted?

"I'm going to grab us a glass of wine. I think we're going to need it. "What happened with Tommy?" she asks as she grabs a bottle of wine and pours us each a glass.

I sit back on the couch. "I got to his dorm and found him having sex with Ashlynn."

She hands me a glass of red wine. "Ashlynn, as in your best friend?"

"The one and only." I tip the glass and take a big drink.

Lana sits down. "Wow."

"Right now, I'm more concerned about what was happening here." I motion around the room.

"I wasn't expecting you to be home." Lana sips her wine before setting it down. "What you saw wasn't what you thought. I mean, it was, but not like you think."

"You were tied up and begging him to stop. It looked like he was hurting you."

She looks up and laughs. "Oh boy, I don't know where to start?"

"How about the beginning?"

"Have you ever heard of BDSM?" She blurts out the question, and I nearly choke on my wine.

"I've read about it in some romance novels. It's all that kinky sex and stuff." Once the words leave my mouth, the realization hits me. "Is that what was going on back there?" I set my wine glass down before I drop it.

"Yes," Lana says and slowly nods her head. "I grew up in the lifestyle. Papa's a Dominant, and Mama is his submissive."

I don't know what I expected her to say, but that wasn't it. "You mean to tell me your dad goes all *Christian Grey* and ties your mom up in the bedroom?" It's a lame joke, but it's all I can manage at the moment.

"Ha, ha. You're so funny." Lana laughs. "That's not exactly how it is in real life. My papa adores Mama, and she him. Their relationship has always been an example of what I hope to find someday." She beams as she talks about her parents.

This is all a bit TMI. "Why would you want to know what your parents get up to in their bedroom?"

"Eww." Svetlana pretends to gag. "We didn't talk about any of *that* stuff. BDSM is about so much more than kinky sex."

Lana explains that BDSM is often a lifestyle choice, not just something limited to what happens in the bedroom. The submissive, man or woman, takes care of the daily wants and needs of their Dominant. The Dominant ensures the safety of their submissive and will lavish their love and attention on them.

I've been to Russia with her to meet her family. I remember thinking their relationship seemed a bit old-fashioned, even more so than my parents. Every day, Mrs. Solonik wore a dress and heels. Her hair and make-up were always perfect. She spent every minute doting on her husband, ensuring he had everything he needed—before he even asked for it. I found myself exhausted just watching her.

But I'll never forget the expression in Mr. Solonik's eyes when he looked at his wife—pure adoration. What really made an impression on me was his openness in showing Mrs. Solonik affection. He was generous with his kisses, caressing touches, and loving pet names. I remember wishing Tommy was half as affectionate with me. I couldn't even get him to hold my hand in public.

"What you walked in on tonight," she hesitates, "was a scene Brandon and I'd been planning for a while. You were supposed to be gone." "Wait a minute. You do this BDSM thing, too?"

She nods. "I'm a submissive."

"How were we roommates for two years, and I never knew?"

"It's not a topic that's easy to bring up. Hi, I'm your new dorm mate. I like to get tied up and whipped."

We both laugh.

Lana explains how she first got into the lifestyle. She was eighteen when she went to her parents and expressed an interest. They had some serious conversations regarding what being in the lifestyle meant.

"Mama wasn't so sure, but I knew I was a submissive. She stressed the importance of being mature enough to put my needs second to someone else's. It isn't as easy as it sounds."

The way she talks about her relationship with her parents so casually makes my heart ache. I could never speak to my parents the way she's able to. My parents' view on sex is it is something you only do after you're married—period, end of story. If they knew I wasn't a virgin, they'd go crazy.

"Mama gave me some books to read and introduced me to a trusted friend who was an experienced submissive. She was my mentor until I went to Moscow to study. That's where I submitted to a Dominant for the first time."

I'm stunned by my friend's confession but also curious. "Do you still happen to have the books she gave you?"

Lana raises her eyebrow. "Why?"

"I figure reading them might come in handy when I graduate." I shrug.

"I've been to Northmeadow." She leans back and crosses her arms. "I don't think your teen clients will be into BDSM."

I'll be working as a school therapist when I return home, but she's right. I highly doubt I'll encounter this topic there. "Maybe *I'm* curious," I say trying to make light of it.

"I'll be right back." Lana walks down the hall and disappears into her bedroom. When she comes back, she's holding an e-reader. "They're loaded on here." She passes me the tablet. "Your turn. Tell me exactly what happened when you got to Mizzou."

The level of betrayal I feel toward Tommy and Ashlynn is indescribable. Maybe my parents were right when they said I shouldn't go to New York City, but would that have changed anything? Were they seeing each other even back then? The thought makes me sick.

Lana listens patiently as I tell her everything.

"Now I have to come up with an excuse to tell my parents," I say through a yawn. "There's no way I'm going back there until I have to."

Lana grabs our empty wine glasses and brings them to the kitchen. "Why don't you sleep on it first. We can come up with something later."

The sun is beginning to rise, and we haven't slept at all. Between being up all night and the wine, my head is spinning.

"You have to promise to tell me more about you being tied up by that hot guy." I grin.

"I just hope he's still interested. Someone scared the shit out of him by calling the police." She links her arm with mine, and we walk to our rooms.

I need to sleep off the worst night of my life.

Natalie

THE FOLLOWING DAY, I CALLED MY PARENTS. AS EXPECTED, THEY WERE upset that I wouldn't be home for Thanksgiving. I made up an excuse, telling them the counseling center I'm interning for asked me to fill in for someone last minute, and I couldn't say no. I need some distance from Northmeadow

Tommy's been calling and texting every day, begging for forgiveness and making every excuse possible for his *indiscretion*. When the tone of the messages shifts to blaming me for coming to New York in the first place, I decide to change my number.

Funny, though, Ashlynn hasn't bothered to call. We've been friends since we were born. We've done everything together, been through everything together. That pain hurts almost worse than Tommy cheating on me.

All of this has forced me to open my eyes to everything in front of me. For the past five years, I've kept one foot in Northmeadow, afraid to let go of everything familiar.

I pick up the picture of my brother Michael and his boyfriend Evan that sits on my dresser. I miss them so much. I can't believe they've been gone seven years. I'm transported back to my junior year in high school when Michael told me about Evan.

"Nat, do you have a few minutes?" Michael asks from my doorway.

I look up and smile. Even though he's only a year older than me, my brother is my hero. I would do anything for him. "I always have a few minutes for you." Closing my math textbook, I jump up and follow Michael outside.

"Let's go for a walk," he says nervously.

He doesn't look at me, and his hands shake as we walk silently down the path into the woods behind our house until we come to the clearing we always played in when we were kids.

When we get there, Evan's waiting for us.

"I thought you'd never get here," Evan says, smiling.

Michael finally looks at me. "I have—we have something to tell you." Michael moves to stand next to Evan.

"Okay." I look back and forth between them.

"I don't know how to tell her," Michael says to Evan.

"I'll do it." He grabs Michael's hand and looks at me. "Natalie, your brother and I are together. I'm in love with him."

I'm surprised by this revelation.

Michael and I grew up with Evan. His family lives on a farm across town. We all played together as children, but as we've grown up, I've seen how they look at each other —it's different from just friends. Michael doesn't know that I know, but I've watched him sneak out his bedroom window late at night to meet Evan. I watched them embrace and kiss, but I didn't say anything. This was Michael's to tell me when he was ready.

"I know," I say with a big smile. "And I'm so happy you guys finally told me."

Michael stands there, his mouth hanging open.

"You know?" Evan asks.

"I've seen you two together," I say, looking at Michael, who's turned pale.

"Do Mom and Dad know?"

"I doubt it. They sleep like the dead."

We share a laugh.

"Are you going to tell them?"

"Yes." Michael shuffles his foot nervously. "We're telling all of them tonight. We want you to know first because things probably won't go well after that."

"I'm glad you told me." I reach out and hug them. "I'm happy for you both."

I run my finger across the picture of Michael's face. He was right. After they told our parents, nothing was the same.

As Michael and Evan come out to our parents, Mom cries hysterically. You would've sworn someone died. Dad yells so loud the dishes in the china closet rattle. Evan's dad passed away when he was young, so it's just his mom.

She's silent for a long time, watching the spectacle my parents are making. Finally, she speaks, "I'm proud of you, boys. There's liable to be a lot of hate coming your way. I'll always be on your side. I love you both so much."

My parents aren't as kind. "Get your things and get out," Dad yells.

Ten minutes later, I'm standing by my bedroom window with tears pouring down my face as I watch my brother walk away. Thankfully, Evan's mom welcomed them into her home.

My eyes fill with tears as I remember what came in the weeks to follow. It was their senior year. It should've been filled with happy memories. Instead, every day was a new level of hell. The entire school turned on them. They were called fags and fairies by kids in the hallway. Messages of hate were posted on their social media accounts. I was alienated from everyone except Ashlynn and Tommy, but I didn't care. I loved my brother and Evan.

Looking back, I think the breaking point for Evan was seeing his mom's car parked in their driveway. One day, when they came home from school, a message was written in soap on the windshield of his mom's car. It read, "You'd be better off dead. Fags not wanted here."

One month after they came out, Evan took his daddy's gun, went into the field, and shot himself. Michael wasn't the same after that.

I wasn't allowed to go to Evan's house. So, the only time I could see Michael was at school. I thought he was still living with Evan's mom. Michael never told me he had moved out and was living in a tent in the woods.

It was graduation night when I realized something was wrong.

"Aren't you going to Michael's graduation ceremony?" I ask my parents.

"No," Dad says and goes back to reading his newspaper.

The only reason I'm allowed to go is that it counts as service hours for school.

When I get to the school, I search for Michael, but he's nowhere to be found. It's not a big graduating class, so I know I didn't miss him. There's no way Michael would miss graduation. Something is terribly wrong.

I called the police, but they refused to file a report because he's over eighteen and not 'officially' missing. Instead, they tell me they'll keep an eye out for him.

The next day, an officer knocks on our door. Before he speaks, I already know. Michael's body was found near his tent in the woods, not far from Evan's house. The officers also found a note addressed to me.

I open the picture frame and carefully take out the worn paper.

Natalie,

I hope one day you'll forgive me for leaving you. The pain is too much. I can't do it anymore. I'm going to find Evan—going to find our happily ever after. Please don't be sad for me. I want you to get out of Northmeadow and live your life to the fullest. Find someone truly worthy of all the love you have to give. I expect you to make your mark on the world. I will always love you and will be watching over you.

Love, Michael.

Tears stream down my face as I sit silently, wishing my older brother were by my side. After re-reading his note, I take a deep breath and carefully fold it, tucking it away safely behind the picture.

"I'm going to make you proud of me, Michael," I say aloud to my brother, hoping he can hear me.

My past hasn't changed. I still have to go back to Northmeadow after I graduate. But right now, I'm living in one of the biggest cities in the world. It's time I embrace everything it has to offer.

I've been reading the books Lana gave me about the lifestyle. At first, I was so horrified that I turned off the e-reader and left it on my desk, where it sat for a few days, taunting me until curiosity got the better of me.

The other night, I turned it back on, determined to keep an open mind, and started reading. The more I read, the more intrigued I became. The ideas about sex are different from anything I've ever known. But the basic principles of a relationship and respect between two people are exactly how I was raised.

After I finish the last book, I search for Lana and find her in the kitchen cooking. Sitting on one of the stools at the island, I tap my fingers on the granite counter.

She turns around, spatula in hand. "You're driving me crazy with the nervous tapping. What's up?"

I'm not used to talking openly about sex, so it takes me a minute to muster the courage before answering. "I was wondering if I could ask you some more questions? You know, about the books I'm reading."

"Sure," she says without hesitation before turning her attention to whatever she's cooking, which smells delicious.

"What're you making?"

"Piroshki. It's kind of my mama's recipe, except I cheated and bought the dough," she says with a smile. "But I don't think that's what you wanted to ask. Dinner's ready. We can eat and talk."

She grabs two plates out of the cupboard and dishes out the food. I get the forks and glasses, pouring a generous portion of wine for each of us before joining Lana at our small dining table.

I love it when she makes one of her mom's dishes. "Oh my god, Lana. This is amazing."

"Thanks, but you're avoiding."

"I want to learn more," I say quickly and take another bite.

Lana laughs. "That's what you were so nervous to say."

I shrug.

She grabs my phone and unlocks the screen. "Here's the club I go to. It's called Fire and Ice." She hands me the phone with a web page pulled up. "They have classes for people who think they might be interested. You should take one."

"I'm not ready for anything like that," I say. "Isn't there anything else I can read?"

She sets her fork down. "There are tons of books, but you'll learn more by taking the class and talking to real people."

"I'll think about it." I bookmark the site and go back to eating. But I know I have no intention of stepping foot in a club.

Natalie

IT'S MID-MORNING ON SATURDAY, AND I'M SITTING CROSS-LEGGED ON the sofa, my face buried in my textbook. Looks like another weekend that I won't be going out. Although I decided to embrace city life, I also have to maintain my grades to keep my scholarship. It's a tricky balance to maintain.

"Are you still studying?" Svetlana grabs the textbook from my hand and reads the title aloud, "Love and Attachment: Adult Relationships." She raises her eyebrows. "You need to get out of this apartment."

"I have a paper." I jump up and swipe at the book, but she's taller than me and holds it out of my reach.

"You can study tomorrow. Tonight, I want you to come out with me."

"But—"

"Come on, Nat." She hands back my book. Her glacier-blue eyes plead with me to say yes.

I resume my sitting position on the sofa and flip through the text to find my place. "I'll go out next weekend, I promise."

"I need you to come out tonight." Lana flops down next to me.

"Why?"

"Well, you remember Brandon, the guy you called the cops on?" Lana smirks.

My cheeks heat from embarrassment. "How could I forget."

"Thankfully, you didn't scare him away."

"That's good because he sure is hot."

"He is, isn't he," she says, a huge smile on her face. "I've finally consented to be his submissive." She pauses, allowing me a minute to digest this new information. "We're doing a scene at the club tonight, and I really want you there."

Now she has my attention. I close my book and set it next to me to give Lana my full attention.

"You're doing a scene? Like getting naked in front of an audience?"

She nods slowly as if she's measuring my response.

"This is what you want?" I ask.

Being naked in a room full of people wouldn't be my first choice. I may not know much about her lifestyle, but I want to make sure she's a completely willing participant.

"I'm so excited about it, but please, I need my best friend there." Lana bats her eyes at me.

"I wouldn't miss it for the world."

She pulls me in for a tight squeeze. "I'm so glad you said yes. You're going to have a great time."

I'm unsure about having a great time. My plan is to go, sit in a quiet corner, and watch Lana do her thing. Tonight should satisfy my curiosity, and then I can move on.

The rest of the afternoon is spent getting ready for our night out. We give each other manicures before I help Lana fix her long brown hair. She says her hair must be up and out of the way.

"There, all done," I say after putting in the last bobby pin.

"Thanks, I love it," Lana says as she checks out her hair in the mirror.

"I need to jump in the shower quick and find something to wear." When I get to my room, I head straight to the closet. I've upgraded my wardrobe over the past few years, but I have no idea what one wears to a sex club. "What do you suggest I wear tonight?" I lean against her doorway.

"I was hoping you'd ask. I have the perfect outfit for you," Lana says, giddy with excitement as she hurries into her walk-in closet. When she comes out, she's holding a hanger with a tiny black scrap of material on it.

"You're kidding, right?"

Lana's stunning. She's tall and fit, with curves in all the right places. Everything she wears looks fantastic on her. I'm five-two, and although I work out, my body looks nothing like hers. There's no way I can wear that dress.

"Nat, you're gorgeous." She pushes the hanger into my hands. "You're going to turn heads tonight."

"Do I want to turn heads?"

"You never know who you might meet," she says as she points me to my room, giving me a nudge forward. "Go shower and get dressed. Now."

"Are you sure you're not a Domme?" I call as I head down the hall. "You're awfully bossy."

My statement is met with Lana's laughter.

When I get to my room, I hold up the hanger and look at the dress—if that's what you can call it. It's black and made of stretchy material with a cutout that will expose my midsection. Two straps hold up the top section that wraps around the neck and crisscrosses in the back.

Peeking my head out, I yell down the hall. "How do I wear a bra with this thing?"

"You don't."

I roll my eyes, close the door, and toss the dress onto the bed. Then, I strip off my sweatpants and t-shirt and step into the shower. My hands shake as I shave my legs, but surprisingly, I don't nick myself. Standing under the hot water, I let it cascade over me, hoping it'll soothe my frayed nerves.

After finishing, I wrap a fluffy towel around my body and stand in front of the bathroom mirror to dry my hair and apply makeup. I style my blonde curls so they cascade softly down my back.

As I walk across the plush carpet in my bedroom, I ignore the dress lying on the bed and instead open my drawer to grab a pair of panties.

I smile as I pull on a sexy thong. Tommy was a fan of sensible cotton bras and underwear. After discovering he was cheating, I emptied them all into the garbage. Lana took me shopping for some adult lingerie. It started as an act of defiance, but I've grown to love wearing something sexy under my clothes. It gives me a sense of confidence I didn't realize I'd been missing.

Holding up the dress, I give myself a pep talk before I step into the black fabric and drag it up my body. The material clings to my curves, leaving little to the imagination. Grabbing a pair of black heels from my closet, I slide my feet into them and slowly turn to face my full-length mirror.

Svetlana appears behind me. "I knew it! You look amazing!" She hugs me tightly.

I've never worn anything like this, but I like what I see.

Suddenly, this all seems too real. "What should I expect tonight?"

"The car's here," Svetlana says. "I'll tell you on the way."

"The car?"

"Brandon sent a car to pick us up. You ready?"

"Yep. Don't want to keep your man waiting."

Alex

IT'S THE WEEKEND, BUT I'M IN THE OFFICE HANDLING A FEW THINGS that can't wait until Monday. I'm in the middle of uploading files when my phone rings.

"Hey, man," Brandon says. "Where are you?"

"At the office."

"On a Saturday? You work too much."

"How did things go with Lana last night?"

Although Brandon and Lana have been playing together for quite some time, they've never formally signed a contract. He's wanted to make their Dom/sub relationship official for quite a while. But for some unknown reason, Lana's been dragging her feet.

"It went well. Can you meet me for a few drinks?"

I've been here all day, and I'm exhausted, but it sounds like Brandon needs to talk. "Text me a time and place, and I'll meet you there."

An hour later, I walk into the bar. I'm only a few steps in when a group of girls approaches me.

"Hey, handsome," the brunette says as she wraps her hands around my arm. "You here alone?"

"I'm meeting someone." I brush her off.

Brandon waves me over.

"Excuse me, ladies," I say and head over to Brandon.

"I bet he's gay," one of the girls says loud enough for me to hear.

"All the gorgeous ones are," another says.

I laugh at their assessment of me. I'm not here to find a date.

There's a beer waiting for me when I sit next to Brandon at the bar.

"You ready to tell me how it went last night?"

"Lana finally consented to be my submissive. After much negotiation, we signed the contract last night."

"Congratulations." I'm really happy for my friend.

"Lana and I are doing a scene at the club in two weeks. It'll be our first public scene, and I'd like you to be there."

"Wouldn't miss it." I slap my friend on the back.

The next few weeks pass by like all the rest.

Wake. Work. Sleep. Repeat.

It's finally Saturday, and I'm out for a run when I get a text from Brandon.

(Brandon) Remember Lana's roommate?

(Me) Yes...

Where's he going with this?

(Brandon) She's coming to the club tonight. I need a favor.

(Me) No.

(Brandon) She needs an escort.

(Me) The same girl who called the cops on you last year?

(Brandon) Yeah.

(Me) And you want me to escort her?

(Brandon) Come on, bro.

Why me? Just what I want to do with my Saturday night. Babysit a college girl who'll be scared out of her mind.

(Brandon) You know I'd do it for you.

(Me) I'm not feeling well. I don't think I can make it.

(Brandon) The fuck you aren't. You're out running right now. Tell me I'm wrong.

Am I that predictable? This is the last thing I want to do tonight.

(Me) Fine. But you owe me.

(Brandon) Thanks, man.

I slip my phone back into my pocket and finish my run. I can't believe I agreed to babysit tonight.

Natalie

THE CAR DROPS US OFF IN FRONT OF A NONDESCRIPT BUILDING. FIRE and Ice is an exclusive club in Chelsea, nestled among traditional businesses. I'm surprised when Lana pulls the door open. I've walked by here many times and never realized there's a sex club here.

Once inside, we're standing in a pretty foyer that could pass for the entrance to any office. A few people are waiting in line. A stunning woman wearing a black latex one-piece that hugs her perfect body stands behind the counter, checking them in.

Feeling insecure, I tug at my dress, trying to give it some length that isn't there.

"Stop fidgeting," Lana scolds while holding back a smile.

"I'm so nervous, but I'm also a bit excited. Is that normal?"

"It's perfectly normal. Don't worry." Lana grabs my hand. "We're going to have a great time tonight."

Trying to distract myself, I shift my focus to the oversized dark wood doors that grant entrance to the club. They look like something from medieval times with their ornate hinges. There's an iron knocker on each door with the BDSM triskelion forged in the center. I recognize it from the books. It represents the three divisions of the lifestyle: bondage and discipline, dominance and submission, sadism, and masochism. It also stands for the motto of *safe, sane, and consensual*. Although simple in its design, the triskelion holds deep meaning for those in the lifestyle.

"When we get to the desk, you'll be checked in as my guest. Mistress Star will give you a colored wristband."

"What's it for?"

"The colors represent a person's status." She points to a sign on the wall.

On it are the colors of the rainbow, each representing a guest's position, whether Dominant or submissive, with a partner or alone, just watching or looking to play.

"You'll get a purple band. It means you're being sponsored by a Dominant, and no one can approach you without asking his permission first."

Although I don't know Brandon, I haven't seen him since the night I called the police. I know Lana trusts him, and that's enough for me. I'm less nervous knowing I'll have a safety net tonight.

"Good evening, Lana."

"Good evening, Mistress. This is my friend, Natalie," Lana says. "She'll be our guest this evening."

"Brandon gave me her information." Mistress Star turns to me. "Has Lana explained our color system?"

"Yes, she has."

"Do you have any questions?"

"No."

"May I have your right arm?" I hold it up and let her snap a wristband on. "You understand you'll have a Dominant responsible for your comfort and safety tonight?"

"I do."

"Are you comfortable with that?"

"Yes, ma'am." It's clear they take informed consent seriously.

"You ladies can go right in. Brandon is waiting for you by stage three. Natalie, I hope you have a wonderful evening. I'll be around all night if you have any questions or concerns."

Lana grabs my arm. "Come on. I'm so excited for you to officially meet Brandon."

As I take my first steps into the club, I'm surprised by what I see.

I imagined we'd be at a seedy nightclub, but it's nothing like that. The expansive main room has a modern, industrial vibe and is brightly lit from overhead. Soft instrumental music plays in the background. I expect to find people naked and engaging in sex acts. Instead, everyone's in casual clothes and appears to be putting the final touches on the setup.

"Things don't start for a few hours. That's when the real fun happens." She waggles her eyebrows, making me laugh.

We walk across the room to where a man stands, his back to us. He's giving directions to several people who are setting up the stage. He must hear us behind him because he turns to greet us.

"Natalie, I'd like you to meet my Dominant, Brandon."

I'm met by his unforgettable gray eyes, but this time, they're soft—not frightened.

"It's nice to meet you," Brandon says.

"It's nice to meet you too." My cheeks heat from embarrassment. "I'm sorry for calling the police."

"Already forgiven." He smiles. "It's good to know Lana has someone looking out for her."

Movement behind Brandon catches my attention. Two muscular men push a giant wooden X onto the stage. Cuffs dangle from the top and bottom.

"What's that thing? It looks like a torture device."

Brandon laughs. "It's a Saint Andrew's Cross. I'll secure Lana to it and use my whip to pleasure her."

"Your whip? Won't that hurt her?" Gruesome visions of my best friend being tied up, her body torn to shreds, run through my mind. I'm ready to grab Lana and get the heck out of here.

"I won't her hurt—much." He winks.

I look at Lana, but she shows no signs of fear.

"Lana likes pain, and I know how to give her what she craves without hurting her." Brandon attempts to reassure me.

"It's okay, Nat. Brandon and I have already talked about everything we're going to do tonight. This is something I want."

"You're sure?" I'm not sold on the idea.

"Positive."

I know Lana knows what she's doing, so I guess I shouldn't freak out—yet.

Brandon looks over my shoulder, and his smile widens. I spin around to see what he's looking at and am captivated by what I see.

A tall, well-groomed man stands inside the doors running his hand through his dark hair while he looks around the room. When he spots Brandon, he starts walking in our direction, exuding confidence with each step. Women and men smile and whisper to each other as he passes by, but he pays them no attention. I'm unable to take my eyes off him.

"Glad you made it," Brandon says as he shakes the man's hand.

"I wouldn't miss it," he says, then turns to Lana. "How are you tonight?"

"I'm fine, thank you," Lana answers, keeping her gaze downward.

I've never seen my best friend act so demure. It's an odd contradiction to the self-assured, outspoken girl I know. It leaves me wondering how she manages to separate these two opposite parts of herself.

"Natalie. I want to introduce you to my best friend, Alex."

Words escape me when I meet the gaze of his soulful blue eyes. I feel like I've been stripped naked, and he sees deep inside me.

"Alex is also a Dominant here. I've asked him to be your escort tonight."

"Oh," I say, surprised. "I thought I'd be staying with you and Lana?" I look at Lana, who's wearing a mischievous grin.

"We won't be available for the entire evening, and because you're a first-time guest, you can't be alone in the club," Brandon explains. "You're in good hands with Alex."

I have a feeling Lana knew about this all along. She and I will be having a chat later.

"I've heard a lot about you," Alex says with a grin.

"You have?" Once again, I look at Lana, who's hiding behind Brandon.

"I have. You're the girl who called the police on my friend here." He slaps Brandon on the back.

"Oh my God. I can't believe you guys told anyone about that." I promised Lana I'd be here tonight, but right now, I want to escape through the nearest exit.

"There's no reason to be embarrassed. I'm sure Brandon appreciated your desire to protect your roommate." Alex chuckles.

"Lana and I have to finish setting up our stage," Brandon interrupts the awkward moment. "We'll see you two later."

Lana waves before she walks away.

"How about I show you around before things get started?" He offers his arm.

"That sounds good," I answer, hesitantly linking my arm with his.

When I do, a current of electricity runs through my body. Did he feel the same thing? I glance at Alex. If he felt it, his expression gives nothing away.

Natalie

"We'll start here. As you can see, all three stages will be used for scenes tonight."

The stages aren't extravagant. Just simple areas set a step above the main floor. Alex and I watch Brandon walk up to the cross, checking the cuffs before picking up his whip and giving it a few practice swings.

"I'm assuming Lana told you what their scene entails?"

"We talked about it. But I still don't understand why anyone would volunteer to be whipped. Seems more like torture to me."

"People find enjoyment in many different ways. What one sees as torture, others see as the ultimate pleasure."

"If you say so."

"Come, there's more to see," Alex says, leading me to the next stage.

Stage two appears much less threatening. A black metal bed sits in the center. Beside it is a matching table. A short, older man with a darker complexion stands, arranging candles into color groups.

A second man with shoulder-length blond hair and crystal blue eyes smiles as he walks past us and steps onto the stage.

So, this is where all the good-looking guys hang out. I almost laugh out loud at my wayward thoughts.

He approaches the older man, who points toward the table, appearing to give him instructions. The blond man looks our way before whispering something in the other man's ear.

The older man turns and walks toward us. "Alexander Montgomery," he says, extending his hand. "It's great to see you."

"Good to see you, Anthony." The men shake hands.

While they talk, I watch what's taking place on the stage. The blond man fits the mattress with a black rubber-like sheet before he finishes setting up the candles.

When he's through, he takes his place at Anthony's side, his head bowed slightly. I stare shamelessly at the two men.

"Natalie, I'd like to introduce you to Anthony and his submissive, Leopold. Tonight, Anthony will demonstrate his skills with wax on his canvas."

I look between the men, my interest piqued. "It's very nice to meet you both."

"I didn't realize you took a new submissive," Anthony says.

"I'm not—"

"Natalie's a guest of Brandon and Lana."

Anthony smiles knowingly. "Well then, I hope you enjoy yourself tonight."

"Let's let these two get back to work." Alex places his hand on my back.

His touch feels natural and familiar as if we've known one another for much longer than a few minutes. As we turn to walk away, a group of women approaches Alex. They're smiling and giggling like school girls.

"Hello, Sir." A pretty brunette bats her eyes at Alex.

I inch closer, feeling a hint of jealousy.

"Ladies," Alex says as he leads me away.

Glancing over my shoulder, I'm met with a glare from the brunette. Alex chuckles as he tightens his arm around my body. His territorial move makes my heart race.

The final area is sectioned off, and chairs are set up. On the stage are a few piles of neatly arranged rope. A man sits on the floor cross-legged in the far corner, his back to us. He appears to be meditating.

"Master Kiyoshi is a guest at the club tonight. He'll be closing the evening with a Shibari demonstration." "I've seen pictures of that online."

"You have?" Alex sounds surprised.

"The art created with humans and rope is beautiful." I debate telling him I like it so much that I have a secret board for it on Pinterest, but decide against it.

"I took the liberty of reserving us two seats." Alex's gaze meets mine, and once again, he takes my breath away. "Let's continue the tour before everything gets started."

We make our way toward a dining area. It's set apart from the rest of the club by a half wall.

"This is the café. It's for club members only."

Inside the café area, employees are hurrying about. Some are putting linens on tables, while others perfect the place settings.

While we're walking around, the club fills with more people. I'm struck by the different ways people present themselves. Some are dressed in nearly formal attire. Others I recognize from earlier who were dressed in street clothes and setting up the stages have changed. Now, I don't feel so out of place in this dress.

As we walk, a couple passes by, the man holding a leash and nodding at Alex. At the end of the leash is a man on all fours, wearing a collar and hood that make him resemble a dog. I watch as the pet kneels patiently by his owner's side whenever he stops walking. I recall reading about pet play in a book, but it's not something that interests me. Nevertheless, the couple seems content with it.

Body shape and size don't seem to matter. Not everyone has a model's figure, yet they still wear revealing outfits, if they're wearing clothes at all. It strikes me that no one appears self-conscious, and there's no whispering, pointing, or judging appearances.

It's a foreign concept to me. When I look in the mirror, I see all my imperfections —I envy the body positivity portrayed around me.

We turn a corner and start walking down a quiet hall. Alex points out the doors on each side. "These rooms are available by reservation for members who want to do a private scene and for aftercare."

"May I see inside one?"

"Sure." Alex takes a card from his pocket and finds the first door that doesn't have a reserved sign. He swipes the card over the reader and pushes the door open. He steps aside, allowing me to enter first.

I take a few tentative steps into the room and pause, giving my imagination and reality time to catch up with each other. I expected to see something resembling a cheap motel-like room, but instead, this is a high-class suite.

One of the first things I notice is the lack of windows. The room's light comes from a beautiful crystal chandelier that casts a soft glow, creating an almost romantic atmosphere. The walls are painted a soothing shade of grey, giving the room a relaxing aesthetic. I continue my exploration, my heels clicking on the tiled floor as I peek inside a slightly ajar door. Inside is a luxurious en suite bathroom with a large soaking tub.

I return to the main room and make my way to the black metal four-poster bed. Folded across the bottom is a plush red blanket. Running my hands up the silky black sheets, I stop at the neatly arranged pillows. A vase with a dozen fresh red roses sits on a small table beside the bed. The attention to even the smallest detail is impressive. This place could easily pass for a five-star hotel.

"It's breathtaking." I turn to face Alex, who's leaning in the doorway, hands in his pockets.

"It is." The deep tone of his voice makes me wonder if he isn't referring only to the room.

I continue my exploration. The wall to my right has downlights showcasing various leather instruments hanging from a wooden shelf. Curious, I walk closer. "What are these?"

"Floggers."

Running my fingers along the leather tails sends a trail of goosebumps up my arm. "What do they feel like?"

"Floggers can offer a sting or a sensual caress, depending on how they're used."

"Will you show me?" Part of me doesn't believe I'm asking this man, who I've only just met, to use a flogger on me. What's with you tonight, Natalie?

He pauses and inhales deeply. "You want me to show you how a flogger feels?"

I nod.

There's something about this man that's doing strange things to me.

Alex pushes off the door frame and stands to his full height. Then, he hits a button showing the room as occupied before he closes the door.

Click.

"They lock automatically from the outside. All you have to do is turn the inside handle, and it'll open."

"That's good to know."

His dominant presence fills the room as he strides toward me. Stepping aside, I watch as he reaches up, his muscles straining the fabric of his black button-down shirt, and removes a flogger from the wall. He turns back to me and runs the purple tails over his palm. His intense gaze never leaves mine.

"You need to have safe words. We'll use yellow and red. Yellow means you're reaching your limit. Red means stop immediately. Do you understand?"

I nod.

"I need a verbal answer, Natalie."

"Yes, I understand."

My heart's racing. Part of me thinks I've lost my mind, and the other part feels as though my whole life has been building toward this moment.

"I'll be gentle." Alex closes the gap between us and runs his knuckles down my cheek. "You're a courageous young woman." Taking my hand, he leads me to the edge of the bed. "Bend over and place your hands above your head." I do as I'm told, and Alex praises me, "Good girl."

Those two words, although simple, make my insides quiver. Why does knowing I've pleased him matter? I'll never see him again after tonight.

"May I pull your dress up?"

Baring myself to a man who's little more than a stranger should scare me, but instead, I'm dripping with arousal.

"Yes."

Alex's hands gently brush the back of my thighs until they find the bottom of my dress. Gently, he drags the fabric up to my waist, exposing my black lace panties.

"You have a beautiful body."

His words catch me off guard. I've always been insecure about my appearance. Tommy played on that by pointing out everything he felt needed to be improved on —and there was a long list. But when I look over my shoulder, there's no sign of Alex being critical of my body. The look on his face is one of sincere appreciation.

"You need to keep your hands above your head and stay still. Don't be afraid to use your safe words," Alex reminds me. "I'm going to start now."

The soft swoosh of the flogger's tails fills the quiet room for a second before I feel their sting across the back of my thighs.

"How was that?"

"It stung, but it felt good."

"Do you want me to do it again?"

"Yes."

No sooner than the word leaves my lips, I feel the sting again. Alex continues his strikes, alternating where the tails of the flogger land. Each time they make contact with my skin, nerve endings come alive, but at the same time, my body relaxes. It's a paradox of feelings that are as confusing as they are arousing.

"We're done," Alex says after several more strikes. Then, just as gently as before, he slides my dress back into place.

I'm so caught up trying to process what my body's feeling that I don't respond.

"Are you okay?" Alex places his hand on my lower back.

His touch grounds me, and I slowly stand. When I turn around, I find myself in his arms.

"That was amazing."

Alex rewards me with a dazzling smile. "I'm glad you enjoyed it, but it's time we head back out."

I remember the reason I'm at the club. "I hope we didn't miss Lana's scene."

I TAKE MY TIME RETURNING THE FLOGGER TO ITS PLACE ON THE RACK. What just happened?

Brandon called a few weeks ago and asked me to stop by tonight to see his scene with Svetlana. I hadn't been to Fire and Ice in a while. I agreed to come to support my friends. At the last minute, he asked me to escort Lana's roommate—the same girl who called the cops on him last year. I envisioned spending a miserable night calming a frantic girl. That thought was enough for me to almost not show up.

I never thought I'd be spending the evening with a beautiful young woman who's not only unafraid, she's curious. She asked me to flog her. The arousal on her sexy lace panties tells me she enjoyed it as much as I did. I busy myself, pretending to straighten out the floggers, giving my arousal time to calm down.

When I return to her, she readily takes my hand and allows me to lead her back to the club's main room. Lana's scene is just starting. She's naked and restrained to the St. Andrews Cross, her back facing the people gathered to watch. Brandon warms up his arm by taking a few practice strokes with his whip.

A few submissives notice me approaching and step aside, allowing me space to stand at the front. I raise my hand, signaling them to stay where they are. Natalie and I have a good view from here. I appreciate the submissives' respect and make a mental note to compliment them later.

Brandon pauses, and the overhead lights in the club go dim, leaving only the stage illuminated. Then, the room goes silent as everyone waits for Brandon's signature move, a loud crack of the whip signaling the start of their scene.

He begins with softer strikes allowing Lana to acclimate to the sensations before increasing the intensity. As he does, Lana's skin turns a beautiful shade of red. Her cries are a mixture of pain and pleasure.

Over and over, the whoosh of the whip's thong fills the room before it connects with Lana's body. Brandon demonstrates his skill by creating an intricate crisscross pattern on his willing sub's skin.

Halfway through the scene, he stops and lays his whip on the table. Moving to the back of the cross, he leans in close to Svetlana.

"What's he doing?" Natalie whispers.

"He's asking her color."

Natalie studies their interactions. She's most likely trying to connect how the man who was leaving welts on his submissive is now feathering kisses on her face and stroking her hair. Brandon and Svetlana may be in a room full of people, but right now, they're only aware of each other's presence. Watching their tender interaction spurs a longing I haven't felt in years. Although I'm a member of Fire and Ice, when I visit, it's usually to observe. I've had offers, sure, but I turn them all down. I haven't had a submissive or even desired one until this evening.

As we stand and watch the scene, I try to make sense of my emotions. The only reason Natalie came tonight was to watch Lana's scene. She's not in the lifestyle. But earlier, there was a connection. I felt it. Did she feel it, too? Should I ask her if she'd be interested in getting to know each other? If I do that, I'm opening myself up to the possibility of getting hurt. I'm at a crossroads, unsure which way to go.

Natalie's soft voice pulls me from my thoughts. "She looks so peaceful."

I shift my attention back to the stage where the action has resumed. Lana's body is now relaxed in the restraints. Her earlier cries only whimpers.

"It looks like she's starting to experience subspace."

"What's subspace?"

"When a submissive experiences extreme pain, it causes their endorphin levels to climb. That can give a person a sense of euphoria. Svetlana tends to be a take-charge kinda person," I say, and Natalie giggles quietly. "This scene, her submission in general, provides a safe space where she can give that control to her Dominant. It's a very freeing experience, I'm told. "

"So, the intense pain becomes her release."

She's already figuring out the intricacy of the pain/pleasure response. That's an uncommon observation from someone inexperienced.

"Being in subspace makes Lana vulnerable," I add.

"How so?"

"Her ability to gauge pain levels may be compromised. Brandon's experienced and recognizes this. That's why he's decreasing the intensity. The scene will be over soon."

Natalie doesn't take her eyes off the stage.

When Brandon's finished, he sets his whip on the table. He moves closer to Lana and runs his fingers over his creation before leaning close, whispering to her while he unlocks the cuffs. Then, he lifts her into his arms. Lana curls into him, resting her head on his chest. We're all privileged to witness such an intimate moment—the intense bond shared between a Dominant and their submissive.

People move aside, allowing Brandon passage through the club.

"Where are they going?"

"He's taking her for aftercare. As her Dominant, his job doesn't end with the scene. It's his responsibility to care for Lana while she comes out of subspace."

"I thought this was all about sex." Natalie quickly puts her hand over her mouth. Her embarrassment at letting her unfiltered thoughts slip is adorable.

"Sex is a part of it, but this world is about so much more."

"I'm beginning to see that."

What else are you beginning to see? I study her face, looking for any clue as to what she's thinking.

Natalie

After Lana's scene ends, the lights in the club come back up. Alex and I stand off to the side while the audience begins to disperse into different areas of the club.

"Excuse me, ladies and gentlemen." Alex gets the attention of a small group walking past us. They stop, heads bowed.

"I appreciate the respect you showed earlier. Your actions didn't go unnoticed."

I'm impressed that Alex took the time to compliment these individuals. It speaks volumes about his character.

"Thank you, Sir," each one says before walking away.

"The next scene will start in a few minutes. Shall we head over to get a spot near the stage?"

"I'd like that." I've never seen wax play, and I'm curious how it works.

We take our place near the front. Anthony and Leopold are already on the stage. Leopold is wearing a black silk robe and is kneeling while Anthony speaks to him. I wish I could hear what he's saying. Leopold finally stands and unties his robe—it falls to the floor.

My mouth hangs open as I take in the tattooed perfection standing completely naked and unashamed on the stage. Anthony looks at his submissive appreciatively before kicking the robe out of the way.

"Lie down," Anthony instructs.

Leopold climbs onto the table and lies on his back. This time, the lights stay on, and New Age music plays through the club's sound system as Anthony lights the candles. With skilled precision, he picks up a yellow candle and drizzles the melted wax onto Leopold's chest. While he works, Anthony gazes lovingly at his submissive, offering caresses and kisses. Leopold looks like he's sleeping. His eyes are closed, and his hands rest at his sides.

"I never realized wax could do such amazing things," I say, unable to take my eyes off the men.

"There are many things that can be used in ways you've never imagined," Alex whispers in my ear.

I don't know what it is about this man, but his words make me want to experience everything this lifestyle offers—with him.

Over the next half hour, Anthony drizzles pink, purple, orange, and yellow wax across his willing canvas. The design, when finished, is a summer sunset. It's exquisite. Then, Anthony turns his attention to Leopold's erection, stroking it up and down. I've never witnessed anything as erotic as this, and I find myself aroused watching them. Leopold moans in ecstasy as his Dominant brings him to orgasm.

I glance at Alex and find him staring at me, his eyes filled with desire. Our gaze stays locked on each other until the applause from the audience interrupts the moment.

"We should head to Master Kiyoshi's stage and get settled."

"Okay." I struggle to get out even that one small word.

Alex takes my hand in his as though it's the most natural thing to do. We walk to the next area, where we meet Mistress Star.

"Are you enjoying your evening, Natalie?"

"Very much."

She glances down at our joined hands and smiles before showing us our seats. "I'm glad to hear that."

Alex points to the stage where Master Kiyoshi and a woman kneel, facing each other. "He chose a female submissive from the club to participate in his demonstration tonight."

"Wow, she's a lucky girl. She must be excited."

"I'm sure she is. Master Kiyoshi is well-known for his Shibari skills. To be chosen by him is an honor."

Several moments later, the lights dim, and the muffled tones of conversation fade. Soft sounds of a bamboo flute fill the room. Master Kiyoshi rises and offers his hand to the submissive, helping her to her feet. Then, he removes her kimono. She's wearing a white bodysuit with a sheer flowing skirt.

I don't have a good poker face, which Alex must notice because he leans over and whispers, "Not everyone has to be unclothed to do a scene."

If I thought he was gorgeous before, he's even more beautiful when he smiles. And I can't help but return it with one of my own.

Our attention is drawn back to the stage when the lights go off, leaving the room dark. A soft spotlight illuminates the submissive standing in the center. Master Kiyoshi begins his work, moving gracefully as he wraps her body in colorful ropes. His movement mimics the flow of the music.

I've read accounts from those who've experienced Shibari. They describe the sensation of the ropes being wrapped around their body and the knots' tightness, allowing them to slow their breathing and relax into the bondage. Knots are often placed on erogenous zones or pressure points, amplifying the extreme sensations. The rope allows them to experience a deep, almost meditative state, something we're witnessing on the stage. The submissive's body is being manipulated into challenging positions. Rather than tensing, her body relaxes into the intricately bound jute.

When the Master ties off the last piece of rope, he steps back and examines his artwork. Once satisfied, he walks to the side of the stage and picks up a rope attached to the submissive. As he pulls it, the woman's body leaves the ground. Suspended in an arabesque position, her sheer skirt flutters around her seemingly weightless form. It's a breathtaking sight.

After allowing her to fly for several minutes, the Master gently lowers his submissive and begins the process of untying her. Rather than being hurried, she's released with great care and grace. While he works, Master Kiyoshi never breaks eye contact with the woman. Their connection is so strong it's almost palpable. Seeing how choreographed the scene was when they've just met was incredible. It speaks to his level of mastery.

Alex places his hand on my shoulder to get my attention. "How about we grab a table and get a bite to eat?"

I didn't realize how hungry I'd gotten over the last few hours.

"That sounds great."

We walk over to the cafe and are seated at an empty table. A male server brings us water and menus.

"What did you think about tonight?" Alex asks.

I take a sip of water while thinking about everything I've experienced this evening.

"Watching Lana get whipped, I know I should've been scared, but I wasn't." I gesture around the room. "All the rest of this, I was expecting to feel uncomfortable, that this was wrong. And maybe I'm crazy, but it feels so right. I'm surprised by my thoughts."

"Surprised? How so?"

"This is all foreign to me. If you knew how I was raised, you'd understand how much. When I walked in on Lana that night—" My face heats with embarrassment, and Alex chuckles. "I read all the books she gave me, but I still had a very different picture in my mind. Being here tonight, it's nothing at all like I imagined. Each couple we watched shared a genuine connection. There was nothing wrong about—"

A pair of arms wrap around my neck, and I nearly fall off my chair.

"I'm so glad you liked it." Lana's excitement pulses through her body.

"Great scene tonight." Alex stands and shakes Brandon's hand. "Grab some chairs and join us."

Brandon borrows two chairs from a nearby empty table and drags them over.

"Are you enjoying your evening?" Brandon asks.

"I've had a great time." I glance at Alex, and my stomach flip-flops. The man beside me is incredibly gorgeous, and I've been the lucky recipient of his attention all night. "I think I'd like to learn more."

"The club has intro classes during the week. You should sign up," Brandon suggests.

Lana told me about the classes a long time ago, but at the time, I wasn't interested. After tonight, I can't imagine just walking away.

Alex

The four of us spend the next few hours talking and laughing. I catch myself staring at Natalie far too often. I didn't think I'd ever want a submissive again, but if she expressed an interest, I'd jump at the chance to be her Dominant.

"Oh, wow, it's almost two a.m. I promised Cinderella here I'd have her home early." Turning to Brandon, she asks, "Sir, do I have permission to leave?"

"You did great tonight." Brandon runs his knuckles lightly down Lana's cheek. "Go, get your friend home."

"Thank you for the tour, Alex."

I stand and kiss her cheek. "It was my pleasure."

The girls turn and head to the door. But my feet remain bolted to the floor, watching Natalie walk away.

"Go after her."

"I don't know if I can." My heart beats furiously, and my palms are sweating.

"You can't just let her walk away," Brandon says as he nudges me forward.

If I don't go now, I'll never get another chance, and I'll regret it. I hurry through the club and catch up with the girls as they sign out.

"Natalie," I call.

"Alex," she replies, turning my direction.

The sound of my name on her lips makes me feel like a schoolboy with his first crush.

"I'm hoping." I fumble for the words. "Can I give you my number? Maybe we could get together again?"

Star chuckles from behind the desk, obviously amused by my awkwardness.

"I guess that would be okay." She pulls her cell from her purse.

"May I?"

Natalie looks to Lana, who nods with her approval before she unlocks the phone and hands it to me. Opening her contacts, I add my name and number. Then I shoot myself a quick text, ensuring I have her number.

"Done." I hand the phone back.

She gives me an awkward smile and slips the phone into her purse. Did I read everything wrong tonight? I'm confused by her reaction. She seemed so receptive until now.

"I guess I'll talk to you soon."

"Yes, you will."

I watch the girls walk out the door and then turn to Star. "That girl is going to be mine."

Natalie

ALEX CALLS ME THE NEXT DAY. HONESTLY, I DIDN'T THINK I'D HEAR from him, but I'm happy he called.

"Have you made a decision about the intro classes?"

"I'm going to call tomorrow and sign up for the next start date."

"I'm glad to hear that." His voice sounds hopeful. "I'd like to keep in touch if that's okay with you?"

"I'd like that too."

I call Fire and Ice on Monday and register for the six-week intro course, which starts the next night.

I'm nervous about going to the club alone and almost tell my driver to turn around at least a dozen times. When I arrive, I'm glad to see our group is small. There are only five of us. Mistress Star and Master Owen, the club's co-owners, lead the class.

The first part of the session is spent getting to know each other and getting to know ourselves. We talk about our personalities and our likes and dislikes. After taking a short break, Mistress Star introduces us to the many different roles people can assume in the BDSM lifestyle. I thought the only options were Dominant and submissive, but I was wrong. A person can be a switch, top, or bottom. And that's just scratching the surface.

Some couples are twenty-four-seven, while others are only in the bedroom. For instance, some people sign a one-night agreement to play at the club. With so many options, there's a place for everyone.

We're sent home with some resources to read before class next week to help determine where each of us feels we might fit within the lifestyle.

From the start, I felt drawn to the role of submissive. It feels like I've been one my whole life but for all the wrong reasons. What really made an impression on me and addressed any doubts I had was the short time I spent alone with Alex. I didn't have to think or worry. Alex had complete control, and I felt special for the first time in a long time. I was in a submissive role, but I still had a voice.

The following week's class focuses on vetting and safety. Given the potential for injury during a scene and the overall level of trust needed between a Dominant and submissive, vetting a new partner is a serious topic. It can take a potential couple of months before they're ready to sign a contract and begin their dynamic. That seems like common sense, but our lesson takes this topic to a depth I didn't consider. The handout we're given provides sample questions to ask a potential partner. I feel my face flush when I read some of the questions—they get very intimate.

It's week four of class. We now have a solid foundation with the basics of the lifestyle and a good idea of where we might fit in. Although I'm not making any commitments, I'm enjoying learning about all this lifestyle offers. Mistress Star calls the class to order and takes her place in front.

"This week, you'll be paired with one of our club members for one-on-one instruction." She gives us each our room assignment, and then I'm off to see who I've been partnered with. I'm shocked at who I find waiting for me when I open the door. "Leopold."

"The one and only," he says, pulling me in for a big hug. "I hope you're not upset you got paired with me."

"I'm thrilled to be with you." I was very impressed by his wax scene, and he's easy on the eyes.

"Me too. Come on and sit down so we can get started." Two modern armchairs are set up with a small table between them. "The first thing we need to do is list any questions you have. That'll give us a starting point." He picks up a pad and pen from the table.

"I can't think of anything off the top of my head."

"That's okay. Tell me about yourself, and we'll go from there."

"There isn't much to tell."

I fill him in about the small town I come from, my brother, and how I ended up in New York City. Leo's laid-back demeanor makes him easy to talk to.

"What about you?" I ask. "How did you get involved in the lifestyle?"

A dark shadow passes over Leo's face. "Life hasn't always been good to me," he shares. "I met Anthony at one of the lowest points. He saved me," he says, meeting my gaze. "He taught me it was okay to trust again."

Leo reminds me so much of my brother. It feels like I'm talking to Michael again. It's both bittersweet and heartwarming.

Tonight's the last class. I'm sad that it's ending, but now I'm armed with a great deal of information.

"I hope to see you all at the club," Mistress Star addresses the class. "Don't hesitate to reach out to Master Owen or me if you need anything."

After we all say our goodbyes, Leo and I head out for dinner and drinks.

Now that class is officially over, I know Leo will ask about Alex and what direction he and I are headed. The problem is, I don't have the answer. Alex and I agreed to keep in touch during my classes but decided we wouldn't see one another. It was a boundary I asked for because I know what my future holds, and I didn't want either of us to get too attached.

"Have you talked to Alex lately?" Leo asks as we drink our margaritas.

"We talk once a week and text almost every day."

"So, things are going well?"

"I guess so." I look down, fiddling with my hands.

"For a girl who says things are going well, your face tells another story. Start talking."

"Last night, Alex asked if I'd be interested in discussing a Dom/sub relationship."

"The problem with that?" He motions for me to keep talking.

"I have to go back to Northmeadow in a few months. I don't want to start something and then have to walk away."

"When you're discussing the contract, you can tell him you want a time limit. That way, there are no unrealistic expectations."

"That's an option, I guess." I play with the straw in my drink to avoid making eye contact with Leo.

"Wait a minute. The problem is you really like the guy and don't want it to end."

"Maybe." I shrug. "Doesn't matter, though. I'm sure he isn't interested in me as anything more than a submissive, and I don't want to put my heart on the line. So, I don't see any use in us getting involved."

"Have you ever heard of a plane?"

"If it were only that easy."

Leo rolls his eyes. "Girl, if that man were interested in me, I'd scoop him up and never look back."

"I bet Anthony would love to hear that," I say, laughing.

"My Master knows I'm completely faithful to him and him only. But he also knows a sexy man when he sees one, and Alex is *all* that. Don't let him get away."

Leo's words repeat in my head for the rest of the evening.

This is my last year of grad school. In a few months, New York City will become a part of my past. I haven't told Alex about my scholarship or the contract that ensures I return to Northmeadow. When I do, I'm sure it'll change everything.

Natalie

ALEX AND I HAVEN'T TALKED MUCH THIS PAST WEEK. NOT ONLY DID I have a huge paper due, but I also picked up a few extra hours at the counseling center where I intern, so I've been swamped.

Thankfully, my paper has been handed in, and now I have time to breathe. I'm lying on my bed when my cell pings with a text.

Alex: Do you have plans tonight?

Me: I'm staying home and ordering a pizza.

Alex: Can I take you out for dinner?

I want to go out with him. Any sane woman would. But I can't get involved with someone right now.

Me: I don't know.

Alex: I pick you up at 6?

I should say no. Just say no, Natalie.

Me: Sure. I'll see you then.

I set the phone down and rest my head in my hands. I can't believe I didn't say no, and now I'm going on a date with Alex. I know he'll ask if I've thought about his question. I haven't stopped thinking or dreaming about it. I think we'd be good together, and I'd love to explore the lifestyle with him, but I can't risk getting my heart involved in something that can never be.

When I check the time, there's less than an hour until he picks me up. I should text him and tell him I changed my mind. Instead, I'm trying on every outfit in my closet before settling on an ankle-length pink dress with open shoulders. I pin my hair up, leaving only a few loose curls that fall softly around my face. The doorbell rings just as I put on my lipstick.

It's been almost two months since the night at the club—the last time I saw Alex. My stomach flip-flops as I pad through the living room and open the door. Alex stands on the other side in black dress pants and a light gray button-down shirt. His

41

dark hair has grown since I last saw him. He's even more handsome than I remember. In his hands is a bouquet of red roses.

"These are for you." He gives me the flowers. "You look gorgeous," he says, his eyes taking in every inch of my body.

"Thank you. Come on in. I'll put these in water before we leave."

Alex follows me into the kitchen while I grab a vase. I can feel his eyes tracking my every movement. Once the flowers are neatly arranged, I set them on the kitchen island.

Offering me his hand, he asks, "Ready to go?"

I thread my fingers in his as we walk to the door, where I get my coat.

"It's not too chilly, and the restaurant is only a few blocks away. Do you mind walking?"

It's mid-December, but the temperature is mild.

"I don't mind at all."

I enjoy the envious glances of the women we pass on the busy New York streets. Sorry, ladies, he's taken. *Woah*. Where did that come from?

Going out for dinner doesn't mean he's mine.

We stroll past Washington Square Park over to MacDougal St. We stop when we reach Italiano Desiderio.

"I hope you like Italian."

"I love it," I reply. "I've been dying to come here, but they're booked solid. How did you get a table?"

"I know the owner," he says with a grin as he opens the door. "After you."

When I step inside, the street noise disappears. The restaurant looks like a scene straight from Italy. The room is long and has a series of arches with ivy growing up the columns. Small lanterns hang from the branches, providing soft lighting for the room. Instrumental music plays softly in the background. If we hadn't just walked through New York City, I'd think we were in Venice.

We wait for the hostess, whose back is turned while she's talking to a server. When she spins around and sees Alex, her eyes light up.

"Mr. Montgomery, so nice to see you tonight," she says, batting her eyes at *my* date.

I don't know what it is that is making me feel so territorial.

"Thank you. Is our table ready?" Alex pays no attention to her blatant flirting.

The hostess glances my way, letting her saccharine smile falter. "Right this way."

I swear she's swaying her hips just a little extra as she leads us through the restaurant to a private room in the back, where there's a small table set for two. The lighting is soft and romantic. There's a beautiful garden space outside, the large windows lit up with soft twinkling lights. It must be incredible during the summer.

Alex pulls my chair out for me to sit before moving around the table and taking his seat.

The hostess hands each of us a menu. "Is there anything else you need?" she asks, placing her hand on Alex's arm.

He stiffens. "No."

She appears annoyed by his further attempts to thwart her flirting. "Your server will be with you shortly," she says before turning and walking away.

"This place is amazing."

"It is. Tony and Leo have done a great job with it."

"Tony and Leo? As in the same Tony and Leo from the club?"

I hear a man's deep laugh behind me.

"Tony, great to see you." Alex shakes his hand. "You remember Natalie?"

"How could I forget such a beautiful woman?" He leans down and wraps me in a hug. I look at Alex, who's shooting a death glare in Tony's direction, making Tony and I laugh. "I'm glad you two could make it tonight. If you allow me, I'd like to offer you a bottle of our finest champagne."

"Thank you. That would be perfect."

Tony motions to a nearby server, who hurries over and pours us both a glass of the bubbly drink.

"Please, relax and enjoy your meal. I'll be back to check on you later."

We're left alone to look over the menu.

"Would you be okay if I ordered for you?"

I lower my menu and look at him, not entirely surprised by his question. This is something Leo and I talked about—ways a Dominant might wish to take charge. He's asking me first, which is appropriate because he isn't my Dominant. But I'm curious to see how this will work.

"I think I'd like that."

"Thank you." Alex smiles and continues looking over the menu.

The server returns a few minutes later and takes our order. I'm impressed with the food choices Alex makes. I also notice the server doesn't seem thrown off by Alex's ordering for both of us. I wonder how often he sees something like this.

"May I offer a toast?" Alex asks. "Congratulations on being one step closer to completing your education."

I'm not sure if he's referring to the classes at Fire and Ice, being in my final year of grad school, or both. We raise our glasses, clinking the crystal together. I bring the flute to my lips and take a sip, savoring the sweet effervescence of the exquisite champagne.

"Have you given my proposition any thought?"

"I have. And I can see myself in this lifestyle."

"You can?" Alex seems intrigued.

"But I don't think the timing's right."

"Why not?"

I've practiced this conversation for weeks, knowing it was something we'd eventually discuss. But now that the moment is here, I've forgotten everything I practiced and struggle to find the right words. Without much thought, I lift my hand and start biting my fingernails. How do I tell him I'm not staying here permanently? Thankfully, our server arrives with our appetizer, a beautiful Caprese salad. I've been granted a reprieve, at least for a short while.

I pick up my fork and cut a piece of tomato and cheese. Alex's eyes follow my movements as I lift the food to my lips and take a bite. The fresh cheese, coupled with the tomatoes' sweetness and the acidity from the balsamic vinegar, explodes in my mouth.

Closing my eyes, I moan in delight. "This is one of my favorite dishes."

"I'm glad to hear that. But you didn't answer my question."

He doesn't miss a beat. "In a perfect world, I'd like to give the lifestyle, give us a try, but—"

"What's holding you back?"

"I'm not sure it fits with my previous obligations." I take another bite before attempting to change the subject. "Tell me more about how you became so successful in marketing."

Alex has mentioned that he owns his own marketing company. I hope to distract him long enough that he'll forget about me not answering. For the moment, he drops his line of questioning and tells me how he opened his firm five years ago with only a few small accounts.

"I struggled for the first few years. I was at the point I thought I'd have to close until the right client walked in. I was incredibly lucky."

With how persistent he's been in getting me to go out with him, something tells me luck is only a small part of his success.

Our meal is served at a leisurely pace, with one decadent dish after another being brought to our table.

"I've never been to Italy, but this is how I imagine the food to be, fresh and rustic," I say as I take a bite of manicotti with truffle shavings.

"That's because it is. Behind the restaurant, Tony has a greenhouse. He grows as many ingredients as possible and makes all the pasta fresh."

"No wonder it's impossible to get a reservation here."

We're served the last course, espresso and cannolis. The dessert looks fantastic, but there's no way I can eat it.

"If you don't like cannoli, we can order something else?"

"I like it very much."

"Then why haven't you touched it?"

"I already overate." I try hard not to bite my nails. "With how I look, I can't eat stuff like this."

"The way you look?" Alex's eyes narrow. "What's that supposed to mean?"

"My weight. I need to watch everything—"

"Stop." He puts his hands flat on the table. "I will not have you talking about yourself that way. You're beautiful. Your body is beautiful."

My eyes are locked on his, ready to challenge him when a man clears his throat.

"I'm sorry for interrupting," Tony says hesitantly. "I can come back in a few minutes."

"No need," Alex says without taking his eyes off me.

"How was your meal?"

"It was incredible. I'm so full I can't manage to eat my dessert. May I have it wrapped?" I glance in Alex's direction.

"Absolutely." Tony smiles, clearly relieved that the tense moment seems to have passed.

"Thank you, Tony," Alex says. "Everything was perfect."

"Anytime. Natalie, I hope I get to see you again soon."

"I'd like that very much."

"Alex will give you my number. Call me anytime you want to come by."

I can see why Leo is head over heels for this man. Tony leaves the table, and our server takes his place to wrap my dessert.

Alex settles our check and offers me his hand. "There's a back exit we can take."

The tension from before melts away slightly, and we walk in silence until we return to Washington Square.

"Can we sit and talk?"

"Sure."

Alex leads me into the park to a bench, where we sit together and spend a long moment watching the people milling about before Alex breaks the silence.

"You said you're interested in the lifestyle, but it doesn't fit with your *obligations*." He searches my face. "Can you tell me what that means?"

"I'm only in the city for school. The scholarship I was awarded came with a five-year work requirement. When I graduate in the spring, I have to return home."

"We still have plenty of time to try it out." Alex takes my hands in his. "When it's time for you to leave, we can re-evaluate if we want to continue together or walk away."

"You'd be okay with a time limit on this?"

"Yes. I'll take any opportunity to explore us as a Dom/sub couple." His smile reaches his beautiful blue eyes.

"Okay," I say, returning his smile with my own.

"Is that a yes?"

"Yes, Sir." I try out the word and am surprised by how natural it feels.

Alex sits up straighter. "Let the negotiations begin."

Natalie

"Last night was like a real-life fairy tale," I tell Lana as we sit at the table drinking coffee. "Alex is amazing."

Lana smiles proudly. "I knew you two would get along."

"How long have you known Alex?"

"A little while."

"How long's a little while?" I have a feeling there's more to this story than she's telling me, but our conversation is interrupted by the doorbell.

Lana jumps up. "I'll get it."

"Saved by the bell," I call. "But this conversation isn't over."

"Alex," Lana says a little louder than necessary. "I didn't know you were coming over."

"Is Natalie here?"

I'm here, but I'm not letting Alex see me like this. I'm wearing the sweatpants and T-shirt I slept in last night. My hair's thrown up in a messy bun, and I haven't even brushed my teeth yet.

"You bet. She's in the kitchen."

I start to get up from the table, hoping to sprint to my room and get dressed, but Alex's voice stops me before I make it to my feet.

"Good afternoon, Natalie."

"Hi. Can you excuse me for a minute? I need to get changed."

"You look perfectly fine to me."

I lift my head and raise an eyebrow.

"I'm going to shower and study," Lana chirps. "I'll leave you two alone." She hurries to her bedroom.

"I wasn't expecting you." My heart's beating rapidly. "Can I get you some coffee?"

"I'd like that," he says. "I brought a contract with me. I hoped we might go over it together."

I almost drop the mug I'm holding. "You have a contract already?"

"It's a standard contract that I made some adjustments to. Since this is your first time as a sub, I kept it very basic."

My fluffy socks cushion my steps as I walk across the kitchen and place the coffee on the table. "Do you take cream or sugar?"

"No." He looks up at me, his blue eyes dancing with excitement. "Thank you, baby girl."

Baby girl? Those words sound so intimate coming from him. I melt as I sit in my chair.

Alex slides a copy of the contract across the table to me and keeps one for himself. "We won't make any final decisions today. But I wanted to read it together in case you have any questions."

This is all new to me, but his statement puts me at ease. I lift the papers and sit back in my chair as I skim through them. Master Owen showed us examples of contracts during class, so I have some idea of what to expect. When I look up, Alex is watching me intently, his hands folded on the table. I imagine this is what he looks like when he's at work conducting a meeting with a client.

Alex was right. The contract reflects my newness to the lifestyle. It details how Alex, as my Dominant, will treat me respectfully and be responsible for my safety. As his submissive, I will treat him respectfully and conduct myself appropriately, as I reflect my Dominant. Although we won't be together twenty-four hours a day, the contract specifies daily check-ins and obligations. Another section details rules and the consequences for breaking them. Some prohibited things are drinking to intoxication, disrespecting my Dominant, and orgasming without his consent.

"No biting my nails?" I ask, looking up at him.

"I'd like to keep that. We can discuss other, less destructive ways to deal with anxiety."

His reasoning isn't what I thought it would be. "I'm open to that."

"On page three, there's a list of things I'd like to do sexually. Can we discuss your experience level first and then review the list? After that, we can address your limits and remove whatever's necessary."

I flip to page three and start skimming the page. Blindfolds, crops, floggers, bondage, anal trainers, gags, and many other things are on the list. Talking openly about sex is still a new concept for me.

"I'm not a virgin," I say quickly. "I've only been with one person, and it was all very *plain*."

Alex laughs. "Plain?"

"Yeah, vanilla, I guess you'd call it. Tommy, my ex-boyfriend, did his thing and never, well, never made sure I got anything from it."

"He never gave you an orgasm?" Alex leans forward.

I shake my head back and forth slowly.

"baby girl," Alex says. "That will not happen between us. Part of my job, and it's a part I love, is to give you pleasure."

His words make me squirm in my seat. I've already had a small taste of how my body responds to Alex's touch from the night at the club. I can't imagine how much more exciting it could be as his submissive.

"I have a question."

"You can ask anything you want." His voice is calm and steady.

"Anal trainers? What are they?"

"I'm assuming anal sex is new to you?"

I nod in agreement.

"They're a series of butt plugs designed to stretch you so I can enter you without causing physical damage. If that's not something you're open to right now, we can take it off the list. I want to help you grow but not push you too far."

Anal sex is something I've always been curious about, but whenever I brought it up to Tommy, he shut me down. "We can leave it there as long as we go slow."

"Deal." Alex smiles.

The way his face lights up when he smiles is a sight I don't think I'll ever grow tired of. We spend the next hour going over everything in the contract. The more we talk, the more comfortable I become. Alex doesn't pressure me or have expectations I feel are unreasonable.

"The contract will expire five months from now, in time for your graduation. We can reevaluate then."

The thought of parting ways already makes me feel sad. It's something I'll have to get used to, though. Whether I want to or not, I have to return to Northmeadow in May.

Alex looks at his watch. "I need to get going. I have to be in the office for a meeting."

"On a Saturday?"

"I try not to, but this is an important client, so I make myself available whenever he requests." Alex stands. "Take some time with the contract. Let me know if you have any more questions or changes, and we'll take care of it."

I walk him to the door. "Is there a deadline on when you need it back?"

"There's no rush. I want you to make a fully informed decision before we continue." Alex leans in and kisses my cheek. "But I do hope I hear from you soon."

Over the past few months, my life has changed dramatically. When I went to the club with Lana, I wasn't looking to meet anyone. And I certainly had no intention of becoming a submissive. But after reading the books and taking the classes, pieces of me I didn't know were missing started falling into place.

Now, here I am, considering signing a contract to be a submissive to a kind and thoughtful, not to mention extremely gorgeous, man. Closing the door, I drop my forehead against it.

"Is he gone?" Lana asks, peeking out from the hallway.

"Yes, he just left. He had to work."

"And?" she asks as she walks into the living room and flops onto the sofa.

"He brought a contract," I sit next to her. "Will you look it over with me?"

"I'd love to."

Alex

I picked up my phone to call her almost every night this week but stopped myself. As much as I want Natalie to sign the contract, I don't want to pressure her. It may be the hardest thing I've ever done, but I need to give her the time and space to make the right decision for herself.

Right now, I'm in my office reviewing some files from Maxim Solonik, Svetlana's father and my biggest client. I owe him everything. I probably would've had to shut my firm down years ago if it weren't for him. I certainly wouldn't be where I am today. Opening the security software, I click the button to encrypt the information before saving it. While the files are saving, I recline in my black leather chair. My mind drifts back to my first meeting with Maxim.

Early in my college career, I decided to double major in marketing and bioethics. Climate change and eco-friendly business practices were beginning to grow in popularity, and I intended to take full advantage.

I'd been left some money when my grandfather passed away. Dad helped me invest it wisely, so I had a small nest egg. Fresh out of school, I said goodbye to my life in Seattle and set off in search of fame and fortune in New York City. I planned to take the city by storm, rebranding businesses and highlighting their eco-friendly efforts.

At the time, I felt office space was more important than living space. So, I used most of the money to secure a prime location and rented a cheap room in a hostel, certain it would be a temporary stop. I figured I'd have a steady cash flow for an apartment within a month or two.

Unfortunately, finding clients wasn't as easy as I expected. Not many businesses wanted to take a chance on the new kid in town. I signed on a few small clients, but they weren't bringing in enough to pay the bills. My ego had taken a hit, and I quickly ran out of money.

My father, who was still recovering from the loss of my mother, suspected I was in trouble and offered to help. But I was too proud to accept it.

I'll never forget that night. It was a Tuesday like any other. I stayed in the office late, trying to figure out how to afford the rent for the office, my room, and food for the week. But no matter how hard I tried, the numbers weren't in my favor. I would have to give up my room and live in my office.

I must've forgotten to lock the door. The jingle of the bells startled me. A man in an expensive tailored suit entered my office and walked directly toward me. He hadn't yet spoken, but something about the way he carried himself made me sit up and take notice.

"Can I help you?".

"My name is Maxim Solonik," he introduces himself and, as if he owns the place, takes a seat. "I have a business proposition for you."

Maxim told me about his company. He was in Russian oil and sought to expand his operations in the US by getting involved in the natural gas pipeline network. His company held technology that would prove helpful in advancing cleaner energy sources.

He had my full attention as we discussed his unique needs at great lengths. We talked until it got late, and Maxim proposed we continue our meeting over food and drink.

That night he made a strong case for why I should take him as a client. We shook hands and have been working together ever since.

Being young and naïve, I didn't ask many questions. All I saw was the chance to save my failing business. I didn't know or really care why he chose me or that our partnership would eventually extend beyond environmental technology.

Meeting him changed everything for me. His involvement ensured my business became more successful than I ever dreamed. And all these years later, it led me to the best thing in my life.

In the beginning, Maxim and I spent a lot of time together, both here in the States and at his home in Russia. We became more than business associates. We also became friends.

One of his trips to New York coincided with the first anniversary of my mother's death.

I'd always admired my parent's relationship as a married couple and a Master/slave. I wanted what they had, so when I turned twenty, I entered the lifestyle. It was everything I wanted and more. Until I witnessed my dad lose everything that mattered to him—my mom. In a reckless move, I left the lifestyle behind. I walked away from my submissive without so much as an explanation. My actions hurt her, something I've made amends for.

My mother's death wrecked me. It left me stumbling blindly through life. I refused to be involved with anyone for fear of falling in love.

That night, after I didn't answer any of his calls, Maxim showed up at the hostel. I was drunk, trying to numb the pain and loss. He stayed with me while my drunken self told him everything I'd been holding in.

Max didn't know my history with BDSM, or so I thought. The following night, he told me we were going out. He brought me to Fire and Ice and introduced me to a submissive. It was a one-night arrangement—no strings attached.

After the night was over, Maxim explained why he chose me.

"Alexander, many years ago, your parents visited a well-known dungeon in Russia. Your father wanted to learn how to wield a bullwhip. It happened to be the same dungeon Irina and I went to. I became your father's teacher."

I sat stunned, listening to his story.

"Over the years, we'd travel to the States, and your parents traveled to Russia to visit one another. They were very dear friends."

Max stayed in the States for several months and mentored me as I cautiously started practicing the lifestyle again. Because of his intervention that night, I not only found myself but eventually found Natalie. I owe Maxim more than I can ever repay.

With the encryption done, I shut my laptop off and push to a standing position. My muscles are tight from sitting in one spot for so long. Before heading out, I check my phone one last time and finally see a text from Natalie.

Natalie: I've gone over the contract and have one request.

Me: What's the request?

Natalie: I'd like to add rope bondage. You know, like Shibari.

I can almost hear her asking the question, and I smile. She's adventurous—I like that. But there's one big problem. I don't know much more than the basics—for her, I'll learn.

Me: Done. Is there anything else you want to add?

Natalie: No, that's everything. I'm ready to sign.

I'm ready to sign.

I read the words over and over, not believing they're real. But, sure enough, the text stays on the screen. Having a submissive is a big responsibility, one I've screwed up in the past. I hope you have your shit together, Alex. You can't mess this up. Natalie deserves only the best.

Me: Do you have plans tonight?

Natalie: Lana's out with Brandon. I just made popcorn, and I'm going to watch a movie.

Me: How about I pick you up? We can grab a bite to eat and watch a movie together at my place.

Natalie: I'd like that.

Me: I'm getting ready to leave the office now. I'll be at your place in about twenty minutes.

Natalie: I'll be ready.

I send one last text to my driver, Viktor, before sliding my phone into my pocket and locking up. When I get outside, Viktor's standing by the passenger door of my black Model 3 Tesla.

"Where to, boss?"

Viktor wasn't with me when I picked Natalie up last time, so I give him the address before getting in. It's a typical Friday evening in the city. Traffic is terrible, and we take longer than my anticipated twenty minutes. When we finally arrive at her building, Viktor waits in the car while I go in to collect my new submissive.

Natalie

I have twenty minutes to get out of my cozy jammies and get ready to see Alex. *You've got this, Nat.* I rush around my room, looking for something comfortable yet sexy. Tonight's a big night. We'll sign the contract and officially start our Dom/sub relationship.

My hands shake as I put on my light pink strapless bra and slide on my cream, off-the-shoulder sweater. Then, I step into my favorite pair of jeans. I had my hair pulled up in two little buns. It's going to have to stay that way, or else my curls will be a frizzy mess. After putting on mascara and lipstick, I look at my reflection in the mirror. I'm unhappy with what I see, but the ringing doorbell interrupts my thoughts.

This is going to be a defining night in my life. For the next few months, I won't be living only for myself. Alex will come first in everything I do. My words and actions will not represent just me but will now also represent my Dominant. With a final breath, I walk to the door and open it. Alex stands on the other side, wearing a black suit. The top button of his white shirt is open, and his red tie hangs loose.

"Hi."

"Hi," he says, his eyes taking me in. "You look beautiful."

"I'm a bit underdressed." I lower my gaze, both uncomfortable with the compliment and embarrassed with the outfit I chose. He puts his finger under my chin and lifts my face so I can't avoid his eyes.

"Don't look away when I compliment you." His tone is stern yet calm. "Let's try this again. You look beautiful, baby girl."

"Thank you, Sir," I say quietly.

"Are you ready to go?"

"I just need to grab my coat."

The warm spell we had a few weeks ago is gone, replaced with more seasonable chilly air. Like a true gentleman, Alex helps me into my coat before offering his arm.

"

Together, we make our way toward a high-end car. A scary-looking man with large muscles and a bald head stands beside it. My body stiffens, thinking we're about to be mugged.

"What's wrong?"

I shift my gaze back to the man.

Alex chuckles. "I'd like to introduce you to Viktor."

Embarrassed by my actions, I debate running back inside. But then I remember I'm a reflection of Alex. "It's nice to meet you."

Viktor nods and opens the car door.

I've never been in a car like this. The seats are made of soft black leather and are heated, a nice addition given how chilly it is outside. Alex slides in next to me, and our legs brush against each other. A sizzle of electricity runs through my body.

Inside, the car is silent as Viktor weaves in and out of traffic. I steal a glance at Alex. His posture is tense. Is he as nervous as I am?

Viktor pulls the car into a lot under a building. Then, Alex leads me to an elevator. He punches in a code before pressing the penthouse button. I'm stunned silent. Why would a man who lives this lifestyle be interested in someone like me? The elevator doors open directly into Alex's apartment. He motions for me to step out first.

"Make yourself at home. Can I get you something to drink?"

"May I have some water, please?" I say almost absentmindedly. I'm distracted by the view from the floor-to-ceiling windows that line two walls. One overlooks his Upper West Side neighborhood, and the other offers a spectacular view of the Hudson River. "The view is stunning."

"The view *is* stunning," Alex says before going to the kitchen to get our drinks. "Come sit. We need to talk." The dark grey sofa is situated by a fireplace, which adds warmth to the room. When I sit down, Alex hands me a glass of ice water. I take a sip before setting it on the glass end table. I fidget with my fingers, bringing one to my mouth to bite my nail. Alex reaches out and takes my hand, placing it in my lap.

"Relax. There's no reason to be nervous."

"Where do we go from here?"

"Before we move any further, I'd like to review the contract one last time. Then, if you're sure you're ready, we'll both sign it."

"I forgot to bring my copy."

"I have one in my office. Wait here."

Alex walks down a hallway. His shoes make a loud clicking sound that seems to echo in the ample space. I silently chastise myself for forgetting something so important. It only takes a minute before he's back with papers and a pen in his hand.

"Here's a copy for you. You'll see, I made the changes you requested."

We take the next few minutes to review everything, ensuring it's written exactly as we both want.

"It looks good," I say, offering him a nervous smile.

"Are you ready to sign?"

Am I ready to sign? Lana and I talked about this for hours the other night. If it were anyone else, she would've advised me to wait—to vet him longer. Because she and Brandon know him so well and have vouched for his character and intentions, I feel safe moving forward so quickly. This is my opportunity to try something new and exciting—to live on my terms.

"Yes, Sir."

He rewards me with a smile that makes my insides quiver. Alex hands me a pen, and I sign both copies. When I finish, I pass the pen back to him, and he does the same. Then, he takes the contracts and sets them aside on the table. The energy in the room suddenly shifts. Sexual tension fills the air. Every time we're together, there's chemistry between us. But until now, we've been unable to act on it.

The first rule Mistress Star drilled into us was not to get physically involved with anyone we were vetting because it could cloud our judgment. Now, the vetting is over, and we can finally act on our feelings.

Alex brushes a strand of hair from my face and tucks it behind my ear. The small amount of contact sends chills down my spine. He leans in for a slow, gentle kiss. His tongue explores my lips before I open, allowing him access to my mouth.

When I do, it's as if a dam spills open. The connection we share explodes. Our kiss turns desperate. He lifts me so I'm straddling his lap.

"Do you feel this between us?" he asks breathlessly. "Do you want me as much as I want you?"

I nod in response.

"I need a verbal answer, Natalie."

"Yes. I want you."

The words no sooner leave my mouth before his lips are back on mine. Then, he stands, lifting me with him.

"Wrap your legs around me." I obey immediately, and he walks us toward his bedroom. He sets me down before stepping back and unbuttoning his shirt, throwing it over a nearby chair.

Following his lead, I pull my sweater off and drop it on the floor.

"You. Are. Beautiful."

Alex makes quick work of his button and zipper before pulling his pants and boxers off. When I see his erection, I gasp.

"This is all for you, baby girl."

With quick strides, he closes the gap between us, his body pushing mine back on the bed as he begins kissing me again. His hands reach around my back, unhooking my bra. He tosses it to the side. His mouth is on one breast, sucking and nipping before switching to the other one, paying it the same attention. Sliding his body down mine, he kisses a trail between my breasts and down my abdomen.

"I need to taste you," he says before unbuttoning my jeans and sliding them off.

Slowly and carefully, he removes my lace panties, feathering kisses along my leg as he does. Then, he spreads my legs and gives an appreciative groan when he sees I'm waxed and smooth, just as he specified in the contract.

"You're so wet for me already," he says before kissing my inner thigh, moving higher and higher. When he reaches my center, his tongue teases my clit, tracing light circles around it.

My hips move of their own accord. Alex pulls back. "Stay still."

"Yes, Sir."

He returns to his task and adds two fingers, sliding them in and out, matching the rhythm of his tongue. I've never had a man's mouth on me before. The feeling is exquisite. It doesn't take long before an orgasm washes over me, and I moan in pleasure. He continues to lick and suck until the waves of my orgasm subside. Then he makes his way back up my body.

"You taste even better than I imagined," he says before kissing me deeply, allowing me to taste myself on him. It's subtle and tangy, like nothing I've tasted before.

"Sir, I need you inside me." My voice is breathy.

He sits back on his knees. "You need to learn some patience." His hand begins stroking his length, up and down. "Is this what you want?"

"Yes, please."

He leans in and drags his cock over my sensitive clit, teasing me before he lines himself up with my opening and slides in ever so slowly. Once he's fully sheathed inside me, he pauses, closing his eyes. "Fuck, you feel so good." Then, he moves slowly, not rushing our first time together.

I reach up and run my fingers through his dark hair before lifting my head to kiss him. Although this is only supposed to be a contractual relationship, my heart is already falling for him. Our bodies move together in a passionate rhythm. Alex's hands slide up my stomach to my breasts. He holds them in his hands, rolling my nipples before giving them a hard squeeze, eliciting a gasp from me.

"Did you like that?"

"Yes." My words are barely a whisper.

"These will look beautiful with clamps on them."

His words only heighten my quickly building arousal.

"I'm so close."

"Do not come yet," he orders as he increases his pace. "Open your eyes. I want you to look at me when you come—to remember who you belong to."

Our eyes remain locked on one another as Alex thrusts harder and faster.

"Come now," he orders.

An orgasm sweeps through my body. With one more thrust, Alex is coming inside me. He kisses me deeply as we ride out the pleasure together. When our orgasms subside, he drops his forehead to mine. The only sound in the room is our mingled breaths.

"We're so good together, baby girl. I'm glad you decided to give us a chance."

Alex rolls onto his back and pulls my body into his. I lay wrapped in his arms, my head on his chest, until I drift off to sleep.

Alex

OVER THE YEARS, I'VE ASSEMBLED TEAMS OF VERY TALENTED individuals who design successful campaigns. Because of this, I've built one of the most sought-after marketing companies on the East Coast.

We've recently signed on with several large companies, which means I've been in back-to-back meetings all day. Where I don't work hands-on with each client, I oversee every project.

I'm sitting in my fourth meeting of the day when an email notification pops up on my phone. A quick swipe of the screen shows it's from Maxim. The subject line reads *New Client Coming Onboard.* This gets my attention, and I sit up straighter. Another client? I'm eager to open the email and read more about it.

"Mr. Montgomery, what are your thoughts on the new campaign slogan?" The team leader interrupts my reading.

"Everything looks good here." I gather the papers in front of me before pushing my chair back and standing. "If you'll excuse me, I just received an email that needs an immediate response. I trust you have this under control." Without waiting for his response, I leave the meeting room and head straight to my office. Once I'm back at my desk, I type in the password to unlock my screen and open the email.

Alexander,
A colleague of mine, Mr. Nicholai Federov, requires your services. He has technology
that will be of interest to alternative energy companies. I want to arrange a meeting
with the three of us to discuss how we wish to proceed. This client will require a great deal
of time but will be mutually beneficial. Attached you will find the proposal. We will
make time to speak next week.
Maxim.

Opening the proposal, I start reading it right away. Nicholai is involved with a company studying Neutrinovoltaic Energy, the latest in renewable energy resources. That's the official business that will go on paper. I have a phone call scheduled with Maxim next week. That's when he'll fill me in on how Nicholai fits into the more sensitive aspects of his business.

When I finally look up, it's dark outside. The sun has long since set. I got so involved in reading the proposal I didn't realize how time had gotten away from me. Grabbing my phone off the desk, I text Viktor letting him know I'll be out shortly. Then I reply to Maxim, acknowledging the receipt of his email.

My house is quiet and lonely when I return after a long day at the office. Coming home after work on Fridays to the smells of dinner cooking and knowing Natalie is waiting for me is something I quickly grew used to. She usually stays over on the weekends, something I've never done before—never shared my home with a submissive. When she's here, it's like we live in our own little bubble. Natalie was initially hesitant but agreed to it as long as we kept it to weekends only. She's holding back because she has to return to Northmeadow and doesn't want to get too attached.

Having her here for a few days at a time has helped us to work out some of the initial kinks. My little sub does well following the rules. I've only had to punish her once. Not biting her nails is a challenge for her.

She takes advantage of my fully stocked kitchen when she's here, ensuring we have a home-cooked meal that we sit and eat together. It reminds me of my childhood. The aromas coming from the kitchen as my mother lovingly prepared dinner for my father, of us sitting down to meals and talking about our days. I didn't realize how important those memories are and how much I desire that in my life.

My biggest concern is knowing Maxim is expanding his operations and wants me to take on another client. It'll bring in a lot of money, but it'll also mean sacrificing personal time. Natalie and I only have a few months together, and I don't want to waste a second of it—I'm torn.

I put my briefcase on the dining table and loosen my tie before walking to the windows. Looking out over the water, I recall the look on Natalie's face the first time she stepped into my apartment. Her green eyes shimmered as she took in the view. Something I had never stopped to appreciate before that moment. I took for granted everything she saw. I miss her presence here and want her back. That thought stops me in my tracks. Natalie's only temporary. The realization causes a stirring in my heart—I don't want her to leave. What is it about this woman that has me turned upside down? Maybe it's her innocence. Even though I've told her very little about my personal life, she's been open about hers.

Losing her brother to suicide greatly impacted her and is the driving force behind her career choice. She's also told me about her ex-boyfriend, the one who broke her heart but is also responsible for her new outlook on life. His loss is my gain.

I'm beginning to care about her as more than just my submissive, which terrifies me. I have to shut those feelings off. We agreed this was nothing more than a few months of fun before she returns home.

Natalie

THE REMAINDER OF THE SEMESTER FLIES BY. FINALS ARE OVER, AND graduation is in two weeks. If you'd asked me last year, I would've said I couldn't wait to graduate. But now, everything's changed. I'm thankful that my schooling is complete and I'll be able to start my career. But at the same time, I feel like I've just started embracing life in the city, and it's ending already.

Then there's Alex.

We've grown close over the past few months. We see each other one or two days during the week and spend weekends together. Every Friday night, he comes home to find me kneeling inside his foyer. His eyes heat the second he sees me. I've learned to keep dinner on warm because we rarely make it to the table before we're naked, and he's inside me.

This wasn't supposed to be anything more than a few months of fun. A chance to try out something new—no strings attached. I should've known that wasn't going to be possible. I'm falling in love with him. Too bad he doesn't feel the same. I have to remind myself his kindness and affection are part of the contract. Nothing more than his responsibilities as my Dominant. Our relationship, just like my time in the city, comes with a rapidly approaching expiration date.

"Nat, your phone's ringing," Lana calls from the living room.

"Who is it?"

"It's Alex," she says in a sing-song voice before answering it.

I hurry down the hall and into the living room.

"Here she is." Lana hands me the phone. "Did you invite him to graduation?" she whispers.

I put my hand over the phone. "Yes."

She nods in acknowledgment. "I'm getting my bag. Brandon will be here any minute. I'll see you at the ceremony."

"Okay, have fun."

Lana's spending the next few weeks at Brandon's. The two of them have been nearly inseparable lately.

"Hello?"

"Hi, baby girl. Did I catch you at a bad time?"

"No. I was saying goodbye to Lana. She's headed to Brandon's."

"He told me she's staying with him for a while. Sounds like they're getting pretty serious."

I feel a pang of jealousy. I'm happy for my best friend but sad for me.

"Are you coming over this weekend?"

It's our last official week together.

"Yes."

"Why don't you spend the week with me?" His voice holds a glimmer of hope.

"I can't. I have to pack and get everything shipped home."

Although that's true, it's more of an excuse. Everything's pretty much already packed. There's no way I can handle spending the whole week with him knowing, in the end, I have to say goodbye.

"We can stay at your place. I can help you."

"I don't think that's a good idea."

"I had to try. I'll have Viktor pick you up Friday?"

"I'll be ready."

I disconnect the call and already feel my heart breaking. How am I going to say goodbye to Alex?

Natalie

I FIGHT BACK THE TEARS AS VIKTOR TAKES MY BAG AND WALKS ME TO the car. It's a quiet drive across town, although that's no different than most days. Viktor doesn't talk much—he's all business. We pull into the parking garage and into the usual spot.

"I'll bring your bags up in a few minutes. I have something I need to take care of."

"Take your time."

The elevator takes me up to Alex's apartment. When the doors open, a trail of roses leads me into the bedroom, where I find a note.

Take a hot bath using the toiletries I left for you. You have one hour, then I expect to find you on my bed wearing only the item provided.

I pick up a red blindfold and run my fingers over the silky material, feeling a shiver of anticipation run through me. What has Alex planned for tonight? My heart pounds with excitement as I imagine the possibilities.

I turn on the hot water and pour some lavender body wash into the tub, watching as it fills with steamy bubbles. Slowly, I strip off my clothes and sink into warm water. The sensation is heavenly, and I close my eyes, letting out a sigh of contentment.

As I soak, my muscles gradually loosen, and my mind drifts. I rarely take the time to relax like this, but I realize how much I need it. When I finally emerge from the bath, I feel rejuvenated.

Drying off, I notice a note resting on top of a fluffy white bathrobe. I wrap myself in the robe, tying it around my waist, and read the card.

Make sure your hair is pulled back and off your shoulders.

I grab a comb and run it through my damp hair, braiding it before pinning it up into a bun. I can't help but wonder what Alex has in store for me tonight.

61

When I glance at the clock, I realize only five minutes are left. I quickly dry myself and lie down on the bed, feeling a rush of excitement and anticipation as I reach for the red blindfold. A thrill runs through me as I slide the silky material over my eyes.

Without my sight, my other senses are heightened. The air is still and quiet, and I try to steady my breathing, waiting for Alex to arrive.

I hear footsteps approaching from the hall. The door opens and closes, and I hear the lock click into place. The room fills with the familiar scent of citrus and sandalwood.

Alex.

Silently, he moves around the room, opening and closing drawers. The atmosphere is charged with excitement, and I can't help but wonder what Alex has in store for me tonight. I jump when I feel something soft being run gently up my leg.

"That tickles," I giggle.

"Shh. There will be no talking."

The same item, a feather, I think, is being dragged over my arms, leaving a trail of goosebumps in its wake.

"Spread your legs," Alex commands.

Without hesitation, I do as he instructs.

"Mmm...so beautiful."

Alex never holds back compliments about my body. At first, they were hard to acknowledge. Slowly, I've been improving on accepting them.

Next, he secures a cuff around one ankle and then the other before attaching them to the hidden clips on his bed. My wrists are next. He ties them over my head and secures the rope to the headboard. I'm completely at his mercy, and I love it.

Following the same path the feather took, there's now what feels like a spiked wheel rolling over my skin. The sharp sensation is such a contrast from the feather. Alex continues dragging it to my abdomen before rolling it across my breasts. My nipples harden in response. The sensation stops as abruptly as it started.

Then there's silence, and I start to panic. "Alex? Are you still here?"

"I'm not going anywhere, baby girl."

Leaning over me, I feel his warm skin on mine. He kisses me before placing a set of headphones over my ears. The sudden hearing loss surprises me, and I pull on my restraints.

He moves one from my ear. "Color?"

"Yellow." I'm finding having both my sight and hearing taken away difficult.

"Do you want to continue?"

"I just need a minute."

He removes the headphones and gently touches my shoulder, kissing me deeper. I lose myself in the passion, and the anxiety dissipates. His hands leave my shoulders, but I can still feel the warmth of his body. I know he's close.

"Can I put the headphones back on?"

"Yes, Sir."

Once he replaces them, everything goes silent. My back arches when something cold swirls around my belly button and down my stomach before he drags it through my slit, where it leaves a trail of burning fire. I thought it was ice, but there was also warmth. The contrast in sensations is intense.

It's not until I feel him suck on my nipple that I'm sure it's ice, and it's been in his mouth the whole time. But just like last time, the object disappears. The silence from the headphones is replaced with soft music.

Alex places feathered kisses down my body, returning me to a state of relaxation. Then, his body is gone again, and I'm left anticipating the next experience. He doesn't make me wait long before I feel something warm and slick on my back entrance, and I tense. We've not had anal sex before, and although I'm open to the idea, I'm also nervous.

Before I have a chance to panic, Alex's fingers begin teasing my clit. My arousal intensifies as an orgasm quickly begins to build. At the same time, I feel something firm yet smooth penetrating the tight muscles. Alex increases the pressure on my clit as he gently eases a toy in and out, allowing my body to adjust to the new sensation. He doesn't rush.

By the time the plug is fully inside, I'm on the edge of an orgasm. He stops abruptly again, and I moan in frustration. I try to pull my legs together to quell the overwhelming sensations, but with the restraints, that's impossible.

The music changes. I don't recognize the song until I hear the lyrics. It's Eminem's "Lose Yourself." This isn't our usual playlist. As if on cue, the toy vibrates a pattern in time to the music. I've never felt anything like this. My body is over-whelmed. It feels as though I'm on the edge of a precipice, but I'm unable to fall off the other side. Alex's fingers begin to tease my clit again. I raise my hips, needing more, but his other hand pushes them down. When I think I can't take it anymore, his tongue penetrates my entrance. It's all I needed to send me over the cliff.

Before my orgasm ends, he slams inside me. At first, it feels like it's too much, and I don't think my body can handle it. Fully sheathed inside me, he doesn't move. Instead, he leans down and kisses me, distracting me from the pain.

Slowly, he begins to rock his hips. What was pain begins to morph into pleasure. The toy continues to pulse, and Alex picks up the pace of his thrusts. My second orgasm rockets through me, leaving me breathless. Alex removes the headphones and the blindfold. It takes a minute for my eyes to adjust, but when they do, I find him staring at me with an intense look on his face.

"You're changing me. You're making me a different man. A man who wants us to be more than just a contract."

As soon as the words leave his mouth, he explodes inside me. I follow right behind him. My body convulses with a climax stronger than I've ever felt.

Then, blackness creeps into my vision, and I'm floating in a quiet, peaceful bliss.

Natalie

The day I've dreaded since Alex and I finalized our contract has come—the end. He asked if we could sit and talk after my shower. Standing under the hot water, I close my eyes and allow it to wash over me while I try to imagine how our conversation will go.

When we signed the contract, we agreed that neither of us wanted a relationship. We were just two people having fun and exploring the lifestyle together. I'd get some firsthand experience, and Alex would have a sub to play with for a few months.

From day one, I began preparing myself to say goodbye. To walk away and leave him in my past. But then, last night, he said something that changed everything. He said he wanted something more than a contract. What am I going to do?

I graduate next week. There's a one-way plane ticket to Missouri sitting on my desk. No matter how much I want to continue exploring this dynamic, I'm tied to Northmeadow for the next five years. I don't have a choice—I signed away my options when I accepted the scholarship.

After I shower, I wrap a fluffy white towel around my body, blow dry my hair, and put on some make-up. I look around and realize I have so much stuff here. It's a good thing I brought a bigger bag. I'm packing everything up now, knowing I plan to return to my apartment after our conversation today.

Alex wants me to spend the week with him, but I can't. I need some time alone to sort out all these mixed-up feelings. Slipping on a pale blue sundress, I look in the mirror. A sad reflection stares back at me. It's time to be strong, Natalie.

Barefoot, I enter the kitchen, where Alex sits at his table waiting for me. He looks up, a gorgeous smile on his face. His eyes hold so much hope. But when he sees me, his smile disappears.

Alex

I retrieved two copies of our contract from my office. Today is the expiration date, the day to reevaluate where we want to go from here. I fully anticipated saying goodbye to Natalie today. I had no intention of this arrangement being anything more than a few months of playtime for her and me.

But something happened. Somewhere along the way, my feelings for her changed, and my heart softened.

Natalie's special. She isn't like any woman I've ever known. So much about her is pure innocence, yet she's wise. Despite having a strict, conservative upbringing, Natalie is curious and open to new experiences. Being a submissive comes naturally to her. She's genuine and beautiful, both inside and out.

I've grown to care about her, and after seeing the look on her face last night when I told her I wanted more, I think she cares about me, too. I can't let her leave without fighting to keep her.

I hear her footsteps as she approaches the kitchen. Excited to share my idea with her, I turn, but the breath is sucked from my body when I see her face. It isn't the face of a girl ready to fight for us. She's prepared to say goodbye. Natalie sits across from me and looks down at her hands.

"I know you're graduating next week and planning to return home. But I don't want us to end. I want to try to make us work however that might look."

"Alex," she says, standing and walking to the windows. It's something she does whenever she's struggling. "Your life is here. Mine is halfway across the country in a small farm town. I don't see how we can be together." She rests her forehead on the glass.

I walk over to her and wrap my arms around her tiny frame. "We can do this in whatever way works for us."

Turning in my arms to face me, she asks, "How?"

"I see two options. First, I own my business and can visit you whenever I want. You'll get vacation days, so you can fly back here, too."

"I won't be making a fancy New York salary. Buying plane tickets to fly back and forth isn't in my future."

"Then let me buy out your contract," I blurt out. "You won't have to leave. We can be together."

Natalie frees herself from my arms. "I will not have my boyfriend, my Dominant, whatever you are, buying out my contract. I made a commitment, and I will see it through."

I'm losing this argument to the beautiful yet stubborn woman standing before me. But as much as I want to, I can't force her to stay—to choose me.

"I don't want to walk away from us either." Her emerald green eyes fill with tears. "I'm so confused right now."

"Natalie, please. Don't walk away from us."

She reaches out and cups my cheek in her hand. "These past few months have been the best of my life." A tear drips down her face. "But it's time to say goodbye. Will you take me back to my apartment?"

Reluctantly, I accept her answer.

Natalie

WE DRIVE IN SILENCE. A HEAVINESS HANGS BETWEEN US. I DON'T WANT to walk away from this—from Alex. But there will be hundreds of miles between us. How could we possibly make that work? I know firsthand the betrayal that can happen when distance is involved. Alex is different. I know that. But I promised myself I wouldn't put my heart on the line again.

"We're here." Alex puts the car in park. For the longest moment, neither of us moves. "We're so good together, baby girl. Please don't give up on us."

The longing in his voice shatters the last shards of my resolve.

"I'll try."

He turns and looks at me. "Will you let me buy out your contract?"

"No. I'm going back to do my job. I'll agree to try this long-distance. But I do have some requests."

"Can I come in? Then, we can discuss them inside."

We walk together to my second-floor apartment. I fumble in my purse for the keys when the door swings open.

Alex pulls me behind him. "Who are you?"

"Who are *you?*" a very familiar voice asks.

I stand on my tip-toes and peer over Alex's shoulder. "Dad? Mom? What're you guys doing here?"

"I decided to close the store for a few days. We wanted to surprise you by coming early." Dad looks from Alex back to me. "Looks like we accomplished our goal."

"That you did." I smile, trying to hide my shock.

"Are you going to introduce us to your friend?" Dad asks.

"Mom. Dad. This is Alex."

Alex reaches out to shake my father's hand.

"Nice to meet you, Mr. Clarke."

"I thought you'd appreciate the help packing your things." Mom reaches around Dad and pulls me in for a hug. "I'm sure you can't wait to get home."

My head is spinning. I can't even form a sentence.

After an awkward silence, Mom says, "Why don't you two come in? I'll put some coffee on." She walks toward my kitchen.

Alex looks at me, and I mouth the words *I'm sorry*. We were supposed to be alone to figure out how to move forward. My request was to keep our relationship a secret from my parents, at least for now. I know how they feel about the city and the people in it. There's no possible way to explain how we met or that he's not my boyfriend but my Dominant. If things work out and we become a real couple, I'll figure out a way to tell them. If not, they'd never need to know. I'm not prepared for this. Tonight could very well end in disaster.

We go to the kitchen, where my mom fumbles around in the cupboards.

"Where do you keep your coffee pot, sweetie?"

I point to the Keurig on the counter. She looks at it and shakes her head disapprovingly. My parents resist anything new.

"I'll take care of it. Please, everyone, sit down."

While I make coffee, my parents start the inquisition.

"How do you know Natalie?" Mom asks.

"I met her through her roommate. I'm a friend of Svetlana's family."

Is that for real or just a story for my parents? I'll have to ask him about that when we're alone.

"What's the nature of your relationship with my daughter?" Dad asks as he leans forward.

I nearly drop the coffee cup I'm holding.

"Dad, please."

"It's okay. We've been seeing each other for the past few months," he answers calmly.

"You realize she has a boyfriend at home?" Mom asks.

"Tommy and I broke up a long time ago," I respond sharply. "Can we please stop this and just have a normal conversation?"

"Natalie tells me you own a pharmacy?" Alex smoothly changes the subject.

Dad's face lights up. He's proud of his business.

"Alex owns a marketing firm, Dad." I place a cup of coffee in front of my father. "Maybe he can give you some ideas for advertising?"

The tension between my father and Alex seems to subside, at least for now. But Mom's a different story. She sits back, arms crossed over her chest. She's not going to let this go.

I'm in awe of Alex's composure. My parents' presence doesn't shake him at all. Actually, he and Dad seem to have hit it off quite well. While Alex and Dad talk, Mom and I discuss what must be done before next week's graduation.

It looks like the evening's gotten away from us," Alex says. "None of us have eaten. I'd love to take you all out for dinner."

I smile at him, appreciating how accommodating he's being.

"Thank you, but we'll be eating in," Mom snips. "We're not much for the chaos out there."

I roll my eyes. "You're more than welcome to stay for dinner."

"I'm afraid I didn't make enough for a guest," Mom says as she stands and walks to the counter, where she turns the oven on.

I overlooked the covered baking pan sitting on the stove until now.

"Mom," I say, appalled by her rude attitude.

"It's okay, Natalie. I'm sure your parents want to catch up with you." He stands. "It was wonderful meeting you both."

Dad stands and shakes Alex's hand. "You, too."

"I'll walk you out." When we get back to his car, I say, "I'm so sorry. I had no idea they were here."

He pulls me close. "It's clear your parents care a great deal about you."

"A bit too much. They tend to go overboard. And that about my ex—"

"I'm not worried about it. I know the truth."

"I should get back upstairs before they come looking for me." I let out a sarcastic laugh.

"That's probably a good idea." Alex threads his hands in my hair as he kisses me goodbye. His kiss is passionate and purposeful. Without using words, his body tells me he doesn't want to let me go. "Text me your stipulations, and we'll figure it out."

"Yes, Sir. I'll try to call you tomorrow."

Alex gets into his car. I stand on the sidewalk and watch him pull away. Even though the air is warm, my body shivers at the loss of his presence. My fingers touch my lips, hoping that the memory of his kiss won't fade.

With a deep breath, I return to my apartment and my waiting parents.

Natalie

Even though I'm not a baseball fan, Yankee Stadium, the site of our commencement ceremony, is quite a sight to behold. Sitting in the bleachers, listening to the inspirational speakers, and then walking the warning track to the stage to receive my diploma is an experience I'll never forget. After the ceremony, I search the crowd trying to find Lana. She spots me first and runs over, wrapping me in a tight hug.

"Can you believe it?"

"We did it!" I squeal.

"My parents insisted your parents ride in the car with them. Alex went with Brandon. He left Viktor to bring us home so we can change," Lana says without taking a breath. "We'll meet everyone at the restaurant."

"Sounds like a good plan." I hug her, suddenly feeling very emotional. "I'm going to miss you."

"You can always change your mind and stay. I know someone else who'd like that, too."

We start walking to the parking area to find Viktor.

"Alex doesn't want us to end. He asked me to stay."

Lana stops dead in her tracks. "And? What did you say?"

"I really like him, but I have to go back. I agreed to try something long-distance, although I don't think it'll work out." I resume walking, and Lana follows. "Please don't say anything about it in front of my parents. They don't need to know."

"I get it. It's too bad, though." Lana puts her arm around me. "Alex hasn't been interested in anyone for a long time. You and he are so good together."

"Alex has women falling all over him. Every time we're at the club, they practically drool when he walks in. He can have anyone he wants."

Lana laughs. "Subs have always tried to turn his head, but it never works."

"There's Viktor." I point in his direction.

We walk the final steps to the car and climb into the backseat. The drive from the stadium back to our apartment takes forever. Traffic is the only thing I won't miss. It's a quiet ride. Neither of us wants to continue our discussion with Viktor present. I stare out the window and get lost in my thoughts.

I can't deny the fun Alex and I have had. Not to mention, he's the hottest guy I've ever met. But where can we go from here? He's not going to wait five years for a girl he only sees now and then. I learned that lesson the hard way, and I don't intend to have a repeat performance.

We finally pull up to our apartment.

"Wait here, Viktor. We won't be too long."

Svetlana amazes me. When she's with Brandon, she's the perfect submissive. She's quiet, subdued, and waits for instructions. But in her day-to-day life, she's anything but submissive.

I've always been envious of her ability to take charge in any situation. But, since becoming Alex's submissive, I envy that even more. We walk into our apartment, and I flop onto our sofa.

"Why did I agree to this? Long-distance relationships don't work." The words slip from my mouth.

Lana sits down and puts her arm around me. "Is there anything I can say to change your mind?"

"You know I can't do that." Even if my heart feels like it's being torn into two. I rest my head on her shoulder. Lana's like the sister I never had. "If I don't go home, I have to pay back the scholarship, and I don't have that kind of money."

"Alex offered to pay for it. Why don't you let him?"

We sit quietly until the buzz of Lana's phone breaks the silence. She pulls it from her purse and glances at the screen.

"It's my dad. I told him we're almost ready to leave."

"Give me a few minutes to get changed."

Five minutes later, we're walking out the door and getting back into the car. This time, I'm thankful for the traffic. It gives me some time to clear my head before we get to the restaurant. With a final turn, the Russian Tea Room comes into view, and so does Brandon, who's outside pacing back and forth.

"You're finally here." He rushes over to Lana as we step out of the car. "I was going to send out a search party to look for you." He laughs.

"Sorry. That was my fault. I needed a few minutes."

"Are you okay?"

"Not really, but I will be." I try to force a smile. "I'm a bit overwhelmed with graduation and all the changes about to happen."

"I'm always here if you need to talk," Brandon offers.

I'm grateful for the friendships I've made here. They're something I'll treasure always.

Walking into the restaurant, I'm surprised to see it's empty except for our families.

Brandon moves closer behind us and whispers, "Mr. Solonik rented the entire place for the evening."

"Somehow, that doesn't surprise me." Lana threads her arm through mine. "Let's go celebrate."

I take a deep breath and put away my melancholy mood. I owe it to everyone here and myself to have a good time tonight.

Mr. Solonik stands as we approach. "Ah, our guests of honor are finally here." He stops and kisses us on both cheeks in greeting. "I am so very proud of both my girls."

"Thank you, Mr. Solonik."

"Natalia, you must call me Maxim. We are family now." He bends closer to whisper in my ear. "Lana tells me you have entered the lifestyle."

My eyes grow wide and dart to my parents, who are beginning to walk toward us.

"Do not worry. Your parents know nothing, and it will remain that way unless you say otherwise."

"Thank you." I sigh in relief.

"Alex tells me—"

Maxim's interrupted by my mother. "Sweetheart, your father and I are so proud of you." She wraps her arms around me and squeezes tight. "The house has been so empty. We can't wait for you to come home."

I try to hide the conflict I'm fighting inside.

"Can we talk about that later? Tonight's for celebrating."

Mom steps back, crossing her arms in disapproval, while Lana shoots me a concerned look from behind her. Maxim's deep, accented voice fills the room.

"Irina and I would like to thank you all for coming to celebrate the girls' graduation. Let us sit down and begin the meal." He signals a nearby server, who turns and enters the kitchen. "I took the liberty of ordering the full menu for tonight's festivities."

"Isn't that wonderful," Mom says with a saccharine smile before taking my arm and leading me away. She whispers in my ear. "Is he always so loud and overbearing?"

The restaurant has been rearranged to make one long table. My parents are sitting on one end. I'm sure trying to stay as far away from the others as possible. There's an empty seat for me between Mom and Alex. When we reach the table, Alex stands and pulls my chair out.

Maxim has spared no expense. He really ordered everything from the menu, complete with a wine pairing for each. He encourages my parents to try tasting at least one of the wines, but they decline. They don't drink alcohol for any reason, something Maxim, being Russian, can't understand.

I try each of the wines with the various courses. I've grown to love both Russian food and wine since living with Lana.

Alex tries to engage with my parents throughout the meal. Dad seems to be enjoying their conversation despite Mom's disapproving glares.

Hoping to ease the tension, I turn to my mom. "Alex put together a small marketing campaign for the store," I say.

"We're doing fine on our own."

"Dad told Alex that business has been slow."

"It'll pick back up. It always does."

"Maybe Alex's ideas can help."

Mom shrugs.

From the look on Dad's face as he talks to Alex, he's excited about the idea. Hopefully, he'll get Mom on board. If only she'd give Alex a chance, I know she'd like him too.

The celebration continues late into the evening. Dessert is just now being served, a Russian Napoleon Cake. I take a bite of the flaky pastry and savor the rich flavors and the crème filling.

"The cake is delicious, isn't it?" I ask Mom.

"It's okay. Although I'm not sure why we couldn't have a more traditional cake."

It takes all my willpower not to roll my eyes. "It's a Russian restaurant, and this is a very traditional Russian cake." I don't understand why my parents, my mother in particular, can never enjoy anything without being critical.

While we eat dessert, a server places a shot glass in front of each of us. Another server follows behind, filling each with a clear liquid that I'm sure is Russian vodka.

"Can I have everyone's attention?" Maxim asks. "I want to propose a toast to two exceptional young ladies." He rounds the table so he's facing us. "Svetlana and Natalia, you have both worked diligently and today, we celebrate that accomplishment. I know you will both meet success in whatever ventures await you." He raises his glass, and we all follow. "*k uspekhu nashikh dvukh baryshen*. To the success of our two young ladies."

Cheers are called out from those around the table as we all take our shots. The burn of the alcohol in my throat causes me to cough. Alex laughs softly next to me. I've done Vodka shots with the Soloniks before, but I have the same reaction every time. Guess I'm a bit of a lightweight.

"Natalie, it's time we head home. We have a flight to catch tomorrow," Mom says as she stands. Dad follows her.

"You guys go ahead. I'm going to stay awhile longer."

"Don't be late, honey," Dad says before Mom can reply.

"I won't."

Maxim and Irina get up to say their goodbyes to my parents.

"I'll send a car to take you to the airport tomorrow," Maxim offers.

"We'll take a cab," Mom replies.

"It was a pleasure meeting you." Irina ignores Mom's icy attitude.

I watch my parents walk out the door and breathe a sigh of relief. Tonight could've gone much worse.

Alex

"Are you ready to go?" I ask Natalie. The party has wound down, and I want to be alone with her before she leaves for Missouri tomorrow.

"Can I say goodbye to Lana first?"

"Take your time." I know saying goodbye isn't going to be easy.

We walk across the room to where Lana and Brandon are standing. The girls embrace each other. Their tears are flowing freely.

"I can come by in the morning to see you off."

"That'll only make it harder to leave." Natalie wipes her face.

"Okay. But call me as soon as you land."

"I will."

Brandon leans in to hug her goodbye. Ordinarily, a Dominant wouldn't touch another Dominant's sub, but this is different. Brandon's like a brother to both Natalie and me.

"Keep in touch. Call us if you need anything."

Lastly, we make our way to Maxim and Irina. It's hard to watch Natalie in pain, especially knowing I could change this if only she'd let me. After the emotional goodbyes, we exit the restaurant. Natalie shivers in the cool evening air. While we wait for Viktor to bring the car around, I remove my jacket and help her slip it on.

It's after midnight when we finally get to my place. Natalie takes my hand and leads me to the bedroom. Tonight isn't about Dominance or submission. It's about showing Natalie I'm in love with her. Tears slide down her face as I help her undress. My hands caress her body, committing every curve to memory.

"No more tears, baby girl."

I make love to her slowly and gently, savoring every second I'm inside her. After we're both sated, I pull her close, and she rests her head on my chest. It doesn't take long until we both fall asleep.

"Alex, wake up." Natalie shakes me. "It's morning. We must've fallen asleep."

I open my eyes and find her rushing around the room, looking for her clothes.

"What are you doing? Come back to bed."

"I have to get back to my apartment. My flight's this afternoon, and my parents —" She checks her phone. "Ten missed calls."

Getting out of bed, I pull on my pants as she frantically swipes across the screen.

"I'm sending them a text."

"Natalie." I place my hands on her shoulders, stilling her movement. "Slow down and breathe. It's a short drive to your apartment. We'll get dressed, and I'll have you back to your place long before you need to leave for the airport."

She visibly relaxes as she leans into my touch. Unfortunately, the ringing of her phone interrupts the moment.

"It's my dad."

"Go ahead and take it. I'll finish getting dressed."

"Hi, Dad. I'm fine. I'm with my friends."

She looks at me for my reaction. I raise an eyebrow.

"We were up late talking. I meant to text you, but I guess we fell asleep."

I watch, impressed, as she slips back into her panties mid-conversation without missing a beat.

"Yes, I know what time it is. I'm already packed. I'm on my way home right now. Okay, bye."

"Are they always this overprotective?"

"They're used to being in a small town where everyone knows everyone. They tend to get a bit jumpy when they're here."

"Are you sure I can't talk you into staying?"

"I'm very sure. I'm going to miss you so much." Her green eyes fill with tears once again.

"We'll talk, and I'll fly out to see you in a few weeks." I kiss her trembling lips.

"Until we see if this will work, can we meet somewhere? I don't want my parents to know I'm still seeing you."

Her words sting, but I understand her hesitation. "I don't like it, but if that's what you need from me, we can do it that way. For now." I'll agree to just about anything not to lose her.

The beginning of our drive is silent. I'm at war with myself. I want to tell Natalie I've fallen in love with her, but I've never said those words to a woman.

"Alex. I'm sorry."

"You have nothing to be sorry for." I reach out and take her hand in mine.

"For not staying."

"There's still time to change that." I glance at her.

"I can't." She turns her head to look out the window.

We pull up to her building. I get out and walk around to help her out of the car.

"We're going to make this work. I'm not letting you get away." I kiss her deeply, wanting to make sure she remembers the feel of my body against hers. Willing her not to forget me—forget us.

"Thank you for last night." With those words, she begins backing away until just our fingertips are touching. "I'll text you when we land."

"I'll be waiting."

Then, she turns and walks toward her building. When she reaches the door, she looks back over her shoulder. Tears are streaming down her face.

It takes every ounce of discipline I possess not to go after her and carry her over my shoulder back to my apartment.

Instead, I stay rooted in place until she's out of sight.

Natalie

I NEARLY TRIP OVER A SUITCASE WHEN I WALK INTO MY APARTMENT. Mom and Dad, who are both sitting at the kitchen table, turn their heads when I walk in. I'm not used to having to answer for my whereabouts, but from the looks on their faces, they aren't going to let this go.

"I'm sorry I didn't call. We were all hanging out, and I guess we fell asleep."

"You had us very worried, young lady." Mom narrows her eyes. "We thought you might've been killed."

I let out a sarcastic laugh. "Alex was there. He'd never let anything happen to me."

"I'm not thrilled either, but she's here now," Dad says and pats Mom's hand. "Safe and sound."

Mom pulls her arm away. "Our taxi will be here any minute. I can't wait to get out of this place. Are you ready to go?"

"I have to grab something. I'll be back in a minute."

Looking around at the stripped-down room fills my heart with sadness. Everything that made it mine has been packed and shipped back to Missouri. All that's left is the furniture. This is the end of what's been one of the best times of my life. Sitting on the bed, I take a minute to reminisce about how Svetlana and I met. I was the quiet girl from a small town struggling to transition to one of the busiest cities in the world. She was a girl from another country, confident and sure of herself, and ready to experience a new culture. We were randomly paired as roommates and have been best friends ever since. I write a quick note and leave it in Lana's room.

Lana,
Thank you for being the best friend I could've ever asked for. You've changed my life in so many ways. I'll be forever grateful to you. I won't say goodbye because our friendship will never end.
~Natalie

Then, I grab my backpack and take a final look around. I can't believe six years of my life have passed so quickly, and now I'm going home.

Home.

I've always considered Northmeadow home, but if that's true, why does it feel like I'm leaving home now? It feels like I'm returning to someplace I'm afraid I'll no longer fit in. So many contradicting thoughts and feelings are a jumbled mess in my head. I slowly make my way back to my parents, who impatiently wait at the door.

"I'm ready," I say and muster a smile.

"Good," Mom says. "Let's go."

When we get outside, the cab is already waiting for us. Dad puts our luggage in the trunk, and the three of us pile into the back seat. I watch out the window as we pull away from my apartment and wipe a stray tear from my face.

"I know you think you don't want to leave this city, but it wasn't that long ago you felt the same about Northmeadow," Mom says.

I nod.

"This was just one chapter, and now it's over. It's time to turn the page and move on." She pats my shoulder as if her words magically make everything better.

"What if I'm not ready for it to be over?"

"Are you talking about that man?" Mom sighs.

"Yes."

"Honey, I understand why you *think* you like him. He's successful and, some would say, handsome. It feels good when a man like that pays attention to you, but he's not like us."

Dad leans forward and peers at me around Mom's shoulder. "Long-distance relationships are difficult, sweetheart."

"I know, but—"

Mom interrupts. "And a certain young man is waiting for you to come home."

"Who?"

"Thomas."

"Tommy Moore?" I roll my eyes. "We broke up, remember?"

"He comes into the pharmacy every week. Thomas has grown into a fine young man, and he can't wait to see you."

Thankfully, we pull up at JFK, and our conversation is interrupted.

I never told my parents why Tommy and I split, and I don't plan to now. I never want to talk about that night again.

I sit in the back of my parent's car as Dad drives the familiar windy roads through the Ozark Mountains. We pass a herd of deer grazing on the side of the road. It's a sight that was once a part of my everyday life but one I haven't seen in a long time. As we get closer to Northmeadow, familiar farms come into view.

Mr. Johnson is tending his cows in the field. When I was a little girl, I loved when we drove by the dairy farms. Dad would slow the car just like he's doing now so I could see the new calves in the fields with their moms.

Then, the scenery changes from farmland to the town's streets. It's late Sunday afternoon, which means nothing's open. The roads are quiet and empty. It's a foreign feeling after living in New York City for so long—it's never quiet there. I pull out my phone to text Alex.

Me: We landed a little while ago. We're almost home.

Alex: Glad you got there safely, but I miss you already.

Me: I miss you too.

Alex: Will you be home at nine?

Me: Small town, remember? Everything's closed today. LOL, I'll be home.

Alex: Good, I'll video call you then.

Me: Can't wait. TTYL

As we make the last turn for home, I shoot a quick text to Lana, letting her know I arrived safely.

Dad pulls into our driveway, and I look up. My mouth hangs open in shock. Strung from end to end on my parent's front porch is a large, brightly colored banner that reads *Welcome Home, Natalie.*

Bouquets of rainbow-colored balloons are tied across the rail. And, there, standing on the steps, is Tommy Moore. He's dressed in dark jeans and his old Northmeadow High Football T-shirt. His dirty blond hair is cut short, and he's wearing a huge grin.

"Surprise." My mother beams with pride.

I'm speechless, and not in a good way.

Natalie

I'M FROZEN IN SHOCK AS TOMMY CONFIDENTLY STRIDES TOWARD THE car and opens my door. He reaches in, grabbing my hands, pulling me out and into him.

"Welcome home, Natalie." He leans in to kiss me, but I turn my head just in time for the kiss to land on my cheek. "I've really missed you." He bounces back without hesitation.

"Umm. Wow. I don't know quite what to say."

Mom gets out of the car and hurries over to Tommy. "You did a great job with the decorations." She pulls him in for a big hug.

"Thanks, Mrs. C. I'm so glad she's finally home."

I watch their interaction. It's like a bad movie playing out in front of me. Except it's not a movie. It's really happening.

"I know you just got home, but can I steal you for a walk?"

"I don't think—"

"Of course you can," Mom answers for me. "It'll give you two kids a chance to catch up."

Tommy grabs my hand, but my feet are lead weights, unwilling to move. His hand holding mine feels wrong. It isn't the hand I want—it isn't Alex. Tommy gives a tug, forcing me to move, leaving my feet with no choice but to obey.

We walk behind my parents' house to a well-worn path alongside fields that used to be farmland. Although they don't look like they've been planted for many years. When we get to a familiar wooded area, I'm hit with an onslaught of memories. All the times Tommy and I snuck off here while we were in high school.

He was my first boyfriend, my first kiss, and the boy I lost my virginity to. Everyone expected we'd get married. Once upon a time, I expected that too, but then he shattered that dream and my heart.

80

Tommy stops walking and turns to face me. "Natalie, I know things ended badly between us."

"You could say that." The hurt I so carefully buried bursts through my chest, reopening old wounds. "At one time, it was you and me against the world," I yell. "Until I came home and found you in bed with my best friend. Seeing the two of you like that ripped my heart out."

He pulls my unwilling body against his. "And I'm sorry for that. I was lonely. It'll never happen again, I swear it."

"You think saying you're sorry will make it go away?" I pull out of his hold.

"It was a long time ago, Nat. I thought we moved past it."

"Tommy, I—"

"You're back now. We're together again." His voice is desperate, pleading. "Things'll be different this time."

"What you and Ashlynn did is unforgivable. We are not *together*, and we never will be." I start walking toward home.

"Natalie, wait."

I spin around and cross my arms in frustration. "What?"

Tommy reaches into his pants pocket and pulls out a prescription bottle. He takes out a tiny white pill and swallows it.

"What did you just take?"

He leans up against a nearby tree. "After we broke up, I got hurt in a game. I couldn't play anymore and lost my scholarship." Tommy holds up the bottle giving it a shake. "Now and then, I need a little something to take the edge off, so I have these guys."

My parents mentioned something about Tommy getting hurt, but I didn't want to hear about him, so I never asked for details. "Have you seen a doctor? I don't think popping pills is a good long-term solution, do you?"

"I've seen a doctor, more than one doctor." He pushes off the tree and closes the distance between us. "There's nothing else they can do. Let it go. I'm fine."

"Whatever you say. I'm going home."

"I'm right behind you."

When we get back to the house, my mother's just putting dinner on the table. "I had your Aunt Delia stop by and throw a casserole in the oven. You two are just in time."

"I'm not hungry. I think I'll go and unpack."

"You'll do no such thing, young lady." My mother scolds me like I'm a child. "You have a dinner guest."

"*You* have a dinner guest," I answer, a hint of sarcasm in my voice.

"Natalie, you'll not speak to your mother like that," Dad says. "You will apologize right now."

In a matter of seconds, I feel myself shrinking back into the subservient girl I was before I went away. The perfect daughter who did as she was told and would never defy her parents.

"I'm sorry for being disrespectful."

Dinner is excruciating. It's my turn to be the silent one, the outcast at the table.

Tommy and my parents carry on as though they haven't missed a beat. It's like they've been talking all this time, pretending we're still a couple. Although I didn't think Tommy would ever leave, dinner finally winds down. He says his goodbyes, promising he'll see me soon.

After Tommy leaves, Dad retires to the living room to watch the nightly news while Mom and I clean up.

"It's so good to have you home, honey," she says as she puts the last plate in the cupboard. "And seeing you back with Tommy, well, everything's perfect now."

"Tommy and I aren't together." I fold the dishrag and set it on the counter. "We broke up a long time ago. I've moved on."

"You left him." Mom reaches behind her, untying her apron. "You should be thankful he still wants you. Most girls around here would jump at the chance to be with Thomas."

"They can have him." I check the time on my phone. It's eight forty-five. "I'm feeling a bit off. Probably jet lag. I'm going to get to bed early."

"Please be smart, Natalie. That man from the city is not right for you." She kisses my cheek. "I love you and want you to be happy. I'm sure you'll see reason after having a good night's rest."

"Night, Mom." I don't argue. She isn't ready to see things my way.

"Night, Daddy." I kiss him on the cheek as I pass through the living room on my way upstairs.

Once I'm in my room, I close the door and lean against it. I feel like I've entered a time warp. I haven't been in my bedroom in nearly two years, yet everything is exactly where I left it. The flowered sheets and pink ruffled bedspread from when I was younger still dress my twin bed. I pick up a pillow and smell the familiar scent of the laundry detergent my mother makes. She must've made sure the sheets were freshly washed.

My stuffed animals and dolls sit neatly on my chair in the corner. I walk to my dresser and run my fingers over the pictures taped to the mirror—pictures of my youth. Carefully, I pull one off to look at it closer.

It's a picture of Tommy and me on the first day of our senior year in high school. He was so handsome, tall, and muscular from working out. I remember how lucky I felt to be dating the starting quarterback. Tommy has his arm around me, and I'm staring up at him, a girl head over heels in love. I set the picture on my dresser and pull another down. This one's from the end of my senior year. I'm standing with a group of my friends, including Ashlynn. We're all in our caps and gowns.

Each of us was young and naïve. And with very different dreams for our futures. None of the girls in this picture ever left Northmeadow. We've led very different lives. I'm not the same girl I was then. Will they like the person I am today? Will they accept me back into their circle? Do I even want to be accepted by them?

My phone buzzes in my pocket, bringing a smile to my face. I set the photo on my dresser and take out my phone to answer the call. Cell service is spotty here, so it takes a second for the image of Alex to pop up on the screen. He's sitting in front of his windows with the city lights illuminating the night sky behind him.

"Hi," I say and sit down on my bed. "Nice view."

"I thought you might be missing it tonight."

"I can't believe how much I miss it already."

"Do you miss anything else?" He raises an eyebrow.

"Hmm—let me think," I tease. "I miss Lana. And there's this guy. I forget his name." I flash him a cheeky grin.

He puts his hand over his heart in mock surprise. "You forgot me already?" I could never forget Alex, and that's part of the problem. If this long-distance thing doesn't work, I don't know how I'll be able to get over him. "How was your flight home?"

"Pretty uneventful. Mom talked my ear off. She made sure I was up to date on all the Northmeadow gossip." I roll my eyes, and Alex laughs.

"What are your plans for tomorrow?"

"For starters." I flip the camera so Alex can see my bedroom. "I need to make this room fit for an adult. Other than that, not much."

Conversation has always come easy for us, but tonight, I'm at a loss for anything to talk about. The divide I was afraid of is already rearing its ugly head. This is why I didn't want to tell anyone about us. I don't see how we can make it work.

"Natalie, stop biting your nails," Alex reprimands.

"Sorry, I didn't even realize I was doing it."

"What's bothering you?" He leans forward, bringing his face closer to the camera.

"Nothing."

"That's not true. Talk to me."

I look down, trying to figure out how to put my feelings into words. "I'm terrified of the distance between us. I don't see how we're going to make this work."

"Right now, we take it one step at a time," Alex reassures me.

"How can I be your submissive when we don't live in the same city, the same state?" I quickly catch my error. "Sorry for raising my voice, Sir."

"I forgive you. We *will* make this work. I told you we can fly to see each other whenever we want."

I remain silent, trying to process his words. He makes it sound so easy, but selfishly, I want more than a weekend visit every now and then. I want the whole experience. I'm not ready to face what that means, so I attempt to change the subject.

"May I ask you a personal question, Sir?" In the few months we've been together, he hasn't told me much about his life or family. I know it isn't typically shared in a contractual relationship. Still, I'm hoping we're at a place where he'll share it with me.

"You can ask me anything." He sits back and relaxes.

"How did you get involved in the lifestyle?"

"My parents. My dad and mom were involved in the lifestyle. Until she passed away."

"I'm sorry." I didn't know he'd lost his mom. My heart hurts seeing the pained look on his face and knowing I'm not there to comfort him. "How old were you?"

"I was twenty-two. She died from breast cancer." He shakes his head. "I knew from an early age I had dominant traits."

I'm starting to think everyone but me was raised in this lifestyle.

"Were you able to talk to your father about it?"

"Yes, my father supported my interest. We lived just outside Seattle, where there are several very active BDSM communities in the area. My father introduced me to his friends. I developed a great respect and appreciation for their ideals and what they stood for. I enjoyed being a part of the lifestyle for several years. Until Mom died. After seeing what Dad went through losing her, I decided I wasn't interested in any relationship—BDSM or otherwise."

"What changed your mind?"

"A few months after I came to New York. Maxim walked into my office and hired me to do a marketing campaign for him."

"Maxim? Lana's dad?"

"Yes, Lana's dad. After I took his account, we spent quite a bit of time together here and in Russia." He closes his eyes as if lost in the memories. "Maxim was the one who reintroduced me to the lifestyle. Helped me find my way."

"Why me?" I don't understand what this amazing man sees in a twenty-four-year-old girl from a small town in Missouri with no real experience in this lifestyle. "Why do you want to do this with me? Especially now that I'm so far away."

"I'm drawn to you. There's a connection between us. Do you feel it, too?"

"I do," I say softly.

What scares me is I feel it too much. I fell in love with him even though he told me this wouldn't become anything more.

"Do you still consent to move forward? I don't know what it'll look like. I wish I had all the answers, but I don't." He shrugs, and I glimpse something I've never seen before in him—uncertainty.

Even though I don't see this working out, I can't say no. I don't want to say no.

"Yes, I consent to that."

"I have some ideas for our Dom/sub dynamic. I emailed you a copy. We don't have to do everything all at once."

I reach over the side of my bed and grab my bag, pulling my laptop out. Once it's fired up, I open my email to see what he sent. There's a list of suggested rules and modifications to our Dom/sub contract. We read through the list and agree on a time for me to call him each morning to let him know my plans for the day. Every night, at nine, we'll video call each other. Alex promises to fly out one weekend a month. My schedule and finances will determine when I can visit him in New York.

"This is a good starting place," Alex says. "Then we can see where it goes on its own.

Having these rules in place makes our relationship feel more stable. I close my laptop and yawn.

"You look tired, baby girl."

"I am. It's been a long day. I don't want to, but I really should go. I have to work at Dad's store for a few hours tomorrow."

"I have a full day, too. I'll call you tomorrow night."

"I can't wait. Night, Alex."

"Sleep well, baby girl."

Natalie

The summer has flown by, and as per usual here, nothing interesting has happened. I've been able to sneak away to see Alex twice—saying goodbye was awful and gets harder each time.

It's August now, and in Missouri, that means oppressive heat and humidity, made worse by the lack of air conditioning in my parent's house. Although I've just showered, I'm already sweating, and my curls are a frizzy mess.

Come on, hair, not today. I struggle to pin up the unruly strands. In an hour, I'm meeting with Mr. Meadows, the principal of Northmeadow High, who also happens to be my new boss.

Finally, I get my hair secured in a loose bun and put on some make-up. I'm attempting to look polished and professional. I'm not sure why I'm going through the trouble. I'm only going to sweat it off.

Since my job at the school doesn't officially start for a few more weeks, I've picked up as many shifts at Dad's pharmacy as possible. Between that and the small amount of money I saved while I was away, I managed to pick up a used car. A 2002 silver Honda Civic I've nicknamed Rhonda the Honda. She's not fancy and doesn't even have power windows, but she runs and gets me where I need to go. Best of all, she's mine. My next goal—an apartment. Living with my parents is not something I can do long-term. Suddenly, I'm a teenager under my parent's thumb again. They question every move I make and give me *advice* on what I should or shouldn't be doing. It's driving me crazy and putting a strain on our relationship. I give myself a once over in the mirror before I head out the door and get into Rhonda.

Aside from the years I was gone for school, I've never lived outside Northmeadow. As I drive through town, I realize absolutely nothing has changed. The same mom-and-pop shops with their run-down storefronts line Main Street. There are no chain stores or restaurants. The residents fought hard to keep them out of town. It's both positive and negative. Small, local-owned businesses have kept their doors open, but just barely.

The summer months bring tourists from Finn Lake. It's that revenue most businesses rely on to get them through the rest of the year. Year-round residents who don't own a business in town work on their farms, often struggling to make ends meet. It's a stark contrast to New York City with its booming companies, crowds of people, and overabundance of money.

I make the turn into the parking lot of my old high school. It feels odd to pull into a spot designated for faculty. Resting my head against the seat, I close my eyes and take a few calming breaths. When I graduated high school, I was the only one in my class leaving the state for college. Heck, I was the only girl pursuing a college degree. Most were content to stay here, marry a local boy, and have his babies. Once upon a time, I planned to marry a local boy, but not until after I had a chance to experience life outside Northmeadow. See how well that worked out, Natalie? This town was once my home, and this was my dream job. I wanted to serve the youth in my community. But things changed—I've changed.

I can't help wondering if I could've served the youth in New York City with the same satisfaction. None of that really matters, though. I'm locked into this position for the next five years. "Six years flew by in the city. These will go by just as fast." I say the words aloud, trying to convince myself they're true. But the excitement I once felt when I imagined this moment is gone. Taking a deep breath, I turn off the ignition, grab my bag, and step out of the car. Using the side view mirror, I straighten my black skirt and silky white blouse. Despite everything, I want to make a favorable impression.

Instinct urges me to use the student entrance, but I continue past and walk to the building's front instead.

I've never stopped and looked at the historic building that houses the school. I shield my eyes from the sun and look up at it. Four sections make up the three-story stone structure. Each floor holds four sets of four windows that sit in perfect symmetry. Drawing the eye to the center of the building are four large columns that flank the sides of the main entrance. The building is typical of classical revival architecture—something I learned about during my time in the city.

One by one, I walk up the granite steps until I reach the main door and pull it open. It's a lot heavier than it looks. Stepping inside, I'm hit with a sense of déjà vu. The familiar school smell brings me back to my student days. It feels like I walked these halls yesterday instead of six years ago. The building is empty, except for a few custodians who appear to be freshening up the paint on some lockers while others clean up the desks. The click of my high-heeled shoes echoes in the hallway as I make my way to the main office.

"Excuse me, miss. Can I help you?" a male voice calls from behind me.

Startled, I turn around. An older and slightly rounder version of the Mr. Meadows I remember from my high school days stands with his hands on his hips, wearing track shorts, a tank top, and a baseball cap. Guess I'm a little overdressed.

"I was just heading to your office." I walk back toward him.

"And you are?"

"Natalie Clarke."

Do I have the wrong day for our appointment?

His forehead wrinkles, and his eyes narrow as he takes in my appearance. "I didn't recognize you."

"I guess it has been a few years."

An awkward silence lingers between us. The warm feelings I initially had when I walked in have disappeared, replaced with an icy unwelcomeness. Ms. Campbell told me she was getting a lot of pushback from adding a therapist to the faculty.

"Your office is this way. Follow me." He turns and takes long strides down the hallway.

I do my best to keep up with him but fall behind. Besides being nearly a foot shorter, I also have a skirt and heels to contend with. We pass classrooms that were once a daily home for me. I peek into them, hoping to rekindle the feeling of belonging. Instead, I'm left feeling like an outsider—an intruder.

"This is your office." He waves his hand at the open door. "You'll notice your window has been frosted. Something about maintaining privacy."

"That's perfect, thank you." I smile.

"It wasn't my doing," he says sharply. Digging into his pocket, he pulls out a key. "This belongs to you."

I reach out to take the key, which he hesitantly hands over before taking the first step into my office. The walls have recently been painted a crisp, clean, and oh-so-plain cream. The smell of fresh paint lingers in the air. Scuff marks from the many shoes that have walked in and out of the room mar the tile floor.

A standard high school-issue metal desk sits in the room's center with a chair on each side. The wall behind the desk boasts a large window overlooking Main Street. It offers the natural light this otherwise poorly lit room needs. I'm surprised at how spacious it is. With a bit of creativity, I'll be able to transform this bare space into something special.

Mr. Meadows walks past me, heading straight toward the chair behind the desk.

"Let's go over the paperwork, shall we?" he says as he lowers himself onto the padded leather chair.

Feeling intimidated, I sit across from him in the simple wooden chair. The same as those found in the hall outside the principal's office. The cushion is worn and has long since disintegrated. I add it to my mental list of things that need to be redone. I'm unsure where to put my bag, so I hold it on my lap and fidget with the straps. It'll help keep me from biting my nails.

Mr. Meadows opens a red binder that's sitting on the desk and takes out a stack of papers. He flips through them, mumbling to himself before he glances up at me.

"Looks like your clearances have come back and are in order. Did you bring a copy of your licensure?"

I reach into my bag and pull out a folder containing my paperwork.

"Here you go."

He quickly skims the paper. "This looks like it's okay. I need your signature on a few pages, and then we'll be done." He slides a stack of papers and a pen across the desk.

Seeing no other choice, I set my bag on the floor to free my hands. I pick up the first paper and begin to read through it.

Tap. Tap. Tap.

The impatient rhythm of Mr. Meadow's pen tapping on the desk urges me to move quickly. I glance up and see Mr. Meadow looking at his watch. Sensing his impatience, I try to read as fast as possible without missing anything important. Don't bite your nails. I struggle to keep my nerves in check.

"Ms. Clarke." His voice is sharp. "These are just your standard employment papers."

"I'm sure they are, but I'd feel more comfortable reading through them before signing. I'm sure you understand."

"As long as this doesn't take too long." He looks at his watch again. "I have another appointment in ten minutes."

I nod in understanding and skim the last few pages, barely reading them. The final paper restates the requirement of remaining employed by the Northmeadow School District for five years, at which time a new contract may be negotiated. Terminating employment before five years will result in immediate repayment of all scholarship money. With trembling hands, I grab the pen and sign my name.

"Very well then," Mr. Meadows says as he grabs the papers and taps them on the desk. "Your schedule and employee handbook are in here." He points to the red binder before making his way to the door.

I follow after him. "Am I able to redecorate the office?"

He spins around with a less-than-amused look on his face. "Isn't it to your liking?"

"It's fine, but it's kinda plain. I was hoping to make it a bit more inviting. Maybe add some artwork to the walls, an area rug, and bean bag seating. To help the kids feel more comfortable."

He crosses his arms in front of him and tilts his head as if trying to figure me out. Ticking from the clock, usually unheard, echoes in the absence of other noise.

"You can do as you see fit." He lowers his hands and begins to walk away, pausing to add, "But it will need to come out of your pocket. We don't supply a *decorating* budget."

"I understand. Thank you." It feels as though I've won a small victory.

He shakes his head and mutters as he walks down the hall. I close the door and lean against it. It doesn't surprise me that Mr. Meadows isn't thrilled with my being added to his faculty. He made that known the day I was offered the scholarship.

It was one week before my high school graduation. Our community was still suffering the devastating effects of both Evan and Michael's suicide the year before. The world was changing, and Northmeadow wasn't immune to those changes. Our young people were experiencing problems the older generations either didn't face or refused to acknowledge, and it was taking its toll.

After losing my brother, I decided I didn't want to work at my dad's pharmacy like we'd planned. Instead, I wanted to pursue psychology with the hopes of working with young people and preventing another tragedy. My sights were set on New York University. In my opinion, it would give me a chance to experience life outside of Northmeadow while getting a solid education. After graduating, I would return, marry Tommy, and work with our young people.

I applied and was accepted. Even though I was eligible for financial aid, it wasn't enough to cover the expenses. My parents weren't supportive of my going away to school and refused to help. I'd just about given up on my dreams until I was summoned to a meeting in the principal's office. When I arrived, Mr. Meadows was there along with Ms. Campbell, the district superintendent. I sat across from them, not knowing the importance of this meeting on my future.

"How are you today, Natalie?" Ms. Campbell asks

"Today's a pretty good day."

"I'm glad to hear that." She smiles. "I'm sure you're wondering why I've asked you here.

"Yes, I am."

After Michael died, Ms. Campbell stepped in as a sort of counselor. She allowed me to talk about Michael and Evan without fear of judgment for my feelings—feelings I could not express at home. I had the best childhood, filled with so many happy memories. The four of us were very close. My parents were never wealthy, but they made sure Michael and I never wanted for anything. My parent's relationship was one I always looked up to. They demonstrated love and respect for each other, but they turned ice-cold after Michael died.

I was lost without my brother, yet I was forbidden to discuss anything about him at home. My parents took his pictures down and even emptied his room. It was like he never existed. I don't know how I would have gotten through that first year without Ms. Campbell's help.

During our meeting, Ms. Campbell told me she'd heard whispers from the student body about other issues, including violence and recreational drug usage. Other young people were struggling with issues related to their sexual orientation—something our conservative religious town found abhorrent.

Our conversation was raw and honest and has remained with me through the years.

"Natalie, as you're all too aware, our young people are struggling," Ms. Campbell says.

"Yes." I look down, trying to hold back the tears threatening to fall.

"Your generation is dealing with issues most of us," –She gestures between Mr. Meadows and herself— "just don't understand."

Mr. Meadows sits back in his chair and crosses his arms. I sense a growing tension between the two adults in the room.

"Would you be willing to share with Mr. Meadows why you're so passionate about pursuing higher education?"

I'm uneasy sharing something so personal with him, but Ms. Campbell gives me an encouraging nod to ease my hesitation.

"I want to study to become a therapist. I don't want anyone else to go through what Michael and Evan did." I pause and swallow over the growing lump in my throat. "I don't want anyone else's family to lose someone they love. I don't share the beliefs of my family or community. I believe the heart can't help who it loves."

Mr. Meadows mumbles under his breath, earning a disapproving glance from Ms. Campbell.

Ms. Campbell sits forward on her chair. "Natalie, if we don't do something, we will lose more youth to tragedies I believe are avoidable."

Mr. Meadows shifts, clearly uncomfortable with the conversation.

Ms. Campbell turns her attention to him. "Jacob, will you excuse us for a few minutes?"

A vein pulses in Mr. Meadow's neck, the only outward sign of his anger. Finally, he walks out of his office, closing the door a little too forcefully.

"Natalie, I know you applied and were accepted to New York University."

"Yes, ma'am."

"Have you replied to your acceptance letter yet?"

"Not yet. But I'm going to have to decline."

"The school board has talked and agreed. We're prepared to make you a generous offer." Her face lights up with excitement. "We're offering a scholarship to cover the full cost of your education in exchange for your agreement to work in the district for five years."

It took a few minutes for her words to sink in fully. "You'll pay for everything?" I ask, still not believing what I think I heard.

"Yes. Tuition, books, room, and board." She pulls a paper from a folder I hadn't noticed lying on the desk. "It's all right here. If you agree, you only need to sign the contract." She hands me the paper.

At the time, I had every intention of living in Northmeadow and marrying Tommy. However, he'd be away at school on a football scholarship, and now I'd also have the opportunity to get my degree. It was a dream come true. Since I was eighteen, I didn't need my parent's permission and didn't think twice. I signed the contract right then and there.

Ms. Campbell has had a significant impact on my life. We've kept in touch over the years. She's the only person, aside from Lana, who knows everything that happened with Tommy. I've told her about Alex, although I've been hesitant to tell her everything. She knows I've been secretly seeing Alex all summer, something neither Alex nor Ms. Campbell is thrilled about. They both think I need to tell my parents the truth. Of course, that's much easier said than done. They don't have to live with them.

I grab my bag off the floor and dig through it to find my cell phone. After taking pictures of my office, I send the images and a text to Lana.

Me: Before pictures. Drab and boring, a typical US high school office.

Lana: Looks similar to my school in St. Petersburg. Please tell me you can change it?

Me: Online shopping is calling my name, LOL. How's it going with the job hunt?

Lana: I have another interview today. Fingers crossed, I get hired soon. Guess what...

Me: What?

Lana: I was going to call you tonight, but I can't wait. Brandon asked me to move in, and I said yes.

Me: OMG! I'm so happy for you.

Although I'm happy for my friend, I'm sad for myself. If I'd stayed in the city, would that be Alex and me?

Lana: How's everything there?

It's awful. My parents are smothering me. My ex-boyfriend won't leave me alone, and the man I love is halfway across the country.

Me: Everything's good. Did you get the invitation to the birthday party my parents are throwing for me?

Lana: I did, but we won't be able to make it.

Me: I knew it was a long shot. It was supposed to be a surprise party, but Dad spilled the beans.

Lana: I wish we were able to fly in. I'm sorry. Is Alex going to be there?

Me: I didn't invite him. They still don't know I'm seeing him, remember?

Lana: Oh yeah. I'm about to walk into an interview. I'll call you tonight, and you can try to explain why you won't tell them.

Me: Good luck.

I sink into the chair behind my desk. It's much more comfortable than the other one, and I set my phone down. The red binder draws my attention.

Opening the cover, I flip through the pages, beginning to familiarize myself with policy and procedure. When I look at my phone, I see two hours have passed. After I mark my page, I close the binder and slide it into my bag.

With a final look around the room, I lock up and head home to do some shopping.

Natalie

THE MINUTE I WALK IN THE DOOR, I KICK OFF MY HEELS AND THROW MY bag on the couch. Moments like this, when both my parents are working, and I have the house to myself, remind me how much I miss living on my own. Another thing I miss—coffee shops. If I want an afternoon pick-me-up, it's either the diner or homebrewed.

Opening the cupboard, I pull out a paper filter and push it into the plastic receptacle of my parents' ancient Mr. Coffee machine. After spooning in the grounds, I turn it on and wait. "Maybe I'll get them a Keurig for Christmas," I say aloud. "As if they'd ever use it."

My parents prefer the tried and true methods of doing things. It was only right before I left for college they stopped using the stainless-steel coffee pot that perks on the stovetop. They haven't thrown it out. It now sits on the windowsill above the kitchen sink with fresh-picked flowers in it.

While the aroma of coffee fills the kitchen, I busy myself putting away the dishes Mom left on the plastic drying rack. I always hated handwashing. It was such a treat when Lana and I got our apartment, and I finally had a dishwasher. Mental note—when apartment shopping, make sure there's a dishwasher.

Ten minutes later, the coffee is finally ready. I pluck my favorite mug off the accordion rack under the cupboards and pour the liquid gold. Add a little sugar and creamer, and the coffee is perfect. Then, I grab my things and go upstairs. Setting everything down on my desk, I strip off my work clothes, exchanging them for shorts and a tank top that exposes my now-toned abdomen.

Several months ago, Lana and I decided to use the gym NYU provides for its students. We started getting up early to work out before class. The physical changes have helped me view my body more positively.

Since being home, I haven't exercised at all. I'll have to get back to it, or I won't be wearing clothes like this for long.

The unpacked boxes in the corner of the room draw my attention. I hoped to have my own place by now, but that hasn't worked out as planned. I've saved enough money to pay for a few months' rent. Unlike in Manhattan, where there's always real estate available, I haven't been able to find an apartment in Northmeadow. But I'm not giving up. Something has to open up eventually.

Meanwhile, somewhere in this mess are books and decorations I want for my office. The goal for this afternoon is to go through the boxes and find everything.

As I stare at the task ahead, I realize I should've done a better job when I packed. At the time, my only thought was to get everything in a box and shipped. I feel overwhelmed looking at the pile of twenty boxes.

Nothing's going to get done just standing here. So, I grab the nearest box and start rummaging through. As I do, I separate things into two piles—one for my office and the second to be repacked. I'm retaping the boxes when my phone chimes. Alex hasn't texted all day, and I'm anxious to talk to him, so I grab the phone quickly.

Unknown: I'm picking you up at five.

Me: I think you have the wrong number.

Unknown: Is this Natalie?

Me: Yes

Unknown: Then I have the right number.

Me: Who is this?

Unknown: It's me.

Me: I'm gonna need a little more to go on than *me*.

Unknown: Tommy

I roll my eyes. Oh my God, go away already.

Me: How did you get my number?

Tommy: Your mom.

She and I will need to talk about not giving out my phone number.

Me: I'm not going out with you tonight.

Tommy: Yes, you are. Be ready by five.

Me: No.

Tommy: I've already talked to your parents. We're going out tonight.

Already talked to my parents. Is he for real?

Me: I'm not in grade school. You can't ask my parents for a play date with me.

Tommy: Already did. You better be ready.

Me: I'm not going out with you.

Tommy: See you soon.

I drop my head in my hands. How do I get rid of him? He obviously doesn't understand that we're over.

Done.

Never getting back together.

I decide not to waste all afternoon arguing with him through texts. I have more important stuff to do. I'll deal with him if he shows up. Until then, I have money to spend and shopping to do.

The sound of gravel crunching in the driveway grabs my attention. Checking my phone, I see it's four fifty-five. Wow, I didn't realize I was shopping for that long.

Curious to see who it is, I pad across the worn-out carpet on my bedroom floor and pull aside the ruffled purple curtains to look outside.

Tommy's beat-up red Chevy pick-up is in front of my house. I race across my room and slam the door. This is ending right now. I take the steps two at a time, intending to stop Tommy before he makes it onto the porch. He can turn that truck right back around because I'm not going anywhere with him.

What I can't see from my room becomes apparent when I open the front door. Tommy's helping my mom out of the passenger seat. Mom looks up. The smile fades from her face when she sees me.

"You aren't going out dressed like that?"

"I'm not going out."

"You and Tommy have a date." She smiles at him.

Tommy leans against the rusty old truck. He wears a smug look as he listens to our exchange.

"Tommy told you wrong." I cross my arms.

"Excuse us a minute, dear," Mom says to Tommy before she hurries up the steps and grabs my arm, forcing me to follow her into the house. "Stop acting like an ungrateful child. That young man out there is crazy about you."

Sure that I've misunderstood her because we've already gone over this at least a hundred times, I ask,

"Excuse me?"

"You don't live in the big city anymore," my mother says, her voice raised. She narrows her eyes. "You need to get off whatever high horse you climbed on while you were off playing house." She uses air quotes to emphasize *playing house*. "You're back home, where you belong, and you need to start acting like it. Now, march upstairs and put on something presentable. You will not keep him waiting."

My mouth hangs open. I'm speechless. I've only been home for a few months, and already I find myself fighting the same battles I'd gone through in my teenage years.

Mom was always strict, but after Michael died, her actions became suffocating. She refused to acknowledge I was an adult and could make my own decisions.

"Now, Natalie." She crosses her arms and taps her foot on the hardwood floor.

At this moment, I wish I was more like Lana. That I had enough confidence to stand my ground, especially with my parents. It was so much easier while I was in the city and had Alex by my side. But I don't have that support now. It's only my parents and me, and I'm all they have left. My downfall has always been not wanting to disappoint them—to a fault.

This time, my upbringing wins. Although I want to scream and stomp, I quietly slip back into the role of a dutiful daughter.

As I walk up the steps and into my childhood bedroom, I feel the independence and self-confidence I'd gained while living in the city slip away. What's worse is I'm helpless to stop it.

Tommy

I FOLLOW CHARLOTTE CLARKE'S GAZE TO HER FRONT PORCH, WHERE Natalie stands in tiny denim shorts and a cutoff shirt. Her body is smoking hot and on display, especially when she crosses her arms, pushing her tits up higher. Even the daggers she shoots my way does nothing to dispel the arousal in my jeans. Tonight's going to be more fun than I anticipated.

Charlotte and Natalie argue while I lean against my truck, amused by the scene. I know I have her parents on my side, which means Natalie will come around. She'd never defy her parents.

While I wait for Natalie to come back out, my hands shake, and sweat forms on my forehead. Yesterday, I saw the doctor and convinced him I'm still suffering. He's a pain in the ass, nagging me to try physical therapy and acupuncture. This time, I was able to use living in Northmeadow and its lack of resources as an excuse with the promise I'd look outside of town for something. I'll spout whatever shit he wants to hear to get a new prescription.

I grab my Oxy bottle and swallow two pills, craving the high they give me. I need to feel good tonight because I'm taking Natalie to the county fair. We used to go every year. I'm sure this will remind Natalie how much she loves me, and if I'm right —and I know I'm right—before the night's over, I'll be buried balls deep between her legs, just like old times.

Natalie doesn't keep me waiting long. Within a few minutes, she's walking down the porch steps in the same denim shorts, but she now wears a black t-shirt instead of her half-shirt. I open the door and offer my hand to help her into my truck. My little wildcat refuses my help and climbs in on her own. Smiling, I close the door behind her, walk around to the driver's side, and get in.

The fair hasn't changed. Food vendors are set up, creating a virtual maze offering anything fried and on a stick. Natalie's favorite was always the stuffed pretzel stand.

"Can I have two steak and cheese stuffed pretzels?" I ask the kid behind the window. He takes my money and hands me the paper-wrapped food.

"Here ya go," I say and proudly hand one to Natalie.

"Thanks," she answers quietly and takes the offered food.

"We'll sit over here and eat." I lead her to an empty table.

She nibbles at the pretzel while staring off into the crowd.

"It must be nice to be home," I say, trying to get her attention. She's acting distant, and I don't know why.

"It's great," she mumbles.

"I'm glad you're back," I say placing my hand on her thigh.

She pulls her leg away. "Tommy, don't."

"You never had a problem with me touching you before."

"You lost that right when you started screwing my best friend." She stands up, throwing away her uneaten food. "I've moved on. I'm seeing someone else."

"Excuse me?" Charlotte didn't tell me this. What the hell?

"I have a boyfriend. Someone I met in the city."

I stand up, knowing I have to plan my next move carefully. It's obvious those people have poisoned her mind, but I'll fix it. I'll fix her.

"Come on." I take her hand. "Let's go ride some rides."

She tries to resist, but I leave her no choice. She's forced to follow me. We stop at the ticket booth, where I buy a few books of tickets.

"Tommy, I don't want to go on any rides," she protests.

"Loosen up. It'll be fun."

Natalie is compliant, something I've always loved about her. Anything I wanted, she always did. I'm confident tonight won't end any differently. We're riding the Ferris Wheel, and it's our turn to be stuck on top.

The entire fairground, surrounded by the mountains, is in full view, but I'm only looking at the view sitting next to me. I put my arm around Natalie and pull her close. This time, she can't resist. She's always been afraid of heights and has nowhere to go. With my other hand, I turn her face to meet mine and kiss her.

"Tommy." She pushes against my chest. "Stop."

"Be quiet. You're going to make a scene."

"If you don't stop. I'll scream."

"Relax," I say and drop my hand.

Patience that's what I need. Patience and a few more pills. I pull the bottle out of my pocket and pop another pill, knowing it will keep my frustration to a minimum.

The sun has set, and although we're walking around, Natalie's still tense. I thought by now, she'd have calmed down and started to enjoy our date. I don't know what's going on with her. I should slip one of my pills into her drink. That'd calm her down.

It's not helping that her phone's been going off for the past hour. I can't see who it is, but I'm happy when she finally powers the damn thing off and sticks it in her back pocket. Now, she can focus on us. I pull out my bottle and swallow another pill.

"Are you in pain? Maybe we should go home?"

"I'm fine."

"Then why do you keep taking pills?" She stops walking and puts her hands on her hips.

"Leave it alone, Natalie," I say, a warning tone in my voice.

"But—"

I grab her arm and drag her to a dark area behind the livestock building, caging her against the brick wall. I'm thankful there's no one around because my temper has reached the boiling point.

"When I say leave it alone." I get up in her face. "I mean it. Leave it alone. Got it?"

She nods. Something about the fearful look in her eyes turns me on. I kick her legs apart and push my erection against her.

"See what you do to me?"

"Please just take me home, Tommy," she whispers. "It's been a long day, and I'm tired."

"Let me kiss you." I press my body harder against hers.

"No." She tries to turn her head.

"Wrong answer, sweetheart." I lean in and take what I want. My tongue forces its way into her mouth, deepening the kiss. She squirms around, trying to get out of my hold. "Don't fight me. You know you want this." I lean in to kiss her again when a light shines on us. I back up to see a security guard holding a flashlight.

"What's going on back here?" he asks.

"Sorry, man," I say, pulling Natalie close. "My girl's just come back from school, and well, I guess I got a little carried away."

"Is that true, miss?" he asks Natalie.

I squeeze her waist tight in a warning.

"Yes, sir," she says sweetly. "This is really embarrassing. We're leaving now. I'm sorry."

"Go on. Get out of here, you two," he says and laughs.

I knew she wouldn't rat me out. It's the proof I needed that she's still mine.

She'll soon forget the city and the people in it. I'll have her back in my bed in no time at all.

Alex

I'VE SPENT THE ENTIRE DAY IN MY OFFICE SETTING UP THE FRAMEWORK for Nicholai's account. I don't have all the specifics yet, but I know enough of the basics to get started. To my employees, it'll look the same as any other ad campaign.

In reality, it's a complicated structure. Everything needs to be encrypted to ensure the underground aspects of Nicholai's dealings remain hidden. I'm the only one here who has access to the data.

I check my phone and see Natalie still hasn't returned any of my texts. She met her new boss earlier and was supposed to tell me how it went, but I haven't heard from her all day. I text Viktor and ask him to get the car ready before slipping my phone into my pocket.

After giving the office a final once over, I lock up and head outside, where Viktor's leaning against my car, waiting. When he sees me approach, he moves to open the door, but I wave him off. I'm grateful for his service, but my pensive mood makes me want to seek solitude.

After sliding into the car, I pull my phone from my pocket. Still nothing. This isn't like her. She usually has her phone on and responds right away. I refresh the screen like a schoolboy desperate to hear from his crush.

Fifteen minutes later, my message is finally read. The three dots dance on the screen, letting me know she's typing.

Natalie: Not a good time. I'll call you tomorrow.

Not a good time? What's that about?

Me: Is everything okay?

Another half-hour passes, and my text isn't read. I'm pacing back and forth in my apartment. It's late, and I'm concerned. No longer willing to wait, I pull up Natalie's number and hit the call button. The phone rings and rings before going to voicemail. I leave a message.

Natalie. What's going on? Is everything okay? Call me. I need to hear your voice.

And then I wait. Nine o'clock comes and goes with no call. My phone doesn't ring until the following morning. Natalie's uneasy during our conversation. Something about it doesn't sit right with me.

"My texts went unanswered all night. Where were you?"

"I was at the fair with some friends," she says hesitantly. "The reception was terrible."

"I see."

"I turned my phone off, and I guess I forgot to turn it on until this morning."

"I'm on my way out for a run. I'll call you later." My tone is cold, and I don't wait for her to say goodbye before disconnecting the call.

I understand Natalie's struggling to fit back in with her town while balancing our relationship.

I've never lived in a small town and feel like my hands are tied, especially when she won't talk to me. When she won't tell me everything. I don't want to fight with her and make things worse. If Natalie's not going to tell me, I'll try Svetlana. Maybe she knows something.

Me: Have you heard from Natalie?

Lana: Not since yesterday afternoon. Why?

Me: She blew me off last night. We just talked, but something's off.

The message shows it's read right away, but her response takes longer than I think it should. I pace back and forth in my kitchen, waiting for a reply. I hold off going for my run as long as possible, but Lana isn't returning my text. I need to go now to run off some of this frustration. Something's going on, and I intend to get to the bottom of it.

I turn the music app on and put my earbuds in. Then, after securing the phone in my back pocket, I ride the elevator down and set off on my run. After I'm a few miles in, I get a text notification. I stop running and pull my phone out.

Lana: She told me everything was okay yesterday, but I get the feeling she's having a hard time readjusting to being home. She isn't saying much, though.

Me: I have that feeling, too. I wish there was something I could do to make it better.

Lana: I'm assuming she didn't mention anything about her birthday party next weekend?

Of course, she didn't tell me. She's still keeping us a secret.

Me: Birthday party?

Lana: I'll take that as a no.

Me: I know it's her birthday Saturday. But she didn't mention a party.

We've only been together for a few months. Most of that time, it was strictly a contractual relationship. I thought she understood I was serious about making us work.

Knowing her past and the damage her ex did by cheating on her, I anticipated she'd struggle with our physical distance. Reluctantly, I agreed with her about keeping us a secret. At least until she felt more secure.

I've flown in twice to visit her. We stayed a few hours away from where she lives. I thought things were going well and we were making progress, but she's still holding off on telling her parents about us. I'm done being patient. If we have a future, we can't be a secret anymore.

I finish my run and take a quick shower before calling Svetlana. She gives me the information about the party and her word that she won't tell Natalie about my plans.

After our call, I make the necessary arrangements for a flight to Missouri on Saturday morning.

My little sub will be getting a surprise visit. It's time to discuss what the path forward will look like.

Natalie

Between what happened with Tommy at the fair and Alex's distant behavior, my nerves have been on edge all week. Today I have this birthday party. It was supposed to be a small get-together, but it turns out my mother has invited half the town.

It's already mid-morning, and I still haven't been able to reach Alex. I'm supposed to call him every morning to check in, but all my calls go straight to voicemail. I wonder where he is? I've been dragging my feet getting ready, hoping to speak to Alex before we have to leave, but I'm running out of time.

Going through my closet, I settle on a pale-yellow sundress. I slide it on before fixing my hair. It's going to be hot today, so I grab a hair tie and pull my hair into a ponytail.

Knowing there probably won't be cell service at the lake, I dial Alex's number one last time. The call goes straight to voicemail again. I've already left two messages and don't want to leave a third.

My body collapses onto my bed. A feeling of dread washes over me. Have I messed everything up by not telling him about Tommy? Maybe this is his way of telling me it's over between us? I knew this wouldn't work. Distance makes it too easy for people to grow apart. And this time, I have no one to blame but myself.

"Natalie, we're ready to go," Dad calls from downstairs.

"Be right down."

Alex said he wants this with me, but he's used to far more than I can ever offer him. Dragging myself off my bed, I stand in front of the mirror.

You're nothing but a small-town girl. You'll never be anything more. You had your fun in the city, but now you're home, back where you belong.

I don't want my parents to be right about Alex, but what if they are? Maybe today needs to be the day I stop resisting and start reacclimating myself into Northmeadow? Grabbing my phone, I slide it into the pocket of my dress before I leave the safety of my room. I make it down the steps just in time to hear my mother call for me from the kitchen.

"Natalie, come give me a hand, dear."

I enter the kitchen and gasp. "Did you buy everything in the store?" I laugh.

"I want the party to be perfect." Mom's eyes gleam with excitement. "Everyone's so happy you're home. They can't wait to see you."

It's been a long time since I've seen her excited about anything. She may be overbearing, but she has put a lot of work into this party. For her sake, I'll try to put my issues aside and share in her joy.

The half-hour drive to Finn Lake is a familiar one. Although we weren't rich, my parents did better financially than many others in Northmeadow. They gave Michael and me a good childhood, including a few weeks each summer spent in a rental cottage at the lake.

Every year, I'd beg my parents to stay longer. Being by the water was magical. But each time, they'd pat me on the head and tell me we had a fine home. Then we'd pack up, leave the water behind, and go back home.

Then, like with everything else, after Michael died, we stopped going.

Before I realize it, Dad turns the car onto Lakeshore Drive, and the pavilion comes into view. It's always been a popular spot for summer parties, even though it's nothing more than a concrete pad and a few wooden posts that hold up a metal roof.

"Who did all this?" I ask when I see the decorations.

"Your mom and Delia Laurel came down early this morning," Dad says.

It doesn't surprise me that Tommy's Aunt Delia had something to do with it. She and Mom have always been close.

"It looks great, Mom."

"Thank you, dear," Mom says and smiles proudly.

She's outdone herself, even if it looks more like a party for a ten-year-old. Purple streamers are draped from each post. A Happy Birthday banner with pastel flowers hangs over the entranceway and waves in the gentle breeze. Purple and pink helium balloons are anchored to each picnic table. Guests are already gathering. They smile as they greet each other, the ease of familiarity written in their actions.

"I told you we should have gotten here earlier, Stanley," Mom scolds Dad.

"Yes, dear," Dad says, appeasing her.

He silently exits the car and begins to unload the food.

I jump out of the backseat. "Let me give you a hand, Dad."

"No, you don't," Mom says as she climbs out of the car. "This is your party. Go, say hi to your friends." She gives me a gentle nudge forward.

I cautiously approach the pavilion, trying to stay hidden behind some trees as I search the sea of faces—people I once knew and who once knew me.

"Well, look who's back," a female voice says from behind me.

My stomach turns at the sound. It's a voice I'll never forget and hoped never to hear again. Slowly, I turn and take in the tall, curvy blonde standing behind me, her hands on her hips.

"Finally realized Northmeadow is where you belong?" she asks mockingly.

"Why are you here, Ashlynn?"

"Your mother invited me." She walks past me, hitting my shoulder on her way. "Didn't think we'd ever see you back again."

Ashlynn and I were inseparable growing up, which didn't surprise anyone since our mothers were best friends. They grew up together, got married within weeks of each other, and were pregnant at the same time. Everyone just assumed we'd follow in their footsteps.

When we were thirteen, Ashlynn's mom died in a car accident. After that, her father struggled with depression and alcoholism. Mom stepped in and filled her best friend's shoes, helping raise Ashlynn through her teen years. My mother loves her like a daughter. I never had the heart to tell her what happened between Ashlynn, Tommy, and me.

"I guess you thought wrong." I attempt to keep a bored tone in my voice while I look over her shoulder for someone, anyone else I recognize—anything to get away from her.

"Don't worry. Your *boyfriend* will be along shortly."

"My boyfriend?" She can't possibly know about Alex.

"Don't act so coy, Natalie." She cocks her hip to the side and places her hand on it.

Then it dawns on me who she's referring to. Seriously, is everyone in this town delusional?

"If you're referring to Tommy, he and I ended a long time ago. I'm sure you remember the circumstances." Just thinking about that night, about their betrayal, makes me feel sick.

"Somebody had to be there for him after you walked away."

"I guess if you like being sloppy seconds, he's all yours," I snap back.

Before Ashlynn can respond, Mom walks up carrying a box filled with party favors, interrupting our conversation.

"I see you found Natalie."

"Yes, I did, Mrs. Clarke," Ashlynn replies in a sickeningly sweet voice.

"It's so nice to see my two girls together again. I'm sure you'll pick up right where you left off." Mom places a kiss on Ashlynn's cheek. "That's the beauty of friendship," she says and walks away.

"Let me give you a hand with those." I move quickly to catch up with her.

I refuse to play Ashlynn's petty games.

Despite my initial reservations, I'm having fun getting reacquainted with old friends. The only thing that could make today better would be having Alex by my side. Would he get along with these people? Would they like him? The lives my friends here lead are so different from my friends' lives in the city. Even though I shouldn't be, I'm shocked to see most of my old girlfriends are married and either already have children, are currently pregnant, or both.

While holding one of their infants, a beautiful baby girl, I can't stop my mind from wandering. If I'd never left, would Tommy and I be married with our own baby? I look up and spot Tommy watching me from across the pavilion. When his eyes meet mine, I see a flash of sadness and quickly break eye contact. Did he share the same thought, or is he finally accepting we're over? When I look up again, the sadness is gone, replaced with something dark and unfathomable. It causes the hairs on my neck to stand on end. I pass the baby back to her mother just as Reverend Miller and his wife Hannah approach.

Much to Mom's dismay, I stopped going to church when I moved to NYC. I was sick of the gossip and hypocritical attitudes I'd witnessed growing up in the church. Organized religion no longer holds any appeal to me. I don't share the same beliefs as my parents. Looking back, I realize I never did. So far, I've gotten a pass on not attending church, but I think my time is about to expire.

"Natalie, it's so good to have you home." Hannah reaches out and hugs me.

I've always liked her. She's a genuinely kind woman who manages to steer clear of the gossip and judgments the people in this town are so good at dishing out. I still don't understand what she sees in her uptight, fire-and-brimstone husband.

"Thank you. It's good to be home." That's the answer everyone expects, so that's the one I give. It's easier that way.

"We haven't seen you at Sunday service," Reverend Miller says, a look of disapproval permanently inscribed across his stern face.

Reverend Miller's placed me on the spot, and I'm unsure how to respond to him. My hands fidget at my sides, and I desperately struggle not to bite my nails—to follow my Dominant's rule.

Hannah puts her hand on her husband's shoulder. "Dear, she's only been home a few months. I'm sure she's still trying to get settled in." She offers me a kind smile.

"Mhm." Reverend Miller nods. "Tomorrow's Sunday. I take it you're settled in now and can attend service?"

"I'll do my best," I reply quietly.

The wind blows, and a familiar scent of citrus and sandalwood permeates the air. "Excuse me, please." I quickly walk away, searching for the source of the fragrance.

I look around but drop my shoulders. Don't be foolish, Natalie. He's not here. I take a few tentative steps before movement outside the pavilion catches my eye.

Standing up against a large River Birch Tree with his hands in his pockets is Alex. Not trusting my eyes, I slowly begin to walk toward the figure. As I get closer, my heart rate speeds up. The realization hits me. He's really here.

He takes his hands from his pockets and opens his arms to me. Without thinking, I run into them. My head settles on his chest as I savor the feeling of his arms wrapped tightly around me. After a few minutes, I pull back and look at him.

"How? Why?"

"Happy Birthday, baby girl." He leans in and kisses me.

"How did you know?" I ask, then answer my question at the same time as Alex.

"Lana."

We share a laugh.

Then his brows draw together, and his mouth tenses. "We have some things we need to talk about."

I drop my gaze and kick my sandaled foot in the loose dirt. He places his finger under my chin, returning my gaze to his. "Don't avert your eyes, Natalie. Talk to me."

"Well, well. Who do we have here?"

My body stiffens at the sound of Tommy's voice. I move out of Alex's embrace and spin around, ready to tell him to get lost. But Alex is already stepping forward, his hand extended.

"I'm Alexander Montgomery, and you are?"

"Thomas Moore, Natalie's boyfriend," he replies, keeping his arms crossed tightly in front of his body.

Alex drops his hand and looks between Tommy and me. The look in his eyes is a mix of hurt and confusion.

I ball my hands into fists at my sides, willing myself not to explode and cause a scene.

"For the millionth time, you are *not* my boyfriend," I snap.

"Very true, sweetheart." Tommy reaches out and grabs my arm, pulling me to his side. His grip is tight and will leave a bruise. "After all this time, we're so much more than that, aren't we?"

Alex's gaze turns cold. "Take your hands off her."

"Or what, city boy?" Tommy puffs up his chest.

I twist my arm from Tommy's grasp. "Tommy, knock it off." I move to Alex and place my hands on his chest. "Can we go somewhere and talk?"

"I think that would be a good idea," he says, not breaking eye contact with Tommy.

The two men stare each other down for what feels like an eternity before Tommy drops his shoulders and takes a step back. "I'll be waiting for you, *sweetheart.*"

Ignoring him, I thread my fingers with Alex's and lead him away from the pavilion and my guests, who've stopped what they're doing to watch this scene.

"Natalie," Mom yells from behind me. "Come back here."

I glance over my shoulder. "I'll be back in a bit."

"Let her go, Charlotte," Dad says, taking Mom by the arm and leading her away. I'm grateful for his intervention.

Alex and I walk silently along the graveled path that winds its way around the lake. Anger rolls off him in waves. I stop when we come to a clearing with a bench overlooking the lake.

"Want to sit here?"

"Yes." His answer is cold and clipped.

I've sat on this bench many times. It's a favorite place for me, tucked far enough away from the swimming areas and houses to give the illusion of being isolated, far from everything and everyone. The view of the lake with the backdrop of the Ozark Mountains is breathtaking. A slight breeze causes the water to lap gently against the rocky shore. The sound has always been calming for me. Right now, I hope it's equally calming for Alex.

After sitting a few minutes, both of us staring at the lake, Alex adjusts his position and leans back on the bench, but his gaze remains fixed ahead of him.

"Alex." I place my hand on his arm. "Tommy's not my boyfriend."

He turns his head. A storm brews in his dark blue eyes. "Care to share why he seems to think otherwise?"

I sit back and throw my hands in the air. "I don't know." How am I supposed to explain something I don't even understand? "I've told him repeatedly that we ended a long time ago. I even told him I moved on with you. He doesn't seem to get it, and my mother keeps encouraging him to come around." I blow out a frustrated breath.

"Were you with him when I called the other night?"

"Yes. I didn't want to be, but there's no arguing with my mother. Tommy was in a bad mood, and I didn't want to cause a scene when you tried calling. I didn't know what else to do." The words spill from my mouth without a breath in between.

Alex sits up and puts his hands on my shoulders. "Natalie, you have to communicate with me. Talk to me. Trust me." His voice softens. "Without communication, this relationship won't work."

"I know."

Seeing the disappointment on his face and knowing I had caused it is too much for me. I try to turn away, but Alex doesn't let me.

"Do you trust me?" he asks.

"Yes, but—"

"You either trust me, or you don't." He searches my face for an answer.

"I trust you."

"Good. Now, tell me everything."

I begin recapping the events of the past few weeks, this time telling Alex the whole story.

"Apartment hunting has been useless," I say and slump back on the bench. "There's absolutely nothing available. So it looks like I'm stuck at my parent's house for the foreseeable future."

"How does Tommy factor into this?"

"My parents are insisting I go out with him. When I try to refuse, they start freaking out. They say as long as I'm at home, I need to follow their rules. Which leads me back to problem number one—I can't find an apartment."

"Where did he take you the other night?"

"The fair." Then I tell him everything that happened that night.

"I'm going to kill him." The anger in Alex's voice startles me.

"I don't want any trouble, Alex. I feel like no one is listening to me and what I want."

"And what is it you want?" He pulls me onto his lap.

"I want you."

He presses his lips to mine and pulls my body against his. I can feel his hardness between my legs.

"I think it's time we tell your parents about us, don't you?

I reach between us and cup his erection. "Right now, there are other things I'd rather do."

"As much as I'd love to stay hidden in the woods with you." He stands and sets me on the ground. "I think we should get back to your party."

"I'd rather stay here with you." I hold onto him.

"We have the rest of the weekend," he says with a mischievous glint in his eyes. "Let's go."

We follow the path back to the party. I get more nervous with each step, knowing we have to face my parents and their questions about why Alex is here.

In a perfect world, they'd welcome him, and all would be well. But I know this world is far from perfect. I only hope they don't cause a scene in front of everyone.

Natalie

With my hand tightly gripping Alex's, we return to the pavilion. My eye is immediately drawn to a picnic table where my mother sits next to Delia. The two women are deep in conversation. Tommy sits across from them, listening carefully. When he spots us, he points over Mom's shoulder. She jumps up and stalks toward us, a grimace on her face.

"Natalie, may I have a word?" Mom asks, not even attempting to hide her disapproval.

I squeeze Alex's hand tighter. "Whatever you have to say, you can say in front of Alex."

"I don't think that's a good idea."

She's infuriating. The last thing I want is a big scene in front of everyone, but she doesn't seem to care.

Thankfully, Alex steps in.

"It's okay, Natalie. I see your Dad over there. If you don't mind, I'll say hi to him while you talk with your Mom."

I nod, letting him know I'll be okay. He kisses my forehead and, with his hands in his pockets, strolls over to where Dad and his buddies are fishing.

"What is he doing here?"

"He came to celebrate my birthday." I try to keep my voice quiet, hoping not to draw attention to our conversation.

"I don't know why you thought it would be okay to invite that man."

"That man has a name. It's Alex."

"He has no business being here." My mother responds sharply.

"Alex is here because I want him here." I pause and readjust the volume of my voice. "I don't want to argue about this in front of everyone."

"Fine. We'll continue this discussion with your father and Thomas later."

I walk away before I explode on the spot. Needing somewhere to calm down, I look around and find a small grove of trees that'll provide shade and protection from my guests' prying eyes and ears. Leaning against a tree, I look up. The sun shines brightly in the vibrant blue sky. White, puffy clouds float with freedom I envy. The view is a necessary distraction, giving me time to re-center myself.

When I feel more in control of my emotions, I push off the tree and head toward the lake. But I notice Alex isn't there anymore.

I look around for him and freeze when I spot him on the other side of the pavilion. The anger I had just worked so hard to dispel is back with a vengeance.

Ashlynn is talking to *my* Alex, her hand on his shoulder and her head thrown back in laughter. Alex stands stiff, not returning her overly friendly behavior but not being outright rude, either.

This party has turned into a disaster of epic proportions. No longer caring if I make a scene, I quickly race across the pavilion to where they're standing and stop behind her. My hands are on my hips, ready for a fight.

"Excuse me," I snap.

The polite and quiet girl has stepped aside, allowing space for a woman on a mission—a woman who wants to rip out Ashlynn's eyeballs for even looking at Alex. Ashlynn turns, a satisfied smile on her face. She knows exactly what she's doing, and I just played right into her hands. Alex removes her hand from his shoulder, walks over to me, and wraps his arm around my waist.

"Is everything okay with your mom?"

"Yes," I say, my sights fixed on Ashlynn. "Why are you over here?"

"Natalie, relax," she says in a condescending tone. "I'm just introducing myself to your friend."

"Ashlynn was telling me stories about the two of you in high school."

"Oh, I bet she was. Did she also tell you—"

"Natalie," my father calls from across the pavilion. "Time to sing Happy Birthday."

"It was nice meeting you, Ashlynn." Alex flattens his palm on my lower back and leads me away.

"How could you talk to her?"

"Relax, baby girl. I know who and what she is. She can try all she wants, but I'm all yours." He flashes me his panty-melting smile as we make our way to where my mother and father stand, a gigantic cake on the table in front of them.

Knowing she's touched Alex makes me want to throw up, but his reassurance helps me see reason.

When we near the table, Dad lights the candles, and my guests break out in the birthday song. Closing my eyes, I make a wish and blow out the candles. My wish has already come true, and he stands next to me with a smile so bright his eyes light up. I love this man with all my heart and want to spend forever by his side.

Thankfully, Ashlynn leaves while I'm opening my presents. My mother sent her off with an extra piece of cake to bring to her father. But Tommy remains lurking along the outskirts of the pavilion. I do my best to ignore him as I introduce Alex to all my old friends.

Together we share laughs over stories from my high school days. Alex doesn't have much in common with these people, but somehow, he blends seamlessly into this part of my life. Seeing him comfortable here, I'm encouraged.

Maybe we can make this work.

With the afternoon winding down, the last guests leave, and we begin to tackle the clean-up. Despite my mother's less-than-welcoming attitude and Tommy's refusal to leave, Alex stays by my side and helps with everything.

"Looks like we got it all," Mom says. "Let's go, Natalie."

I look between her and Alex. "Alex is in town for the rest of the weekend. I'm going to stop by the house and grab some clothes. I'll be staying with him."

My mother's face turns red, and her nostrils flare. "You are an unmarried woman. You will not be spending the night with him."

"Mom, this has to stop. I'm a grown woman, not a child."

Mom stands silent. Her arms are by her side, and her body is tense with anger. Dad walks over to us with a less-than-pleased look on his face. Behind them, Tommy sits on top of a picnic table. He shakes a few pills into his hand and swallows them, silently watching the confrontation.

Alex moves to my side. "It was a wonderful party, Mr. and Mrs. Clarke." He turns to me. "Are you ready to go?"

"I am."

Leaving the stunned trio behind, Alex and I walk hand-in-hand to his car.

"If we hurry, we can get to the house and grab some stuff before they get home."

Once I'm in the safety of his car, I'm able to take a deep breath. That wasn't easy, but it went better than I anticipated. Alex pulls out of the parking lot, and I look out the window. My parents appear to be arguing, my mom's hands flailing in the air—Tommy is shooting daggers in our direction. Dread fills my stomach.

We may have avoided a confrontation this time, but we aren't going to be able to avoid it forever.

I'm thankful to be driving Natalie away from that scene. It's clear her parents, especially her mother, don't want me around. Her father's been friendly with me, but I have a feeling that won't last much longer.

Dealing with them is going to be a tricky situation. I don't want to step in and take over. Enough people are trying to do that already. Natalie must be allowed to use her voice—to make her own decisions. But if they try to silence her in front of me, I'll have no choice but to step in. I'm hoping that won't happen.

There's also Tommy. If he comes near her again, so help me, he won't live long enough to be able to regret it.

"I'm very proud of you, baby girl."

She looks at me, a sad smile on her face.

"I'm tired, Alex. I'm sick of having this same argument with them."

"We're going to figure this out. Together."

"When I didn't hear from you. I thought the worst. I thought you were done with me."

"I could never be done with you." The words *I love you* sit on the tip of my tongue, but I hesitate too long, and the moment passes.

I pull in front of her house instead of in the driveway. With our head start, we got here first. Parking on the street ensures we won't get blocked in.

"Wait here. I'm just gonna run inside and grab a bag." She gives me a quick peck on the cheek.

I watch her run up the front porch steps and disappear into the house. It's been nearly a month since I last saw her, and I miss her in more ways than one. Although we video chat and play, I miss the feel of her body beneath mine. But before we can get to that, she has a punishment coming for lying to me earlier in the week.

After being hurt, having a long-distance relationship is hard for her. However, honesty and trust are two crucial elements that our relationship must have. Now that

I'm here, I see the extreme stress she's under and realize my punishment will need to change some, but I can't let her totally off the hook.

While I wait, I get out and walk around the property. Her parents have a rather large house. At one point, I'm sure it was a beautiful home, but today, it sits in a state of disrepair. Like they've given up. The paint on the white wood siding is peeling, and the black shutters are faded. Their front porch is quintessential farmhouse style and wraps around the side of the house. Near the steps and door, the boards look to have been recently replaced but were left unstained.

The flower boxes that hang from the porch rails catch my attention. I recognize the petunias. They were one of my mother's favorites.

Walking around the side of the house, I spot a rusted swing set. It must have been Natalie and her brother's. The vision of a young Natalie, her blonde pigtails flying in the air as she swings back and forth, brings a smile to my face.

I imagine our little girl with Natalie's blonde curls and my blue eyes, giggling as I push her on a swing.

Our little girl? The thought catches me off guard.

Beyond the swing set is a large vegetable garden. Between the flower boxes and vegetables, someone is clearly skilled at gardening. I wander back to my car, taking another look at the house. A little TLC and it could be beautiful again. My phone buzzes with a text alert.

Brandon: Just checking to make sure you made it in one piece.

Me: I did.

Brandon: How's it going?

Me: She's not happy, man. The old boyfriend is still sniffing around, and her parents are smothering her.

Brandon: Lana's told me a bit.

Me: Speaking of parents, they just pulled up. Gotta go.

Natalie steps through the front door as her parents pull into the driveway. My instincts tell me things are about to explode. I hurry to meet Natalie at the steps. Her eyes lock with mine.

Just keep looking at me, baby girl. We've got this.

Her father's the first out of the car. "Alex, son. I don't know how they do things where you come from, but girls don't just run off and spend the night with strange men around here."

"Mr. Clarke. With all due respect, Natalie's a grown woman. She's fully capable of making decisions for herself." I hold my hand out, allowing her to make the choice. She willingly threads her fingers with mine.

"Natalie, you're making a mistake," her mother pleads. "People will talk."

"Do you think I'm the only girl having sex with her boyfriend?"

"Watch your tone, young lady," her father corrects her.

"Mom, Dad, I love you both," she says, her grip tightening on my hand. "I'll see you in a few days."

I'm filled with pride, seeing the woman at my side stand up for herself. Taking the bag from her, I lead her to my waiting car, help her in, and shut the door. Her parents stand side by side, their postures stiff.

"I'll have her home Monday," I say as I put her bag in the trunk.

As if unable to watch, Stanley Clarke turns his back while his wife holds her hand over her chest. This might have been the first time Natalie has ever willingly defied them.

I don't want her relationship with her parents ruined, but they have to allow her the space to make her own choices, and right now, I'm her choice. When no other words are exchanged, I get in the car, and we drive away.

After a few minutes, I reach across the console and hold Natalie's trembling hands. With us being apart, I've missed the feel of her soft skin and how her tiny hand fits inside my grasp. She's mine to care for—to protect.

"I know that was hard for you. I'm so proud of you."

"That was the hardest thing I've ever done. I wouldn't have been able to do it without you by my side."

"I'll always be by your side."

I turn on the radio and allow the soft sounds of music to fill the car.

"Where are we staying?"

"Water's Edge Bed and Breakfast."

When I googled the Northmeadow area, I was surprised to find there were no hotel chains within a fifty-mile radius. A few motels were on the outskirts of town, and several lake houses were still available to rent for the weekend. But then I found this bed and breakfast. It looked like the perfect place for a romantic weekend getaway.

"Mrs. Wilson's place." Natalie smiles.

"You're familiar with it?"

"I've seen it from the outside, but I've never stayed here."

Perfect. A first, we'll share in her hometown.

Hopefully, it's a first of many.

Alex

After the half-hour ride back to the lake, we pull into a small gravel parking lot. The pictures online don't do this place justice. The three-story log cabin structure is ideally situated just steps from the lake.

Lining the expansive porch are wooden rocking chairs that sit under large ceiling fans, giving the place a homey, inviting feel. Just inside the foyer is the check-in desk. Behind it sits an older woman. Her white hair pinned neatly on her head.

"Hello, ma'am. I called earlier in the week and reserved a room."

She stands up and peers at us over her silver-rimmed glasses that sit low on her nose. "Your name?"

"Alexander Montgomery."

There's no computer to check for the reservation. Instead, the woman has a spiral-bound notebook in front of her. She flips through a few pages. "There you are." Glancing up, she looks between us. "Two nights?"

"That's correct."

"Here's your key. Your room is on the third floor. It's the second door on the left," she explains and points behind us. "Unfortunately, we don't have an elevator. Enjoy your stay."

"Thank you, we will."

I smile politely and place my hand on Natalie's back as we make our way to the ornate oak staircase with a hand-carved knotty pine railing. As we walk away, I can feel the woman's eyes boring into our backs. The judgmental attitudes in this town are unbelievable. Having always lived in a bigger city, I've never experienced anything like this. I'm getting a taste of what Natalie has lived with all her life.

As we climb the two flights of steps, we admire the candid photos of couples and families enjoying the bed and breakfast and the small beach. They add to the charm of the place.

We make it to the third floor and walk down the hall to the door of our suite. I place the key in the lock, and with a click, it opens. Natalie ventures in first.

"I've always wondered what these rooms looked like."

The woodsy feel of the outside has been carefully balanced to create a warm, country atmosphere. Our room overlooks the lake with large windows and a balcony. The doors are open, allowing the evening breeze to flow through the room. The hardwood floors creak as we walk into the room. I set the bags down, and we begin exploring. A small table and chairs are situated to the side under one of the windows. They have the same carvings as the handrail on the steps. When I look more closely at the intricate design, I see the carvings mimic the mountains and lakes in the region. They are indeed a piece of art.

A four-poster canopy bed is along the side wall, with sheer curtains flowing in the breeze. A handmade quilt stretches across the bed, with various pillows arranged neatly at the top. Next to the sides of the bed are tall, mahogany-stained tables, each holding a small lamp.

The back wall is home to an expansive wood armoire, allowing guests a place to unpack. The antique furniture and country décor add to the quaint and welcoming feeling one expects from a bed and breakfast.

On the other side of the room, there's a sitting area with a vintage sofa arranged across from a large stone fireplace. That must be incredible on a chilly winter night. The table in front of the couch is constructed from a reclaimed crate. A large vase of lilacs sits on top of it—their fragrance fills the room.

Natalie walks onto the balcony, and I follow. "When I was growing up, we spent every summer in a rental cottage." She points off to the right, where I can see the lights from a few small cottages in the tree line along the lake. "Michael and I would see couples standing on these balconies, and we'd make up stories for them. I always thought it would be romantic to stay here."

I love hearing stories about her childhood.

Natalie sighs. "Things were so different back then."

I move beside her and look at the lake illuminated by the bright moonlight.

"Are you happy here?"

"Yes. No. I don't know. Nothing is like I remembered it. Maybe I changed too much while I was away?"

"You don't have to stay. You can come back to the city with me and get a job there."

"You know I can't do that."

I push off the rail and stand in front of her. "I can get you out of the contract. I'll pay the money for the scholarship. You can come back home with me."

In my mind, this is easy. With a quick phone call, the money will be transferred, and this can be done.

"We've already been over this. You are not paying my way out of it." She laughs and shakes her head. "That would make me nothing more than your whore."

"Natalie." I reach out to her, but she steps out of my grasp.

"No, Alex."

"You are not a whore, and I will not tolerate you speaking about yourself like that."

"What else would you call it if I allow the man I'm sleeping with to pay my way through life just so I can leave town with him?"

I'm taken aback by her words. I'd hoped I was more to her than just the man she's sleeping with.

"I'd call it a man who's in love with you and would move heaven and earth to be with you."

I walk toward her slowly, closing the gap between us.

"A man who's in love with me?"

"Yes. I'm in love with you, Natalie Clarke. And I want you to come home."

Her shoulders relax, and her eyes soften. "Alex." She walks into my arms. "I love you too."

I wrap my arms around her, needing to feel her body next to mine.

"I don't want to sound ungrateful, Sir. But I can't accept your offer. I'm sorry."

Although I hate her answer, I respect her decision.

My arms don't want to let go, but there's a matter that needs to be taken care of before we can move on. I take a step back, breaking our connection.

"We need to address the issue of your lying to me earlier this week."

She looks down. "Yes, Sir. There is that."

I walk back inside the room and over to my bag. Unzipping it, I pull out a black leather riding crop. "Come here."

Although hesitant, she enters the room and stands before me. When I point down, Natalie lowers herself to her knees. My cock comes to life, watching her willingly submit to me.

We don't need anyone watching what's about to happen, so I shut the balcony doors and draw the curtains closed. Holding my palm out, I hit the crop across it, allowing the sound of the sharp crack to fill the room.

Natalie gasps. The crop's painless across my palm but will cause a stinging bite when used on the delicate skin of her ass. The punishment won't be too much, but it will remind her of her responsibilities in this relationship.

"Natalie, this lifestyle and commitment between us require nothing less than complete honesty. If we can't trust one another. If I have to question your honesty, this—" I motioned between us. "This won't work." Her gaze drops to the floor. "When we entered this relationship, we discussed punishments and why they're necessary. Do you understand why you're being punished?" Another silent nod. "You need to use your voice, baby girl."

"I wasn't honest with you. I lied about where I was and who I was with."

A Dominant is only as good as his word. No matter how much I hate giving out punishments or how difficult it will be, it's my responsibility to follow through. If I don't, what's the sense of having rules?

I sit on the nearest chair and hold the crop across my lap. "Stand and strip."

Natalie gracefully gets up. Although her hands tremble, she unzips her sundress before slipping the thin straps off her shoulders. The dress slides down her body, exposing her sun-kissed skin inch by inch. My sweet, innocent sub acts like a sexy minx, even though she's stripping for punishment.

Natalie turns and looks back at me. Her emerald eyes smolder with desire as she unclasps her white lace bra, letting it fall to the ground by her dress. My eyes follow her hand as she slides it down her body to her lace thong. The fabric glides down her legs. She bends over, her ass on full display, as she picks them up from the floor. Slowly, she turns to face me again. With a mischievous smile, she tosses her panties to me.

I catch them and bring them to my nose, inhaling her sweet scent. "These are coming home with me."

She runs her tongue along her lower lip.

I take a minute to appreciate her body before calling her to me. "Come here." My voice is sure and steady, betraying none of my emotions. "Lie over my lap."

She folds her body across my legs. I run my hand over the globes of her ass before dragging my finger between her legs. She's wet—aroused.

"You will receive ten strikes."

Without warning, I raise my arm. The swoosh of the crop fills the air, followed by the sound of it cracking across first one side of her ass, then the other. She whimpers from the sting of the leather. After three more strikes, she begins to cry. I don't know how thick the walls are in these rooms.

"You need to remain quiet. Or I'll have to gag you. Do you understand?"

"Yes, Sir," she says through her tears.

I've disciplined my past subs but never felt anything when they cried. Natalie's cry and knowing she's in pain twist my heart. I know my submissive earned her punishment, but the man in me wants to throw the crop down and gather her in my arms. The depth of my feelings is as terrifying as it is thrilling. She's obedient and doesn't make another sound as I continue, alternating sides of her ass.

After the last strike, I drop the crop and inspect her red skin. It's a beautiful sight. My skill ensures no permanent damage, but she'll remember this when she sits down tonight. I help her up, and she curls against my chest, crying softly.

"I'm sorry I lied to you, Sir. It won't happen again."

"I forgive you, baby girl." I use my thumbs to wipe the tears from her face before pulling her in for a kiss.

With her punishment over, I can concentrate on giving her pleasure. I place her gently on her feet.

"Don't move."

That command used to be difficult for her. She was always concerned with covering her nakedness, ashamed of her body. Now, my beautiful sub stands proudly before me, allowing me an unobstructed view.

"Yes, Sir."

Reaching into my bag, I pull out a wrapped gift. When she sees it, her eyes light up.

"Happy Birthday."

"May I open it now?"

"Yes."

She wastes no time ripping the shiny paper.

"Oh, Sir, it's beautiful," she says as she runs her fingers over the length of soft jute I had dyed purple for her.

"When we first negotiated our contract, you said you wanted to include rope play."

"Yes."

"You probably thought I forgot about it."

"I did." She giggles.

"Other than a few rudimentary ties to restrain a sub, I didn't know anything about Shibari," I confess.

But, over the past few months, I've been taking online instructional classes with Master Kiyoshi.

"Most were video lessons. Last month, he visited Fire and Ice to teach some classes. So I was able to get some hands-on learning."

"Oh," she says quietly.

"Look at me." I place my finger under her chin, raising her face. "They were private lessons between the Master and myself. I'm not an expert, but I'd be honored if you'd allow me to show you what I've learned."

She stands on her tiptoes and kisses me. "I couldn't think of a better present, Sir. Thank you."

"What are your safewords?" I ask, making sure they're at the forefront of her mind. An injury can happen too easily, even with simple bondage.

"Yellow and red, Sir."

I begin at the top of one arm. Using a single column to make a diamond pattern with the rope, stopping right before her wrist. With a separate piece, I do the same on her other arm. With both arms harnessed, I stop to check in.

"Does everything feel okay?"

She closes her eyes as if doing a mental inventory. "Yes, it feels good."

I return to my bag and pull out more rope. "Give me your hands."

She raises them, and I position her palms together. Using a double-column tie, I wrap the jute around her wrists twice and loop it through the middle. It's only a beginner's harness. But with each twist of the rope, I feel Natalie's body relaxing, submitting to my control.

This experience may be my present to her, but she's gifting me something even more special—freedom over her willing body.

Having that control over her is an incredibly intimate connection I've never shared with another. When I finish tying, I check to ensure the rope is taught but not tight. Then, I check in one final time.

"Is everything still okay? Nothing's too tight?"

She tries to pull her hands apart, testing the tension. "It feels good."

Grabbing the rope, I lead her to the bed.

"Lie on your stomach."

I help her onto the bed and stretch her arms above her head. Using the rope's tail, I thread it through the thick wood spindle of the headboard and tie it off. I tug at it to ensure it won't slip. Satisfied with my work, I walk to the bottom of the bed. Natalie wiggles, trying to turn her head, but comes up short.

"Good try, baby girl." I chuckle, watching her squirm.

I'm standing just out of her line of sight while I pull my shirt over my head and toss it on the chair. It lands next to her discarded panties.

"You need to stay quiet."

"Yes, Sir."

Moving closer to the bed, I push her up on her knees, legs spread wide. Her head and chest remain on the bed with her arms stretched out before her. I stand back for a second to admire her positioning.

"You're wet for me already."

"Very."

The desire dripping from her words only encourages my already throbbing dick. But as much as I want to sink into her tight, wet center, I still have other plans. My dick will have to wait. I pull one last item out of my bag and turn it on. A vibrating hum fills the air.

"What's that?" she asks as she tries to look over her shoulder.

"Have you ever used a magic wand?"

"No, Sir."

"Well, then, I'm happy to introduce you."

I crawl onto the bed, kneel behind her, and place the wand directly on her clit. She's already aroused from the crop and gasps at the intense sensation. Her first orgasm will be quick.

"You are so fucking beautiful."

The words barely leave my mouth when she throws her head back in ecstasy. Her legs collapse from under her. I use my free arm to hold her up while I keep the wand firmly in place, not allowing her body a chance to come down from its high.

"Alex, I can't," she pants.

"Relax, you can." I turn the wand on high and continue massaging her overly sensitive center. "I want to see you come again."

Her breathing increases as her body prepares itself for a second release.

"Come for me, Natalie." Her back arches and her body explodes with another orgasm before going limp in my arms. I quickly release her arms and untie the rest of the rope. Climbing in bed, I pull her into me and pull the blankets over our bodies.

"I love you, baby girl," I whisper to her while she experiences the freedom of subspace.

Natalie

I'VE LEFT MY BODY AND AM FLOATING THROUGH A SEA OF VIBRANT colors.

Weightless.

Peaceful.

Worries are no more.

I'm free.

Whispered words of love float through the air. I want to remain here forever, but my eyes blink open.

The room is dark and quiet. My head rests on Alex's chest. His arm is around me, holding me close. It takes a few minutes for the fogginess to clear. When I'm able to push up on my elbow, I study Alex. Even in sleep, there's an inherent strength in his face.

My fingers trace the dark stubble on his jaw from not shaving before my gaze travels down his chest. I admire the defined muscles in his abdomen and the trail of dark hair, where his jeans sit low on his hips. I struggle between wanting to open his pants and give him pleasure or letting him sleep.

"Welcome back, beautiful," he whispers.

"Hi." I lean in, kissing him.

"It's nice to have you back."

"That was an incredible experience."

He rewards me with a sexy smile, and I find myself aroused again. I can't believe this man is here with me. That he loves me. As I lower my hand to unbutton his jeans, my stomach grumbles.

"I guess I'm a little hungry."

"I think we missed dinner."

I continue to reach for his button. "I'd rather have you."

He grabs my hand. "And I would love that, but first, you need to eat. I know it's late, but is there any place we can get some food?"

"What time is it?"

Alex grabs his phone off the bedside table. "It's almost eleven."

"There's a pizza place down the road that might still be open."

I pull up their page on the web browser. Alex calls and places an order.

"They were about to close but took the order as long as I agreed to go right over to pick it up." He throws his legs over the side of the bed and gets dressed.

I lean on my elbows, allowing the sheets to slide down, earning a throaty growl. When Alex's dressed, he comes back to the bed. Leaning over, he takes a nipple into his mouth, nipping and sucking before letting go.

"I'll be back in a little bit."

I let myself fall back onto the pillow and blow out a frustrated breath. How can I be so turned on after all the orgasms he already gave me? Alex is a generous lover. He always places my needs first. When he gets back, I'll give him the pleasure he deserves.

After he leaves, I jump in the shower to clean up and then slip into one of his T-shirts. I find a switch that illuminates the balcony with soft lighting. While I wait for Alex to return, I sit on one of the wooden chairs and allow the warm breeze to dry my damp hair.

Tommy

I PULL INTO HER PARENT'S DRIVEWAY, BUT I'M TOO LATE. CHARLOTTE tells me Natalie left with Alex about ten minutes ago. She isn't sure where they're staying, only that Natalie said she'll be home Monday.

That guy isn't going to stay in a cheap motel. Other than a lake house, the only place to stay is at Old Lady Wilson's, so I take a chance and drive there.

Sure enough, there's a fancy rental car parked in the lot. I pull my truck into the driveway of an empty cottage next door. The moon is bright tonight, but the trees lining the property will keep me hidden. I open the glove box, pull out my gun, and make sure it's loaded. Then, I set it on the seat next to my night vision binoculars. Reaching into my pocket, I pull out my pill bottle and swallow two pills. I'm craving their high more and more.

I don't have a plan yet, but I'll be damned if I let this guy waltz into town and take Natalie away from me. It takes a few hours before movement in the lot catches my eye. Alex gets into the car and pulls away. Once I'm sure he's gone, I grab the binoculars and tuck the gun into the waistband of my pants. A path leads through the trees to a few outbuildings that allow me to stay undetected while also looking for any sign of Natalie.

I'm about to give up hope when the lights of a third-floor balcony turn on, and Natalie walks out. Looking through my lens, I see her hair's damp, and she's wearing a man's T-shirt that hangs to her mid-thigh. From the way her nipples poke through the fabric, I know she's not wearing anything underneath, and that makes me hard as fuck. Using the camera feature in the binoculars, I snap some pictures. I'll be getting off to these tonight.

While I'm figuring out my next move, Alex pulls back into the parking lot. I move further behind the building to stay hidden and continue watching. A few minutes later, he walks onto the balcony. Natalie stands up and wraps her arms around him.

Her ass peeks out from underneath the shirt. I take more pictures before going back to my truck.

I need to come up with a way to get rid of him once and for all.

When I return to our room, I find the balcony door open. Walking across the room, I place the pizza box and sodas on the table and stand in the doorway, watching Natalie. She sits on a wooden chair with her legs tucked under her. The warm breeze blows her damp blonde curls in her face. She tucks the wayward hair behind her ear and stares into the dark.

My heart aches knowing she's struggling, but she's so much stronger than she realizes. I have two days to remind her of her strength.

"Hungry?"

The sound of my voice startles her. When her eyes reach mine, she runs her tongue across her bottom lip before untucking her legs and standing. Slowly, she walks across the spacious balcony wearing only my T-shirt.

"Starved."

The meaning behind her answer is not lost on me as she wraps her arms around my neck and kisses me. My cock stirs, but once again, it'll have to wait.

"Let's eat out here. It's a beautiful night."

Natalie steps back. "Yes, Sir. I'll go make your plate."

She gives me a sexy pout as she walks past me, swaying her hips. I smack my little temptress on her ass, making her giggle. While she makes my plate, I lean on the balcony rail. It's easy to see how Natalie got lost in her thoughts.

Unlike the noisy city, the only sounds I hear are the chirp of crickets and the occasional croak of a toad. Replacing the artificial city lights is a beautiful night sky with thousands of twinkling stars. It's so different from my daily life, but the tranquil feeling of being immersed in nature is something I could quickly get used to. Maybe we'll have to look at getting a place by the water?

We.

That's something I never imagined I'd be saying, but I've been thinking in those terms more and more.

My mind drifts to the night I first met Natalie at Fire and Ice. I've always had experienced subs. I never thought I'd be attracted to someone new to the lifestyle. I wasn't even looking for a submissive, but then *she* came along.

Natalie's special. She's the perfect mix of naïve and curious. She has a playful side I adore. It sets her apart from others who believe being in a Dom/sub relationship has to be all rules and formality.

Quite the opposite. In addition to following the protocols of our lifestyle, I enjoy laughing and having fun with her. Unknowingly, she's challenged me to be a better Dominant and a better man. I was running from my past, from love—until her. She changed my life.

Her smile, the one that lights up her emerald eyes, melted the ice that had formed a prison around my heart.

I see a future with her—a forever with her.

Natalie interrupts my thoughts. "I have your dinner, Sir."

I sit in one of the Adirondack chairs and take the offered plate. Before she goes back in, she drags over a small white table and sets my soda can on it.

When she returns, she sits next to me, tucking her legs back under her. My shirt rides up, exposing the top of her leg, and I see she's naked underneath. Natalie looks at me and bites her lower lip, my lust reflecting in her eyes. For a brief moment, I consider putting my plate aside and fucking her on the balcony, but she needs to get some nourishment before I bring her back to bed and have my way with her.

It isn't until I take my first bite that my sub begins to eat. The mood shifts from the lightheartedness we shared just a few minutes ago to one filled with tension.

While she eats, Natalie's gaze again drifts back toward the water. When she's stressed, she tends to withdraw. I desperately want to know her every thought.

"What are you thinking about?"

She sets her plate on her lap. Her brow creases with worry.

"It's harder being back here than I thought."

"Harder, how?"

"When I first left for school, I was an insecure girl who'd lived a very sheltered life. I blindly did as I was told. It was all I knew. I did a lot of growing up while I was away. A lot of changing."

My heart aches to see the conflict on her face, but I stay quiet and let her finish.

"For the first time, I was able to live life on my terms and make my own decisions. Coming back home—" She looks down at her lap. "I feel like I'm losing myself, my voice, and I don't know how to stop it."

I can make this situation go away for her, but she won't let me. It's frustrating, but I understand why. She's an independent woman who went to New York City with a plan for her future. Unfortunately, life had other plans for her. Now, she's stuck in a situation where she's unhappy.

It would be easy to buy out her contract and bring her home with me. She could have a career there, and we'd come back here to visit. It would be a win for everyone. But if I force that on her, I'll be just like everyone else in her life. As difficult as this is, my role as her Dominant is not to take away her voice.

"What can I do to help you?"

"I don't know that there's anything you *can* do. Other than being here for me."

"I'll always be here for you." I set my plate on the table and turn to face her.

"As your Dominant and the man who loves you, I'll stand beside you. I'll fight for you. I'll support your decisions and catch you if you fall."

"Alex—"

"You're my world, baby girl. My whole universe. There's nothing you could say or do that would change my feelings for you." I reach over and cup her face in my palm. "I love you, Natalie."

At this moment, I finally understand the love my parents shared and why my father didn't regret a second of loving my mom, even though she left him too soon.

I want the same with Natalie and am willing to risk everything to get it.

Natalie

Last night, something shifted between Alex and me. Barriers we'd both erected from our pasts began crumbling. When we finally finished eating, he took me to bed and made love to me all night. We fell asleep, our bodies entwined, just before the sun rose over the horizon.

By the time we wake up, it's nearly noon. We dress in a hurry, hoping to make it in time for lunch downstairs. And we do. Mrs. Wilson is just putting the food on the table as we walk into the dining room. A young couple follows shortly after and joins us at the table. As soon as the food is served, Mrs. Wilson excuses herself, leaving us to eat.

"Do you two live around here?" Alex asks.

"Alma and I were just married two days ago. We're on our way to California."

"Miguel was offered a job there," Alma explains. "So we're having a cross-country honeymoon." She smiles lovingly at her husband.

The couple tells us they're only twenty years old—high school sweethearts who decided to throw caution to the wind.

"We have a few weeks before my job starts, so we decided to drive across the country. We've been stopping in small out-of-the-way towns along the way," Miguel says

We enjoy chatting with the couple as they tell us about their experiences so far. Throughout lunch, they continually touch each other, their love sweet and uncomplicated. After they finish eating, they quickly excuse themselves from the table.

Even as they walk away, the young bride leans into her husband's embrace—they don't have a care in the world. Only excitement at starting their new life together.

A pang of jealousy stabs my heart, and I find it hard to swallow my next bite of food. I had a high school sweetheart. A boy I once shared dreams with. Someone I was supposed to marry—until he betrayed me.

Watching them walk away, I wonder what my life would look like today if things had worked out as initially planned. Tommy and I would be married right now. I'd be living the life my parents arranged for me. That thought makes me pause. Would I have resented my life because it wasn't mine but one forced on me since childhood?

The day I found Tommy and Ashlynn together, I lost two people who'd meant the world to me. But it was also the catalyst for my change. For me to figure out who I am and what I want—I found myself.

After returning to New York, I took Michael's advice. I allowed myself to start living my life rather than just going through the motions. I stopped worrying about pleasing others or what they thought about me. Instead, I chose to do things that made me happy. For the first time, I was content with who I was.

What I thought was the worst thing that could happen to me turned out to be the start of this incredible new journey. The one that eventually led me to the man sitting next to me.

Alex places his hand over mine. "How about we grab one of the boats and spend the day on the water?"

"You know how to row a boat?"

"Nope." He flashes me his sexy grin. "Do you?"

I return his smile with one of my own. "Of course I do."

"Well then, baby girl." He stands and pulls my chair out for me. "Why don't you show me your skills?"

We walk through the yard of the bed and breakfast, stopping to admire the lush flower gardens before making our way to the beach. Families are set up on blankets, some under umbrellas that shield them from the hot sun. Children splash and play on the water's edge.

"Do you want children?"

"Someday, sure," Alex says. "What about you?"

"Yes, I'd love to be a mother."

He wraps his arm around my waist, and I imagine a time in the future when we're here playing with our children. The thought fills me with warmth. We make our way to the dock, where Alex makes the arrangements, and then we're led to a waiting rowboat. Alex takes a tentative step down and quickly grabs the dock to steady himself from rocking back and forth.

Having done this before, I'm sure of my footing and step safely into the boat. I go to sit in the rowing seat, but Alex scoots me out of the way.

"I've got this. How hard can it be?"

I gladly move to the bench in front and kick my feet up. I can't wait to see my city boy in action. The employee unties us from the dock and gives us a little push. I bite my lip, holding in my laughter as Alex struggles. We go in circles for a few minutes until he gets a feel for the oars and the boat's movement.

"I'm impressed, Mr. Montgomery. You catch on quick."

"I'm a man of many talents," he smirks. "Which way are we headed?"

I point out the direction to take. "There's a quiet cove with a sandy beach where we can relax."

Alex rows us across the lake with what looks like practiced ease. Finally, we enter the shallow water of the cove. I slip off my sandals and hop out, pulling the boat onto the sand. Alex climbs out behind me, ensuring the boat is far enough out of the water that it won't float away.

The beach is a small, secluded area surrounded by trees. It's a spot not many people know about, so I'm confident we're not likely to see any other people while we're here. Alex sits on the sand, and I lie with my head on his lap. The August sun shines warm, making the water look like crystals dancing across the surface. Small waves lap gently on the rocks. The sounds of birds chirping fill the air. For the longest time, we enjoy the sounds of nature.

"I told my father about you," Alex says while he plays with my hair.

"Oh?" I'm surprised by his revelation.

Alex has told me a little about his family. But, with us not being a typical couple, I didn't know if we were something Alex would talk to his dad about.

"He'd like to meet you." He stops moving his hand and looks down at me, a hopeful expression on his face.

What must he think about how we met? Has he met all of Alex's subs?

As if he's sensing my wayward thoughts, he adds. "Even though my father lives in Seattle, we're close. He knows the nature of how our relationship started."

"Have you introduced him to your other subs?"

"No. I've never brought anyone to meet my family." He looks down at me. "I told him you're more than just my submissive, that I'm in love with you."

I sit up. Alex only told me last night that he loves me. I'm still getting used to this new part of our relationship. But knowing he's already told his father his feelings makes this between us feel like so much more.

"I'd love to meet him."

Alex lets go of the breath he's holding. "I'll arrange a trip to Seattle."

"I'd like that very much."

Alex reclines back on his hands, a carefree look on his face. Then, he begins telling me about his childhood.

"I'm an only child. My parents had just about given up on having a baby. And then, surprise, I came along."

I like this youthful side of him.

"My mom had a free spirit. She believed in letting children play and explore." He stares off as he speaks. "She encouraged me to pursue anything I was interested in. That's how I got involved in martial arts and became interested in Eastern philosophy. Many of those principles I carry with me today."

I can easily see that in the way he approaches life. He's disciplined, yet I also recognize his mother's free spirit.

"Mom would've adored you."

"I wish I could've met her."

We sit in silence for a while. Alex appears lost in his memories. I recline between his legs, my back against his chest, as he wraps his arms around me. Inside, I feel warm and content. The doubts I once had about our relationship fade with each day that passes.

Alone on the beach, we continue to share stories of our childhoods. We've come from very different worlds, but somehow, fate played a role and brought us together. The sun is beginning to set, casting vibrant colors over the horizon.

"We should start heading back," Alex says as he stands and dusts the sand off his shorts. He offers me his hand, helping me up. "I don't want to get stuck on the lake in the dark."

"You aren't scared, are you? There hasn't been a monster sighting in—"

Alex scoops me up and tosses me over his shoulder. "Shall we get in the water and find out?"

I hit his back with my fists in mock protest. "Put me down." I barely manage to say between fits of laughter.

"As you command." He motions like he'll toss me into the water before gently setting me on my feet in the boat. "You should've seen your face." He laughs, and the sound is music to my ears.

I sit while Alex pushes the boat back onto the water. Then, he climbs in, trying to be careful, but we rock back and forth anyway. Good thing we're still in shallow water, or we'd both be soaked right now.

We arrive back at the dock just as the last of the sun begins to fall below the horizon. The attendant sees us approaching and jumps up from where he's sitting. I toss him the rope, and he ties us to the cleat. The boat rocks back and forth again as Alex stands. I hold my breath, hoping he doesn't end up in the lake. Instead, he easily climbs onto the dock. With a grin on his face, he offers me a hand, pulling me up next to him.

"Let's find a place to eat and celebrate not capsizing."

"Good morning, beautiful," Alex says from the table, where he's sitting with a cup of coffee in his hand, his laptop in front of him.

"You're up early." I sit up and rub the sleep from my eyes.

"I have a meeting with a client when I get back today." He sets his cup down and comes over to sit on the bed. "I was getting some last-minute details in place."

He bends over and kisses me. I wrap my arms around his neck.

"I don't want you to go."

"My offer still stands."

All it would take is one phone call. I could be on a plane going back to New York with him today. He's waiting for me to say yes, but I can't. When I accepted the scholarship, I also accepted the commitment that came with it. It's important to me that I honor my commitment. But it doesn't make saying goodbye any easier. I can't say the words, so I shake my head.

"Come shower with me." He pulls off his shirt as he walks to the bathroom.

I climb out of bed and follow him, appreciating the view of his muscular back and how his jeans sit low on his hips. A part of me still can't believe this man is mine. I'm waiting for the bubble to burst. For him to decide I'm not what he wants.

Alex turns on the hot water, and steam quickly fills the small bathroom. Turning to face me, he grabs the hem of my shirt and pulls it over my head. His knuckles graze my nipples. They harden in response.

I step into the shower, and he follows, closing the glass door behind him. Water sluices over his muscular body. He stares at me like a predator about to pounce on its prey. In one move, he lifts me, and I wrap my legs around his waist. Then his mouth is on mine, his tongue seeking entrance.

The kiss is different—desperate. He walks us until my back is against the tiled wall, then slides his hard length into me. His movements are rough, almost primal, as he tugs at my hair, forcing my head up and giving him access to my neck. My orgasm builds, and I tighten my legs around Alex's waist, encouraging him to go even deeper.

I can't hold back any longer. An orgasm rips through my body, and I ride wave after wave of intense pleasure. Alex increases the intensity of his thrusts until he comes with a deep growl in his throat.

He lowers his forehead, resting it against mine. "Change your mind. Come home with me."

The desperation in his voice is almost my undoing. Instead, I unwrap my legs from his waist and slide down his body until my feet touch the ground. Reaching around him, I grab the small bottle of body wash and pour some into my hands. I wash his body, gliding my hands over the taut muscles in his abdomen and chest before moving lower. I leave no part of his body untouched.

After our shower, we dress and pack in silence. The ride back to my parents' house is tense. I spend most of the drive worrying about all the possible outcomes of the conversation that'll happen later. My heart is heavy. Saying goodbye gets harder with each visit. Knowing I'll have to face my parents tonight makes this goodbye the hardest.

"Stop biting your nails."

"Sorry, Sir." I put my hands under my legs.

"I can reschedule the meeting and stay with you. You don't have to do this alone."

"I appreciate the offer. But I have to do this myself."

We pull up to the house, and Alex shuts the car off. Neither of us moves, not wanting the weekend to end—not wanting to say goodbye.

Reluctantly, I turn to him. "If you don't go now, you'll miss your flight."

"That wouldn't be such a horrible thing."

I lean over the center console and kiss him. "I love you." My voice cracks. Reaching into the backseat, I grab my bag and turn to get out of the car. Alex reaches out and grabs my arm.

"Are you sure you won't change your mind?" His eyes plead with me.

"Call me when you land?" I open the door and step out.

"I will," he says, a sad smile on his face.

I close the car door and step back.

Watching Alex drive away, I feel small and alone.

The minute his car is out of sight, the tears I've held back roll down my cheeks.

Natalie

INSECURITY ABOUT NOT PLEASING MY PARENTS HAS PLAGUED ME ALL MY life. My earliest memories revolve around trying to be the perfect daughter. It got worse after Michael died. I felt I owed it to my parents to always say and do the right thing—to do what they wanted—even if it meant I hid what I felt inside.

It wasn't until I found out Tommy was cheating on me that I realized I wasn't living. I was merely existing, continually trying to please someone else. The encouragement Michael left for me in his note urging me to live my life to the fullest finally made sense. So, I started fresh and created a new Natalie—the Natalie I wanted to be. And I was happy with that person.

I neglected planning how to continue being that girl once I returned to Northmeadow. I ignored it. It was easier to pretend my time in the city wouldn't end. But unfortunately, it did end, and I'm already losing the independence and confidence I had just a few months ago. I've regressed to the insecure girl who ignores her wants and desires in exchange for her parent's approval.

I love my parents. That doesn't change just because I have different thoughts and desires. Somehow, I have to make them understand that. When they get home, I need to be the woman who isn't afraid to stand up for herself. But will I be able to do this? Will my parents understand? Wiping the tears from my face, I walk up the sidewalk and into the house.

My parents are both at work, so I have the afternoon to myself. I go upstairs to my room and sit on my bed. I need a plan. Somehow, I have to get them to let go of the notion that Tommy and I are a couple. I need to convince them to keep an open mind about Alex. If they do, I know they'll see what I see. But how do I do it?

I grab my phone and call Lana. She'll know what to do.

"Hello?"

"Hey, girlie. Thanks for telling Alex about my party."

"Phew," she laughs. "When I didn't hear from you, I assumed you were mad at me."

"I could never be mad at you."

"How did your parents take him being there?"

"Not well. Mom freaked out when she saw him. They were even more furious when I left with him for the weekend. I haven't seen them since. That's why I'm calling. I need your help."

"Anything. You name it."

We spend the next half hour planning how to approach my parents. The goal is to focus on the positives. To show them Alex is a wonderful, caring man. That he's a hard worker and successful. He might live in a big city, but where a person lives doesn't have any bearing on their character. That thought is ridiculous. What matters is how he treats me and how we feel about each other. I need them to see how happy Alex makes me.

"Thanks, Lan. I knew you'd be able to help."

"Call me later and let me know how it goes, ok?"

"I will. Love ya."

After I unpack, I decide to make good use of my time and cook dinner.

"Maybe that'll ease things up later," I say to no one as I walk downstairs and into the kitchen. I take my phone out, tap my screen for the music app, and turn the volume up. Singing my favorite songs, I look through the kitchen for dinner ingredients. I decide on steak, fresh potatoes, and a salad from the garden.

I have many fond memories of gardening with my mother.

During the summer, our backyard was transformed into a thriving vegetable garden. Each day, Mom would don her coveralls and slip on her green garden gloves. She'd spend hours keeping the garden weed-free while Michael and I played.

Throughout the summer, we had fresh vegetables with our dinner every night. Then, in the early fall, we'd help her harvest what we hadn't used and preserve it, ensuring we had homegrown food all winter.

Because of my mom's love of gardening, I also grew to love it. While I lived in the city, I wasn't able to garden. Outdoor space comes at a premium. Lana and I had a small balcony where I managed to grow a few herbs, but it wasn't quite the same.

The afternoon has gone by quickly. It's almost time for my parents to get home, so I fire up the grill and start cooking. While I sit in one of our old lawn chairs, I practice what I'll say to them. I imagine how it might go and prepare answers to what I think they'll ask. The conversation plays over and over in my head. This has to work because I don't know what else to do if it doesn't.

The food is nearly done when I hear my parents' car pull into the driveway. I listen for them to come into the house. When they finally reach the kitchen, I open the door and peek in. "Dinner will be ready in a few minutes."

There's no response.

As soon as the food is done, I carry it inside. The salad I'd left on the counter is now on the table. My father sits in his usual chair, a muscle twitching in his clenched jaw. Mom sits to his right, her mouth drawn in a tight line, her eyes narrowed. With shaking hands, I set the food down and take my seat. I thought I was ready for this, but now I'm not feeling quite as confident.

Dad says grace and then quietly makes his plate and begins eating. Mom continues to glare at me.

"I hope you guys like it." I try my best to sound cheerful, hoping it'll break the suffocating tension in the room.

"Do you know how you've caused people to talk this weekend?" Mom asks, disapproval dripping from every word.

I sit up straighter and pull my shoulders back, steeling myself for the conversation.

"Surely I'm not the first unmarried girl who's spent a weekend with her boyfriend?"

"You're ruining your reputation in this town. You're ruining *our* reputation." She folds her hands in front of her. "And you're going to ruin your chances with Thomas. Then where will you be? Who will you marry?"

I laugh out loud. Mom and Dad stop and stare at me like I've gone mad.

"Ruin my chances with Tommy? Mom, do you hear yourself? I've tried to tell you I'm not interested in Tommy, but you won't listen. You aren't hearing me."

"What can you possibly say to make this okay?" Mom asks.

I look back and forth between them. This is the moment I've practiced for all day. When they meet my gaze, disapproval is evident in their eyes. My instincts try to force me to back down and cave to their demands. Why was I so stubborn when Alex asked to stay? I wish he were here now. But, no, this is something I have to do for myself.

I can do this. It's now or never. "I've been seeing Alex since I came home from school."

They remain stoic.

"The trips I've been taking weren't for work. I was with Alex."

Their angry stares pierce through me. But they say nothing.

"Alex is a good man. He's a hard worker, and he treats me well. He makes me happy. I plan to continue seeing him. I'm in love with him."

"That's enough." My father slams his hands on the table, startling me. "You're not to see that man again."

"What? You can't be serious?" I raise my voice.

"Natalie." Mom's tone is condescending. "I understand you think you love him, but he isn't right for you. Once you are away from him, you'll see that too."

It feels like I've been punched in the stomach. I struggle to take my next breath. Is this how Michael felt when he told them he loved Evan? The flicker of hope I had inside, the one that believed they'd see reason, maybe even give me their blessing, has extinguished. I'm alone in the darkness.

"So that's it?"

"I'm done talking," dad says. "Whatever you think you had with him is over." He picks up his fork and resumes eating as if nothing happened.

They expect me to do as I'm told, with no questions, no arguments—it's what I was raised to do. It's what I've always done. But I can't do that anymore. I refuse to be that person again.

This is about my future—my happiness.

I'm sure they believe what they're doing is best for me. Maybe they're trying to save me from heartache? But, where I appreciate that they care about me and want to protect me, I'm an adult now. I have to be allowed to make my own choices. I don't want the same things they want for me.

Why are they refusing to support me? Just once, I'd love for them to cheer me on. Celebrate with me when I succeed, and be there when I fail. Somehow, I have to make them see reason.

"I love you both very much. You've always been there for me. You've guided me, taught me, and raised me well. We've been through a lot, especially losing Michael." The ache in my soul comes back just as strong as the day we lost him, and I struggle to continue. "I thought being the perfect daughter would make our family whole again, but it hasn't. While I was away, I learned a lot about myself. Who I am and what I want. I understand Alex isn't your choice for me, but who I love isn't your choice. That doesn't mean I don't respect you or your input. I do." I pause to swallow the lump in my throat.

"Even if you disagree with my choices, I need you both to see me as a capable adult and at least try to respect them. All I'm asking is that you give Alex a chance. Spend some time with him and get to know him. He's wonderful—"

"That's enough. This is my home. As long as you live under my roof, you will obey my rules." Dad's voice is stern and leaves no room to argue.

I can't believe this is happening. My parents did the same thing with Michael. They shut off and refused to give even an inch. The next thing I say takes even me by surprise.

"I think it's best for all of us if I leave."

It's a move I've been planning to make, but I didn't envision it would happen like this. My father nods in agreement, ending the conversation.

No one speaks through the rest of dinner. The only sound in the room is my parents' forks and knives clinking off their plates. How can they carry on as if nothing happened? Is this my punishment for not obeying? My appetite is gone—nausea bubbles in my stomach. Instead of eating, I push the food around.

After Dad finishes his dinner, he walks into the living room and sits on the couch to read the evening newspaper. Mom goes to the kitchen to clean up. I decide to follow Mom, hoping if it's just her and I alone, we can talk. Maybe we can come to a better resolution.

"Mom."

"No, Natalie. You heard your father. The conversation is over." She turns her back on me.

It feels like I'm reliving the night Michael left home, except this time, it's me that's going. My knees buckle, and I grab the counter for support. I don't want to lose my family, but I refuse to give up Alex. It shouldn't have to be a choice. Why can't I have both? I put my dishes in the sink and quietly walk through the living room. Dad doesn't even look up from the paper.

One by one, I walk up the steps, noticing every creak and crack. I pause when I reach the top and look at the scene downstairs. My parents continue their nightly routine as though nothing's happened.

Once I get into my room, I grab my laptop and sit on my bed to start the search. But like every other time I've looked, there isn't anything available to rent in Northmeadow. I check the listings for a short-term rental at the lake, but with Labor Day in two weeks, everything's booked solid.

I don't know where to look next, so I call Alex. His plane should've landed by now, but my call goes straight to voicemail. I leave a message asking him to call me as soon as possible.

My next call is to Lana.

"How did it go?"

"Awful," I say, barely keeping my composure. "Dad said as long as I live in their house, I have to follow their rules. They actually forbid me to see Alex."

"You've got to be kidding. I'm sorry they're being awful."

"Trust me, I know. I told them I was moving out, but there aren't any available apartments. I even checked the lake for a rental, but there's nothing. I don't know what to do."

"Let me think. What about a hotel?"

"I didn't think about that."

I do a quick search for a hotel that's nearby. Rhonda's old and not in great condition. She's won't make a long commute to work every day.

"I think I found something. The Lakeview Motel. They have cheap rooms, and they rent by the week."

"That sounds perfect."

"It does. Thanks, Lana."

"Anytime."

We hang up, and I make an online reservation. My savings will be enough to cover the room until school starts.

My phone ringing wakes me up. I rub my eyes and strain to read the time. It's three a.m.

"Hello?" I answer, my voice groggy.

"I'm sorry to wake you, baby girl."

"I'm glad you did. You didn't just get home, did you?"

"My flight was rerouted because of a storm." He yawns.

"Oh no, you missed your meeting?"

"I ended up having it online in a quiet corner of the airport café."

"I'm sure that wasn't—" A yawn interrupts my talking. "—ideal. I'm glad you're home safe."

"I got your message. How did things go with your parents?"

"I told them everything. I asked them to give you a chance, but they refused. They forbid me from seeing you as long as I live in their house. So, I told them I'm moving out."

"I'm so sorry, Nat." He pauses before hesitantly asking. "Do you need money?"

"I appreciate your generosity, but I have some saved. I was able to find a small place. The rent is cheap, and they don't require a security deposit." For now, it's best he doesn't know it's a motel room.

"That's one positive thing about not living in New York. It's late. Go back to sleep. I'll call you tomorrow."

"Yes, Sir." The words fall easily from my lips. "Alex?"

"Yes?"

Silence hangs between us as I go to war with myself. Will you rescue me? Will you buy out my contract and bring me back to New York? The words dance on the tip of my tongue but won't come out. Instead, I say, "Thank you for coming this weekend. I love you."

"I love you too, baby girl. Sleep well."

Natalie

After hanging up with Alex, I couldn't fall back to sleep. Every time I closed my eyes, the scene at the dinner table replayed like a bad movie on repeat. My alarm didn't have the chance to wake me since I was already out of bed packing my things.

Today's the day I move out. This whole time I had the silly notion it would be a happy occasion. I thought I'd have the support of my family, but that's not how it's turning out.

After I shove the last of my clothes in, I zip my suitcase and move it to the floor. Then I pull the sheets and blankets up, leaving my bed neatly made. Some habits are hard to break. Most of my things will have to stay here until I find an actual apartment.

Although this option isn't ideal, it's making it possible for me to move out right away. I stuff some essentials in another bag and then grab my suitcase and walk down the steps, setting it by the front door.

Dad's already left for work. Mom's in the kitchen, going through her weekly cleaning routine. Before I leave, I have to try one more time.

"Mom."

She turns around, her reply curt. "What?"

"I found a place to stay. I'm taking some things with me today." My voice cracks as I speak. "But I'm going to leave most of my stuff here for now. I hope that's okay."

For a brief second, Mom drops her mask, and I see the sadness in her eyes. But just as quickly, it's gone. "That'll be fine."

She doesn't even ask where I'm moving to. I step closer, hoping to at least hug her goodbye, but she turns her back on me. "Mom, please," I beg. "I don't want to leave things this way."

"Are you ready to cut that man out of your life?"

"No."

"Then, I think it's best if you leave now."

"Yes, ma'am."

Walking away, I look around the house. A lifetime of memories washes over me. My first day of school. Mom braiding my hair, and Dad tying my saddle shoes. Christmas mornings when Michael and I would sneak down the steps to peek at our presents.

Although tears fill my eyes, I don't let them fall. Everything happens for a reason.

I grab my things and walk out the front door with my head held high.

The mid-morning sun shines brightly as I drive the half-hour to the Lakeview Motel. My commute to work just got longer. Hopefully, Rhonda makes the drive every day without any issues. I pull into a guest parking spot and turn off the car.

There are only two other vehicles in the lot. That doesn't surprise me, as the place isn't exactly a five-star establishment. The planters contain the dead remains of the summer's flowers, and cigarette butts litter the walkways. The outside looks rundown, but it's all I can afford.

"It's only for a few weeks." I remind myself as I get out of the car and go to the main office to get my key.

When I open the glass door, I find myself standing in a dingy, smoke-filled room. To my right are two wooden chairs with torn vinyl seats and a small table littered with magazines. In front of me, there's a tall counter with dark brown paneling. I walk up and peer over it.

A man sits, his back to me, a cigarette in his hand. He's watching a Cardinals game on a flat-screen TV that hangs on the wall. The volume's so loud he hasn't heard me come in.

"Excuse me," I shout to be heard over the television.

The man spins around on his chair. His eyes open wide when he sees me.

"Hello, little lady. How can I help you?"

He stands and takes a puff of his cigarette. The smoke blows in my direction, and I cough. Do I really want to stay here, or will I be safer sleeping in my car?

"Hi," I say, trying to sound more confident than I feel. "I booked a room online last night."

He nods and types on an old desktop computer behind the counter.

"Natalie Clarke?"

"Yes."

"I put you in room seven. You're staying for one week?"

"Your webpage said the rooms could be rented long-term?"

"That's correct." He takes a final puff of his cigarette before snuffing it in the ashtray on the counter.

"Do I pay online for additional weeks?"

"No need." He checks the game over his shoulder before returning his attention to me. "Stop in here, and we can process the payment."

Keys hang on a pegboard next to his computer. I guess this place doesn't do key cards. He grabs the key that hangs under the number seven and walks around the counter, dangling it in the air.

"Can I show you to your room?"

"I think I can find it on my own."

This guy's creeping me out a bit.

"Suit yourself. If you need anything, there's a phone in your room. My name's Marshall. Press #11 to call me."

"Thanks." I take the key and walk out of the office.

I stop by my car, grab my suitcase, and then make my way to the red metal door with the number seven. The lock takes a little jiggling to get it to move, but finally, it clicks open. Pushing the door open, I take my first steps into my new home.

As soon as I enter the room, I gag from the overwhelming musty smell. Clearly, this room hasn't seen the light of day in a long time. The heavy drapes are closed, keeping the room dark. A shiny gold floor lamp, typical cheap motel style, stands in the corner.

I switch the light on and then close the door behind me. This will stay locked at all times. When I go to latch the security chain, I notice it's missing a screw. I'll have to ask Marshall to get it fixed. In the meantime, I grab one of the chairs and wedge it under the doorknob—a little extra security.

Hesitantly, I step further into the room. The carpet is worn and stained, probably where most of the smell comes from. I don't want to know what's stained it. There's a double bed on the wall to my right. Walking by, I run my hand over the ugly floral bedspread. On the wall over the bed hangs two pictures, each in a cheap plastic gold frame. The photos must be from the 1980s, with bright colors and geometric patterns. The amount of dust on them must be from the '80s as well.

Across from the bed is a wooden dresser. Sitting on top of it is an old television. Good thing I don't watch much TV.

The last place to explore is the bathroom. I'm almost afraid to look, but curiosity gets the better of me. Pushing open the squeaky door, I walk into the small space. The first thing I notice is there's no window, only an overhead light with one light bulb burned out. I have to close the door to access the white pedestal sink. On the wall above it hangs a cracked mirror held together by a strip of tape. Opposite the sink is a toilet, and on the back wall is a walk-in shower—no tub.

"That's okay. I can live with only having a shower," I say aloud.

Closing the door to the bathroom, I go back into the main room and sit on the bed. It takes a few minutes for me to get my thoughts together and come up with a plan. First things first. I need some cleaning products to disinfect the room, and then I'll buy my own sheets and a new comforter. That should help the space feel more like home.

This room needs some fresh air and sunlight. I head to the window and pull open the drapes. Dust flies everywhere, making me sneeze. But now, the bright midday sun is shining in the room. It makes the place feel better already. The hand crank on the window is stuck. I struggle with it for a few minutes before it finally gives way, allowing the window to open and fresh air to flow into the room. I make a mental note to buy an air freshener.

It's not the apartment I shared with Lana in the city, but it's not that bad. I can make it work until I find a real place.

I pull up Alex's contact in my phone. He won't like this, but I know he'll at least try to respect my decision. I tap the video call button and wait for him to answer.

"Hi. I didn't expect you to call so soon."

"I told you I'd call when I was settled."

Alex gives me a quizzical look. "It's barely been two hours. You've moved in already?"

"Well—" I hesitate. "I didn't find an apartment, exactly."

"Natalie, turn the camera around. I want to see where you are."

"Yes, Sir." I take a deep breath, tap the icon to reverse the camera, and pan around the room.

"Where the hell are you?" Alex yells.

His tone catches me off guard. He's never yelled at me before.

"It's a little motel outside of Northmeadow." I flip the camera back to me.

"A motel? It looks like a dump. Is it even safe?"

"Safe enough." I shrug.

"Safe enough? I'm getting you a room somewhere better."

"It's only for a few weeks. I'll be okay, I promise."

The heated discussion continues with a lot of back and forth. I know Alex has the means to get me something better, and although he begs me to see reason, he doesn't force his will on me. That's one of the things I love about him.

Alex never uses his authority to take away my voice. He's reasonable and fair and understands the importance of allowing me to make this choice. He doesn't like it, but he respects it—respects me.

"It's only for a few weeks. A month tops. I'll keep looking for an apartment. I promise."

"Fine. But promise me you'll keep the door locked and chained."

Neither of us wants to say goodbye, but he has to get back to work, and I have to run into the office for a few hours to do some last-minute prep before school starts.

"I have meetings the rest of the afternoon. I'll text you if I'm running late."

I see the stress on his face. This new client account is taking up a lot of his time.

"I'll be here when you get home." I smile, hoping to ease some of his worries. "Talk to you later." I reluctantly tap the screen, making Alex's image disappear.

So much has changed over the past few days. Alex showing up at my party was the best thing that could've happened to me—to us. I don't know how I would've found the courage to tell my parents everything without it. Keeping him a secret was hard on our relationship. Looking back, I see how unfair it was to him. It makes me even more thankful that he stuck around and gave me a chance.

When I left New York, I was uncertain if Alex and I could have a future together. Now, I can't imagine a future without him.

Alex

I KEPT MY COMPOSURE, MOSTLY, UNTIL WE HUNG UP. NOW, I'M PACING around my office, talking to myself like a man gone mad. A motel? There's tons of work begging for my attention, but I can't focus on any of it. My mind is in Northmeadow with a certain young lady. I need to talk to Brandon. He's not in the office this week, so I call him.

"Hey, Alex. What's up?"

"What the hell is she thinking?" I yell.

"Slow down. Who are we talking about?"

"Natalie. She had a fight with her parents."

"Lana told me about it."

"She can't find an apartment. So she's staying at some cheap motel." I rub the back of my neck.

Brandon's like a brother to me and always manages to talk me off the cliff. Right now, I need his advice because I'm teetering on the edge.

"Let me get this straight. The town she lives in is so small there are no apartments for rent?"

"It's hard to imagine. But I checked for myself while we were talking. There's really nothing."

"Shit. That *is* a small town."

"What do I do? Because right now, I'm ready to get on a plane and drag her back here."

"You need to give her some space."

"Space?" I ask, raising my voice once again. "How do I take care of her by giving her space?"

"Relax. You told me her parents were smothering her, trying to dictate her life?"

"Yes." I tap my fingers on my desk.

"Now you want to go there and bulldoze her with your agenda. That makes you no different than anyone else in her life. As her Dominant, that isn't your role. I promise it'll backfire on you."

I think about his words for a minute. As much as I hate to admit it, he's right.

"I don't know what to do." I drop my head into my hands.

"Are you in love with her?"

Brandon knows my history. He knows I didn't want to get involved with a sub, let alone fall in love with someone. When I took Natalie as a sub, he was happy for me. We've been so busy going in opposite directions at work. When I'm in the office, Brandon's traveling, and he's in the office when I'm traveling. And when I'm alone at night, he's with Svetlana. I haven't had the chance to tell him about my feelings for Natalie. Do I tell him now?

"Yes." A single word.

"I'm happy for you, brother."

"Thanks. But what do I do? How do I fix this for her?"

I'm out of my league. I'm a Dominant. I know how to make a submissive bend to my will—and enjoy it. What I don't know is how to be a Dominant and a boyfriend at the same time. The rules are different, and I'm struggling to keep up.

"Right now, the best thing you can do is be there for her. Listen when she needs someone to talk to. Support her, but unless it's something you've already agreed on, you can't control her decisions."

We talk until my secretary buzzes that my next client is on the line and ready for our conference call.

"I have a meeting I need to be in. Thanks, Brand. I appreciate your help."

Natalie

I CAN'T BELIEVE LABOR DAY WEEKEND HAS COME AND GONE, AND I spent it holed up in my room. The hot, humid summer air is already starting to change, ushering in the crispness of autumn—which is spectacular in Northmeadow.

The leaves on the trees color the mountains in shades of red, yellow, and orange. Being gone for so long, I forgot how beautiful it is and can't wait to see nature's show.

Living at the motel isn't all that bad, either. Now that I have everything clean and smelling fresh, it feels like a home. Marshall even let me get a small fridge and a microwave for my room. I can't make gourmet meals, but it beats eating out every night.

With the change of seasons also comes the start of school.

My alarm goes off as planned, allowing me enough time to shower before leaving for work. As usual, the water is lukewarm, but that's something else I've gotten used to, and now I take a very efficient shower.

After I wrap myself in a towel, I grab my phone and read the messages from my friends back in the city wishing me good luck. I love that they haven't forgotten about me. With my phone in hand, I walk to the full-length mirror I purchased. The bathroom's cracked mirror is useless. It's the one thing Marshall hasn't fixed. I grab my comb and run it through my hair before applying some product. Then, I take my time applying make-up while texting Lana in between.

Dropping my towel to the floor, I slip into a lacy bra and panty set. I snap a picture and text it to Alex. He loves it when I send sexy pictures of myself. I'm wearing the outfit I picked out weeks ago—a black pencil skirt and a soft blue blouse. When I turn to face the mirror, the image reflecting back at me is that of a professional woman—put together and confident. If only my hands will stop shaking.

The time on my phone reads seven-thirty. If I don't get on the road, I won't make it on time. I grab my bag, slip into my black heels, and walk out the door. The holiday weekend has brought a lot of people to the motel, although I'm not sure why.

When I got home yesterday, the lot was full, and I had to park at the far end. I make my way across the parking lot when I spot Marshall leaning against the brick wall outside his office, a cigarette in his hand. I laugh when I think back to the day I first met him. Over the past few weeks, I've gotten to know him better. We've shared lunches at the picnic table in the grassy area outside his office a few times.

He's in his mid-thirties and has never been married. Marshall bought this place a few years ago, hoping to make it a place tourists want to stay rather than a place they settle on when everything else is booked. He intended to fix it, but it's more expensive than anticipated. I've offered to speak to Alex for him and see if he can do anything to help marketing-wise. But Marshall refuses to accept a handout.

"You're all dressed up today," Marshall calls across the parking lot.

"First day of work."

"Knock 'em dead, kid."

"Thank you." I smile and get into my car.

The drive into Northmeadow feels like it takes forever. I miss the convenience of hopping on a subway or being able to walk wherever I need to go. Despite continually checking the listings for an apartment in town, there's still nothing available. I've even looked into renting a lake house, but most owners are closing them up. I'm already dreading this drive when winter comes. My phone rings just as I pull into the busy school parking lot. I smile when I see who it is.

"Alex. I didn't think I'd hear from you until tonight."

"Did you think I'd let you start a new job without wishing you good luck?"

Although I can't see him, from the tone of his voice, I know he's smiling. I let my head fall back on the headrest and close my eyes.

"I'm so nervous. I hope I can do this."

I've studied and trained for this job for the past six years. I know I have the right skills, but self-doubt has crept in again.

"Take a deep breath and relax." His voice is deep and sexy, causing my thoughts to drift elsewhere. "I know you and how invested you are in this. You're going to do terrific. They're lucky to have you."

"I have to get inside before I'm late. Love you. Talk to you later."

After hanging up, I step out of my car and walk through the busy parking lot toward my old high school. This time, it's not as a student but as a faculty member.

The parking lot is buzzing with activity. Students are milling about greeting each other before filing into the side entrances of the building. No one seems to pay me any attention as I walk past them to the teacher's entrance.

I climb the main steps and pause before opening the heavy wooden door. When I take the next step, my heel catches in a crack, and I trip over the threshold. I stumble right into Mr. Meadows.

"Oh my gosh, I'm so sorry."

"Good morning, Ms. Clarke." Mr. Meadows frowns as he gives my appearance a once over. "I guess you didn't take my advice on your style of dress. In the future, remember this is a small farm town, not the fancy city."

A few students walking by snicker. My cheeks heat with embarrassment at his public reprimand.

"Yes, sir. I'll try to keep that in mind."

I didn't think my outfit was too fancy until I glance at the other teachers' clothes and realize I don't fit in. The male teachers, including Mr. Meadows, wear khaki pants or jeans with a polo-type shirt. Some female teachers wear slacks, the polyester variety, with a blouse buttoned up high. Two female teachers are wearing skirts that go to their ankles. My clothes aren't revealing by any standard, but I stand out compared to my colleagues' overly conservative outfits.

When I was a student, I never paid attention to what my teachers were wearing. When I interned in the city, my current outfit was standard. I'll have to stop by my parent's house after work and grab some of my old clothes.

I mumble an awkward good morning to the faculty members standing nearby, watching the encounter before lowering my eyes and walking away. I hear my name whispered, but I refuse to turn around. The last thing I need is for them to think they've got to me.

Ms. Campbell tried to warn me. She suspected I might not receive a warm welcome. She'd heard whispers that my support of Michael and Evan wasn't forgiven or forgotten. I listened to what she said but convinced myself that enough years had passed. There was no way the community could possibly still hold that against me. Guess I was wrong.

As I walk the long hallway, weaving my way between students, many thoughts race through my head. I remind myself that none of that matters. It doesn't change my reason for being here. I'm here for one reason—to help the kids who feel they don't have a voice.

When I get to my office, I reach into my pocket, grab my key, and place it in the lock. But when I turn it, I realize the door is already open. That's odd. I'm sure I locked it when I left yesterday.

Pushing the door open, I'm met with the sweet fragrance of flowers. On my desk sits a beautiful bouquet of red roses. I grab my phone from my bag before tossing it onto my chair. Snapping a picture, I send a text to Alex.

Me: Thank you for the flowers. They're beautiful.

Alex: They are beautiful, but they aren't from me.

If they aren't from him, then who are they from? I search the bouquet for the card.

Natalie,
Roses are beautiful, but they're nothing compared to you. Good luck on your first day.
I'll see you tonight.
Love Tommy.

Furious, I rip up the card and dump the flowers into a trashcan in the hallway.

Alex: Was there a card?

Me: Yes.

Alex: And? Who are they from?

Me: Tommy. They're in the trash. I'll call you later.

After recovering from the shock of the flowers, it's time to put my game face on and get to work. Today and every day this week, I'll be stopping in several classrooms to introduce myself to the students and tell them about the new counseling programs available.

After each classroom visit, I leave pamphlets the students can take and read on their own time. It's important they know I'm here for them no matter what they want to talk about.

When I return to my office, I leave the door open and sit at my desk. I'm very proud of how the room turned out. I still have the chair with a worn-out cushion, but now it has a brightly colored rainbow-shaped pillow. The other side of the room is much less formal. The old floor is covered by a circular rug with the yin/yang symbol. A few tie-dyed bean bag chairs are arranged on the floor around the rug.

Against the far wall, under the windows, is a small bookshelf. My psychology-themed books are on the top two shelves. The bottom shelf has various fidgets, including Rubik's cubes, stress balls, adult coloring books, gel pens, putty, and other sensory things. In the far corner is a white noise box that quietly plays the sound of ocean waves in the background.

I've tried to create a relaxed and welcoming environment. I hope my future clients feel the same way.

I'm looking over some files I was given for students considered to be high-risk when there's a knock on my door. I look up and spot a female student is standing in the doorway. I close the file I'm reading and set it aside.

"Come on in. Grab a seat wherever you're comfortable."

She closes the door behind her before taking tentative steps into my office. Her eyes open wide when she notices the bean bag chairs. "May I?"

"Absolutely. I'm Natalie."

"My name's Mary," she says quietly.

Mary. She looks very familiar, but I can't quite place why.

"It's nice to meet you."

"Thanks. My brother said you'd be nice and that you're safe to talk to."

"Your brother? May I ask his name?"

"Billy Simmons. He was two years behind you in high school."

Oh my goodness, this is little Mary Simmons, although she's not little anymore.

"I remember your brother. How is he?"

"He's doing good. Now."

"Please tell him I said hi. And thank him for the good reference."

"When I get to talk to him again, I will." Mary looks down at her lap and fidgets with her fingers.

It's clear she's nervous, so I get up from behind my desk and walk over to a bean bag chair.

"Mind if I sit?" She shakes her head, and I sit easily despite wearing a skirt. It's a skill I perfected while working at an after-school program in the city. I grab two plastic containers of putty from the shelf.

"Want one?"

"Sure," she says, smiling.

I toss one, and she catches it easily. We work the putty through our fingers while chatting about what grade she's in her favorite subject—the easy stuff. After getting a little more comfortable with each other, I ask, "What's brought you in today?"

She stops playing with her putty momentarily and looks up at me. "Do you know about my brother and everything that happened to him?"

"No. Are you comfortable telling me?"

Mary explains when Billy was sixteen, he told their parents he was gay.

"They freaked out." She stands up and begins pacing the room. "They told him he needed to be cured of his evil ways, so they sent him away to get conversion therapy."

Flashbacks of the night Michael and Evan came out play in my head. Now's not the time to get lost in those memories. I stand up from my bean bag and walk over to my desk, leaning against the edge.

Mary's still pacing, her face red with anger. She has a death grip on the putty. "Two years," she says louder. "Billy was there for two years while they did unspeakable things to him. As soon as he turned eighteen, he signed himself out. He wasn't the same for a long time after that." She quickly wipes her tears.

"I'm very sorry that happened."

Mary stops, pushes her shoulders back, and looks me straight in the eyes. "I was born female, but I don't identify as one. I have a girlfriend I'm in love with. Eventually, I want to have gender reassignment surgery. Other than Billy and my girlfriend, you're the only one who knows. I'm sick of pretending. Sick of hiding. I'm ready to come out," she says without breathing.

"Thank you for trusting me with your story. I'm glad to hear you're ready to tell everyone, and I will support you through that process. But first, I'd like to try talking about it. Maybe put a plan together. Would that be okay?"

She grabs the rainbow pillow from the chair before sitting down. "Yes."

"Good." I smile and take a seat behind my desk. "Before we get too far ahead of ourselves, there's some paperwork we have to do. We have about ten minutes before lunch is over. We can start it now if you want. Then we can set up a regular time to meet. I'll let your teacher know and have you excused from class."

Mary agrees, and we start the intake paperwork. "What are your pronouns?" I ask, wanting to make sure I address them correctly and respectfully.

"They/them," Mary replies.

"Thank you for sharing," I say with a nod. "It's important to me that you feel seen and respected here."

Mary shifts slightly in their chair, their lips pressing together as if considering my words. "I guess I'm not really used to that," they admit quietly, their gaze flickering to the floor before meeting mine again. "But thank you." There's a hint of vulnerability in their voice, as though the acknowledgment catches them off guard but means more than they expected.

We get about halfway through it before the bell rings. Then, we agree on a regular day and time to meet.

"I'll get the info to your teacher. So you know, everything we talk about here is confidential. The same goes for your teacher knowing about your sessions. She can't tell anyone. Your parents will not be informed without your consent."

"Good. I don't want them to know I'm talking to you yet."

We say our goodbyes, and Mary heads back out into the hall. I watch as she easily blends back into the matriculation of students. No one notices or cares that she's just left my office.

My first day is busier than I ever imagined it would be. Besides Mary, three other students stopped in and signed up for counseling appointments. A few others stopped by and asked for more information on available services. After the final bell, I pack up my stuff and make sure to lock the door.

Before I go back to the motel, I need to swing by my parents' house. I'm glad they aren't there, and I use my key to let myself in. I grab some clothes and throw them into a small suitcase. I hate putting these back on. It feels like a huge step backward, but I have to choose my battles. Then I hurry out. I'm not ready for another confrontation with my parents.

After leaving their house, I stop at a grocery store to grab a few microwave meals and sodas. They don't make the best dinners, but it's much cheaper than eating out. I'm trying to save every penny I can to put toward an apartment when one opens up.

When I get back to my room, I put the groceries away. Even though it's early, I'm exhausted. I change into comfy pajamas before I microwave some dinner.

For the rest of the evening, I work on the intake paperwork for my newest clients. The district has finally gone digital, so I can access the kids' files from home instead of staying late at school. Good thing I have a mobile hotspot on my phone because the rooms don't have wifi.

I'm startled when my phone rings. I didn't realize it was already nine. I swipe to accept the video call request, a pattern that's become familiar these past few months.

"Hey, baby girl."

"Hi, handsome," I reply and blow him a kiss.

"How was your first official day?"

"Great. I had a total of four students sign up for counseling. Can you believe it?"

"Of course, I believe it." His eyes fill with pride as he speaks.

"I know, but I wasn't sure." I lean back on my pillows. "The adults in this town are so close-minded. I wasn't sure how much of that had been passed down to the kids. But I think I have an opportunity to help them."

"I'm very proud of you."

"Thank you, Sir." Knowing I've pleased him fills me with pride. "How was your day?"

"Busy." Alex takes a deep breath and rakes his hand through his hair. His face is etched with concern.

"What's wrong?" I ask, suddenly filled with worry.

"It's the new account I've been working on."

"Did something happen?" I sit up, alarmed. I know this account is important to his firm.

"No, it's all good. It's just that this account comes with some travel obligations."

It isn't unusual for Alex to travel, especially for his important clients.

"Where do you have to go?"

"Russia."

"Did you just say Russia?"

Turmoil swirls in his blue eyes. "Yes."

"When do you leave?"

"In two days."

"How long will you be gone?" I ask quietly, afraid of his answer.

"I'll be there until mid-December."

Until December? That's nearly three months. He's never had to travel for that long.

Alex is quiet, watching and waiting for my response. I see how much he's struggling with this, so I try to put on a brave face.

"I'm sad you'll be gone for so long, but I know this is a huge opportunity." I try to find a positive in this situation. "And you'll be home before Christmas."

Over the next two hours, I ask him all about his upcoming trip. He seems to relax some as he tells me more about it. On Maxim's insistence, he'll be staying with the Soloniks.

I stayed there when I visited with Lana. Their home is as grand as a hotel. The trip will be long, but this account is huge for him. It'll be the second-largest account his firm holds, Maxim's being the largest.

Alex tries to explain the company's new energy-efficient technology. I don't understand what it all means or why a Russian company wants to advertise in the U.S. When I asked, Alex told me there are confidential parts of the business. Proprietary stuff, I guess.

"It's going to mean a lot more travel. I'm hoping you'll accompany me on some of the trips."

His eyes hold so much hope as he waits for my answer. I want to say yes, that I'd follow him anywhere, but my schedule isn't as fluid as his.

"If it's a school holiday or I can get some time off, I'd love to travel with you."

The smile he gives melts my heart. Unfortunately, it's gotten late for both of us. This is the part I hate the most—saying goodbye. Each time, it gets more and more difficult.

After we hang up, my brave façade slips away. Being a few states away is hard enough, but at least we get to see each other every few weeks. This will be different. He'll be on the other side of the world, and we won't see each other for three months.

I grab Alex's T-shirt, the one I kept from our last weekend together, and hold it close as I fall asleep.

I left for Russia two weeks ago. Although it killed me to put more physical distance between us, especially with how much Natalie's struggling, I had no choice. My business with Maxim and Nicholai can't wait. Natalie was understanding, although I could see the sadness in her eyes.

The eight-hour time difference has made things more challenging. Daily contact is important to both Natalie and me. We have our video calls when Natalie gets home from work, which is about midnight. I'm trying to keep things creative, so every afternoon, I text her a sexy challenge for our call that evening. It's not the same as being together in person, but we're doing our best to make it work.

"Hi, baby girl," I say when the video comes to life.

"Hello, Sir."

She obeyed today's challenge and is kneeling beside her bed, wearing only a tiny pair of red lacy panties.

"You look gorgeous."

"Thank you, Sir."

"You may get up and sit on the bed. There are some things I want to talk about."

Natalie stands and readjusts her laptop before crawling across the bed. I'm treated to a fantastic view of her breasts through the camera lens. I groan, wishing I was there. Natalie giggles before she sits and gets comfortable.

Seeing her topless, her nipples erect, and begging for attention makes it difficult to concentrate on the conversation we need to have. I didn't think my request for so little clothing through. This will be a lesson in self-restraint for me as well.

"Obviously, we both want to continue working on our dynamic. So, I've been trying to come up with things we can do even while we're so far apart. I want to add some daily tasks to keep us connected."

"I like the sound of that."

"I've come up with a few activities we can do individually, and then we can talk about them on our video calls. I'd also like to know if you have anything you want to add."

"This is a great idea."

"I found a journaling app. I'd like you to write in it every day. I can access it from here and will write back to you."

Finding a solution to address Natalie's emotional struggle was a challenge. We're in nearly opposite time zones, so often, when she needs me, I'm not available. I'm hopeful having a place to write her concerns, struggles, and victories will be an avenue to increase our communication.

"I haven't been exercising like I should since I've been home."

"I've been lax with it as well. Especially since being over here."

Natalie asks to add daily exercise to our tasks. It was never a rule, just something she and I used to do together. We write up a plan that we both promise to stick to. Then, I send her the link to the journal.

"I didn't realize there was anything like that available."

"I'm hoping this will become an important tool in keeping us connected."

"I don't know how you came up with this idea, but it's perfect."

"You know what else is perfect?"

"What, Sir?" She bites her lip.

"You. Now, take off your panties, and let me see you."

I stroke myself while I watch Natalie. My body is jealous of her fingers. It wants to be the one touching her soft, wet skin. To be the one giving her pleasure. Natalie throws her head back as her orgasm hits. My body follows. As good as it feels, it's not the same as being with her.

Natalie

Alex's idea of using this journal app is perfect. So often during the day, I want to grab my phone to text or call him. Then I remember the time difference. Having the journal makes it feel like I have more access to Alex while he's gone. I open the app on my laptop and type a note for him.

I'm really missing you today. Work is a double-edged sword. The kids seem to be embracing my services with open arms, but I'm not making any friends with the staff. But that's okay. Who am I kidding? It's not okay. It's lonely—I'm lonely. I'd like to have even one person here to talk to. Maybe someone to sit with at lunch. I've taken to staying in my office and eating at my desk instead.

I have to remind myself that I'm here for the kids, not the staff. I think I'm making a difference with them, especially with M. They're strong and brave. They know what they want and are not afraid to go after it. I love their tenacious spirit.

You asked if things were any better with my parents. Mom calls once a week. I'm hopeful our relationship is beginning to heal, even if just a little.

Tensions are still high with Dad. He and I haven't talked much. He's furious that I chose to defy him, but I haven't lost hope that he'll come around eventually. I've tried to bring up the subject of you and me. When I do, Mom shuts it right down. I'm trying not to push but not to let it be forgotten, either.

One good thing she's stopped bringing up Tommy. Hopefully, she's realized that's a dead end. I know they'll come around and see what we have is real.

I have to get back to work. Lunch is over. I love you.

~Natalie

I close the app and sit back in my chair. This separation was a bit rocky at first, but Alex and I have fallen into a routine uniquely our own. The journal has been a big part of that. I can write to him whenever I need, and I know he'll read it. Getting his notes back is equally as exciting. It's adding another dimension to our relationship. It's helped make the distance a little easier. But I still can't wait until he's home and we can be together again.

The rest of the afternoon goes by slowly. I don't have any more appointments today. I'm sitting in my office, finishing some paperwork, waiting for three-thirty when my phone rings.

"Hi, Mom," I answer cheerfully.

"Natalie, your father isn't feeling well. We had to close the pharmacy counter early, but we didn't want to close the rest of the store. Can you come in and work until close?"

"Yes, of course. Is Dad alright?"

"I think he has the flu. He's been working himself too hard."

My father never gets sick, but I'm thankful Mom reached out to me. This is the first time since I moved out that they've asked me to work. I'm sure this is a good sign.

"I'm done here in a half-hour. I'll come right over."

"Mrs. Smith will stay until you get there," Mom pauses. "Thank you, Natalie."

"You don't have to thank me. Tell Dad I hope he feels better."

The phone disconnects. I hold it in my hand, savoring the brief moment where it felt like things were okay between us—like nothing bad had ever happened. I drop Alex a quick text letting him know I won't be able to call him after work. I'm going to miss talking to him, but I'm also glad for something to do. It gets lonely sitting in that motel room every night.

Finally, the bell rings, ending the school day. I grab my stuff and am one of the first out of the building and to my car. The pharmacy is only a few blocks down the street, so it doesn't take me long to get there. Dad's store is small, unlike the two-story Duane Reade pharmacies all over New York City.

Clarke's Pharmacy is more of an old-fashioned operation. My parents know all their customers by name and still offer personal lines of credit to them. Dad carries only the tried-and-true essentials. He rarely orders anything new. *'The people in this town don't like to try new things. They stick to what they know works,'* is the motto he lives by.

While that may be true, Dad seems to ignore the fact that Northmeadow sees a lot of tourists during the summer. In my opinion, many sales opportunities are missed because of that.

Coming to the pharmacy is almost like coming home. I grew up helping my parents in the store, so much of my life is connected to it. My Grandpa Clarke opened it when he was about my age. My father followed in his footsteps. He always hoped Michael would continue the family tradition, but Michael wasn't interested.

I was their Plan B, but they discouraged me from becoming a pharmacist because I'm a girl. I didn't fight them. I wasn't interested in that career path anyway. That's where Tommy came in.

My parents focused on their future son-in-law, encouraging him to pursue a PharmD so he could take over the store for them. I don't know what their plans are now that Tommy didn't finish school.

The bells on the door jingle when I pull it open and step into the store. Mrs.

Smith is in a tizzy and barely gives me time to get behind the register before rushing to gather her things.

"It's about time," she says.

"I got here as soon as I could."

I try to stay out of her way as I watch her hurrying about.

She stops and gives me a cross-look. "You wouldn't understand, Natalie," she says as if reading my thoughts.

"What do you mean?"

She crosses her arms.

"Things like making sure to be home and having dinner on the table for your husband as soon as he's home from work. Old fashioned values that your generation has written off."

Her words sting, but I bite my tongue. Arguing with her will do no good. I remain quiet while she grabs her purse, says a quick goodbye, and hurries out the door.

I lean back against the counter. Mrs. Smith's words play over and over in my head. Alex may not be my husband, but I understand and embrace putting him first. It's the heart of my relationship with him. Everything I do as a submissive is meant to put Alex's needs ahead of mine. Our relationship isn't that much different than so many of the relationships in this town—my parents included. I laugh out loud. Except for what we do in the bedroom, *that* is much different.

An idea pops into my head. Maybe this is the angle I need to take with my parents. All they've ever wanted is for me to be in a relationship that mimics theirs. Being with Alex isn't how they assumed it would happen, but if they see it in action, it could change the game. I'll ask Alex if he's willing to come in for a weekend when he gets back from Russia. We can plan to spend some time with my parents. It'll give us a chance to show them that part of our relationship—the *old-fashioned* part. If they see the similarities, they won't have an argument against it anymore. This could be the key to getting them to accept us.

The store is pretty much dead. Only two customers come in. Finally, it's nine o'clock, time to close up. I lock the front door and grab the register drawer. As I walk to the back of the store, I peek down the aisles, ensuring everything is neat and organized for the morning. Then, I lock the drawer in the safe and let myself out the employee door around the back.

Tommy

I'VE BEEN WATCHING NATALIE FROM A DISTANCE FOR THE PAST FEW weeks. She doesn't know I have a second car, which allows me to stay undetected. It's been easy to learn Natalie's schedule. She's so predictable. In the morning, she goes to work. A couple times a week, she stops at the grocery store before going back to that dump of a motel where she's staying.

Speaking of the motel, I stopped by last week—uninvited, of course. I was outside Natalie's door, about to let myself in.

"What the hell do you think you're doing?" A male voice asked from behind me.

I spun around and quickly slid the lock pick into my back pocket.

"I'm a friend of Natalie's. I stopped by to see if she was home."

"I've seen you sitting across the street watching her. And picking a lock isn't the usual way to see if someone's home."

"I was just trying to surprise my girl. You know, trying to be romantic."

"If I see you here again, there won't be time for a nice conversation like this. It'll be a one-way conversation." He pulled a gun from his waistband. "Now, I suggest you get the hell off my property."

I lifted my hands. "No harm done, man," I said and slowly backed away.

He screwed up my plans for her at the motel, but at least I still have her parents in my corner. Charlotte called me earlier to let me know Natalie was working at the pharmacy tonight, just in case I wanted to stop by to see her.

As a matter of fact, I do want to pay her a visit. I park across the street from the pharmacy, in the lot for the grocery store, and wait. It's almost nine. Natalie will be getting ready to lock up soon. This is my chance. The streets are deserted as usual, but that works in my favor tonight.

Even still, I'm careful to check my surroundings before getting out of my car and crossing the street. I walk around the back of the pharmacy to the employee entrance, waiting for Natalie to come out.

My prescription ran out, and the damn doctor won't give me another one. He had the nerve to accuse me of being an addict. Suggested I seek treatment for my *problem*. Screw him. I'll find another doctor who'll give me what I need. I've done it before. It takes time, though.

The problem is that I took my last pill earlier today, and it's worn off. The withdrawal is making my eyes water and my hands tremble. Sweat is pouring off me even though I'm not hot. I need some pills to hold me over for a few days. Stanley always spots me a few until I get a new prescription, but he's not here tonight. Natalie will do it. She'd never tell me no.

Movement catches my eye. The door is starting to open. Quietly, I move in closer. She doesn't hear me. She's focused on locking the door. I walk up behind her and place my hands on her shoulders. She screams, and I put my hand over her mouth.

"Relax, it's just me," I say, trying to calm my girl down.

She spins around to face me. "You almost gave me a heart attack."

"I'm sorry." I reach out and tuck a loose curl behind her ear.

She tries to move away, but I place my arms on both sides of her head, caging her against the door.

"I need to get some pills."

"Dad's not here tonight. You'll have to come back in the morning." She tries to duck under my arms, but I don't let her move.

"I can't wait, Nat. I need them tonight." I rock back and forth on my feet, fighting waves of nausea.

"I've already closed up and can't fill a prescription even if I wanted to." She pushes at my arms, but I don't budge. "Please let me go."

"My prescription ran out. I need a few pills to hold me over."

"I can't help you, Tommy." She squirms, trying to get away. "Please just move out of the way and come back in the morning."

Why is she making this more complicated than it has to be?

"I'm not asking, Natalie. Open the damn door and get me some pills."

I know I'm scaring her. I don't want to do that, but I need her to cooperate. I place my hands on her shoulders and turn her to face the door.

"Unlock it." I hold her firmly until she puts the key in the lock and pulls the door open.

With my hands on her shoulders, I force her body forward. She reaches to turn the lights back on, but I stop her.

"No lights. We don't need any unnecessary attention, do we?"

She shakes her head but doesn't make a sound. I guide her to the pharmacy area.

"I don't know Dad's code for the lockbox."

Natalie must think I'm stupid. She's worked here since she was a kid and knows how to access everything. Hell, she could be the damn pharmacist if she wanted to.

I lean close and whisper, "Don't play dumb, sweetheart. I know you know the code." Her body is trembling. She's afraid. I have to admit, her fear turns me on. I lean in and kiss her neck.

She tries to pull away, and I snicker. "Open it and get the Oxy." She doesn't move. "Now."

I give her a small push forward, encouraging her to comply.

Slowly, she punches in the code to the lockbox where Stanley keeps the pain meds. She moves her head slightly, eyeing the silent alarm button only a few feet away.

"Don't even think about it, Natalie. Just take out a few pills and hand them to me. Then we can both go home." I'm beginning to run out of patience.

Without turning around, she says, "You aren't going to get away with this. There are cameras."

"I knocked them offline, and you aren't going to say anything." I know exactly how to play her. I know her weaknesses. "If you do, your parents will get some rather revealing pictures."

"What pictures?"

"Pictures, I know you don't want your parents seeing."

"Where did you get—"

"Don't worry about where. Just know I have them, and I'll use them."

She reaches into the safe and pulls out the bottle. "Three pills, Tommy. That's all you're getting."

"Four. Or your parents get the pictures."

"Fine." With how quickly she's complied, I know I got lucky.

She's hiding something.

There's gotta be dirt on either her or that guy that's hanging around. I'll call my buddy in the police department and have him do some digging for me. Natalie hands me the pills before replacing the bottle and closing the safe.

"I gave you what you want. Now get out."

I'm not taking any chances with her pressing the alarm.

"We'll leave together."

She shakes my hand off her arm and rolls her eyes.

I can't wait to get her back under me in bed. I like this feisty, grown-up version of her. She was always a good lay, and now she'll be even better.

"After you," she says, holding the door open.

I walk past her, not letting her get too far from me. She locks up again and looks around.

"How did you get here? I don't see your truck."

"I walked. You're going to drive me home."

I'll get a ride back to get my car tomorrow. Right now, I have the chance to spend more time with Natalie, and I'm not going to pass that up.

"I'm not driving you anywhere." She crosses her arms. "You walked here. You can walk home."

"Not a chance." I grab her hand and drag her to her car. "My place is on your way."

"Fine." She pulls her hand free. "I'll drive you home. But this is it. You need to leave me alone."

I raise my hands in mock surrender. "Whatever you say, sweetheart."

If she thinks we're through, she has another thing coming.

We're just getting started.

Natalie

My hands tremble as I drive Tommy to his house and drop him off. I make it a mile down the road before I pull over and vomit. There's no way that just happened. I lean my head on the headrest and take a few breaths, trying to calm my racing heart.

Tommy threatened to show my parents pictures of me. Alex and I have exchanged photos in texts and video calls, but I don't see how Tommy could have gotten access to them. Either way, I can't take the chance. I can't tell my parents what happened and risk Tommy showing them anything Alex and I have done. They'd never understand. I'd lose any chance I might have of getting them to accept him.

Once I'm calmer, I pull back onto the road and finish driving to the motel. By the time I make it home, it's late, and I'm mentally and physically exhausted. I text Alex, knowing he'll be getting up any time now. I let him know I'm home safe and will talk to him tomorrow. I can't tell him what happened tonight, either. He's got a lot on his plate with work. I don't want to add to his stress.

My stomach is in knots, so I don't bother eating. I get into pajamas and crawl into bed, hoping to sleep off the night's events.

Alex

I MISSED TALKING TO NATALIE LAST NIGHT, BUT I'M GLAD SHE WAS ABLE to work at the pharmacy. Mending her relationship with her parents is important to her. Hopefully, this is a good sign.

I've been up for a while. I took an early morning run and had a shower. There's some time before I need to be in Maxim's office, so I leave Natalie a note in our journal.

baby girl,

I missed talking to you last night. This distance is killing me. I can't wait to be home and have you in my arms. The things I want to do to you. Next time I have to be gone for so long, you're coming with me.

Have you heard about the days you requested for Christmas? I'll book the flight as soon as you get word. My client just got here, so I have to cut this short.

Be naked and ready for my call tonight.

I love you.
-Sir

Natalie

Farming is a big part of Northmeadow's economy, so school closes for two weeks during the Thanksgiving holiday. This allows the kids to be home to help harvest the fields and prepare their family's farms for winter. Vacation is coming at the perfect time because I'm exhausted. I've been plagued with nightmares since my run-in with Tommy.

In every dream, he has a gun pointed at someone, but I can't see their face. I wake up just as he pulls the trigger. Part of the problem is that I'm keeping the encounter bottled up. I still haven't told Alex what happened. I don't want to waste the precious time we get to talk. And I don't want him worried about me.

I can't tell my parents about it because Tommy can do no wrong in their eyes. I fear if I bring up what happened, it'll only make things with them more tense. The ice is just starting to melt, and I don't want to refreeze the situation. I need to shake the whole thing off. Tommy's addicted to pain meds, and although the other night was unsettling, he'd never harm anyone.

Thanksgiving's in a few days, and I have no plans. Lana and Brandon invited me to spend Thanksgiving with them, but I couldn't bear the thought of going to NYC without Alex being there. While I'm lying on the bed watching a rerun of *Friends*, my phone rings.

"Hi, Mom. How are you?"

"I'm doing well. Busy getting ready for the holiday. Dad and I would like to invite you home for Thanksgiving."

I sit up, shocked by the invitation. Although we've been talking, it's been superficial conversations. I wasn't expecting this.

"Why don't you come early on Wednesday. We'll bake pies, and you can spend the night."

"Thank you. I think that would be nice."

After we hang up, I write a note to Alex.

Sir,

I'm in shock. Mom called and invited me home for Thanksgiving. Can you believe it? I'm going to spend the night on Wednesday. This has to be a step in the right direction. A sign that they're beginning to accept me—and soon us.

I wish you were here. Only two more weeks. I'm counting the hours.

I got the vacation days I requested so I can fly out and spend Christmas with you. I can't wait!

I love you.
~Natalie

I close my laptop but am too excited to sit still. So, I get up and take a shower.

When I was growing up, we affectionately called the day before Thanksgiving 'Pie Day.' Michael, Mom, and I would make apple, pumpkin, and pecan pies. Dad would beg Michael to go to Northmeadow High's big football game, but he always said no. He wasn't into sports. Michael was content to spend the day making intricate designs with pie crust. Together, the three of us made not only delicious but beautiful pies for our holiday meal.

I haven't been home for Thanksgiving in years. I'm excited to have this back.

Natalie

After another restless night's sleep, this time more from excitement than fear, I give up on sleeping and get up. I grab a bowl of cereal and then take a quick shower. I have some time to kill before heading to my parent's house, so I busy myself with checking emails and then packing my overnight bag. The holiday is going to be near perfect. The only thing missing is Alex. I wish he could be here to spend the holiday with us. Next year.

Dad's still at the pharmacy when I get there, so there's room in the driveway, but I don't want to take his spot, so I park on the street. My nerves kick in full force when I shut the car off. I haven't been back home in almost four months. I decide to go into the house with no expectations and take things as they come. Hopefully, everything will go smoothly. I knock on the door before opening it.

"Hi, Mom, it's me," I call.

"Come on in. I'm in the kitchen."

I drop my bag by the door and head straight in. The scent of spiced pecans cooking makes my mouth water.

"It smells delicious in here." I kiss Mom on the cheek.

She's standing at the stove, wearing her ruffled apron with pumpkins on it. Tomorrow, she'll wear her turkey apron. The sight brings back many happy memories.

She points to a chair at the table. "I've made you an apron. I hope you like it."

Walking over to the chair, I spot the apron. It's made from the same fabric as Mom's.

"You didn't have to do that," I say as I hold it up.

Mom's a terrific seamstress. It's an exact replica of hers. But she *really* didn't have to do this. I'm not much for wearing aprons.

"Don't be silly," she says as she pours the cooked pecans onto the waiting wax paper. "The fabric was your grandmother's. She made my apron when I first got married." She wipes her hands off on a dishtowel. "I've saved it all these years waiting for you to be married. But, well, never mind that. It's time you had your own."

"Thank you. I love it." I may not love the apron, but I love the thought and time she put into it. "Can you help me tie it?"

We keep busy in the kitchen the rest of the afternoon, making tomorrow's desserts. Each pie is made from scratch, the crust decorated, and the pie baked to perfection.

In my naivety, I assumed today would be like old times, carefree and easy. But instead, there's an unspoken tension lying just beneath the surface. Conversation is limited, interrupted by uncomfortable periods of silence. I try to ignore the awkward moments, choosing to focus on the spirit of the day. Like when I was a child, I sample the filling for each pie before Mom pours it into the shell.

Michael and I used to fight over who got to lick the mixing bowls. He'd always tease me, reminding me he was the firstborn, so he was entitled to lick the bowl. I'd cross my arms and pout. Then, Mom would get me a second spoon so Michael and I could both scrape the mixing bowls clean. Days like today make Michael's death hurt all over again.

"One day, you'll be doing this with your children," Mom says with a dreamy look.

"I don't think that'll be happening any time soon."

"Well, you aren't getting any younger," Mom says as she puts the last pie in the oven.

"Alex and I have talked about having children."

"Alex? You're still seeing him?"

"Yes, I am." I put the bowl in the sink. "He's in Russia for work right now, but he's planning to spend a weekend here when he gets back. Maybe we can all get together for dinner?"

Mom ignores my question. "We need to clean the kitchen before your father gets home. You know how much Dad hates a mess."

I won't force the issue. I put it out there, and now she can think about it. We clean in silence, getting it done in record time. Per family tradition, Mom calls and orders Chinese take-out. Then, with the table set, we wait for Dad to get home.

He strolls into the house twenty minutes later, food bags in hand. Dad's talkative tonight, something I wasn't expecting.

"How's the job going?".

"Things are going really good. I have a nearly full caseload."

"I'm glad to hear it. You've worked hard for this."

"Alex told me he sent you his marketing plans for the store. Did you have a chance to look at them?"

"I got them. But it's not something I'm interested in."

"Is there something you'd like changed? I can ask Alex—"

"I've run this store on my own for over thirty years. I don't need some young hotshot coming in thinking he knows better than I do."

"I understand.".

I was hoping bringing up something Dad was invested in and that Alex could help with would be a safe topic. But, obviously, I was wrong. Thankfully, the rest of dinner goes by without any more issues.

After we clean up, Mom cooks popcorn on the stovetop. Then, we settle in for another family tradition that started when Michael and I were little.

The town would start putting the Christmas decorations on the lampposts downtown before Thanksgiving. The stores put out their Christmas displays and turned on their Christmas music. We got our parts for the yearly nativity in Sunday school and started rehearsals. Christmas was all around us, making it easy for Michael and me to catch the Christmas spirit.

We'd come home and beg our parents to put up the Christmas tree. Every year, they'd tell us a firm *no*. We had to celebrate Thanksgiving before we could move on to Christmas. But on the night before Thanksgiving, Mom would make popcorn and homemade hot chocolate while Michael and I spread blankets on the living room floor. Then we'd all sit down and watch *Miracle on 34th Street*.

It was just a little taste, enough to get Michael and me through what we thought was the boring holiday that stood between Christmas and us.

"The parade is even better in person," I tell them when we get to that part of the movie. "Maybe you guys can come to New York next year, and we can all go together?"

"I don't think so," Mom answers. "I've seen enough of that city for a lifetime."

"I know it isn't your favorite place. But the parade is something extraordinary. We can have Thanksgiving dinner at Alex's apartment, maybe start some new traditions."

"The answer is no. Dad and I aren't looking for new traditions."

"What happens when Alex and I have children? Won't you want to visit the city and spend the holidays with us?"

Dad lets out a frustrated breath. "I see you haven't gotten over your ridiculous notion of a future with that man."

"It's not ridiculous. We're hoping you'd both be open to spending time with us when Alex gets home." I hesitate before continuing. "I love him. We both want you to be a part of our lives."

"Please don't ruin tonight with any more nonsense," Mom says. "This conversation is over."

They're infuriating.

Even though it's still early when the movie ends, Mom and Dad say goodnight. They'll be up before the sun to start cooking the turkey.

"I'll be up shortly. It's a beautiful evening. I'm going to sit on the porch for a little bit."

It's unseasonably warm, and Alex told me to call after the movie, even though it's the early morning hours in Russia.

"Don't be up late," Mom reminds me. "Tomorrow's going to be a busy day."

"I won't." I shake my head as I walk out the front door. Some things will never change, I guess.

Alex's voice is groggy when he answers the phone. I know I woke him up.

"You should go back to sleep. I can call you later."

"No, I want you to tell me about your day."

I try to condense everything into as short of a story as possible. I can hear how tired he is. He has a big day ahead of him, too. Even though Russians don't celebrate Thanksgiving, the Soloniks are having a special dinner to commemorate the day for Alex.

Irina's never made a turkey before, but she bought one and plans to cook it herself. She even has Alex's mom's recipe for the stuffing. They're such a thoughtful family. Part of me wishes I was there with him.

After we say our goodbyes, I head to bed, my heart heavy. I'm envious of Lana's family. I'd give anything for my parents to be half as open as Maxim and Irina.

Is it possible to love my parents and at the same time wish I had a different family?

Alex

∞

After hanging up with Natalie, I try to fall back to sleep, but that doesn't happen. So, I head to the kitchen and grab a very early breakfast. Maybe I'll get a run in before everyone gets up? Not wanting to wake anyone, I pad through the house quietly. As I move down the hallway toward the kitchen, I spot the library door cracked open. The light is on.

I get closer and peek inside. Maxim's sitting in one of the brown leather wingback chairs in the center of the room. In front of him is a wooden table with an open bottle of vodka sitting on top. A shot glass is in his hand.

"Come in, Alexander." Maxim's voice echoes in the silence.

"I'm sorry. I didn't mean to intrude."

"Get a glass and sit down."

"Yes, sir." It's way too early to drink. The sun isn't even up. But the pained look on Maxim's face implores me to do as I'm told. Walking over to the bar at the back of the room, I grab a shot glass before returning to the chairs and sitting down. Maxim picks up the bottle of vodka and fills our glasses. We share a shot.

I've never seen Maxim like this. His eyes are red, not from alcohol but from tears. Something has gravely upset him, but I'm afraid to ask questions.

"Today would have been Jelena's twenty-fifth birthday."

"I'm sorry, Max."

"As a parent, it is a wonder to see how different your children are. Svetlana was always spirited. She loved to steal the show. But Jelena was quiet. Content to stay in the background."

I listen as Maxim continues.

"I used every contact I had to find my Jelena. I went days without sleep trying to find my little girl. But Jelena was young and still a virgin. She was a sought-after prize and was sold right away." His haunted eyes fill with tears. "By the time we found the

167

man who bought her, it was too late. They raped and tortured my daughter before they killed her."

I can't imagine the heartache of losing a child, but how Jelena died is unimaginable. No parent should ever have to experience that. Maxim avenged his daughter's brutal murder by taking the lives of the men responsible for her death.

"Did you know opening Jelena's Hope was Svetlana's idea?"

"I didn't."

Maxim explains how a young Svetlana approached him with her desire to help other people who were trafficked. "She wanted to make sure they could heal. As difficult as she can be at times. *Moya babochka* has a good heart."

When Lana first came to live with me, I seriously doubted my sanity. Saying she was challenging is putting it mildly. She was infuriating. It took some heart-to-heart conversations with Pyotr to see past her prickly exterior to the scared little girl underneath. That's when I started to see her differently. But it was Brandon who really made a difference for her.

"Alami, that bastard, knew we were coming for Jelena. He had eyes all over and got a tip that my men were coming for him. We missed it, Alexander." His face twists in pain, and he pours himself another shot. "Jelena died because of me."

"That's not true, Max. You did everything you could."

"Some of them are in horrible condition," Max continues. "This is the most dangerous time for a recovered victim. They struggle with finding the will to live again. We lost one young woman in the very beginning. I will never forgive myself for that."

"I see." I know my response is lacking. I'm struggling to keep up and process all this information.

"I know we are fortunate we were at least able to bring her body home. Many families do not get that much closure. That is why I vowed to hunt the scum that preys on innocents until the day I die. It will never bring back my Jelena, but I will ensure her death was not in vain."

My respect for Maxim grows exponentially. "I'll always be available in any way to help you win this war."

I'm honored Maxim chose me.

This is a fight for a worthy cause, one that's part of making the world a safer place.

Natalie

At seven a.m., my alarm goes off. With my eyes still closed, I reach out, trying to find my cell phone to turn the noise off. I'd hoped to sleep in on my vacation, but that's not happening today. Instead, I sit up and stretch. I don't know if it was the comfort and safety of my old bedroom, but for the first time in weeks, I slept all night and didn't have any nightmares.

Climbing out of bed, I throw on sweatpants and a T-shirt, my chosen outfit for the day. As soon as I open the bedroom door, my mouth waters. The fragrant aroma of the turkey has already filled the house. I hurry downstairs to the kitchen, knowing I'll find a familiar sight.

My parents have music on and don't hear me outside the room, so I'm able to quietly watch them. It's like a vignette from my childhood. Dad sits at the kitchen table, cutting the ingredients for his famous stuffing. Mom's at the stove working on her cranberry sauce. In past years, neighbors have placed orders for it ahead of time. I can almost see Michael's ghost at the counter with the Kitchen Aid making home-made whipped cream for the pies.

Michael loved baking and had an exceptional talent for decorating his baked goods. He'd spend hours in the kitchen making decorated cookies in all shapes and designs. He made several birthday cakes for kids' parties. His dream was to open his own bakery. Before I get too emotional, I make my presence known.

"Morning," I say and head straight to the coffee pot.

"Good morning, Natalie," Mom chirps.

"Morning, Dad." I set my cup on the table and kiss his cheek.

"Morning," he grumbles. "You overslept. We've been up for hours working on dinner."

I shrug, refusing to engage.

"There are fresh biscuits and sausage gravy keeping warm on the stove."

"I haven't had that in years." I lift the lid off the pan to take in the aroma of the delicious Southern goodness. I grab a few biscuits and ladle a generous helping of gravy over them before sitting down to eat.

"Can you give me the recipe for this, Mom?"

"Sure, dear."

"I'd like to make this for Alex," I say and quickly take another bite.

"When you're done, can you start setting the dining table?"

"Sure."

"I got everything out. Do you remember how to set up the centerpiece?"

"Of course I do."

We never had company for Thanksgiving, but it didn't matter. It was one of the few days of the year we ate in the formal dining room. Mom would take out her China and set an elaborate table for the holiday. The focal point of the centerpiece was a wicker cornucopia she and Dad made when they were first married.

When Michael and I were kids, our parents made a big deal of filling the empty horn. Each year, Mom would sit down to tell us the history of the cornucopia and how it symbolized abundance. She'd have a bowl full of vegetables, flowers, and decorative gourds we spent all summer growing. Michael and I would take turns stuffing the horn full until the bounty of our work began to overflow into the table. Then, we'd take turns saying things we were thankful for.

It's a memory I treasure deeply.

When I'm finished eating, I wash my dishes and go to the dining room. On the table is Mom's China, but with many more settings than we need for the three of us. I peek my head into the kitchen. "Don't you have too many plates out?"

"No, dear. We're having company."

"Company?" We've never had company for Thanksgiving.

"It's a tradition we started while you were away."

"Who's coming?"

"Reverend Miller and Hannah, Ashlynn and her dad, Delia, and a few others who don't have a family to spend the holiday with," Mom says. "You'll need to change your clothes before we eat. Put on something a bit nicer."

"Please tell me Tommy isn't coming."

"Delia and Tommy are with us every year. You will be on your best behavior."

I can deal with Ashlynn being here. My parents don't know anything about why we're not friends anymore. But Tommy. They know I don't want to be near him, yet they didn't mention he would be here. They should've said something, given me the choice. I guess it's partially my fault for not asking, but I had no reason to believe Thanksgiving had changed so much.

Today's a day for being thankful, not for fighting. I repeat my mantra while I set the table. I will not let Tommy's presence ruin this holiday for me.

The afternoon has flown by while we've been busy with the preparations. By the time I look at the clock, it's after two. We always eat early, so it comes as no surprise when the doorbell rings, announcing the first guests' arrival. I look down and realize I haven't changed yet.

While mom answers the door, I race up the steps and find a dress that should be more appropriate. I make quick work of washing up before I get dressed and fix my hair. The doorbell rings again just as I'm coming down the steps.

"Can you grab that?" Mom calls from the other room.

"Sure." I open the door and freeze.

Delia and Tommy are standing on the other side. Even though I knew they were coming, I'm still shocked at their presence.

"Hello, Natalie, dear." Mrs. Laurel smiles and walks past me, carrying her casserole dish.

Tommy remains in the doorway, holding a bouquet of roses. He's smiling from ear to ear, clearly amused by the situation.

I, however, am not amused.

"Aren't you going to say hi?" Tommy asks.

"Hi," I say sharply and turn to walk away, but Tommy grabs my arm.

"That's not a very polite way to welcome a guest. These are for you." He pushes the flowers toward me. When I don't reach out to accept them, he squeezes my arm tighter. "Take your flowers like a good little girl."

Grudgingly, I take the bouquet before walking into the kitchen. Tommy follows close behind.

"Look at the beautiful roses. Are they from Tommy?" Mom asks.

"Yes," I say and drop them on the counter.

I start to walk away, but Mom stops me.

"Natalie, don't be rude. Put your flowers in a vase and set it on the buffet." She makes her way to Tommy and kisses him on the cheek. "That was so thoughtful of you."

Everyone's already seated at the table when I walk in and set the vase down. Our guests murmur their appreciation for the *romantic gesture.* I struggle not to roll my eyes.

Moments later, Dad comes into the room carrying a silver tray with the golden-brown turkey proudly displayed. He sets it on the table and then takes his seat at the head of the table. Mom sits to his right, leaving one empty chair for me next to Tommy. He's wearing a smug look on his face as I sit down.

"Let us join hands as we say a blessing for the meal," Reverend Miller says.

My stomach turns as I place my hand in Tommy's. He finishes his lengthy prayer, and there's a chorus of 'amens.' I quickly pull my hand away, ready to start the meal, when Tommy stands.

"Before we eat, there's something I'd like to say."

This time, I roll my eyes, earning a reprimanding glare from my mother.

Tommy turns to me. "Natalie, you and I have known each other for as long as I can remember. And I think I've loved you for just as long."

There's no way he's doing this. My heart rate skyrockets and my eyes dart around the room, looking for a quick escape.

"I know we've had some problems. Every couple does." He glances at Ashlynn.

She looks down, her eyes filled with tears. Does she actually care about him?

"Things were rough when you went away for school. But since you've come home, any doubts I had are gone. It's clear what I want." Tommy reaches into his pocket and pulls out a small velvet-covered box.

Looking around the table, I realize no one's surprised at the scene unfolding before them. Reverend Miller and Hannah are holding hands. Mom's dabbing at the tears in her eyes, but there's a smile on her face. Nausea bubbles in my stomach. My palms are clammy, and sweat forms on my brow.

Tommy gets down on one knee.

"Natalie Clarke, will you do me the honor of being my wife?" He opens the box and takes out a ring. "Marry me?"

I can't move—can't breathe.

I don't know what to do.

I thought Tommy understood there isn't an *us*.

When I moved out, I assumed my parents understood it was because I was serious about Alex. When they invited me home for the holiday, I figured they'd finally accepted there'd be nothing with Tommy. Even if they weren't ready to accept Alex yet. But looking around the table now, it's clear no one has moved on except me.

"Tommy, I—"

He grabs my hand and tries to slip the ring on my finger.

"No." I pull my hand away. "I'm not marrying you."

He gets up quickly, trying to keep a smile on his face, but I see the anger boiling over in his eyes.

"Natalie, how dare you," Mom snaps.

When I'm finally able to move, I jump from my chair, horrified at the situation.

"How dare I? How dare you. All of you." I point at the shocked faces around the table. "You all knew about this, didn't you?"

My parents' guests squirm in their seats.

"I've tried telling you, Tommy and I aren't a couple. We haven't been for years. We haven't been since he cheated on me."

Mom gasps.

"Natalie, don't," Tommy whispers in my ear. "Shut up and put the ring on your finger."

He grabs my hand, but I pull away.

"Don't touch me. I'm done. I refuse to do this any longer. I've kept the truth to myself for too long, but it's time you all hear it. I was in my first year of grad school and finished my mid-terms sooner than expected." I look pointedly at my parents.

"Do you remember I was supposed to come home? Instead, I called and told you there was a last-minute change of plans, and I had to work."

They stare at me but don't react.

"I was here. I flew in a few days early and went to Mizzou. I wanted to surprise Tommy. So, I went to his dorm. God, I was so excited. Until I opened the door."

The pain of that moment rips through me as if it happened yesterday. At this moment, I have a decision to make. I can tell everyone I caught Tommy and Ashlynn together.

But what will that do?

What good will come of it?

I let my gaze wander to where Ashlynn sits across from me. She looks at me, her eyes wide and pleading. I could be vindictive and hurt her as badly as she hurt me, but I don't want that. There's been enough hurt.

I just want to be heard.

"I found him in bed, having sex with another girl."

Our guests begin to whisper amongst themselves.

"I couldn't handle the betrayal, so I found the next flight to New York, and I left." I begin to back away from the table. "These past few years, I've tried to protect Tommy. I didn't want to ruin his precious reputation, so I kept it to myself. I thought it was the right thing to do." I let out a sarcastic laugh.

"Instead, everyone turned on *me*." I hit my chest. "My own parents refuse to accept I've moved on. That I'm in love with someone else. A man who's kind and treats me well. Someone honest and trustworthy who would never hurt me. A man who loves me. I naively thought I'd find support from my friends, and I thought my parents would be happy for me." I turn to face them.

"But you're content to trick me. To make a fool of me."

"Natalie, you will stop this instant," Dad yells.

"I'm sorry, Daddy, but this is too much. I can't do this anymore."

I turn and nearly trip over my chair as I hurry to leave the room.

"Natalie, child." Reverend Miller stands up, blocking my path. "Let's sit down and discuss this calmly."

"Move out of my way." My voice comes out in a roar.

He must sense the depth of my fury because he steps aside, clearing the path to the door. Tommy's right on my heels, and before I can get to the door, he grabs my arm. His voice is low, so only I can hear.

"If you walk out, I'll show them the pictures."

I pull free from his grip. "You know what? Do it. Get it over with. I don't care anymore."

"Natalie, if you walk out that door again, you won't be asked to come back," Mom says in an even, calm tone.

I look up and see my parents standing in the archway that separates the dining room from the living room.

"I wasn't planning on coming back."

I grab my purse from where it hangs by the door and, with hurried steps, rush out of the house. I'm thankful for the forethought of parking on the street. My tires squeal as I pull away.

I can't believe I was so stupid to think everything was okay. I thought my parents had accepted my choices, even if they disagreed. By the look on everyone's faces when Tommy stood up to make his awful proposal, they all knew what was happening. This was planned behind my back. Did they think I would say yes just because everyone was sitting there? That I'd cave to the pressure?

"Ha. They probably did," I say aloud.

Well, this time, they got the message. And, come to think of it, so did I.

But I'm not that girl anymore.

Alex

I'VE BEEN CALLING NATALIE ALL NIGHT, BUT MY CALLS KEEP GOING straight to voicemail, and my texts are all unread. I tried Lana, but she hasn't heard from Natalie either. She was supposed to call me after her family had dinner.

That was five hours ago.

Where are you, baby girl?

I traded sleep for pacing the house all night, waiting for her call. A new day has dawned, and I still haven't heard from her. I'm on the other side of the world and completely helpless. It's a feeling I'm not used to and one I don't like.

It's only seven in the morning, and I'm already on my third cup of coffee. Between my anxiety and the caffeine overload, I can't sit still. I pace back and forth in the dining room, willing my phone to ring.

"Alexander, you look terrible. Did you not sleep well?" Maxim asks as he walks into the room.

I run my hands through my disheveled hair.

"Natalie never called. Her phone's going straight to voicemail." My words come out hurried. I recheck my phone—nothing.

Maxim, never one to rush a response, pours his coffee and then sits in his chair at the head of the table.

"Have you tried calling her parents?"

"I called her father's cell. He didn't answer, and their landline is unlisted." I don't stop moving while I speak.

"Alexander, sit down," Maxim says with authority. "You are going to wear out my floor."

Although sitting still feels like an impossibility, Maxim's command leaves no room for argument. I sit at the table and pour myself another cup of coffee. The kitchen door opens, and Maxim's staff serves our breakfast. As delicious as the kasha smells, my stomach is in knots. I can't eat.

Maxim pulls his phone from a pocket inside his suit jacket and types out a message. After setting the phone on the table, he begins eating.

"I don't know what to do." I drop my head in my hands. "I need to go to Missouri. I need to find her, but I can't leave yet."

Maxim continues eating his breakfast, seemingly unfazed by my rambling. I dial Natalie's number, and again, no answer. Hanging up, I put the phone back on the table.

"I shouldn't have come. I shouldn't have left Natalie alone."

Maxim's phone vibrates. He lifts it and looks at the screen, but his face gives nothing away. A few seconds later, my text alert sounds. I rush to check it, hoping it's finally Natalie, but it's a text from Maxim instead.

"Her parents' phone number," he says calmly.

"How did you?"

"I have my sources, Alexander. Call them."

Pulling up the keypad, I input the numbers and tap the green call button. The line connects and begins to ring.

"Hello?"

"Mr. Clarke?"

"Who is this?"

"It's Alex Montgomery. I'm trying to find Natalie. Is she there?"

There's no response. I pull the phone away from my ear to check the screen, ensuring the connection didn't drop.

"She's not here."

"Do you know where—"

With a click, the line goes dead.

"He hung up on me." My hands shake from a mix of fear and anger. "What do I do now?"

Maxim stands, his demeanor eerily calm. "I am going to my office to make a few calls. We will find Natalia."

With confident strides, he walks away. And once again, I'm left alone with my thoughts. I know Maxim's reach is long. I'm hoping it's long enough to find Natalie. Because as much as I want to get on the next plane back to the States, I can't. I have a meeting with Nicholai in an hour.

I don't know Nicholai's story, but I assume it's similar to Maxim's, making these two men a formidable force in their fight against trafficking. Today's meeting is to set up the framework for a second treatment center in another part of Russia. Identifying a victim and getting them to safety is only the first step.

Yesterday, after our Thanksgiving meal, Maxim and Irina brought me to Jelena's Hope. It's the first time I've been at their facility. What I witnessed will not soon be forgotten.

The people brought to the center are often severely injured physically, which turns out to be the easiest of the wounds to heal. The mental and emotional trauma is the most difficult to treat. It's often a long and bumpy road to recovery. These concerns need to be addressed before they're reunited with their families.

Sadly, some of the victims don't have a family. Worse yet are the ones whose families choose to no longer accept them. Maxim and Irina ensure they're set up with a new life and a support system. They'll never be unwanted again.

As we walked through the facility, I pictured Natalie working alongside Irina, helping to heal the broken. Her caring nature and her professional skills would be valuable.

I finish my coffee before going to my room for a hot shower. There's work to be done, so I need to put on my game face. When I'm dressed, I leave my room on the second floor and take the grand staircase to the first floor. Maxim's office is down a hallway near the front of the house. I arrive at a closed door. Usually, Maxim's guard, Timur, is here, but since he isn't, I knock.

"Come in."

Maxim's office is impressive. The exterior wall is lined with windows that overlook the front of his property. Larch wood, native to Russia, was used to build the massive desk in the room's center. Behind it are built-in bookshelves filled with centuries-old books on Russian history. A pair of ornately carved, neoclassical armchairs that date back to 1820 sits opposite the desk.

"Viktor is on a plane heading to Northmeadow. He will call as soon as he locates Natalia," Maxim reassures me.

I lower myself into one of the armchairs and allow myself to breathe. Viktor's been loyal to me for years. I'm confident he'll find her and keep her safe. But it does little to stop the ache in my heart that I can't be there myself.

"Thank you." The words don't seem enough, but they're all I have.

The office door opens, and Maxim's guard announces Nicholai's arrival.

Nicholai's an older man. I'm guessing close to Maxim's age. He always arrives in a tailored suit and carries the same air of power and danger as Maxim. During our first few meetings, he was guarded—distrusting. We've spent a great deal of time together over the past few weeks. I've earned his trust, and he's beginning to open up.

Although I've seen a kinder side of Nicholai, make no mistake, he's a dangerous man—I wouldn't want to be on his hit list. His bodyguard steps aside when Maxim approaches. I follow, shaking Nicholai's hand.

"Good to see you this morning, Mr. Federov."

"Nicholai, please," he reminds me again.

"Let us sit down and get to work," Maxim says, nodding to Timur, who closes the office doors. Nicholai's guard remains inside by the door.

I'm forced to set my personal issues aside for the time being and give this project my full attention.

With innocent people's lives at stake, every minor detail of this account is essential and must be done correctly.

Natalie

Once again, I find myself running from Tommy and the mess he's created. My only thought is getting away—putting as much distance between them and me as possible. Not wanting to be found, I turn off my phone and drive without conscious direction. But I find myself pulling up at Finn Lake. It doesn't surprise me. I'm always drawn to the water. Tourist season is over, and with it also being Thanksgiving, there's no one here.

I set off on the path I've come to so many times when I needed to clear my head and think. When I come to the bench, I nearly collapse from physical and emotional exhaustion.

The rhythmic sound of the water lapping on the shore has always helped ground me, but today, it does nothing to calm the thoughts rushing through my head.

Hours pass while I try to make sense of what happened, but I'm no closer now than when I got here.

What sort of alternate universe is Tommy living in to imagine that I might accept his ludicrous proposal? It seems like he's not the only one living there, either. I keep replaying the scene and come to the same conclusion each time. Except for Ashlynn, who looked just as shocked as me, no one else was surprised. They all knew what Tommy had planned. I've never felt so betrayed—so unseen.

"Michael, why did you leave me?" I yell. "I need you, and you're not here."

I drop my head in my hands and cry until my tears run out. A chill runs through my body, and I reach for my jacket. That's when I realize I don't have it. I didn't grab any of my things in the rush to leave.

With the sun now setting, it's getting too chilly to stay outside. I push my weary body to a stand and walk back to my car, shuffling my feet through the leaves that litter the path on my way.

Then, I begin the long, lonely drive back to my motel room.

Natalie

Although it's three in the afternoon, the curtains are still drawn tight. I was up all night, and now I'm exhausted. My hair is a mess, and I haven't bothered to get dressed. I'm lying on my bed, hoping sleep will pull me under, when banging on the door startles me.

"Natalie, are you in there?" I recognize the voice immediately. What's Viktor doing here? I jump out of bed and hurry to unlock the door, throwing it open. "Is Alex okay?"

Without waiting for an invitation, Viktor walks into my room.

"I've got her. She's right here, sir. It's for you." He hands me the phone

"Alex? Are you okay?"

"Am I okay? Where have you been?"

"I've been in my room."

Then it dawns on me that I never turned my phone back on after leaving my parents' house yesterday.

"I've been worried sick about you? Are you okay?"

"Yes. No." Fresh tears fall, making it hard to speak.

"Put Viktor back on."

Even though I know Alex can't see me, I nod and pass the phone back. Although I can't make out his exact words, it's clear from the volume of his voice that he's upset. Unable to handle more yelling, I drag my feet across the carpet and curl into a ball on the bed.

"She looks unharmed." Viktor's silent as he listens. "I'll stay with her and find out." He nods while Alex continues to vent. "Sir, if I may, please calm down. I'm here, and I won't leave her." More silence. "I'll have her call you as soon as she calms down."

Finally, he disconnects the call and slides the phone into his pocket.

A few minutes pass as he stands, arms crossed over his broad chest. His form is large and imposing in the small room. Then, he swipes his hand across his shaved head, looking uncertain, before grabbing a chair from the table and dragging it next to the bed.

Viktor sits silently beside me, his presence steady and unspoken. He places a hand gently on my arm, a quiet reassurance that I'm not alone.

The sound of the microwave beeping wakes me.

"Good evening, sleepyhead," Viktor says before opening the microwave and removing what smells like chicken soup. He places a bowl on the table. "Come over here. You need to eat."

I sit up and throw my legs over the side of the bed. My head pounds from all the crying I've done over the past twenty-four hours.

"What time is it?"

"Nearly nine," he says as he pulls out a chair for me before he goes back to the microwave to put another bowl in. "You cried yourself to sleep. By the way, you look like shit." He chuckles.

"Thanks, you're too kind." I roll my eyes as I stand up and walk to the mirror. I do look like shit.

What used to be a bun has fallen out, and now my hair is poking up in all directions. My face is blotchy. My eyes are swollen and bloodshot. Whatever. I continue my trek to the table and sit. "I'm not hungry." I push the bowl away.

"You can eat on your own, or I'll feed you. Alex's orders."

"He's so bossy, even from halfway around the world."

The microwave beeps again. Viktor grabs his bowl and sits across from me. My stomach betrays me by growling loudly.

"Eat." He points to the bowl of soup. "And start talking. What happened?"

Grudgingly, I pull the bowl to me and take a few spoonfuls of the warm chicken noodle soup before I gather the courage to relay the disaster that was Thanksgiving.

Viktor listens intently, and although his face shows no signs of emotion, his tightly clenched fists give away his anger. When I finish, he picks up his phone.

"Who are you calling?"

"Alex."

"Let me tell him, please."

I don't want to tell the story again, but he needs to hear it from me. Viktor hands me the phone. It's already ringing.

"Thank you," I whisper.

Viktor offers me a rare smile. "I'll just be outside."

"Hello?"

"Alex."

"It's me, baby girl."

Unlike earlier, his voice is now calm and gentle.

"Yesterday was awful." I struggle with the still-raw emotions. "And then I left. I turned my phone off because I didn't want my mom or dad calling me, and I forgot to turn it back on." He stays quiet for so long that I think the line may have disconnected. "Are you still there?"

The sound of his breathing is the only thing I hear.

"I'm sorry doesn't feel like enough. I feel useless. You need me, and I'm stuck here."

"Please don't do that."

I don't want him to feel responsible for this mess. It's not his burden to bear. The fault lies solely with the individuals sitting around that table yesterday.

"You're mine to protect. And I'm not there when you need me."

The pain in his voice is palpable, even through the phone.

"You're here now."

"No, I'm not. I'm half a world away." There's a raw edge to his words.

I close my eyes, fighting the tears threatening to spill once again.

"I know you're not here physically, but at least we can talk. And you'll be back soon."

"I'm assuming I can't talk you into going straight to New York?"

"You assume right. I have to work. But I'll be there in three weeks, and then I'm all yours until after the new year."

He sighs deeply. "Viktor will be staying with you until then."

"That's not necessary."

"This is non-negotiable. I can't do what I need to here while constantly worrying about you there. Viktor will be by your side until you get back home."

My Dominant is back, and I don't miss his use of the word *home*.

"Yes, Sir."

There's no use arguing with him, and honestly, I'm not sure I want to. I've been looking over my shoulder since that night at the store with Tommy. Something I still haven't told Alex about. It might be nice to have Viktor around for protection and some company. Glancing at the clock on the nightstand, I see it's nearly midnight, which means it's eight in the morning in Russia.

"It's late. You've been on the phone with me all night."

"I can stay on the phone as long as you need me, baby girl."

I smile, knowing I'm the luckiest girl on earth.

"I appreciate that, but it's late for both of us."

"Let me talk to Viktor. He has my card. I want him to get the room next to yours."

This isn't going to go over well.

"He'll have to stay in my room for the weekend." I hold my breath, waiting for the explosion on the other end.

"That's not going to happen," Alex growls.

"Marshall closed the motel for the weekend and went on his own vacation. He won't be back until Monday."

With tourist season over, the motel is a ghost town. Marshall knew I had nowhere to go, so he let me stay and left me his number for emergencies. I hardly consider this worth interrupting his time off.

"He'll sleep in the car."

"Don't be ridiculous." I let out a sarcastic laugh. "He'll stay in my room."

"Natalie—"

I ignore the warning in his voice and open the door. Viktor is outside, leaning against the wall. I motion for him to come back in and put the phone on speaker. I know I'm pushing Alex on this, but I'm not letting Viktor sleep in his car.

"Alex would like you to stay in Northmeadow until I leave for vacation," I say, addressing both men.

"Not a problem, boss. I'll—"

I raise my hand, interrupting him.

"The motel office is closed for the weekend. You and I'll be roomies until Monday." I sit down and cross my legs in mock victory.

Viktor's mouth hangs open. His eyes grow wide.

"Viktor," Alex yells. "Take the phone off speaker, now."

I swear the walls in the room shake. Maybe I shouldn't have pushed him *that* far. Viktor shoots me a warning look as he grabs the phone from my hand and once again steps outside the room. I've just managed to upset two powerful men.

Oh well, what's done is done. While they hash it out, I decide to take a much-needed shower.

After I dry off and get dressed, I crack open the bathroom door, trying to gauge the situation. Viktor's turned the chair to face this direction. He's sitting back, legs spread, arms crossed over his chest. Cautiously, I step into the main room. I give a slight shrug and attempt a smile.

"It's a good thing that man of yours is in another country. Let's hope, for both our sakes, that he calms down before he gets home." He shakes his head, clearly not amused.

The past forty-eight hours hit me all at once. Exhaustion permeates my entire being, and all I want to do is sleep.

Knowing I'm safe with Viktor, I ask, "So, what side of the bed do you want?"

Viktor cocks his head to the side.

"Neither. I'll take the floor."

"That's ridiculous."

"Maybe so, but I want to remain alive and keep my job."

Remain alive? He's a bit overdramatic.

But I concede and am happy he at least lets me give him a pillow and blanket.

Natalie

First thing Monday morning, Viktor's standing outside the motel office waiting for Marshall to arrive. He's now my neighbor in room six, which means I'm alone tonight. Alex video calls to ensure I'm appropriately punished for my behavior the other night.

"Undress for me, slowly," Alex instructs.

Climbing off my bed, I turn the laptop so Alex can watch as I strip. I remove each piece of clothing as slowly and seductively as possible.

"Pull a chair over and sit."

While I'm getting the chair, I hear the sound of his zipper. When I turn around, he's sliding his hand up and down his hard length. Unable to take my eyes off him, I stumble when I go to sit on the chair.

"Open your legs. I want to see you," he demands.

I do as I'm told, even though I don't see how this is supposed to be a punishment.

"Touch yourself."

I drag my finger through the wetness between my legs and rub small circles on my already sensitive center. Watching Alex stroke himself intensifies my arousal. With my free hand, I pinch my hardened nipple and moan at the sensation.

"That's it, baby girl." Alex encourages me. "You look so hot right now."

"I'm so close."

"Keep your eyes open and look at me."

"Yes, Sir"

Alex increases his pace as he chases his release.

"Alex, I'm going to—"

"Stop," he commands.

My hand stills, and I watch as he brings himself to orgasm, ribbons of cum landing on his shirt. He doesn't speak until the last of his contractions stop.

"Do not touch yourself until I give you permission."

I'm so close it's painful. My thighs squeeze together, trying to take the edge off. I'm ready to drop to my knees and beg Alex to let me finish, but I know he won't allow it. Denying an orgasm is my punishment.

"My little sub, you need to learn not to push me, especially in front of another man."

I lower my gaze. The knowledge that my actions disappointed him hurts more than being denied pleasure.

"I'm sorry, Sir."

"Look at me."

I raise my eyes to meet his.

"I forgive you." The edge that was in his voice is gone.

Punishment within a relationship is something I've had to get used to. I try to avoid it, but I know it serves a purpose. Alex is an experienced Dominant. His discipline challenges me but doesn't push me past my limits.

The most beautiful part is the complete forgiveness Alex gives me. There are no arguments or grudges held. It's just over.

The hardest part is forgiving myself—that's still a work in progress.

Tommy

Natalie's behavior on Thanksgiving has anger pulsing through my veins like red, hot lava.

"What the hell was she thinking telling me no?" I pound the steering wheel.

The box with her diamond ring lies like a lead weight in my pocket. She left me standing in front of everyone, looking like a fool. I haven't figured out exactly how, but she'll pay.

For now, I'm back to following her from a distance. Since that motel guy found me outside her room and threatened me at gunpoint, I've had to watch my step. I found a secluded area where I could park my truck where it wouldn't be seen.

It's a half-mile walk through the woods until I'm across from the hotel, where I sit hidden in the tree line. I use my binoculars to keep an eye on her room. I'm gonna need a new plan soon. It's getting too cold to stay outside.

Natalie's been a naughty little girl, a thought that makes me hard for her. While her *boyfriend* is out of town, it seems she's keeping company with another man. He follows her around like a lost puppy. They do everything together, and I've got the pictures to prove it. I'll make sure her boyfriend knows what she's up to when his back is turned. She'll have no one to turn to, and she'll be forced to come back to me. I pull the ring out of my pocket.

"Then I'll slip this onto her pretty little finger, and she'll be mine once and for all."

It's my lucky night. The curtains are still open in her room. She and that guy are sitting at the table playing happy little family. I use the zoom lens on the built-in camera to snap some pictures before packing up and trekking back to the truck. It gives me time to think about all the changes since Natalie's tantrum.

Stanley hired me to work full-time at the pharmacy. That puts me one step closer to our original plan. I was supposed to follow in Stanley's footsteps and become a pharmacist. Natalie was going to have my babies and work part-time at the store.

When her parents were ready to retire, the store would be given to us. That was until she screwed everything up when she took off for New York.

This arrangement works in my favor, though. Stanley was concerned that his new security system went offline a few weeks ago. So, I played hero by setting up new firewalls and security codes. Which means I have access to them, and her folks are none the wiser.

It's a handy bit of information to have since I haven't found a doctor who'll give me another prescription. I drove three hours to Kansas City to see a new doctor. But as soon as he accessed my records, he refused to give me meds. Said I had to go for some tests and other shit. Fuck that.

Instead, I found a seller online and got some pills. But they come at a high price. Now that I'm working at the pharmacy and have been given the code for the safe, I can grab a few pills now and then.

So far, Stanley hasn't caught on, and I plan to keep it that way.

Natalie

It took a week to get past the awkwardness of having Viktor around all the time. Once I broke through his tough exterior, I learned he's a lot of fun, and we've fallen into a comfortable pattern. Although I've tried to explain to both him and Alex that it's unnecessary, Viktor insists on driving me to work every morning and even stands guard outside my office door. After my punishment the other night, I learned my lesson about pushing Alex too far.

Every evening, Viktor and I eat dinner together and play a highly competitive game of rummy. It's not his typical assignment, I'm sure.

This morning, I woke to find a voicemail from my father telling me I have one week to remove my belongings from their house or they'll be put in the trash.

Mondays are bad enough without adding this to the mix. How am I going to move everything out this week? Where am I going to store my stuff?

Like clockwork, I receive a text followed by a knock on my door—Viktor's right on time. Usually, I am too, but today I'm running behind. I unchain the door and let him in.

"Good morning," he says and hands me a cup of coffee.

He brings one every morning. The man is a saint.

"You're going to make some woman very happy," I say as I reach out and take the cup.

His mouth twitches with amusement.

"Have a seat. I'll be ready in a few minutes."

"No problem." He lowers himself onto the chair and pulls out his phone.

"Can we stop by my parent's house after work today?" I lower my mascara wand and glance at him in the mirror.

"Why?"

"I have to get some things."

"We'll go shopping. I have Alex's card for anything you need."

After I finish applying my lipstick, I take a seat opposite him.

"There's nothing I *need*, exactly." I play with my coffee cup nervously. "My dad called to let me know I have until the end of the week to move out my stuff, or else they're getting rid of it."

"Well, isn't that fucking fantastic of him."

I shrug, unsure what else to say.

Everything I'd once thought about my parents lies scattered in a debris field, and I've yet to sort through the remains. Is there any truth to my memories, or have they been this way all along? Perhaps because I never challenged them, I didn't see it. I'm not ready to face what I might find, so I place everything in a neat little box in the back of my mind. My main focus is making it through the next few weeks until I leave for New York. Maybe I'll be strong enough to face the hurt once some time has passed.

"Would you mind going with me and giving me a hand? It's just some clothes, books—"

"You don't have to ask. We'll go and get everything you need." He offers me a reassuring smile.

"Thanks."

"Just doing my job."

"Well, I appreciate you just doing your job."

"Right." He stands and heads for the door. "You ready to go?"

I laugh at his reaction, knowing he's operating in uncharted territory. I know Alex threatened Viktor within an inch of his life about being here alone with me. It's a little much, but Alex is my overprotective alpha Dominant. And secretly, I do love it.

"I'm right behind you." I slip on my winter coat, grab my bag, and follow him out the door.

Winter seems to have settled in early this year. Snow flurries are dancing in the cold breeze. I reach into my pocket for my mittens and pull them on.

"Cold?" Viktor asks in a playful tone.

"Freezing." I almost forgot how much I hate the bitterly cold Missouri winters. And it's only the second week of December, not even really winter yet. "Don't tell me. You aren't cold?"

"This is nothing compared to a Ukrainian winter," Viktor says as he opens the door for me. "I've already warmed the car. Can't call my boss and tell him I let his woman freeze to death now, can I?"

I punch him lightly in the arm as I get in. Shaking his head, he rubs his arm and laughs before shutting my door.

Viktor seems to be in a good mood this morning. There's something I've been wanting to ask him about, but every time I go to say it, I chicken out. Since we're in the car, where I can't back out once I start, I decide it's now or never.

"Viktor?"

"Yes?"

"Would you help me with a surprise for Alex?"

He glances my way, lifting an eyebrow. "Depends on what you're planning."

"I want to change our plane tickets. I have some personal days that I took off. I'm hoping we can leave for the city a few days early so I can get everything ready for Christmas before Alex gets home. But you can't tell him. Can we do that?"

Viktor's face remains stoic, his eyes focused on the road ahead. I bite my nails, nervous he's going to say no. I need him to go along with this.

"Yes."

"Yes? I'm so happy I could hug you right now."

"You'll do no such thing." The edge of Viktor's mouth turns up in a small smile. "I'll change our flight this afternoon."

The adrenaline rush from the mix of excitement and nervousness makes it hard to sit still. For the rest of the drive, I make a mental list of everything that needs to be done. I'm going to have to call Lana and enlist her help. This is Alex and my first Christmas together. I want to be sure it's extra special.

When we pull up at the school, there's a group of kids outside with boxes of lights and ornaments. Some are already decorating the trees that line the sidewalk. Others are taking selfies.

"What are they doing?" Viktor asks.

Memories of my last year in high school rush to the surface.

"The Santa Parade is this weekend. Every year, the senior class decorates the trees for the parade. Businesses up and down Main Street do the same."

He nods as he continues to watch the kids stringing lights and garlands. It's clear they're having a terrific time, and as much as I'd love to sit here and watch them, I can't. I have to get into my office before the bell rings and I'm late. I don't need to give Mr. Meadows any ammunition to use against me. I reach for the handle on the door, but Viktor grabs my arm.

"Wait." He motions over my shoulder.

Turning to look out the window, I see Tommy leaning against his parked car across the street.

"What's he doing here?"

"Don't know." Viktor turns off the car and unbuckles his safety belt.

My eyes stay fixed on Tommy while I wait for Viktor to come to my side. Tommy crosses his arms over his chest, undaunted by my staring. Viktor opens the door and steps into my line of sight. But I still hesitate to get out.

"It's okay. He won't get near you."

Viktor's reassurance is enough to give me the courage to leave the safety of the car. But I still grasp his hand for support. His body tenses at the contact.

"Thank you," I say softly.

I can feel Tommy's eyes boring into my back the whole walk up the steps and into the building. Viktor talks to me the entire time, reminding me to be brave and not look back. I'm relieved when we get inside the door.

Tommy's appearance this morning spooked me, and I've been jumpy and distracted all day. Since his proposal, he's becoming more and more unraveled. Now, I hear he's working at my parents' pharmacy.

After everything that's happened, I know I shouldn't care, but I do. My parents are hard workers, and I don't want them to lose everything because they refuse to see what's right in front of their faces. This time, it's on them. I can't—no, I won't step in and fix it.

"Miss Natalie." Mary's voice cuts through my wayward thoughts.

"I'm sorry, Mary," I say, embarrassed by my lack of professionalism. "Can you repeat what you said?"

"Is everything okay?"

I school my features, hoping to relieve some of the worries I see on their face.

"I'm just getting excited for Christmas. Do you have any plans for break?" I ask, switching the focus back to them.

They study me for a minute before answering. "Oh yeah, big plans." They huff a laugh. "Billy's coming over. He'll leave his boyfriend home because, well, you know why." Mary rolls their eyes.

I know exactly why Billy won't be bringing Todd with him. Mary continues to tell their story matter-of-factly.

"It's all about appearances. Mom'll be busy trying to make the perfect dinner. Dad'll be watching TV until Billy gets there. Then all hell will break loose. They'll start screaming at each other. I'll go to my room, and then Billy will leave." They look at me with grief-filled eyes. "I miss him."

"I understand." My heart goes out to Mary.

Even though there's a five-year age gap between the siblings, they grew up close. Billy always looked out for Mary. He still does. A few months ago, Billy gave Mary a cell phone, so they could talk to one another, and he tries to visit as often as he can. He's an essential part of their support system.

"Last session, we discussed how and when to tell your parents. We listed the pros and cons of telling them now or waiting until after your birthday. Have you thought about it at all?"

"I've thought a lot about it. Heck, I can't stop thinking about it. I can't go through the things Billy did. I decided it was best to wait until after my birthday. It's only a few more weeks." Mary looks down at their hands.

"That's a very mature decision."

When Mary first started sessions with me, they were fueled by anger and on their way toward a head-on collision with their parents. However, Mary's made a lot of progress over the past few months and is doing a great job responding rather than reacting. Mary accepts they can't change what their parents do when they tell them about their sexual identity, but it will change how Mary responds to them.

"I'd like to take your suggestion about inviting them to a session. Can we still do that?"

"Yes, we can. You'll need to sign a few papers permitting me to talk to your parents."

"Thank you for helping me. At least I'll be eighteen, and they won't be able to force me into therapy, too," Mary says with a sad smile.

We spend the rest of the half-hour session making a safety plan. Something they may need after they tell their parents.

If they kick Mary out, which is highly probable, I want to ensure they have somewhere safe to stay and can finish high school.

"Did you talk to Billy?"

"I did. He's glad I'm waiting to tell them, too. He and Todd said I can live with them as long as needed. They're already getting a bedroom ready."

I'm relieved to know Mary has somewhere to go. Over the coming weeks, we'll talk more about how they want the session to happen. My role will be to facilitate, ensure it remains productive, and be there for Mary in the aftermath.

Unfortunately, stories like Mary's are all too familiar in this community. But, unlike in generations past, these kids have access to the whole world via the internet and social media. As a result, they've seen ways of life different than what North-meadow offers. Many of them hope to take advantage of the opportunities that await them because they know they won't have the support of their parents. Something I'm all too familiar with.

I see myself in so many of these kids. But unlike when I was in high school and felt alone, these kids have found each other. They've been my teachers in many ways, as they model bravery and self-confidence. They still have a long road ahead of them, and I refuse to lose any of them like I lost Michael and Evan.

When the dust settles, they'll need someone in their corner, and that someone will be me.

Natalie

The energy throughout Northmeadow High has been building all week in anticipation of the upcoming holiday break. The students only have one more week of class, but today is my last day. After the bell rings, Viktor and I are going to the airport to catch our flight to New York City. I'm trying to finish all my paperwork when there's a knock on my door.

"Come in."

The door opens a crack, and Ms. Campbell peeks her head in. "Am I interrupting?"

"Not at all." I close the file and push it to the side. "Have a seat."

"I wanted to see you before the holiday break." She takes a seat across from me. "I'm very pleased with the work you're doing. I know it isn't easy around here. But you're doing great."

Ms. Campbell's one of my only allies in this place. Her compliment means the world to me. I sit back in my chair and let my guard down for a few minutes.

"It hasn't been easy. You're right about that. But the kids make it worth it."

"I hope I'm not overstepping. But with everything that's happened with your family, I wondered if you had plans for the holiday? If not, I'd like to extend an invitation to my home for Christmas."

"Thank you so much." Her offer genuinely touches me. "I have plans already, though."

"Do those plans involve that handsome man you keep telling me about?"

"They do. I'm leaving today to spend the holidays with him."

"I'm glad you're getting away. But I'll miss seeing that hot man standing outside your door every day."

We both laugh.

Ms. Campbell blushes as she stands and walks to the door. "I won't keep you. Have a safe trip and a wonderful holiday."

"Same to you."

I'm anxious for the day to end, but I swear the clock moves slower than usual. Having difficulty focusing on paperwork, I walk across the room to the window and look out. Snow is falling softly. It's beginning to coat the decorated trees in white, making it look like a Winter Wonderland. A few people walk down the street. It's clear from the packages in their hands they've been shopping. Tommy's appearance last week still has me shaken, but today everything appears normal.

My cell phone dings. Confident that everything outside is status quo, I walk back to the desk to see who's texting.

Viktor: I'm not in the hall. I ducked out a few minutes early to warm the car up. I'll be out front.

Me: Thank you. As soon as the bell rings, I'm outta here.

Viktor: Text me when you're on your way.

Even though my mind is already on vacation, I force myself to sit and finish my notes. I refuse to bring any work home over the holidays. With the last file done, I place them in the bottom drawer of my desk, making sure it's locked.

Almost as if on cue, the bell finally rings. I toss my phone into my bag and take one last look around the room. Then, I turn off the lights, locking the door behind me. I'm in a hurry to leave and begin my vacation.

I start walking toward the side entrance, texting Viktor as I go. A few students call out goodbyes. I wave and keep moving. I'm trying to get out of the building as quickly as possible. When I push the exit door open, I slam into a solid wall of muscle and let out a shriek as two large hands rest on my shoulders.

"I'm sorry I startled you," Viktor says, "Tommy showed up."

I look around Viktor's imposing frame, and there, in front of the school, is Tommy. He's sitting in his car—watching.

"He wasn't out there a few minutes ago. Why is he doing this?"

"He's trying to intimidate you. But we aren't going to let him. We're going to walk to my car like nothing's wrong."

"Right, focus on walking to the car parked behind Tommy's. Got it."

This time, Viktor grabs *my* hand. "I'm right here. I won't let anything happen to you."

I squeeze his hand tight as we start walking to the car. Viktor's calm and cool, the exact opposite of how I feel. He chats with me as though we're out for a casual afternoon stroll.

"Do you have everything you need, or do we need to make any stops before we get on the highway?"

It takes a second to slow my irrational thoughts and answer. "I packed everything last night."

"Good, then we can leave right away. We'll stop to eat once we're farther from here."

My gaze drifts to where Tommy's parked.

"Eyes on me. Not him."

Out of the corner of my eye, I see Tommy get out of the car. He's walking straight to us. My heart beats so loudly I'm shocked Viktor can't hear it.

"Get in the car, Natalie."

I'm sick of being ordered around. Everything moves in slow motion as I step out from behind Viktor's protective stance and confront Tommy. "What are you doing here?"

"I want to talk to you."

"You did enough talking with that ridiculous proposal. Don't you think?"

"Get in the car now," Viktor orders.

Ignoring Viktor once again, I step closer to Tommy. "This time, you're going to listen to me." I point my finger at him. "I'm done being a pawn in whatever game you're playing. It stops now."

"Sweetheart, you're just upset. You need to calm down." Tommy reaches out to grab my arm.

"Do not touch her." Viktor steps between us.

"Back off," Tommy sneers.

I place my hand on Viktor's arm. Our eyes lock in a silent battle before he steps aside.

"Once upon a time, you were my everything. I was in love with you. Until I walked into your dorm room and saw you and Ashlynn together. God, Tommy, you broke my heart." I close my eyes for a brief second. "I was lost and angry. So very angry. I hated you. I hated you both."

"I said I was sorry. It was a mistake. What else do you want from me?"

I put my hand up to silence him. "I forgave you long before you apologized."

Tommy smiles and puffs out his chest.

"It wasn't about you. I forgave you for myself." I watch the smile disappear from his face. "That afternoon, when I ran, I thought my life was over. I couldn't figure out how to pick up the broken pieces of my heart. I should thank you. That day marked a changing point for me. It ended up being the best thing that ever happened to me. It forced me to change how I viewed life. It was when I decided to start living for me." I point to my chest.

"There will never be an us again. I respect myself far too much for that. Whatever this is you're doing, hanging around watching me. It stops now. You're never going to win me back. You and everyone else in this town need to back off and let me live my life."

Having said my piece, I turn my back on Tommy and walk away.

"You're going to regret this, little girl," he sneers.

I spin around to face him. "You don't scare me, Thomas Moore."

Without another word, I get into the car. Tommy stands on the sidewalk, legs spread, arms crossed. His eyes are dark as he stares at me through the window. Viktor starts the car, and we drive away.

Like so many years before, I don't bother looking back. Except this time, my heart isn't broken. I'm proud of the stand I just took for myself.

Anger rolls off Viktor in waves. Neither of us says a word until we're out of Northmeadow and onto the highway.

"I didn't appreciate you ignoring my directive back there. But the way you stood up to him. I'm proud of you."

"Do you think he got the hint?"

"Let's hope so."

It isn't until the plane's wheels leave the ground that I breathe a sigh of relief.

Holding up my ear pods, I ask, "Do you mind?"

Viktor looks up from whatever he's reading on his phone. "Not at all. Try to relax."

And for the first time in weeks, I feel like I can actually do that.

I put the earbuds in and open my playlist before laying my head back and closing my eyes.

Natalie

I thought the Branson airport was busy, but JFK is bursting at the seams. By the time we disembark and get our luggage, it's after midnight. Between the nap on the flight and the chilly New York air, I'm now wide awake.

"Do we need to get a ride?"

"Nope. Alex's car is here."

"You left the car parked here while you were in Northmeadow? It's going to cost you a fortune."

"It's going to cost Alex a fortune." Viktor laughs. "He made it clear. Your safety is worth more than any dollar amount."

The knowledge that Alex cares so deeply about me that he'll do whatever it takes to keep me safe makes me feel cherished.

We finally get to the car and get on the road for the last part of our trip home. While Viktor drives, I pull out my phone and double-check the list I made. I need to get a tree, decorate, bake, and do all my shopping before Alex gets home on Wednesday. That only leaves me five days. I sure hope Lana's up for the task.

When I look up, I'm surprised we're heading toward the Queensboro Bridge. I'm about to say something, but Viktor beats me to it.

"Alex told me this is your favorite way to drive into the city."

I'm amazed that Alex doesn't miss the smallest detail, even from so far away. The skyline, with all its twinkling lights, is a breathtaking sight. I have to hold in a squeal of excitement as we cross the bridge into Manhattan.

I'm almost home.

That's an unexpected feeling but not an unwelcome one. I've spent so much time focusing on settling back into Northmeadow that I haven't let myself think about returning to the city or calling it home again.

But as we drive through the brightly lit streets, my mind paints a picture of me living here with Alex. Of being his submissive full-time. Of us getting married and having a family.

Slow down, Natalie.

Alex said he loves me and mentioned wanting something long-term, but he's never talked about marriage. Don't imagine things that aren't going to happen. You'll end up hurt—again.

We make our final turn into the parking garage. I look at Viktor, unable to hide the smile on my face.

"Thank you. For everything."

"You aren't getting rid of me yet." He gets out of the car.

"What do you mean?" I follow him. "I'll be fine here."

"If I leave you alone and word gets back to Maxim, well, I'd rather avoid that unpleasantness."

"What does Maxim have to do with anything?"

He hesitates for a minute before responding. "He signs my paycheck."

With a click of a button, the trunk opens. I reach to grab my suitcase, but Viktor removes my hand.

"I've got them."

Although his voice holds no humor, I laugh anyway and raise my hands in surrender. It's not a battle I choose to fight. But I do manage to close the trunk before hurrying to the elevator. Without having to wheel a suitcase, I have the advantage of speed. We are just walking into the apartment when my phone rings. Alex is requesting a video call.

"Shit," I whisper.

Viktor laughs. "Didn't plan for this part, did ya?"

I have to think quick and come up with a story. I decline the video request and answer it as a voice call.

"Hello, Sir." The pitch of my voice is higher than I'd like. I hope it doesn't betray me.

"Why isn't your camera on?"

"My phone's acting up. The camera won't turn on."

Viktor shakes his head as he walks past me.

"Use my card and have Viktor take you to get a new phone."

"Okay, I'll do that."

"Finally, I don't get an argument." Alex's laughter is a warm, rich sound that makes me miss him even more.

"What do you have planned for today?"

"Maxim and I are meeting with Nicholai. We're finalizing the details of his account."

"I'm glad to hear that. I can't wait until you come home." Being here without Alex is making me miss him even more. I'm counting the minutes until he gets back.

"Me either," Alex says softly. "I asked Brandon to put up a job listing for a management position. My attention needs to be focused on Maxim and Nicholai's accounts. And having another manager will free me up to spend more time in Northmeadow with you."

"Really? You'd spend more time in Northmeadow?"

"I was thinking about buying a house for us there."

"I don't even know what to say."

"Nicholai just arrived. I have to go," Alex says, cutting our conversation short.

He's thinking about buying a house in Northmeadow? I'm on cloud nine as I walk to our bedroom, where Viktor has already put my suitcase on the bed. I take a few minutes to unpack, filling the drawers and closet space Alex left empty for me. Then, I change into my pajamas and crawl into bed, but I can't sleep. The energy in the city is contagious.

Even though it's nearly two in the morning, I call Lana, knowing she'll be awake.

"You're back," she squeals so loud I have to pull the phone away from my ear.

"I am. Are you free for breakfast and shopping tomorrow?"

"Absolutely. I'll meet you at your place."

"Sounds like a plan. I can't wait to see you."

We chat for a few minutes until Brandon calls for her.

"Gotta go. I'll see you in the morning."

Natalie

Something—or rather someone—jumping on the bed startles me awake.

"You're home." Lana giggles. "I missed you so much."

"Oh my God, you scared me. What time is it?"

"It's after one. Viktor told me to let you sleep, but I'm starving and couldn't wait any longer."

"I can't believe I slept so late." I jump out of bed. "Give me a few minutes to get dressed, and we'll head out."

I grab jeans and a sweater from the closet and go into the bathroom. While I get ready, Lana sits cross-legged on the bed, telling me about her new job. After I slip on my black chucks, I turn to her, "Ready to go?"

Lana pulls her phone out. "I just have to let Brandon know we're headed out."

"He can come too."

Her fingers fly across the screen. A few seconds later, she gets a reply.

"He said no. It's a girl's day, and he'll see you soon."

I grab her hand. "Let's go, then. We have a lot to do."

It's been a long time since I've spent a day in the city with Lana. I can't contain my excitement any longer.

"We're on our way out," I call to Viktor, who's in the office.

We're about to step into the elevator when Viktor appears behind us.

Lana spins to face him. "Girl's Day, Vik. I have my car."

"No can do, ladies."

Lana rolls her eyes. "You're kidding, right?" He opens his mouth to speak, but she holds up her hand, stopping him. "Never mind, I know you don't kid around."

Watching their interaction is comical. Lana's so bossy with him. My laugh slips out at her comment on his inability to joke around.

"Viktor knows—"

"Knows how serious keeping you safe is." He raises his eyebrows.

I'll keep his secret. It's the least I can do for everything he's done for me over the past few weeks.

Our first stop is the Christmas tree lot on the corner. Lana and I pick the perfect tree and pay the delivery fee. It'll be waiting for us at the apartment when we get back.

"I'm starving. I need food," Lana says.

The next stop is a corner café. Viktor refuses to join us at our table. He's back to his serious, all-business demeanor.

Lana and I place our order at the counter and find a table in the corner.

"How was Tony and Leo's collaring ceremony last night?"

"I wish you could've been there. It was amazing."

"I'm so happy for them."

We stop talking when the waiter arrives with our sandwiches and coffee.

"I hope we get to the club while I'm here. I miss seeing everyone."

After we finish eating, we get down to business.

"Where do you want to start?" Lana asks.

"I thought we could head to the Holiday Shops in Bryant Park. We can figure out where else to go after that."

We walk around the market, marveling at the products made by talented artisans. I find a handmade ornament with two penguins kissing under the mistletoe that I have personalized for Alex and me. It'll look adorable on our tree.

When we're done at the market, Viktor drives us downtown to do more shopping. We spend the rest of the afternoon filling the trunk with packages and bags.

When we leave the last store, Viktor asks, "Where to now, ladies?"

I can tell he's holding back from rolling his eyes. He's been a great sport today.

"Can you drop me off at Fire and Ice? I told Brandon I'd meet him there. Wanna come? Leo and Anthony will be there."

"I'd love to, but I need to get home. I have a lot of wrapping to do."

I might have gone a little overboard with the presents. When we pull up at the club, I hug Lana.

"I missed this. I'll call you after Alex gets home, and we'll make plans for Christmas Day."

"Something tells me you might be a little tied up." We share a laugh.

Lana grabs her bags and, with a wave, heads into the club.

Viktor and I head back to the apartment.

Alex

I can't wait to see Natalie's face when I show up in Northmeadow tomorrow. Before I can get on the plane, I have to finish the most important task on this trip—picking up Natalie's engagement ring.

My driver pulls the car to a stop in front of a small jewelry store. According to Maxim, Yegor is the best jeweler in St. Petersburg. I take a minute to get my emotions under control. This ring is a symbol of both my past and my future. The conversation with my mom when she gave it to me is as clear today as it was all those years ago.

"Alex, I want you to have this." She slid her engagement ring from her finger and placed it in the palm of my hand.

I tried to give it back, tried to make her put it back on.

"You're going to beat this, mom."

"Alexander." She placed her frail hand on my arm. "I'm tired. My body can't fight anymore. Listen to me, please."

Reluctantly, I sat quietly as she spoke.

"Your father gave this to me when I was a young woman—a symbol of his promise to love and care for me. He and I have discussed this. I want you to have it. One day, you'll meet someone. Someone who'll turn your world upside-down. A woman who'll love you just as much as you love her. When you're ready to make the promise of forever, put this ring on her finger. Love her the same way your Father has loved me."

I put the ring away and tried to forget about it. For so many years, it only represented what I'd lost—what Dad lost. Mom wasn't supposed to give up. She was supposed to keep fighting and beat cancer.

It took me a long time to accept that she didn't quit. That everything happened the way they were supposed to. It took Natalie coming into my life to understand what my parents shared and what the ring truly symbolized.

Before I left for Russia, I took the ring out and visited my mom's grave for the

"

first time since she died. I apologized for being angry with her for leaving us. After nearly ten years, I finally made peace with my mother's death.

My parents' love story will always be a part of the ring, but I decided to redesign it, adding our love story to it.

I take a deep breath, trying to hide my nerves as I walk into the jeweler. Yegor greets me with a kiss on both cheeks. He speaks very little English. Thankfully, I speak enough Russian to conduct a conversation. He motions for me to sit in a high wooden chair in front of the glass showcase before holding up a finger, letting me know he'll be a minute.

I perch on the edge of the chair and watch him walk into the back room. When he returns, he's holding a small jewelry box. He stands across from me and places it on the glass.

"Your ring, *Gospodin* Montgomery." He pushes the box to me.

With shaking hands, I carefully lift the lid and pick up the ring. Even though I drew up the design, what I see is nothing short of amazing.

Yegor has transformed my mother's solitaire round stone into a heart set on a platinum band twisted like a vine. One row of the vine is lined with diamond pieces that were removed from the original stone. The other is lined with black diamonds.

"It's exquisite."

"I'm pleased," he says, bringing his hand over his heart. Another man, a young version of Yegor, joins us.

"The ring is beautiful, sir."

"Your father did an amazing job with it," I say, still in awe of the ring.

"It will look beautiful on your *nevesta's* finger."

I pause at his words. *Nevesta—my fiancée, my future wife.*

I examine the ring one more time before setting it back in the box.

Yegor speaks his native tongue, but I don't understand enough to keep up. His son translates for me.

"I see many beautiful stones come through here, but none more beautiful than my wife. Treasure yours, and you will share many happy years."

"I plan to do exactly that."

Once the transaction is complete, I leave the store, knowing I'm the luckiest man on earth.

Sixteen hours after takeoff, the plane's wheels hit the ground at JFK. I have a two-hour layover until my flight to Missouri leaves. I'm exhausted from the long plane ride, so I grab a coffee and find a quiet corner to wait.

When I turn my phone on, I see three missed calls from Natalie. I can't risk her hearing the background noises and questioning my whereabouts, so I settle for texting.

Alex: I'm in a meeting. I'll call you later.

I don't like being dishonest with her, but it's the only way to keep my surprise. It'll be worth it when she's in my arms. A few hours and another flight later, I'm finally in the Branson airport, weaving through people to get to the rental car counter.

While waiting in line, I text Viktor, asking if Natalie's at the motel. I'm expecting a return text, but instead, my phone rings.

"Hello?"

"Hey, boss." Viktor's voice is uncharacteristically nervous.

"Is Natalie in her room?"

"Why?"

"Because I want to know where she is."

He hesitates a bit too long for my liking. "Not exactly."

"Viktor." My voice rumbles. "Where's Natalie?"

"She's safe, boss. She's just busy right now."

"Busy?"

What's going on? He knows better than to evade my questions.

"Where the hell is she?"

"Shit. She wanted to surprise you. We're at your place."

"Natalie's in New York?" I laugh out loud. People look at me like I'm crazy and try to avoid me as they walk past.

"Alex, you okay?"

"I wanted to surprise her. I'm in Missouri."

Viktor lets out an audible sigh of relief.

"Guess my plans are changing." Excusing myself from the rental car line, I walk the opposite way and get in line at a ticket counter. "I'll book a flight and see you guys soon. And Viktor?"

"Yes, boss?"

"Don't tell her I'm coming."

With my new ticket, I get ready to board a plane back to New York. But first, I text my flight information to Viktor and instruct him to make sure she stays home.

One way or another, I'm surprising Natalie today.

Natalie

THE APARTMENT SMELLS SO YUMMY FROM THE CHOCOLATE CHIP cookies in the oven. Viktor said he would help me with the decorating, but he got a phone call, and his mood went sour. He's been hiding in the office ever since. It's taken longer than I thought, but finally, I'm hanging the last wreath above the fireplace. The only thing left to do is for Alex to put the star on the tree when he gets home.

Climbing off the chair, I look around at my work and smile. Everything's perfect. When the timer on the oven goes off, I pull out the last tray of cookies. They look delicious, and my stomach growls in response. I didn't realize how late it got. I'm hungry, but I don't feel like cooking after baking all day. I'll grab Viktor, and we'll get some dinner. I walk down the hall and knock on the closed office door.

"Come in."

I take a few steps into the room. "Let's go out and get a bite to eat."

"You can order in," he says without even looking up.

"I'd like to go out."

"No."

"No?" I cross my arms, annoyed. "Why not?"

"I have things to do. Just order something in, okay?"

I'm confused by his cold response. What's gotten into him? I don't stick around long enough to find out. I storm out of the room, slamming the door behind me. Part of me wants to go out anyway. The heck with him. But I know word will get back to Alex, and that'll end badly. I go back to the kitchen and grab my phone.

Opening the food delivery app, I scroll through my options and settle on Chinese take-out. Despite his bad mood, I order dinner for Viktor and me.

While I'm waiting for the food to arrive, I grab my book and get comfy on the couch. I'm in the middle of a page when Viktor walks into the room.

"I'm going down to my apartment."

"I ordered dinner for us. It'll be here shortly."

"I'm not hungry. I'll see you in the morning."

"Whatever," I mumble and go back to reading. I don't know what's wrong with him today.

A half-hour later, I hear the elevator signal its arrival. I'm not expecting company, and the delivery person doesn't have the code to get up here. I pull up Viktor's contact on my phone just as the elevator doors open. It takes a moment for the message to travel from my brain to my legs. When it does, I jump off the couch and run to the foyer. My eyes didn't deceive me. Alex is standing there holding a food bag in one hand and his suitcase in the other.

"Did someone order take-out?" he says with a huge grin.

"Alex? It's really you."

He sets the bag on the credenza and drops his suitcase before opening his arms. "It's me, baby girl."

I run into his embrace. "You weren't supposed to be home for two more days."

"And *you* were supposed to be in Northmeadow."

He doesn't give me time to respond before his mouth lands on mine, his tongue parting my lips. He lifts me as we kiss, and I wrap my legs around his waist. Alex carries me into his bedroom and kicks the door shut behind him.

"I've missed you so much," he says, lowering me until my feet touch the floor.

"Why didn't you tell me you were coming home early?"

"Why didn't *you* tell *me* you were coming home early?"

The amusement in his eyes a moment ago quickly shifts to something dark and hungry.

"We'll talk about that later. Right now, I need to be inside you."

I don't waste a second before tugging my shirt over my head. Reaching out, I begin unbuttoning his dark blue dress shirt. My hands explore the toned muscles of his abdomen before moving lower to undo the button and zipper on his pants.

"Natalie." My name falls from his lips like a prayer.

My hands slide his pants and boxers down, freeing his erection as I lower to my knees. Alex stares at me with lust-filled eyes. I fist his hard length, earning a low growl of approval. It's a powerful feeling knowing I'm causing this reaction in him.

My tongue circles his velvety soft tip, teasing him. I look up and see his head thrown back and his eyes closed. Starting at the base of his cock, I flatten my tongue and drag it up his swollen length. When I reach the tip, I blow across it before running my tongue through his slit, tasting his salty essence. Alex grabs my hair, tilting my head up.

With our eyes locked on each other, I open my lips and slide my mouth down to the base. My hands cup his balls and massage them gently as I move up and down his shaft in a steady rhythm.

"You're mouth feels amazing. I'm not going to last long." His body trembles as he fights to not lose control.

Without warning, I take him deep into my throat. His grip on my hair tightens. I relax, allowing him to take control of the pace. Within seconds, his balls draw up, and I know he's close.

"Fuck." He loses himself, shooting waves of cum down my throat. I greedily swallow everything he has to give before dragging my tongue up his length one last time.

Alex grabs my arms and lifts me so I'm standing in front of him. I unhook my black lace bra, tossing it to the side. The move only intensifies his desire. I step backward, and Alex advances on me like a predator stalking its prey. I keep moving until my legs hit the bed, and I fall back.

Leaning up on my elbows, I watch him as he slides my pants down my legs. His breath catches when he sees I'm not wearing panties. He spreads my legs and drops to his knees.

"My turn." He gives me a wicked grin.

Alex wastes no time as he drags his tongue slowly along my slit. My back bows off the bed from the intense sensation. He licks and sucks like a starving man, and I'm the meal that'll save him. He knows exactly how to play my body, and my orgasm builds quickly.

"Alex," I whisper his name as waves of pleasure pulse through my body.

He doesn't stop until I'm lying limp on the bed.

"I've missed you," he says before flipping me over on all fours.

He rubs himself back and forth through my wetness, teasing me. He's rock-hard again.

"I need you."

"Where do you need me?"

"Inside me, please."

I'm already wet and needy. My body is ready to make up for our time apart.

"As you wish."

He lines his erection up with my opening, and with one thrust, he's fully sheathed inside me. Then, he grabs my hips, his fingers digging in deep. Alex isn't gentle. He takes me hard and fast.

Reaching his arm around my body, he rubs my clit, intensifying the pleasure. His fingers pinch hard, and my orgasm crashes into me. His movements become frantic until I feel him explode inside me.

"I missed you so fucking much."

He lays on his back, and I curl up against him, my head on his chest. I lose track of time as we lie together, touching and talking to one another.

"We should go heat up dinner," Alex suggests. "Then I'm bringing you back to bed. I have a lot of time to make up for."

I WAKE NATALIE A FEW TIMES DURING THE NIGHT. WE'VE BEEN APART too long, and I can't get enough of her. Between our marathon sex and the jet lag, it isn't surprising that although it's nearly noon on Christmas Eve, I'm just waking up. Natalie's still asleep next to me, snoring softly.

Careful not to wake her, I get out of bed and throw on sweatpants and a T-shirt. Barefoot, I pad down the hallway and into my gourmet kitchen. I haven't eaten at home in months, ever since Natalie returned to Northmeadow. I'm thankful Natalie got here early and restocked the kitchen because I plan to start our day with a home-cooked meal.

Bacon sizzles in the frying pan while I flip the French toast. I'm in my own little world until I feel two slender arms wrap around my waist.

"That smells delicious," she says, resting her head on my back.

"I was hoping to surprise you with a late breakfast in bed." I put my free arm around her, pulling her to my side.

"I don't think we would've gotten much eating done there."

"Why don't you make the coffee while I finish cooking."

Seeing her in nothing but my T-shirt makes me want to go all caveman, tossing her over my shoulder and dragging her back to bed. That needs to wait because today, I have other plans.

Natalie's setting the coffee mugs on the breakfast bar while I fill our plates. Then, we sit and enjoy our late breakfast. There's so much I've missed about her, but I missed these simple moments the most.

"I didn't get a chance last night to tell you how beautiful the decorations are." I've always lived alone and never decorated for Christmas. But Natalie's transformed the apartment into a Christmas wonderland.

"Oh, that reminds me." She sets her fork down and reaches for her phone. "I told

Lana I'd call her today and let her know what time they should come over tomorrow."

"I already talked to Brandon. We're all set for tomorrow. As soon as we finish eating, we're heading out."

Her eyes light up. "Where are we going?"

"You're not the only one who can plan a surprise." I motion to her almost empty plate. "Eat up."

After we finish our last few bites, Natalie starts gathering the dishes.

"I'll get them. You go start getting ready."

"Are you sure?"

"Positive. And leave your phone at home. We're going off-grid."

While she heads to the bedroom, I throw the dishes in the sink. I'll deal with them later. Then, I text Viktor and ask him to have the car waiting. Thankfully, Natalie isn't a girl who needs hours to get ready. Ten minutes later, we're dressed and in the elevator.

"Now, will you tell me where we're going?"

"Nope." I laugh, knowing how impatient my sub can be.

I'm thankful we got out so quickly. With the holiday, the traffic downtown is worse than usual. When we near our destination, I see the recognition in her eyes.

"Are we going to Radio City?" She beams with excitement. "Did you know I've never been to the Christmas show?"

"I know. A little elf told me."

Natalie's green eyes are wide and sparkling with pure joy as we walk into the historic building.

"There's so much to see. I don't know where to look first." Her eyes dart from the terrazzo floor to the majestic chandeliers that hang from the four-story-high ceiling. "Wow," she murmurs.

I take her hand and lead her into the auditorium that's already filled with people. She spins around, taking in the three levels of mezzanines before turning toward the Great Stage.

I understand her excitement. Although I've been here many times, the opulence of this building never grows old. There's always something new to discover.

For the next hour and a half, the stage comes to life with Christmas magic. Natalie's totally immersed in the show, and I'm totally engrossed in watching her. When the curtain closes, she grabs my face and kisses me.

"Alex, that was incredible."

"I'm glad you liked it. Let's go. There's more to do."

"More?"

Our next stop, the Rockefeller Christmas Tree, is right around the corner. It's still daytime, but the tree is lit up with thousands of colored lights. Tourists from all over the world are here taking in the splendid sight. Being a New Yorker, sometimes I forget the magnificence of the city. But not today. I pull out my phone.

"I thought you said we're off the grid today," she says with a hand on her hip.

I show her my screen. "Airplane mode."

She laughs softly before cuddling close for our selfie.

For the next few hours, we pretend we're tourists visiting many of the iconic

Christmas sites in the city to take selfies. We stop at the oversized Christmas ornaments before going to Fifth Avenue to see the holiday window displays. They are all incredible, but Macy's outshines them all.

Natalie and I take selfies everywhere we go. I want to have the pictures to look back at and show our children one day when we retell our love story.

"I'm told you've been missing New York pizza," I say as Viktor approaches our favorite pizza place.

"You have no idea. Pizza isn't the same anywhere else."

We're seated by a window in the front, where we're treated to a view of people bustling about doing last-minute shopping for tomorrow. When we finish, I check the time on my phone. "If we don't get going, we'll be late."

"Late for what?"

"You'll see soon enough. Come on."

Hand-in-hand, we walk the few blocks to Central Park, where the final surprise waits. I'm filled with a mix of nervousness and excitement, knowing what lies ahead. I haven't decided exactly when to ask her. I'm counting on fate to lend a hand.

When we round the corner, a white horse standing in front of a white carriage comes into view. Both the horse and the carriage are decorated with red bows. When the driver sees us approaching, he climbs down from his seat. Natalie squeezes my hand tightly.

"Mr. Montgomery?"

"Alex, please." I shake the man's hand.

"My name's Seamus and this is my horse, Storm," he says with a lilting brogue. "We're ready to go if you are."

I look at Natalie. "Are we ready?"

She returns my gaze, her eyes sparkling with excitement. "I'm so ready."

I help Natalie into the carriage and then climb in behind her. The sun is setting, and the air has a chilly bite. Once we're seated, I pull the woolen blanket over her lap. The carriage starts moving and enters Central Park just as the Christmas lights turn on.

"I've walked through this park so many times. But something about tonight feels different—magical." She rests her head on my shoulder.

I pull her close as we listen to the clip-clop of the horse as she prances her way through the park's lit-up trees.

Snow begins to fall in delicate flakes as we approach Bow Bridge. On one side, a group of carolers sings, their voices enchanting a small, attentive crowd.

"Can you stop right up there?" I ask the driver.

He nods.

When the carriage stops, I hop out first and help Natalie down. Taking her mittened hand in mine, we walk onto the bridge and listen as the carolers sing, "I'll Be Home for Christmas." My free hand is in my pocket, holding the ring box while I say a silent thank you. Fate has done her job and provided me the perfect moment. Without letting go of Natalie's hand, I turn to face her.

"Natalie, last year, I was asked to escort a young lady for the evening at the club. I wasn't looking forward to it and almost didn't show up. I'm so glad I went because that night changed my life. It was the night I met you." I pause, swallowing over the lump in my throat, and pull the ring box out of my pocket.

Natalie gasps when I let go of her hand and get down on one knee.

"These past few months apart have been challenging, to say the least. But I learned an important lesson—I never want to be without you again. Natalie Clarke, you're my world, my heart. The very breath I breathe. I don't want to spend another day without knowing you'll be by my side forever. Will you marry me?"

Natalie brings her mittened hands over her mouth. Tears are streaming down her face.

Her voice is barely a whisper. "Yes, I'll marry you."

She said yes. I blink back my tears as I stand up and take her left hand in mine. I pull off her mitten and slide the ring onto her finger. It fits perfectly. Then I pull her close and kiss her. I don't even realize we've drawn an audience until they clap and call out their wishes of congratulations. Natalie looks down at the diamond on her finger.

"Alex. It's the most beautiful ring I've ever seen."

"It was originally my mother's. I had a jeweler in St. Petersburg redesign it."

Movement catches my eye, and I look up. Sitting on a branch in a nearby tree is a Cardinal. I look toward heaven, knowing my mother is sharing the moment with us.

"I love it." She wraps her arms around me.

I lift her from the ground and kiss her again.

At this moment, everything is perfect.

In my arms is the woman who will soon be my wife.

Natalie

After the proposal, we listen to a few more carols before climbing back into the carriage. We sit close, wrapped in each other's arms. It's as if the rest of the city is silent—there's only Alex and me. The reality of what happened is still sinking in. Alex asked me to marry him. I'm going to be his wife.

As the carriage ride comes to a close, I see Viktor standing outside the car. His head is down, and he's looking at his phone. When he hears us approaching, he lifts his head and gives Alex a questioning glance. Alex nods in response. Viktor's serious demeanor cracks, and he smiles.

"He was in on this too?"

"I couldn't have done it without him."

When we get to the car, Viktor slaps Alex on the back. "Congratulations, boss."

"Thank you."

"Congratulations, ma'am."

Viktor hugs me, and I swear I hear Alex growl.

"Ma'am? What happened to Natalie?"

Viktor doesn't answer, but his smile tells me all I need to know.

When we get back to the apartment, I take Alex's hand and lead him to the bedroom, where I remove his clothes before doing the same with mine.

"Lie down. Tonight, I'm going to take my time with you, Natalie."

And he does.

Slowly and passionately, my Dominant, my fiancé, makes love to me.

Cutting through the most beautiful dream I've ever had is the sound of my phone ringing. I wake up momentarily confused. Alex grumbles next to me. I'm slightly annoyed when I roll over and reach for the phone. Who would call before dawn on Christmas morning? When I look at the screen, I see my mom's number. I debate sending the call to voicemail. At the last second, I swipe the screen to accept the call.

"Natalie?"

"Yeah, it's me."

Why is she calling me at four a.m.?

"There was a—" She doesn't finish her sentence before she bursts into tears.

"Mom?"

Alex rolls over. "What's wrong?"

"I don't know." I get out of bed. "Mom, are you still there?"

"Ms. Clarke?" A male voice asks.

"Yes?"

"My name's Officer Cooper. I'm with the Northmeadow police department." His voice is calm and steady, unlike my heart, which is beating wildly. "There was a break-in at your family's pharmacy."

"Oh my God. When? What happened?"

"Shortly after midnight. Your father recently had a silent alarm installed. He was notified the alarm had been triggered."

"Someone broke in? What did they take?"

"It appears the perpetrator was after prescription medication."

My stomach turns. I don't need to ask who did it. I already know the answer.

"Was anyone hurt?"

"Your parents arrived before we got to the scene. There was an altercation, and your father was shot."

My legs nearly give out beneath me, and I clutch the bed for support. Alex is at my side in an instant, steadying me as he guides me to sit down. Gently, he takes the phone from my trembling hand.

"This is Alexander Montgomery, Natalie's fiancé. Can you tell me what's going on?"

Alex walks toward the window. He's silent, listening to whatever the officer is explaining.

"What's his condition?" Another long pause. "We'll be on the next flight out. Please give this number to the hospital and ask them to contact us with any updates." He drops his head against the window.

I'm cold, and my body shakes uncontrollably. As much as I want Alex to tell me what the officer said, I'm equally afraid to hear more.

It feels like an eternity before he turns from the window and slowly walks across the room to sit beside me. He takes my hands while he relays the officer's story.

Dad noticed that the pill count on some controlled substances had been off several times over the past few weeks. Although he already had a security system, he suspected it might be an employee. So, he secretly had a silent alarm installed.

"They were at church for the Christmas Eve service when Stanley got a notification on his cell that the alarm was triggered. He and Charlotte figured it was a false alarm and left the church to turn it off. When they got there, Stanley noticed the employee entrance was propped open. Instead of waiting for the police to arrive, he went inside. A few seconds later, Charlotte heard a gunshot."

According to the officer, she got scared and crouched down in the car. When she heard the metal door slam off the brick building, she tried to peek out the window, but all she saw was the back of a man running away.

"The police arrived within minutes and called for an ambulance." Alex rubs my hands gently as he speaks. "Your father sustained a gunshot to his chest. All the officer could tell me was he was life-flighted to a trauma hospital in Branson."

Bile rises in my throat. I run to the bathroom, making it just in time to vomit in the toilet. Alex follows behind me and holds my hair. When I'm sure my stomach is empty, I lean against the wall and stare at the ceiling. Alex wipes my face with a warm washcloth and sits next to me.

"Is he alive?" I barely get the words out before sobs wrack my body.

"He's in surgery. The officer said things don't look good."

I drop my head in my hands as guilt washes over me. "This is my fault." If I had said something weeks ago, I could've prevented this.

"Look at me," Alex demands. "This is not your fault. You had nothing to do with this."

"But I did."

It takes a minute to calm myself enough to tell Alex about the night Tommy showed up at the store. The further I get into the story, the more tense Alex becomes.

"I'm sorry. Please tell me you forgive me."

"Of course, I forgive you."

He pulls me onto his lap, and I tuck my head into his chest. Alex rocks me back and forth, whispering soothing words while I cry.

We stay like this until I have no more tears to shed.

I'VE NEVER EXPERIENCED PURE RAGE BEFORE, BUT ALL I SEE IS RED WHEN Natalie tells me how Tommy dragged her into the store and forced her to give him pills. He laid his filthy hands on what wasn't his to touch.

It takes every ounce of self-control I possess to remain calm while she finishes her story. Her heart's hurting enough. I don't need to add to it by acting on the rage pulsing through my veins.

Once her crying subsides, I help her up.

"Let me make you a cup of tea."

She doesn't respond as I lead her down the hall into the living room, get her settled on the couch, and cover her with her favorite blanket. Her eyes are filled with so much pain. It nearly brings me to my knees. But right now, I have to be strong for her.

"I'll be right back."

I call Viktor and quietly relay the information. "Book three tickets to Branson on the next available flight."

"I'll be up in a minute." He hesitates before asking, "Boss, is she okay?"

I know he's grown fond of Natalie after all the time they've spent together. I look to where she sits, tears silently streaming down her face. "I don't know."

"Take care of your girl. I'll handle the details," he says and disconnects the phone.

Viktor's become more than just a trusted employee. He's also a friend. If he says he'll take care of it, I can be confident, knowing this is one thing I don't have to worry about. Next, I send a text to Maxim.

Me: We have a problem. Call me on the secure line.

While I wait for his response, I finish making Natalie's tea and bring it to her.

"Thank you," she whispers, taking the cup from my outstretched hand.

"Viktor's making flight arrangements." I brush a curl from her face. "He'll be up as soon as he has the tickets."

I get a text and check it quickly.

Maxim: I am heading to my office now.

"I have to make a call. I'll only be a few minutes."

I don't want to leave Natalie's side, but I have to talk to Maxim. The phone is already ringing when I get there. I hurry to my desk and lift the receiver.

"What is wrong?" Maxim asks, his voice cold and severe.

He knows I wouldn't ask for a secure call unless there were extreme circumstances. I relay every detail I was given by the police and the information from Natalie.

"Is her father alive?"

"So far. But the prognosis is grim." I rub the back of my neck.

"And they have not arrested Thomas Moore yet?"

"No," I growl. The rage I thought I had under control rushes through me once again. "The security cameras were down. The police are going through the crime scene looking for evidence."

"Send me his picture. I will get things in motion." His keyboard clicks in the background. "Irina is already packing, and my jet is being fueled."

"I wouldn't ask—"

"I know. We will find Thomas, and he will pay." The line goes dead.

I drop my head into my hands and grab my hair. I promised myself I'd never cross that line—never ask Maxim to step in like this. But there's also never been anyone I've loved so much that I'd want to kill another for hurting them. I'm at war inside myself.

"Alex."

I hear Natalie's soft voice and look up. She's standing in the doorway, eyes puffy and red, and wrapped in my blanket. I push up from my chair and go to her.

"Viktor's here."

I hold her petite frame against me. "Let's go find out when we leave."

"I didn't think you'd go back with me after the way my parents treated you."

I freeze mid-step and put my finger under her chin, forcing her to look at me.

"None of that matters now. Stanley and Charlotte are your family, and they need you—they need us, and we'll be there."

Her eyes fill with tears again as she lays her head against my chest. "Thank you, Sir."

"You don't need to thank me. That's what family does." I take her hand. "Let's go see what Viktor has for us."

Tommy

I just needed a few pills, that's all.

They were supposed to be in church.

Easy in, easy out.

I had the bottle in my hand. I was just about to grab the pills when Stanley came in.

"Tommy? Is that you?" he called from the door. "What are you doing, son?"

I didn't think. I pulled the gun from my waistband and pointed it at Stanley.

"Don't come any closer."

His eyes moved to my other hand, where I held the bottle of Oxy. Recognition came across his face.

"You're the one taking the pills."

"Shut the fuck up," I yelled. "Move out of my way, and this can all be over with."

"Thomas, let's talk about this. Just put the gun away and—"

Everything happened so fast.

Stanley took a step toward me. I didn't realize I had pulled the trigger until his body fell at my feet. A pool of red quickly formed around him.

I shot him.

I'll never forget his eyes, the way they stared at me—blank and lifeless.

And the blood—

There was so much blood.

The bottle fell from my hand.

All I wanted was a few pills. Now I've killed someone.

I ran for the door to the only person I could think of.

Natalie

Viktor got us a flight at eleven. It doesn't give us much time to pack before we have to leave for JFK. We'll be cutting it close, but Alex is confident we'll make it on time.

On the way, Alex calls Brandon to let them know what happened. Lana wants to talk to me, but I can't handle talking to anyone right now. Alex promises her I'll call her as soon as I can.

Thankfully, we get through airport security in record time. Before I know it, we're en route to Missouri.

"Try to close your eyes," Alex encourages me.

"I can't. Every time I close them, I see Tommy pointing a gun at my father." The nightmare I've been having for months is now a reality.

There's no longer a blank face. I know who the gun was aimed at—my father. I put my head on Alex's shoulder.

"He must've been so scared." Tears slip down my cheeks.

"Don't go there, Natalie," Alex says softly.

Although I nod, I can't stop thinking about it. My dad's been shot. My parents and I haven't spoken in a month. I don't know what will happen when we get to the hospital. Will Mom even want me there? What will she say when she sees Alex is with me? So many questions keep going through my mind. So many unknowns. I'm thankful I won't have to wait much longer to get the answers—one way or another.

We finally land, and the feeling is surreal. Viktor and I came through this same airport a few days ago. When everything was okay. I'm thankful Alex and Viktor are here to take care of everything. All I can do is smile when appropriate and nod when spoken to. How did things change so quickly?

Alex leads me out of the airport, where Viktor is waiting in a rental car. None of us talk as we drive to the hospital. The only sound is the dinging of Alex's phone with an incoming text. He checks it and types a quick return.

"Is that Lana and Brandon?" I ask.

"Uh-huh," Alex mumbles, distracted by another incoming message.

I turn my attention out the window. Although nature has provided a beautiful Christmas backdrop, I only see the heavy snow load the trees' branches are forced to carry. It feels much like the weight on my shoulders right now.

"We're here," Alex says, his tone somber.

We're here—the hospital.

A war rages inside me. I want to rush in, hold my father's hand, and know he's still with us. But I'm struggling with anger and hurt. How do I reconcile my feelings? I don't have time to answer that because Alex is already out of the car, giving my hand a light tug.

My body moves of its own accord, following Alex's lead. He doesn't let go of my hand as we enter the hospital and take the elevator to the ICU floor. This part of the hospital is quiet and filled with the heaviness of the lives hanging in the balance. As we round the corner, the waiting room comes into view. Mom sits in the far corner. She looks weary and alone.

"Mom," I say softly.

She raises her head, and tears begin rolling down her cheeks, but she does not move toward us.

"We're here. You aren't alone now."

As if my words give her permission to move, she walks over.

"I'm so scared, Natalie," she says between sobs.

"I know, Mom. So am I," I say, my voice cracking. "Is Dad okay?"

"I don't know. The nurse said they'd update me when he's out of surgery."

"He's still in surgery?" Panic rises.

He's been in there almost all day. Something must be very wrong.

Mom turns to Alex. "I'm so sorry."

"No apologies necessary, Mrs. Clarke," he says, taking her hands in his. "We're here now, and we'll face this together."

We wait for what feels like forever until we finally hear footsteps on the tiled floor that are coming closer. I look up and see a tall man with dark skin walking in our direction. He's pulling his surgical cap off. His shoulders slump, and I prepare myself for the bad news.

"Mrs. Clarke?"

"Yes."

"I'm Dr. Fitzgerald. I operated on your husband."

"This is my daughter Natalie and her boyfriend, Alexander."

We exchange handshakes before the doctor motions to the nearby chairs. "Let's sit."

We each take a seat in the waiting room chairs. The doctor takes his time explaining my father's injuries to us.

"Mr. Clarke sustained a gunshot to his right lung. The bullet lodged itself in the lower lobe. The damage caused his uninjured lung to fill with blood, which had to drain slowly," Dr. Fitzgerald explains.

"Because the injured lung wasn't functioning, he was placed on a heart-lung bypass machine for the past twelve hours while we operated. This allowed time for the wounded lung to be repaired and re-aerate."

"Is he going to be okay?" Mom asks, desperation in her voice.

"He's currently on a ventilator. We're keeping him in a medically induced coma to allow his body some time to rest from the trauma. The next few hours are critical." Dr. Fitzgerald pauses.

"Tomorrow, we'll try to take him off the ventilator and see if he can breathe on his own. If he does, that's a good sign."

"And if he doesn't?"

"If he doesn't, we'll be forced to consider a lung transplant. Because of his injury and the amount of blood loss, we'll only consider that as a last resort. So for now, we watch and wait."

"Can we see him?" Mom asks.

The doctor looks between us. "We can only allow two people at a time."

"Mrs. Clarke and Natalie will go. They're his family," Alex interjects before anyone can answer. "I have a few calls to make. I'll be out here if you need me."

Mom and I follow the doctor to the room. When I look in, I freeze. Dad's hooked up to so many wires and tubes I can hardly see his face.

"It's okay," Dr. Fitzgerald places his hand on my shoulder. "You can go closer."

I look up at the doctor, who nods in encouragement.

Dad's body is still and pale—he looks lifeless. The steady cadence of the monitor is a comforting sound, letting me know he's still alive. Dr. Fitzgerald checks Dad's monitors and makes a few notes in his chart.

"We'll watch him closely tonight, and I'll be back tomorrow to wake him up."

"Can he hear us?"

"I believe he can. Talk to him. Let him know you're here."

I move closer to the bed and grab Dad's hand— it's warm.

"Daddy, I'm here." Tears pour down my cheeks when there's no response.

What did I expect? Did I think he'd hear my voice and open his eyes? Mom walks over and puts her arm around me. I rest my head on her shoulder and allow my tears to fall.

Mom and I whisper to Dad for the next few hours, hoping that wherever he is, he hears us and knows he's not alone.

Alex

While Natalie and her mom visit Stanley, I go back outside to
search for Viktor. I want an update. I find him standing a short distance from the
walkway where people meander in and out of the main door. Even though his back is
to me, I see he's on the phone. When I walk up to him, he nods, acknowledging my
presence.

"Keep me updated," he says and disconnects the call.

His face shows no trace of kindness. "Maxim's in the air. He's called some local
contacts who've dispatched a team and are in Northmeadow now."

"Have they found Tommy yet?"

"They checked cameras near the pharmacy and know he got away on foot. They
tracked him for a few blocks but lost him when he entered the woods."

"Dammit." I pace back and forth.

"We'll find him, Alex."

"Did you have any luck with the other part?"

"Yes. Ms. Campbell wasn't happy that my phone call interrupted her Christmas
dinner. At first, she refused, but after some insistence, she relented. Everything's been
taken care of."

"Good." I'm done taking chances with Natalie's safety.

"Get back up to her, boss. I'll let you know as soon as I hear something. He can't
stay hidden forever."

I take a minute to gather my thoughts before returning upstairs. Before going to
the waiting room, I check with the nurses' station to see if Natalie and her mom are
still with Stanley. The nurse informs me that Charlotte is in the family room and has
asked to see me. She points me in the right direction, and I walk down the hall.

Although the door is cracked open, I knock.

"Come in."

I step into the room and close the door behind me.

"Please sit for a minute, Alex. We need to talk."

I take a seat across from the hospital bed where she's reclining.

"I was exhausted. The nurses insisted I come in here and try to rest." She shakes her head. "I don't know how they expect me to do that."

"You'll need your strength for when Stanley wakes up."

"Alexander," she says and fidgets with her fingers in her lap.

I see where Natalie gets that habit from.

"Stanley and I were wrong about you."

"Mrs. Clarke, we don't have to do this right now."

"Yes, we do. And please call me Charlotte." She sits up.

For the next half-hour, we discuss everything that's transpired over the past few months.

"We've known Tommy since he was born. His mom left him when he was a toddler. She never told anyone who his father was. His Aunt Delia raised him. He and Natalie grew up together. Everyone just assumed they'd get married. We never knew why they broke up. Tommy told us one story, and Natalie told us nothing. She just stopped coming home." Charlotte wipes the fresh tears that are falling.

"Stanley and I have always lived in Northmeadow. It's all we know. First, we lost Michael." Her voice catches on a sob. "Then Natalie refused to come home. We were scared. We just wanted things to go back to the way they were. We never saw this coming."

"It's okay, Charlotte." The devastation on her face is too much. She's alone and hurting. I get up and walk to the bed. "May I?" She nods. I sit beside her and take her shaking hands in mine. "Natalie and I are here now. You don't have to go through this alone."

"We listened to Tommy and believed his lies. We were so unfair to Natalie and so wrong about you. Can you ever forgive us?"

"Already done. I want you to know I love your daughter very much."

"I see that now. I hope it's not too late to fix things with Natalie."

"It's never too late," I reassure her. "And when Stanley recovers, we'll have a lot to celebrate."

I hope our happy news will give Charlotte something positive to hold onto.

"Yesterday, I asked Natalie to marry me, and she said yes."

"My little girl is getting married." She brings her hands to her mouth in surprise.

Taking the phone from my pocket, I open the photo gallery and show her the pictures from yesterday.

"Natalie looks so happy." Charlotte smiles through her tears.

"When Mr. Clarke wakes, I'd like to ask him for his—"

She stops me mid-sentence. "You already have our blessing."

I know how important it is for Natalie to have the love and support of her family. I hate that it's taken a tragedy for this healing to happen. I wrap my arms around Charlotte. My move catches her off guard, and her body remains stiff briefly before she relaxes and returns the hug.

"Would you mind walking me back to my husband's room?"

"I'd be glad to." I stand and offer her my arm.

We walk down the hall in companionable silence. As we near the room, my phone starts ringing.

"I have to take this. Excuse me, please."

I watch as she steps into Stanley's room before I answer my phone.

"Viktor?"

"We got him, boss."

"Where is he?" I ask as I pick up my pace, heading to the elevator.

"I have the address. Maxim just arrived. He and his men are waiting for us there."

"I'm on my way down."

I hang up and text Natalie.

Me: I'm going to book a hotel room for us. I'll be back in a little while. Text me if you need anything.

I can't tell her where I'm really going.

Natalie: Okay. I love you.

Me: I love you, too.

When I get outside, Viktor's waiting at the main entrance in the running car.

"In an old fishing shack."

"How did they find him there?"

"Some girl name Ash something."

"Ashlynn. Natalie's supposed best friend." My hand pounds the car door. "What did she have to do with this?"

"Ashlynn saw Maxim's men at the motel and stopped them. She explained who she was and that she knew where Tommy was. She brought them to him," Viktor explains. "I think she's trying to make amends."

"It's the least she could do for all the pain she's caused, Natalie."

I don't know where Viktor is taking us, but it's far from civilization. Finally, we turn onto a gravel road and drive for a few more miles until a small wooden cabin comes into view.

"Where the hell are we?"

"It's a safe house. It belongs to one of Maxim's contacts."

I'm amazed at the lengths Maxim's reach goes. Viktor barely has the car in park before I open the door and jump out. Maxim steps out the front door as I approach.

"Where is he?" I'm anxious to get my hands on him, to instill the same fear in him that he caused Natalie. Then, I'll watch the life drain from his eyes.

"Alexander." Maxim places his hands on my shoulders. "First, you must calm down."

He stops me from entering the building. When I look at him, I see he's the picture of calm. He's dressed in a perfectly pressed shirt and black pants. How is he so put together right now?

"I need to see him. He needs to pay for what he's done."

"And you will. But first, we need to talk. Come with me."

We walk away from the building instead of going inside.

"I'm going to kill him."

"Alexander, you have never taken a life before. It changes you. You do not have to worry about legal implications. I will take care of that."

He stops walking and turns to face me. His eyes are cold. It's something I've only witnessed once before. They're dark and tell the story of a man who's seen the worst humanity has to offer and who's done things that aren't spoken about.

"You need to worry about what happens here." He puts his hand on my heart. "That man hurt your submissive. He tried to kill her father. So it is only right that I give you the choice of taking his life by your hand. But you need to understand it *will* change you. It is a decision you can never undo."

I haven't thought about what happens after or how I'll explain to Natalie that I've killed someone. I've only considered the hate I'm feeling and the vengeance I wish to extract.

Suddenly every high and low I've experienced since yesterday rushes to the surface, and a primal yell explodes. I sink to my knees and drop my head into my hands.

When I look up, Maxim stands before me. His face is void of all emotion.

"I want to see him."

"It is time. Let us go."

Viktor's waiting in front of the door. When he sees us approaching, he opens it and steps aside, allowing us to enter. The inside isn't what I thought. Bright lights illuminate the room, but you'd never know it from the outside. The windows must have a privacy coating on them.

Inside there are no walls. The only piece of furniture is an old wooden chair, and tied to that chair is Tommy. When I step closer, I see Maxim's men have already taken a turn with him. His nose is broken, and one eye is swollen shut.

He raises his head and meets my stare. "Well, well," The asshole has the nerve to snarl at me. "Looks like the man of the hour is finally here."

His cocky attitude pushes me past my breaking point. I pick up the pace of my strides and punch him in the gut. The air leaves him in a woosh, and he struggles to catch his breath. This is my moment. I can snuff the life out of this bastard for what he's done. I turn my back on him but make no move to walk away.

"You should die for what you've done to Natalie. But I've decided to give you one chance. First, you will turn yourself in and plead guilty to all charges. Then, you will waive your right to a hearing and accept the sentence you're given." I turn to one of Maxim's men. "Give me your gun."

He looks to Maxim, who gives his approval, before handing it to me.

"Otherwise." I walk back to Tommy and point the gun at his head, my finger on the trigger poised to shoot. "You die now."

There's a long pause before realization washes over Tommy, and his shoulders slump. The only way he's walking out of here alive is if he turns himself in.

"Fine, I'll do it."

I lower the gun and pull out my phone to dial Officer Cooper's number. When the officer answers, I put the phone on speaker. Tommy identifies himself and makes arrangements for where and when he'll turn himself in. Then, I disconnect the phone and hand the gun to Maxim before walking out. A few minutes later, I watch Maxim's men drag Tommy from the building and push him into the back of their car.

"Come, Alexander," Maxim says. "I'll ride with you."

Viktor trails the car that's transporting Tommy to the assigned location. After being ejected from the vehicle, Tommy is abandoned to await the arrival of the police. We watch from a nearby vantage point, ensuring he upholds his end of the bargain. Otherwise, his life is over.

When the officers arrive, Tommy's handcuffed and shoved into the back of a police car. Officer Cooper looks around like he can sense he's being watched. When he finds no one, he returns to his car and drives away with Tommy in the backseat.

It's only then that I'm able to breathe again.

"That was a brave decision that only a man of great integrity would make. I am proud of you, Alexander."

I don't know how to respond, so I say nothing.

"Let's get you back to the hospital."

On the long drive back to the hospital, I call and reserve a hotel room.

Natalie

Mom and I are sitting in Dad's room when my phone rings.

"Is this Natalie?"

"It is."

"I'm Office Cooper. We spoke last night."

"Yes. I remember."

"I wanted to let you know that Thomas Moore is in custody."

"He is?"

"Thomas contacted me about an hour ago and confessed. He also turned himself in and waived his right to a trial."

I struggle to wrap my head around the information. "Thank you for letting me know."

"Don't hesitate to get in touch if you have any questions."

After wishing my father a speedy recovery, we hang up.

When Alex finally returns, I tell him about the call. "Do you know something about this?"

"Be thankful he's in custody, and don't overthink it."

Now, I'm certain Alex had something to do with it, but I can't figure out how.

We stay until visiting hours are over. Mom refuses to leave the hospital, opting to remain in the family room. Alex and I say goodnight and promise to be back first thing in the morning.

The next day, we're gathered in Dad's room with Dr. Fitzgerald and his team. Dad's vitals were stable through the night, so they're moving ahead with the plan to remove the ventilator this afternoon. Alex wraps his arm around me, holding me tight.

The room is silent, except for the soft murmuring between the doctor and the staff. They adjust Dad's IV and remove the tube from his throat. The monitor keeps a steady rhythm, but his eyes don't open. Dr. Fitzgerald assures us Dad's breathing on his own and that we've crossed a huge hurdle.

As the hours pass with no improvement, it becomes increasingly more difficult to take solace in the doctor's confidence. I lay my head on Alex's shoulder.

"You should try talking to him, Charlotte. Maybe if he hears your voice, it'll encourage him to wake up."

Mom moves to the edge of Dad's bed. "Stanley, can you hear me? It's time to wake up."

We wait and watch, but there's no change.

"Stanley, I said it's time to wake up." Her tone is more forceful.

"Mom. He's not going to want to wake up if he's being yelled at." I laugh, and Mom cracks a smile.

This time, when Mom looks at him, her features soften. She takes his hand and begins stroking it with her thumb. It's the first time in many years I've witnessed her showing Dad affection. "Stanley, I need you to wake up," she says quietly. "Our little girl got engaged. She's here with her fiancé, and they want to tell you all about it."

I look at Alex, who's standing next to me. "How does she know?" I whisper. Before he can respond, Dad begins to stir. "It's okay, Daddy. Take your time."

"I'll let the nurses know he's awake," Alex says and hurries out the door.

A few minutes later, Alex returns with a nurse and Dr. Fitzgerald. The room is a whirlwind of activity as they take Dad's vitals and assess his pain level.

"Do the police—" Dad tries to speak but stops to catch his breath.

"It's over. Tommy turned himself in. He's going to jail."

"I saw Michael. He told me I've been wrong about how I treated you." Dad reaches for my hand. "I'm sorry."

I'm unable to hold back my tears. Thank you, Michael.

I kiss Dad's cheek. "I forgive you."

It's been three days since Dad woke up. Because he's stable and no longer needs all the services of the ICU, he's being moved to a step-down unit. Dad's lung sustained significant damage, and he has a long road ahead of him, but Dr. Fitzgerald is optimistic that he'll make a full recovery.

This near tragedy repaired my relationship with my parents. They've finally accepted that Alex and I are together and have given their blessing for our marriage. My mom even bought bridal magazines from the hospital gift shop to start planning our wedding.

Alex and Dad have become co-conspirators on something.

They spend hours every day on the computer whispering to one another. Whenever I ask what they're looking at, I'm told I need to be patient.

The night of the shooting, Mom came to the hospital with nothing but the clothes she was wearing. Mom hasn't left Dad's side since the night of the accident.

The nurses have been giving her scrubs, but since Dad will be in the hospital for quite a while, she needs her own clothes.

Alex and I are making the two-hour round trip to pack her a suitcase. I hope we make it back to the hospital tonight. School goes back next week, and then I'll only be able to visit my father on weekends. So, I want to spend as much time with him now as possible.

We're making good time and arrive in Northmeadow right around lunchtime.

"Why don't we stop at the diner and grab something to eat?" Alex suggests.

"That sounds good. It'll be nice to eat somewhere other than the hospital café."

The diner's parking lot is packed. Apparently, everyone else in town had the same idea. Knowing how gossip travels, I prepare myself for the onslaught of questions that are about to occur.

Leslie, the diner's owner, spots us as soon as we walk in. She doesn't waste a second before coming over. "How's your dad, honey?"

"He's doing okay. Anxious to get home."

She leads us to our table. "I couldn't believe it when I heard Tommy Moore shot him. Mrs. Smith was in yesterday. She told me Tommy was after drugs."

"What happened was a tragedy. Thankfully, Dad's on the mend, and we can put this behind us."

I don't ignore the comments about Tommy. I refuse to take part in town gossip.

"Well, let him know we're all pulling for him." She hands us our menus. "I'll be back in a minute to take your order."

"Well done, baby girl. You handled that like a pro."

"I've had years of practice."

Alex excuses himself to use the restroom. While I wait, I look over the menu even though I already know what I'm ordering. The shadow of someone approaching comes over my menu, and I look up. Mr. Meadows is standing over me. I can't deal with anything else right now.

"May I?" He gestures to the empty chair.

"Alex will be back in a minute."

Despite my warning, Mr. Meadows sits anyway. I set the menu on the table in front of me. His actions put me on high alert.

"I'm glad I ran into you today. We need to arrange for you to come by the school and clean out your office." He sits back, a satisfied look on his face. "Figured you wouldn't stick around very long."

"Clean out my office? Why would I need to do that?" That doesn't make any sense.

"Your resignation was handed in, and your contract was paid in full."

"Resignation?"

"We've already started the process of hiring your replacement."

I'm about to ask him what he's talking about when Alex returns.

"Excuse me. I believe that's my seat."

Mr. Meadows stands, chest to chest, like he's ready to challenge Alex. But there's no comparison between the men. Where Alex is tall and well-built, Mr. Meadows is short and overweight. Even more noticeable is the confidence Alex exudes.

"It was lovely to see you, Ms. Clarke." Mr. Meadows shoots me a cocky grin as he walks away.

"What did he want?"

I stare at Alex, who's sitting across from me, looking at his menu.

"Did you buy out my contract?"

"Yes."

"How could you? We talked about this."

"Natalie." Alex reaches across the table for my hands, but I pull away.

"No." I push my chair back, nearly knocking it over in my hurry to get up. "You know how much this job means to me."

"Sit down," he says in a low tone.

"You took it away from me without even asking."

I grab the sides of my head, which is now pounding. The walls feel like they're closing in on me.

"I have to get out of here."

"Natalie, wait," Alex calls after me.

With hurried steps, I reach the door and go outside. I don't know where I'm going or how to get there. I just need to leave. Alex quickly catches up and takes my hand.

"After what happened, you can't stay here any longer."

"You went behind my back and ended my career without asking me." I pull my hand from his. "My staying here and working—we agreed on it. Those kids depend on me. Leaving without warning, without saying goodbye, could ruin all the progress they've made. I can't believe you did this. Just go."

"You don't mean that. Let's go somewhere private to talk."

Our argument in the middle of the diner's parking lot has caught the attention of several bystanders.

"You should've thought about that first. This is over." Slipping the engagement ring off my finger, I force it into his palm. "I want you to leave."

"Natalie, please. Let's get in the car and—"

"Red."

It's the one word I hoped I'd never have to use. Alex freezes as soon as the single syllable falls from my lips. Although he says nothing, his eyes reflect the horror he sees in mine. We're frozen in time. Both of us are afraid to move, fearful of what comes next.

I know the moment when what's just happened hits him—his shoulders fall, and he walks away. As angry as I am, I can't watch him leave. I turn my back to him and listen to his retreating footsteps.

I will myself not to change my mind, but I'm losing the battle. His name is on the tip of my tongue, but when I spin around, he's already in his car, driving away.

Alex is gone.

It's over.

I keep my emotions in check long enough to call a cab. Thankfully, it's a short ride to my parent's house because I can't hold back the tears much longer. I pay the fare and slowly drag my feet up the sidewalk and into the house.

After closing the door behind me, I slide down the wall, and the dam lets loose. Tears pour down my face.

I've been so naive, thinking me, a small-town girl with nothing to offer, could have a man like Alex. I talked myself into believing he was different. That he truly respected my boundaries. What a fool I've been.

Desperate for someone to talk to, I call Lana.

"Hello?"

"It's me."

"Is your Dad ok?"

"He will be."

"Are you okay? You don't sound like yourself."

I search for the right words, but there are none, so I blurt, "I called my safeword and told Alex to leave."

"What? Why?"

"He knew I said no, and he did it anyway. He ruined my career," I say between sobs. "I don't even think he cared."

"Nat, you know that's not true. Alex was scared, too. He did what he thought was necessary to protect you."

"He went too far."

Svetlana is *my* best friend. She's supposed to be on my side, but she's defending him instead.

"Listen, I have to go. I have to get some things and get back to the hospital. I'll talk to you later."

I hang up without giving her a chance to respond. Lana tries calling back, but I send her call to voicemail and turn off my phone.

Once again, I find myself alone.

Alex

I need her to listen to me. To try to understand from my viewpoint why I bought out her contract. When she told me what Moore did that night, I realized Natalie could've easily been the one lying in that hospital bed. I was terrified.

Red.

She calls her safeword.

I already did enough damage with the contract. I can't ignore her safeword.

Walking away isn't easy. It's the hardest damn thing I've ever had to do. I'm leaving a piece of my heart standing alone in a parking lot.

I drive until I'm far enough away that I won't be tempted to go back, and then I pull off the road. Grabbing my cell, I try to buy a plane ticket, but I can't go through with it. I can't leave Missouri.

Instead, I drive back to Branson and get another hotel room. Until I figure out what to do, at least I'll still be close to her.

Once I get settled, I call Brandon.

"Hello?"

"I fucked up. Natalie safeworded. She left me." Then something unfamiliar happens—tears fall.

"What happened?"

"I bought out her contract and handed her resignation to the school district."

"Shit, Alex. I thought we talked about giving Natalie the freedom to make her own choices?"

"That was before her psycho ex almost killed her father." I cover my face with my hand. "What do I do now? I can't go after her. My hands are tied."

"You really dug yourself a hole this time."

"I was terrified and reacted. I realize it was too far now, but I don't know how to fix it. I need to get her back. I don't want a life without Natalie in it."

"Where are you?"
"I'm in Branson. I can't leave."
"Let me talk to Lana, and I'll call you back. We'll figure this out."

Natalie

WHEN THE HOLIDAY BREAK IS OVER, I VISIT MS. CAMPBELL'S OFFICE.

"Is there any way you'll reconsider and allow me to keep my job?" It's a long shot, but I have to try.

"I'm sorry, but that's not possible. The district already hired a replacement." She hesitates a moment. "May I say something personal?"

"Of course."

"I know you're disappointed. Angry even. But I also understand why Mr. Montgomery did what he did. Only a man in love with a woman would have gone to such lengths to keep her safe."

She's trying to comfort me, but I can't reconcile Alex's words with his actions.

"Can I see my students and say goodbye?"

"Unfortunately, you're no longer an employee, and I can't allow that. Why don't you write them each a note? If you leave them on your desk, I'll ensure they get them."

"Thank you. I'll get the office cleaned out and be on my way."

"Natalie."

"Yes?"

"Please use me as a reference when you're looking for another position. I'm going to miss you. But I know you're destined for greater things."

When I get to the office, I spot a cardboard box on my chair. "I guess that's for my things." The problem is, everything I put in here was for the students, not me. I can't take this stuff away from them. I move the box off my chair and sit. I fight back the tears as I write a personal note to each student, assuring them they'll be in good hands.

The letter to Mary is the hardest to write. We were supposed to meet with her parents next week. I have to trust I'm leaving them with enough tools to successfully navigate the rough waters ahead.

My heart is heavy as I walk out of Northmeadow High.

Another chapter in my life has closed.

Over the past few weeks, Dad's had a few setbacks. He developed pneumonia in the damaged lung and returned to the ICU for a while. There were some scary nights, but finally, he's on the road to recovery. Dad will be in the hospital for a while longer to ensure the infection fully clears up. Even still, the doctors are amazed at his progress.

Unfortunately, this ordeal has taken a drastic toll on his body. Dad's very weak and, at this point, can't walk. They've started physical therapy in the hospital. Eventually, when he's discharged, a mobile therapist will come to their house a few days a week to continue his treatment.

Mom will have her hands full, caring for him and keeping the store running. I can't leave her to handle all that alone, so I decide to move home. It'll be easier if I'm there to help out.

Marshall's been helping me pack all afternoon. "I'm gonna miss you here, kid," he says as he loads the last of my things into the car.

"I never thought I'd say this, but I'm gonna miss it here too."

"I'm sorry things didn't work out with that guy. But, hey, if you're ever free, I'd love to take you out."

"That's a very nice offer, but I'm going to have to pass."

"Can't blame a guy for trying." He gives a slight shrug.

I reach out and hug him. "Thank you for everything."

"Keep in touch." He smiles.

Marshall's turned out to be a good friend. I wave goodbye as I pull out of the parking lot, unsure if this move is a step back or a step forward.

<h1 style="text-align:center">*Natalie*</h1>

I'm having lunch with my parents in Dad's hospital room.

"Explain to me why you broke off the engagement?" Dad asks for the millionth time.

"Alex bought out my contract even though we agreed I'd work the five years. He made me lose my job." I feel like a broken record. "We agreed on this months ago."

"That was before," Mom says. "I think the circumstances are different now, don't you?"

"No." I take a bite of my sandwich.

"And you haven't heard from him at all?" Dad asks.

I can't tell them about our contractual relationship and that I safeworded. I ended it. There's no reason for Alex to call me.

"I think you should try to call him," Mom says. "Talk to him. Give him a second chance."

"Says the person who didn't want me with him in the first place."

"We were wrong about him. That man loves you."

Even if that's true, he crossed a line. I've resigned myself to the fact that I'm probably meant to be single.

Mom has remained in Branson so she can be near Dad. But I've had to return to Northmeadow to keep the store running. We've been gone for weeks, and there's no food in the house. The first thing I have to do is restock the kitchen. What I hoped would be a quick shopping trip has taken over an hour. In every aisle, I'm met with people asking questions about Dad. Wanting to know what happened and why Tommy would do such a thing. I can't wait to get out of here.

As I near the house, I see an unfamiliar car parked out front. "What now?" I pull into our driveway and shut the car off. Maybe if I wait a minute, they'll leave. But instead of going, they get out.

I glance in the rearview mirror and almost can't believe my eyes. I throw the door open and jump out. Lana runs over to meet me and squeezes me in a hug. Brandon stands to the side, watching us.

"What are you guys doing here?"

"We're here for an intervention. Can we come in?"

An intervention? I don't like where this is going.

"All we ask is that you hear us out," Brandon says. "If it doesn't change your mind, we won't say another word about it."

"Okay." I agree. Although, I'm confident there's nothing Lana can say that will change the situation.

Opening the trunk, I grab a few grocery bags. Brandon gets the rest, and they follow me into the house.

"Just put them on the table."

I put the perishables away before asking, "Can I get you guys something to drink?"

"Water would be great," Brandon says.

I grab three glasses and fill them with ice water. Lana helps me carry them into the living room, where Brandon sits on the couch. She hands a glass to Brandon and takes the spot next to him. I choose the chair across from them, hoping this will be over fast.

"Alex is miserable," Lana says. "And you aren't much better."

Dark circles stain my face under my eyes from not sleeping. I'm exhausted between managing the store and driving back and forth to the hospital.

"It's been a rough few weeks. But, it'll get better, eventually."

Lana looks at Brandon. He responds with an encouraging smile.

Sadness comes over her face. "I need to tell you a story. It's not something I like talking about, but you need to hear it."

Whatever this is, it's very important to Lana.

"I'm not sure where to start. So, I guess I just say it. Papa is the *pakhan*, the boss of a group in the Bratva."

"You expect me to believe Maxim's in the Russian mafia?" I laugh at the absurdity of the idea.

"Yes," she says without a hint of amusement.

"And I thought there wasn't anything more you could tell me about Maxim that'd surprise me. But what does that have to do with Alex?"

"I had a sister," Lana continues, a far-off look in her eyes. "Jelena was five years older than me. She was smart and beautiful. I wanted to be just like her. I was ten years old when she was taken.

We were walking down the street when two men jumped out of a van and grabbed her—we were holding hands, and they ripped her away. Jelena yelled at me to run and not look back." Lana uses the back of her hand to wipe the tears from her face.

"I had no idea. I'm so sorry."

"They were traffickers. Papa searched day and night, but even with all his connections, it was too late when he found her. She'd already been sold and killed. Since then, Papa has used his position in the Bratva to fight the traffickers. He couldn't save Jelena, but he has saved many others."

I'm stunned and don't know what to say.

"It's made him very overprotective of me. When I approached Papa and told him I wanted to come to America to study, he went crazy." She laughs. "He wouldn't be able to protect me here, which was unacceptable to him."

"I'm sure he was terrified something would happen to you. But I still don't see what this has to do—"

She puts her finger up. "Hang on. I'm getting to the part about Alex."

I take a drink of my water, trying to be patient.

"Papa didn't want to hold me back, so he arranged for me to stay with a business associate of his who lived in New York. This is where Alex comes in." Lana grins. "My parents and Alex's parents had been friends for many years. Which is how Papa started working with him in the first place."

I readjust my position on the chair. This story just got more interesting.

"Papa's responsible for reintroducing Alex to the lifestyle. He knew that after Alex's Mom passed away, he lost his focus—his direction. The first anniversary of his mom's passing was a particularly bad time for Alex. Papa found him drunk in his room. He was concerned about him and stayed with Alex the rest of the night. The following morning, he told Alex about his friendship with his parents and invited Alex to the club. Initially, Alex was resistant. He wasn't interested in having a sub. But, my papa can be persuasive, and Alex finally gave in."

"That's how Alex got involved at Fire and Ice." The pieces are finally starting to fall into place.

"It is. Fast forward a few years. The businessman Papa went to visit was Alex. Papa asked if he would step in and become my Dominant."

The familiar feelings of betrayal creep up. Secrets. I hate them. "You and Alex were a couple?"

"Alex and me?" Lana wrinkles her nose. "He's a great guy, but he's not my type. We were *never* a couple."

Brandon steps in to continue the story. "What Lana's trying to explain." He pats her leg. "Is that Maxim asked Alex if he'd be willing to be responsible for Lana's safety. To allow her to wear his collar of protection."

"Doesn't wearing a collar symbolize a relationship—ownership?" I'm bewildered and still not sure I like where this is going.

"In some cases, yes, but there're other kinds of collars," Brandon explains. "Lana was young and would be alone in a big city—in a foreign country. She was also a submissive who would be playing at a new club. Maxim wanted to ensure Lana had someone willing to protect her in his absence. A protection collar doesn't represent a partnership but rather a Dominant's commitment to be responsible for another's safety. It also meant any Dominants interested in Lana couldn't approach her without getting Alex's permission."

"So, you and Alex were never *together*?" I really hope the answer is no. I can't lose any more people I love.

"Nope, never a couple. Never played together."

Reaching into her purse, she pulls out a thin silver chain with a pendant hanging from it. Tentatively, I accept it and examine it closely.

"That was my collar. On the charm, you can see Alex's initials and the lowercase p to show I was under his protection."

I remember seeing this. "You wore this when I first met you."

"I wore it for almost six months." She smiles fondly. "I was so lonely until Alex showed me the city and introduced me to his friends at the club. Without him, I probably would have packed up and gone back to Russia. But it wasn't always smooth sailing. Alex can be a bit overprotective. He made decisions for me that I didn't always agree with."

Brandon laughs a full belly laugh. "Alex and Svetlana became famous at the club for their *very* heated disagreements. Star and Owen had to step in on more than one occasion."

She and Alex still fight like they're siblings.

"The thing is, he saw things and knew things I didn't. It was hard, but I had to learn to trust his decisions. And in the end, he was always right."

"This isn't the same, Lana."

"It is, Nat." She comes over and sits on the arm of the chair. "You may not see the big picture. Actually, I know you don't see it."

"When Alex lost his mother, he gave up. He closed himself off from everyone around him. He was afraid of caring about someone and losing them, too. Then you came into his life, and his carefully constructed walls crumbled," Brandon says.

"All those fears rushed to the surface when your Dad was shot. When you told him what Tommy did to you that night, it pushed him over the edge. I'll admit, he made some rash decisions."

"That's an understatement," I add sarcastically. "Alex and I had an agreement, and he broke it."

"I agree with you, Natalie. Alex and I have discussed what happened. He knows he was wrong and understands that he should've approached things differently. Alex is a Dominant, a protector—sometimes to a fault." Brandon pauses.

"He's also only human, and sometimes he screws up. But Alex is a good man. All he was thinking was that he couldn't risk losing you. I know you disagree—"

"Disagree? I more than disagree."

"That man loves you." Brandon's expression changes. The Dominant in him rises to the surface. "Do you love him?"

"Yes," I say softly.

"Do you trust him?"

"Brandon—"

"This lifestyle revolves around trust. Do you trust Alex as your future husband and, more importantly, as your Dominant?"

I look down at my hands. My mind goes back to the first night we met. How I allowed Alex to use a flogger on me when I didn't know him at all—I trusted my instincts.

Over the past year, we've shared many experiences. Alex has never given me a reason to distrust him.

On the contrary, he's always been there for me, even when I didn't deserve him. Finally, I look up and meet Brandon's intense gaze. "Yes, I trust him."

"Get your coats, girls." He stands. "We're going for a ride."

Lana jumps up and grabs her coat, but I don't move.

"Where are we going?"

"This time, you have to trust me." Brandon shoots me a wicked grin as he heads toward the door. "Get up. Let's go."

Lana grabs my hand, and I reluctantly follow. A semi-willing participant in whatever crazy scheme they've come up with.

Once we're in the car, Brandon turns around. "One more thing. You need to put this on." He holds out a blindfold.

"You're seriously crazy. You know that?"

I play along with their game and take the offered blindfold, slipping it over my eyes.

"Good girl. Sit back and relax."

He and Lana share a laugh. I'm beginning to question the sanity of my friends. I try to pay attention to the turns we're taking, hoping to figure out where we're going. But unlike in the movies, it only takes a few minutes before I'm all turned around. We drive for what feels like forever before the car stops.

"You may remove the blindfold now," Brandon says.

It takes my eyes a few seconds to focus. We're at the lake, sitting in the driveway of a sweet little stone cottage. Luminaires line each side of a path leading to the front door.

"It's gorgeous. But what are we doing here?"

"Go knock on the door," Brandon says.

"But I don't—"

"Stop questioning and just trust me," Brandon chastises me. "Get out and go knock on the door."

I leave the car's safety and take a few tentative steps toward the house. But then I stop, unsure if I should keep going or turn around. A car door opens.

"Keep moving forward," Brandon instructs.

Reluctantly, I continue walking and find myself at the door.

Natalie

I RAISE MY HAND TO KNOCK, BUT THE DOOR OPENS BEFORE I GET THE chance. Alex stands in the doorway wearing jeans and a dark blue T-shirt that clings to his muscles. Despite everything that's happened, I'm still drawn to him. My gaze travels up his body until it meets his eyes. The usual sparkle in his blue eyes is gone. All I see is sadness—loneliness.

"Come in before you freeze out there." He steps aside, and I walk into the house.

Before closing the door, he waves to Brandon and Lana, who drive away.

The inside looks like it was recently remodeled. The quaint country feel of the cottage is mixed with modern touches.

"Do you like it?" Alex asks nervously.

"It's beautiful. But what are you doing here?"

"I bought this for us. It was going to be a Christmas present. This is part of why I came back early, but you were in New York."

He bought this for us?

"This was supposed to be our home while you finished your contract. Then I thought we'd live in the city and use this as our vacation home."

My mind is struggling to keep up with what he's telling me.

"Natalie, I didn't mean to hurt or betray your trust. That was never my intention. After you told me what Tommy did to you and then seeing what he did to your father. I was scared. I couldn't take any more chances. I was terrified of losing—"

"I know."

"Can we sit and talk?"

I follow him into the living room and sit on the couch. When I look closer, I notice the small, personal details like the framed pictures of us sitting on the mantle over the fireplace. My favorite blanket from his apartment is folded over the back of a chair. I'm not sure what to think. I have so many questions right now, but I have to stay focused. We have some serious issues to discuss.

"Natalie, when we signed our Dom/sub contract, I had every intention of keeping my emotions out of it. I wasn't looking for a relationship and thought putting an ending date on us would protect us both. But the closer that date came, the more I realized I didn't want to let you go. I fell in love with you and couldn't imagine my life without you in it. I still can't picture my life without you."

Alex stands and starts pacing, his nervous habit of choice.

"I understand our falling in love complicates everything. But we agreed I was staying to finish my contract, and then we'd reevaluate our next steps. Alex, as your submissive, I put my full trust in you. But, then, you went behind my back and crossed a line."

"I overstepped a boundary and screwed up. I can't argue with that—I was wrong, and my actions forced you to use your safeword." He comes back and sits next to me. The expression on his face is pained and wrought with regret.

"That's a position I never wanted to put you in. I was wrong, and I'm sorry." He hesitantly reaches for my hands.

"I forgive you." I place my hands in his. "But, where do we go from here? Is it possible to try again?"

"As a man and as your Dominant, the last thing I wanted to do was hurt you. I want to be the one you can always count on and always believe in. The only thing I can do is ask if you'd give me another chance. Let me prove to you that you're everything to me. That I'm worthy of your submission."

"I didn't think there was an option to try again," I whisper.

"I put you in that position, baby girl. That's on me, not you. Whether or not we move forward is your decision."

I know his apology was genuine, but I also don't want to let him off the hook that easily. Instead of answering, I get up and walk to the window. "I'm sure the view of the lake is stunning from here."

"It is."

I stand silently, looking into the night for a few minutes before slowly turning to face him. "I guess we have some renegotiating to do."

He raises an eyebrow. "You have the floor, Ms. Clarke."

I return to my place on the sofa next to him.

"As your submissive, I agree to place my full trust in you to make decisions in my best interest. However, where my career is concerned, we will discuss everything openly. My voice *will* be heard. You will not make any decisions behind my back."

"And as your Dominant, I promise to be the man you expect me to be. I will honor the trust you place in me. I'll work to prove myself to you every day. I promise I'll never again break a boundary we've put in place together. I'll always listen to you before making a decision. But when the final decision has been made, I need to know you'll trust me enough to accept it."

"No more secrets?"

"No more secrets." Alex agrees.

Without warning, he slides from his spot and kneels before me. "You make me a better man, baby girl. Will you agree to be my submissive?"

"Yes, I agree."

He takes the ring from his pocket. "Will you still marry me?"

Alex is the strongest and most honorable man I've ever known.
Is he perfect? No. But he's perfect for me.
He owns my heart.
He's my soulmate.
"Yes, Sir. I'd love to marry you."
He slides the ring back onto my finger.
"Mine," he says as he pulls me against him.
I place a kiss on his lips.
"Always and forever, Yours."
THE END

Acknowledgments

There are so many people who have been an integral part of my writing this story. First and most important, my husband, George. You believed in me long before i believed in myself. You've been my rock throughout this journey and have held me up when i was unable to stand on my own. You dried my tears (on more than one occasion), and you celebrated each success with me. i can't believe how much things have changed in one year. Finally, we have Alex and Natalie's story back where it belongs. i love working side-by-side with You. Thank You for Your love, support, and endless patience, especially as you listened to revision after revision. i love You more than words can say. i can't wait to continue this writing journey and every other journey in life with You.

To my children—you have been my cheering section through this whole writing process. I love that you all come to my signings to support me—it means the world to me. George—thank you for finally agreeing to take one of my pens, even though you have more than enough pens. I do appreciate your support and encouragement. I can't wait until we publish your book too! Jacob—your tech skills have saved me more than once. I wouldn't have a website or any other digital form if it wasn't for you. I'm so proud of you. Kayla—your critics and edits are something I'll never forget. Literally will never forget—I saved the pages, and they will be part of my book wall. Thank you for always being willing to read and give me your critiques. I love you, Sweetpea. Rebekah—your unwavering support helped make this all possible. You always saw the rainbows when all I could see were clouds. I love you, princess. Jonathan—Thank you for loving my daughter and for coming on this crazy ride with us. One day I'll make enough to employ you as my merchandise manager. I love you and can't wait until you make yourself an official member of the family.

Max—You taught me some of my first and most important lessons in writing. You asked me to take my hurt and put it on paper—that changed my life. Your encouragement and support mean the world to me. I'm proud to call you my teacher and friend.

Jay—You've been with me since almost day one. You've been through my successes and failures. You cheered me on and gave me pep talks when I needed them. I can't wait until your book is born.

Norman and Nancy—Your friendship and beta reading helped shape this book into what it is today. I value the friendship I've found in you both.

Dr. C—the inspiration and brains behind Dr. Fitzgerald's character. You literally saved Stanley Clarke's life with your rock star trauma surgeon skills.

Last but certainly not least, Paul. As a professor, you are the toughest there is, but that toughness comes from a place of wanting to see your students do their absolute best. At the beginning of my classes, I thought I was giving the best. But with each assignment, you asked for more. You forced me to dig deep inside myself, to get out of my comfort zone. Your influence has allowed me to grow as a writer. I can't thank you enough for the lessons I carry with me today. It's been a bumpy road, but I'm loving every minute of it. I'm honored and privileged to now call you my friend.

Greg- As soon as we all heard your audition (yep, the whole family listened to it over a tray of pizza) we knew you were meant to be the voice of this book. Thank you for taking a chance on a new author and a new series. I'm so happy you've brought Submitting to Him to life.

PART TWO

His Fight

EVERY DAY WITHOUT NATALIE IN MY LIFE WAS A LIVING HELL. OUT OF fear, I made decisions that broke us. But fear isn't an excuse for wrongdoing. What I did is on me, and I've been paying the price for it. I haven't been able to eat or sleep.

My life has been empty—meaningless. I can never repay our friends for stepping in to help. If it wasn't for their intervention, I don't know what I would've done. I screwed up and came very close to losing Natalie for good—that's something I won't let happen again.

Last night, my mouth and hands explored Natalie's body as if it were our first time. I missed her quiet mewls of pleasure, the way her body comes to life from the simplest touch. Over and over, I brought her to orgasm until she was unable to keep her eyes open. I held her in my arms all night, fearing if I let go, I'd wake and find it was all a dream.

But when I open my eyes, Natalie's body is still curled against mine. I watch my angel as she sleeps, her blonde hair fanned over her pillow as I gently rub my knuckles down her cheek. Natalie stirs and looks at me with a sleepy smile.

"Good morning," she whispers.

"Good morning, baby girl." I kiss her lips. "I missed waking up next to you." And I plan to show her exactly how much. Rolling her onto her back, I position myself over her before sliding my erection into her tight, wet body. Natalie's back arches, pushing her breasts up. Her pert nipples beg for attention, which I gladly lavish on each one. "Do you feel how much I missed you?" I ask as I pull all the way out.

She whimpers at the loss of contact and lifts her hips, trying to find me.

"Always my impatient sub. Tell me what you want." I rub the tip of my cock through her wet folds, teasing her.

"You." Her voice is breathy and wanting.

That's all the confirmation I need to push in, balls deep. "And this time, I'm never letting you go. Tell me you're mine." I need to hear her say the words.

"I'm yours, Sir," she says, wrapping her legs tight around me.

Her show of possessiveness fuels my desire, and I growl in appreciation. I roll us over. Natalie now straddles my body, giving me the most perfect view of her breasts as she rides me. I want her to come with me. My fingers find her clit circling it until I know she's getting close. Then, I grab her hips, taking charge of the pace.

"Come with me." It's all the permission she needs. Natalie throws her head back as her body tightens around my cock. One more thrust, and I follow her into ecstasy. I hold her to me until our bodies come down from their high. I pull her next to me. She lays her head on my chest, and I run my fingers through her hair.

"What time is your dad being discharged today?"

She pushes up on her elbow. "How did you know?"

The loneliness from the past few months hits.

"I never went back to New York," I confess. "I moved in here and kept in touch with your parents."

"I had no idea."

"I couldn't leave."

Natalie lays her head back on my chest. "Thank you for not giving up on us." She places a kiss over my heart.

I don't know what I did to deserve this amazing woman, but I know I'm never letting her get away again. I play with her long blonde curls, trying to postpone the inevitable. It might be our first day back together, but we won't be able to spend it how I'd like. There are things we can't ignore. "As much as I want to spend the day in bed. We need to get up and shower."

Natalie groans as I sit up. "Are you sure we can't stay here?"

Stanley hasn't been home since he was shot on Christmas morning. Last month, he was transferred to the hospital's rehabilitation facility. They've been working tirelessly on his daily living skills—things he needs to be able to do to go home. It's taken a long time, but he's finally strong enough to be discharged. "Your parents are expecting you to pick them up. It's a big day for your dad. We don't want to miss it."

<h1 style="text-align:center;">Natalie</h1>

Alex leads me into our en-suite bathroom. He offered a full house tour last night, but I opted out, preferring to spend my time getting reacquainted with his body.

Like the rest of the house, the bathroom has been skillfully renovated, combining a rustic farmhouse feel with a modern vibe. The ceiling is covered in wood planks that Alex tells me are reclaimed from a hundred-year-old barn that once stood in town. Across the room, under a large window overlooking the lake, is a freestanding soaking tub.

"The window's tinted from the outside. So we have complete privacy in here."

"I was wondering how that would work."

As much as I love the tub, it's the walk-in shower that steals the show. Ombre glass tiles that transition from a dark charcoal grey at the top and fade into pure white line the walls. It's exquisite. I lean against the counter and watch Alex turn on the water. His muscles flex with each move. Hot water rains down from the ceiling. Alex steps in, and I follow, closing the glass door behind me. I position myself under the hot water so it cascades over my body.

"I missed you, baby girl."

"I missed you more."

The words barely leave my lips before Alex lifts me and presses my back against the tile. Instinctively, I wrap my legs around his waist for support as he takes me in the shower. This isn't slow or gentle, and I don't want it to be. He's marking me, laying claim to my body and my heart.

"Promise me you'll never leave again." He rests his forehead against mine.

"I promise, Sir. I'm yours always and forever."

Alex lowers me, keeping his arm around my waist until I'm sure of my footing. He reaches behind me and grabs the shampoo bottle, squeezing some into his hand.

"Turn around." Alex washes my hair, his fingers massaging my scalp. A soft moan escapes my lips. "Don't make those sounds, baby girl."

"Then don't make me feel so good."

He slaps my ass.

"Cheeky little thing today, aren't you?" His voice is playful and light.

After Alex rinses my hair, he uses his hands to wash my body. He takes his time reacquainting himself with every curve before allowing me to step under the water to rinse.

"Go start getting ready. I'll be out in a minute."

"Do I have to?" I drag my finger down his chest and abdomen, teasing him.

"Natalie." He grabs my hand. "Go, or we'll never leave the house."

I step out of the shower and blow him a kiss. Without grabbing a towel to cover my body, I walk out of the bathroom, swaying my hips.

"Just wait until tonight, my little temptress."

Natalie

"I'M LEAVING NOW," I SAY TO MY MOM. "I'LL BE THERE IN ABOUT AN hour."

"Please drive safely, honey. I hate the thought of you on the highway alone."

Alex and I decided to surprise my parents today. They'll be thrilled to see us together. Over the past few months, they haven't stopped begging me to call him—to work things out. It's a complete turnaround from several months ago when they begged me to stay away from him.

"I'll be fine. I could do this drive with my eyes closed."

"Don't do that," Mom shrieks.

"It was a joke." I laugh. "I'll see you guys soon."

Alex locks the front door, and together, we walk the stone path to his car, which is now parked in the driveway.

"This wasn't here last night."

I know everything happened in a whirlwind, but I wouldn't have missed his car sitting in the driveway. Would I?

"No, it wasn't." Alex opens the door for me. "Brandon and Lana brought it over early this morning."

I'm relieved I didn't miss something as obvious as a car. I'm also thankful for Brandon and Lana. They went to great lengths to make sure Alex and I got back together. If not for them, I would've lost the best thing in my life. I need to find some way to thank them.

Alex slowly maneuvers the gravel driveway until we reach the main road. Then, we start the all too familiar drive to Branson. It's been a long three months of driving back and forth while juggling my responsibilities here. Knowing this is the last time we'll need to make this drive is a huge relief.

Dad cleared a significant hurdle when he was released from the hospital to a lower level of care. Unfortunately, there are no in-patient rehabilitation centers in Northmeadow. As a result, my parents were forced to remain in Branson while Dad continued his physical therapy. Mom insisted on staying to be near her husband. I don't know how they were able to afford the hotel room for all these months. Every time I asked, my parents changed the subject.

"I'm worried about how to help my parents pay off their credit cards. This stay in Branson must've cost a fortune."

"You don't need to worry about that."

"Of course I do, Alex. They're my parents. There's no way they can afford—"

"I was hoping this didn't come up." Alex glances my way. "I paid for her hotel room and expenses."

"You did?"

"Charlotte and Stanley are your family, which makes them my family. I couldn't stand by and do nothing when I had the means to help them."

"Thank you doesn't feel like enough."

"I have you. That's all I need."

We drive in silence for a few minutes. The knowledge of what Alex did is still sinking in. I safeworded. Ended our relationship. But Alex not only stayed, he took care of my parents for the past few months. I don't deserve this man sitting next to me.

"I'm sure once Charlotte sees us together, the first thing she'll want to know is if we set a wedding date yet," Alex says, breaking the silence. "I want to get married as soon as possible."

The selfish part of me thinks we should elope, but the little girl in me wants the fairy tale wedding I've always dreamed of. And then there's the adult me who's holding back. My head and heart are at war with each other.

When I don't respond, Alex asks, "What's wrong?"

I fidget with my fingers in my lap. "I don't want to get married until my dad can walk me down the aisle."

Alex reaches over, grabbing my hand. "As much as I don't want to wait for you to be my wife, that's a compromise I can live with."

"Really?"

"baby girl, I want our wedding day to be perfect. But perfect isn't only about what I want. It's also what you want. Why don't we talk to his physical therapist and see if she has an idea of a timeline? Then, we can pick a date from there."

"Thank you."

"You don't have to thank me."

With my biggest concern addressed, we spend the rest of the drive sharing ideas for the wedding.

"I'd like to keep it simple and inexpensive."

"Money isn't an issue," Alex reminds me. "Whatever you want, we'll get."

When I was a little girl, I'd spend hours sitting on the floor in front of the magazine display at Dad's store. One by one, I'd go through every bridal magazine, pretending it was me in one of the beautiful dresses. As an adult, my love of weddings hasn't changed. Now, instead of magazines, I use the internet to save pictures and wedding-themed ideas.

"I don't want us to spend a fortune—"

"We get one chance at this. I want it to be everything you dreamed of and more."

He glances my way, a sexy smile on his face. Will there ever be a day this man won't cause me to feel like a schoolgirl with her crush? I certainly hope not.

"I've been wondering. Do you think Anthony would let us have the ceremony in his garden at the restaurant?"

"I'm sure he will. Once we have a date in mind, we'll give him a call to make the reservation. Have you thought about who you want in the wedding party?"

"Lana's my maid of honor." That's a foregone conclusion. "I'd like to ask Leo to be my man of honor. Would you be okay with that?"

"I couldn't see it any other way." Alex doesn't flinch at my non-traditional request. "Your parents might have something to say about it, though."

"I'm sure they'll be shocked. But this is our wedding. They'll have to keep an open mind."

"Very open," Alex chuckles. "I've asked Brandon to be my best man, and I was thinking of asking Tony to be a groomsman."

"Two couples. That's perfect."

With the wedding party agreed upon, I move on to my next concern.

"Who's going to marry us?"

Neither of us subscribes to a particular religion, so having a minister wouldn't be a good fit.

"I have an idea about that," Alex says as he pulls into the rehab parking lot. "If you don't like it, we can come up with something else."

"What's your idea?"

"Viktor." He watches me carefully for a reaction.

"You want Viktor to marry us?"

"Yes. All he has to do is go online and fill out a registration."

Obviously, Alex has already thought this through.

"Do you think he'll do it?"

"I think he'd do anything for you."

Alex's face tightens. He gets out of the car and comes around to open my door.

"Are you jealous, Sir?"

"Insanely and irrationally."

I exit the car and smile at the alpha man standing next to me.

"Let's ask him."

Hand-in-hand, we walk down the long hallway to Dad's room. The door is shut, so I knock.

"Come in," Mom calls.

Alex steps aside, "You go first."

I push the door and walk in. A second later, Alex follows.

"Alex." Mom jumps up from her chair. "Does this mean you two are together again?"

Walking over to her, I kiss her cheek. "Yes, Mom. We're back together."

Mom brings her hands to her chest. "I'm so happy. Come here, Alex. Let me hug you."

Alex offers a warm smile before he wraps Mom in a hug. Dad sits on the bed, his eyes glimmering with excitement.

As I watch the scene unfold before me, the progress we've made as a family is evident. We've made great strides in our communication with one another. Instead of rushing to judgment, we've learned to listen with compassion. To try to understand the other's point of view. My parents don't always agree with my decisions. But instead of treating me like a child and fighting me at every turn, they've learned to respect my choices.

As a result, we're a happy family for the first time in a very long time. That knowledge brings a smile to my face. Our family is finally functioning like the loving and supportive unit Michael and I wished for so many years ago. Yet, the pain of his death feels raw, as if he left only yesterday. Grief is a complex process. It's something that really never ends. It changes with time. How I wish Michael were here to experience our love.

Alex returns to my side and wraps his arm around my waist. "Are you okay, baby girl?"

With Alex by my side and my family in my life, I'm confident with my answer.

"I am."

Alex

With the discharge papers in hand, we prepare to leave the rehabilitation center. The sun shines bright, but a chill remains in the early spring air. I leave the Clarkes with Natalie while I get the car and pull it up to the main doors. Natalie pushes her father's wheelchair to the car while I open the front door. I try to help Stanley into the front seat, but he insists on sitting in the back with his wife. When we get them settled in, I fold his wheelchair and put it in the trunk before circling to the driver's side.

"Are we all set to go home?"

I never thought I'd say it, but the small country town and even its nosey residents have grown on me. It won't be our permanent residence, but our cottage in North-meadow has become a comfortable second home.

"I've been ready for weeks," Stanley mutters.

He makes me laugh. Stanley's been pestering the doctors to discharge him for months. Unfortunately, his lung sustained severe damage. Although he initially seemed okay, he suffered quite a few setbacks. Stanley was readmitted to the ICU at one point because he developed pneumonia. The doctor's prognosis was grim, but the man is a fighter. Despite everything, he beat the odds. It's clear where Natalie gets her tenacity.

"Let's get on the road, then."

Almost as if on cue, Charlotte asks, "Have you two chosen a wedding date?"

Natalie and I look at each other and laugh. We took bets on how long it would take for the wedding questions to start. Looks like Natalie won this one.

"What's so funny? Can you blame me for being excited that you're finally getting married? Maybe I'll even get a grandchild."

"Mom." Natalie looks back at her mother.

I interrupt before that conversation gets out of hand. "I'd like to marry Natalie tomorrow. But we've decided to wait until Stanley can walk her down the aisle."

"I think that's a wonderful plan," Charlotte says, "In the meantime, Natalie and I can start planning the wedding. We'll need to go dress shopping, choose the colors, pick flowers, and make decorations," she says, finally taking a breath. "I'll call Reverend—"

"The wedding isn't going to be in Northmeadow," Natalie interrupts.

"What do you mean?"

Natalie looks at me with trepidation in her eyes.

"We're going to get married in New York," I say calmly. "We have a venue already chosen. I have pictures on my phone if you want to see them."

Anthony hired my firm to promote his restaurant and their new wedding venue. Our photographer sent me the shots the other day. The place looks incredible. Using the rearview mirror, I glance in the backseat. It's clear from the look on Charlotte's face she's struggling with her next move. I give her a few minutes to work things out for herself. I hope she'll tamper down her usually overbearing nature and allow Natalie the freedom to plan our wedding.

"That sounds like a great idea." Stanley jumps in. "All I need is a date, so I have a goal to work toward. There's nothing that can stop me from walking my little girl down the aisle."

"We wouldn't have it any other way. Let's talk with your physical therapist, and we'll set a date from there."

"That's fair, son," Stanley says, satisfied.

While I'm driving, I continue telling them more about the venue. "It's an Italian restaurant. They have a brand-new space in Manhattan."

"You're getting married in a restaurant?" Charlotte shrieks.

"Not exactly," I reply calmly. "Our friend, Anthony, owns the restaurant. Recently, he purchased a large outdoor space that he's transformed into an exclusive wedding venue. Natalie, will you pull up the pictures for your parents?"

She grabs my phone from the center console, opens the digital album, and hands the phone to her mom.

"What will the menu be?" Charlotte asks as she swipes through the pictures. "Will you get to sample the food?"

"Natalie and I have sampled Tony's food on several occasions." I chuckle. "How about I call him and see if I can arrange to fly him in so you and Stanley can taste it, too?"

"You don't have to go through all that trouble for us."

"It's no trouble at all. Once we're settled at home, I'll give him a call and set something up."

"It's charming," Charlotte says, passing the phone back. "But it isn't a church. Will you at least have a minister?"

"We're asking a close friend to be the officiant," Natalie says calmly, leaving no room for argument.

"No church. No minister." Charlotte's voice grows in volume.

"Charlotte. Let's not let the little things put a wedge between Natalie and us again."

"Thank you, Dad." Natalie's voice is quiet. "Would you like to see some of the dresses I'm looking at, Mom?"

Six months ago, this conversation would've turned into a huge fight. But instead, my girl did a great job standing her ground yet staying calm. Now, she has successfully changed the subject to something less controversial.

Charlotte passes my phone back to Natalie. "Yes, honey. I'd love to see them."

"I have a bunch saved on Pinterest," she says excitedly.

"What's a Pinterest?"

Natalie laughs. "It's like an online magazine."

She turns in her seat so she can see her mom. "You swipe just like when you're looking at pictures," Natalie explains as she passes her phone to her mom. "Obviously, I'm not paying for the designer price tag." She glances my way with a raised eyebrow. "But I'm hoping we can find something with a similar style to Grandma's dress."

For the remainder of the car ride, Natalie and her mom chat about planning a bridal shower, dress styles, wedding colors, flowers, and cakes.

Each time we make this drive, it feels longer than the one before. I'm thankful when I make the final turn and pull into the Clarke's driveway. I get out first to get the wheelchair. Natalie quickly follows me.

"Thank you for being so patient with mom. I know she can be a lot sometimes."

I reach out and cup her delicate face in my hand. "There's nothing I won't do for you, baby girl." I place a kiss on her forehead. "Let's get your parents inside so I can get you home."

"Yes, Sir." She turns to walk away, but not before I give her ass a quick swat making her giggle.

After I've helped Stanley into the chair, I wheel him up the newly installed ramp.

"This wasn't necessary," Stanley says quietly.

"It's not permanent," I reassure him.

As a man, I understand his reluctance to be dependent on others. It's a defeating feeling.

"You'll be on your feet in no time."

"Yes, I will." Stanley straightens his posture and holds his head high.

"Welcome home, Daddy," Natalie says as she opens the front door.

After months of recovery, her family is back in their home where they belong, and life can begin moving forward again.

Natalie

Spring is in full bloom. Mother Nature has done her job of waking the natural world from its winter slumber. The early pink and white tree buds have been replaced with vibrant green leaves. In the wooded area surrounding our lake house, we've had the pleasure of watching newborn fawns, still with their spotted fur, ambling close to their mamas as they learn to navigate their new surroundings.

On the left side of our patio stands a magnificent oak tree that's now adorned with bird feeders. I set them up, hoping to lure in some of the lovely feathered creatures inhabiting the nearby lake. My efforts paid off. A family of bluebirds has taken up residence in the tree's shelter. Over the past weeks, the mother bird diligently brooded over her eggs, guarding and nurturing them until they finally hatched a week ago.

Each day, I watch her as she lovingly cares for her newborn hatchlings. She tirelessly tends to her young by feeding and nurturing them, prioritizing their well-being over her own. Her vigilant male partner watches from afar, safeguarding her and their nest.

My heart swells with emotion at the sight of her devoted mate, bringing her small tokens of nourishment in the form of insects. As I watch this feathered family, I am startled when Alex quietly comes up behind me, wrapping his arms around my waist.

"Watching the birds again?"

"It's fascinating the way they care for their family."

Alex laughs softly, and I turn in his arms.

"Do you want children?"

We discussed birth control options at great length when we negotiated our contract. But other than one conversation in passing, we've never seriously discussed if or when we'd have children.

"Someday. But not right now." He pauses and searches my face. "Do you want a baby now?"

If someone had asked me that question a few years ago, I would've had an immediate answer. Yes, I want children—a lot of them.

Growing up, especially while Tommy and I were dating, I was surrounded by people who had similar dreams. My girlfriends and I planned to settle down with a boy from town and become mothers. During high school, I babysat as much as possible. I loved caring for newborns and playing with rambunctious toddlers. I figured it would give me the experience I'd need when I had my own children. Even though I dreamt of school and a career, children were always in the picture.

Since I've been with Alex, I haven't given much thought to the question of children. Our relationship began as nothing more than a contract between a Dominant and submissive. It was agreed there was no room for children within that arrangement.

Everything is different now. We're still Dominant and submissive, but our relationship has evolved into more. We're in love and will be married. This is something we didn't talk about in our class. I'm not sure where the line begins and ends. We're still very much involved in a lifestyle in which I have no idea how to raise a child.

"I'd like a baby, maybe a few babies. Someday."

"Someday. That's good." He visibly relaxes. "Right now, I have some work I need to catch up on before your parents get here." He pushes a wayward strand of hair behind my ear before leaning in and kissing me.

"I'm going to watch the birds for a while longer. Then I'll be in to start dinner."

"I'll be in my office if you need anything," he says, flashing his sexy smile.

Standing outside, I get lost in a daydream about *someday*.

A day when Alex and I are happily married. He beams with pride and love while holding our newborn baby in his arms. The smile on my face falters when I think about Alex's reaction.

Someday doesn't mean soon.

And with that, I leave my daydream behind and head into the kitchen to prepare dinner.

Babies once again infiltrate my thoughts while I'm chopping vegetables for the salad. How does a couple have a child while they're focused on their Dom/sub relationship? So much of our daily life is wrapped up in the lifestyle. Would we have to hide it or stop it completely? I don't know how we'd adapt if such a big part of our identity as a couple was suddenly gone.

Then I think about how busy my life is right now. Since Dad can't work and Mom has to care for him, I've taken on the responsibility of managing the pharmacy. The first thing I did was close for a week while we updated and rearranged the store's layout. Without Dad, we had no pharmacist, so I hired two recent pharmacy graduates, Donna and Reuben. Mrs. Smith has agreed to stay on and help oversee a few of the high school students I hired to work part-time after school. Until I can hire someone to manage the store, I have to work a few hours every day.

Alex worked his magic on some simple marketing ideas. We now have a fresh look both inside and out. Despite some initial resistance from my parents, Clarke's Pharmacy also carries souvenirs and other items tourists are always looking for. It's been a big transition, but business is steadily picking up.

My parents are like a full-time job all by themselves. I had hoped things would settle down once they returned home, but that hasn't been the case. In fact, life has become even more chaotic. What used to be weekend trips to Branson has transformed into daily trips to assist Mom with household chores or take Dad to various appointments. I'm grateful to have Alex by my side. He's always more than willing to lend a hand whenever possible.

Dad's a physical therapy rock star. In the month he's been home, he's gone from being totally wheelchair-bound to being able to walk short distances with his walker. Alex and I spoke to his physical therapist, hoping she had a timeline for when she thinks Dad will walk independently. She felt a safe time frame would be about a year. Seeing Dad's accomplishments, I'm confident he'll be ready to walk me down the aisle for our wedding next spring.

Right now, the biggest obstacle Dad has to overcome is himself. He's always been a proud, self-sufficient man who provided for his family. But since the shooting, he's had to rely on Mom, Alex, or me for nearly everything. Dad refuses to go anywhere other than the doctor. His rationale is that he doesn't want anyone to see him in *this condition*.

The knife slips, and I nearly cut myself. There's no room in your life for a baby right now, maybe ever. That's a reality I have to face, but not right now. What I need to focus on is dinner. My parents will be here in a few hours. It's taken weeks of begging, but I finally convinced Dad to let Mom bring him over. Neither of them has been here yet. I'm excited to show my father the result of all his sneaking around with Alex.

After dinner, Mom's hoping we can start planning my bridal shower. I wanted it to be in the city, but she begged me to let her host it in Northmeadow. It's a concession I'm willing to make, especially since they aren't giving us a hard time about getting married in the city.

After cutting the salad ingredients, I toss them together in a bowl and stick them in the fridge to chill until later. Then, I start assembling the lasagna. It's four-thirty, and the lasagna needs to cook for an hour. Mom and Dad said they'll be here about six, so I have plenty of time to get it in the oven and shower quickly.

After putting on clean clothes and make-up, I head down the hall and poke my head into Alex's office. "Are you almost done?"

Alex doesn't look up from his computer screen. "Mhm."

I walk over and wrap my arms around him. "Is everything okay, Sir?"

"Yeah, I think so," he says and lets out a deep breath. "There are some irregularities in the system I'm trying to figure out."

I rub his shoulders, trying to relieve some of the tension he's holding there. "Irregularities?"

He grabs my arm and leads me around his body, pulling me onto his lap. Then, pointing at the screen, he says, "I received an alert. There was a failed attempt to access my encrypted folders."

"Do you think it's something to worry about?"

"I don't think so." He continues to stare at his screen. "Probably an employee that tried to access the wrong file." He closes the laptop. "Dinner smells delicious."

"Thank you." His compliment fills me with pride. "My parents will be here any minute."

"What time is it?"

"It's almost six."

"Damn," he says and helps me to my feet. "I didn't intend to be in here so long."

"It's okay. I have everything under control."

The doorbell rings, interrupting our conversation.

"I'll get it. I'm sure Charlotte's going to need help with the wheelchair."

While Alex answers the door, I go back to the kitchen to finish dinner. I'm setting the table when Mom comes into the room. "Natalie," she gushes. "Your home is beautiful."

"Thank you." I stop to hug her. "Alex did a great job with it."

"Don't forget I helped," Dad chimes in.

"Daddy." I throw my arms around him. "I'm so happy you're both here."

"So are we," Dad says. "I hope dinner's ready. I'm starving."

"I'm just about to take it out of the oven."

Grabbing oven mitts, I carefully remove the steaming tray and set it on the stovetop.

"Please, make yourselves at home." Alex holds up a bottle of Merlot. "Can I interest anyone in a glass?"

"I guess it couldn't hurt to have a little taste," Mom says, shocking all of us. "It's a very special occasion, after all."

Alex fills the glasses while I put the food on the table. Then, we sit down and have our first family dinner in our cottage. Looking around the table, I realize how lucky we are to be together. It wasn't that long ago that my parents refused to accept Alex. Then Dad got shot, and Alex and I broke up. This past year has been hell. But thankfully, we've come out the other side and can look forward to what this next year will bring.

"I'm thinking of a late summer bridal shower," Mom says between bites.

"That'd be great. We have a lot of out-of-town guests that'll need time to make travel arrangements."

"My dad and his girlfriend are planning on flying in as well," Alex adds.

I adore Sam Montgomery and his sub, Luna. The week after Dad was released from the hospital, Alex insisted I needed a break. He conspired with my parents and hired an in-home nurse to stay with them. Then, he booked plane tickets for us to fly to Seattle to spend a long weekend with Sam and Luna. Even though we'd spoken on video chats, I was nervous about meeting them in person, especially Luna. She's a free spirit, kind of a hippie. I've never met anyone like her.

Alex and Luna have a friendly relationship. He respects her and her place in his dad's life, but she's not his mom. Luna respects that and has never tried to take her place. Alex doesn't talk about her much, and I assumed they weren't close. I wasn't sure where that put me as far as a relationship with her. Was I okay to consider her my future mother-in-law, or would that be disrespectful to Alex's mom? He and I talked a lot about it before we flew out. He gave me his blessing to develop my relationship with her, to let it naturally become whatever it's meant to be.

I was shocked to learn Luna isn't her given name. It's actually Esther. Luna is the name she chose when she was in her early twenties. That's when she decided to leave conventional life behind, trading it for a more bohemian lifestyle. She embraced a vegan lifestyle and studied natural medicine. While we were there, she gave me some supplements to aid my dad's recovery.

Luna and I have similar backgrounds. She also comes from a very conservative, religious family in a small town. That commonality helped us form an instant connection. It's hard not to be affected by her peaceful soul. She's become a treasured friend. Since our trip, she and I try to talk at least once a week. Luna understands where I'm coming from and has been a help with balancing both parts of my life. I'm excited knowing they're coming in for our shower.

Alex's phone rings. "I need to take this."

He excuses himself from the table and quickly makes his way to his office, closing the door.

"Let me clean off the table. Then I'll get my notebook so we can go over the guest list."

"Is everything okay?" Dad asks.

"There's a small issue at his office."

"I hope it's nothing serious," Mom adds.

"I don't think so." But, even as I say the words, a small voice inside tells me it's more serious than it appears. "I'm going to grab the notebook. "I'll be right back."

The notebook's in Alex's office. From outside the door, I hear his raised voice. Not wanting to interrupt, I knock and wait for a reply.

"Come in," he calls sharply.

"I'm sorry to interrupt. I just need to grab something."

"Hold on a minute, Viktor." Alex lowers the phone from his ear. "I have to fly out to New York tomorrow."

"Why?"

"Something's going on in the office. I need to be there to get to the bottom of it."

This news shouldn't come as a surprise. We both knew there'd be times he'd have to fly back and forth, but I didn't think it would be this soon.

"I'd prefer if you came with me."

His face is serious, leaving little room for argument, but I proceed anyway.

"I can't leave. I have to oversee the pharmacy, and my parents aren't ready to be alone yet."

"I'll hire an in-home aide."

"You're kidding, right." I cross my arms.

That was okay for the weekend, but going back to New York will be longer than a few days. I know my parents, and they aren't going to be comfortable having a stranger in their home for a longer-term stay.

"Natalie—" Alex issues a warning.

This isn't a topic I plan to give in on. The fact that he's exerting himself as my Dominant right now has me frustrated. I swipe my notebook from the desk.

"Can we talk about this later, *Sir*?" The title comes out harsher than I intend.

The look on his face tells me I've overstepped and I'll have consequences later. "I have to finish this call."

There's more I want to say, but I'm already in trouble, so I do the smart thing and walk out of the office. Closing the door, I lean against it, holding the notebook against my chest. Alex is worried about whatever is happening within his company, but that doesn't give him the right to nearly demand I go with him to New York. Or does it?

He's my Dominant, and I understand that, but I'd like him to at least listen to my concerns and take them into account before he goes all caveman on me. Now's not the time to worry. My parents don't need to be stressed about it, so after taking a few calming breaths, I put a smile on my face and walk back into the kitchen.

"Got it." I hold up the notebook.

"Oh, good." Mom reaches for it. "Let's get started on the fun stuff."

While Mom flips through a few pages, I make everyone a cup of coffee. Mom and I are squabbling over the guest list when Alex returns to the kitchen.

"Everything okay, son?"

"What did I miss here?" Alex avoids the question, taking his seat next to me.

"Mom just finished showing me her guest list for the shower. I'm trying to tell her there are too many people."

"We can have as many people as she'd like."

Seeing as she's won this battle, Mom smiles proudly.

"Now, let's look at your list." When she turns the page, her eyes grow wide. "Natalie, a bridal shower is for women." She points to the page. "You have men's names on here."

"We're planning a co-ed bridal shower."

"Co-ed?"

My patience is running thin. "Co-ed, as in both men and women."

Mom stares at me. Her mouth hangs open.

"Times are changing, Charlotte." Dad pats her hand.

"I guess so."

"How about we move on to the food." Alex pulls a menu from the back of the notebook, handing it to Mom. "Anthony has graciously offered to cater the bridal shower for us."

"We talked to him about having a tasting," I add. "He and Leo are going to come in for the July Fourth holiday. We'll have a party and tasting all in one."

It's been months since I've seen Leo in person. Of course, we keep in touch through video chats, but it isn't the same.

"Who's Leo?" Mom asks.

I look to Alex, knowing my next words won't go over well.

"Leo is Anthony's partner."

"Oh, Leo's a chef too."

Alex chuckles. "No, not his business partner. Leo's Anthony's fiancé, soon-to-be husband."

The color drains from Mom's face. "He's gay?" she asks in a hushed tone.

"Yes, Mom. He's gay."

Alex senses my frustration and squeezes my leg under the table, letting me know I need to relax.

"We love them both, so please try to keep an open mind."

"I'm trying." Mom takes the last sip of wine from her glass before raising it. "May I have a refill?"

Her question makes us all laugh, breaking the tension.

"Of course." Alex doesn't miss a beat and pours her another glass of merlot.

We all watch in silence as she takes a big drink. When she realizes we're staring, she sets her glass down and shrugs.

Alex steers the topic away from Tony and Leo's relationship and back to our food choices. Once we decide on the menu, he takes a picture of the list and texts Tony.

"I think it's time we head home." Dad yawns. "It's almost eleven, and I'm pretty tired."

"I'm sorry. I didn't even look at the time."

"Don't apologize, sweetheart. I've enjoyed myself tonight."

Mom gathers their things, including the container of lasagna I made for them to bring home. I try to make extra of all our meals so she doesn't have to worry about cooking. Between the ladies from church and me, they have a freezer full of pre-prepared meals.

"Thank you both for coming," Alex shakes Dad's hand and hugs mom. "Drive safely, Charlotte."

"Thanks for having us."

"Call me when you get home." Now I sound like the parent.

"We will."

Alex steps back and wraps his arm around me as we watch my parents drive away.

Alex

Once her parents' car is out of sight, I lead Natalie back into the house. There's an unsettled matter of her coming to New York with me to discuss.

"Viktor booked plane tickets. We leave tomorrow."

"I'm not going to New York right now."

"You aren't staying here alone."

"Tommy's in jail. There's no danger."

"I'm not taking any chances."

"What happened to talking things through?"

I walk over to her and place my hands on her shoulders. "Where your safety is concerned, there's no conversation."

"Can we come to some sort of a compromise, Sir?"

I drop my hands and walk over to the window overlooking the lake. Natalie's right, I know she is, but my overprotective nature doesn't want to compromise. My rational self realizes Tommy isn't a threat, but what if something else happens? I'm not leaving her behind. I refuse to risk losing her again. But if I force this, am I going to do precisely what I'm trying to avoid? So, instead of pressing the issue, I relent.

"I shouldn't be more than a few weeks," I say. "Viktor will stay with you while I'm gone."

When I bought this cottage, I also purchased the one right next door. Viktor lives there and can monitor our security system while giving us privacy.

Natalie comes up behind me and wraps her slender arms around my waist.

"Thank you, Sir."

I reach my arm around her, bringing her to my front and holding her close.

"Now, there's this little matter of your attitude earlier this evening."

She smiles and bats her eyelashes.

265

"I don't know what you mean, Sir."

"You have one minute. After that, I expect you to be naked and on the bed, waiting for me."

Giggling, she hurries to our bedroom.

Natalie looks beautiful. She's laid out before me with her arms bound over her head and her legs spread and restrained to the bed. Since this is our last night together for a few weeks, I plan to make it one she won't forget anytime soon. She watches me as I walk around the bed silently, examining her body from all angles. Her face gives away her curiosity. She's dying to know what her punishment is. But I'm not ready to let her know yet.

Leaving her in the bedroom, I go to the kitchen for a glass of water. The ice cubes will prove useful for what I have in mind. When I return, Natalie lifts her head and bites her lip. I return her stare with a smile, take a drink, and put the glass on the nightstand before sitting beside her.

Leaning over with the ice cube between my teeth, I tease her nipple. Natalie gasps from the cold. I trail the melting cube lightly down the valley between her breasts, over her toned abdomen, and down to her bare pussy. She squirms from the contact, but I hold her waist, steadying her. The ice cube makes contact with her clit, heightening her responsiveness. While the ice melts, I add two fingers, sliding them in and out. She's wet and panting, climbing closer and closer to an orgasm. Then, I pull my fingers out.

"Why did you stop? I was so close."

Bringing my fingers to my mouth, I suck each one, tasting her arousal before answering, "I know."

Without further explanation, I release her wrists and ankles from their bondage.

She sits up. "What are you doing?"

"I'm going to my office. I told Viktor I'd call him after your parents left." I make my way to the bedroom door. "You are not to touch yourself."

Natalie blows out a frustrated breath. Without another word, I leave the bedroom and head to my office. This punishment will remind her to keep her attitude in check when we're having a conversation. What she doesn't know is I don't intend to let the night go by without giving her multiple orgasms.

I call Viktor, who assures me he's checked into the access attempts.

"They all came from an IP address inside the company," he explains.

"I'm glad it's not an outside threat, but I'm going to need to get to the bottom of it when I get to New York."

Taking a few more minutes, I email Brandon to make him aware of the potential in-office issues. He's in the office every day while I'm in Missouri. I want him to investigate this and give me a report when I get there tomorrow. If something is going on, I want to know about it.

Natalie is still sound asleep when I get back to the bedroom. It's time to wake up my submissive. After I strip my clothes and climb into bed, I return to my earlier mission of feasting between her legs. My tongue flicks her clit, waking her. The rest of the night is spent giving each other pleasure over and over until we're both exhausted, and she falls asleep in my arms.

Natalie

Leaning against our parked car, my heart aches as I watch Alex disappear inside the airport. I know this won't be like last time, but that doesn't stop my tears. Using the back of my hand, I wipe my face.

"Chin up," Viktor nudges my shoulder. "I'm still here."

"Just like old times." I smile sadly at the man who's seen me through so many hard times.

"Come on. Let's grab some lunch."

"Can we stop by the store first? I need to check in."

Mrs. Smith is working today. She has experience, but the majority of the employees are still new. I'm usually there for at least a few hours a day to ensure everyone is adequately trained and the store runs smoothly. Once Dad's on his feet, he and Mom can take over. But for now, that responsibility falls on me.

"No problem," Viktor says when we return to the car. "First the store, then food."

"Hungry?" I don't know why I ask. I already know the answer.

"Always." He grins.

While Viktor drives into town, I sulk in the passenger seat. Alex has only been gone for a few minutes, but I already miss him like crazy.

Alex spent all morning reassuring me this would be a short trip, a few weeks at most. That the attempts at accessing the encrypted files were just an employee accidentally trying to get into the wrong file. An innocent mistake. As much as I wanted to believe him, I saw the stress on his face. There's more to the story than he's telling me.

"Do you know what's going on with Alex's company?"

Viktor tenses. "Yes."

"Will you tell me?"

"No."

I roll my eyes and look out the window.

"Can you just tell me if it's serious?"

I know I shouldn't push. I should trust Alex instead of trying to extract information from Viktor, but I can't help myself. I don't particularly appreciate being kept in the dark. If there's something serious going on, I want to know.

"What did Alex tell you?"

"Just that an employee tried to access his encrypted files." I shift in my seat to look at Viktor. "But that it was only an accident, possibly from one of the new hires."

"Then that's all you need to know."

"There's more, though, I can tell." I continue to pry.

"Natalie." He shoots a glare in my direction. "If Alex wanted you to know more, he would've told you himself. You need to stop. Now."

"Fine." I cross my arms and return to staring out the window.

There's an uncomfortable tension between us, and we remain silent for the rest of the ride. It's my fault. I pushed too hard again.

Viktor pulls into the pharmacy's parking lot and turns the car off. Neither of us makes a move to get out.

"I'm sorry."

"I forgive you," Viktor says, his features softening. "Alex will tell you what you need to know and when. You need to trust him."

"I know. I'm trying." I open the car door and get out. "Are you coming in with me?"

"I'm right behind you."

Knowing Viktor has my back is a comforting thought. At nearly six and a half feet tall, he's an imposing solid wall of muscle. His build, combined with his shaved head and Russian-sounding accent, tends to intimidate most people. If they only knew what a teddy bear he really is, his status as my bodyguard would be useless. I'll never let that secret out. I quite enjoy seeing people scurry when he comes their way. Viktor takes a step ahead of me so he can grab the door. Always a gentleman.

"Good afternoon, Mrs. Smith," I say with a big smile. "How's everything today?"

"Running smoothly," she answers without looking up.

She finishes with her customer before looking at me. Her body tenses when she notices Viktor behind me. Mrs. Smith has made it perfectly clear she is not a Viktor fan.

"How are the new managers working out?"

"Very well." She looks over my shoulder. "Alex is gone again, I take it?" she asks, her eyebrows pinched.

I pretend I don't hear her prying question or see the disdain on her face and walk away. I didn't come here to engage with Mrs. Smith. Just seeing me with Viktor gives her enough ammunition to start the rumor mill turning. I've heard it all since we've been here. Whispers about me living with two men. That something's going on between the three of us.

Honestly, the stories they come up with make me laugh. The opinions of the people in town no longer matter to me. Let them think what they may.

"I'll never understand these people," Viktor mumbles as we walk to the back of the store.

"I quit trying to figure them out," I reply, shrugging my shoulders.

When we get to the pharmacy area, there's a small line. Reuben, our newest pharmacist, is working the register.

"Good afternoon, Ms. Clarke." He offers me a cheery smile.

"How's everything going? Looks busy today."

"It's been steady all day."

"Do you need help out here?" I have no problem jumping on the other register to give him a hand.

"Nope. I'm enjoying meeting all our customers." He glances at Viktor. "Good afternoon, Mr. V."

Keeping up his tough-guy exterior, Viktor crosses his arms and nods. I bite my lip to keep from laughing.

"I'll catch up with you when you're not as busy."

Using my key, I unlock the door leading to the pharmacy area. Donna's back is to us. She appears to be concentrating on the prescription she's filling.

"Hi," I say, coming up behind her.

She jumps and drops the pill bottle in her hand.

"I'm sorry. I didn't mean to scare you."

"It's okay." She laughs nervously. "I didn't hear the door open." When Donna sees Viktor, her eyes light up. "Hi. I mean, hello, Viktor." She stumbles over her words.

Women are constantly falling all over themselves to get Viktor's attention. But at least when he's with me, he's all business and doesn't indulge their attempts.

"I'm just checking in. How's Reuben doing?"

He looks pretty engaging with the customers. Donna started a few weeks before him, so I'm interested in her opinion.

"He's easy to work with, and as you can see, the customers love him," Donna replies. "I think he's a good fit."

A sense of relief washes over me. Once Reuben's fully trained, he'll be the pharmacist for the night shift. That will ease Donna's schedule and allow us to have the pharmacy counter open for longer hours. It's one step closer to getting the store back to being fully functioning. Aside from Dad getting back on his feet, keeping the store running is my biggest concern. My new managers need to be able to handle everything on their own, with minimal help from my parents, before Alex and I can move back to the city.

"How are the new part-timers working out?"

"The kids are doing great," Reuben says, joining the conversation. "Mary really stands out."

"I agree," Donna adds. "Mary will make a great assistant manager after they graduate."

A few months back, Billy, Mary's older brother, came into the pharmacy looking for me. He explained that things didn't go well for Mary after they talked to their parents. Something that unfortunately didn't come as a surprise to either of us. Thankfully, Billy and his now-husband, Todd, were prepared. They had a bedroom ready and waiting to welcome Mary into their home. Although their parents' reaction wasn't unexpected, Mary was struggling with it, so Billy sought me out. He wanted to see if I'd be willing to talk with them. I knew it'd be walking a fine line, but I agreed anyway.

I invited Mary to spend an afternoon with me at the cottage. They didn't need a therapist as much as they needed a friend. And that I could be. It also allowed me to offer her a part-time job at the store while Mary finished the last few months of high school.

"I'm not sure what their plans are after graduation, but I'll talk to them about it." I put a reminder in my phone.

Mary and I talk frequently, and I know they're considering leaving North-meadow for a bigger city. But that isn't my secret to tell. I'll offer the promotion to Mary so they know they have options should they consider staying.

"Tourist season will start with the Memorial Day holiday in a few weeks." I return to my original plan for this visit. "We've been doing a lot of advertising with the rental companies and other businesses by the lake. I'm hoping it draws more customers into the store. Do you feel prepared for an increase in customers?"

"Yes, we are," Donna answers quickly.

Her confidence inspires me. "I'm glad to hear that."

We take a few minutes to review the inventory order forms, cross-referencing them with our sales figures to ensure accuracy. Though it can be tedious, I need to know they can perform this task when I'm not present.

As we pore over the paperwork, Viktor remains by our side, silently observing. Catching his eye, I signal that I'll wrap up soon. Once we've completed our review, I pass the documents back to Donna. "If you guys don't need anything else, I'm going to head out. Keep up the great work."

Viktor opens the pharmacy door allowing me to exit first. Donna and Reuben stay behind, whispering about the *scary but oh-so-hot* man who's accompanying me.

"We can hear you," I say and laugh as we keep walking.

Donna and Reuben giggle. Both of them have expressed an interest in my body-guard, but I'm not in the habit of playing matchmaker.

"Ready for lunch?" I ask.

"I thought you'd never ask."

Viktor and I take advantage of the beautiful spring day and walk the few blocks to the diner.

It's been almost three weeks since I left Northmeadow and returned to New York City. Part of me missed the constant hustle and bustle the city offers. The other part longs to be back in my quiet cottage, hidden away from everything with Natalie.

For the time being, I need to be present in the office. Brandon's done a great job gathering information for me. Since I've been here, I've been paying attention to the office gossip channels. It's incredible what a person can learn hanging around the break room. It seems there are a few upper-level executives who've taken advantage of my extended absence.

Two of my employees have decided to branch out and start their own business, a move I usually applaud. Instead of going about it professionally, they chose to access my personal files, trying to lure my clients to their firm. Unfortunately, they gave their plan away when they tried to access the encrypted files.

Now, more than ever, I'm thankful Brandon and I work together. He had no experience in advertising, but that was easily taught. What was more important to me was having someone I could trust implicitly by my side.

As we went about business as usual, we waited and watched. Our patience paid off because now we have enough evidence to expose the guilty parties. Brandon and I are meeting outside the office tonight to formalize our next step. I plan to send a strong message to the two offenders and the rest of my employees not to fuck with my company or me.

While there seems to be nothing more nefarious going on, I'm not letting my guard down. The information in those files is too important to risk. I contacted Dimitri, the head of Maxim's tech team. He sent an upgrade for the security system on my computer. While I'm waiting for the update to finish, my cell rings. I'm hoping it's Natalie, but when I pick it up, I see it's my father.

"Dad. How are you?"

"I'm doing well. How's Natalie? Is she there so we can say hi?"

Dad and Luna fell in love with Natalie when we visited. Whenever he calls, he always asks to talk to her first.

"What happened to *how are you, Alex*?" I laugh.

Dad joins me in laughing. "Hi, Alex. How are you? Where's Natalie so we can say hi to her?"

"I'm doing okay. Natalie isn't with me right now."

"Where are you?"

"I'm in New York." The update finishes, and I close my laptop. "There's an issue in the office."

Because of his friendship with Maxim, my father is aware of the work we do together. I suspect he's more involved than he lets on and that he at least has his hand in the financials, but some things are better left unsaid.

"What kind of an issue? And why didn't Natalie go with you?"

"A few employees attempted to access my files, trying to poach my clients. I needed to be here to handle it in person. I knew it would take a few weeks, at least. Natalie didn't want to leave an aide with her parents that long, so she stayed behind with Viktor."

"Are you sure there's nothing more to this?" The concern in his voice is evident.

"We thoroughly checked it out. The IP addresses were from in the office."

Having that reassurance coupled with the evidence on my desk, I'm confident it's nothing more. I don't want to discuss this topic any longer, so I shift the conversation to wedding planning.

"We have a date for the shower and the wedding."

"Wait a minute. Let me get Luna." Dad covers the phone and calls his submissive into the room with him. "You're on speaker now."

"Hi, Luna. How are you?"

"I'm well. How are you and Natalie?"

"We're doing good. We decided on a date for the bridal shower. August nineteenth, the day after Natalie's birthday."

"That's perfect," Luna says. "We'll get to celebrate both occasions."

"That's the hope. And the wedding is set for May seventeenth."

The physical therapist is confident Stanley will be on his feet in plenty of time.

"I wish we could see you before then." Dad sighs. "August seems so far away."

"Tony and Leo are coming in for the July Fourth holiday. We'd love it if you'd come in, too."

"I'll book our plane tickets right now." Dad's excitement is palpable even through the phone.

After we hang up, I call Natalie to let her know we're getting more company for the holiday.

It's a balmy June evening as I walk down the sidewalk to the familiar corner bar a few blocks from my apartment. It's Thursday, so there isn't a large crowd. Looking around, I spot Brandon sitting at our usual table in the back corner. I walk across the small, dimly lit room, ignoring the whispers from a group of women standing by the bar.

"Looks like you've attracted some attention." Brandon laughs.

"Lucky me," I answer wryly.

Brandon waves, signaling the bartender, who comes over and drops off two cold beers.

"You look like shit."

"Thanks for the compliment." I take a long drink from the bottle.

"We have everything needed for tomorrow's meeting."

"I can't wait to see the look on those bastard's faces," Brandon says. "They aren't going to know what's hit them."

"That's the plan."

Over the next hour, we have a few more drinks, and I fill him in on my plan for the meeting. I'm not taking the chance of someone figuring out that Brandon and I are on to them, which is why we're meeting at a bar instead of my office.

"We'll have our typical Friday wrap-up. While we're in the meeting, a scheduled email will be sent to my advertising contacts. The guilty parties won't have a chance to undermine us. They'll never find another job in this town—or any other once I'm done."

"Justice will be served." Brandon raises his bottle in a toast. "Lana tells me the wedding plans are moving along nicely."

"They are." With the change of subject, the tension drains from my body. "The bridal shower's in August and the wedding in May."

"Tony told Lana they'll be in Northmeadow for July Fourth." Brandon raises an eyebrow.

"He's coming to do a tasting for Natalie's parents. Kind of a concession for the wedding being here."

"That ought to be interesting."

"Dad and Luna are flying in. You and Lana should come too."

Brandon laughs. "This get-together is something I have to see. We'll be there."

For Natalie's sake, I'm hoping the holiday won't be the circus Brandon's expecting.

It's gotten late. We finish the last of our beers, pay our tab, and walk out together.

"Thanks, Bran." I clasp his shoulder. "I needed a distraction tonight."

His ride pulls up to the curb. "Get a good night's sleep. You're going to need it tomorrow."

I take a slow walk back to my apartment. It's late and, at least in this section of town, quiet.

Tomorrow, I'll rectify the situation at work and take the first flight back to Natalie.

Natalie

Today marks a significant milestone in Dad's physical therapy journey. He's preparing to overcome a final hurdle - venturing out in public. Despite everyone's relentless efforts, he's been apprehensive about going out in public with his walker. His therapist has decided that the time has come.

We arranged to meet her at a small park in town so he could practice walking outside. This exercise will not only put his physical abilities to the test but will also be a mental challenge for him.

Viktor helps me get Dad into the car. He's unfazed despite my father's constant mumbling and grumbling. Dad's behaving like a toddler who's been denied their coveted lollipop from the store. I try to keep my distance so I don't make anything worse. After safely stowing away his wheelchair and walker in the trunk, I make my way to the driver's door.

"I'm driving." Viktor tries to get to the door handle before I do.

"Not today," I say, laughing when I beat him to it. "I promised Dad I'd drive. You get to sit in the back."

"You've got to be kidding." Viktor leans down and peeks into the backseat. "I'm not going to fit back there."

"It's a short drive.," I say as I get behind the wheel.

Reluctantly, Viktor folds his large frame into the backseat. Great, now I have two pouty men to contend with. Let them sulk. I plan to have a lovely afternoon at the park.

"Thank you for talking your mother into staying home," Dad says. "Too bad you couldn't get *him* to stay home too." He gestures with his thumb toward Viktor.

"You're welcome." I glance at Viktor in the rearview mirror. What I see makes me laugh.

Viktor's long legs are tightly bent. I'm pretty sure the lump in my back is his knee hitting my seat. I told him to stay home, but no way was that happening. I'm lucky I managed to drive. Returning my focus to my father, I say, "I still think you should've let Mom come."

"Maybe next time." He turns his head to look out the window.

"There's nothing to be ashamed of, Daddy." I place my hand on his shoulder.

"I'm not the man she married," he says quietly. "I can't do anything myself. I'm useless."

"Dad, that's enough." I don't like raising my voice, especially to my father, but something needs to snap him out of this self-pity. "What happened was a tragic accident. Yes, you need some help for now. But you're working hard and getting stronger every day."

He doesn't answer. Instead, he continues staring out the window, ignoring me for the rest of the ride.

The park is situated on the opposite side of town. During the latter part of the summer, local farmers set up an outdoor market. Today, the park is mostly empty except for a man walking his dog. "I'll get your walker."

Viktor beats me to it and has the walker by Dad's door before I'm barely out of the car. Opening Dad's door, I extend my hand.

"Ready?"

"No." But he accepts my help anyway.

After getting him situated with his walker, I look around for his therapist and spot her sitting on a bench a short distance away.

"You coming?" I ask Viktor.

"I'll wait here." He leans back against the car, crossing his arms.

Dad's therapist sees us and starts heading our way. We walk slowly, meeting her on the path.

"Hello there, Stanley," she chirps. "It's a beautiful day for a walk, isn't it?"

"I guess," Dad mumbles.

"Someone's grumpy today." She looks at me over Dad's shoulder.

I shrug, not knowing what to say or do.

"Why don't you hang out here while Stanley and I take a few laps around the park."

"No problem." I smile, glad to let her handle my grumpy parent. "I'll be at the car keeping Viktor company."

It's hard to watch my hero, my father, using a walker to steady himself while he slowly shuffles his feet. He's always been strong and able. Sadness grips my heart like a vice, knowing in one thoughtless, drug-fueled move, Tommy caused this.

"He's a fighter like you," Viktor says as he appears at my side.

I wave him off, hoping to stave off the tears threatening to fall.

"Dad's so stubborn sometimes."

"Explains where his daughter gets it from," he smirks.

"Shocking, isn't it?" We share a laugh and walk back to the car together. "Have you heard from Alex?" I ask as I pull out my phone. "There was a text when I woke up this morning. But when I tried calling him, it went straight to voicemail."

"Not since last night."

"I hope his meeting goes well today."
"I have no doubt he's handling it," Viktor says matter-of-factly.
Alex is probably busy, and I don't want to interrupt him with a phone call.
Me: Sorry I missed you earlier. Good luck with your meeting today. i love You.

My phone vibrates with a text from Natalie. I texted her early this morning, knowing she'd get it when she woke. I miss hearing her voice. We're both on different schedules and haven't talked since yesterday. She tried calling this morning after reading my text, but I was in a meeting with a new client and had to send her to voicemail.

Me: I got your voicemail. I'm sorry I couldn't answer. I've been swamped all day. I love you, too.

After I hit send, I slide my phone into my pocket. It's almost go time, and I need to keep my head in the game. At precisely four p.m., I send a reminder that the wrap-up meeting is in ten minutes. It's the usual course of events for a Friday, except this meeting will end with fireworks.

Once everyone is comfortable in my conference room, my security team will take their place outside. Their task is to escort my soon-to-be-former employees out of the building. Powering off my laptop, I put it in my leather messenger bag and go through the door that leads from my office to the private conference room.

Within minutes, my employees stream in and sit around the expansive glass-topped table. Several employees stop to shake my hand as they pass by. Brandon's the last one in. He closes the door behind him before taking his spot on my right.

"If everyone can take their seats. I want to keep this short so we can start our weekend early."

My employees settle in and give me their full attention.

"First, I'd like to congratulate Cameron and Morgan on signing two new clients to the agency this week."

A round of applause fills the room.

Once it's quiet again, I continue, "I want to thank Brandon for steering the ship while I was out of town. Everyone's done a great job keeping the day-to-day operations running seamlessly. I appreciate you all. I'll open the floor for any questions."

A few employees have concerns I'm able to address quickly and easily. "Anyone else?" I look around the room, but no one moves to speak. "I have one more thing, and then you can go." I smile. "It's come to my attention that several of your colleagues are branching out from Montgomery Advertising to start their own company."

It's not the first time I've had employees who possess an entrepreneurial spirit and work to start their own companies. It's a move I typically applaud and even give assistance with, so it's not surprising there are smiles around the table.

"Ben and Michelle, please make your way up here." I motion to the front of the room.

The pair rises from their seats with proud smiles. They've been fooled into thinking their efforts will be praised and offered the standard package I typically give. That makes what's about to happen even sweeter.

"These two employees came to my company fresh out of college. Over the years, they've worked hard and have achieved a remarkable amount of success." I pause, allowing them time to bask in their deceit. "Typically, I support employees taking the next step and opening their own company. But that isn't going to happen."

Their smiles fade as those words leave my lips. A hushed murmur emanates from their colleagues. I can sense that everyone is curious about why I'm unwilling to support Ben and Michelle. I have no intention of letting them off the hook. No one in my company will attempt to undermine me and get away with it. I stride towards the conference room door, yank it open, and summon the security team inside. The room falls silent, and a few employees shift uneasily in their seats.

With measured steps, I return to the head of the table. Brandon takes his place at my side—a united front.

"Ben and Michelle made the mistake of trying to steal my clients." I look at Ben, who refuses to make eye contact with me, and Michelle looks down. "Your personal belongings are waiting at reception. Security will escort you out of the building."

By taking this decisive action, I am confident nobody else will dare to entertain the idea of undermining me. Scanning the room, it's clear that my employees are taken aback by my bold move, and I'm satisfied that my message has been delivered loud and clear. The room remains quiet while the duo exits.

As Ben walks past me, he grumbles under his breath. Michelle avoids eye contact and trails behind him towards the door. With my security team in tow, I watch as they leave the room and hear the door click shut. Turning to Brandon, I exchange a satisfied look, knowing justice has been served.

"Now that that's out of the way," Brandon smiles, addressing the room. "Does anyone have anything to add before we wrap up?"

It takes a minute for what happened to sink in and for the employees to relax. Then, a chorus of *no sirs* echoes throughout the room.

"In that case, have a great weekend."

With that, everyone gathers their belongings and says their goodbyes on their way out.

"That went well," Brandon says once we're alone.

Sinking into my chair, I put my head back and close my eyes. "I'm just glad it's over."

"Lana's out with the girls tonight." Brandon puts the files in his bag. "I'll drive you to the airport."

"I appreciate that." I reach into my pocket and fish out my cell phone to text Natalie.

Me: I'm just leaving for the airport. I'll be home in a few hours.

Natalie: I can't wait to see you.

Me: You better be well-rested. I don't plan on letting you get much sleep tonight.

Natalie: I'm going for a nap now.

Viktor's at the small airport terminal in Northmeadow, waiting for me. There's no traffic at this late hour, so we make good time returning home.

"Everything go okay today, boss?"

"It went exactly as planned. They're no longer employed and won't work in advertising again."

"Dimitri gave me the rundown on the system update," Viktor explains. "I've also applied the same update to the systems at the lake."

Although it was only a pair of foolish individuals who believed they could destroy my business through theft, I find comfort in the fact that our security measures have been upgraded.

"Was Maxim apprised of the situation?"

"There's no need to alert him." My pulse quickens. Viktor knows better than to second-guess me.

"Sorry, boss. I'm just doing my job."

"Lose the *boss*, would you? And it's fine," I quip. "It was an internal issue, and it's been handled."

Viktor makes the final turn onto the narrow gravel road leading to the cottage. My body buzzes, knowing I'm only moments away from being with Natalie. I hate these separations. Next time I go to the city, she'll be by my side—we'll be going home together.

We both get out of the car, the beep signaling the doors are locked.

"Thank you for staying with her."

"My pleasure, *Alex*." He makes a point of stressing my name.

"It better not have been too much of a pleasure." I laugh, trying to ease some of the earlier tension between us.

Viktor's my right-hand man, and I trust him with my life. But, more importantly, I trust him with Natalie's life.

"Night, boss," Viktor says and walks toward his cabin.

I do what I've been waiting all day for. I go to my waiting sub.

ALEX: I'LL BE HOME IN LESS THAN AN HOUR. YOU'RE TO BE WEARING something sexy and kneeling by the bed when I get home.

My pulse races with excitement. I don't waste a second taking a shower and fixing my hair. I choose to remain topless, only putting on sexy black lace panties. When I check the clock, I see forty-five minutes have passed. Alex should be here any second.

Right on cue, the sound of gravel crushing under the car's tires reaches my ears. I drop to my knees, placing my palms on my parted thighs, eagerly anticipating the arrival of my Dominant. I hear the front door open and shut, and he takes his time meandering through the house before heading in my direction. The measured and unhurried rhythm of his footsteps draws nearer to our bedroom door.

As the doorknob turns, I lower my gaze. Out of the corner of my eye, I catch a glimpse of Alex placing his bag next to the dresser before he sits at the edge of the bed, his movements fluid as he removes his shoes and socks with relaxed ease.

Although he's yet to speak to me, I feel his intense stare taking in every inch of my body, which only heightens my arousal. I glance up and watch as he stands with his back to me and strips his clothes. His muscles flex with each step as he walks to the bathroom and leaves the door open. Alex turns the hot water on and steps into the shower.

My nipples harden, and wetness pools between my legs as I watch him lather his body. My hands itch to be rubbing themselves over every inch of his skin. He steps under the hot water, allowing it to rinse away the soap. Alex takes his time drying off before going to the dresser and slipping on a pair of boxers that hang low on his hips. I return my gaze to the floor, hoping he comes to me. The anticipation is driving me crazy.

Alex

I'VE BEEN AWAY FOR THREE WEEKS, AND EVEN THOUGH WE'VE PLAYED over video chat, it's never the same as being here, able to run my hands over her soft skin and hear her mewls of pleasure. So, rather than rushing our reunion, as my erection encourages me to, I take my time.

Patience is difficult for my submissive, and I know my silence is pushing Natalie's boundaries. But I'm not ready to show my hand yet. Walking past her, I go straight to our closet, where we store our toys. I grab the few things I want and return to the bedroom, where I set a step stool in front of where Natalie kneels.

During the house renovation, I strategically installed several suspension hooks on our bedroom ceiling. Using the step stool, I carefully secure the swing. When I glance down at Natalie, I notice her biting her lower lip. She's beginning to sense what I have in store for her tonight.

With no words exchanged, I retreat to the closet again and emerge with bundles of jute rope in various colors, which I lay on the bed behind her. Then, I pull up the playlist that Master Kiyoshi sent me, featuring soft sounds from a bamboo flute that Natalie would undoubtedly recognize from the night we met.

With sure steps, I move to my place before my sub.

"Remove your panties."

Natalie stands and hooks her fingers in the black lace, sliding them down her legs. I extend my hand, and she places the tiny piece of fabric in my palm. Bringing it to my face, I smell her arousal, a move that nearly forces me to abandon my original plan and sink into her wet heat right now. Tossing the panties onto the dresser, I take a minute to refocus. The past three weeks of separation have been stressful. I don't want to rush tonight. Natalie and I desperately need this time to reconnect. Taking a step closer to her, I trace the seam of her lips with my thumb before kissing her.

"You're so beautiful."

"Thank you, Sir."

"Lie down on the bed."

She spins around and lets out a tiny gasp when she spots the rope. "How do you want me, Sir?"

"On your back, baby girl."

She lies next to the rope, propping herself on her elbows. Then, she spreads her legs just enough so I can see her glistening arousal.

Taking one of her feet in my hands, I begin massaging it.

Her head falls back. "That feels so good."

My hands make their way up her leg as I continue rubbing her muscles. Then, I repeat the action on her other leg. Natalie's body relaxes under my touch. "Ready for the rope?"

"Mhm."

Starting with the purple rope, I anchor it around her toe and proceed to wrap it around her foot. At the front of each loop, I create a lark's head knot to add to the beauty of the pattern. Continuing this action, I make an intricate design of wraps and hitches up the length of her leg. Afterward, I tie the rope off on the outside of her thigh and repeat the same pattern on her other leg. Before proceeding any further, I check in with her. "Color?"

"Green," she breathes.

"I need you to stand." I take her by the hand and help her up.

Taking hold of the black rope, I start tying a chest harness. My ties tonight aren't about restraint. I planned this design to help Natalie unwind and relax into the sensation of the jute material gliding against her skin. Beginning below her breasts, I skillfully wrap the rope around her torso and loop it around the back, gently trailing it along her flesh.

Next, I create an intricate crisscross pattern between her breasts before draping it over her shoulders to form a bikini-style harness. Stepping back, I take a moment to assess my handiwork. Despite my best efforts, the ties are not flawless, but that doesn't inhibit me from becoming aroused. Her breasts are held tight, and her nipples beg to be sucked. I adjust the erection, tenting my boxers.

"Come with me." I lead her to the front of the swing.

Placing my hands on her waist, I lift Natalie and help her settle into the reclined position of the swing. Then, I put her feet into the restraints keeping her legs spread and allowing me a view of her beautiful pussy. I drag my finger over her outer lips, teasing her. She whimpers when I take my finger away. Returning to the bed, I grab the last two bundles of pink rope. Setting it next to her, I take her arm, lift it above her head, and run a length of rope up her arm before making a loop and bringing it back to her wrist, tying off the strap on the swing. Then, I repeat the process on her other arm. With her fully tied, I check in once more. "Color?"

"Very green, Sir."

Now the fun begins.

I circle the swing, coming back to Natalie's spread legs. It's time for a taste. I feather kisses up her leg and pause to blow gently on her. She tries to squirm, but with her arms and legs restrained, she has nowhere to go. "Hold still, baby girl," I remind.

Steadying the swing, I lick her long and slow before plunging my tongue inside her fucking her slowly while I rub gentle circles around her clit. She moans in response to my ministrations. With a final taste, I stand up, not wanting her to come yet.

Leaving her on the swing, I walk back into the closet. This time, I come out with the magic wand. I turn it on while I'm still behind her, allowing her to hear it before she sees it. "Do you want me to let you come, baby girl?" I whisper in her ear as I round the swing.

"Yes. Please, Sir."

I press the wand against her swollen clit. It only takes seconds before she's screaming in pleasure. Wave after wave pulses through her body, yet I don't move the wand.

"I can't."

"You can." I turn the wand up to its highest setting.

Natalie's orgasm explodes, and she writhes in pleasure. When I know she's had enough, I remove the wand and set it on the dresser. Then, I make quick work of stripping off my boxers. I'm harder than I think I've ever been as I approach her. Natalie lifts her head, watching me fist my erection. My hand moves up and down as pre-cum drips from the tip.

Without wasting another second, I slide into her inch by slow inch, relishing her tight, wet warmth as it wraps around me. Once I'm fully sheathed, I stop. "I missed you so much." I caress her face. "Promise me that's the last time we'll be separated."

"I promise, Sir."

With her promise given, I begin to move. I alternate between sliding in and out and rolling my hips. Natalie comes two more times before I can no longer hold back.

"Come with me, baby girl." I rub her clit faster and harder, keeping pace with the increased speed of my thrusts. "Now."

Her body rhythmically squeezes my cock as I come inside her. The pleasure of our perfectly timed orgasms is intense. "You're amazing," I say before I pull out slowly and go into the bathroom to get a warm washcloth to clean her off.

The act of unbinding is done with care. My movements are slow and steady as my hands gently caress her skin. I leave the ropes in the swing and lift Natalie, cradling her in my arms. She rests her head on my chest as I carry her to the bed. With one hand, I pull back the blankets and lay her down. I take her twice more before she's worn out.

Only then, knowing that the most important person in my life is safe in my arms, do I allow myself to drift to sleep.

Natalie

"They're ten minutes away," I call to Alex, who's across the hall in his office, as I finish putting the finishing touches on our guest room for Tony and Leo. The sound of a car beeping sends my heart rate into overdrive—they're here! I put the last pillow on the bed and hurry to greet our guests at the front door. But Alex beats me to it and is already outside when I arrive.

"Pixie," Tony says, scooping me in a hug and lifting me from my feet.

"I can't believe you guys are here," I squeal.

"You can put my sub down any time now," Alex jokes.

"She's cute." Tony sets me down as Leo sidles up next to him, suitcases in hand. "But I brought my own sub with me."

"Leo." I squeeze him in a hug. "I can't believe you're here."

"I can't believe we're here either." He kisses my cheek and then looks around cautiously. "You really live in the middle of nowhere."

"Wait until nighttime. It gets so dark you can see all the stars," I say dreamily.

"And risk getting eaten by a wild animal." Leo shakes his head. "I'll take a pass."

Leo's a city boy through and through.

"Let's go inside. Natalie will show you to your room so you can get settled in."

I grab Alex's hand, squeezing tightly as we take our guests into our house.

"It's this way." I motion to Leo to follow me to their bedroom while Tony and Alex make their way into the kitchen.

"This place is gorgeous," Leo gushes. "Your pictures don't do it justice, girl."

"Alex has a great eye for design. I'll miss this place when we go back to the city."

We arrive at the door to the guestroom, and I step aside, letting Leo go in first.

"Look at that view," Leo drops the suitcases and heads straight for the windows that overlook the lake.

The azure blue sky is cloudless, and the temperature is mild. A gentle breeze has been blowing from the water, prompting me to leave my windows open to fully enjoy its benefits. It's the perfect summer afternoon.

I make my way to Leo's side.

"I've missed you. But I can see why you've been holed up here. Even I might be able to get used to this."

The idyllic scene mesmerizes us as we watch several boats bobbing on the water, the small waves rippling onto the rocky shore.

"You guys are welcome here anytime." I rest my head on Leo's chest, enjoying the familiarity of his company.

"Natalie. Leopold. We need you both out here," Alex calls.

"Coming."

"That sounds suspicious," Leo grins.

"It sure does. I wonder what's going on?"

"Let's go find out." Leo grabs my hand.

When we enter the living room, I'm surprised to see it's been transformed. The furniture is pushed to the side, and a black fleece blanket is spread out on the floor. Next to the blanket are candles, arranged by color. Alex and Anthony stand beside the candles, arms crossed over their chests—their dominance fills the empty space in the room. The hungry look in Alex's eyes takes my breath away.

"Go change." He hands me a pair of tiny shorts and a bra-like top.

"Yes, Sir."

With the clothes in hand, I hurry to our bedroom. I hear footsteps and look over my shoulder. Leo's right behind me, also carrying a pair of shorts.

"Looks like we're about to have some fun," Leo says before disappearing inside the guest room.

I quickly change and somehow make it back to the living room before Leo. When he enters, he takes his place on his knees beside me.

Alex and I have never done a scene with another couple. Not knowing what he has planned fills me with nervous anticipation.

"Anthony has graciously offered to give us an early wedding present." Alex strokes my hair. "Are you willing to allow him to create a wax design on you?"

I want to squeal in delight but force myself to remain composed. Since the first night I visited Fire and Ice, I've been enthralled with Tony's art. Alex and I have played with wax, but Tony is a master of design. I'm honored he'll be creating a design on me.

"Yes, Sir. I'd love that."

"You and Leo will lie next to one another, and you will remain clothed." Alex raises an eyebrow.

Alex is territorial and possessive. From day one, he made it perfectly clear that he would never allow another man to touch or see me naked. Something I was thankful for.

"Leo, I want you on your stomach," Anthony instructs. "Pixie, lie on your back with your arm and leg against Leo's."

While we get into position, Anthony lights the candles. "Alex tells me you two have played with wax."

"Yes."

"My wax is similar in burn temperature to what you've used," Tony explains. "However, if you're uncomfortable in any way, you are to use your safewords. What are they?"

"Yellow and red."

"First, we're going to prepare your skin. It'll help with removing the wax later."

Alex kneels next to me, a bottle in his hand. He pours some oil into his palm before passing the bottle to Anthony, kneeling beside Leo. While Alex rubs the oil over my abdomen, he lowers his head, whispering what he plans to do with me later. His words, combined with his sensual touch, set my body on fire.

"Ready?" Anthony asks.

Alex brushes his knuckles across my cheek. "I'm ready."

"Let's have some fun." Anthony lifts the first candle, and chills run up and down my body, anticipating what's to come. "Your Dominant is going to be my assistant. I'm going to teach him how to be an artist."

His statement is followed by Alex's laughter. My Dominant might have an eye for design, but an artist, he is not. Anthony hands the dark green candle to Alex and instructs him where to drip the wax. Alex alternates between Leo and me, drizzling streams of wax across my abdomen. It feels pleasantly warm on my skin. I lift my head, trying to get a peek at the design they're creating.

"Head down," Alex instructs. "You'll see it when it's time."

"May I have a hint?"

"No." Both men say in unison. I blow out a frustrated breath.

"Patience, little pixie. Relax and enjoy this."

Following my instructions, I shut my eyes and surrender myself to the various sensations. The initial warmth of the wax as it touches my skin, followed by its swift cooling and solidifying. Lost in this dreamlike state, I don't know how much time has passed until Anthony's voice jolts me back to reality. "It's done."

My eyelids are heavy. I have to blink a few times before they cooperate and remain open. Turning my head, I see Leo struggling the same way. "Alex, can you grab the black light from my bag?"

Alex rummages through the duffle while Tony pulls the black-out curtains closed. The room is bathed in darkness. I lift my head slightly, hoping to get a glimpse of the design. I gasp when I see the wax glowing.

"Shh," Anthony admonishes me.

I feel a twinge of guilt for disobeying and trying to peek—again. Tonight, Anthony's gifting Alex and me something extraordinary, and I don't want my impatience to spoil the grand gesture. As a submissive, I know that cultivating patience is essential, and I need to work on it.

As Leo and I lie covered in the luminous wax, Alex reaches for his camera and starts snapping pictures from different perspectives, the sound of the shutter clicking filling the air.

"I think I got enough," Alex says as he scrolls through the pictures.

"It's time to lift the wax. Hopefully, we can get it off in one piece."

Our Dominants return to our sides.

"You look gorgeous covered in so many colors, baby girl." Lust swirls in Alex's blue eyes.

The men work together to remove the design. The oil underneath helps their efforts, and they remove the wax with minimal cracking. Then, they set it carefully on our dining table. Alex offers his hand and helps me to a seated position. My body is a little stiff from lying still so long. He notices right away and gently rubs my arms and legs before helping me to stand.

"Ready to see it?"

"I'm so ready." The double meaning behind my words isn't lost on Alex.

He places his hand on the small of my back and leads me to the table. What I see there is beyond anything I imagined. Together, the men created a colorful meadow of flowers. The design flows until it turns into the shimmering turquoise water of the lake. It's all set to the backdrop of a purple and pink sky depicting the sunset over the lake.

"Is that glitter?" I ask and run my finger gently over the wax that makes up the water.

"It is. Do you like it?" Tony asks.

"Like it? It's the most beautiful thing I've ever seen." I kiss his cheek. "Thank you so much. I'll treasure this always."

"I have a custom frame for it in the car. Leo and I will arrange it in the frame for you before we leave."

Alex clasps Tony's shoulder. "Thank you. This means a lot to both Natalie and me."

"It's my pleasure," he says before turning to Leo and me. "You two go get cleaned up so we can eat."

Leo and I make our way back to the bedrooms. He follows me into my room so I can wash the oil from his back before he goes to his room to get dressed.

I'm in the bathroom with the water running when I hear the door open again.

"Did you forget something?" I call over my shoulder, but there's no answer.

Maybe I'm hearing things? I return to washing the oil from my skin when strong arms wrap around my naked body, hands teasing my pebbled nipples.

"I didn't forget a thing," Alex says between kisses. "Bend over."

I lean over, resting my arms on the marble counter. Looking over my shoulder, I watch as Alex lowers his zipper.

"I've wanted to do this since I rubbed that oil on you." He lets his pants and boxer briefs fall to the floor. "I'm going to fuck you hard and fast. Hold on and do not make a sound."

In one swift motion, he's inside me. I swallow a moan and grip the counter, bracing myself against his punishing pace. My head drops, and I close my eyes.

"Pick your head up," Alex demands. "I want you watching as I come inside you."

I lift my head and meet his piercing gaze in the mirror. He's focused on his task as he continues his pounding rhythm. The first waves of my orgasm catch me off guard, and I struggle to keep my eyes focused. My whole body shakes from the intensity of the pleasure rocketing through me. Alex's eyes remain locked on mine as he ruts wildly before coming with a deep groan. His expression is one of complete ecstasy. When the last waves of his orgasm subside, he folds his body over mine, placing kisses along my back.

"Don't move," he instructs.

He gently washes between my legs and then tosses the washcloth into the sink. When he finishes, I turn to face him. Alex pins me to the counter, caging me in with his arms.

"You're amazing, baby girl," he says before leaning down and kissing me slowly and seductively. A direct contrast to the way he just fucked me. Despite having just had an orgasm, my body is ready for more. But he ends the kiss. "Go get dressed. We have company waiting."

"Something tells me our company may be preoccupied as well."

"Possibly. But I did promise them dinner."

After I get dressed, Alex and I go back to the living room. I grab a bag and start cleaning up the bits of leftover wax. Anthony and Leo join us a few minutes later.

"Here, let me help." Leo takes over the task, and I pick up the blanket from the floor.

"Shall I put this in the washer, Tony?"

"That would be great."

While I go to the laundry room, the three men work together, putting the furniture back into its rightful places.

Instead of cooking, Tony and Alex decide to order take-out. The four of us share our meal outside on the patio, watching the last few minutes of the sunset transition to a star-filled sky. Fireflies dance in the grassy area while bullfrogs croak by the water's edge.

I already know this weekend will be one I'll never forget.

Alex

The following day, I wake up early to pick up my father and Luna from the local airport. Brandon and Svetlana arrived in Branson last night and are en route to our location. Stanley and Charlotte are expected to arrive later in the afternoon. I hope they will get along with our eclectic mix of family and friends.

Careful not to disturb Natalie, I slip out of bed and throw on a pair of shorts. Natalie rarely sleeps in, so I want to give her the luxury of doing so today. When I walk into the kitchen, I find Anthony and Leo well into their preparations for tonight's meal.

"Good morning," Tony says while stirring a pot on the stove.

"Can I make you a cup of coffee?" Leo asks.

"Thanks. That'd be great."

"Have a seat, and I'll get your breakfast."

"I wasn't expecting this, but okay."

I sit at the table, and Leo brings me a steaming mug. A second later, he places the sugar and creamer in front of me. Then he fills my plate with French toast and bacon. After serving me, Leo returns to Tony's side, and I scroll through the morning's news stories on my phone while eating.

I'm taking my last bite when Viktor strolls into the kitchen. "Ready to go, boss?"

"I am." I stand and move to clean up my plate.

"I've got it." Leo rushes over, taking it from me.

"Thank you, Leo." Anthony has his subimmisive impeccably trained. "When Natalie gets up, will you tell her I've left for the airport?"

"Will do," Anthony replies. "Drive safe."

Viktor has the car already started. I get in, and we drive down the bumpy gravel driveway. "Remind me to get some estimates to get this paved."

"Gladly." Viktor laughs.

We discuss the rest of the day's events on our drive. With some of the strong personalities that'll be in attendance, there's a good chance things might blow up in our faces before the night's over.

"Everything will be fine," Viktor reassures me.

"That's what I'm hoping."

My phone chimes, alerting me to a message. "Natalie must be awake." I pull the phone out of my pocket. When I see the screen, I freeze.

"What's wrong? Is Natalie okay?"

"There was another attempt on Maxim's files."

Dread fills my entire being while I process what this might mean. It has to be Ben and Michelle. That's what I tell myself because I can't accept the alternative.

"Alex," Viktor says, glancing my way. "I think it's time to call Maxim."

I want to argue with him and deny that it's anything more than the actions of vindictive ex-employees. But I know there's no possible way for Ben and Michelle to access my system. "Call the security team," I relent. "This stays between us for now. I don't want to upset Natalie."

"Yes, boss."

There's a palpable silence between us. Viktor's just as lost in thought as I am, contemplating all the potential outcomes of the situation. Unfortunately, my mind can't imagine any positive scenarios, and I'm left with a growing sense of unease.

Viktor pulls the car up to the sidewalk in front of the airport's only terminal. "I'll make the call while you're inside." His tone is calm. The only sign of nerves is his white-knuckle grip on the steering wheel.

"Their plane is scheduled to land any minute. I shouldn't be long."

The small airport is bustling with last-minute travelers for the summer holiday.

"Alex," a familiar voice call my name.

Turning around, I spot Dad and Luna hurrying toward me.

"Did I have the wrong flight time?" I hug my father.

"We had a tailwind and landed early."

"It's so good to see you." I hug Luna before grabbing her bag. "Come on, Viktor's outside with the car."

"Where's Natalie? I thought she'd be with you," Luna asks.

"I didn't want to wake her." We get outside, and I search the parking lot for Viktor. It takes a few minutes, but finally, I spot him leaning against the car, talking on his cell phone.

When he sees us coming, he ends the call and rushes over to take the bag from my father. "Mr. Montgomery. Luna. It's a pleasure to see you both."

"Good to see you again." Dad shakes Viktor's free hand.

We get their luggage situated in the trunk and pile into the car. I send a text to Natalie, hoping she's awake.

Me: The plane landed early. We're on our way home. There's French toast waiting for you in the kitchen.

She texts back immediately.

Natalie: Thank you for letting me sleep in, Sir. French toast, yum! Be careful, and I'll see you soon.

Natalie

I roll over and reach out to Alex, but he's not there. When I open my eyes, I find a note on his pillow.

baby girl,
I didn't want to wake you. I've gone to pick up Dad and Luna. See you soon.
Sir

Swinging my legs over the bed, a surge of excitement mixed with fear courses through my body. It's the first time my parents are meeting our friends and Alex's family. I'm worried my parents won't find anything in common with anyone. There's a very real chance today might end in disaster. I quickly push that thought aside and try to focus on the positives—everyone I love will be here today.

As I push open the bedroom door, a mouthwatering aroma wafts through the air and fills my nostrils, pulling me toward the kitchen. Walking down the hallway, I step lightly, my bare feet soundless on the hardwood floor. I stand quietly in the kitchen archway and watch Leo wash the dishes. Anthony stands closely behind, nuzzling his neck.

Witnessing such an intimate moment feels almost intrusive, but I can't help being drawn in. The obstacles they've faced and conquered make their love all the more potent and inspiring.

"Good morning," I chirp. Feeling like I need to make my presence known. "It smells so good in here."

"Good morning, pixie. Hungry?"

"Very," I grin. "Alex mentioned something about French toast."

"Have a seat," Leo says. "I'll make your plate."

"I can get it. You guys look pretty busy." I motion at the food in various steps of preparation all over the kitchen.

"Sit." Anthony points to the chair. "Today, Leo waits on you."

"Yes, sir," I chuckle and sit at the table.

Leo serves me a plate of French toast dripping with fresh maple syrup, crispy bacon strips, and a cup of coffee. He kisses the top of my head before returning to his task of washing dishes. I start eating, thoroughly enjoying my breakfast. Why does food always taste better when someone else cooks?

While I eat, I can't help but be captivated by the perfectly choreographed routine of Anthony and his staff. Their movements are precisely timed, ensuring their work doesn't stop.

"Do you have a lot more to cook?" I ask in between bites.

"We're just about done with all the prep work. Later, we'll put the finishing touches on the dishes."

"You're amazing."

"You're too kind, baby girl." Alex's arms wrap around me, startling me. I drop my fork on the floor. "I didn't mean to scare you." Leo quickly picks it up and replaces it with a clean one.

"Where's Sam and Luna?"

"Viktor's showing them to their room. They'll be along in a few minutes. You should go get dressed."

I take my final bite. "Give me a few minutes, and I'll be ready."

I hurry to our bedroom and look through the closet, pulling out several different outfits before settling on a pair of jean shorts and a black tank top. I pull my hair into a half ponytail and put on mascara and lip gloss.

"You going to be in there all day?" A familiar female voice calls from the other side of the door.

Opening the door, I find Lana with a massive smile on her face. I squeal and wrap my arms around my best friend.

"I can't believe you're here!"

"I wouldn't miss this for anything in the world." She squeezes me back. "Your parents were just pulling up when we walked into the house."

"Lana, I'm so nervous. What if they hate everyone?"

"Not even Charlotte could hate Leo."

We both laugh.

"I hope you're right." I grab her hand. "Come on, let's go say hi."

Everyone's seated at our outdoor table, enjoying the delicious food the guys prepared for us. Lana was right. I had nothing to worry about. Tony and Leo charmed my parents in a matter of minutes. And what's not to love about Sam and Luna?

"Anthony, dear," Mom says. "Your food is exquisite."

"Thank you, ma'am."

"Our wedding guests will be getting a real treat."

Tony smiles proudly.

Sam stands. "I'd like to propose a toast to the future Mr. and Mrs. Montgomery."

A round of cheers and the clinking of glasses sound around us. I sip my champagne and grab Alex's hand under the table. I'm overwhelmed at the realization of how incredibly lucky I am—every one of my dreams is coming true.

Alex

THE AFTERNOON COULDN'T HAVE GONE ANY SMOOTHER. DESPITE THE various personalities around the table today, everyone's getting along. Tony's culinary creations impressed all. Our guests are currently indulging in a selection of delectable desserts. Meanwhile, nature puts on a show in the sky with a beautiful sunset preceding tonight's fireworks. Viktor catches my eye from the back door and signals for me to come inside. He must have heard from Maxim.

"I got a text from Dimitri."

"And?"

"At first glance, it looked like another internal issue. But that didn't make any sense, especially with the updated security. Alex, it didn't come from inside the office."

Shit. My stomach turns.

"Dimitri went back to compare the attacks. The IP address appears to match your internal system—an innocent mistake like we first thought. It was when he attempted to trace it back to a specific computer that he found the anomaly. This is a professional job. Someone outside the company made it look like an accident, and we missed it."

"Fuck." I run my hand through my hair. "Max is going to kill me for not calling him sooner."

"Alex." In a rare display of emotion, Viktor puts his hand on my shoulder. "It's a highly constructed attack. They got lucky with their timing because of the issues with the employees. Even Dimitri missed it."

I pace back and forth, wondering what will happen next. It only takes a minute for my phone to ring. I know who it is even before I look.

"Maxim."

"I just got all the information. I do not want to discuss it over the phone. My jet is enroute to JFK. I want everyone here immediately."

"Max. I'm sorry."

"There is no need to apologize. But until we know who is behind this, everyone needs to be at the compound."

"Everyone's at my house for the holiday."

"I will speak to Svetlana. She and Brandon will need to change their plans and stay at yours or Viktor's home tonight," Maxim instructs. "There is no need to ruin your gathering tonight. You will need to leave first thing in the morning, though."

"We'll see you soon."

"*Do Svidaniya*." Maxim ends the call.

I slip the phone back into my pocket and look outside at my family and friends. Everyone's enjoying a relaxing evening. Little do they know the potential danger in store for us.

"Natalie is so happy right now. I don't want to spoil any of this for her," I say softly.

"You heard Maxim. Go back out and enjoy the evening."

"I can't. I need to arrange for Charlotte and Stanley to have an in-home a—"

"I'll make the arrangements. All you need to do tonight is enjoy your family. Let me worry about everything else."

"Thank you." I school my features and walk back outside.

As soon as I take my seat, the fireworks light up the sky. Natalie's emerald eyes are filled with questions as she looks at me. I grasp her hand and pull her onto my lap, hoping my pounding heart doesn't betray my nerves.

Lana pulls out her phone and reads a message. Her expression gives nothing away. She's been down this road before and knows how to handle it. Lana looks my way and gives me a nod of understanding before turning her attention back to the fireworks.

The thought of breaking Natalie's heart by delaying our wedding planning and forcing her to travel to Russia weighs heavily on me. Unlike Lana, Natalie's not used to the dangers Maxim faces, and in turn, I face. This won't be an easy conversation to have, but I'm left with no other choice.

After the fireworks show, Natalie's parents leave, bidding us farewell before driving out of sight. We return to the gathering, where our other guests are gathered around the fire, chatting quietly. I sit, hoping to put off what needs to be done for a while longer, but Natalie stands before me with her arms folded. She's clearly upset.

"Are you going to tell me what's going on now?"

"No," I say calmly. "Sit down. We have guests."

She ignores my quiet warning. "I saw the look between you and Lana earlier. What's going on?"

Anthony stretches and forces a yawn. "I think it's time we turn in."

"You don't have to." My anger builds. "Don't let my wayward sub chase you away." I narrow my gaze at her, warning her to stop.

"It's really okay," he says and motions to Leo, who's kneeling at his feet. "It's time for us to turn in anyway."

Lana pulls Natalie aside, whispering in her ear. I'm sure she's letting her know she stepped out of bounds. Natalie doesn't take her eyes off me as she shrugs.

"Lana, we should go too," Brandon adds.

"No, you two need to stay."

"Oh?" Brandon looks at me, searching for a hint, but I give him none.

"Dad, I need you to stay too."

He gets the hint by what I haven't said. "Luna, go to bed. I'll be in shortly."

Although Luna looks concerned, she doesn't question her Dominant. She says goodnight and makes a quick exit. I wish my submissive was as obedient.

"Let's move this inside," I say, standing. "I'll get Viktor and meet you in the living room." I need the distance to compose myself. When I get into the office, Viktor's s.

"Have you made any progress?"

"I hired the same aide the Clarkes had when you went to Seattle. She'll arrive tomorrow afternoon. I've also arranged for a discreet security team."

"Are you ready to share the good news?" I ask sarcastically.

"Can't wait."

Viktor follows me back to the living room, where everyone's gathered. Natalie's standing by the window, looking out into the darkness. I sit opposite Brandon and Lana on the sofa to keep an eye on Natalie while I talk.

"There was another attempt at accessing the encrypted files earlier today." I take a deep breath. "I was wrong from the beginning. The files weren't being accessed from within the company."

"It wasn't the employees you fired?" Dad asks.

"No. The timing of everything was purely coincidental."

"Is Max aware?" Dad looks concerned.

"Yes. He called earlier. His jet is enroute to JFK. We're leaving in the morning for an extended stay in Russia."

"We're what?" Natalie spins around. "We can't do that. My parents. Our bridal shower." She's nearing hysterics.

I hurry over and grab her shoulders. "We don't have a choice."

She pulls from my hold. "I'm not going to Russia."

I'm usually very patient, but my blood's boiling right now. I don't want to have this argument in front of everyone. "Come with me." Taking her by the arm, I lead her outside.

Once we're out of the house, she pulls out of my hold. "I can't just leave. I have to oversee the store and my dad's therapy—"

"Do you think I want to drop everything and go?"

She turns away, ignoring me. I knew she wouldn't take the news well, but by arguing with me in front of our company and disrespecting my authority, she's pushed too far. As her Dominant, it's my responsibility to maintain the balance between discipline and caring for her emotional state.

"baby girl." I wrap my arms around her waist, but instead of relaxing into my touch, she stiffens in my arms. "I know this is a shock and not what either of us wants. Whoever's behind this could pose a great danger to us. We need to be at Maxim's until we have more information."

"What about my parents?"

"I don't believe they're in danger." I turn her to face me. "But Viktor arranged for a security team, just in case. They'll remain out of sight so we don't alarm your parents. Viktor also rehired the same aide. She'll be there tomorrow."

"I don't like this."

"Neither do I." I tuck a stray curl behind her ear. "But we have to ."

"Yes, Sir."

I'm thankful she's accepted the inevitable, but I can't let her attitude slide. "We need to address your earlier behavior. Not only did you disrespect me. You were also rude to our guests." Natalie lowers her head. "I'll administer your punishment when we're alone."

Taking her by the hand, I lead her back into our now-empty living room. Everyone must've gone next door with Viktor. Since we're alone now, I continue walking to our bedroom. "Take your clothes off and kneel."

While she strips, I go to the closet to retrieve the paddle. Our current guests won't be concerned if they hear the punishment that's about to happen. I prefer privacy, which is why I have soundproofed the bedrooms.

Returning to the main bedroom, I stop and take in the sight. Natalie's naked on her knees with her head bowed and her palms resting on her slightly spread legs. The view makes me rock hard, but I push those thoughts aside. Although I dislike administering punishments, it's an integral part of our Dom/sub dynamic.

"Do you know why I'm disciplining you?"

"Because I disrespected you and our guests, Sir."

"Stand and bend over the bed," I instruct. "You will receive ten strikes."

Natalie rises from the floor, averting her eyes. She leans over the bed, resting her cheek on her arms.

"Count aloud." I don't give any warning before landing the first strike.

She gasps. "One."

I don't care to draw this out any longer than necessary. Each strike comes in quick succession, but Natalie keeps the count. By the end, her ass is bright red. She'll be uncomfortable on the flight in the morning. However, I'm confident she's learned a lesson and will grow in her submission from this experience. "Stay here."

"Yes, Sir." Her words come out quietly between sobs.

Once I put the paddle back in its place, I pick up the soothing balm. Even though this was a punishment, I'm responsible for properly caring for my sub. I squeeze some of the lotion onto my hand and apply it gently to her skin. Natalie flinches. "I know it stings, but it will help." When I finish, I toss the tube onto the dresser and lift Natalie into my arms. She buries her head into my chest as her tears continue to fall.

"I'm sorry for my behavior. I'm so scared, Alex."

"I know, baby girl," I murmur and wipe her tears. "I won't let anything happen to you, I promise."

Natalie

"We're on the way to the airport now." It's no surprise my mom isn't taking the news of our sudden departure well. "I know this isn't ideal."

"Why such a hurry? Couldn't you at least wait until after your bridal shower to take a trip?"

"Maxim surprised us at the last minute." I don't want her to think this is more than a spur-of-the-moment vacation.

"But why do you have to go right now?" Mom persists.

I repeat the story Alex and I came up with last night. "Maxim and Irina aren't able to make it to the shower. You know they're like family to Alex. They want to celebrate our upcoming wedding with us. This is their way of doing so."

I look to Alex for support. He nods in approval.

"That Maxim is always trying to outshine everyone," Mom complains.

Her comment makes me laugh. "Please try to understand. We'll be home in a few days. There'll be plenty of time for anything that comes up last minute."

"Okay, dear."

I spend the remainder of the drive explaining that Dad's aide will arrive this afternoon. I remind her that Sam and Luna are leaving tomorrow, but Tony and Leo will be staying for the rest of the week. "We just pulled into the airport. I have to go."

"Have a safe trip," she says reluctantly.

"We will. Give Daddy a hug and kiss for me."

When I get out of the car, my stomach turns, and a wave of dizziness washes over me. I grab Alex's arm for support.

"Are you okay?"

"I'm really nervous," I admit.

"Relax, baby girl. Everything will be okay," he says, trying to soothe me.

I can only hope Alex is right because, at the moment, nothing feels okay.

The men grab our bags and walk into the airport ahead of Lana and me.

"What's wrong?" Lana asks.

"This is all very sudden."

"It's part of the territory." She waves her hand as if having to drop everything and go to Russia is entirely normal. "Dad will find out where the threat is coming from and stop it. Then, we can all return to life as usual."

"Doesn't this bother you at all?"

"I grew up in this life, remember? Consider it a vacation before the wedding planning really starts." She skips ahead to catch up with Brandon.

Lana may have grown up amidst danger, but I didn't. When I learned about Alex's involvement with Maxim, I didn't stop to think about the possible repercussions. Now that I'm getting a first-hand taste, I don't like it. I know what he and Maxim do is important, but does Alex have to be involved? That's ridiculous. I can't ask Alex to walk away.

After an uneventful two-hour flight, we land at JFK, where Max's security team meets us. We're whisked away to a private hangar where Maxim's jet waits. One of the men reaches out to take my bag, and his jacket shifts, revealing the gun strapped to his waist. Another wave of dizziness washes over me, and I stumble.

Alex grabs me by the waist, steadying me. "I'm texting Maxim. I want a doctor waiting to examine you when we land."

"I'm fine. I didn't eat before we left, and all this"–I motion to Viktor and the rest of the security team, who are hurrying to get everything ready for what I'm sure will be an imminent take-off—"is a lot."

"I want you to get checked out anyway." I resist rolling my eyes at my overprotective Dominant.

Hand in hand, Alex and I ascend the steps into the luxurious airplane, and he guides me to a plush leather sofa. Across from us, Brandon and Lana are seated. Lana offers me a reassuring smile. Viktor and another gentleman are engrossed in something displayed on the laptop screen before them.

"Who's he?" I whisper to Alex.

"Dimitri. He's the head of the tech security team." I've heard his name mentioned several times over the past twenty-four hours, but I wasn't expecting him to be on the flight with us.

The pilot announces we're ready for take-off as the jet engines roar to life, and we start our taxi down the runway. The plane's wheels leave the ground in one of the smoothest takeoffs I've ever felt. Before I know it, we're high above the clouds, flying over the ocean on our way to Russia.

A pretty blonde flight attendant, who only speaks Russian, emerges from the back of the plane. I don't miss how she bats her eyes at Alex, trying to get his attention. His body tenses before he entwines his fingers with mine.

After a short conversation with Lana, she momentarily disappears. When she returns, she's pushing a cart full of food. We're each served appetizers of fresh figs and a selection of cheeses, followed by the main course of Chicken Kyiv. My stomach growls from skipping breakfast, and I quickly finish everything on my plate.

After the dishes have been cleared, Alex stands and takes my hand. "Come with me."

"Where are we going?"

"To the bedroom. You barely slept last night."

"I'm fine." I wave him off.

"It's a long flight. I want you to get some rest."

I've been on this plane before but have never been in the bedroom. I'm surprised at how big it is. There's even a king-size bed.

"The bathroom's over there." Alex points to another door.

"This is incredible."

"Maxim's a very wealthy man who prefers to travel in comfort."

"I guess so." I move closer to Alex and reach for the button on his pants, but he grabs my hands.

"Sleep." He points to the bed.

"Can't blame a girl for trying."

Alex pulls the blankets back, and I crawl into bed, appreciating the feel of the bamboo sheets caressing my skin. He climbs in and lays next to me, pulling me close. It doesn't take more than a few minutes for my eyes to close and my body to give way to sleep.

Natalie

I STARTLE AWAKE, MY HEART BEATING FURIOUSLY FROM THE TERRIBLE nightmare I was having. I'm momentarily disoriented and push up on my elbows to take in my surroundings—I'm on Maxim's plane. We're in the bedroom, which is mostly dark except for the sliver of light coming from the bathroom door that's cracked open. Alex lies next to me, his breathing soft and even. Gently, I run my fingers along the dark stubble on his jaw.

"Did you sleep well, baby girl?"

"I did," I answer before crawling over him, straddling his body, and rocking my hips gently.

Grabbing the hem of my sundress, I pull it over my head and toss it to the side. Alex groans in response. Reaching between us, I open his pants, freeing his erection. This time, instead of stopping me, he lifts his hips, allowing me to slide his pants down his muscular legs.

He reaches behind me to unclasp my bra. The straps slide down my arms, exposing my breasts to him. He removes the lace fabric from my arms and drops it off the side of the bed. Alex stares at me, his eyes full of lust, before leaning in and taking a nipple in his mouth. My head falls back, and I moan in pleasure. He releases it with a pop and lavishes the same attention on my other breast.

"You're so beautiful," Alex's voice is deep and seductive. "Can you be quiet?"

"Yes, Sir." He slips his fingers into the thin fabric of my panties and pulls, tearing them. "They were one of my favorite pairs." I pretend to pout.

"I'll buy you more."

Placing his hands on my hips, he lifts me, and I position myself over him. Then, I lower my body slowly, allowing it time to stretch and take every inch of his long, hard length. His face tightens in concentration. Alex is used to being in control, but right now, he's allowing me to set the pace. I lean close, my breasts pushing against his chest as I roll my hips, teasing him. He grabs my ass in frustration.

"Is there something wrong, Sir?" I ask coyly.

He lifts his hips, encouraging me to move. Pushing on his chest, I lean back onto my knees before quickly sinking onto his cock. He palms my breasts as I continue the rhythmic motion. Without warning, he flips us, and I'm underneath him.

Alex sets a pounding rhythm, an unspoken message of need and want being exchanged between our bodies. Wrapping my legs around him, I pull him deeper. Encouraging him to let go and lose control. To consume every part of me.

"Come for me," he growls.

And I do. He kisses me deeply, muffling my cries of pleasure as his body trembles with the force of his orgasm—our bodies pulsing as one.

"You're amazing. Let's hope we didn't wake the whole plane."

Although I laugh at his comment, I'd be mortified if they heard us.

Alex rolls off me and grabs his cell phone to check the time. Turning on the light, he says, "We should be landing soon. Get dressed so we can get back to our seats."

I collect my clothes from where they landed on the floor. "What do I do with this?" I hold up the torn lace.

"I'll take that." He swipes the shredded panties from my hand and balls them in his fist. "I'll be out in a few minutes."

I take my time washing up before I get dressed and run my fingers through my hair. Opening the door, I peek my head around, "Alex?"

"What is it?"

"Do you think they heard us?"

His laugh fills the room. "No, I don't think they heard us. Let's go."

We make our way back out into the main seating area just as everyone is getting settled. Alex and I retake our seats on the sofa. He reaches across my lap and fastens my safety belt, pulling it tight. This time, when the pilot's voice comes through the speakers, he's announcing our landing.

The plane descends from the sky, landing in the dark at the Pulkovo Airport in St. Petersburg. When the plane's door opens, we're met by a group of large and very intimidating men standing in front of a lineup of black SUVs. Alex walks ahead and shakes hands with one of the men.

"What is all this?" I ask Viktor, who remains at my side.

"Part of Maxim's army." There's no trace of humor in his voice.

"Are we in that much danger?"

"Maxim's ensured our safety. There's no need for concern."

"A small army of your clones has met us, but I shouldn't be concerned?"

"Exactly. Come on, let's go."

Viktor escorts me to one of the waiting vehicles and opens the door. I slide onto the back seat, and Alex gets in after me. Viktor rounds the car and sits on my other side.

One by one, each vehicle in the convoy starts to move. We're officially on our way to the Soloniks' home.

Alex

I settle in for the two-hour drive to Maxim's compound. Natalie pulls out her cell phone.

"Don't turn that on." I grab the device from her hand.

"Why not? I texted my parents after we landed. I wanted to see if they texted back."

Shit. I toss the phone to Viktor, who quickly powers it off and puts it in his pocket. Natalie looks between us, silently questioning our actions.

"What's going on?"

I'm not ready to disclose how serious the problem is.

I reiterate the only version of the story I'm willing to tell her. "There were attempts to access Maxim's files from outside my company. Maxim wants us here as a precaution until he discovers who's behind this cyberattack."

"And as a *precaution*, Maxim sends his army of Viktor-look-alikes to escort us to his home. As what, a welcoming committee?"

Viktor bursts out laughing, and I follow, which only frustrates Natalie more.

"I'm glad you two think this is funny." She crosses her arms, trying to protest, but even she can't keep a straight face.

"You know Maxim. He likes to go over and above."

"Why can't I use my phone?"

"Until we know who's behind this," Viktor explains. "We'll only use burner phones or the secure line at Maxim's—something that can't be traced."

"So, I can call them when we get to the house?"

"Yes."

Viktor throws a disapproving look at me over Natalies's shoulder. I can't bring myself to tell her we're not going to Maxim's house. Instead, I wrap my arm around her and draw her close as we ride silently until we arrive at the heavily fortified gates of the Soloniks' compound.

Natalie lifts her head and looks out the window. "Where are we?"

"Maxim's compound," I mutter without looking at her.

"Maxim's what? I thought we were going to their house?"

"No, baby girl." I grab her hand and rub circles on it with my thumb. "Because of the security threat, we'll be staying here."

"Behind gates and walls?" She pulls her hand from my grasp before returning her gaze out the window, watching as the SUV makes its way up the long drive. "With guards and guns?"

"Yes."

"Alex—"

"No more questions," I say, cutting her off. "Right now, you need to trust me."

I hate silencing her. The lack of communication is already putting distance between us. But until we know more of what's happening, there's nothing else I can tell her.

Our vehicle comes to a stop in front of the expansive mansion. I've been through this before, so I understand at least some of the thoughts going through Natalie's head. My previous stay was a false alarm, and we were able to resume our normal lives within a few days. I only hope this time is the same.

I open the car door, and we step out. The smell of seawater wafts in the air. We round the car and are greeted by Maxim and Irina, who are waiting at the front door. Lana runs up and is wrapped in the arms of her parents. Brandon's right behind her and shakes Max's hand before being pulled in for a hug by Irina.

"I've missed you both so much," Irina gushes over her daughter and Brandon. "Go, get settled in your room."

"Thanks, Mama."

"Food will be served in a half-hour in the dining room," Irina calls after the couple. "Don't be late."

Natalie and I approach next. Irina reaches out to hug Natalie while I shake Max's hand.

"We're so glad you made it." Irina looks at Natalie. "Alex told us you were ill?"

"I didn't sleep well and skipped breakfast," Natalie answers.

"Come, I'll show you to your room."

Natalie looks over her shoulder to me for permission. "Go ahead. I need to speak with Max. I'll see you in the dining room."

Natalie follows Irina into the house.

"Let us go to my office," Maxim says.

He leads the way down the cavernous hallway. Unlike his residential home, which is traditional and full of history, the compound has clean lines and a modern design. Its sole purpose is for the maximum protection of its inhabitants. Timur, one of Maxim's guards, stands outside the large double doors that lead to his office. When we approach, he steps aside.

Maxim sits behind his desk. "Have a seat." He motions to the tufted armchairs opposite him. Resting his elbows on the desk with his fingers steepled, he studies his computer monitor before he speaks. "My men have been working non-stop since Viktor called yesterday." The stress and exhaustion of the past twenty-four hours are evident on his face. It's not like Max to reveal his emotions like this. That fact alone has me concerned. "Whoever is behind this attack is using an intricate network of proxy servers to conceal their identity."

"This is all my fault. I'm sorry. I thought it was just my wayward employees. If I'd had any idea—"

"Alexander," Maxim interrupts. "I am not angry with you. This is a high-level attack made to look like an innocent attempt from within your office. The fact that it happened simultaneously with your actual internal issues is purely coincidental. Whoever it is got lucky."

"I let you down." Insecurity and fear eat away at me.

"You did no such thing." Maxim pushes from his chair and walks around his desk to stand before me. "You are a good steward of this information. Do not doubt your integrity or ability."

"Yes, sir," I reply, even though I disagree with him. I don't have the energy to argue, though.

Maxim flips his computer screen around so we can all see. On the monitor is a map marked with dozens of red flags. I lean forward, trying to make sense of it all, but I'm not a tech genius. I don't know what any of it means. I look to Dimitri for an explanation.

"These," Dimitri explains as he points to the screen. "Are the locations the hacker's IP address has pinged off. My team is still trying to determine the actual origin of the attack, but each time it looks like we're reaching the end of the trail, a new group pops up."

I turn to look at Viktor, who's sitting back in his chair, arms crossed and an impassive expression on his face.

"So, what now?" I ask.

"We stay here and keep working until we find out who is behind this," Maxim says.

"That's my cue." Dimitri stands. "If you don't need me here, I'm going to head back to the tech room."

"Where do you want me, sir?" Viktor asks.

"Your priority is Natalie. If Alexander cannot be with her, you will be. When you are not with her, you are to be in the tech room."

"Understood. Text me when you need me, boss." He clasps my shoulder on his way out of the office.

Once we're alone, I ask, "Do you have any idea who's behind this?"

"Not yet."

My stomach sinks at his revelation.

Maxim points to the monitor as we discuss the next steps in the plan. In addition to Dimitri and the tech team here, Maxim has his contacts around the globe working on this. Until the threat is neutralized, the compound is on code red—complete lockdown.

"We are safe here. Everyone is free to come and go within the compound's walls." Maxim concludes the briefing. "Now, let us move to the dining room and eat."

It's after midnight, and although I'm not hungry, I'm wide awake. Maxim and I make our way through the halls to rejoin the group.

Natalie

"Here's your room. Your bags will be brought up shortly," Irina says as she opens the door to a suite that's the size of an apartment. "I hope you will be comfortable here." Irina's voice is warm and welcoming despite the less-than-desirable circumstances. Walking into the room, the first thing I notice is the wall of windows. In the center is a set of open glass doors.

I'm drawn to the balcony, where I can hear the sound of ocean waves in the distance. Looking out into the night, I see nothing but blackness. Even the moon is hiding behind the thick cloud cover.

Irina steps out next to me. "The compound sits on cliffs overlooking the Baltic Sea. In the daylight, you will have an extraordinary view."

I give her a sad smile before returning inside to look around the room. This place, although magnificent in design, feels uninviting and cold. It's a direct contrast to the welcoming feel of the Soloniks' home.

"I don't mean to sound ungrateful," I say quietly. "I'm still trying to process all of this."

"I understand, honey. I felt the same way the first time I had to go to a safe house," she explains. "This life can be a lot to handle sometimes. But you must trust Maxim and his men to handle the situation and keep us safe."

"Safe from what?" I ask desperately wanting to understand.

"We don't need to know the details," she says with a slight shrug.

But I want to know the details. I need to understand why we had to drop everything and come to Russia.

"Alex was very concerned about you when he texted Max." Irina quickly changes the subject.

"I told him he was overreacting. Once things settled down, and I had some food on the plane, I was fine."

"In any case, the doctor will be here in the morning. Why don't you take a few minutes to settle in." She walks to the door, her high heels muffled by the plush carpet. "I'll return shortly to show you to the dining room." Irina closes the door gently behind her.

Now that I'm alone, I take the time to look around the room, which really is more like an apartment. There's a sitting area complete with a marble-tiled fireplace and a kitchen. When I open the fridge, I find it fully stocked with our preferred foods and drinks. Somehow, even with very short notice, every detail has been taken care of.

As I scan the room, I notice two doors, and I immediately decide one must be a closet and the other a bathroom. After careful consideration, I try the door on the right. Upon opening it, I discover a spacious walk-in closet with glossy white wardrobes and drawers lining the walls on both sides. At the far end of the room, I spot floor-to-ceiling shelves designed to house a vast shoe collection.

After exploring the closet, I head towards the remaining door, which leads me into the en suite bathroom. The room mirrors the luxurious decor of the bedroom, with an entire wall of windows. One side of the bathroom features a massive walk-in shower with two rainheads suspended from the ceiling and strategically positioned body jets. While admiring the shower, I find a touchpad mounted on the wall, indicating that it controls the various functions.

On the other side of the room, a white vanity houses double sinks. A purple orchid sits on the counter between the sinks, adding a touch of nature to the otherwise sterile space.

I feel like I'm intruding on someone's private space, but I open the drawers anyway. What I find makes it look like we're staying in a fancy hotel. There are brand-new toothbrushes, hairbrushes, and all the toiletries one might need for an extended stay. If they're here, I may as well use them to freshen up. While I'm in the bathroom, I hear a knock on the bedroom door.

"Come in."

"It's just me. Are you ready to go to the dining room?"

As Irina and I stroll through the compound, she points down various hallways, showing me where everyone's rooms are. "Don't worry. After a few days, you'll know your way around. Until then, Alex will get you where you need to go. He's stayed here before."

"I'm hoping we're only here for a few days." I don't want to be hidden behind the compound walls any longer than that.

It doesn't go unnoticed that Irina fails to respond to my comment.

I'm filled with a sense of dread that we may be here much longer than I hope. As we approach what I assume is the dining room, I hear familiar voices laughing and chatting like we're here for a vacation. Am I the only one who sees the abnormality of this situation?

When Alex notices me, he stands and pulls out the chair next to him. "I've missed you."

"Me too."

"Make yourself a plate, Natalia."

Despite my reservations, Maxim's Russian use of my name always makes me smile. The food laid out looks and smells fantastic. It's been hours since I ate last, and my stomach growls in response. I fill my plate and start eating. Alex places his hand on my thigh under the table and makes lazy circles with his thumb. I allow myself to relax and join the conversation and laughter, pretending that everything is okay, at least for now. But I fully intend to interrogate Alex when we're alone.

I don't know how long we've been talking or even what time it is when I find myself yawning.

"Are you tired, baby girl?" Alex whispers in my ear.

"I am."

"It's time for Natalie and me to get to bed." Alex stands, offering me his hand. "We'll see everyone in the morning."

Irina was correct. Alex is sure of his steps as we walk hand-in-hand back to our room. I wonder how many times he's been here. I'm just about to ask when he opens the door to our room, but I get distracted. "Our bed's turned down?"

"Maxim's staff is nothing if not efficient," Alex says.

When I peek in the closet, I find that not only has our luggage been delivered, but our clothes have been put away as well.

"I'm going to get changed for bed." I grab a pair of my satin pajamas and spin around, finding myself in Alex's arms.

"I know this isn't ideal, but please try to relax and enjoy yourself."

"Relax?" I pull out of his arms. "We're in a mansion. No, a walled fortress with heavily armed guards because of a threat to our safety. And what I'm gathering, from what's not being said, is that we may be here for an extended stay," I say, my voice rising with frustration. "Yet, you're asking me to relax?"

Alex places his hands on my arms. "I know this is hard, but you'll see it's not so bad. We have everything we could possibly want at our disposal. Tomorrow, I'll take you for a walk around the grounds. It's beautiful. I know you'll love it."

"I don't know about love it."

"Please try to keep an open mind," Alex pleads. "As soon as the threat is dealt with, we'll be on the first flight home."

"Promise?"

"I promise." Alex leans in and kisses me.

Despite the nagging feeling that it won't be that simple, I promise to keep an open mind about our impromptu *vacation*.

Natalie

My mind and body drift in the blissful place between sleep and awake—where the lines separating dreaming and reality are blurred.

Sensation.

Pleasure.

Wetness.

My eyes flutter open, and I find Alex's head between my legs, his tongue circling my clit. I run my hands through his dark hair, and he looks up at me, his blue eyes full of sensuous longing.

"Good morning, baby girl." He smiles, his sexy dimple giving him a mischievous look.

"Good morning." I barely manage to get out before he's back to licking and sucking, working me quickly toward an orgasm.

I fist the sheets and arch my back as I come undone. Alex doesn't stop until he's sucked every last bit of pleasure from me. Then he crawls up my body and kisses me. Tasting my arousal on his tongue only turns me on more.

"I need you," I say, the three words holding so much meaning. I need more than just a connection with his body. My soul needs to connect with his. I need his strength to quell the fear that's plaguing me.

Slowly, he slides inside. I raise my hips, trying to make him go faster, but he stills.

"Patience." He nips at my lower lip.

When I relax, he moves again, still achingly slow.

"Please. I need more."

"You need more, do you?" He pulls out, and I blow out a frustrated breath.

"Always so impatient."

Then, he grabs my hands, putting them up over my head. I hear one click and then another. When I try to move, I find they've been restrained to the headboard. Knowing I'm at his mercy, entirely dependent on him for my pleasure and safety, allows me to relax. I need the freedom to still my thoughts and focus only on Alex and this moment.

After he's given me more orgasms than I can count, we take a shower and dress. We're on our way out of our room when we bump into Lana and Brandon in the hall.

"Good afternoon, sleepyheads," Lana says, linking her arm with mine. "Planning on joining us for lunch?"

"I wouldn't miss it. I'm starving."

"Did you sleep well?"

"Surprisingly, yes."

"Good, I'm glad to hear it. I know how nervous you were yesterday."

"Alexander. Natalia." Maxim's booming voice fills the hall, startling me. "I was just coming to get you."

Maxim's heading in our direction with a well-dressed woman at his side.

"Natalia, this is Dr. Turova. She is one of the physicians who volunteers her time at Jelena's Hope."

"You didn't have to go through all this trouble." I can only imagine what it costs to have a doctor do a house call on a weekend.

"It'll give me peace of mind if you let her look you over," Alex says. "Then we'll eat and go for a walk."

I look back and forth between Alex and the doctor, who smiles warmly at me.

"It'll only take a few minutes," she says.

"Natalia, do you know the way back to your room?" Max asks.

"I'm pretty sure I can get us there."

"I'll see you shortly." Alex kisses my cheek.

"I don't know how to get back to the dining room, though." Irina showed me last night, but this place is enormous. I lost track of where we were and how we got there.

"It's okay. I do," Dr. Turova answers.

Alex and the others continue to the dining room while Dr. Turova and I make our way back to the bedroom.

"I'm really okay, doctor. Yesterday was just very stressful."

"Please call me Karina." She motions to the sofa. "How about we just sit and talk?"

I take a minute to study her. She's wearing a dark blue dress and high heels. Her hair and makeup are done like she's dressed for a night, not a medical visit. I nod in agreement and take a seat on the sofa. Karina chooses to sit on the chair across from me.

"Sorry, I don't know why I'm so nervous. As I said, this trip was very sudden, and I'm feeling a bit out of sorts."

"That's understandable, given the circumstances. Would you be willing to tell me what happened yesterday that caused Alex concern?" Her demeanor is calm and serene, putting me at ease.

"Well, I've had my hands full running my parent's store and helping my mom care for my dad as he recovers. We're also planning my bridal shower and wedding. I've been working on very little sleep. Then there was the news that we had to drop everything and fly to Russia. I was nervous and didn't eat breakfast. Then, I had a dizzy spell. I don't know. Maybe I had a panic attack or something."

"I see. It sounds like you have a lot going on right now."

"I do."

"Since I'm here, do you mind if I give you a quick exam? It will save me a lot of explaining to Maxim if you'd agree."

I don't want Maxim to think I'm ungrateful for his help, and I certainly don't want to get Karina in trouble with him.

"I guess it wouldn't hurt."

While she examines me, she asks the typical doctor questions. Whether I have any health problems or take any medications.

"The only thing I take is a birth control pill." That's when panic sets in. "I run out next week and didn't have time to fill my prescription."

"I can get it and have it delivered." After Karina finishes her exam, she asks, "Are you ready to head down to the dining room?"

My hands are still shaking, and I can only manage a nod.

I follow her back through the hallways, my head a chaotic mess of thoughts and emotions.

Alex

It seems to take forever before Natalie returns to the dining room with Karina at her side. As soon as I see her, my stomach drops. She's white as a ghost and trembling.

"What's wrong?" I hurry to her and grab her arm.

"Nothing."

I look at Dr. Turova, who offers a reassuring smile. "Other than being a bit worn out from all the stress she's been under, Natalie's completely healthy. All she needs is some rest and proper nutrition."

"Thank you, doctor." I turn to Natalie. "Are you sure you're up for a walk?"

"Absolutely. You promised me a tour, remember?"

"You have my number, Natalie. I'll be in touch," Dr. Turova says. "I'll see myself out."

"Where is everyone?"

"They've all eaten and gone their separate ways. You don't mind a quiet lunch with just me, do you?"

"Never."

"Let's go then."

"I thought we were eating?" she asks, confused.

"We are."

I lead her outside to start our tour. It isn't until we walk along a trail that overlooks the sea that Natalie begins to relax. I knew the fresh air and sheer amount of outdoor space would help her feel less confined.

"What's this?" she asks when we come to a laid-out blanket with a basket in the center.

"It's our lunch."

While she was with the doctor, I arranged for a picnic to be set up. Natalie loves being outside, especially by the water. I'm hoping this will provide a bit of normalcy.

We sit together, and I unpack the basket. The cook prepared some American sandwiches and Natalie's favorite, Olivier salad, along with a variety of snacks.

"It's beautiful here," Natalie says as she looks out over the cerulean water.

"I know you weren't happy about coming, but I need you to understand there was no other choice."

"I'm sorry about the way I reacted." She reaches out to cup my cheek in her tiny hand. "I do understand."

We eat our lunch quietly. Natalie may be physically present, but her thoughts are a million miles away. I let her go for a while, hoping she'll tell me what's on her mind without my having to ask. When she finishes her sandwich, she walks to the lookout spot, her gaze fixed on the water. I follow and stand next to her.

"Alex," she says quietly. "I have something I need to tell you."

"What is it, baby girl?" She looks up at me, tears in her eyes. "I'm afraid to say it. I don't know—"

"You don't have to be afraid to tell me anything."

"I'm pregnant."

My world stops.

Alex

"I'm sorry." There's a desperate plea in her voice. "I took all my pills. I don't know how it happened. Karina said sometimes—"

I lift her chin with my finger. "You're pregnant?"

She nods.

I place my hand on her belly. "You have a child, our child, growing inside you right now."

"I do." She covers my hand with hers. "Are you mad?"

"Is that what you thought? That I'd be mad?" I wipe the tears from her cheeks with my thumbs.

"I wasn't sure. I didn't know."

"Shh." I place my finger over her lips.

This baby wasn't planned. It wasn't something I even knew I wanted, but the second she blurted out the words *I'm pregnant*, my heart filled with an all-consuming love for this little life growing inside her.

"We didn't plan this." Tears are now streaming down her face.

"No, we didn't. But I don't care. I love you, and I love our baby."

"You do?"

"How could I not love something you and I created together?" I wrap my arms around her, never wanting to let her go. "Dr. Turova checked you and the baby? You're both healthy?" Thinking about the stress of the past few days fills me with worry.

"Yes."

"How far along are you?"

"I haven't gotten my period in months from being on the pill, so I'm not exactly sure." Natalie pulls her cell phone from her pocket. "Karina felt my uterus and estimates I'm about probably about twelve weeks pregnant." She opens a recorded video on her phone. "Listen."

Swoosh. Swoosh. Swoosh.

"Is that our baby's heartbeat?" I ask, swallowing over the lump in my throat.

"It is."

I drop to my knees, humbled by the knowledge we created a new life. My head lowers as my tears fall like rain. Natalie drops down next to me.

"Alex." Her voice is small and unsure. "What's wrong? Are you ok?"

The feeling in my chest is unlike anything I've ever experienced. I'm going to be a father. A new life is going to come into this world, entirely dependent on Natalie and me. No longer will life be just about us. We'll have a child, a mix of the best of us to protect and love.

It's even more critical now that we find out who's behind the cyber-attack.

"This is the best gift you could ever give me." I smile through my tears at this amazing woman.

<h1 style="text-align:center">Natalie</h1>

We walk back to the compound, each with puffy red eyes from our happy tears. My heart is so much lighter knowing Alex is happy about this baby. His face is alight with a smile. He has a secret he's bursting to tell, and he won't have to wait long. We're heading straight to Maxim's office to discuss my visit with Dr. Turova.

Everything's quiet when we get back inside. Alex leads me down a hallway I haven't seen yet.

"The security rooms are down there." Alex points to the end of the hall. "And this is Max's office."

A guard is stationed outside of the double doors. He looks up when he sees us approaching.

"*Kak vy segodnya?*"

"*U menya vse khorosho a u tebya?*"

"I'm doing well. Timur, this is my fiancé, Natalie."

"Pleasure to meet you, ma'am," Timur answers in perfect English.

I smile in return, suddenly too nauseous to speak. The elation I was feeling has given way to nerves. My pregnancy is going to complicate an already difficult situation. I know Maxim will be happy about the baby. What I don't know is what his reaction will be when we ask him to leave the compound.

"Is Maxim available?"

"He's finishing up a phone call. Is he expecting you, Mr. Montgomery?"

"He isn't. But something's come up, and it's imperative I speak with him right away."

The guard nods in acknowledgment before opening the doors and disappearing inside. My stomach is doing tumble saults. I've known Lana's family for many years. But things feel very different here—less like a family and more like a business.

Instead of Max being the kind, approachable man I know him to be, he's distant, almost cold. His eyes don't hold their usual warmth. In its place is a dark ruthlessness that, if I'm honest, scares me. I'm just about to ask Alex if we can wait to tell him when the doors open.

"He'll see you both now," Timur says, stepping aside so we can enter the office.

Max's office is ultra-modern. The room is sparsely furnished, with only the shiny black desk Maxim is currently sitting behind and several grey leather chairs opposite him. Like most of the other rooms, there's a wall of windows allowing natural light and scenic views outside.

Yesterday, Irina assured me all of the glass is bulletproof, and each window is equipped with steel shields that activate by the press of a button in the case of an emergency. I don't know whether that knowledge helped or made me more afraid of what sort of threat requires that much of a response.

"It is a pleasure to see you both. What brings you by this afternoon?" Concern appears on his face. "Did everything go well with the doctor?"

I sit next to Alex with my hands folded tightly in my lap. I'm hoping to hide how badly they're shaking.

"That's what we came to talk to you about," Alex says.

The room is silent for what feels like hours. My heart's beating so fast and loud I'm sure Maxim can hear it.

"We have good news to share with you." Alex takes my hand. "Natalie and I are going to have a baby."

Maxim's face lights up. "I am going to be a *dedushka*," he exclaims as he jumps from his seat and rounds the desk.

Alex stands and extends his hand, but Maxim ignores it and pulls him in for a hug instead. Then, he leans down, grabbing my face in his strong hands, kissing both cheeks before wrapping me in a Maxim-style bear hug.

"This is indeed wonderful news, my sweet girl. We must celebrate tonight."

"I have something I need to ask," I interrupt.

"What is it?"

This lighthearted version of Maxim is the one I'm used to and comfortable with. It helps dissipate some of my nerves, although I'm still unsure of his answer.

"Karina wants to do an ultrasound to determine how far along the pregnancy is and to check on the baby's health. But we need to leave the compound to do it."

Maxim leans back on the edge of his desk with his arms crossed over his chest. Alex returns to his seat next to me. We sit in silence, watching Maxim deliberate his answer.

"We wouldn't ask if Karina didn't think it was necessary."

"I know. I will not stand in the way of Natalia and *moya vnuchka* getting the medical care they need," Maxim says thoughtfully.

"Granddaughter?" Alex asks, raising an eyebrow.

"*Da.*"

"What if it's a grandson?" I ask.

"I will love this baby either way. But you will see, this baby is a girl." The love he already has for our child fills me with warmth. "When is your appointment?"

"Karina told me to call after we spoke to you."

"I'm assuming Viktor will accompany us?" Alex asks.

"No. Viktor is not familiar enough with the area. Timur will escort you."

"Your guard?" I ask, surprised.

"Yes. You and your child will have only the best protection." Maxim returns to his seat behind his desk. "Set up the appointment, and I will arrange to get you there and back safely."

"Thank you, Max."

"Thank you, Natalia. You have brought much-needed joy to my life."

Alex and I leave his office together. With that hurdle crossed, a weight lifts off my shoulders.

"How are you feeling?"

"It was a long day yesterday. With the time change, I'm kinda tired. I was thinking about going to lie down for a bit."

"You go ahead. I'll be along shortly. I have to check in with Viktor." Alex kisses my forehead, and we part ways.

Once I'm back in our room, I take the card Karina left with her contact information from my pocket and lift the receiver to place the call.

"Hello, Ms. Clarke," a man's voice answers. "Can I help you?"

I wasn't expecting to get a live person. "Yes. I need to make a phone call."

"Who do you need to reach?"

I give the information to the unknown man on the other end, and the line rings.

"Hello?" Dr. Turova answers.

"Hi. It's Natalie Clarke."

"How are you?"

"Tired, but well."

"How did Alex take the news?"

I recount our afternoon, telling her how delighted Alex is. "We got the okay to leave the compound for the ultrasound."

"I'm glad to hear that." Karina goes silent, and I hear the click of keys on a keyboard. "Let's do Monday at seven p.m. The clinic will be closed then. I think that will be best."

"Okay, I'll let Maxim know."

"See you then."

With that taken care of, I hang up the phone, crawl into bed, and fall asleep.

After seeing Natalie off, I go directly to the security room. When I get there, the door's open.

"What brings you this way, boss?" Viktor asks.

"I'm just checking on the progress. Any updates?"

Viktor motions for me to take a seat next to him. He's sitting with one of the men on the tech team, someone I'm unfamiliar with. They're looking at several computer screens, each with an image similar to the one Maxim showed us when we first arrived. More than we saw yesterday, red flags dot locations on a map that's now spread across the globe.

"Whoever it is clearly doesn't want to be found," Viktor says.

"How do you even make sense of that?"

"It's a slow process," Viktor says as he leans back in his chair. "It's taking more time than we'd hoped, but we won't stop until we uncover who's responsible for this."

"Alexander, I was hoping to find you here." Maxim walks into the room.

"Did we forget something?"

"*Nyet*. I did not want to say anything that might upset Natalia."

I appreciate his thoughtfulness. Natalie doesn't need to worry about anything more than necessary, especially now.

"I was on the phone with Nicholai when you came to the office. Unfortunately, his computer system sustained a series of attempted cyberattacks overnight," Maxim explains. "They were unsuccessful, but this raises my level of concern. Whoever is behind this is serious about getting our information."

His words are like a punch to my stomach, knocking the wind out of me. "We aren't going home anytime soon, are we?"

"I am afraid not."

I close my eyes, absorbing the information and making a quick plan to tell Natalie.

"I spoke to my staff," Maxim adds. "Everything is set for tonight."

Viktor looks at me curiously. "Did I miss something?"

"All will be revealed later." Maxim turns to leave the room. "I will be in my office."

I shrug, pretending not to know what he's talking about. "I'm going to go talk to Natalie. Keep me updated."

When I get to our room, I find Natalie sound asleep. Quietly, I pull a chair next to the bed to watch over her while she rests. My girl looks so peaceful sleeping—she's radiant. Her arms draped across her still flat belly. In a few weeks, her body will begin changing as our unborn child grows. The image makes my pulse accelerate with excitement.

She stirs as if she can sense me staring at her.

"Hi," she says, her voice quiet.

"I hope I didn't wake you."

"You didn't. Come lay with me?"

I slip my shoes off and get in bed, pulling her into my arms. She lays her head on my chest. I've never felt as emotional as I do right now, holding my whole world, the two people I love most, in my arms. My heart aches, knowing I'm going to spoil the moment with the news I'm about to deliver.

"Viktor briefed me on the tech team's progress."

"Have they found whoever is responsible?" Natalie pulls back to look at me. Hope fills her eyes.

"No." Watching disappointment wash over her is hard. "Nicholai called," I continue and force myself not to look away as I tell her the rest of the update. "His systems are being attacked as well."

"What does that mean?"

"This attack is more sophisticated than we first thought. We're going to be here longer than we planned."

"What about the bridal shower?"

"We need to call your parents. It's going to have to be postponed."

Natalie doesn't answer. She lays her head back on my chest and begins to cry. All I can do is hold her and tell her everything will be okay. I don't know how or when, but I have to trust it will.

"Can't we have dinner in our room?" Natalie sits on the edge of the bed. "I want to be alone."

"We can't do that to Maxim. He's excited to tell everyone our news." I look at her through the mirror while I finish straightening my tie. Maxim requested formal dress for tonight's dinner. "It would be disrespectful if we didn't show up."

"I know." She shrugs. "I just don't feel much like celebrating."

I walk over and stoop down before her. "I know you're disappointed, and so am I. But we're together, and we have this." I place my hand on her belly. "The news of your pregnancy is exactly what everyone needs to hear right now."

"I can't believe we're having a baby."

"You're going to be a wonderful mother." My heart overflows with so many emotions.

Elation.

Awe.

Fear.

Fear is the biggest one. The one I'm trying to hide from Natalie.

I don't know how long we'll have to stay in Russia. Although we're safe at the compound, I want to get Natalie home as soon as possible so we can move up our wedding date. Then, our focus will be on preparing for our little one's arrival.

"Should we call your parents before dinner?"

"Can you tell them, please?"

"Of course, baby girl. I'll take care of everything."

I'm connected to her parent's line, and after we get past the formalities, I break the bad news.

"Postpone the shower?" Charlotte screeches so loud I have to pull the phone away from my ear.

"I'm afraid so," I reply calmly. "I've had some important business matters come up that require my attention. I need to see them through before we fly home." Charlotte knows I do business internationally, so this story won't raise any red flags.

"Can't Natalie fly home on her own?"

"We discussed that option and decided against it."

"How am I going to cancel everything?"

"We aren't canceling, just postponing," I say as I take Natalie's hand in mine. "We don't have good cell service here. If you can make the calls for us and let everyone know, we'll get back to them with a new date as soon as we're home."

"Where's Natalie? I want to speak to her." Charlotte's tone is clipped.

"She and Lana went into town to do some shopping."

"I'll give her a call."

"Unfortunately, she left her cell phone here." I don't like being dishonest with her, but my priority will always be to protect Natalie. And right now, the less her parents know, the better. "I'll have her call you when they get back."

"I don't like this one bit, Alexander."

"We're disappointed too. But Natalie and I discussed it and agreed that since we're already here, we should stay and get this handled now. Otherwise, this will be hanging over our heads, and we won't get to enjoy planning our wedding."

"I don't understand all this business stuff." Charlotte blows a frustrated breath into the phone. "Just have Natalie call me."

"I will. Have a good afternoon." Natalie lays her head on my shoulder. She's under too much stress. It can't be good for her or the baby. "I know that was hard. I'm sorry for all this."

She doesn't respond.

I close my eyes and, for the first time, wonder if getting involved with Maxim was a mistake. At the time, I had no one to think about other than myself. Now I have Natalie and a baby on the way. If I could go back, would I change anything? My thoughts are interrupted when there's a knock on the door.

"You guys in there?" Lana calls.

Natalie answers the door. "We're here."

"What's wrong?"

"Just disappointed about having to postpone my bridal shower."

Lana wraps Natalie in a hug. "I'm so sorry. But, on the bright side, you get to spend more time hanging out with me."

I check the time on my watch. "Ladies, we need to get to the dining room. If we're late, Maxim will have our heads."

"What's up with him tonight anyway?" Lana spins around, showing off her evening dress.

"I guess we need to get to dinner and find out." I take Natalie's hand in mine. "Let's go."

Natalie

BRANDON JOINS OUR TRIO AS WE MAKE OUR WAY THROUGH THE labyrinth of hallways. While we walk, Lana chatters away about how lucky we are to get this extended vacation. I smile and nod in agreement. She doesn't seem to notice my lack of enthusiasm as she prattles on about spending afternoons swimming and exploring the many paths on the property.

I love my best friend, but I'm relieved when we arrive at the dining room, and she takes her seat across the large table next to Brandon.

Alex leans over and whispers, "Lana's used to coming here. Growing up, Maxim would periodically bring her and Irina here to make it seem normal. Now, it's no big deal to her."

I meet his gaze. Looking back at me are eyes filled with so much love and devotion.

"I'll be okay. Everything will work out the way it's supposed to." Alex offers me a reassuring smile.

I'm surprised when Viktor and Timur join us at the table. Viktor takes the empty seat next to me, and Timur sits across from him. Looking around the table at this unexpected mix of people that's become my second family takes away some of my sadness. Maxim signals to a member of his staff standing near the kitchen entrance. She disappears behind the door. Seconds later, several staff members enter the room, carrying plates of mouthwatering food they set before us.

"Are you going to tell us why we had to get all dressed up tonight?" Lana asks.

"All in due time, *moya babochka*." Maxim grins.

Lana huffs a loud sigh and rolls her eyes, to which Brandon gives a warning glare. I'm amused watching their dynamic silently play out.

Despite the circumstances of our being here, the conversation is light and easy throughout the remainder of the meal. I don't think I could ever get used to this or consider it *normal.* But even I can't stop myself from enjoying the company of my friends. It isn't until drinks and dessert have been served that Maxim winks at me and stands.

"I know you are wondering why I have called for formal attire at this evening's meal."

I look across the table at Lana, who sits silently with her hands folded in her lap.

"We have had little to celebrate the past few days, but that all changed with some news I received today," Maxim says, motioning for his wife to stand next to him. "Irina and I are going to be grandparents," he announces proudly.

Brandon's eyes grow huge as he looks between Maxim and Lana. "What?"

"I have no idea what he's talking about," Lana says, her face going pale.

Maxim chuckles. He's enjoying the confusion around the table. Irina gives him a subtle look, imploring him to finish the story.

"Alexander and Natalia, although neither of you is our child by birth, Irina and I have come to love you as family. We are so excited that you will be adding to your own family."

His sentiment brings tears to my eyes.

"You're pregnant?" Lana squeals as she jumps from her seat and rounds the table. "I'm going to be an aunt?" She grabs me from my seat and pulls me into a tight hug.

"You're not going to get to be an aunt if you squeeze the life out of her," Alex jokes.

Lana grabs my shoulders. "Oh my God. I'm so sorry. Did I hurt you?"

"You didn't hurt me," I giggle.

Brandon walks around the table. Alex extends his hand, but Brandon pulls him in for a bro hug. Then he turns and hugs me. Timur is the last to congratulate me before I sit and resume eating dessert. Viktor mindlessly drags his fork through his *Ptichye Moloko* cake. It surprises me that he didn't offer his congratulations. Instead, he remains sitting, a serious look on his face.

"What's wrong?" I ask quietly, putting my hand on his shoulder.

"Nothing."

"That's not true. Please, tell me."

"I'm happy for you. But you know me, always thinking about safety and logistics." He offers me a strained smile.

I put my hand on my stomach. "I've got it covered for now."

"I'm going to take my cake with me and get back to work," Viktor says quietly and kisses my cheek. "Congratulations."

"Where are you going to so soon?" Maxim asks.

"I told Dimitri I wouldn't be gone long. I need to get back to work."

Maxim nods, not at all bothered by my bodyguard's sudden exit. But I can't shake the feeling that there's more to Viktor's mood than he's letting on. Maxim must notice my concern.

"Do not worry, Natalia. He has a lot on his mind right now."

"Yes, he does." Although I'm not convinced, that's the whole story.

Lana moves to Viktor's vacated seat and dives right into planning everything we need to do before the baby's born. She's only known for a few minutes, and already she has a list a mile long. I'm forced to put my concerns about Viktor aside.

As the evening progresses, Maxim and Irina entertain us with parenting stories—they had their hands full with Lana as a young child.

It's very late when we finally return to our room. Despite my initial reservations about tonight, I'm glad Alex forced me to have dinner with everyone. It ended up being a fantastic evening that filled me with joy.

Natalie

Once again, I've slept well into the afternoon, a luxury I haven't been afforded in months. The sheets on Alex's side of the bed are cold. He must've been up for hours. I'm sure he and Maxim are planning out each and every detail for our appointment with Karina this evening.

I swing my legs over the edge of the bed and sit up slowly, hoping to avoid the nausea I've been experiencing if I get up too fast. Once I'm sure my stomach will remain calm, I shower quickly before heading out of our bedroom, searching for food and Alex—in that order.

The dining room is empty, which doesn't surprise me since I slept through breakfast and lunch. Carefully, I open the kitchen door. I've never been in here before. I'm not sure if I'm even allowed in here. I stand just inside the doorway and watch the chefs busy at work preparing what I assume will be tonight's dinner.

"Excuse me," I say, hoping to get someone's attention.

An older woman looks up from her task.

"I know I missed mealtime, but is it possible I can make myself a quick bite to eat?"

"*Nyet*." The woman leaves her stool where she's cutting vegetables and ushers me out of the kitchen.

My stomach growls in protest. "I'll stay out of your way. I just need to make—"

She takes my arm. "Sit," she says with a heavy accent. "I will feed you."

"You don't have to go to any trouble."

She puts her finger to her lips, silencing me. "Stay."

With that, she turns and disappears into the kitchen. A few minutes later, she comes out carrying a bowl of *Okroshka*, a cold soup with potatoes, eggs, and cucumbers. I thank her and begin eating, savoring the fresh ingredients. She returns with a Charcuterie Board filled with cheeses, meats, crackers, and fruits. I laugh at the vast amount of food she's laid out.

"I hope you plan to stay to help me eat all this."

"Eat." She points to my tummy. "For *malysh*."

"*Spasibo*." I thank her in Russian, bringing a big smile to her face.

Then, I do my best to put a dent in the food that's been prepared for me. While I'm eating, Alex comes into the room.

"There you are," he says, kissing me before sitting down. "I've been looking all over for you."

"I was going to come find you after I got something to eat." I gesture to the food. "Want some?"

He plucks a few grapes from the tray and pops one in his mouth.

"I assumed you'd be busy with Maxim. I didn't want to interrupt you."

"You're never an interruption, baby girl. Maxim's taken care of every detail. We'll go, get our baby's first picture, and return for a late dinner. Unfortunately," Alex says as he stands up. "I have some work to do before we leave."

"That's okay. I'm going to find Lana and see if she wants to spend the rest of the afternoon at the pool."

When it's time to leave for the clinic, Viktor walks us outside, where Timur waits in one of the black SUVs we arrived in.

"Natalie, give Viktor your engagement ring to hold until we return," Alex instructs.

"Why?" I haven't taken the ring off since we got back together.

"We're going into a section of town where the ring could draw unwanted attention. It'll be safer for us if you leave it here."

I slide the ring off my finger and place it in Viktor's palm.

"I'll keep it safe until you get back."

I feel naked without my ring. But I have no doubt Viktor will take care of it until we get back.

We get in the car and slowly start to pull away. I wave goodbye to Viktor. Surprisingly, he returns it with a wave and an unexpected smile.

I didn't realize how far away from everything we actually are at the compound. It took almost three hours for us to get to the clinic. Finally, Timur pulls around the back of a nondescript building into a private parking lot.

"Wait here," Timur instructs before taking his gun from the seat next to him. He steps out of the car and scans the area.

I grab Alex's hand. "I'm scared."

"Maxim took care of everything. Timur's just being extra cautious."

We wait while Timur makes a call on his cell. As soon as he slides the phone into his pocket, the back door of the clinic opens. Karina stands in the doorway, smiling as she motions for us to come in.

Timur turns and opens the car door. "Everything's all clear." He offers his hand to help me while Alex gets out on his side. Together, we make our way inside the clinic.

"I'll wait here, sir," Timur says, closing the door.

"It's so good to see you again, Natalie." Karina kisses me on both cheeks. "How are you feeling?"

"Other than tired and a bit nervous, I'm okay."

"There's nothing to be nervous about. The clinic is a secure location."

"How are you this evening, Alex?"

"Doing well, thank you for asking."

She escorts us into a small, dimly lit room. Inside is a twin bed covered in a beautiful bedspread with several fluffy pillows arranged at the top. Sitting next to the bed is a plush armchair. On the opposite side, the ultrasound equipment is set up. Despite the room's purpose being for a medical procedure, it has a comfortable, homey feel.

"If you could lie down, we'll get started."

I get on the bed and lay back, finding a comfortable spot on the pillows. Alex sits on the chair next to me.

Karina turns a large TV-like screen in our direction.

"I'm going to put some gel on your tummy, and we'll get started." She places the wand on my stomach and starts moving it around.

The screen comes to life with a fuzzy, grey-and-white picture that doesn't look like much of anything to me.

"I'm just doing some measurements," she explains as she pauses the screen and clicks some buttons. I strain my eyes, trying to find something that looks like a baby, but I can't decipher the grainy image on the screen. "Now we get to the fun part."

Suddenly, the room is filled with the rapid swooshing of our baby's heartbeat. Then, with the click of a button, the image on the screen changes.

"Is that?" Alex's voice cracks.

"Yes. That's your baby." She explains the 4D images we see on the screen. "From my measurements, I'd say you're about thirteen weeks pregnant. As you can see, the baby still looks a bit like an alien at this stage." We all laugh at her comment.

She continues moving the wand around, giving us different views of our little one. I'm amazed at how active the baby is as it kicks its little feet and moves its hands close to its face.

"Is the baby sucking its thumb?"

"Yes, it is." Karina freezes the screen on the image.

I turn and look at Alex. Tears are streaming down his face, his gaze fixed on the screen. Seeing my Dominant so humbled by our unborn child leaves an indelible imprint on my heart.

"How is this even possible, though? I was on the pill. I never missed a day."

"Did you make sure to take it at the same time every day?"

"Yes."

"Except for the weekend we visited my father. I got you, um—" Alex clears his throat. "Sidetracked. And you forgot your pill that night, remember?"

My cheeks blush. "Yes, but I took two the next night."

"That could do it," Karina says.

"And that was about thirteen weeks ago." Alex smiles.

Karina gives us a pregnancy book to read about the changes my body will be going through. She also provides us with a bottle of prenatal vitamins. We finish our appointment and are about to walk out the back door when Karina rushes over. "Don't forget these." She hands me a small stack of black and white photos. "Baby's first pictures."

"Thank you so much."

"Please let me know if you need anything else while you're here."

Alex

Timur's standing guard outside. When he sees us, he grabs the door and holds it as Natalie and I walk through. "All set, sir?"

"Yes. We're ready to go."

Natalie shows him the ultrasound pictures as we walk to the parked car. He nods and smiles, pretending to be looking, but his eyes never stop scanning our surroundings. I'm feeling lighter than air as I help Natalie into the car.

I figured we might have a child eventually.

Someday.

But when I saw my unborn child on the screen, nothing else mattered other than the unconditional and all-consuming love I felt for our child. I can't imagine my life any different.

Timur starts the car and pulls onto the main road to begin the drive back to the safety of Maxim's compound. Natalie and I are immersed in our child's photos and looking through the thick paperback book Dr. Turova gave us.

"What the fuck?" Timur's voice startles me.

"What's wrong?"

"It's the police. They're pulling us over."

I hadn't even realized they were behind us, let alone that they had their lights on.

"What's going on?" Natalie asks, panic filling her voice.

"Don't worry, baby girl." I grab her hand. "I'm sure it's nothing more than a routine stop."

I meet Timur's worried eyes in the mirror. He puts his gun under his leg before signaling and pulling to the side of the poorly lit road. A million scenarios run through my head. This shouldn't be happening. Maxim called his contact in the police department. We were cleared for travel without interference. "Don't worry. Timur will handle this, and we'll be on our way."

An officer dressed in a black uniform walks up to Timur's rolled-down window.

"Can I help you, officer?" he asks in Russian.

"Turn the car off and step out of the vehicle."

"Did I do something wrong?"

"Turn it off and step out of the vehicle," the officer repeats.

Timur slides the gun between the seats before opening the door and stepping outside the car.

"Alex, I'm scared," Natalie whispers.

Another car drives by and pulls in front of us, blocking us in. That's all the confirmation I need to know that this isn't a routine stop. Something's wrong. I lean forward to grab the gun, and at the same time, the doors of our car are pulled open.

"Get out of the car," a masked man orders.

"Alex," Natalie yells as a second masked man pulls her from my grasp.

I jump out of the car. "Get your fucking hands off her."

I find myself forcefully dragged toward the rear of our car, where I'm placed next to Timur and held at gunpoint by our captors. The officer in charge is currently occupied with a cellphone conversation. I take a quick look around to assess the situation. Natalie is at the front of the car, but I can't see who is holding her or if they are armed.

Despite having some knowledge of hand-to-hand combat, I am not as skilled as Timur. However, we exchange a meaningful glance and decide to make a move against the men standing in front of us.

Timur nods, and in a sudden motion, one of the men falls to the ground. I quickly take advantage of the opportunity to pin him down while delivering a powerful right hook to his face, causing him to drop his weapon. I kick the gun out of his reach. However, he regains his strength and overpowers me, causing me to fall to the ground. Meanwhile, I hear the sounds of a struggle between Timur and the officer next to me.

A gunshot rings out.

Time stands still.

Timur's body falls to the ground next to me—lifeless.

Somewhere in the distance, Natalie's screams fill the night.

I scramble to my feet. "Let her go."

Momentarily, I forget about the man I'm fighting. My only goal is to get to Natalie, but it's dark. I know she's near the front of the car, but I can't see her. My feet struggle to find purchase when the sound of a gun's safety being removed stops me in my tracks.

"If you continue to fight, we'll shoot the girl." A gun digs into my temple.

"Alex," Natalie whimpers.

The police vehicle's lights turn on. That's when I see the man holding Natalie with one arm around her waist. In his other hand is a gun pointed at her head.

I stop struggling, paralyzed by fear. "Don't hurt her,.

3+ and I'll do whatever you say."

The officer barks out instructions in Russian. The man holding Natalie grabs her arm, pulling her to the car in the front.

"Where's he taking her?"

Natalie struggles, trying to grab anything to keep from being taken. She loses the fight when the man grabs her hair and drags her toward the waiting car.

"Get your fucking hands off her."

Crack.

My world goes black.

Natalie

THE DOOR IS YANKED OPEN, AND I AM FORCEFULLY PULLED FROM THE car by a pair of gloved hands. During my struggle to break free from the grip of the masked assailant, my unborn baby's ultrasound photograph tumbled to the ground.

The police car no longer has its lights on, rendering the area pitch black. I'm unable to locate Alex and Timur, but their grunts are audible. Alex yells for the masked man to release me.

A gunshot echoes into the stillness of the night, startling birds that take flight from a nearby tree.

"No," I scream. My world moves in slow motion.

The police car's blazing lights create a surreal world around me. A pool of blood surrounds Timur, who is lying on the ground. My eyes shift to Alex, who's being held at gunpoint. His eyes widen in terror, and he freezes in place.

Suddenly, I feel the chill of metal pressed against my temple, and I silently beg Alex to rescue me. The officer barks orders in Russian, and the man holding me yanks my hair, throwing me off balance as he drags me towards their car.

Alex struggles again, fighting to reach me. The police officer coolly approaches him and slams the butt of his gun into Alex's head. He falls motionless beside Timur. Panic grips me, and I attempt to scream, but no sound comes out.

I'm no match against the man's force, and he drags me toward the second vehicle while the other men toss Alex's lifeless body into the police car. Seeing them taking Alex rather than leaving him dead beside Timur gives me a flicker of hope he may still be alive.

I'm shoved into the backseat of the second car. "Alex," I call, tears pouring down my face as the masked man takes his place beside me. The door barely shuts before the driver squeals the tires, tearing away from the scene.

"If you don't shut up. You'll meet the same fate as your boyfriend," the driver says in perfect English.

I don't listen and fight with every ounce of my strength, yanking at the door handles, doing everything in my power to break free and escape.

"Do it," the driver orders.

The man beside me pulls a syringe from his pocket. Before I can react, he jabs it into my neck.

My baby.

Darkness creeps into my vision, and I fall into the black abyss.

My thoughts are jumbled, and confusion engulfs me. Where am I? Why does it feel like I'm in motion? My eyes flicker open for a fleeting moment, and a flood of memories rushes back. I force myself to shut them once more and remain motionless. The reality hits me hard - Timur is dead, Alex's fate is unknown, and I have been taken.

With deliberate slowness, I reach for my pocket, hoping my phone is still there, but I find nothing. It must have fallen during the struggle. Panic rises within me, knowing the phone was my only link to the people who could save us.

"I know you're awake. You may as well open your eyes."

It takes a few moments for my eyes to adjust and focus. We're no longer on the desolate highway. Instead, bright lights surround us, forcing me to squint. The presence of other cars suggests we're in a city of some sort. When we arrived, we landed in St. Petersburg. That's at least a two-hour drive from the compound and in the opposite direction of the clinic. How long was I knocked out? Could we really be in St. Petersburg?

Suddenly, the sound of a low-flying airplane catches my attention, and I sit up to look out of the window. My heart races as I see the familiar airport. My mind races as I try to make sense of the situation. The driver takes us to a small building far from the main terminals and opens my door without turning off the engine. But I stay rooted in place, making no move to follow.

"Get out." I refuse to move. The man forcibly pulls me out of the car.

A tall man with bronzed skin steps out from the shadows. He's well-dressed in an expensive tailored suit. His hair is dark, sprinkled with strands of grey. Soulless black eyes stare at me. "She's lovely. She'll command a handsome price."

Oh my God, they plan to sell me.

In a panic, I scan the surroundings for a means of escape. The entrance we drove through is now closed, and the only other exit is blocked by this new man standing in front of me. It's an impossible task for me to make it past him. I can't think clearly. My head is still fuzzy from the drugs they administered. Did they harm my unborn child? I push the thought aside for now. I have to remain level-headed, prioritize the safety of my baby, and preserve my strength until a real opportunity to flee arises.

The well-dressed man reaches into his suit jacket, pulls out an envelope, and hands it to the driver, who tears it open. Inside is a large stack of cash. I gasp as I watch the man quickly count the money. When he's done, he nods and gets in the car. The garage door opens, allowing him to speed away before it slams closed.

My body trembles as I stand face to face with this stranger.

"Who are you? What do you want with me?"

"Tsk, tsk," the man sneers. "A trained submissive should know her place, which is silent unless spoken to. It seems we'll have to do some more training with you."

How does he know I'm a submissive?

"Alex is going to come after you. You won't get away with this."

"Silence. It's time to go." He grabs my arm.

I struggle to match his long strides as we exit the building through a black door. Before us sits a large, unmarked jet. My feet anchor to their spot as I resist his pull. For a fleeting moment, his grip loosens. Boarding that jet is not an option. If I let them take me, I'll vanish without a trace, and I refuse to become a statistic. I quickly scan my surroundings and spot the main terminal in the distance. It's a long shot, but it's my only chance. I have no choice but to take it.

The night air is filled with the man's menacing laugh. "What do you think you're doing?"

Without wasting another second, I sprint toward the terminal, hoping to put as much distance between myself and the plane as possible.

"Fuck," he yells.

I have a split-second head start, but the man's heavy footsteps catch up quickly. I will my feet to move faster. My lungs burn, but I don't give up. I have to get away. Then, a heavy weight tackles me from behind. My body crashes to the ground, and I'm rolled onto my back. The man straddles me.

With a burst of adrenaline, I fight back, using all the strength I have left. I claw at his face, and he grunts in pain, but his grip only tightens. My heart races as I struggle to break free. I refuse to give up, even as he overpowers me.

"Your fight only turns me on."

His erection pressed against my stomach makes me nauseous. My stomach churns, and I can't stop the urge to vomit. I turn my head to the side and empty my stomach onto the ground.

The man's laughter echoes in my ears. I feel his hand on my shoulder, pulling me back to my feet. He retrieves a white handkerchief from his suit pocket and holds it out to me. "Clean yourself up," he says with a twisted smirk.

Reluctantly, I take it and wipe the vomit from my face before dropping the white fabric to the ground.

"You will be punished for that." Then, without wasting any time, he lifts me and tosses me over his shoulder.

"Put me down." I kick and scream, trying to get out of his hold.

He slaps me hard—the impact reverberates through my body.

"Hold still," he orders. "If you fight, your punishment will be worse."

As much as I want to keep fighting, I must think about the baby. Protecting them is my number one goal. I can't take any more foolish chances.

With that in mind, I stop fighting, surrendering to the man who easily carries me up the jet's stairs, taking me away from Alex and everyone who can save me.

ANXIETY GNAWS AT ME AS I PACE OUTSIDE THE FRONT DOOR OF THE compound, my eyes glued to the driveway. If I concentrate hard enough, maybe I can make the SUV appear.

Alex texted me over three hours ago, saying they were on their way back, but they're nowhere in sight. They should've been here by now. I've tried calling and texting them, but there's been no response. My calls go straight to voicemail.

Frustrated, I pull out my phone to check the SUV's GPS, and my heart sinks. "What the hell?" I punch the side of the house in frustration. Shoving my phone into my picket, I burst through the front door and storm into Maxim's office without bothering to knock. The doors slam against the walls, echoing through the quiet halls.

Maxim's face flushes with anger from my rude intrusion into his office. "What's the meaning of this?" he demands.

"There's a problem."

My head pounds from the most wicked headache I've ever had. Men's voices echo around me, the sound so loud I have to fight the urge to vomit. I force myself to wade through the fog and concentrate on my surroundings. That's when I feel the unmistakable rumble of the engine beneath me.

I'm on a plane, and we're in the air. Staying quiet and keeping my breathing even, I continue to assess the situation. The feeling is just beginning to return to my limbs. I attempt to wiggle my fingers but realize my wrists are secured to the armrests. Testing my feet, I find they are also restrained with chains. I'm completely immobilized.

The sound of men's voices gradually comes into focus, drawing my attention to the two figures sitting across from me. Though they speak English, their elongated vowels and rapid speech suggest Mexican heritage. My heart races when I hear them mention a *guera*. They must be referring to Natalie, but I don't hear her voice. If they've hurt her in any way, I'll make sure every one of them suffers a slow and painful death.

"You're finally awake," one of the men says, kicking my leg.

I slowly open my eyes and survey my surroundings. The sun is just beginning to peek over the horizon, revealing a seemingly endless expanse of water—we're flying over an ocean. Inside the jet, I'm seated on a plush caramel-colored chair. The two men facing me wear chino pants and dingy button-down shirts that hang open, revealing their white undershirts. The tattoo on their necks, a dagger piercing a rose with a drop of red blood, strikes fear in my soul.

Suddenly, everything falls into place: the attempts to hack into encrypted files, the complex network of IP addresses, and my abduction. The tattoo branding the men's skin is the infamous mark of *El Tomador*, a notorious figure in the world of human trafficking. I also don't have to question where we're going. We're headed to Mexico.

"Where's the girl?" I ask.

"The pretty blonde? She's in good hands." They elbow one another and laugh.

"Where the fuck is she?" I struggle, but it's a futile effort. I can't get free.

"If you're a good boy, maybe you'll get to see her before the boss sells her." The man gets up and moves closer so we're face to face. His breath smells rancid when he speaks. "Give us any trouble, and we make a call that ends her life now. It's up to you." He shrugs casually and walks past me.

I clench my jaw, forcing myself to stay silent and not make any more demands. It's a struggle, but the thought of Natalie and the baby's safety gives me the strength to hold back.

The remainder of the flight passes in relative quiet. The men alternate between napping and texting. When they do speak, it's in Spanish, a language I only have a basic understanding of.

When the plane begins its descent, I strain to catch a glimpse of anything outside the window that could give me a clue to our exact whereabouts. But all I see are nondescript buildings and an unremarkable landscape passing by.

Finally, the wheels touch the ground, and I straighten in my seat, eager to get a better view. We come to a halt in a small airport. The engines power down, and the men rise from their seats.

The taller of the two, who also has a shaved head, pulls out his gun, pointing it at my head. "Don't do anything stupid."

I nod, showing I'll cooperate—for now.

The second man, who's very thin and has greasy hair that hangs over his face, pulls out a pocketknife and approaches my seat. He cuts one zip tie and slaps a handcuff on that wrist before cutting the other free. Then, he pushes me forward, cuffing my hands together behind my back.

"Let's go." The bald man waves the gun.

Standing is difficult, and walking with the short chain around my ankles is clumsy. Greasy hair man grabs my arm and drags me as I stumble to keep up. We're met on the tarmac by what looks like an older model tan military vehicle.

The bald man opens the door, and I'm pushed in. I fall on the seat and try to right myself. A difficult task without the use of my hands. Greasy hair guy gets in after me, shutting the door. We start moving. He pulls me to a sitting position and puts a black hood over my head.

I'm restrained, helpless, and at the mercy of dangerous criminals.

Please be okay, baby girl.

Just hang on.

I *will* find you.

Natalie

Despite my current situation and the adrenaline running through my system, I'm exhausted. The last thing I wanted to do was fall asleep on the plane, flying to who knows where with a madman sitting next to me. My body has other plans and screams for rest. My eyes close of their own accord, and I'm lost to sleep.

"Wake up, beautiful. We've landed." I feel the light caress of knuckles against my cheek and the warm whisper of his breath against my ear. The words are gentle, but the voice is all wrong.

It's not Alex.

I startle awake. Plucked from the sweetest dream and dropped into the nightmare that's become my reality. Leaning in closer, the man tries to kiss me, but I turn my head and pull away before his lips meet mine.

"Don't touch me," I snarl.

"*Mi pequeña mascota*," he says smoothly. "Soon, you'll be begging me to touch you."

"Never."

"You are not to speak unless given permission." He grabs my hand. "Come, *mascota*. We don't want to be late."

I pull against him, refusing to stand. "Where's Alex?"

He spins around to face me. "I warned you about speaking out of turn. I'm going to enjoy punishing you very much." His black eyes twinkle with eerie delight. I open my mouth to let this guy know what I think about him, but his warning glare makes me think twice, and I remain silent.

"Good girl," he croons.

His words send shivers down my spine. This time, when he pulls my hand, I follow him out of the plane. We walk to a black stretch Escalade where a man holding a large gun across his chest waits.

"I hope you had a good flight, sir," the man says as he opens the door.

"It was a smooth flight," my captor responds. "Get in, pet."

I slide across the black leather seat, moving as far away as possible.

The man gets in and laughs when he sees me. "Sit closer. I won't bite—yet."

I inch closer, still leaving distance between us. He pulls me the rest of the way until our legs are touching.

"When I give instructions, you will reply *yes, Master*. Is that clear?"

He expects me to call him Master?

"Answer me." His raised voice bounces off the walls of the car.

"Yes, Master." The disgusting words slip from my mouth.

"That's a good girl." He pulls out his cell phone. "Now, sit quietly. I have work to do."

He spends the rest of the drive on the phone while he strokes my thigh with his free hand. I try to distract myself from his touch by looking out the window and seeking any clue about our location. Because I fell asleep, I lost track of how long the flight was.

Wherever we are, the sun is still well above the horizon. It won't set for at least a few hours. It isn't until we've been driving on a highway for quite some time that I finally see a sign. Although the words are in Spanish, I recognize the town's name, Juarez.

Oh my God, we're in Mexico.

The driver takes an unmarked exit, and the surroundings begin to change. The city's buildings disappear. All signs of civilization are now behind us as we drive down a single-lane road through the desert.

Alex, where are you?

I haven't seen or heard mention of him since I watched those men toss his lifeless body into the back of the police car. Is he still in Russia, or did they bring him here, too? Our drive comes to a stop when we pull up to a tall chain-link fence with razor wire on top. Heavily armed guards nod at the driver and then slide the gate open, allowing us to pass through.

The driver takes us on a series of roads that weave in and out of warehouse-like buildings. Outside of each building are several armed guards patrolling the perimeter. Is this place some sort of prison?

We wind our way up a gentle slope until we stop in front of a sprawling estate. The building looks as though it's been standing for centuries, and it is made of a combination of crème-colored stone and stucco. Multiple archways grace the front of the structure, and the red Spanish-style roof boasts a terrace with intricately adorned white railings.

The property is surrounded by lush gardens that lend it an almost magical quality as if it were taken straight from a fairy tale. Except in this fairy tale, this is where the villain resides.

"Welcome to my home." I look between him and the estate, my mind reeling with unasked questions. "You may speak."

"What is this place? Where am I?" The questions are rapid-fire. "Who are you?"

"My name is Silverio Moreno."

"What is this place?"

He gets out of the car, pulling me along with him. "This." He motions around us. "Is my headquarters."

"Excuse me?"

"I specialize in the delivery of human commodities."

I can't believe what I've just heard. Looking around at the rusty corrugated metal buildings, the gravity of the situation threatens to drown me. The highly guarded buildings are filled with people—people being trafficked.

"You, *mascota*, are fortunate." He strokes my arm. "You will be staying with me as my special guest."

"Where's Alex?"

"He'll be along shortly." Silverio's menacing laugh fills the otherwise quiet space. "Come, let's go inside."

The last thing I want to do is go inside, but I have no choice but to play with his sick little game until I can find Alex.

<h1 style="text-align:center">Viktor</h1>

"The GPS was tracking their location—everything was fine." I shove my phone in his face. "But then we lost the signal."

Maxim calls Dimitri and orders him to figure out what's happening.

"I can't stay here. I'm going to look for them." It's not a question, and I'm not seeking his approval.

"Take one of the guards with you," Maxim says. "I am trusting you to find them."

On my way to the weapons room, I call the guardhouse, letting them know I need their best man weaponed up and ready to go in five minutes. I grab enough ammo to take out a small town before going to the garage to get a vehicle. Misha, another one of the guards, is waiting there with the keys in hand.

I exceed every speed limit on the way to the GPS's final destination. Legal repercussions can wait. All that matters now is ensuring the safety of my boss and his fiancée. "Over there." Misha points out the SUV that was carrying Natalie and Alex. It's been abandoned on the side of the road.

I swerve across the grassy divider that separates the two directions of travel. This route was chosen because it's not a highly traveled road. But now it looks like that's backfired on us. My tires screech to a stop behind the SUV, and I jump out.

The scene I find confirms my worst suspicions. The car's empty. To anyone driving by, they'd assume the unfortunate motorists had mechanical issues and abandoned their vehicle to get help. I know that's not the case, and I inspect the scene closer. There are several tiny drops of dried blood on the ground outside the driver's door.

"Get Maxim on the phone, now," I yell over my shoulder to Misha, who's just getting out of the car.

My feet stop dead in their tracks when I get to the back passenger door. Scattered on the ground are pictures from Natalie's ultrasound. My hands tremble as I pick one up. The image of their unborn child is crystal clear. I gather all the discarded pictures and carefully put them in my pocket—the same pocket that holds her engagement ring.

Misha hands me the phone.

"They're gone." I slam the side of the SUV. "Where the fuck are they?"

"I have all my men on it. We will find them."

I disconnect the call to search for more clues.

"Viktor, over here," Misha calls from where he's crouched in the high grass.

I rush over and find Timur lying in a puddle of blood. "Is he alive?"

"His pulse is weak, but he's still with us."

I drop down next to his motionless body. "Timur, can you hear me?"

Misha rips open his shirt to locate the source of the blood and finds a gunshot wound in his chest. He tears his own shirt off and uses it to apply pressure to the injury. Timur groans in response but doesn't open his eyes.

"Hang in there. You're going to be okay," I reassure him.

He has to be okay.

He's the only person who can tell us what happened—our best chance of finding Alex and Natalie.

The hood is ripped off, and after a quick look around, I know exactly where we are—The Chihuahuan Desert. If I had any doubt, our current location, combined with the tattoos, confirms Silverio Moreno, one of the most prominent and dangerous men in the trafficking world, is behind all of this.

We're in deep shit.

My first priority is finding Natalie and making sure she's unharmed. Then I must figure out how to get us out of this highly guarded fortress alive.

I'm sickened as we drive past warehouse-like buildings, most with no windows, knowing that countless numbers of men, women, and children are being held against their will. Innocent people were swiped from the streets, plucked from their families, never to be seen again.

We don't stop at any of them. Instead, we head straight for the sprawling hacienda atop the hill.

"Get out," greasy hair man orders and pushes me out of the car door.

My feet hit the ground, and my head spins. I'm sure I have a concussion from the hit I sustained. "Where's Natalie?" I growl.

"She's with the boss," one of the men says as they elbow each other and laugh. "They're busy."

Murderous rage boils through me. If anyone touches her, I'll kill them. I'll kill them all.

I'm pushed through the front door of the house, my legs tangle around the chain, and I fall to my knees. A pair of leather boots appears in front of me. When I look up, I recognize their owner. Silverio Moreno, better known to his associates as *el Tomador* or *The Taker*. He stands in his tailored suit, arms crossed over his chest, and a sinister smile on his face.

"It's nice of you to join us, Alejandro," he drawls. "Your beautiful girlfriend has been asking about you."

"Where is she?"

He lowers his hands to his sides and smiles. "She's a little tied up at the moment. We've been waiting for your arrival to get started."

"If you touch her—"

Moreno fists the top of my shirt, pulling me to my feet. His face is only inches from mine. "I suggest you consider your next words very carefully. Your girlfriend will pay for every threat you make. Do you understand?"

"Yes." The single word comes out with a snarl.

"Uncuff our guest," Moreno orders before dismissing the men who dragged me in here. They're replaced by Moreno's guards. "Now, if you'll join me in the courtyard, I have a little something waiting for us."

One of the guards shoves his gun between my shoulder blades. A little encouragement to follow their boss. We walk down an open-air hallway with tall, arched ceilings. It would be beautiful if evil didn't permeate every inch of the place.

Moreno approaches an archway and stops walking. When I look into the center courtyard, my stomach turns. Natalie is naked. She's been positioned on her hands and knees and restrained to a bench.

"Your submissive is a stunning woman." His eyes never leave what's mine.

"What the fuck?" I roar.

"Alex?" Natalie pulls against her restraints, trying to look behind her.

"It's me. I'm here." My heart feels as though it's being ripped from my chest.

Moreno strolls over to Natalie and runs his fingers up her spine. "Sit him down. Struggle, and her punishment will be worse."

The guards firmly grasp each of my arms and force me onto a hard wooden bench, positioning me to face Natalie from behind. Dread fills me as I realize I'm about to witness whatever evil intentions Moreno has in store for her. Moreno positions himself in front of Natalie and begins stroking her hair.

She flinches and attempts to avoid his touch. Rage builds within me. Suddenly, Moreno bends down to pick up an object. I can't see what it is until it's flying through the air, producing a deafening crack that echoes throughout the courtyard.

"No," I yell and jump from my seat. The guards grab me, shoving me back down.

"You've just added another lash," he says with a maniacal laugh.

Natalie's never experienced a whip. She doesn't like pain. Yes, she's received punishments, but never at the hands of an animal. I can't let him do this. She's pregnant. "Punish me instead of her."

"That would be too easy. My *mascota* earned her punishment and will accept every lash. Won't you?" He leans close to her neck and nips at her ear.

"Yes, Master." Natalie's voice is small.

Hearing her call him *Master* makes my body shudder violently.

Without further delay, he flicks his wrist, and the tail of the whip soars through the air. It lands with a crack across Natalie's upper back. The impact reverberates through her body.

"One," she says through tears.

Again, he wields his whip. A second lash marks Natalie's perfect skin.

"Two," she chokes out.

Moreno doesn't stop until he reaches ten strikes, each delivered with the same intensity as the last. Natalie's back, upper thighs, and ass are now crisscrossed with angry welts. Thankfully, he hasn't drawn blood, but that does little to stop her cries that echo throughout the courtyard. I can barely contain my own tears as I witness her pain. I can't let my feelings get the best of me. I have to stay focused and keep a clear head, no matter how difficult it may be.

He removes the restraints from Natalie's wrists and ankles. "Kneel," he commands.

Gingerly, Natalie slides off the bench. Each move looks like agony. She turns in my direction, only sparing me a quick glance, but it's enough time for me to see the tears pouring down her face. Then, like a dutiful submissive, she lowers to her knees.

Moreno stands beside her while he addresses me. "*Mascota* did not understand her place when we first became acquainted." He strokes her hair. "However, she appears to be a quick learner and has since pleased her new Master."

"You will never be her master," I growl through clenched teeth.

He fists Natalie's hair, forcing her to look at him.

"Who is your Master?"

"You are, Master." Natalie's voice shakes.

He pushes her head back down before looking at me with a cocky smile.

"As I was saying. You're probably wondering why you're here." He walks over to me. His leather cowboy boots click on the stone walkway. "You have information I want."

"What information could I possibly have that you want?"

The guard to my right lands a fist on my jaw, snapping my head to the side.

Natalie gasps.

"Let's try that again. You have information that I want, and you're going to get it for me."

"I'm listening." I meet his stare, not showing any of the fear threatening to suffocate me.

"I want Solonik and Federov's files." He turns his back on me, returning to Natalie. "He and his minions have been getting in the way of business and making my life difficult lately. You are going to help me take them down."

"And why would I help you?"

Once again, he grabs Natalie's hair, pulling her to her feet. "Because if you don't. She'll disappear, and you'll never see her again."

Natalie's terrified green eyes meet mine. I want to run to her. Console her. Promise her everything will be okay, but I can't. I need to play this carefully, or we're fucked for sure.

"If you expect me to cooperate, I need your word that she'll remain untouched."

Moreno drags his finger between her breasts and down her abdomen. Natalie tenses, and I give her a slight shake of my head, trying to warn her not to flinch. Not to give him any reason to deliver punishment to her abdomen. She can't let on that she's trying to protect her stomach and the life growing inside.

My brave girl fights through her fear and remains still despite having Moreno's hands on her. My eyes zero in on where his hand hovers. If he touches her, I'll cut his hands off myself.

"As much as I'm dying to taste her." He licks his lips. "I will guarantee she remains untouched as long as you get me what I want."

I don't trust Moreno or his word, but it's the only assurance I have right now.

"We have a deal. I'll get you whatever you want."

Natalie

Knowing Alex was behind me, watching me stripped naked and whipped by this monster, split my heart in two. I didn't want to give this bastard my tears, but the pain was unbearable, and I couldn't stop them from falling.

I hate being naked in front of all these men. Silverio's hands on me as he drags his perfectly manicured finger down the front of my body, lower and lower, make me sick. Alex shakes his head, a subtle warning for me not to move.

The baby.

Pulling from a strength hidden deep within, I force myself to remain poised, never breaking the connection of my Dominant's determined stare.

I don't want Alex to work with Silverio, even if it's just a means to buy us some time. I understand his reasoning, but I hate the proud look on Silverio's face. Now, I can only hope that he'll hold up his end of the bargain. But those hopes are quickly dashed when he pulls something from his pocket.

"Every *mascota* needs a collar so they don't get lost." Silverio wraps the piece of leather around my neck and fastens it with a click. Reaching into his pocket again, he pulls out a thin chain that he attaches to the collar. He tests the leash, giving it a light tug. With Silverio in front of me, I can't see Alex. But I can hear his growl from where he sits. "Come, *mascota*. Time to eat."

Silverio pulls the leash like I'm an animal, leading me away from Alex. I catch one last glance at him over my shoulder until we turn a corner, and he's out of sight. We keep walking through the estate, most of which appears to be open-air, a feature that would be appealing if we weren't in the middle of hell. Finally, we turn into what appears to be a small dining room. In the center is a table set for one. My captor sits in the chair and pulls my leash, forcing me to kneel on the floor next to him.

Within seconds, a young girl wearing a tiny white lace dress carries out a plate of food, which she sets on the table in front of Silverio. She's so young, she can't be more than fourteen or fifteen. It appears she's been here a while. She's already trained to keep her head down, her body almost folded in on itself.

The girl rounds the table and gasps when she spots me on the floor. I meet her eyes, offering a small smile, hoping in some way to comfort her. Silverio clears his throat loudly, startling the child, who scurries away.

Without a word, he picks up the fork and knife, cuts into the juicy steak on his plate, and takes a bite. He takes his time before cutting a second piece and bringing the fork to my mouth. My stubbornness says to resist that I'm not some animal to be fed on the floor. But I have to think of my baby first. They need nourishment, so despite my reservations, I open my mouth and take the offered food.

"Good girl," he croons and then offers me another bite. This time, it's vegetables.

After I swallow, he holds a glass of water to my lips. I hate how much I enjoy the cool liquid that slides down my throat. The remainder of the meal continues in the same fashion. Silverio takes a few bites, and when he chooses, he offers some to me. It's degrading to be treated like an animal, but each time I open my mouth to accept the food, I remind myself I'm doing this for my baby.

As soon as he finishes, the young girl returns, clearing his empty plate.

"Get up."

I struggle to get to my feet. My legs are numb from kneeling for so long. Silverio doesn't allow me to work out the pins and needles. He's already on the move, pulling me along behind him.

We retrace our steps until we come to a grand staircase. Silverio takes the steps quickly, and I struggle to keep up. Then, we walk down a long hallway lined with doors on both sides until we stop at the last entrance. He doesn't have to open it for me to know where we're going—his bedroom.

Inside, the room is dark and soulless, just like its inhabitants. Being alone with a madman makes my heart pound. I fight the fear that threatens to paralyze me. Looking around, I quickly search for anything that can be used as a weapon. For any possible means of escape. It comes as no surprise there's nothing. Silverio wastes no time stripping his clothes before walking over to me and nuzzling his face in my neck.

"All evening, I've imagined how delicious you'll taste. Pity I gave Alejandro my word that I wouldn't touch you, for now." He snickers before grabbing the end of the leash.

I follow him around the bed, where I see a pillow and blanket on the floor. He leans down and attaches the leash to a lock.

"I can't risk my *mascota* getting away overnight."

As though this scenario is normal, he crawls into bed and, using a remote control, turns off the lights, leaving the room in complete darkness. I feel around on the floor until I find the blanket. It may be thin, but it covers my nakedness—a small amount of comfort.

Lying down, the silence of the night is suffocating. When I close my eyes, images of the past few days play like a movie.

Timur being shot. His dead body was left lying in a ditch.

Alex knocked unconscious. His lifeless body dragged away.

My relief at seeing Alex alive and my heartache when I saw him restrained. Knowing he had to watch Moreno whip me and hear me call him master.

And the worst horror of all was being injected with an unknown drug and not knowing if it harmed my baby. If their life ended before they even had a chance to live.

I wrap my arms around my stomach and cry until sleep pulls me under.

We've been at Moreno's compound for two weeks. I haven't laid eyes on Natalie since the first night we got here. My new routine is ingrained in my being, my existence reduced to that of a prisoner held in a metal box. Holes have been drilled along the top of the walls. They serve as both ventilation and lighting.

It's almost a relief each day when the guards come for me and shackle my ankles. Although the desert heat is scorching, I relish the minutes I'm outside walking from my cell to the concrete building that I've figured out is their tech headquarters.

Once inside, I'm deposited in a tiny room with nothing more than a metal table and a chair. My shackles are locked on the chair's legs, ensuring I don't challenge the guards or attempt an escape. Like all the other buildings, there are no windows.

The light source is a lone bulb dangling from a frayed wire on the ceiling. In direct contrast is a state-of-the-art laptop that sits on the table. I've spent hours trying to access Maxim and Nicholai's files. Unfortunately, nothing I'm doing is working. The security codes have all been changed again.

"Fuck," I yell and slam my fists on the table.

The guard throws the door open. "What's going on in here?"

I run my fingers through my filthy, matted hair. "Where's your boss?"

"Do you have the files?"

"I want to see him."

I'm certain Moreno's patience is running thin. I need to see Natalie. I have to know he's holding to our agreement. That she's unharmed.

"Until I see him, I stop working."

"*El Tomador* doesn't take well to demands."

"I don't take well to not seeing Natalie."

He leaves the room without another word—the lock clicks into place. I drop my head into my hands. I've been trying to keep it together, trying to stay level-headed, but who am I kidding? Natalie's in the hands of a madman who's threatened to sell her to the highest bidder.

I'm locked out of the encrypted files and unable to deliver the promised information. My plan to access the files and leave Dimitri a message has proved futile. Timur was the only one who knew what happened, and now he's dead.

No one knows where we are or who's holding us captive—no rescue is coming.

I'm Natalie's Dominant, the one responsible for her safety. But look at me. Look at what I've been reduced to. A chained-up prisoner helpless to do anything. It's my fault we're in this situation and may never get out. I'm slipping into a familiar black hole of depression.

After I finish berating myself, I do the only thing I can. I get back on the laptop and keep trying to access the files. The one thing I know is that Dimitri can see all the attempts I'm making.

Although I don't know whether my continued failures will help their efforts to locate the source or if it's wasting their time, sending them on yet another wild goose chase. It doesn't matter. I have to keep trying. I'm hanging on by a thread to the only hope I have left.

Not having a window, I don't know how much time has passed before the door is wrenched open. Like every day, I'm released from the chair and brought outside. The sun hangs low along the horizon, giving a much-needed break from the brutal desert heat. I'm ready for the daily trading of one cell for another. But instead of heading the usual way, the guards lead me in the opposite direction. Today, we stop at a building on the outskirts of the property.

The door opens with a creak, and I find myself standing in a room resembling a nightclub. The walls are dark charcoal, and the lights are set low. My skin prickles from the evil permeating the space. Like all the other buildings, there are no windows, yet the air is crisp and cool from the air conditioning vents in the ceiling.

At the far end of the room is a large stage that's currently empty. The reality of what happens in this room sickens me. This place is where men, women, and children are sold to the highest bidder. On auction nights, each attendee has a private booth with a door and walls high enough to ensure they remain anonymous.

But anonymity isn't mandatory. If the guests are comfortable, they are free to leave their booths to socialize with one another. This place is exactly how Moreno's undercover buyers described it.

As we walk toward the stage, I notice the doors on the booths are open, and I glance inside. There's a leather armchair with a small table next to it. Hanging on the wall is a flat-screen monitor. Each booth we pass has the same setup. At the end of the rows, I see Moreno sitting in his black leather chair. He acts like a king sitting on his throne overlooking my submissive, who's kneeling at his feet, The collar still around her neck and the leash clipped to the wall.

"Alejandro," he says, dragging out each syllable. "Come join me."

Each time he utters my name in his native tongue, it fuels my desire to tear his heart from his chest. A heart that I'm not convinced exists. My hands, which the guards have left out of cuffs, ball into fists. The only thing that stops me is knowing that even if I could get my hands on Moreno, the guards will kill Natalie before I could get the job done.

I can't take my eyes off Natalie, scanning her body to ensure she's unharmed and willing her to look up at me. But she remains still. Her eyes never leave the floor in front of her.

"Glad you could join us today. Please have a seat." He motions to a chair across from him.

I sit, my eyes remaining fixed on Natalie.

"Why is she naked?"

"My *mascota* is training for when you fail, and she's sold." Moreno stares at me. His black eyes are empty of all humanness. "It's a pity she's already used. She would've brought in top dollar. However, she'll still command a high price with her body and excellent obedience skills."

Rage burns hot, and despite the consequences, I lunge at him. I don't even make it to my feet before his guards push me back down. The click of guns being readied to shoot fills the otherwise silent room.

"Please don't hurt him," Natalie screams.

"And what are you willing to do to keep him safe?"

"Do not answer him," I warn, but she ignores me.

"I'll do whatever you demand, Master. Just please don't hurt him."

"Come closer to your Master, *mascota*." Natalie crawls to him, and he pets her hair, making my stomach turn. "Have you made any progress with your task?"

"Not yet. Their security has been upgraded. It locked me out. Let me send them a message. We both know they'll never pinpoint the source. I'll demand they give me the files." As hard as I try, I can't hide the desperation in my voice.

Moreno laughs. "Do you think I'm stupid? Even if I allowed you to contact them, I have no reason to believe they'd hand over that information. Tomorrow, this room will be filled with men who wish to sample my merchandise. By the end of the weekend, they'll be ready to pay whatever price I demand for the opportunity to own one of my products."

"And what does that have to do with us?" I don't know why I asked. I already know the intention of his thinly veiled threat.

"I plan to show off my latest acquisition. A beautiful slave who'll be available to purchase by the end of the weekend."

"I'm doing everything I said I would. You agreed not to lay a finger on her."

Moreno stands, rising to his full height before me. "This is my kingdom. I'm the only one who makes the demands here." He taps the gold watch on his wrist. "Your time is just about up, Alejandro. My little *mascota* will be the star of the show. By the end of the weekend, men will be willing to do anything I ask to have a chance at owning her."

Grabbing Natalie's hair, he pulls her to her feet. That's when I see how thin and pale she is.

"Feed her. She'll be useless to you if she's not nourished and able to perform in your little show. Nobody wants to buy a sick slave."

Natalie doesn't look up. Doesn't react to my words. It's as if she's given up.

Don't quit on me.

Keep fighting, baby girl.

"This is my kingdom," he reminds me. "And *mascota's* part of it now. She'll eat when and if I choose."

Motioning to one of the guards, he hands Natalie's leash off, instructing him to return her to his room. His eyes never leave Natalie's body as she walks away. When he turns back to me, the sick bastard adjusts his erection. We don't scene in public for this reason. I won't tolerate anyone looking at or getting off on what's mine.

For now, I'm forced to tamp down my rage. Forced to offer something I never thought I'd do, but this is for our survival. It's bad enough that men will look at her and lust for her, but I'll be damned if I allow anyone other than me to touch her. If sceneing in public is part of his twisted plan, *I* will be the Master of it. Natalie may hate me for it. But right now, I don't see any other option.

"I'll do the scene." I'm not asking for permission. "I know her body better than anyone. If I'm her Master, her body will respond to me. Your clients will get a show they'll never forget."

Several long minutes pass while he paces back and forth, considering my proposition.

"Fine," he concedes. "You will do it, but it will be a scene of my design." He stops in front of me. "And if you don't follow it exactly, I will step in and finish the job for you."

Without any further conversation, he turns and strides to the exit.

I'm escorted back to my cell and left to worry about what he'll require of me tomorrow.

Viktor

I'm in the tech room pouring through the data with Dimitri and his team. We're looking for any clue or any weakness in the IP encryption when I get the text I've been waiting for. Pushing my chair out, I get to my feet quickly. "Timur's awake."

The men look up from their screens, knowing this could be the break we've all been waiting for.

"Does he have any intel?" Dimitri asks.

"I'll let you know as soon as I find out," I call as I hurry out of the room.

I'm more hopeful than I've been in weeks. I pray Timur has the information we need and that we're not too late. I break into a sprint and don't stop until I get to the medical wing of the compound. The door to Timur's room is open. Maxim's sitting at his bedside, where the two men are talking quietly.

Timur looks up as I walk into the room. "I'm sorry, Viktor. I did everything I could to stop them."

"I know." I take the seat next to Maxim. "Can you tell me what happened?"

Although Timur's weak, he recounts the events from the night they were ambushed. He explains that he was pulled over by *Politseyskiy*.

"I found it odd," he struggles to speak. "We were cleared to travel undeterred." Timur stops to catch his breath.

Maxim continues for him. "We got the description of the officer. I have already dispatched a team to extract information from him. And after we get it, he will be made an example of."

"When the second car pulled up, I knew we were in trouble," Timur adds.

I can see how taxing this is on him, but I need him to tell me every detail he remembers.

"The officer made me get out of the car. I slid the gun back, hoping Alex had enough time to get it, but we were outnumbered. They grabbed him and Natalie so fast." He closes his eyes as if he's reliving that night. "I fought hard, boss," he says, looking between Maxim and me. "Then they shot me. I was in and out of consciousness but didn't open my eyes or move. I let them believe I was dead. Then, I heard them threatening to kill Natalie," Timur says, his voice pained.

My blood pressure spikes. Natalie is my responsibility to protect. If we don't get them back, I'll never forgive myself for not fighting harder to accompany them.

"Do you remember anything else?"

"I don't know if it was real or a dream. But I thought I heard them mention *El Tomador*."

I freeze. Silverio Moreno. If Timur heard them correctly, we have a clusterfuck of epic proportions on our hands.

"You did well." Maxim lays his hand over Timur's, reassuring him. "You did real good."

"They were so happy talking about their baby." He closes his eyes again. "Natalie was showing me pictures—" Timur's voice trails off as he drifts to sleep.

"I'm going to find them and bring them home." I'll move heaven and hell to bring them back.

Pulling my cell phone out, I shoot a text to Dimitri.

Me: I need all the recent intel on Moreno's operations.

Dimitri: Fuck. We're on it now.

Maxim and I leave Timur's room, quietly closing the door.

"Boss—"

"Do not say anything more." Maxim knows as well as I do the danger Alex and Natalie are in. "I have some calls to make," he says as he walks away.

Natalie

I wasn't sure how much time had passed since I last saw Alex. It wasn't until he was brought into the auction room the other day that I had confirmation he was still alive. I was so relieved to see him, although he looked awful. He's still wearing the pants and polo shirt he wore the day of the ultrasound, but now his clothes are torn and dirty. And he's so thin and pale. Dark circles weigh down his blue eyes, which have lost their usual sparkle.

Seeing him in that condition was heartbreaking, but I'm holding onto the knowledge he's still alive.

Thankfully, Silverio was generous today and chose to feed me. I don't know how much longer I could've gone without food. This forced starvation can't be good for my baby if they are still alive. Stop, Natalie. If I let myself go down that rabbit hole, I'm not sure I'll make it back out.

I've spent most of the day in my capture's office. Silverio's been busy taking phone calls and doing things on his computer. He's made sure my back is to the desk while I kneel at his feet, so I've been unable to see anything. A knock on the door breaks the silence.

"Enter," he calls.

I hear footsteps but don't see who's come in.

"Get up." He jerks my leash, forcing me to stand.

I lose my balance from moving so quickly and stumble. Before I hit the floor, Moreno catches me, pulling me onto his lap. My body stiffens as he brushes my hair aside and licks my neck.

"You smell so good, *moscata*. I should forget the deal I made and fuck you right now. But you're in luck. I have more important things to do." He shoves me off his lap.

A guard is waiting in front of his desk, and next to him is the same girl who serves Moreno's meals.

"Take these two back to my room," he orders the guard before turning to me. "You will prepare your body for your debut tonight. *esclava*, you will help."

"Yes, Master." Her voice is no more than a whisper.

"Behave, *mascota,* or you will suffer." He unlocks my leash from his desk and hands it to the guard. "When they are ready. Escort them to the club."

"Yes, sir."

We trail behind the guard as he leads us back to Silverio's bedroom. Once we're inside, he faces me and tugs the leash tight. His eyes take in every inch of my body.

"I'd like to fuck every hole you have. Too bad the boss said you're off-limits."

I'm relieved when he leaves the room and locks the door. For the first time since I was brought here, I'm alone in a room without Silverio. It's just the girl and me.

"What's your name?" Her stormy blue-grey eyes dart around the room. "It's okay. You can talk to me. I won't hurt you." I smile, trying to reassure her.

"Amelia," she whispers.

"That's a pretty name. My name's Natalie."

She looks at me briefly before returning her gaze to the floor.

"I'll draw you a bath, miss. We mustn't waste time." She hurries into the bathroom, where she begins to run the water.

Although she hasn't spoken much, I hear a distinct accent. "Are you from Australia?"

She nods.

"Do you have family looking for you?"

She shakes her head.

"Get in, please," she says.

I step into the coconut and vanilla-scented water. For a moment, I'm distracted from our conversation as I allow my stressed body to slide into the warm water. Relaxing, if only for a few minutes, is a luxury.

I don't know how long we'll be alone to talk. And although I hate throwing so many questions at her, I want to get as many answers as possible. "How old are you?"

"Fifteen," Amelia whispers as she dunks me under the water to wet my hair.

My heart shatters. She's the same age Jelena was when she was taken. Where is this girl's family? How did this happen to her? What horrors has she endured while being held captive by this monster?

She helps me wash and rinse my hair before giving me a razor and instructing me to prepare my body.

"Prepare my body? For what?"

Ignoring my question, she instructs, "When you're done with the razor, I'll give it back to the guard." Amelia looks up at the camera as if to warn me not to do anything stupid.

I finish my task and step out of the tub. Amelia offers me a fluffy towel, which I gladly accept. Besides the blanket at bedtime, this is the only time I've had something to cover my naked body.

"Do you have a family?"

"My parents died in a car accident. Since I didn't have any other family, I was put into a foster home. The family I lived with had a son," she hesitates, "I hated it there and ran away. For a while, I lived on the streets. One night, a man grabbed me." Her voice catches on a sob. "I should've stayed in the foster home."

I reach out to embrace her, but she jumps away from my touch. "Everything's going to be okay. We're going to get out of here. My fiancé will make sure of that."

"We shouldn't be talking." She puts her walls back up and turns away from me.

Realizing I've pushed her enough, for now, I grab the comb that's on the counter and carefully work to untangle the knots in my hair.

"We're almost out of time," Amelia says, grabbing the razor and taking it out of the bathroom.

I follow her back into the bedroom and watch as she knocks on the door. It opens a crack just enough for her to hand the razor over to the guard. Then she hurries across the room and disappears into Silverio's closet. When she reemerges, she has a white silk robe draped over her arm and a pair of silver heels in her hand.

"Put this on." She holds out the robe for me to slide my arms into.

The sensation of the silk against my skin feels foreign. It takes me a few minutes to become reacquainted with the feel of clothing before I'm able to tie it closed. Amelia helps me fasten the straps on the silver heels.

"It's time to go." She returns to the door and knocks.

A few seconds later, the door opens wide, and Amelia scurries down the hall. It's only now that I'm alone with the guard that I allow fear to creep into my consciousness. What have I just readied my body for?

The guard attaches my leash and escorts me out of the house to a waiting car.

"Where are we going?"

"You'd be smart to shut up. Unless you wish to meet *Tomador's* whip."

I shut my mouth, holding back my next question. I never want to feel the sting of a whip again.

The sun is setting over the horizon as we drive past all the warehouse buildings and stop outside Moreno's club.

"Let's go." The guard grabs my arm. Without a center console, he easily pulls me across the seat.

Music and men's voices drift from inside the building when he opens the backdoor. Fear, as I've never experienced, hits me. We're out of time. Moreno's going to sell me. My legs threaten to give out.

The guard sees my hesitation and tugs on my leash, forcing me through the backdoor and into a new level of hell.

Last night was a nightmare. The heat in my room was oppressive and coupled with my fears about our fate, I couldn't sleep. Every time I closed my eyes and tried to drift off, the horrors of what might happen tonight jolted me back to reality. I'm awake and sitting up against one of the concrete walls when a guard brings a breakfast tray.

Today's meal is slightly more substantial than usual. I devour the oatmeal, almost licking the bowl clean before drinking the water. I need all the strength I can muster to get Natalie and me through the night.

When the guard returns to collect me, I'm prepared. I anticipate being led on the usual walk to the tech building. Instead, we veer off and enter one of the warehouse buildings. As we walk down the hall, I hear the cries of innocent victims coming from behind the closed doors. The depravity of this place only strengthens my resolve to get us out of here alive and then burn this hellhole to the ground.

We stop in an open shower room where the guard unchains my hands and feet. With the stakes so high, Moreno and his minions must feel confident that I won't attempt an escape.

"Shower and put those on." He points to a pile of black clothes folded off to the side.

The water is cool, but I don't care. It's been weeks since I last took a shower. Being able to wash the grime from my body is a relief. After my shower, I find a thin, tattered towel that I use to dry myself. Then, I dress in black pants, a black button-down shirt, and the black boots left for me.

I expect to be restrained, so it comes as a surprise when my guard motions for me to walk without them. Even with the sun setting, it's still a long walk across the facility's grounds in the scorching heat. As we get closer to the club building, I see there's already a line of cars, all with tinted windows lined up. Inside the high-end vehicles are men who'll be in attendance tonight. From reading Maxim's files, I know that some of the world's wealthiest men, from both the private and government sectors, attend these functions.

One at a time, the cars are brought around the side of the building to a special entrance, ensuring each man retains their anonymity. We enter through a back door and walk down a deserted hallway until we come to an office.

"*El Tomador* is expecting you."

I enter the office with my shoulders back and head held high. I've already been apprised of what's expected of me tonight. And as hard as it's going to be, I refuse to cower in fear in front of Moreno. Tonight, the tables will turn. Moreno may think he's in control because he gave orders. But on that stage, I'm Natalie's Dominant. It's me who's in control of the scene and her safety. That puts me in a power position.

"Sit, Alejandro."

His voice makes my skin crawl, but I keep my composure. Taking a seat, I spread my legs and cross my arms over my chest. I'm in full Dom mode and am prepared to beat Moreno at his own game.

"I take it you're ready to entertain my guests this evening?"

The only response he gets is a slight shrug.

"Let's get right to this then." He closes his laptop, giving me his full attention. "There are a few things we didn't discuss at our last meeting. You are to remain silent during tonight's scene, and you will wear this." He reaches into his drawer and tosses something at me. I hold up the black hood with cutouts for my eyes and mouth. "We don't want your identity to spoil things, do we?"

I ball the hood in my fist. I'd hoped Natalie would at least be reassured that I was behind the torture. This disguise and the order to stay silent are going to change my plan. Think Alex. I have to find another way to let her know it's me. It's the only way it'll be bearable for her.

Moreno picks up his phone and makes a call. "Bring it in now."

A guard appears carrying a black lacquered box. Almost reverently, he sets it on the desk in front of Moreno before leaving the room.

On the top of the box is an intricate etching of a pewter dagger spearing a red crown. Carved into the crown is the name *Moreno*. What's inside the still-closed box is something that many tell tales about but few have ever seen.

"It's time for a history lesson, Alejandro." Moreno places his hands on the lid. "This box has been passed down in my family for many generations, each having carved their initials inside." Then, he opens the top and lifts out the infamous dagger.

My eyes land on the metal as it glints in the light. Seeing it before me gives credibility to everything I've been told.

"I see you've heard the stories." His laugh is sinister. "You will be one of the few outside the Moreno family to have the privilege of using this."

Moreno continues schooling me on the history and features of his implement of torture. The knife has a contoured, hand-carved walnut hilt with bronzed edging. The hand-forged blade boasts an intricate carving of two ravens perched on a castle's turret—the Moreno family crest.

"For many generations, my family has enjoyed carving the skin of our slaves. Tonight, you will give my guests what they desire. The tears and screams of a slave.

And if you do not perform to my liking, *I* will replace you as *mascota's* Master tonight."

I won't allow that to happen. I'll give Moreno the show he's demanding and deal with the repercussions when we make it out alive.

I'm locked in a holding room backstage. Knowing men are gathering in the audience, ready to purchase a human. An innocent person who they will take pleasure in maiming and torturing until their life is ended makes me sick.

I've always supported Maxim's efforts to take down trafficking rings and rescue the victims. But being here and experiencing this personally has given me a different perspective. When we get out of here, I need to do more than provide a network to transfer information. I plan to step up and take an active role in wiping these animals from the face of the earth.

The monitor on the wall of my holding room comes to life. Moreno sits on his throne in the front as a man steps onto the stage.

"Before tonight's auction, our host has a special performance. So please, sit back and enjoy the show."

The lights dim, and the curtains open. A masked man dressed in all black holds the end of Natalie's leash. He leads her onto the stage, where a large Saint Andrew's cross is set up. He comes to a stop in front of it.

Despite the circumstances, I can't help but admire how beautiful Natalie is wearing a white silk robe and high-heeled shoes. Her long blonde curls hang loose down her back. My girl is so brave. She doesn't cringe at her surroundings. Instead, she stands proud and unafraid, even though, unbeknownst to her, she's the innocent lamb being prepared for slaughter.

"Strip," the man commands.

Despite the terror I know she must feel, she doesn't hesitate. Pulling at the knot, her robe opens, revealing her naked body. My stomach turns when I hear the catcalls and whistles from the sick bastards hiding in their booths. But I refuse to take my eyes off Natalie. The only outward sign of her nerves is the slight tremble of her hands.

A second man steps onto the stage and takes the robe before quickly exiting. Then, the hooded man unclips her collar and sets the leash on a table next to the apparatus. He pushes her from behind, forcing her to step up to the cross.

The camera view switches, allowing me to see Natalie as she's bound, facing the cross. I can only imagine what she's thinking, knowing this position is typically associated with being whipped. She'd be correct, but she doesn't know that tonight will be much worse. After she's fully restrained, the man steps up to her. In a move that makes my pulse spike, he presses his body against hers.

"Open," he commands.

Natalie opens her mouth, and a ball gag is shoved in and fastened behind her head. One of her hard limits is being gagged. I know she's going to hate it, and she may hate me for it. But it was my one demand for tonight. What's about to happen is going to be torture. The gag will give her something to bite down on. To absorb her screams—something to help us both get through this. Before he steps away, he secures a blindfold over her eyes.

With a loud squeal of metal, the door to my room is wrenched open.

"Let's go."

I'm led onto the stage and am standing behind my sub. Natalie's body is now shaking—she's terrified. I want to reach out and caress her. To tell her it's me, and she's going to get through this, but I can't. Doing so will give Moreno the excuse he's looking for to step in and take my place. If I don't approach this with a cold, heartless exterior, I'll never make it—the consequences of which I won't be able to live with.

The hooded man returns with the black box in his hands. He removes the lid in front of me, and I take the dagger out. In my hand, I hold a weapon, a symbol of power passed down through generations of traffickers. It's been used to mutilate the bodies of countless people for nothing more than the pleasure of the sadistic man wielding it. It's a symbol of the worst humanity has to offer.

Tonight, I'm being forced to use it. Not to torture or kill but to mar the flesh of my submissive. It sickens me, but I have no choice. This is buying us a little more time for me to continue searching for any weakness, any chink in the armor. Anything to get us out of here.

The room is deadly silent. Straining to see through the darkness of the club, the only thing I can make out is the silhouette of Moreno sitting in his chair. I don't need to see his face to know he's waiting for me to screw up so he can take my place on this stage. But the joke's on him. I won't be making any mistakes.

I turn back to face Natalie and lift the dagger, holding it flat. She doesn't move as I drag the cold blade down her back. Turning it, I press the sharp edge against her perfect skin. It's her first hint at what's to come. Without putting too much pressure, I make my first cut—her body tenses.

I continue my task, making shallow cuts that, once they heal, won't scar. It does little to lessen the pain she's suffering each time I drag the knife's edge down her back. Time loses all meaning as I continue making cuts.

Moreno's voice pierces the silence, "I want to see blood. Hear her scream."

His comment is followed by the whistles of the cowards hiding behind the walls.

"Cut her deeper, or I'll come up and show you how it's done."

Natalie shakes her head back and forth violently. The words she's trying to say are garbled by the gag. I lift the dagger to the area by her shoulder blade and press, slicing her skin open. Her blood-curdling scream fills the room, and cheers erupt from the audience. This is the show they came to see.

Movement from the side of the stage catches my eye. Once again, the hooded man is walking toward me. This time, with a white cloth over his hands. It's my cue. One more cut, baby girl. This torture's almost over. Parallel to the deep slice I made, I drag the dagger down her body.

Rivulets of blood follow its path. Her screams fill the room again, shattering the remaining pieces of my heart. Turning, I place the dagger in the man's hands. The white fabric soaks up the blood, turning it red. My stomach turns, and I nearly vomit. The guard sees my disgust and snickers exiting the stage.

Natalie's out of energy. Out of endurance. But we aren't done yet. The biggest challenge is still ahead of us. I have to fuck her on stage, knowing Moreno and his buyers are watching. This disgusts me. It's a part of our relationship we never wanted on public display.

When she finds out it was me behind all this—cutting her and fucking her in front of an audience it might be the very thing that causes her to walk away from us. Losing her will ruin me, but I have to do this. It's the only way I can keep her alive.

My body brushes against her mangled back, and she hisses in pain. I bring my hands up and release the restraints from her wrists and then her ankles. Taking her hands, I place them on the center of the cross and push on her back, bending her over. Then I open the button and unzip my pants, leaving them hanging low on my hips.

When she hears the zipper, she tries to stand—she knows what's about to happen. But I force her back down. Even with the gag in place, I hear her crying as she shakes her head back and forth. She thinks she's about to be raped by an unknown evil man. Please forgive me.

Fisting my erection, I take the final steps forward and impale her in one hard thrust. She cries out from the violent intrusion. I close my eyes and put all thoughts of where we are and who's watching out of my head. I need to fuck her hard and fast to end this charade.

"Take the gag off. I want to hear her scream," Moreno calls from the audience.

Leaning over her back, I grab the strap of the gag. "I'm so sorry, baby girl," I whisper. Natalie freezes. "Keep fighting and screaming. Do not let on you know it's me."

Our lives depend on her continued fight. After discarding the gag on the floor, I pull out and thrust in hard. I don't stop the punishing pace as Natalie screams and thrashes about, forcing me to hold her in place.

No longer is she fighting against me. Now, she's fighting with me.

Tonight isn't about her pleasure. The men in the room don't care if she's allowed to orgasm. Giving her a release is the least I can do. Reaching around her waist, I find her clit. She shakes her head back and forth, yelling for me to stop, but I don't. I know her body and how to make it respond to me, even against her will. I rub fast, hard circles while I pump in and out of her.

Regardless of our circumstances, I'm right there with her. She's fighting it, but her body is readying itself for an orgasm. I pinch her clit hard. Natalie screams as her body jolts with the force of her orgasm. Her inner walls squeeze my cock tight, and I let go, spilling inside her.

Natalie falls limp in my arms.

Applause fills the room.

Fuck, what did I just do?

I pull my pants up with my free hand and then lift her into my arms, cradling her against my chest. Then, I hurry off the stage. "Where can I bring her?" I ask the guard standing there, but he doesn't answer. I look around, panicked, but there's nowhere to go.

"Alejandro, very well done." Moreno appears backstage. "My guests are already asking how much she'll cost."

"Fuck you," I spit. "I need to take her somewhere for aftercare."

"I don't engage in aftercare with my pets."

"As long as I'm breathing, she's still mine." My eyes lock on his. "Where can I take her?"

"I will give you this only because you followed my instructions with your performance. Take them to a room," Moreno orders. "You have one hour."

We're led down a dark hallway. Natalie hasn't opened her eyes or moved. The guard pulls the door open, and I brush past him to go inside. The room is dark and dingy. A single lightbulb overhead offers a small amount of illumination. Across the room is a bed with a metal frame. Cuffs hang from both the headboard and footboard. I can't stop to think of the atrocities that occur in this room.

Using one hand, I pull back the blanket and lay Natalie down before ripping the hood off and looking around. There's a doorway without a door that leads to a small bathroom. Inside, I find a towel and washcloth, presumably Moreno's attempt at hospitality for his *guests*. Grabbing the cloth, I let the water in the tap run, hoping it gets warm, but it doesn't. I settle for cool.

When I return to bed, I find Natalie still passed out. I roll her onto her side and gently clean off her back, wiping away as much blood as possible. Then, I spread the towel on the mattress and carefully place her on her back. Leaving her once again, I rinse off the cloth. When I return, I wipe between her legs. When I pull the cloth away, it's covered in blood.

No. Oh my God. No.

I drop the washcloth onto the floor and crawl on the bed, pulling Natalie into my lap.

"baby girl, it's time to wake up," I say softly as I rock her back and forth. "Please wake up."

It feels like an eternity before she begins to stir in my arms.

"I'm here, baby girl." I kiss her forehead. "Everything's okay. I'm here."

"Alex? Is it really you?"

She cries in my arms as I stroke her hair gently.

"I'm here. You're safe," I whisper.

Unable to hold back any longer, my tears silently fall. I'm holding my whole world in my arms. But my heart is heavy knowing I've ended our unborn child's life tonight.

Several men burst into the room. "Time's up."

"It hasn't been an hour," I yell.

"And I care?" He reaches for Natalie.

"Get the hell away from her."

Natalie grabs onto me. "Please, Alex. Don't let them take me."

"Shut up, bitch," the hooded man snarls and reaches out to refasten the leash onto her collar.

"Get away from me." She slaps his hand.

"That was a mistake." He goes to grab her hair.

"Keep your fucking hands off her," I yell and shift my body, trying to keep her away from him.

The sound of the safety being taken off a gun rings in my ear. The cold metal presses against my head.

"I said time's up."

This time, I have no choice but to let her go.

She struggles with all her might.

"Natalie," I yell, getting her attention. "Stop fighting and go with them."

She looks at me, tears streaming down her face as she's dragged away. My eyes go to the blood dripping down her legs.

Then, with a final look over her shoulder, she whispers, "i love You."

I'm frozen on the edge of the bed, unable to move or speak as I watch her disappear.

Natalie

THE SKY IS DARK AND CLOUDY. THE ONLY ILLUMINATION COMES FROM lights that line the driveway leading back to Silverio's estate. My body is in agony, so I don't resist when the guard pulls my arm, forcing me out of the car. My torn flesh rips from the leather seats, causing another wave of pain to roll through me.

"You made quite an impression tonight, *mascota*," Silverio's slimy voice startles me.

I look up and find him leaning against a tree outside the entrance to his home. He's still wearing the suit he had on at the club, but his tie is loosened, and the first few buttons of his shirt are undone. The guard transfers ownership of the leash back to Silverio.

"*Gracias por devolver mi mascotita.*"

The guard nods before returning to the car and pulling away.

"I've received many lucrative offers to purchase you this evening. Seems you're in high demand." He runs his knuckles down my cheek."

"I'm not for sale."

"I'll let that indiscretion pass this time." He pulls my leash. My bare feet scrape on the pavement as I struggle to keep up with him. "On your knees, *mascota*," he commands once we're inside.

I'm sore and tired. My muscles scream in pain each time I miss a step as I crawl back to the bedroom. The scene tonight was grueling—unlike anything I've ever experienced.

All the while the man was cutting me, I silently cursed him. Wished he'd die for unleashing his violence on my body. Then, I heard him open his pants, and I knew I was about to be raped by one of Moreno's depraved men. Instead of wishing for my death, I imagined the many ways I could end his life.

Then the man leaned in and whispered to me.

Natalie

It took a second for my mind to accept it was really Alex. He insisted I keep fighting. Which wasn't hard to do because even though it was my Dominant, I didn't want to be fucked in a roomful of sick men. Men I knew were getting off on what was happening on that stage.

The fear and regret I heard in Alex's voice hurt so much more than the physical wounds. What he was doing was beyond his control. Alex is a puppet in Moreno's sick and twisted world. What he did was necessary to keep us alive.

Afterward, as Alex held me, he tried to hide that he was crying. His tears fell on my skin, betraying his secret. But then the men came too soon. They dragged me away from Alex before I got to talk to him. To tell him I knew none of it was his fault. That I didn't blame him. I only hope my silent declaration of love was enough.

Silverio drags me through his bedroom into his bathroom. The collar pulls tight around my neck as Silverio unclips the leash. Then, turning the shower on, he opens the glass door and pushes me in.

"Wash him off you. I don't want to smell another man on what's mine," he growls in disgust before storming out of the bathroom.

Reluctantly, I step under the water, knowing it'll sting the cuts on my back. And it does. Red-tinged water sluices down my body from the cuts on my back. From the amount of blood coming off my body, I can only imagine what my back must look like. I find a bottle of shower gel. It turns my stomach because it smells like Silverio. But it's all that's in here, and I don't want to waste the opportunity to clean up, so I squirt some into my hand and begin to wash. I wipe my hand between my legs, but when I pull it away, it's covered in fresh blood. I do it again and find more. This blood isn't from the cuts on my back. My hand flies out to the wall, steadying myself.

My baby.

Oh my God, there's so much blood.

I'm losing my baby.

As I watch the steady stream of red wash down the drain, a part of me dies along with the life inside me.

"I didn't think he had it in him," Silverio's eerie laugh startles me.

I look up at him and hope he sees the hate in my eyes. He's the monster responsible for this.

"He made you bleed. Maybe I'll keep him on after I sell you. Alejandro might prove useful in breaking in new acquisitions."

Silverio's words, coupled with the knowledge of what I'm losing, are too much. I vomit in the shower. My body retches until my stomach is empty, and I'm on my knees.

This is too much to handle, and my world goes black again.

Natalie

I DON'T KNOW HOW LONG I'VE BEEN OUT, BUT WHEN I WAKE, I'M chained to my *bed* on the floor of Silverio's suite. Sunlight streams in from the open window, letting me know a new day has dawned. Grief overcomes me. I wish I didn't wake up. Lowering my hand to my abdomen, I feel something unfamiliar—fabric. I'm wearing underwear.

"I cleaned and dressed you." Amelia kneels next to me. "I think you were injured in the scene last night. But when it didn't stop, Master believed it was your time of the month, and he doesn't like when a woman bleeds from *that*. You were also given a birth control shot last night, so Master isn't inconvenienced again."

My eyes fill with tears as I grab her hands. This time, she doesn't pull away.

"I'll get the guard to unlock you so you can go to the bathroom and change your —" She motions to the underwear.

As usual, the guard takes his time answering. "What do you want?"

Amelia's reply is so quiet I can't make out her words. The man pushes her out of the way and heads straight to me, unlocking the leash.

"Hurry up," he says gruffly.

I'm only given privacy in the bathroom because there's one door and nowhere to run. I use the toilet and change the pad, thankful for the little bit of humanness I've been allotted. After washing my hands, I work up the courage to look at my back.

Turning slightly to see my reflection in the mirror, I examine the marred flesh. Most of the shallow cuts have stopped bleeding and should heal without scarring. However, the two deeper wounds on my shoulder blade are red and angry. They look like they need stitches, but I don't think properly caring for my wounds is on Silverio's agenda.

The door flies open. "You've had enough time. Let's go."

He grabs my leash and returns me to my place on the floor, where I wait for a plate with food and a bottle of water. I look around for Amelia, but she's no longer in the room. My heart drops. I was hoping to have her company for a bit longer.

"*El Tomador* expects you to eat the lunch he's left," the man says as he reattaches my leash to the lock on the floor.

I nod, grateful for the food and for being allowed to feed myself.

Days pass without seeing Silverio. The only person I see is the guard who unlocks me twice daily to use the bathroom. The solitude is a welcome relief. The only person I wish was here is Alex. I need his arms to hold me. To grieve the loss of our baby together. This routine continues for the next week until the bleeding finally stops.

"Wake up, *mascota*." I'm kicked in the side.

Instead of opening my eyes to escape a nightmare, I wake to find I've been thrust back into the same one. Silverio stands above me, my leash in his hand.

"I'm told the inconvenience of your *condition* is finally over." He wears an evil smile.

As far as he's concerned, the bleeding was from an injury during the scene. I'll never tell him. Never allow him the opportunity to claim the victory that would come with knowing he killed my baby.

"Get up. We have work to do."

I don't give him the satisfaction of a reaction as I stand from the floor. Once I stopped bleeding, the small amount of coverage I had been allowed was taken from me. Once again, I'm paraded through the estate naked. Forced to endure the lustful stares of the guards we pass in the hallways. When we get to his office, I take my usual spot on my knees. Instead of going onto his computer or phone like usual, he spins his chair to face me and leans forward, resting his elbows on his spread legs.

"Look at me, *mascota*," Silverio commands.

I raise my eyes and meet his dark stare.

"Tomorrow will be an exciting night for us. Do you want to know what happens tomorrow?"

Not knowing what day it is gives me no reference for what tomorrow is. Either way, no, I don't want to know. I don't care what happens tomorrow. But if I don't play along and indulge him, I know I'll be punished.

"What happens tomorrow, Master?" I ask.

He runs his fingers through my hair before grabbing a fistful and tugging. "Tomorrow, while Alejandro watches, I will finally taste you and use every hole until I have my fill. And after you're done screaming my name, you'll take your place on my stage with the other *putas* to be sold."

"You can't do that," I yell. "You made a deal with Alex."

Silverio's hand strikes my face with a loud crack. Instantly, my cheek is on fire. I bring my hand up to cover it.

"Watch your mouth, *mascota*. Unless you'd like to experience my whip again?" He raises an eyebrow, watching for my decision.

I drop my shoulders and lower my gaze to the floor.

Knowing he's won, Silverio swivels his chair to face his laptop, turning it on before returning his attention to me.

"Your dominant failed. He didn't get me the information I wanted. Which means you are now mine to do with as I please."

The horror of his statement sends ice through my blood. First, he's going to rape me and then sell me. I'll never see Alex or my family again. I can't just let this happen. I have to do something.

"Master," I say quietly.

"What?"

"If it pleases you." I nearly choke on my words. "Would you keep me? Allow me to serve only you?"

If I'm not sold, Silverio will keep me here. It's the only chance I have of being rescued. His laugh fills the room.

"After I have my fill, I'll have no use for you. I have my sights set on a much younger slave to amuse me. Now shut up. I have work to do."

He hasn't said her name, but I know who he has his sights set on—Amelia.

I vow to myself that before he has the chance to lay his filthy hands on her, I'll find a way to kill him myself.

Alex

THE DAY IS IRRELEVANT. EACH BLENDS INTO THE NEXT AS IF THERE'S NO beginning or end. It's been nearly two weeks since I last saw Natalie. Since the night, I was forced to carve her body. Two weeks since my vicious claiming—the act that killed our unborn child.

It physically hurts knowing the heartache Natalie's experiencing right now—alone. I've demanded to see her, but my demands were met with refusals and beatings. There have been no other deviations from my daily routine.

Each day, I'm hauled to the tech building and chained to a chair, where I spend hours unsuccessfully trying to access Maxim's files. According to the clock on the computer screen, it's now twelve-thirty p.m. Moreno gave me until noon to deliver the information, and I failed. Our agreement has expired.

My time's up.

Leaning forward in my chair, I drop my head into my hands. I feel utterly hopeless. I pick up the laptop from the table and throw it at the metal wall.

"Fuck," I yell, my anguish echoing in the small room.

The laptop screen shatters. Shards of plastic pieces and electronics scatter across the floor. The guard throws the door open, slamming it against the wall. He looks around at the destroyed components of the laptop.

"You'll pay for that," he snarls and cuffs my hands.

I don't resist. There's no reason to fight anymore. My worst nightmare is about to happen tonight, and I have no way to stop it. Moreno's going to force me to watch as he rapes my fiancee. Then he's going to parade her across the stage and sell her to the highest bidder. It'll be as though Natalie never existed. She'll disappear. The future she deserves will be over. We'll never marry.

She won't get a second chance at becoming a mother. Instead, she'll be subjected to the twisted desires the sick fucks Moreno sells women to like. Rather than being treasured, she'll be repeatedly raped and tortured until her owner decides to put her out of her misery.

I don't want to live in a world without Natalie. My hope is Moreno kills me, too.

Finally, I'm dragged from the computer room. We go past the warehouse facilities to a building that sparks terror in my core—Moreno's club. Once inside, I'm put in a room similar to the one I was in the night of our scene. Except tonight, I won't be going out to Natalie. Instead, I'll watch Moreno do unspeakable things to her before he auctions her.

Alone and depressed, I slide my body down the wall. While I'm sitting on the floor, I reminisce about our relationship.

I came so close to not showing up at Fire and Ice that night. The last thing I wanted to do was babysit the girl who called the cops on my best friend. But my promise to Brandon ended up being the driving force behind why I went. I'll never forget my first glance at her from across the room.

God, she took my breath away. From our first touch, there was electricity between us. And she was so curious. Despite everything I'd previously thought, I was drawn to her. After that, I couldn't walk away.

The day she finally agreed to sign the contract and give a Dom/sub relationship a try was the first day I really started living again. And that silly expiration date. She insisted on it, but I knew that wouldn't be the end—it couldn't be. We were so good together.

I remember the look on her face when I proposed to her in Central Park—it had been the best day of my life. And just a few weeks later, the worst day of my life—when she safeworded.

I worked hard to fix myself and earn her trust again.

We were going to be parents.

We haven't had enough time together.

The lock clicks and the door opens. I don't have to look up to know Moreno and his guards have entered the room.

"You don't look so good, Alejandro," Moreno says with a sly smile.

When I don't respond, I'm kicked in the stomach, causing me to double over.

"I was informed that not only did you fail to get me the information." He crouches down in front of me. "You also destroyed one of my computers."

"As if it matters," I sneer. "I'm sure you won't even miss it."

A fist strikes my jaw. The physical pain doesn't compare to the emotional agony I'm in.

"Get up," Moreno orders as he backs away.

Before I'm fully standing, one of the guards delivers a series of punches to my front, cracking at least one rib. The pain is so intense that I fall to my knees. While I'm down, they continue their assault on my body. I don't bother to protect myself. Death would be a welcome respite.

"Enough," Moreno yells. "I want him alive to watch me fuck his girlfriend tonight."

They leave me lying on the floor, broken but unfortunately alive.

Viktor

Between the combination of the name Timur gave us and the continuing efforts of someone trying to access our system, we finally caught a break. Dimitri and his men were able to trace the location of the cyberattacks, confirming Silverio Moreno is the man responsible for everything. Last week, Maxim and I assembled a select team of security and medical professionals. We flew to Alex's apartment in New York City, where we set up a home base for our next step—rescue.

Maxim's been trying to bring Moreno down for years. Creating a profile and history for Salvador and Paul, the two plants, was a painstaking process. Their backgrounds had to be iron-clad to pass Moreno's security tests, which are some of the most advanced in the world.

It's taken nearly two years for them to gain trust and work their way into Moreno's buyers' circle. They showed up and played the part, purchasing trafficked women. Only these women were the lucky ones. Instead of living a life of sexual slavery and torture, they were brought to Jelena's Hope, where they received medical and psychological care to recover from their trauma. Some were able to be reunited with family. Others were set up with a new life.

Salvador and Paul got a message to us last week. They were invited to a special get-together two weeks ago. Moreno had a new acquisition he wanted to show off to a select group of buyers. After being shown pictures, our men confirmed his *acquisition* was Natalie and that she was the victim of a brutal scene at the hands of one of Moreno's men—one that will be dead as soon as I find him.

According to Paul, Moreno spent the rest of the evening bragging about his new *pet*. He was already taking preliminary bids for her and said she'd be available for purchase at his next auction, which is tonight.

Unfortunately, we don't have confirmation of Alex's whereabouts. Moreno mentioned he found a potential new slave trainer, but neither of our men could confirm his identity.

After receiving the information, Maxim hired the best private rescue team money could buy. It's a mix of American and Ukrainian ex-special forces—a team that operates in the grey area of legalities. Given the short timeline, we've been working around the clock. The plan is to infiltrate Moreno's desert compound and extract Natalie and hopefully Alex—alive.

While we're there, we'll also take out Moreno and his men, shutting down his operation. Then, the teams from Jelena's Hope will step in to care for the victims we identify.

Right now, we're on the ground in Mexico, sitting in a dump of a motel outside Juarez, about a half-hour from Moreno's headquarters. It's an easy place to hide in plain sight. This area is used to wealthy men waltzing in either looking for cheap thrills or as a stopover before going to Moreno's. People here have learned to keep their heads down and their mouths shut. No one's even spared us a second glance.

We've rented several rooms, one of which has been turned into our tech room. Dimitri set up his equipment, ensuring we maintain a constant connection with the rest of his team, including Timur, who is back in New York City.

As soon as Timur could sit up, he insisted on being a part of this mission. But he's still weak and would be a liability. The doctors compromised and cleared him to fly to New York, where he's heading the communications. It's not exactly what he wanted, but he's thankful he wasn't left behind.

So far, everything's going as planned. Paul and Salvador received their text earlier, gauging their interest in making a purchase at tonight's auction. They responded by paying the minimum buy-in amount of half a million dollars. So now we are waiting for a confirmation text granting admission. They expect to receive it any minute.

"Got it," Paul says, holding up his cell.

"Mine's here too," Salvador confirms. "It's go time."

We have less than four hours to finalize a very intricate plan. If anything goes wrong, we'll lose our only chance to get Natalie and Alex out alive. Anything other than perfection is unacceptable.

Moreno allows the buyers to bring their cell phones in for the sole purpose of using an app specifically designed for his auctions. Once inside the gates, all cell and Wi-Fi signals are scrambled, rendering the phones useless to contact anyone outside. When the auction starts, one of several recycled internal frequencies is chosen randomly so buyers can use the app to bid and pay for their acquisitions.

Paul and Salvador, who are also tech geniuses, are going in equipped with a high-tech phone case they designed that will easily pass Moreno's strict security measures. Once the internal frequency is turned on, they'll activate the satellite phone feature embedded in the case to contact Timur, who will direct me and the army of men assembled outside the compound. They've tested their system at previous auctions and have remained undetected.

Once inside, our goal is to take the perimeter guards down quickly and quietly, hopefully keeping our presence undetected. At the same time, Timur will scramble the guards' frequency, ensuring they can't communicate with each other while. We'll make our way through the warehouse buildings, taking out the guards one at a time.

As long as we're successful, the club will proceed as usual. Our goal is to eliminate any reinforcements Moreno may try to call when we enter the club.

On our team are trained mercenaries who will have several tasks, including eliminating everyone inside, finding Alex, and detaining Moreno.

Maxim has given strict instructions to do everything possible to secure Moreno alive. A swift and painless death is too good for him.

My job—locate Natalie and get her to safety.

Our task is nearly impossible, but with Alex and Natalie's lives on the line, failure is not an option.

Natalie

Silverio dropped his bomb on me, then continued his work as usual. On the other hand, I had nothing but time on my hands to think about every possible scenario for tonight. The problem is, I know the worst I can imagine is nowhere near as bad as it will be.

"Well, *mascota*. It's time for you to get ready for our date tonight." He pulls me to my feet, which are numb from kneeling for hours.

I wiggle as the numbness quickly switches to pins and needles. The movement of my body causes my naked breasts to bounce. Silverio takes the opportunity to grab one.

"I've wanted to touch these since the first time I saw them," he says, twisting and pinching my nipple roughly. "Do you see what you do to me?" He adjusts the erection tenting his pants with his free hand. "I should try out your throat now, a little appetizer before tonight. Would you like that little *mascota*?"

"Go to hell." My words earn a slap across my face.

Silverio pulls my leash, forcing me onto his lap. "You will behave like the perfect little *mascota* for my guests tonight. You will open your mouth when I tell you to suck me." He runs his thumb along my lips before pushing it inside. "You will take all of what I give you. And you will thank your Master for it when I'm done."

I have nothing left to lose and snap my teeth down on Silverio's thumb, infuriating him.

"You bitch," he yells as he wraps his other hand around my throat, squeezing tight. "For that move, you'll get twenty lashes before I fuck you. When I'm done, I'll make sure you're sold to someone who'll make you wish you were dead." He laughs and shoves me off his lap.

I'm delivered to Silverio's room by one of his guards, where Amelia waits to help ready me for tonight. She's already drawn my bath and poured aromatic oils in. But, this time, when I slip into the warm water, there's no enjoyment, no relief. Instead, my tears fall, landing like raindrops on the water.

"I'm so sorry, miss." Amelia does her best to console me.

Even though she knows the fate that awaits her, Amelia puts on a brave face and apologizes to me.

"Alex will save us," I say, but this time, my words lack the conviction they held the first time I uttered them. There are only two of us against Silverio and all his men. We're severely outnumbered, and I have no idea where Alex is.

Reality has set in. I'm going to get out of here, but not with Alex. Our lives are about to be permanently altered. Our future, the one that just a few weeks ago was everything we could've ever asked for, no longer holds the promise of happiness.

"I heard the guards talking. From what I could hear, they beat your Alex today. He destroyed something that belonged to Master," Amelia says quietly.

"What else did you hear? Is he okay?" I want to force her to tell me every detail, but she walks away, returning with a towel.

"You need to finish getting ready."

"Please, Amelia. Did they say anything more?"

"They stopped talking when I entered the room."

I take the offered towel and wrap it around my body.

"Alex is strong. I know he's okay," I say, trying to convince myself more than Amelia.

"Yes, miss." She offers me a sad smile.

No other words are spoken as I finish getting ready for the unavoidable night in store for me. Until this moment, I had never felt true hopelessness. After drying my hair, I return to the bedroom to find the same white silk robe on the bed. A pair of white strappy heels sits on the floor.

"What's the point in even putting this on? We all know I won't be wearing it for long."

Amelia doesn't react. She silently holds the robe for me as I slide my arms into the sleeves and tie it shut before putting on the shoes.

"I'll get the guard."

Natalie

THE SCENE PLAYS ON REPEAT. WE ENTER THE CLUB THROUGH THE backdoor. But this time, we're not alone. Walking down the hall, I hear crying behind the closed doors. There are different guards, men I've not seen, milling around and staring as we walk by. But no one says a word or makes a move to touch me.

Finally, I'm brought to the stage. The curtains are closed, but I can hear the low murmurings of the men gathering on the other side. Tonight, the stage is set to look like a dungeon. There are several pieces of furniture, including a spanking bench, a pillar with chains hanging from the ceiling, and a bondage bed.

"Strip. Except for the shoes. *El Tomador* wants those on."

My fate may be sealed, but I refuse to cower in fear. With my head held high, I untie the belt and allow the robe to slide off my arms. It falls into a puddle on the floor. The guard kicks it aside and steps closer, removing the leash. He takes me by the arm, leading me to the pillar.

"Turn around and bend over," he barks before grabbing my hands and wrapping them around the pillar. He secures them to the chains that hang overhead. Then he reaches into his pocket and pulls out a black piece of satin, which he wraps tightly over my eyes, stripping me of my vision.

"Don't do this," I whisper. "I'll tell Alex not to harm you. He'll let you go if you help us get out of here." He doesn't answer. Instead, he kicks my feet apart, attaching them to chains fastened to the floor. "Please," I beg.

The bravery I felt earlier disappears and is replaced with desperation. I can't help it. I'll plead and promise. Anything to get out of here untouched and alive. I feel his body against mine, his erection pressing into my ass.

"Your begging turns me on, princess," he says as he unzips his pants. "I think I'll have a piece of this before—"

"What the fuck do you think you're doing?" Silverio's voice booms across the stage.

"*Tomador*. I didn't. I mean, I wasn't."

"Take him to a cell," Silverio orders. "I'll deal with him later."

There's a scuffle behind me. I hear the man begging as he's dragged away. What does it say about me that I don't feel an ounce of pity for what I'm sure will happen to him later?

Silverio steps up to me. "It's understandable why Julio couldn't keep his hands off you. Bent over on display like this, you're a sight to behold." He runs his fingers between my spread legs. "Just a little while longer, and I'll be able to sink my cock into you." His fingers tease the outside of my folds. "I'll be back for you soon, *mascota*."

His footsteps retreat, leaving me alone on the stage, and I pray for a miracle.

The announcer instructs everyone to take their seats. The voices I heard earlier begin to subside until the room is silent. The master of ceremonies then describes the evening's events. Once again, it seems I'm the top bill. Following it will be the auction. A feeling of overwhelming dread courses through me. I've run out of time.

The sound of a loud detonation makes my ears ring. The floor below my feet shakes from the impact.

Pop. Pop. Pop.

Gunshots and yelling come from the other side of the curtain.

Everything happens so fast.

A warm body comes up close behind me. I scream and struggle to get free. "Natalie, hold still."

"Viktor?"

"It's me." I feel his warm breath on my neck. "Stop fighting. We need to get out of here fast."

"Where's Alex?"

"I don't know." Viktor releases my hands and then moves to my ankles. I slowly stand up and remove the blindfold, not that it helps me see anything. It's pitch black in here. "Take these off," Viktor instructs and helps me out of my high heels.

The commotion on the other side of the curtains is escalating. It sounds like an army has invaded. Men are yelling in both English and Spanish. Gunshots are exchanged back and forth.

Viktor lifts me into his arms. "Stay quiet. We're getting out of here."

Grabbing his shirt, I tuck my head into his muscular chest.

I'm putting my complete trust in the man who is no longer just my bodyguard and friend. He's the rescue I hoped for but didn't think would come.

Alex

∞

The monitor flickers to life. I'm helplessly staring at the scene unfurling in the club's main room. Moreno has the stage set up like a dungeon with several pieces of BDSM furniture. The more sinister items are hidden behind a black curtain where a guard is walking with Natalie.

Several whips are laid out on the table, some relatively innocent, others more destructive. The worst of which is the cat-o-nines made of chains with barbs on the end. Moreno intends to tear Natalie apart.

This is my fault—I failed. And Natalie's about to pay with her life.

Natalie's stripped and positioned bent over. Then she's restrained to the pillar.

The guard reaches for his zipper and pushes himself up against her. "What the fuck?"

Just as he steps up to mount her, Moreno storms onto the stage. He's livid and barking orders. The man is dragged off—his time remaining on the earth isn't long.

Moreno moves in close to Natalie and slips his hand between her legs. It's almost too much to watch, yet I can't take my eyes off the screen. My body vibrates from uncontrolled rage. How am I going to get through tonight?

"I'm so sorry I couldn't save you, baby girl," I say aloud, even though I know she can't hear me.

The room plunges into darkness, leaving me alone and disoriented in the sound-proof chamber. Clutching my aching ribs, I cautiously crawl towards the far corner, fumbling in the pitch-black void. A series of thuds reverberate against the door, followed by a burst of sparks, and the door forcefully swings open. The hallway beyond is also shrouded in darkness, indicating that the entire building has lost power.

Crouched in silence, I hope to remain unnoticed, using the darkness to my advantage. My efforts are interrupted by gunfire and shouting emanating from some-where in the distance. Panic sets in as I realize the club is under attack. Natalie is out

385

there, a helpless target on the stage, in grave danger. As heavy footsteps approach my hiding place, I hold my breath and brace for the worst.

"There's someone in here," a male voice says. "On the floor, back right corner." I don't move. "Alex? Is that you?"

"Who are you?"

"Maxim sent us. Come on. We're getting you out of here."

I'm sure I must've misheard, so I ask again. "Who are you?"

"We don't have time for that now."

A hand grabs my arm, pulling me up. I groan in pain.

"Can you walk?"

"I think so." I try to take a step, but the pain from my broken ribs makes breathing difficult.

They're going to waste too much time on me. "Leave me here. Natalie's on the stage. Go get her instead."

"Viktor's got her. We're getting you out of here." The hand stays firmly attached to my arm. I'm nearly dragged from the room and out of the building.

Once outside, we take cover against the club's back wall. The scope of what's happening around us is overwhelming. An army has invaded Moreno's compound. Gunshots ring out from all directions, and explosions light up the night sky. Now, I understand how rescuers found me in the pitch black. They're wearing night vision goggles, which are now flipped up on their helmets. I lean back and try to catch my breath.

"Name's Michael," The man still holding my arms says. "You doing okay?"

"I'm fine. Where's Natalie?"

"She's with Viktor. They left through the side entrance. He's taking her off the property."

"Where are we going?"

"To the main estate. They're holding Moreno there for you."

Viktor

I hold Natalie's trembling body tight against me as we quickly escape through a side door. I set her down as soon as we're out of the building.

"Don't leave me, Viktor." She fists my shirt, holding it tight.

"I'm not going anywhere," I reassure her. Without removing my arm from her waist, I use my free hand to take off my night vision goggles, tossing them over my shoulder into my backpack.

"Fuck, you're naked." I was in such a hurry to get her out that I didn't think about her lack of clothes. Despite her protest, I let her go and rip the pack off, dropping it on the ground. With my hands free, I pull my T-shirt off. "Put this on." I help her into my shirt. "Are you hurt?" I scan her for any apparent injuries.

"No," she says softly.

I click a button on the earpiece I'm wearing. "Boss?"

"Do you have her?" Maxim asks.

"She's safe. I've got her," I say and listen closely to the orders Max gives me. "Yes, sir. I'll call when we get there."

"Where's Alex?" she asks.

"He's with another group from our team," I explain.

"Will you bring me to him? Please?" she begs as tears stream down her face.

I lift her again, cradling her against my chest. "You and I are leaving. They'll bring Alex as soon as he's ready."

"I can't go without Alex." She punches my chest and tries to wiggle out of my hold.

"Natalie, stop." I know she's scared, but there's fighting all around us. I have to get her out of here and back to safety.

"I'm not leaving without him or Amelia. I promised we'd keep her safe."

"Who's Amelia?" I stop with my back against the side of a building while I scan the area.

"She's a young girl. In Silverio's house. Promise me you'll save her."

"I promise." I adjust my grasp on Natalie. "But right now, you and I are getting out of here."

Satisfied with my answer, she tucks her head back into my chest. I tighten my hold and break into a sprint, heading to the black SUV waiting outside the gates.

Alex

AFTER WHAT SEEMED LIKE AN ETERNITY, THE SOUNDS OF WAR FINALLY subside. The scent of gunpowder lingers heavily in the warm night air. Flanked by Michael's team, we walk toward Moreno's estate. I struggle to catch my breath and keep up with the group.

Looking around, I can't help but wonder how Maxim had managed to orchestrate such a successful raid. Not only did they infiltrate Moreno's facility, but they also took out all of his men. Within the span of an hour, Maxim shut down the entire operation.

Michael hands me a cell phone. "It's the boss, sir."

"Hello?"

"Alexander. It is good to hear you," Maxim says, relief evident in his voice. "Before you ask. Viktor has Natalia. She is safe and off the compound."

"How?"

"We will discuss that once we get you home. Right now, your only priority is getting to the villa safely. My men are holding Moreno," Maxim says, pausing momentarily before continuing. "I know you remember our discussion about Thomas. Your actions tonight will have life-changing consequences."

"Moreno's going to die tonight. A slow, painful death."

"Make him pay for what he has done. Then you will be brought to Natalia."

I disconnect the call and pass the phone back to Michael.

"Have a seat," he says, pointing to a stone bench near a fountain outside the front door to Moreno's estate. "We need to wait for the power to be restored before going in."

I slump onto the bench. Our respite allows me to catch my breath after the grueling walk up the hill.

"What happens now?" I motion in the direction of the buildings still bathed in darkness.

"Several recovery teams will go through each warehouse and scan every individual for trackers, which they'll remove and destroy," he explains, gazing out over the vast grounds. "Any person requiring emergency treatment will be transported by helicopter to secure medical facilities tonight. The rest will wait until morning to be transferred. It'll be a long night for everyone." He pauses for a moment before continuing.

"Tomorrow, recovery teams will arrive and assess the needs of those still remaining. They'll gather as much identifying information as possible for each person. Once everyone has been accounted for, they will be transferred to specialized facilities for recovered trafficking victims."

Michael's cell rings, interrupting our conversation. "I have to take this."

While I'm waiting, the power is restored to the desert compound. The haze is just beginning to clear, giving way to a cloudless, star-filled sky. Despite the atrocities that have occurred here, it's a relief knowing the compound is now under Maxim's control. Moreno's reign coming to an end seems to have cleared the evil presence that filled the space just a short time ago.

"I just received confirmation that your fiancé is safely back at the motel with Viktor," Michael says. "She informed Viktor a young girl was being held somewhere in the estate. I'm sending a few of my men to search for her." He places his hand on my shoulder. "Are you ready to pay Moreno a visit?"

I close my eyes and try to take a deep breath. Unfortunately, my broken ribs prevent that from happening, and I wince in pain.

"Do you want me to tape those up before we go in?" he offers.

"No," I say firmly. "I've already waited too long for this."

WHEN WE ENTER THE ESTATE, WE'RE MET WITH A FLURRY OF ACTIVITY as armed men, all under Maxim's control, move about.

"Did you get the description I sent out?" Michael asks one of the soldiers standing guard at the bottom of the staircase.

"Affirmative. I forwarded it to the teams inside. If she's here, we'll find her."

"Keep me updated."

"Will do, Mike."

We continue walking past the entrance to Moreno's office to the end of the hall, where a hole is blown open. "There used to be a door opened only by retina scan. My guys did a little redesigning to make it more accessible." Michael grins.

The air temperature noticeably cools as we descend a wooden staircase that brings us underground. A chill runs up my spine.

"Moreno had an intricate series of tunnels dug under his estate," Michael explains as we walk. "He hosted special events down here that only select individuals were invited to. It took Salvador several years, but he was finally able to infiltrate that inner circle." We stop at an open door. "Unfortunately, if a girl was brought here, she didn't make it out alive."

As I make my way through the building, I unwittingly walk into a windowless room. Despite its emptiness, my mind conjures up images of the unspeakable horrors that have occurred there. The modern lighting fixtures seem out of place amidst the ghastly surroundings.

Hooks are installed at various points on the walls, with some still holding cuffs. The ceiling is rigged with an intricate track system, complete with chains and suspension bars dangling from it. Bloodstains still mark the floor. My hands shoot out and clutch the door frame for support. There are no words to describe the depravity of a man like Moreno. But tonight, the tables have, and he won't be leaving alive.

I follow Michael to the end of the tunnel, where we stop in front of a medieval-looking door. It's easily eight feet tall and made of vertical wood planks secured by horizontal braces. Iron hinges hold it to the stone that makes up the arched doorway.

"Ready?" Michael turns to me.

Am I ready? The knowledge that once I choose to walk through this door, my life will never be the same isn't lost on me. I'm transported back to the day I stood before a different door, one with Thomas Moore sitting behind it.

After what he did to Natalie and her family, I couldn't see past my rage. Killing him was the only option I could imagine. It was Maxim who impressed on me the life-altering implications of taking the life of another. In the end, I found a small amount of compassion and decided to spare his life in exchange for him going to prison.

But at this moment, as I prepare to face Moreno, I have no compassion. There's no excuse for the hell he's put not just Natalie and me through but also countless others. There will be no bargains made. Moreno will suffer, and then he'll pay with his life. I meet Michael's steely gaze. "I've never been more ready."

I cringe as the metal latch scrapes across its housing, followed by the groaning of the hinges from the weight of the door as it's pulled open. Fighting the searing pain in my ribs, I pull my shoulders back and step across the threshold, prepared to come face to face with the devil himself. This room is more rudimentary than most of the others we saw. If it can even be called a room. The walls are made of brick, and the floor is dirt. It smells musty and stale.

My eyes scan my surroundings. Various whips hang on the walls, not the typical kind one would expect to find in a BDSM club. The sole purpose of these whips is to maim the person on the receiving end of their punishing strikes. On the opposite wall are knives and daggers of various sizes. It hits me like a punch to the gut. This is the room where Moreno carves the skin of his slaves.

Then I turn my attention to Moreno himself. Walking further into the room, I stop a few feet in front of him and inspect the job Maxim's men have already done. Blood drips from the corner of his mouth, and his right eye is swollen shut. Heavy chains attached to a pulley system, the same one that's held countless innocent victims, now bind his wrists above his head. Moreno's body is strung, so only the tips of his toes brush the floor.

"Where's the dagger?"

"Fuck you, Alejandro." Moreno spits at my feet.

"Michael, can you—"

"Already on it," he answers before I finish the question.

With my back to Moreno, I walk to his wall of whips and inspect each one. I'm looking for the one that will cause the maximum amount of pain. The same one he was prepared to use on Natalie tonight.

"You aren't man enough to wield one of my tools," Moreno snarls.

Oomph.

I spin around. "Stop," I bark, freezing one of our men mid-punch. "Let him say what he wants. He won't have the option of talking much longer."

He steps back.

Returning my attention to the task at hand, I remove a bullwhip from where it's placed on the wall and test the feel of the dark wood handle in my hand. I run the whip's thong across my palm, noting the quality of the plaited leather. As I reach the end, I examine the sharp razors intricately woven into the fall. This whip has one purpose—maximum destruction of flesh.

I cock my wrist back, pausing briefly, my stare directed at Moreno, whose one good eye is locked on the whip. I'm sure he's wielded this instrument of torture many times on innocent women. He's basked in their screams each time the razors hit their skin. Then, he turns his attention back to me.

Fear swirls in his eyes. Moreno knows what's about to happen. As I flick my wrist back, the tail of the whip flies through the air, landing across his chest with a loud crack. Without pausing, I land several more strikes across his torso and down his legs, tearing the expensive fabric of his clothing and ripping through his flesh. He flinches each time the razors connect with his body. Curses fall from his lips.

"How does it feel to be powerless?"

I begin another round of ruthless strikes, allowing the razor's edges to slice through his flesh. Moreno's wails of pain fill the room. With each lash, I feel my humanness slip further and further away. Knowing the weapon I'm wielding holds the power of life and death is a dangerous and heady feeling.

When I'm satisfied with the thoroughness of my assault, I return the whip, now dripping with blood, to its place on the wall.

Turning to Michael, I ask, "Can someone get me a bucket of cold water?"

Michael directs two of his mercenaries to complete the task.

"You know," I walk closer to Moreno. "Now I understand the high you get from using your whips."

"Fuck you, Montgomery." His breathing is labored.

I land a punch to Moreno's jaw, whipping his head to the side. Blood splatters fly from his mouth, landing on the wall. His head lolls forward as he battles to stay conscious.

Michael's phone rings. He exits the room just as two men enter, carrying buckets of ice water.

"You're just in time. Dump one on the bastard. We don't want him checking out just yet."

The men approach Moreno to carry out my order while I briefly exit the room and search for Michael. I find him standing at the end of the hall, talking on his cell phone. While I wait, I lean against the wall and close my eyes. Pain radiates across my chest. Each breath is more painful than the last.

"Are you holding up okay? We can get you to medical if—"

"I'm fine," I say, pushing off the wall.

He holds up his phone. "My men found the girl in a hidden room off Moreno's bedroom."

"Is she okay?"

"They're bringing her for medical attention," Michael says, sliding the phone into his pocket. "The guys said she's just a kid."

"Fuck. I need your gun."

Without question, Michael pulls his pistol from the holster on his waist and hands it to me.

"Take your time with him. Make him suffer." He motions with his chin over my shoulder. "My team wired the estate with explosives. When you're through, we're going to blow Moreno and this house of horrors apart."

With the gun in my hand, I return to Moreno. "Did you miss me?"

He doesn't look up. Doesn't answer.

"We're going to take a trip down memory lane, you and I," I say as I prowl around him like a predator stalking his prey. "Let's go back to our first day as your *guests*. Do you remember what you did to my submissive?"

"I took great joy in whipping her." An evil grin spreads across his face. "I should've fucked her then."

"You touched what didn't belong to you." Clicking the safety off, I raise the gun and aim it at his right hand. The one he used to hold the whip he marked Natalie with and pull the trigger.

Moreno's screams echo in the small room. His body shakes from the excruciating pain, but I don't look away. Instead, I stand and watch the blood that spills from the carnage that used to be his hand—and I feel nothing. Over the next few hours, I alternate between inflicting pain and dousing Moreno with cold water to keep him from losing consciousness.

Between my malnourishment and injuries, I'm utterly exhausted. My body pleads with me to rest, but my mind refuses to slow down. I settle for taking a break and walk out of the room, with Michael following closely behind. I make my way back through the tunnels and take the steps two at a time, not stopping until I reach the front door of the estate. I open the door and stumble into the cool early morning air, which does little to alleviate the stench of death that still lingers in my nose.

Taking a few steps away from the house, I fall to my knees as my stomach involuntarily empties itself, not realizing there's nothing in it. Each heave sends searing pain through my chest. I try to push myself back up to my feet, but the blackness creeping into my vision causes me to fall once more.

"It's a given Moreno's going to die. I don't want you dying too. Let's get you to a doctor." Michael grabs my arm, helping to steady me.

Losing all self-control, I tear my arm from his grasp and yell, "You don't understand everything he's taken from me. He stole my fiancée. Then, that bastard paraded her around naked and tethered to a leash—treated her as if she were an animal." I point in the direction of the house. "Because of him, my unborn child is dead." My emotions are a jumbled mess. I'm unable to separate one from the other.

"Dammit. I had no idea. I'm sorry we can't give back what you've lost." Michael puts a hand on my shoulder. "Let's go finish him and get you back to your girl. She's going to need you."

Using the back of my hands, I wipe the tears from my face and try to catch my breath. Before going back in, I tell Michael exactly how I want this to end.

As we approach the door, one of the men steps forward, holding out the black box that contains Moreno's prized dagger. The group falls silent as I take the box and slowly open it, revealing the weapon within. I lift the blade from its resting place, and my hand trembles as memories from the last time I held it flood back. I force them from my mind and focus on what I must do.

For generations, this dagger has represented the purest form of evil in the world. The man who possessed it had used it to extract screams of pain from their victims, all for their own sick pleasure.

The reign of the Moreno family ends today.

Never again will this weapon be used to harm an innocent person.

The soldiers guarding the doors pull them open. Then, with the dagger firmly in my grasp, I walk up to Moreno. "Look at me, you son of a bitch." He slowly lifts his head, a snarling grin on his face. "Do you have any last words?"

"Go to hell," he spits.

"You first."

Lifting the dagger, I drive it into Moreno's chest. His piercing scream fills the room as I drag the blade down his torso—bones crack, and blood pours out. I reach into his chest with my free hand. Moreno has a flash of recognition. Terror oozes from his pores as I wrap my hand around his heart and rip it from his chest.

In my hand, I hold the useless organ as it pulses.

Once.

Twice.

It quivers.

Moreno's life ends.

Viktor

We made it out of Moreno's fortress and are being driven back to the motel. Natalie's weak and scared. Her body trembles as I cradle her on my lap and rub her back softly. Once we're parked, the driver comes around and opens the back door of the SUV. I slide out with Natalie still in my arms. We're under the cover of darkness and in a seedy town. No one notices or cares that I'm carrying an almost lifeless woman into a motel room.

"We need to get some food into you," I say as I try to set her down.

"Don't let me go." She wraps her arms around my neck, holding on as if her life depends on it.

"It's okay. I won't leave you." I kiss the top of her head, trying to console her.

Without letting go, I grab the blanket folded at the bottom of the bed and sit with her on my lap. She holds me tightly while I open the blanket and cover her before pulling her close to me once again. Then, her tears start to fall.

"Shh. I've got you," I whisper. "I won't let anything happen to you." I gently stroke her hair and quietly hum the haunting lullaby *Bayu Bayushki Bayu*. It's the song my mama sang to me when I was a little boy and would wake from nightmares.

When Natalie's tears finally subside, I turn her so I can see her face. My eyes are drawn to her neck and the leather collar that's locked on it. How the hell did I miss that? I touch it, looking for a clasp or a lock, but find nothing.

"Moreno put it on me," she says over a sob.

I reach into my pocket and grab my knife. "I'm taking it off." Angling her head away, I slide the blade under the collar and carefully slice through the leather, freeing her. She runs her hand along her neck. I take both the collar and knife and slide them into my pocket. "Why don't you take a bath and get washed up? I'll have one of my men get us something to eat."

"I don't want to be alone."

"I'll be right outside the bathroom door," I reassure her.

"No. Don't close it. You can't leave me alone." Natalie's body trembles from fear.

I take a second to try to figure this out. "I'm going to move you off my lap and go talk to one of my men." I point to the door of our room. "I won't go out, but I need to ask them to get us some food. I'll come right back to you."

"Okay," she says softly.

I shift her off my lap, and she pulls the blanket tight around her. Every few steps, I look back and remind her I'm still here and not leaving. Natalie's eyes remain fixed on my every move. When I open the door, I give one of the men instructions to find us food. The other is to stay on guard outside the door.

"We didn't want to interrupt. But we were told to relay a message that the girl, Amelia, was found. The kid was beaten and raped. She's been brought for a medical evaluation. But they expect her to be okay."

"Thank you." I close and lock the door before returning to Natalie.

Her hair falls over her face, and I gently brush the blonde curls behind her ear.

Natalie

Viktor's my rock, my safe place, and the only thing keeping me from falling apart. I know he's uncomfortable being in here while I bathe. But I need him. I can't be alone. Although I've grown accustomed to my nakedness, Viktor's anything but comfortable with it. He's busying himself with straightening towels and toiletries, anything to keep from looking at me while remaining close.

I slide down the tub until my head goes underwater, shutting out everything except the racing thoughts inside my head. Where's Alex? Is he okay? Why isn't he here yet? How am I going to tell him about our baby? Gasping for air, I shoot up. Water splashes over the sides of the tub from my sudden movement.

"Are you okay?" Viktor rushes over and drops to his knees.

I meet his cerulean blue eyes that are swirling with concern. There's an avalanche of emotions at the precipice of crashing down and burying me. I wrap my arms around my abdomen.

"What's wrong?" he asks, grabbing my shoulders. "Is the baby okay? Fuck, I need to get a doctor here." He starts to get to his feet.

"There is no baby." It's the first time I have uttered the words aloud, and I'm not prepared for the onslaught of grief acknowledging my loss brings.

"What do you mean?" Viktor freezes.

"A few weeks ago. Moreno made Alex—" I choke on a sob. "There was so much blood. I lost the baby."

He pulls me close, holding me tightly. In that moment, the magnitude of our emotions is indescribable. Wrapped in a cocoon of deafening silence, we share a bond of grief I have never felt before. For a brief moment, I allow myself to be lost in the warmth and strength of his embrace.

"The water's getting cold," he says, pulling away suddenly. "Let me get you a towel."

Viktor leaves, and I shiver from the loss of his heat. When he returns, he's holding a towel out for me. I feel a little stronger, so I stand up and step out of the tub alone. He averts his gaze while I squeeze the excess water from my hair and wrap the towel around my body. Viktor holds my arm to steady me as he leads me back to the bed.

"Sit." I perch on the edge of the bed, holding the towel close, and watch as he opens one of the duffle bags sitting on the motel's dresser. "We thought you might appreciate having your own things." He shrugs as if he's unsure of his actions.

"That was very thoughtful. Thank you."

He approaches the bed with my hairbrush in his hand.

"Turn around." I sit with my legs crossed and my back to him. His touch is gentle yet sure as he combes the tangles from my hair.

"You've done this before?"

"Never."

While he brushes my hair, I realize I don't know much about Viktor's personal life. He's never told me about his family or if he's had any serious relationships. Although I want to ask, I know right now isn't the time for my questions. There's a rapping sound on our door. I jump and almost lose my grasp on the towel.

"Wait here."

Viktor pulls his gun from the holster on his waist as he approaches the door. His muscles visibly relax when he looks through the peephole, and he returns the weapon to its place before looking back at me. "It's our food." He cracks the door, exchanging hushed words with whoever is on the other side before closing it and securing the locks. "Dinner?" He holds up the bag and grins.

His smile is contagious, and despite my sadness, I can't help but return it with one of my own. Viktor returns to the bed, sets the bag down, and begins rummaging through its contents.

"We're in luck. They found a street vendor," Viktor says as he pulls the food from the bag. "There's tacos, quesadillas, elotes, and fresh fruit. They even managed to score some churros if you're in the mood for something sweet."

My stomach turns at the thought of eating any of the spicy offerings. "I think I'll stick to this," I say and grab a banana.

Viktor frowns. "You need to eat more than that."

"I haven't had anything more than beans and rice for weeks. And even that was only if he decided to let me eat."

"Death isn't good enough for that bastard."

I put my hand on his arm. "It's over now. Thanks to you, I'm safe." I set the banana down. "Before I eat, can I get dressed?"

"Shit. Your clothes." Viktor hurries over to grab the duffle bag. "I don't know what Irina packed for you."

He pulls out a variety of shirts, shorts, and pants. I grab one of Alex's T-shirts and bring it to my face. It smells like him. Needing to feel close to him, I slip it over my head before grabbing a pair of yoga pants. Without removing the towel, I put my feet in and pull them up. Then I unfasten the towel and slide it out from under my shirt.

"Impressive." Viktor chuckles and claps his hands.

I pretend to bow. "Thank you." Having my clothes helps me feel a bit more like myself. "Do you know when Alex will get here?"

Viktor tenses. "He's with one of the teams. They'll be here in a bit."

There's more he isn't telling me, and I wait for him to elaborate.

"Eat your banana." He motions to the fruit lying on the bed and then passes me a bottle of water. "You need to get some nourishment, and then you need to rest."

Reluctantly, I take the piece of fruit and take a small bite while Viktor grabs a taco and sits next to me. "Did you ever think we'd be having dinner in a motel room again?"

"It seems to be our thing."

Several silent minutes pass as we share the comfortable familiarity of a meal together.

"Thank you, Viktor. I thought Silverio was going to—"

"Don't go there," Viktor interrupts. "And don't thank me. It's my job."

I resist the urge to roll my eyes at his comment. "Well, thank you anyway." A yawn escapes.

Viktor finishes the last bite of his taco, crumbling the wrapper in his hand.

"You should lay down."

He scrambles to clean up the food packages, putting the garbage in a small wastebasket by the dresser.

I look toward the door. "I was hoping to wait for Alex."

"It's been a long day. You need to sleep. I promise I'll wake you as soon as he gets here."

Viktor pulls the blankets down and motions for me to get in bed.

"You promise you won't leave?"

"I'll be right here." He goes to sit in an armchair in the corner of the room.

"Can you lay with me?"

"You know I can't."

"I need to feel you next to me. To remind me I'm safe. Please," I beg.

He drops his head in defeat before walking to the far side of the bed. "Alright. I'll stay next to you."

My limbs are heavy, and as much as I want to stay awake until Alex gets here, sleep beckons me. Unable to resist any longer, I crawl into bed. Despite the lumps in the old mattress, it feels like heaven compared to sleeping on the floor.

Viktor pulls the blankets up to cover me, and I slide close, resting my head on his chest. He tenses. His heart is racing. I'm sure he's worried about Alex's reaction, but I'm not concerned. All Alex will care about is that I'm safe.

Viktor puts his arm around me. "Close your eyes. I've got you."

Alex

It's as if we're frozen in time. No one moves or makes a sound. I remain rooted where I stand in the middle of the room. Staring at the lifeless body hanging from the ceiling—the dagger tightly gripped in one hand. Moreno's useless heart in the other.

Michael comes over to me. "He's dead, Alex. It's over."

I let my fingers fall slack, and the dead organ drops to the dirt floor.

"It's time to go."

My legs are lead weights beneath me, anchoring me to this spot.

"Come on. Let's blow this place up."

Silently, the men file out of the room.

I don't move. An unknown force is holding me here, and I can't leave.

Michael tugs my arm, urging me to go with him. Without conscious thought, my legs move, following him. When we reach the doorway, I look over my shoulder at the carnage behind us. I should be happy that bastard's dead. That there's one less piece of scum walking the earth.

It was justice.

A life for a life.

Killing him was supposed to piece the shattered pieces of my heart back together. But I feel nothing.

We climb the rudimentary stairs, taking our final steps toward the exit. The sun is cresting the horizon, illuminating the once-dark night. As we move away from Moreno's estate, the warehouses come into view. Those who were once prisoners, facing a bleak future, now move freely within the compound's gates.

When we reach a safe distance, we come to a stop, and our group turns to face the villa. A man to my left begins a quiet countdown. "Three. Two. One."

The explosion's deafening sound shatters the desert's silence. Stone blasts apart, and glass shatters. Debris flies high into the air as the ground shakes beneath our feet from the sheer force of the explosion. Transfixed, I watch as the rubble falls into piles and the dust begins to settle. In just minutes, the entire estate is destroyed.

Around us, men and women gather in small groups, clutching each other for support. The sound of children's cries fills the air. Moreno's reign of terror is over, but my soul feels no relief. I am nothing more than a cold, dead shell of a man.

"Alex." Michael's voice slices through the dark fog in my head. "Our ride's here. Let's get you back to Natalie."

Silently, I follow him to a black SUV that's waiting for us. As we drive, Michael and the driver talk to one another. Although I hear their voices, their words are nothing more than unrecognizable sounds. I stare out the window, watching the landscape pass by in a blur.

I don't know where we're going, only that Natalie is there and she's safe. I should be happy. All I've wanted is to be reunited with her, but after everything I've just done, I'm scared.

In the past few weeks, I've killed two people. The first a heinous monster. I did things I never imagined I was capable of—and I enjoyed them. I took pleasure in administering even a fraction of the torture Moreno has inflicted on countless people. I watched as the life drained from his eyes and felt no remorse for being the one to snuff it out.

The other, my unborn son or daughter, once the symbol of new life and hope, now a victim of my actions. As a father, my role was to protect my child, yet I caused mortal harm. I would give my own life if it meant I could give our child back to Natalie. How can she ever forgive me for taking our baby from her? I am a murderer, a monster. Why would Natalie ever want me now?

The vehicle stops in a dirt parking lot at a rundown motel. Michael leads me to the door of a room.

"It's time to give this to me." Michael reaches for the dagger, but I pull my arm away. "Sasha's going to take it and get it cleaned up." He points to the other man standing with us and then tries to take it again, but I don't release my hold.

This dagger is my lifeline. The only thing connecting me to reality. If I let it go, I fear I'll fall into the black abyss lurking in the shadows, waiting to swallow me whole.

"Alex, if Natalie sees this, it'll scare her. You don't want that, right?" Michael places his hand on top of the dagger's handle. We're stuck in a silent battle. Finally, my fingers open, allowing him to take it. "I'll make sure you get it back."

Michael opens the door. Shuffling my feet, I walk into the room. I'm expecting to see Natalie, but there's no one here.

"Before we go to Natalie, you need to shower and get into some clean clothes."

I walk into the bathroom, my movements robotic, and I stop in front of the mirror. Looking back at me is a stranger, wearing the same black outfit I was forced to wear weeks ago when I committed unforgivable acts. The torn and filthy clothing hangs from my body, and my hair is disheveled, almost matted. My face is covered in coarse, dark hair from not shaving in weeks. Another man's blood is smeared on me from head to toe. Part of me recognizes that it's my image, but the rest feels like I'm viewing everything from outside my body.

Slowly, I strip off my clothes, letting them fall on the cracked tile floor before turning on the shower's knob. Water spurts from the small showerhead. I turn it as hot as it will go before stepping under the stream, hoping it will rinse the filth from me.

My body is hyper-alert, sensing movement outside the shower. I'm at a disadvantage and have no weapons to fight with. Carefully, I move the edge of the shower curtain to see who's there, unsure of what threat I'm about to face.

"It's just me," Michael says calmly. "I'm taking your dirty clothes and leaving clean ones right here." He points to the pile of clothes neatly folded on the counter by the sink.

Quickly, I close the curtain and lean back against the wall. It takes a few minutes for me to catch my breath and stop my body from shaking. When I finally compose myself, I grab the soap and washcloth to cleanse myself of the horrors I've endured. But no matter how hard I scrub, the feelings and memories won't disappear.

Desperate, I get more soap and try again. Over and over, I attempt to wash away the guilt, the memories, and the filth. My skin is red and raw when I finally give up and shut the water off.

While I dress, I listen to the voices on the other side of the door. I hear Michael and an unknown woman's voice. When I open the door, they stop talking and turn my way.

"Alex, this is Milina. She's one of our medics. She's going to tape up your ribs and check you for any other injuries."

"Come sit on the bed so I can look at those cuts on your face." Milina sets a black bag on the bed.

Instead of sitting, I walk to the door. I don't care about my injuries. Regardless of whether she'll reject me or not, I need to see with my own eyes that Natalie's safe.

Michael blocks my path. "As soon as we get you patched up, I'll bring you to her."

My mind screams no, but my body lets him lead me to the bed.

"This is going to sting," Milina says before using an alcohol wipe to clean the cut over my eye. "I'm going to need to stitch this one. Can you grab my suture kit, Mike?"

Michael digs through the bag, gathering the required supplies. He lays them out on the bed. Milina grabs a vial and a needle, filling it with a clear liquid.

"I'm going to numb it first," she explains as she injects it into the area around the cut.

It may numb the pain from the U-shaped needle she uses to stitch up my head, but it does nothing for the ache deep in my soul.

"Alex?" Milina leans down, coming eye-to-eye with me. "Did you hear me?" Her words float around outside me, but I can't grasp them. Can't respond to them. "Has he spoken at all?"

"No. Not since we left that bastard's house."

"I'm concerned he's in shock." Milina gently removes my shirt and presses on my ribs.

Red-hot pain shoots through me. It's hard to breathe.

"Maxim has a medical team waiting in New York."

"I don't think he should wait that long," she says as she wraps tape around my chest. "He needs to be evaluated now."

I rip the tape from her hand and toss it onto the bed before putting my shirt back on.

Michael looks between Milina and me. "What he needs is his fiancée."

"Michael." Milina crosses her arms in protest. "He needs medical and psychological treatment."

These two can keep arguing. I'm done waiting. I shove past Milina and head for the door.

Michael follows me. "Let's go. I'll take you to Natalie's room."

Alex

Michael's talking. I see his lips moving and how he looks at me, waiting for a response. But the thoughts swirling in my head are too loud. I'm unable to hear what he's saying. I can't respond. It's early afternoon, and the heat in this godforsaken place is already oppressive. Beads of sweat run down my face as we walk along the cracked concrete sidewalk littered with cigarette butts and garbage. How the hell did they find this dump? How much farther is Natalie? I want to ask, but words don't come.

We finally get to another rusty white door with two guards posted outside. Michael stops to talk to them, but my focus is past them. It's on the woman inside the room. My heart jackhammers in my chest, and I'm certain it's about to explode. I desperately want to see Natalie, but I also fear her rejection. How will I go on without her in my life?

One of the men knocks, and we wait. Finally, the door swings wide open. Viktor stands there, a huge smile on his face. "Good to see you, Alex."

I walk past him without acknowledging his greeting.

"I didn't want to wake her. She—"

His voice fades into the background. My entire being is laser-focused on Natalie. She's asleep on the bed, her blonde hair fanned out on the pillow around her. Carefully, I sit on the bed, trying not to wake her, but she stirs anyway.

"Viktor?" She reaches across the bed, her eyes still closed.

Viktor? Why the hell is she asking for him?

I thought my heart couldn't break anymore, but I was wrong. It hurts. Pain sears through my chest. Natalie knows, and she doesn't want me anymore. Her hand feels around the bed and comes up empty. Then, she opens her eyes and sits up quickly.

"Alex?" she asks, her green eyes blinking a few times as if in disbelief. "Is it really you?"

I'm frozen in time, waiting to see the disgust on her face. Waiting to be rejected.

"You're here." She throws her arms around my neck, holding me tight. "It's over. It's really over."

Natalie's tears run down my neck as she cries, and I feel the weight of her sadness. Her sobs are the catalyst that breaks through my numbness, allowing me to feel. I break. Tears stream down my face, and my body trembles from the sheer force of emotions I can no longer hold back."

"I'm sorry. I'm so sorry, baby girl. I ruined your body. I scarred you. And our child—I killed our baby." I choke on a sob. "It's my fault. This is all my fault. I don't know how to fix this. I don't know how to fix us."

She pulls back and holds my face in her hands. "Alex. Stop."

"I should've fought harder. I should've done more to protect you. I ruined everything. I failed." I'm unable to stop the purge of emotions.

"Everything you did was to protect me." Natalie wipes my tears. "I'm alive because of you."

"But our baby." I drop my head. "I don't expect you ever to forgive me."

"Look at me," she says softly.

I don't look up. I'm afraid to see the hate in her eyes—the pain I've caused.

"Please, Sir."

Slowly, I lift my face and nearly drown in the depths of her emerald gaze. Because instead of hate, all I see is love and compassion.

"I'm so sorry, baby girl."

"There's nothing to apologize for." She caresses my cheek with her tiny hand. Her skin is so soft against mine. "Alex, we were forced into an unimaginable situation. The choices you were given were impossible. But you acted as my Dominant and did everything in your power to protect me from Moreno's depravity." She takes my shaking hands in hers. "You made sure it was you on the stage that night instead of him. You did that to protect me—to make sure I lived. What happened after that was out of our control."

"I should've—"

"You can't blame yourself."

She wraps her arms around me again, and I cling to her as if my life depends on it. And it does. Without her strength. Without her love. I'm going to fall back into the black abyss.

"I love you, Alex. We're together, and we're safe." She rains kisses on me. "Everything's going to be okay now."

Natalie

ALEX IS SITTING ON THE BED, I THINK. I'VE HAD THIS DREAM SO MANY nights that I'm afraid to believe it's real. He doesn't answer when I say his name. I'm scared when I go to touch him, his image will disintegrate as it has so many times before. But this time, when I reach out, I feel the warmth of his body. It's really him. He's still here. The nightmare is finally over.

Then he shatters in my arms. His body trembles as he cries and apologizes over and over. He's broken. I look over Alex's shoulder and see the concerned look on Viktor's face. The man standing next to him whispers something. Then, with one last glance, they leave, closing the door softly behind them.

It's just us.

Alex's expression is tortured as he pours his heart out. He's blaming himself for everything. Hearing the agony in his voice is killing me. Everything that happened was Silverio's doing. He's the only one responsible for the heartache we're both experiencing. Knowing I lost our baby has been indescribable grief.

An emptiness like I've never imagined possible. But not even for a second did I blame Alex. I don't know what to do other than tell him how much I love him and hold him. I'm hoping my love breaks through the grief he's experiencing.

Alex finally lifts his head. His blue eyes, still filled with tears, meet mine.

"I love you, Alex. Nothing will ever change that," I say one more time before he relaxes and begins to accept the truth of my words.

He leans in and kisses me. It's different from any kiss we've shared. It's desperate like he's drowning, and I'm his air. His lifeline—the only person who can save him.

"I don't deserve you," he says between kisses.

His words tear my heart in two. "Don't say that. I was made to be yours." My lips meet his once again. I pull him with me as I lay back on the bed. He winces. "Are you hurt?"

"I'm fine. Don't stop."

Grabbing his shirt, I lift it up, revealing his chest. It's wrapped tightly in medical tape, and he has sutures above his eye. I was so concerned with his emotional state I didn't notice them before. "What happened?"

He pulls his shirt down. "It's nothing, just a few broken ribs."

"A few broken ribs? That's not nothing." I don't want to hurt him, so I try to pull away.

"It's not important." He holds me tight. "It's over. Moreno's dead."

Moreno's dead? I want to ask him more. I want to know how Silverio died. But Alex's eyes plead with me not to question him. That right now, what he needs is my love. I take the shirt I'm wearing and pull it over my head. Alex palms my breasts, kneading them before rolling my already hard nipples. His hands skate down my sides to the top of my pants. I lift my hips as he slides them down my legs, tossing them off to the side before he leans over me, kissing me deeply.

Grabbing the hem of his shirt, I carefully help him take it off. It lands near my pants on the floor. Carefully, Alex stands up. Each move looks stiff and painful. He kicks off his shoes before unbuttoning his jeans removing them and his boxers. My eyes scan his body, assessing each and every cut and bruise. He was beaten, and given the different colors of the bruises that cover his body, he was beaten more than once. Tears fill my eyes at the thought of him being hurt.

"It's over. No more tears, Natalie."

I close my eyes, trying to rid myself of the sadness.

Alex takes the opportunity to position his body over mine. I've missed this feeling. There were many days I didn't think I'd ever experience being loved by Alex again. His lips caressing my lips. His hands roaming my body, touching every inch as he reacquaints himself.

"I've missed you so goddamn much, baby girl."

"I need you." I lift my hips, encouraging him.

He runs his fingers between my legs and gives me his sexy smile. I'm already wet and ready for him. Then he slides his erection in ever so slowly. Stretching me inch by inch until he's fully sheathed. He closes his eyes for a long moment.

"You feel so good."

I moan in appreciation, loving the way our bodies fit together as if we were made only for one another. Alex begins to move in a gentle rhythm as he makes love to me. I pour every ounce of emotion I have into each movement and each kiss, using my body to convey my love for him. We climax at the same time, solidifying our reunion.

Carefully, Alex moves off me. We lay together, wrapped in each other's arms, our legs entwined. The nightmare we were forced to live in is finally over. I'm drifting in and out of sleep when a knock on the door startles me.

"Stay here." Alex gets out of bed and slips his pants on. Then, padding to the door, he looks out the peephole before opening it.

"I'm sorry to interrupt, boss."

I release the breath I'm holding when I hear Viktor's voice. Sitting up, I hold the blankets against me to keep myself covered.

"Maxim's jet is ready. We need to leave for the airport."

"Give us a few minutes."

"You got it." Viktor reaches out and clasps Alex's shoulder. "Glad to have you back, boss."

"Thank you." Alex glances back at me. "And thank you for taking care of Natalie."

Viktor's blue eyes meet mine from across the room. "It's my job, sir."

That simple statement, everything he isn't saying, holds so much meaning. We've formed a friendship unlike any other. I owe him something I can never repay—my life.

Alex closes the door, and I climb out of bed and gather my clothes to get dressed.

"Are you ready to go?"

"I never thought I'd hear you say that." I smile. "Let's go home."

Alex

A PARADE OF BLACK SUVs ACCOMPANIES US TO A PRIVATE HANGAR AT the Abraham Gonzalez Airport. Viktor helps the rest of the men load everyone's bags onto the plane.

Michael walks over to where I'm standing. "This is where we part ways."

"I can't thank you enough for everything you've done." I motion for Natalie to come over. "Michael, I'd like to introduce you to my fiancée, Natalie."

"I've heard a lot about you." He smiles and reaches to shake her hand, but she surprises us both when she hugs him instead.

"You brought Alex back to me. Saying thank you doesn't feel like enough."

"It's my job, ma'am."

Natalie giggles. "I've heard that somewhere before." She glances in Viktor's direction.

"Did you get—"

"It's all taken care of. Viktor has it."

Natalie looks at me curiously, but I'm not ready to talk about the dagger and what I did. I don't know if or when I'll ever be ready.

"Where are you headed now?" I assumed Michael and his team would accompany us back to New York, but they don't seem to be getting on the plane.

"We're off to our next job."

"Mike, you ready to go?" a man calls from one of the other vehicles.

"Be there in a minute." Michael shakes my hand. "I'm glad to see you're doing better. You two have a safe flight."

I wrap my arm around Natalie's waist and watch Michael walk away. "Let's go home."

Together, we climb the stairs into Maxim's jet and get settled in our seats. Viktor, Sasha, and a few more of Maxim's men board the plane after us. We're taxiing down the runway within minutes, and the wheels lift off the ground. I didn't think this moment would ever come, but finally, this whole nightmare will be in our past.

It isn't until the plane touches down at JFK that I can breathe easily again. We're home, and we're safe. It's really over.

"Maxim sent a driver and a car. He's waiting at your apartment," Viktor says as we prepare to exit the plane.

"How did you find us?" I'm trying to put the pieces of our rescue together.

"It wasn't until after Timur woke up. He told us he heard the name *El Tomador*," he explains as we walk across the tarmac to the waiting car. "That was the break we desperately needed."

"Timur's alive? He was so still, and there was so much blood." Natalie's voice quivers. "I thought he was dead."

"He got lucky. The bullet missed his heart by a few inches."

We slide into the car's back seat and sandwich Natalie between us. The lights from the skyline illuminating the night come into view. It's a welcome sight. I put my arm around Natalie, and she lays her head on my shoulder.

"Tired?" I kiss the top of her head.

"My body doesn't know if it's day or night." She yawns.

"I'm sure you haven't slept well in weeks." I know I haven't slept a full night since we were taken. But now that we can finally let our guard down, I feel like I could sleep for a week. And even that probably wouldn't be enough.

"I texted Maxim," Viktor says as we pull into the underground parking garage. "They're awake and can't wait to see you both."

"You shouldn't have woken them.".

"Maxim gave me orders. Take it up with him."

Something's off with Viktor. He's been distant since we left for the airport. I'm sure he's trying to process everything. It can be argued he had the most critical job—Natalie. Finding her tied up on that stage must have been hard for him. And then he was the first one she told about miscarrying.

Viktor has a lot of responsibility on his shoulders. Usually, he handles it well. He rarely lets his emotions show. Knowing Viktor, he wanted to be in that room with Moreno. Maybe he needs some time off after this to decompress? I make a mental note to speak to Maxim about it later.

We climb out of the car and make our way to the elevator, where I punch in the code for the penthouse.

We're finally home.

Natalie

If this is a dream, I never want to wake up. The three of us are in the elevator, an everyday occurrence I've taken for granted. As I look between the two men who mean the world to me, I'm filled with gratitude. It's hard to believe that I'd said my silent goodbyes to them just yesterday, thinking I'd never see either one again. But now we're safe, and we're home. The elevator doors don't have a chance to open all the way before Maxim grabs us, pulling us in for a hug.

"Alexander. Natalia." His voice cracks. "Welcome home."

"Natalie," Irina says, wrapping me in a hug before pulling back and appraising me. "You're so thin and pale. How are you feeling?"

Did anyone tell them? I look to Alex. He offers me a slight shrug as if he doesn't know what to say either. My gaze turns to Viktor, and he shakes his head no.

"I think we're all tired." I choose an evasive answer, not wanting to ruin our homecoming with the news of our loss.

Movement from the kitchen catches my eye, startling me. I let out a small gasp.

"It's Dr. Turova," Irina says, touching my arm.

"Welcome home, Natalie," Karina says.

"Thank you."

Alex doesn't leave my side as we make our way into the apartment.

"I know you've just gotten in, and I'm sure you're exhausted," Karina says quietly. "But I'd like to examine you right away."

My body trembles. "I, um—"

"Why don't we take Karina to our room," Alex suggests. "We can talk more there."

I nod, trying to hold back my tears. Alex places his hand on the small of my back as the three of us walk to our bedroom.

"I hope you don't mind. Maxim had me set up in here."

The ultrasound machine sits next to the bed, taunting me with the memories of our visit with the doctor. We were so happy watching our tiny baby move inside me. Everything was perfect. Then we left her office, thinking we were heading back to the safety of the compound.

The lights. The sounds. The blood. Horrific memories resurface, and I grab Alex for support.

He leads me to the bed. "Sit," he says, his voice firm yet gentle. "Doctor, while we were being held, I did some terrible things." I cover his hand with mine for support. His voice cracks as he says, "I caused Natalie to lose the baby," Alex admits and then walks over to the large window, keeping his back to us.

"Can you tell me exactly what happened?" Karina sits beside me.

Although the story is painful, I do my best to recount the events of that fateful night. "While I showered, there was so much blood. I continued to bleed for over a week." I wipe the tears from my face.

"I'd like to do an ultrasound."

"Why?" I don't want to see an empty uterus.

"Diagnostically, it's important I check."

Alex spins around and comes back to my side. "Don't you think she's been through enough without putting her through this too?"

"Mr. Montgomery," Karina says patiently. "I understand your concerns, but I have a medical responsibility to my patient. And right now, that involves an ultrasound examination."

"Alex, it's okay." I do my best to reassure him. "If it's too much for you, you can wait—"

"You were forced to grieve this loss alone. I'm not leaving you to do this without me, too. Let's get this over with." He glares at the doctor.

She appears unphased by his outburst. I pull up Alex's T-shirt so she has access to my abdomen.

"The gel is going to be a little cold. I apologize."

She places the wand on my stomach, and I turn away from the screen. I can't bear to watch. To see an empty place where my baby should be. Alex keeps his eyes locked with mine as he holds my hand tight. His presence gives me the strength to get through this. Karina's silent as she moves the wand across my abdomen. She clicks a button on the machine, filling the room with a familiar sound.

Swoosh. Swoosh. Swoosh.

I snap my head to the screen. My mind can't process what I'm hearing or seeing.

"Your baby is alive and well," Karina announces.

"I don't understand."

She moves the wand a little lower. "This." She points at the screen. "Is your placenta. It's typically lower in early pregnancy and moves higher as your uterus grows. Yours is still very low."

"What are you saying?" Alex asks.

"What Natalie described didn't sound like a typical miscarriage, but I didn't want to say anything until I confirmed my suspicions. Natalie most likely suffered cervical trauma, which upset the low-lying placenta and caused the bleeding," she explains. "The fact that you were forced to stay off your feet for a few days following the episode was a good thing. It allowed your body to heal."

"I didn't lose the baby?" My head can't wrap itself around what she's saying or what I'm seeing.

Karina smiles. "Your baby's heartbeat is strong and healthy. It measures right on track at almost eighteen weeks."

"Our baby's okay?" I ask again.

"Your baby looks perfect." Karina looks between Alex and me. "Do you want to know if you're having a boy or a girl?"

"Do you want to know?" Alex asks me.

"Yes, please."

Karina moves the wand until she gets the angle she's seeking and then pauses the image on the screen. "It looks like you're having a girl."

For the past few weeks, I believed our baby had died. It was a loss unlike anything I'd ever felt. Finding out our baby is alive has brought back a part of me I feared was gone forever. I'm laughing and crying as I look at the crystal-clear image of our baby girl's tiny hands and feet as she kicks and wiggles around.

"That's my daughter?" Alex asks in disbelief.

I watch Alex's expression as he gazes at the image of our little girl on the screen. The light that had been missing from his eyes has rekindled. Learning our baby is alive has aided in healing the broken fragments inside him. Grateful for our miracle, I redirect my attention to the screen. Karina prints off a fresh set of photographs. The last one she hands us says *It's a girl* in pink ink.

"Wait until Maxim sees this. He'll never let us forget he was right." Alex laughs.

It's been so long since I've heard him carefree. It's a beautiful sound.

After I wipe the gel off, we move to the sitting area in our room to complete the rest of our visit. I've suffered from malnutrition and have lost a significant amount of weight, which explains why I'm not showing. Karina gives me some new prenatal vitamins, and we discuss a diet plan that includes extra nutrition and calories so I can slowly gain back the weight I lost.

"I fully anticipate the placenta to continue moving to exactly where it should be. But I'd still like you to take it easy the next few weeks."

"I'll make sure she does. I'll see you out."

"Alex?"

He turns to me.

"Can you get Viktor? I want to show him our daughter."

Viktor

THE LOOK ON NATALIE'S FACE WHEN THE DOCTOR SAID SHE WANTED TO examine her nearly killed me. I watch helplessly as she and Alex bring Karina to their room. I hate that Natalie's already suffered so much, and now she must endure this.

My nerves are on a hairpin trigger, and I need to be alone so I don't snap. I stalk down the hall to Alex's office, closing the door behind me. Lowering myself onto the desk chair, I unlock the bottom drawer and take out the gift box with the pink and blue bows.

The night Misha and I found their abandoned car, I saved Natalie's ultrasound pictures. Even managed to get them into a little photo album. These pictures are special, and I knew Natalie would be happy that I was able to save them. But now, I don't know what to do with the reminder of what could've been. I drop my head into my hands.

I'm startled when the door opens and quickly sweep the box into the drawer, slamming it shut.

"Is everything okay?" Alex asks.

I jump up from my seat. "Yeah, all good. Did you need something?"

"Natalie asked to see you. She's in our bedroom."

I walk down the hall to their room. Even though the door is open, I knock.

"Come in," she calls softly.

I find Natalie reclining on several fluffy pink pillows—her tear-stained face tugs at my heart.

"Hey," she says.

"Hey yourself," I say awkwardly and stop just inside the doorway. And after our interactions in Mexico, I'm unsure what to do or how to act. It's a foreign feeling.

"Come here." Natalie pats the bed.

I cock my head slightly before taking hesitant steps to her side. She slides over, making room for me to sit next to her.

"Are you okay?"

Natalie pulls out a piece of paper she had hiding under the pillow next to her and hands it to me.

I hold the paper, momentarily shocked at what I'm seeing. "Is this?"

"Yes. It's my baby." She smiles, and her eyes light up.

My thoughts return to yesterday. How I held her while she cried in my arms, mourning the loss of her child. The look of torment in her eyes was too much to bear. But right now, her beautiful green eyes are glistening with excitement as she explains everything Dr. Turova told her about what caused the bleeding. "But the baby is alive and healthy."

"Wait here." I jump up and hurry to the door.

"Where are you going?"

"I'll be right back." I hurry back to the office and retrieve the box from the drawer. The thought of giving Natalie this gift fills me with joy. After everything they've gone through, they truly deserve a happy ending. "This is for you." I pass her the box.

"What is it?"

"Open it." I smile.

Carefully, Natalie unties the ribbons and lifts the lid off. She picks up the photo album and looks at me before opening it and flipping through a few pages.

"Viktor," she says as tears fill her eyes. "Where did you find these?"

"You must've dropped them during the struggle. I salvaged what I could. I don't know if I did this right." I shrug. "But I thought it might be a nice surprise when you got home."

"I couldn't imagine anything better." She wraps her arms around me. "It's perfect."

"I'm glad you like it."

"I love it." She releases me and sits back. "Will you help me put these in?"

I take the book from her, flip to the next empty page, and arrange the pictures. When I get to the last photo, I freeze. "It's a girl?"

"It is." She beams with pride.

"Maxim's never going to let you forget he was right." Natalie joins me, laughing. Then my focus shifts back to her and how thin she's gotten. I don't know anything about pregnancy or babies, but I can assume her severe weight loss isn't good. "Are you hungry? Can I get you something to eat or drink? I can order—"

"Viktor. It's the middle of the night. I need to get some sleep before you try to fatten me up."

"She's right," Alex says as he walks into the room. "It's time to sleep so your body can focus on growing our little girl."

"I'm going to go down to my place. A hot shower and my bed sound really good right about now." I clasp Alex's shoulder. "Congratulations, boss. I'm happy for you both."

"Thank you. We'll see you later today."

It looks like everyone's already gone to bed. The house is quiet as I make my way to the elevator to go down to my apartment. It's time to wash away this nightmare and get a few hours of sleep.

Alex

∞

The morning sun's just beginning to peek over the horizon, dispelling the darkness we've been living in these past few weeks.

"What's that?" I point to the box next to her.

"Viktor found the ultrasound pictures I dropped. He made us a photo album."

After all the time they spent together in Northmeadow, he and Natalie formed a close friendship. It seems their bond grew even stronger after their experience in Mexico. They care about each other. I understand that, but part of me hates what they share and wants to put an end to it—I'm territorial and jealous. The rational side of me realizes they've shared some traumatic experiences. It only makes sense that they're going to be close. I try my best to hide the conflicting emotions. "It seems he's already smitten with our little girl."

"I think he is."

"Let's shower. Then we need to get some sleep." My eyes are glued to her as she strips, making a small pile of clothes on the floor next to her. Until now, I never understood what people meant when they said a woman glows when she's pregnant. Natalie's absolutely radiant.

"I never thought I'd be so excited to do something as mundane as showering." She grabs her clothes and turns to bring them to the hamper.

The happiness I felt seconds ago fades when I see her back. It's a stark reminder of what we've been through—what I did to her. Natalie continues talking while I stare at the two cuts that are still in the beginning stages of healing. They were deep and needed stitches, but she wasn't allowed medical care. Now, she's going to be left with jagged scars that will serve as a permanent reminder of what I did to her. She spins around, and I know she sees right through me, straight to the feelings of inadequacy and guilt that are assaulting me.

"Alex, don't. They're just cuts that'll heal. You kept us safe. That's all that matters."

The love that's reflected in her eyes rights every wrong.

She twists, looking over her shoulder in the mirror. "I was thinking maybe I could get a tattoo after it's healed."

"I think that's a great idea."

"Maybe we can pick a design together?"

"Of course, baby girl."

Once we're in the shower, Natalie lets her hands roam my body, her lips following their path.

I'm rock hard in an instant, but I pull back. "Dr. Turova said no sex for three weeks."

"She didn't say I can't make you feel good." Natalie begins to lower herself to her knees, but I grab her elbows, holding her up.

"I'll wait as long as I have to for us to be together," I say. "I will not use you for my pleasure."

I don't know what triggers it, but Natalie starts crying. "I was so scared, Alex."

"I know, baby girl. I was scared, too. But it's over. I'll never let anyone hurt you again."

We continue our shower, and there isn't a minute where our bodies aren't touching. Natalie's touch is tender as she washes my bruised body. Then, it's my turn. My hands glide over her, reacquainting themselves with every curve. I've never experienced something so sensual and intimate outside of sex.

After we're dry, I close the blackout curtains and climb into bed. I've spent the past month in a primitive cell, forced to lie on a dirty floor. Our soft sheets and fluffy comforter feel like heaven. It's a luxury I'll never take for granted again.

"Please don't let me go. I'm afraid if I close my eyes, you'll disappear."

"I'm not going anywhere," I say as I stretch my arm out, and she snuggles close.

I wait until her body relaxes and her breathing calms before closing my eyes. But for me, sleep never comes.

The clock on the nightstand reads eleven a.m. Natalie's still sound asleep in my arms. As much as I want to, I can't lay here any longer. There's work to be done. I'm certain Maxim's waiting to debrief us. Slowly, I pull my arm out from underneath her. She stirs slightly but thankfully doesn't wake. Viktor warned me about her reactions to having a closed door, so I leave it cracked open.

Before going to the kitchen, I have an important task to take care of in my office. Sitting in my chair, I open the top drawer and take out paper and a pen. Before meeting Natalie, I never thought about the potential risks of working with Maxim.

My life is different now, and after what we've just lived through, it's something I realize I must do. As I put pen to paper, I know this will be the hardest thing I've ever done.

After shredding at least five sheets of paper, I'm finally satisfied with the words I've penned. The letter gets sealed in an envelope with Natalie's name and placed with the other essential documents she'll need if anything ever happens to me. With that out of the way, there's one final step I need to take.

On my way down the hall, I check in on Natalie, who's still sound asleep. Then, I go to the kitchen, where I find Viktor sitting at the island drinking a cup of coffee.

"I wasn't sure if you'd be up yet." I walk past him and grab a mug from the cupboard.

"Couldn't sleep," he mutters.

"Me either." I push the button on the Keurig, and with a hiss, the machine comes to life.

Viktor glances down the hall. "Is Natalie still sleeping?"

"She is," I reply as I add sugar and creamer before I take a seat next to him. "We need to talk."

"Okay," Viktor says and turns slightly to look at me.

"Natalie is my world. I owe you everything for rescuing her."

"I was just doing my job."

"Cut the shit, Viktor." He always blows off his actions as *just his job*, but I know this is more personal to him. "Natalie is more than just a job to you. I know you care about her."

"Alex, if you're implying—"

"I trust you with her life," I interrupt him. "And I know you'll always put her first."

"What are you getting at?"

"I need you to promise me something."

"What kind of promise?"

"If anything ever happens to me. I need you to step in and take my place with Natalie and the baby."

"Boss, I know you've just been through hell, but we've got everything handled."

"This situation was a rude awakening. All these years, I've ignored the danger working with Maxim could present. That was fine when it was just me, but there are two more people I need to protect now. It'll give me peace of mind moving forward, knowing you'll be with them if anything happens to me."

Viktor studies my face before running his hand over his shaved head. The thought of Natalie being with someone else makes me feel sick, but I need this commitment from him. He's the only one I know I can trust with their lives.

Several long minutes pass before he speaks. "I promise, boss."

"Thank you."

It's both a relief and a promise I hope to never have to rely on.

Natalie

I WAKE DISORIENTED, MY HEART POUNDING. SQUEEZING MY EYES closed, I try to take a few deep breaths, but my body doesn't cooperate. Panic is rushing through me like a freight train. I can't breathe. I'm suffocating. "You can control this. Find something to ground yourself," I say the steps aloud.

Opening my eyes, I look around the room and find something to focus on—the picture of Alex and me on the dresser from Christmas Eve. It's a selfie of us in Central Park right after he proposed. Sitting up, I swing my legs off the bed and touch them to the cool wood floor. Then, I run my hands along the soft blankets next to me. Slowly, the familiarity of the objects helps to calm my over-stimulated senses.

"My name is Natalie Clarke. I'm in my apartment in New York City. I'm safe and loved. I am strong," I speak the affirming words repeatedly, anchoring myself to the present. Little by little, my body begins to regulate itself. My breaths come easier.

Next, I focus on the auditory senses. I hear familiar sounds—Maxim's boisterous voice, Viktor's deep timbre, and Alex's carefree laugh. The full realization washes over me, filling me with an all-consuming peace—I'm home.

After a quick trip to the bathroom, I put on a silk robe, tying the belt in a knot before padding down the hall to the kitchen to join everyone.

"Good afternoon, sleepyhead," Alex says when he sees me.

"You should've woken me up." I sit next to him at the island.

"You looked too peaceful to wake. Besides, Karina said you need to rest."

"Oh good, you're awake." Irina hurries into the kitchen. "I hope you're hungry. I made lunch."

"Lunch sounds wonderful. I'm starving."

"Perfect." Irina grabs a plate and starts dishing out food.

"She's been out here all morning cooking," Viktor whispers conspiratorially. "You'd think she was making food for an army."

Out of the corner of my eye, I see the silhouette of a man coming around the corner. "Timur," I squeal. Jumping off my seat, I run over to him, wrapping him in a tight hug. His body stiffens, and I let go quickly. "Did I hurt you? I'm so sorry."

"It's okay." He smiles stiffly.

"I thought we'd lost you."

"It'll take more than a bullet to get rid of me." He winks.

"It's time we get to work," Maxim interrupts.

"Where are you going?" Alex tries to stand, but I grab his arm, stopping him.

"I'll just be in my office. Come and get me when you're done eating." He kisses the top of my head.

"Yes, Sir." I don't want him to return to work already, but I'm sure they have important things to discuss. I watch the men exit the room, leaving Irina and me alone in the kitchen. She wastes no time setting a plate of cucumber and tomato salad before me.

"This looks heavenly." I moan, seeing the fresh food.

"That's just a start, dear." She opens the oven and pulls out a tray.

"Did you make *piroshki*?"

"I know how much you love it."

"You must've been up with the sun to get all this done." I take a bite of my salad, savoring the flavors.

"I couldn't sleep," Irina says before opening the refrigerator and pulling out another plate.

This time, the platter has what looks like buns with open centers. Some appear to be filled with cream cheese, others with apples.

"What are they?"

"These are called *Vatrushka*. It's sweet dough with a filling. I used my *babushka's* recipe."

"I don't know what to eat first." I giggle, looking at the decadent foods set out for me.

"Now that it's just us." Irina sits next to me. "How are you, honey?"

I set my fork down and finish chewing my bite of food. I'm trying to buy myself some time before I'm forced to answer. My eyes dart around the room, avoiding eye contact with her for fear that she'll see right through me.

She places her hand over mine. "You don't have to put a brave face on. It is okay to not be okay."

I blink back the tears that once again fill my eyes. "I had a panic attack when I woke up." When I finally give in and look at her, I find her gray eyes filled with compassion. "We're home and safe, but I can't shake this fear. I'm afraid to trust that it's really over. It's like something bad is lurking in the dark, just waiting for me to let my guard down."

"That's perfectly normal." She rubs my hand gently, soothing me like a parent would a young child. "You've experienced significant trauma. It's normal to struggle with your emotions."

"I know all of that."

"Yes, you've learned how to help others from a textbook," she agrees. "But living through it and finding your own healing is very different."

Tears slide down my cheeks. "Silverio forced Alex to do awful things to me. There was so much blood. I was certain I lost the baby."

"But Alex told us the baby was okay." Irina looks confused.

"Karina did an ultrasound last night. She explained my placenta was low, which was the most likely cause of the bleeding episode. That's when I found out the baby was okay."

"I'm sorry you had to go through that."

"I know I'm lucky. For the most part, I was spared the horrors most of the people there had to endure." I swallow over the lump in my throat.

"You must not compare your trauma with that of anyone else."

I take another bite of my lunch and let her words sink in.

She's right.

My trauma isn't any more or less. It's unique to me. I'm going to have to learn how to live with it.

"I'd like to put you in touch with a therapist from Jelena's Hope," Irina offers. "It will be helpful with your recovery."

"I think that might be a good idea."

Irina is easy to talk to, especially about these difficult subjects. I find myself sharing more details about the night in the club with Alex and the scars it left on my back. Then I tell her how close I came to being raped and sold.

"If Viktor hadn't come." My voice trails off.

"The important thing is he did."

I nod in agreement, unable to think about what might've happened. But then, a forgotten detail surfaces and the panic I thought I had under control rears its ugly head. "There was a young girl. She lived in the house with us."

"Amelia?" Irina asks.

"Yes. Have you heard anything about her?"

"She was brought to a secure clinic just over the Mexican border. She's being treated for some—" Irina hesitates. "Injuries."

"Injuries? What kind of injuries?" She's leaving something out.

"Amelia was raped."

"No. Please tell me that's not true. I promised Amelia she'd be taken care of."

"Viktor told me everything. As soon as she's medically cleared, Maxim and I will fly her to Jelena's Hope, where I will personally make sure she's cared for."

"Thank you." I throw my arms around Irina.

"Right now, you only need to be concerned with resting and getting stronger."

Natalie

After filling my tummy with all the delicious foods Irina made for me, I return to our bedroom to get dressed. It's a hot August afternoon, so I choose a loose sundress, put on some makeup, and pull my hair half-back.

"You look beautiful, baby girl," Alex says from the doorway.

"Thank you." A blush creeps up my cheeks.

"It's a good thing it was me walking past the open door while you were dressing, though."

"I'm sorry. I can't be in a room with the door closed."

"I'm not angry." Alex comes up behind me. "It'll take time for us to get over what happened." I rest my head on his chest. "I have something for you."

"You do?"

Alex takes my engagement ring from his pocket. "I hope you still want to marry me."

"There's nothing that can make me change my mind about becoming your wife."

He slides the ring back on my finger, pausing to look at it. "There's something we have to do today."

"Oh?"

"Your parents have been calling. Everyday."

"What are we supposed to tell them?" Panic begins to come to the surface once again.

"First, you need to relax. You and the baby don't need any more stress." Alex takes my hand and leads me to the bed. "Viktor has been speaking to them. They think we went on an extended earlymoon."

"An earlymoon?"

"Yes, an earlymoon." Alex grins. "You know, a honeymoon before the wedding."

"I see."

"We left our phones at the Soloniks' and went off-grid to spend some quality time together."

"Is that what we're calling spending time with a madman?" I give a sarcastic laugh.

"For this purpose, yes." Alex leans in and kisses my nose. "We took an earlymoon because we found out we were pregnant and knew we wouldn't be able to take a honeymoon."

The smile on his face tells me he's proud of the story he's come up with, and although I hate to admit it, I think it might work.

"Do we have time to call them now?"

"I think now is a perfect time." He reaches into his pocket and pulls out my phone. "Viktor kept it while we were gone."

Darkness clouds his eyes as if he's disappeared into the memories of our past few weeks.

"Hey." I take his hand. "I'm right here."

Shaking his head, he returns his focus to me. "Let's call your parents and give them the good news."

I pull up their contact and touch the green call button.

"Natalie?" My mom answers on the first ring. "Is that you?"

"Hi. Mom. You're on speaker. Alex is here too."

"Stanley," Mom yells. "It's Natalie and Alex. Where have you two been? We've been worried sick about you."

"Alex and I went on an earlymoon." I try to stifle a laugh.

"So we were told," Dad says.

"Hi. Dad." I keep my voice as carefree as possible. "How are you feeling?"

"Better now that we've heard from you."

"I'm sorry, Mr. and Mrs. Clarke," Alex chimes in. "It was a spur-of-the-moment decision. I was in such a hurry and wanted to surprise Natalie. Looking back, I realize I should've called to give a heads up."

"That would've been nice," Mom says, a sarcastic edge in her tone.

"I'm sorry, Mom."

"Where did you two run off to anyway?" she asks.

"Alex arranged for us to use Max's remote cabin," I tell them all about Maxim's compound without telling them we were actually hiding in a heavily guarded fortress before being kidnapped. Instead, I describe a beautiful cabin atop the Baltic Sea's cliffs. "The place is totally off-grid. No phone or internet. It was wonderful." I look to Alex, who nods in approval.

"I'm glad you had a nice time," Dad says, "But please, don't disappear and scare us like that again."

Disappear.

My father says the word so casually, not knowing how close we came to truly disappearing. It's something they never need to know.

"We won't." It's time to change the topic of conversation. I open a text message on the phone and attach one of our ultrasound pictures. "I just sent you a text. Can you check it out?"

I grab Alex's hand, trying to hold back a swirling mix of nerves and excitement.

"What is it?" Mom asks, her voice laced with confusion.

"We're having a baby." I squeal.

"That's why we went away early," Alex explains. "We knew we wouldn't have a honeymoon after the wedding."

I hear crying. "Mom. Are you okay?"

"I wasn't expecting something like this. It isn't right."

"This wasn't something we planned."

"How did it happen then?" Mom snips. "And what am I supposed to tell our friends?"

"I suppose you'll tell them you're going to be a grandmother."

"I can't believe my little girl is going to be a mom," Dad says.

"I am, Daddy. Alex and I are thrilled. We hope you both will be as well."

"Well, we weren't expecting this, so it's going to take a little time to get used to the idea," Dad says calmly. "But I'm sure we'll be just fine once the shock wears off."

"We need to reschedule the bridal shower. When are you coming home?" Mom's tone is clipped.

"We just got back to New York yesterday," Alex says. "Natalie had a few complications—"

"What kind of complications?" Mom interrupts.

"I had some bleeding. I've seen an excellent doctor who assured us that everything is okay. I have to take it easy for a few weeks, but she and I are healthy."

"She?" Dad asks.

"We're having a baby girl."

"As soon as Natalie gets the all-clear, we'll fly out."

"Do whatever you need to keep my daughter and granddaughter safe."

"You know I will, Mr. Clarke."

A yawn slips out.

"You sound tired," Mom says, her voice softening slightly. "Alexander, make sure Natalie's getting enough rest."

"I will. We'll call you tomorrow."

Alex

"You heard your mom." I wag my finger, trying to do my best impression of Charlotte. "It's time for your nap."

Natalie laughs at my poor comedy skills.

"I've barely been up a few hours," she protests.

"Doesn't matter. You need to rest."

"Can I interest you in *resting* with me?" She bats her eyelashes.

"I have to go out for a bit."

"Please don't leave me." Natalie clings to my shirt.

"Hey, baby girl." I move her back so I can see her face. "I won't be gone long, I promise."

"I don't want to be alone," she begs.

"Lie down." I pull the light blanket from the bottom of our bed over her. "I'll get Viktor and have him stay here with you until I get back."

"Thank you, Sir."

"I'll be back soon." I lean down and kiss her. "I love you."

"I love you too."

Leaving the bedroom door open, I search for Viktor and find him still in the office with Maxim and Timur.

"Can I steal Viktor for a little while?"

Viktor looks to Max, who gives a nod of approval before joining me in the hall.

"I have some errands to do. Natalie's lying down but doesn't want to be alone."

"I'll stay with her," he answers before I ask him.

"Thank you. I shouldn't be long."

I pull into the parking lot for the businesses in Chelsea. My destination—Fire and Ice. Shortly after we got back together, I designed a collar for Natalie and was planning a ceremony. But then we ended up in Russia, and everything spiraled downhill. Shake it off, Alex. I silently remind myself as I pull open the door to the club.

It's a Wednesday evening. The only thing going on is a beginner class in the main room. I quietly walk in just as Star prepares to dismiss the students into their small groups. She smiles and holds up a finger. When the last of her students exit the room, she walks across the club's wood floor—her stiletto heels clicking with each step.

"Alex." She hugs me. "I'm so glad you're back. How's Natalie?"

"She's pretty shaken up. But she'll be okay."

"When Anthony told me." She puts her hand over her heart. "I'm just glad Maxim was able to get you two back."

"Actually, he brought three of us back." I grin.

"Three?"

"Natalie's pregnant." It's the first time I've told anyone outside our family.

"Oh, Alex. I'm so happy for you both. Let's go to my office to talk."

We continue chatting. "It was a surprise for the both of us, but we're thrilled."

"When is she due?"

"The beginning of January."

Star has a huge office space. Half of the room is a typical setup with a desk where she conducts the club's business. The other half is a sleek sitting area with red leather furniture. She sits on the sofa and motions for me to sit across from her.

"Do you know what you're having?"

"It's a little girl." I beam with pride.

"You're so screwed." Star laughs. "She's going to have you wrapped around her little finger the second she's born."

I laugh along with her. But the reality is we came so close to losing the baby. I already know I'll do anything to make sure she's not only well-cared for but also safe and happy.

"I'm assuming you're here about something else, though." She raises an eyebrow at me.

"Do you have the collar?"

"I do." The experienced Dominatrix rises gracefully. She pulls a small key from her pocket and unlocks one of the desk drawers. Reaching in, she takes out a black jewelry box. "I hope you don't mind that I peeked."

"What did you think?"

"It's breathtaking." She passes me the box and returns to her spot on the sofa, crossing her legs.

Instead of opening it, I set the box on the glass table in front of me.

"What's wrong?"

A sick feeling stirs in the pit of my stomach as flashbacks of Moreno play in my mind. "He put a collar on her," I grit out the words. "He put her on a leash and made her crawl around. He treated her like an animal." I drop my head in my hands.

"I'm so sorry, Alex," Star says quietly. "Look at me." I can't lift my head. The memories are too much. "Alexander," she says sternly. "Raise your head and look at me."

Slowly, I lift my head. My vision is blurry from the tears that are now falling.

"That collar meant nothing." Star perches on the edge of the table and picks up the jewelry box. "This has meaning. This collar represents the Dom/sub bond you and Natalie share."

"I know, but—"

"There are no buts, Alex. Moreno will get what's coming to him. I'm sure Maxim will see to that."

"He's already dead. I killed him."

Star nods, undaunted by my admission. "Good." She pushes the box into my hands. "Open it."

With a deep breath, I lift the lid. "It's stunning."

The collar is a silver chain, not much thicker than a traditional necklace. It's discreet in appearance, so Natalie can wear it every day without garnering unwanted attention. Set in one end of the chain are two gemstones: a Peridot, Natalie's birthstone, and an Amethyst, my birthstone. The ends of the chain attach to a heart lock with the words *baby girl* inscribed on it. Once it's secured, it won't come off without the key I'll be wearing.

"She's going to love it," Star assures me.

"Do you think I'm doing the right thing? Given what's happened, should I wait?"

"What does your heart say?"

Rarely do I listen to my heart. It's a foreign feeling to make a decision based on pure emotion. "It tells me to do it now. To replace the terrible memories with something wonderful."

"Then you already have your answer."

"I'll call Anthony and tell him we're a go for Friday night. Can you make sure Brandon gets this for the ceremony?" I hand the box to Star.

"I'll take care of the rest of the details," Star reassures me.

Natalie and I are lucky to have such a supportive community to rally around us.

Alex

"Everything's all set. We'll see you Friday." I disconnect the call with Anthony before getting into the elevator. The collaring ceremony is in two days. It's last minute, but I shoot a quick text to my father. He's been on cloud nine since my earlier text about the baby.

Me: Natalie's collaring ceremony is Friday evening at Tony's place. I know it's last minute, but is there any chance you and Luna can fly in?

Dad: I'll do everything I can to get us there.

Everyone's sitting in the living room when I get upstairs.

"How was your nap?" I go straight to Natalie.

"It was good. I feel much better now."

"I'm glad to hear that."

"Where did you go?" she asks.

"My impatient little sub. You'll find out soon enough."

Natalie sticks her lip out in a pout.

"You're cute." I kiss her forehead. "But that won't work. Something smells delicious." I change the subject.

"That is my wife working her magic in your kitchen," Maxim says proudly.

"I offered to help, but she refused. I'll go crazy if all I can do is sit with my feet up for the next few months."

"Rest now, Natalia," Maxim advises. "When that little one comes, you will no longer have the luxury of rest."

"Dinner's ready," Irina calls from the kitchen.

"Let us eat." Maxim stands and, as usual, is the first one in the kitchen.

I offer my hand to Natalie, helping her from the couch. "You're glowing, baby girl."

"I'm so happy to be home and to know our little girl is okay." She places her hand on her stomach.

We join our extended family in the dining room. Irina is a master in the kitchen and has filled the table with various mouthwatering Russian dishes.

"I can't thank you enough for this." I motion toward the spread of food.

"It's my pleasure," Irina says before taking her seat next to Maxim.

Natalie waits while Irina makes Maxim's plate, showing deference to his place in the lifestyle before she makes mine.

When she's through, Maxim announces, "Everyone, please make your plate."

Viktor and Timur don't waste a second piling their plates high.

"Should we tell them now?" I whisper to Natalie.

"Yes." Her eyes light up.

"We have an announcement to make." I get everyone's attention.

The room grows quiet. All eyes are now on me.

"As you know, we had an ultrasound yesterday." I place my hand on Natalie's thigh under the table. "Dr. Turova assured us our baby is strong and healthy. She also informed us we're having a little girl." My heart swells with pride.

"A *vnuchka*," Maxim boasts. "I knew it."

"I don't know how." Natalie laughs. "But you were right."

"We didn't officially find out the gender of our babies before they were born. But Maxim knew both times."

"Somehow, that doesn't surprise me."

The rest of the meal is filled with baby talk and all the shopping Irina and Natalie plan to do before the Solonik's return to Russia.

"It sounds like I need to start converting one of the guest rooms to a nursery sooner rather than later," I say to my fiancé, who is absolutely radiant.

When I bought this penthouse, I never imagined I'd share it with a woman, let alone a child. But now that it's happening, I can't imagine my life any other way.

Natalie

Being back in New York is like a dream come true. It's taken a few weeks, but we're finally falling back into a familiar routine—something that's helped keep my anxiety at bay. Yesterday, I had my first video session with my therapist from Jelena's Hope.

Even skimming the surface of what I endured was hard to do. However, my therapist assures me we'll work through it at my pace and that I'll be okay. Recovery will be a bumpy road. It always is. But I'm confident that with the help of my support system, I'll triumph over my fears.

After my session, we had quite an online shopping spree for baby Montgomery. Irina is taking her role as *Babushka* seriously. While we're shopping, I get a text from Alex.

Alex: Don't worry about cooking. We're going out tonight for a farewell dinner.

Maxim, Timur, and Irina are leaving for Russia tomorrow. I don't want them to go, but I understand they have lives to return to.

Me: Where are we going?

Alex: It's a surprise.

A surprise means the unknown, and the unknown is terrifying. I lived nearly a month of my life with *surprises*. I put my phone away and try to concentrate on baby shopping instead of the fear clawing at my insides.

I've just finished my shower and am standing in front of the mirror, wrapped in a towel, attempting to apply my makeup.

"You're shaking. What's wrong?" Alex asks when he walks into our room.

I push the mascara wand back into its tube and set it on the dresser. "Not knowing where we're going is messing with my head. I know you want it to be a surprise—"

"A surprise isn't meant to scare you," he says patiently. "We're going to *Italiano Desiderio.*"

"You didn't have to tell me." I look down, disappointed with myself.

"I know I didn't." He pulls me into his arms. "It won't be scary forever. We both have some issues to work through, and we'll get through them together."

"But I've ruined your surprise."

"Oh, baby girl," he says with a sexy grin. "You haven't ruined anything. Now, put on your black lace dress so we can get to dinner."

"I love you, Sir." I plant a kiss on his lips.

"I love you too, baby girl."

This time, my hands are steady as I apply my mascara. I style my hair in a simple updo, leaving some loose curls to hang softly around my face. Then, I find the dress, a mermaid style, floor-length evening gown Alex told me to wear, and put it on.

Solid black lace covers me to my knees, where the fabric transitions to sheer lace. It's sexy yet not overly revealing. As I slide it on, I notice my breasts are already fuller than usual, enhancing the tightly fitted bodice and the deep V neckline.

"Can you help me zip this?"

"Sure." I turn around, and Alex slides the zipper up slowly.

"It feels a bit tighter than usual." I run my hand over my stomach.

Alex puts his hands over mine. "You've never looked more beautiful than you do right now," he says and kisses my neck softly before returning to buttoning his shirt.

When we're finished, we head out to the living room, where our guests are dressed equally as fancy.

"Everyone ready?" Alex asks.

We make our way to the garage. Maxim and Irina go with Timur in their rented car, and Viktor drives our vehicle as we head to the restaurant for our goodbye dinner.

Alex

Everything's all set for the ceremony tonight. Natalie thinks we're going out to have a farewell dinner for our Russian family. Instead, everyone's coming to celebrate us. Dad and Luna were able to get a flight in late last night. Lana and Brandon flew in earlier in the week. They've laid low since Natalie thinks they're still visiting Lana's extended family in Russia.

Collaring a submissive is a significant step in a Dom/sub relationship. It's not to be taken lightly. In many ways, this step is more serious than our upcoming marriage. I'm more nervous than I've ever been. I want everything to be perfect tonight.

"There's no one here," Natalie remarks as we enter the empty restaurant.

"Must be a slow night." I shrug, feigning indifference.

"Alex. Natalie." Anthony comes around the corner. "It's so good to see you both."

He wraps Natalie in a hug. "I hear congratulations are in order."

"They are." Natalie smiles. "Thank you."

"It's good to have you back." Tony reaches to shake my hand but decides to go for a hug instead.

"It's good to be back," I assure him.

Tony exchanges greetings with Max and Irina before turning back to us.

"Since it's such a beautiful night. I took the liberty of setting your table in the garden. Follow me."

Am I doing the right thing? Or is it too soon? My heart pounds as I place my hand on the small of Natalie's back. We follow Anthony through the restaurant and out the glass doors leading to the garden.

<h1 style="text-align:center">Natalie</h1>

W HEN WE GET TO THE RESTAURANT, IT'S EMPTY. I'D BE MORE suspicious if we weren't out with Maxim. He has a habit of booking out entire venues to avoid crowds and security issues. But after what we've just been through, I have a newfound appreciation for his actions. Tony leads us to the outdoor seating area, but instead of stopping, we turn in the opposite direction.

"Where are we going?" I ask Alex quietly.

"You'll see."

I squeeze Alex's hand, fighting the anxiety that's trying to steal this moment. It takes a conscious effort to remain grounded in the present. I try to focus on everything around me, like the flagstone path we're walking on. The creeping thyme with its delicate purple flowers growing between the stones. I'm careful where I step, trying to avoid sinking my heels in the dirt.

On both sides of the walkway are lush gardens of all-white flowers. The blooms are meant to be shown off by the moon's light. I recognize the Japanese lilacs, night-blooming Jasmine, and gardenia, among many others. Their sweet fragrance fills the air. Behind the flowers are miniature trees adorned with soft, twinkling lights.

"It's a moon garden," I murmur.

"Do you like it?" Anthony asks.

"It's magical. I love it."

A tall wrought iron gate stands at the end of the path, guarded by two imposing men. I recognize them as the security guards from Fire and Ice. When we approach, they pull the gates open, letting us pass. The metal clangs behind us. I look over my shoulder and find the gate is closed, and the men have resumed their post.

We stop walking and are shrouded by darkness. I look around but can't see anything. Why are we here? Chills creep up my spine as I try to convince myself the dark isn't going to swallow me whole.

"Are you ready?" Alex's warm breath tickles my neck.

"Ready for what?"

The second the words leave my mouth, lights flicker on, illuminating the open space. We're standing in a circular garden, and all our friends from Fire and Ice are lining the circle's edge. The Dominants are standing with their submissives kneeling at their feet. Maxim and Irina step out from behind us and take their place by Sam and Luna. Brandon and Lana are next to us, completing the circle.

"What's going on, Sir?"

"No more talking, baby girl."

Alex steps away from me and walks to the center of the circle.

"Natalie, please join your Dominant," Brandon instructs.

Lana grabs my hand and squeezes it as I pass by.

Alex motions toward a small black silk blanket on the ground in front of him. "Kneel." He reaches out to steady me as I lower to my knees before him, my gaze cast downward.

"Look at me." Alex's voice is deep and commanding.

I lift my eyes and meet the loving gaze of my Dominant.

Brandon walks up to Alex and hands him a black box. He stays next to Alex as he lifts the lid so I can see what's inside.

I gasp when I see the beautiful collar displayed on the black velvet. In the center of the box is a heart-shaped lock inscribed with the words *baby girl*.

A deluge of emotions, both good and bad, overwhelms me. I close my eyes and try to regain control over my thoughts. Before we were taken, Alex and I talked about me wearing his collar. It was the next step in our Dom/sub relationship, and we were both looking forward to it.

Then, a few weeks ago, that monster unwillingly locked a collar around my neck and paraded me around like an animal. I know this isn't the same, but after everything we went through, after being forced to wear a collar I didn't want, am I ready for this?

Alex clears his throat before he speaks. "I'm thankful for each of you who came tonight to share this special evening with us. The last few weeks have been the scariest of my life. Not only was I unsure if I'd live to see another day, but my submissive, the most precious person in my life, was in grave danger. Even though we're back safely, we're both still healing." Alex's voice cracks.

"I had this collar made before all that happened. Since we've been back, I've struggled with how to proceed. I wasn't sure if I should let more time pass before offering a collar to my submissive, fearing it would trigger her."

Tears are sliding down my face, listening to Alex speak. When he looks at me, he reaches down and wipes my tears.

"I sought the advice of a wise friend." He looks up and smiles at someone behind me. "Who explained to me that the piece of leather Natalie was forced to wear was meaningless—it held no significance in our lifestyle or relationship.

This collar is the one that holds meaning and commitment, the only one that matters. I decided to take a chance and seize the moment because no one is guaranteed a tomorrow. I didn't want to let another day go by without my submissive knowing how much I treasure her. How much it will mean to me if she accepts my collar."

My eyes follow his every movement as Alex takes the collar and lock from their place and hands the box to Brandon. He takes it and returns to his place in the circle.

"Natalie, as your Dominant, your heart, your safety, and your life are mine to care for. I'm honored that you've chosen to submit to me. I cherish that submission. Tonight, I'm asking you to take your commitment to us one step further. I'm asking you to wear my collar." I cling to his every word.

"By accepting this collar, you demonstrate your commitment to our relationship and your willingness to submit to me both physically and emotionally. You promise to obey me and accept my guidance, knowing I will care for and protect you in every way. Moreover, this collar represents my commitment to continue to train and support you, always respecting your boundaries and helping you grow in your submission. Above all, I promise to cherish and protect you for as long as we live. So, Natalie, I ask you now. Will you accept this collar and all the promises it symbolizes?"

His words weave deep into my heart, knitting together every broken piece. "Yes, Sir. I will."

Alex places the silver chain of the collar around my neck. He attaches the heart lock on the front and snaps it closed. "Thank you for your gift of submission, baby girl."

I place my hands in his as he helps me to my feet. Tears stream down his face as he says, "You are mine."

"i am Yours, Sir."

Alex pulls me tight against him, wrapping me in the strength and love of his embrace.

Our guests approach, offering their support and congratulations. These people are our chosen family, a strong community that has rallied around us and shelters us with their love and support.

After we get through the last of the line, Tony announces the food is being served. He motions for everyone to follow him through a pergola overflowing with white wisteria. The other side opens to a reception area where tables are set under a tent. Fairy lights are strung on the tent roof, twinkling in the night, and soft music fills the air.

"It's the wedding reception venue. Alex, this is incredible. How did you do all this?"

"Star was instrumental in helping me."

"Remind me to thank her later."

Alex leads me to our table, which is set apart from the rest. In the center of the table is a vase with a single white rose. Alex pulls my chair out just as Anthony approaches our table to personally serve our food.

"We'll be having a traditional seven-course meal," he says as he sets down our first plate.

It's a beautiful antipasto for two, complete with fresh meats, cheeses, and several varieties of olives. Alex and I taste some of each. I can't decide which is my favorite. Tony approaches with our next course. He sets a bowl of soup in front of us.

"This is my creamy tortellini soup."

I taste the first spoonful and moan in delight. "Tony, this is the best thing I've ever tasted. I'm going to want this every day."

"I can make that happen." He smiles and leaves us to finish.

The next course is shrimp fettuccine alfredo, followed by a Caprese salad—two of my favorite dishes.

"I don't know if I can eat another bite," I say. "I feel like I'm going to explode."

I'm still having a hard time increasing my calorie count. Tonight's meal is the most food I've been able to eat.

"That was the bulk of the meal. Only do what you can," Alex says, taking my hand.

The next course is a light offering of fresh fruits. Followed by dessert, cannoli, and coffee.

Once the meal is over, we're treated to exhibitions from some Dom/sub couples from the club. My favorite is the fire play display.

"Have you ever tried fire play?" I ask Alex.

"No. Why?"

"I really like it."

Fire play wasn't something we discussed when we negotiated our contract, so I'm not sure about Alex's thoughts on it.

"I'm not super comfortable doing it, but I'm willing to talk about it. After you have the baby."

"I can live with that."

What I assumed would be a simple farewell dinner turned out to be an unforgettable night that will stay with me forever. As I run my fingers over my collar, any doubts or uncertainties I had are dispelled. Wearing Alex's collar around my neck fills me with pride and serves as a constant reminder that I belong to him. It's a beautiful and meaningful symbol of our bond, and I'll cherish it forever.

LIFE APPEARS TO HAVE RETURNED TO NORMAL OR AT LEAST A NEW normal. While I go into the office, Viktor stays with Natalie. It's the only way I can walk out of the house without worrying about her safety.

I'm grateful that Brandon, even from Russia, was able to keep the business up and running. Especially after I disappeared without warning. Being back in the office the past few weeks, I've come to a new realization. My heart is no longer in advertising. I've been toying around with the idea of a major career change. I think I'm finally ready to talk to Natalie about it.

Right now, I'm supposed to meet Natalie at her obstetrician's office. It's her twenty-week ultrasound and check-up. When I rush into the waiting room, she's already there with Viktor at her side.

"I'm sorry I'm late." I kiss her cheek. "I got stuck on a call."

"It's okay. The doctor's running late."

The office door opens. "Natalie?"

"That's us." She smiles as she stands. "Do you want to come in for the ultrasound, Viktor?"

His face pales. "No thanks. If it's okay, I'll head back to the apartment. There are some things I need to get done."

"Sounds good. We'll see you later."

Viktor exits the waiting room as we go into the back office with the nurse. After checking Natalie's vitals and weight, we get settled in the ultrasound room to wait for the doctor.

"Do you think everything's okay yet?"

"I sure hope so. Because I don't know how much longer I can keep my hands off you." I adjust my erection, and Natalie laughs.

There's a knock on the door a second before it opens. "Good afternoon," Dr. Young greets us. "Are you two kids ready to take a peek at your little one today?"

"We sure are," I answer.

Natalie adjusts her clothes so the doctor can access her tummy. She's followed Dr. Turova's advice to the letter and is slowly gaining back the weight she lost. She's now sporting an adorable baby bump.

"Have you felt any movement yet?" he asks while setting up the scan.

"Sometimes it feels like there are butterflies in there. The books say that's the baby moving?" she asks, unsure.

"That's what they tell me, too." He chuckles.

The doctor starts with the routine part of the exam—all the measurements to make sure the baby is growing appropriately.

"Here's what we're looking for." He points to the screen. "The placenta is nice and high, right where it's supposed to be."

Natalie sighs in relief.

With the diagnostic portion of the ultrasound done, Dr. Young switches the view to 4D.

The image of my baby daughter is crystal clear. I'm in awe. "Look at her little nose. She's beautiful, like her mama."

Natalie laughs as our daughter does acrobatics. "She's sucking on her toe."

"You've got quite an active little girl in there," The doctor says as he finishes the ultrasound and hands me the printed pictures.

Baby Montgomery is going to fill her entire photo album before she's even born.

"I'll give you a minute to clean off, and then we'll talk in my office." With that, he exits the room.

Natalie uses the provided towels to wipe off her tummy before fixing her pants and shirt. Then we go to Dr. Young's office, where he's already behind his desk waiting for us.

"Everything looks great. The placenta previa is completely resolved, and the baby's growth is right on track."

"Am I able to travel now?" Natalie asks in a hopeful tone.

"Yes, this would be the perfect time to take any trips you have planned."

"What about sex?" I ask.

Natalie's cheeks turn red at my candor.

Dr. Young chuckles. "You're clear for sex. Natalie may be uncomfortable at first, so go slow."

"I'll be cautious," I assure him.

"Do you two have any other questions?"

Natalie looks at me. Uncertainty is written on her face.

"Yes, we do," I say confidently. "We were referred to you because you're a kink-friendly physician."

"Yes, that's true." The doctor leans back in his chair, steepling his fingers. "Let me reassure you both that this is a judgment-free place. I want you to feel comfortable speaking freely and asking your questions."

"We're in a BDSM relationship. As her Dominant, I have to be certain that anything we do is safe for her and the baby."

"The first thing I advise all my expectant couples is to practice good communication. It's even more important now than pre-pregnancy," the doctor explains.

"Natalie, your body's going through many rapid changes, which will impact your comfort level. Things you were previously okay with may not be okay right now. And things you are okay with today may not be okay in the coming weeks."

"Are there any activities that are off-limits while she's pregnant?"

"Do you have anything specific in mind?"

"Is bondage okay?" Natalie asks.

"Yes. With some modifications."

Dr. Young explains the obvious areas, like Natalie's abdomen, must be excluded to not restrict blood flow to the uterus. Refraining from having her fully on her back or tummy is also important. "I'd suggest you avoid full suspension because it puts too much pressure on your limbs and could cause serious complications. Those are the most important things to consider. Other than that, use common sense, communicate openly, and you'll be okay."

"What about impact play?" I inquire.

"Impact play is safe." The doctor smiles. "Again, the abdomen is off-limits, as is her lower back. Any area that may impact the uterus."

"Thank you, doctor." I'm surprised by how few restrictions there are. "We appreciate you taking the time to answer our questions. I think that's all we have right now." I look to Natalie, who nods in agreement.

"If anything comes up before your next appointment, you have my number."

"Do you want to grab a bite to eat?" I ask Natalie on the way out of the doctor's office.

"These days, I'm always hungry."

"There's a quiet little place a few blocks from here. Are you up for a walk?"

"I'd love that."

The air is beginning to change. The heat of the summer is starting to give way to early fall. Hand-in-hand, we walk down the busy Manhattan streets until we find a corner café. It isn't a tourist destination like many other restaurants in the city, so there aren't any crowds. We should be able to talk in relative quiet.

"You get us a table, and I'll order."

Natalie chooses a secluded table in the back corner. It's perfect. The conversation we're about to have is important, and I don't want to be interrupted.

While we eat, an awkward silence stretches between us. I'm struggling to find the right words for what I'm about to propose. I don't know if there's a perfect way to say it, so I blurt it out. "The past few weeks, I've had a lot on my mind."

"Okay." Natalie sets her sandwich down. "Is everything alright?"

"Yes," I assure her.

Her shoulders relax.

"I'm going to be stepping away from my company."

"Oh?" Natalie cocks her head. "I thought you loved your job?"

"I do. I did." I stammer over my words. "But my heart's no longer in it. I'll still hold the majority of the shares, but I'll be putting Brandon in charge of the day-to-day operations. That'll leave me free to pursue other ventures."

"Such as?"

My palms are sweating, and I wipe them on my pants. Here goes nothing. "I want to open a recovery center, a branch of Jelena's Hope, but here in New York."

Natalie's expression gives nothing away, and I hold my breath in nervous anticipation.

Natalie

I'm speechless. Alex wants to walk away from the company he worked so hard to build and to make a success so he can help others.

"I thought maybe it was something we could do together. I'll use my business skills, and maybe you'd be willing to use your training as a therapist."

The idea of using the skills we both have and being able to use our experience to help others is more than I could've ever imagined.

"You are an amazing man, Alexander Montgomery," I say, reaching across the table to take his hand. "You have the most generous heart, and I'm in complete awe. I would love to do this together."

The tension falls from his face, replaced with his sexy smile.

"It's going to be a big change for us. I wasn't sure what you were going to say. I didn't know if—" he hesitates, "if, after everything, it would be too much for you."

"We're going to see the after-effects of the worst of humanity. I'm not going to lie and say I think it's going to be easy. There'll be many hard days," I say and place my hand on my tummy. "But if we can make this world a little safer for her, it's something we have an obligation to do."

"I love you, Natalie Clarke," Alex confesses.

"And I love you."

"I'd like to talk to Brandon right away. Would you call and see if they're available to come over tonight?" Alex pulls out his phone. "While you do that, I'll book a flight to Missouri.

I grab my cell and call Lana.

"Hey, girlfriend. How did your appointment go?"

"Everything's great. I got the all-clear."

"That's awesome." She puts her hand over the phone and relays the message to Brandon. "Does that mean you'll be leaving us to visit your parents?"

"Alex is booking the flight now." I can't take my eyes off the incredibly sexy man across from me. "Are you and Brandon free to come over for dinner tonight?"

"Hang on, let me ask." Lana puts me on mute. "We're free. What time?"

We decide on a time and say our goodbyes.

"Flights booked." Alex puts his phone away.

While we finish our lunch, Alex excitedly tells me about his ideas for the recovery center. It'll be a huge undertaking, especially with a baby coming in a few months, but I have no doubt we'll be able to handle it. I'm impressed with the amount of research he's done. He's already started applying for the permits and licenses we'll need to get started.

"I've been looking at real estate," he says as we walk back to the car. "One building, in particular, stands out. It would allow us to have our office and primary residential spaces in one place. I'd like to show you on our way home."

I share his excitement. My mind's already racing with the possible services we can offer the survivors. All the different therapy options we can use to help them recover from their trauma and begin a new life—a free life.

It takes nearly forty-five minutes for us to drive a few miles across town. Finally, Alex pulls the car to the side and points out a 1930s Art Deco-style building overlooking Central Park West.

"The building has round-the-clock security at the door and a state-of-the-art video surveillance system. There's enough space on one floor to set up administrative offices, medical rooms, and therapy rooms. The top three floors of the building will be used for residential units."

"I see one problem," I say, looking out my window at the tall building.

"What is it?"

"Real estate in this area costs millions. We don't have that kind of money at our disposal."

"I've already spoken to Maxim. He's willing to front the costs."

"Wow." I knew Maxim had money. I guess I never thought about how much. "That's very generous of him." I look at the building, the sunlight reflecting off its windows. "I love it. When the survivors first get here, they'll be very vulnerable. Being able to stay within the protective walls of the center to access all their treatments is important."

"Exactly. And as they progress in their treatment, they'll move to transitional housing," Alex adds.

"Allowing them to learn to maneuver in the world while still having protection." It's a great plan. "How do we buy the space?"

"I'll call the realtor and attorney and have them start the process."

It's hard to believe it was only two years ago when I came back from Northmeadow heartbroken and stumbled upon Brandon and Lana in our apartment. At the time, I could never have imagined being here right now. I'm collared and engaged to the most amazing man in the world. And I'm pregnant with his child and about to embark on a life-changing adventure.

My mind drifts back to the cab driver, Shusuke. I'll never forget the kind man and the words he said, *"Your heart is broken now. It is blessing when wrong person leaves your life. Don't let hurt turn to anger. Tonight is start of new journey. Now right person comes.*" I'll admit, I didn't believe him. I wish I could find him and tell him how right he was.

We start the drive back to our apartment. Alex calls Maxim from the car and lets him know Jelena's Hope NYC is a go. Maxim assures Alex he'll take care of the financial end and get the necessary paperwork to the attorney.

"Natalia. I have someone here who has been asking to speak to you."

"Who is it?"

"She is an impatient little sub, Alexander." Maxim laughs.

"Natalie?" I hear a sweet little voice with an Australian accent.

"Amelia? Is that you?"

"It's me," she says. "I'm in Russia with Mr. Max and Miss Irina."

"How are you, sweetheart?" Being pregnant has my emotions on hyper-drive. My eyes fill with tears—happy tears.

"I have good days and bad days. Therapy's hard, but it's helping. And Miss Irina's very nice."

"They're good people, Amelia."

"Mr. Max scared me at first," she whispers her confession.

"He can be big and loud. But he's one of the kindest men you'll ever meet. He and Irina will make sure you're never hurt again."

"It's the first time I've felt safe in a long time. Almost like I have a family."

"I'm so happy for you, honey."

"Mr. Max said he's going to get me a cell phone, so I can call you whenever I want." She hesitates. "If that's okay with you?"

"I would love that."

"Okay. Mr. Max says he'd like to speak to you again. Catch you later."

"I thought you might like to hear from her." Maxim comes back on the line.

"Thank you, Max. It means a lot to me. What's going to happen to her?"

"Irina and I would like to formally adopt her," Max says.

"For real?" I squeal.

"For real," Maxim chuckles. "We have spoken to her therapist about the best way to bring it up. We will be speaking with Amelia about it soon."

"I don't know what to say. Thank you doesn't seem like enough."

"It is I who should be thanking you." Maxim's tone turns serious. "Amelia cannot replace my Jelena, but adopting her gives my wife and me a second chance at parenting. We have the resources to give this young lady opportunities she did not have just a few weeks ago. We will also assure her a safe and happy future."

I wipe at my tears. Since I've gotten pregnant, it seems I cry at everything.

"We're so happy for your family," Alex says. "I'll let my attorney know to look for your email, and we'll be in touch soon."

When we get home, we cuddle on the couch to watch a movie. As usual, Natalie falls asleep halfway through. Her nap is perfectly timed. I need to make a phone call without her overhearing, so I grab the blanket off the chair and cover her before going to my office.

"Alex," Charlotte answers the phone. "How did Natalie's appointment go today? Is everything okay?"

Charlotte has been slowly warming up to the idea of becoming a nana.

"Everything went great. The doctor said everything is exactly where it should be, and she's clear to travel."

"Oh, thank God," she says, relieved. "I've been praying for that."

"Thank you." I may not be a religious man, but I won't turn away her mom's prayers. "I have us booked on a flight for Sunday."

"Stanley and I can't wait to see you both."

"I have a favor I'd like your help with. But I don't want Natalie to know."

"Okay," Charlotte says hesitantly.

I give her the details of my plans, and although it'll be a lot of work, Charlotte's totally on board.

"I'll start working on it immediately," she assures me.

"Thanks. If you need anything, please call."

With that handled, I open the food delivery app and order dinner. It's already been a long day, and I don't want Natalie to have to cook for everyone tonight.

Last week, my attorney drew up the necessary paperwork to allow Brandon to step in as the CEO of Montgomery Advertising. All he has to do is say yes and sign his name to make it official. I grab the folder containing the contract and go to wake Natalie. Brandon and Lana should be here any minute. When I get back into the room, I see Natalie beginning to stir.

"What time is it?" she asks.

"Almost seven."

"Oh my God, Alex." She jumps up, and the blanket falls to the floor. "Why didn't you wake me? I have to get something ready for dinner."

"Relax, baby girl." I walk over and pick up the blanket. "I ordered take-out."

"Still." She pouts. "You shouldn't have let me sleep all afternoon."

"You need—"

"I know." She rolls her eyes. "I need to rest."

"Did you just roll your eyes?" I set the folded blanket on the back of the chair.

"Maybe." She bats her lashes.

"It's a good thing you napped." I take slow, measured steps in her direction. "Because you're going to need it after our guests leave tonight. It's been a long time since we've been together." I pull her close to me so she can feel my erection. "I plan—"

The ding of the elevator's arrival interrupts us.

"Saved by the bell." She smiles and sashays to the foyer to greet our guests.

THE KITCHEN ISLAND IS FULL OF STEAMING CHINESE TAKE-OUT cartons. Brandon and I shoot the breeze while Lana and Natalie gush over Baby Montgomery's newest photos.

"This is so good." Natalie groans after taking a mouthful of noodles and vegetables.

Lana laughs. "I've never seen you enjoy food so much."

"I am eating for two." Natalie grins.

"Lana said you two are leaving for Missouri this weekend. How long are you staying?" Brandon asks.

"Only a few weeks. We promised Charlotte she could have a small bridal shower while we're there."

"Has she settled down about the baby yet?" Lana asks.

"Kind of," Natalie says between bites. "Mainly, she avoids the topic, and that's fine. Right now, I don't need any more stress."

When we're done eating, the girls clean up, and I grab the folder before moving to the living room. Brandon and Lana take the loveseat while Natalie and I sit on the couch.

"This is the real reason I asked you over tonight." I hold up the manilla folder.

"What is it?"

I take out the paperwork and pass it to him, giving him a few minutes to read it.

"You're kidding, right?" He sets the packet on the glass coffee table.

"I'm dead serious."

"What is it?" Lana asks.

"Alex wants to step down from his company, and he wants me to take over as the CEO."

"Are you kidding?" Lana looks between Natalie and me.

"I'm not kidding. We're planning to start a new venture together."

"Care to elaborate?"

"We're opening Jelena's Hope NYC."

"I don't know what to say." Brandon looks stunned.

"All you have to say is yes and sign the contract." I pull a pen from my pants pocket and slide it across the table to him.

"Aren't you afraid this might put a target on your back?"

"Judging by recent events, I think the target's already there. But for this, there'll be state-of-the-art security in place. Dimitri's already on it. So I have no doubts about our safety."

Brandon picks up the pen and clicks it nervously. I don't know why he's stalling.

"The new position comes with a raise. If that helps sweeten the deal." I quirk my eyebrow.

He flips through the packet with overexaggerated movements until he reaches the signature page and signs with a flourish. "I would have signed either way."

We all share a laugh.

In all seriousness, I'm relieved. Brandon's been by my side since day one. Under his leadership, I have no concerns about the company's future. This frees me to give my full attention to getting Jelena's Hope NYC off the ground. It's bittersweet happiness I'm feeling. I'm excited to work side-by-side with Natalie. But I wish there wasn't a need for such a place.

The sad reality is human trafficking remains a lucrative business for those who seek to steal and destroy lives. As long as people, and I use that term loosely, are willing to pay, trafficking will never cease to exist. There'll be a continued need for people like Maxim and Nicholai, fighters who seek to shut down as many rings as possible. And there'll be a need for places like Jelena's Hope to exist so that identified survivors can access the treatment they need to heal.

"What does the timetable look like?" Brandon asks, handing me the pen.

"I plan to speak to the employees and contact my personal clients over the next few weeks." I lean forward to sign the contract and make the transaction official. "By the six-week mark, the transition will be complete."

"That sounds doable."

"Are you planning on working at the center, Nat?" Lana asks.

"We haven't talked about all the details. But yes, I plan to be on the staff as much as I'm able."

"I'm so proud of you. You could've let your experience in Mexico ruin you, but instead, you're going to change so many lives because of it." The admiration in Lana's voice is genuine.

"It hasn't been easy," Natalie says quietly.

It hasn't been easy.

The truth is Natalie has had a tough time. Everyday things like dark rooms and closed doors are triggers for her and have caused major panic attacks. We've also been working through her apprehension with blindfolds, starting with a few seconds and allowing her to remove it without needing permission.

She needs me to be strong, so I hide my fears. But each night, I wake from nightmares that put me right back in Moreno's club, hurting her. Over and over, I see the blood on my hands and relive the feeling of killing our unborn daughter.

"I know Silverio's dead, but the memories can be so vivid—so real. Every day, sometimes more than once a day, I have to make a conscious decision not to let the memories get the best of me." Natalie swipes at a lone tear making its way down her cheek. "I have to be stronger than the memories."

Witnessing Natalie struggle is a heart-wrenching experience. As a man and a Dominant, I feel a responsibility to shoulder her burden even though I know it's impossible to erase the pain she's endured. The first few days after our ordeal, she pleaded with me to pack our bags and flee to a remote island in the Caribbean, where we'd be safe from harm. I hated telling her no, that running away would not solve anything. We might be physically safe, but it wouldn't erase the memories.

Instead of living in constant fear, we've decided to turn our harrowing experience into something positive. We've realized that we can no longer ignore the evil that exists in the world and assume that others will take care of it. Maxim, Nicholai, and many others are fighting against trafficking, but we must also do our part.

Although my company helps transfer information, it's not enough now. The fight has become personal, and it has led to the creation of Jelena's Hope NYC.

Rather than cower in fear, we want to turn our trauma into a force for good and make a meaningful difference in the world. We know it won't be easy, but we're committed to the cause and won't stop until we see an end to trafficking crimes.

I have a baby daughter coming into this world in a few short months. I owe it to her to do everything I can to make the world a safer place to live.

Alex

"Natalie," I call from the kitchen. "Are you ready? If we don't leave now, we'll miss our flight." I pace back and forth. Nervous energy pulses through my veins, and I'm ready to explode like a pressure valve.

"I'm ready." Natalie strolls into the room, wheeling her suitcase behind her.

"Let me take that." I grab the handle.

Viktor gets up from the couch. "Let's get this show on the road."

Thankfully, the traffic isn't too bad, and we're able to make up some time. While Viktor arranges long-term parking with the valet, I get our bags out of the car.

As we're hurrying to our terminal, I break the news. "We're going to have to stay at your parent's house."

"What? Why?"

"Your mom texted this morning. She went to the cottage to air it out and found it infested with spiders."

"Eww." Natalie shivers.

"She called an exterminator, but they can't come out until Wednesday. Then we have to wait twenty-four to forty-eight hours to go back in."

"Why can't we stay in Viktor's cottage?"

"Same story there. Spiders. Lots of them."

"Where's Viktor going to stay?"

"Your mom offered me her couch."

"The couch?" Natalie shakes her head in disbelief. "This trip is going to be a disaster."

Oh, baby girl, if you only knew. The last thing this is going to be is a disaster.

The weather was great, and we had a smooth flight. Now, we're in our rental car on our way to the Clarke's house. It's a good thing Viktor's driving because I'm busy answering non-stop messages.

"Who's texting you so much?"

"It's the attorney. He's making sure he has all the details for the transition." That's not totally untrue. This particular text is the attorney. She doesn't need to know about all the other texts.

Viktor pulls into the Clarke's driveway and turns the car off. Natalie leans forward to grab the door handle and freezes. Her hands quickly go to her abdomen.

"What's wrong?"

Natalie grabs my hand and puts it on her stomach.

"Do you feel it?" She looks at me expectantly.

My gaze shoots to where my hand presses against her stomach. Soft bumps hit my hand from the inside. I'm awestruck as more little thumps hit my hand.

"Alex? Do you feel the baby kicking?"

"I do." I finally manage to get words out. "That was incredible."

"That was the first time I've felt her kick so strong."

I've been addicted to this woman since I first met her. Soon after, I learned she struggled with her body image due to Tommy's inability to appreciate her inner and outer beauty. Over the past two years, I've worshiped her body, teaching her that every inch of her is beautiful.

Thankfully, she's finally accepted it and has confidence in her appearance. But this, what her body's doing now as it's growing our baby, is beyond comprehension. "You're amazing." I lean over and kiss her.

"What do you mean? I didn't do anything."

I put my hand back on her belly. "You're growing our child. That's the most incredible thing in the world." I don't break eye contact, mesmerized by the depth of the green in her eyes. "I hope our daughter gets your eyes."

Tapping on the window interrupts the moment we're sharing.

"Are you two ever getting out?" Charlotte is bent down, hands cupped over her eyes as she peers into the car.

Viktor's behind her, shaking his head. Even he can't stop the force that is Charlotte Clarke.

"Maybe we should've called Marshall?" Natalie laughs.

I kiss her one more time before opening the car door and stepping out. "Charlotte. It's so nice to see you." I hug her.

"We're so glad you two are here." She squeezes me back and whispers, "Everything's going as planned."

Natalie comes around the car before I can respond.

"Look at you. You're positively glowing." Charlotte hugs Natalie. "I'm still not thrilled about your order of events," she says and dabs at her eyes with a tissue. "But

I'm excited that I'm going to be a Nana. Wait until you see the blanket I'm crocheting."

"Thank you, Mom. I'm sure it's beautiful."

"Come on." Charlotte takes her arm. "Dad's inside and can't wait to see you."

Charlotte's already going a mile a minute and is dragging Natalie into the house. Viktor and I stay behind to grab the bags.

"You sure about this, boss?"

"It'll all be worth it on Friday."

Alex

WHAT WAS I THINKING, AGREEING TO SPEND THE WEEK AT HER PARENT'S house? Natalie was right. I should've called Marshall. He and I have kept in touch and now have a business relationship.

Marshall had a dream for his motel but couldn't secure the funds to make it happen. So, as a thank you for him taking care of Natalie while she stayed there, I invested in his motel. The rooms were remodeled during the off-season, and I designed an advertising campaign to attract tourists.

He's doing a great job running his now clean and modern motel. I should've gotten rooms there. But, instead, I'm going crazy here. The walls in this old house are paper-thin, and Natalie's bedroom is next door to her parents. And did I mention she only has a twin bed? Sleeping in rather uncomfortable positions has been the only thing on the menu.

When I come downstairs, Viktor is already waiting in the living room. He follows me as I go in search of Natalie. I find her sitting on the front porch swing, enjoying a glass of sweet tea with her dad.

"Viktor and I are going to head over to the cottage to check on the progress." I kiss her on the cheek. "We shouldn't be too long."

"Are you sure it's safe?"

"They fogged yesterday. Hopefully, it's gotten rid of the pests." I keep up the ruse. "We'll check it out and open the windows to air it out."

"See you boys later," Stanley calls after us.

"She's really buying the spider thing," Viktor says dryly.

"Natalie hates spiders. It was a guarantee she wouldn't want to be anywhere near the place if there was even a chance at coming in contact with them." I chuckle.

"Tony texted. They landed safe and are already at the lake."

"Perfect." Somehow, even on short notice, everything's coming together seamlessly.

We pull up to a flurry of activity at the lake house. Leo's in the driveway directing people who are unloading their vehicles to set up for tonight.

"You guys look busy."

"There's a lot of work to be done in a short time," Tony says between directing people carrying food into the house. "Someone keeps scheduling these big events at the last minute." He chuckles.

"On that note, I'm going to head to the security room to check on everything." Viktor doesn't wait for a response before hurrying off.

"Since I'm that someone, where can I help?"

Tony pulls out his phone and unlocks the screen before handing it to me. "I have pictures of the flowers. I need you to take a look and give your okay."

"Svetlana really came through on these," I say as I scroll through the pictures. "Good thing she had access to Natalie's *kinkterest* boards."

Tony freezes mid-movement. "Her what?" His brows furrow. I don't know whether it's from confusion or extreme interest.

"Pinterest." I nearly double over laughing. "Those two manage to find some pretty kinky stuff on there."

"Damn. I thought I was missing out on something new." Anthony shakes his head and returns to his task while I look through the pictures.

The first photos showcase the tables and centerpieces, which feature three vases of different heights filled with clear crushed glass and illuminated by tiny LED lights at the bottom. Purple orchids are beautifully arranged in a vase that's filled with water. A small floating candle adds an extra touch of elegance.

The following image is Lana's simple yet classy bouquet made of purple orchids. When I swipe to the next picture, I admire the bride's stunning bouquet, featuring a mix of purple orchids in varying shades and white Calla lilies cascading down in an elegant design. Lastly, we see the boutonnieres for the men, each adorned with a single deep purple orchid.

"They're perfect." I hand the phone back to Tony.

"Excellent." He swipes his fingers over the onscreen keyboard. "I just gave the final approval to the florist. The flowers will be delivered first thing in the morning."

"Have you heard from Brandon and my dad?"

"Yes. Both have landed and are en route as we speak."

"I can't believe this is actually happening." This surprise wedding will be considerably smaller than the ceremony we had planned for next year, but I couldn't wait. I don't want another day to start and finish without Natalie being my wife. "She was okay with the surprise collaring ceremony. I hope I didn't go too far planning a surprise wedding."

"Natalie's going to love it," Tony reassures me.

Several tables have been arranged on the patio, each adorned with a single white rose, just like the beautiful centerpieces we used for our collaring ceremony. To provide warmth and illumination as the evening air cools, faux stone propane fire columns have been strategically placed around the area. It appears that the finishing touches are being applied to the tables in preparation for tonight's dinner. "How much longer do you need?"

"Give me an hour to finish the food," Tony answers confidently.

"Sounds good. I'm going to make sure the guest rooms are ready."

Tony starts walking away, then stops. "Alex," he calls over his shoulder.

"Yeah?"

"Stay out of your bedroom. Natalie's dress is in there."

I text Charlotte with an update.

Me: We'll be ready for you in an hour.

Charlotte: I'll let Stanley know.

Next, I send a text to Natalie.

Me: The cottage has been cleared for us to go in.

Natalie: Are you sure there are no spiders?

Me: I'm positive.

Natalie: What about the chemicals? Are you sure it's safe?

Me: The exterminator said your mom overexaggerated the infestation. He didn't have to do as much as he anticipated. He left the windows open to air it out overnight. We just hung up, and he gave the all-clear.

Natalie: I don't know. Maybe we should wait, just in case?

Me: Do you trust me?

Natalie: Of course, Sir. It's the spiders I don't trust.

I laugh aloud, drawing a few curious looks from people walking past.

Me: I wouldn't tell you to come back if there were still spiders or any danger from the chemicals. Your parents agreed to drive you over so I can get our room ready. I'll send Viktor back to get our things later. Oh, and wear that pretty new dress you bought. The one thing we don't have here is food. We'll go out for dinner tonight.

Natalie: Yes, Sir. See you soon.

With that done, I start toward the guest rooms to ensure we're ready for our company.

Natalie

"It was Alex." I set the phone in my lap. "He said the cottage is spider-free, and we're staying there tonight." I fiddle with my hands nervously.

"That's good news."

"I guess so."

"What's wrong?"

"Do you think they got rid of all the spiders?"

My dad nearly doubles over in his seat, laughing. "I don't think your overprotective fiancé would let you go back if there were still spiders."

"I know." I scrunch my face. "But spiders, eww." I shiver, then stand and kiss my dad on the cheek. "I'm going to go change. Alex said we're going out for dinner."

"That sounds like a great idea. I think I'll take your mom out, too."

When I get to my room, I find the soft pink maternity dress Alex requested I wear. It's a thin, gauzy fabric that hangs loose and stops just above my knee. Looking in the mirror, I run my hands down my front, pulling the fabric tight to emphasize my little round tummy.

"You're starting to make your presence known, Baby Montgomery." I rub my hands over my belly and am rewarded with a kick. "I can't wait to meet you, sweet girl."

My curls are a bit unruly today, so I pull my hair back into a long ponytail, grab my sandals, and head downstairs to see when we're leaving.

Mom and Dad are sitting on the porch. "Are we ready to go?"

"As soon as we finish our coffee," Mom says, picking up a mug and taking a sip. "It's such a beautiful afternoon, isn't it?"

"Yes." Now that I know Alex is waiting for me, I want to go to him right away, but my parents are dilly-dallying with coffee. "Maybe I should call Viktor to come and get me?"

"Don't be silly." Mom waves me off. "Your father and I are looking forward to the ride, but there's no hurry. Sit down and relax for a few minutes. I made you chamomile tea." She points to a cup on the little metal table next to her.

I sigh loudly, not trying to hide my impatience as I plunk into the wooden rocker. "Thank you."

My parents chat back and forth, sharing all the latest Northmeadow gossip while drinking their coffees ever so slowly.

Me: Are you sure you or Viktor can't come to get me? My parents don't seem to want to move.

Alex: There's no hurry. Anyway, it'll do them good to get out for a while.

Me: At the rate they're moving, we won't be leaving until after the baby is born.

Alex: LOL Enjoy your time alone with them. It's going to be the last trip here for a while.

I gently rub my tummy. The next time we're here, our baby will be with us. The thought fills me with both excitement and trepidation. The realization of how much our lives are about to change hits me like a ton of bricks. Once Baby Montgomery arrives, our days of impulsive outings will be gone. We'll have to plan for another little human being, packing and bringing along all the things babies need, even for short outings. We'll have to schedule our days around her nap and feeding schedules.

As I touch the lock on my collar, I wonder how we'll maintain our lifestyle. I have no idea how other Dom/sub couples balance their relationship as a couple with their responsibilities as parents. It seems daunting. We won't be free to go to Fire and Ice clubs or do scenes whenever we please. Our focus will be on our little girl. Her needs will always come first.

I know we're not the first Dom/sub couple to become parents, but the thought overwhelms me. I wish there were classes or resources available to help guide us through this transition. Maybe I can reach out to Irina for advice. She and Max raised Lana while living the lifestyle. I'm sure she could offer some valuable guidance as we prepare for this new chapter in our lives.

"Natalie." Mom's voice startles me.

"Yes?"

"Daydreaming about your little girl already?"

"I am." That and so much more.

"Dad and I are ready to go."

I jump up before they change their minds. "I'll get these." I grab our cups and bring them to the sink.

Mom helps Dad into the car. He's stronger than he was the last time we were here. He can walk short distances in the house with his walker, and he's able to get into the car with minimal assistance. As soon as I get into the back, Mom pulls the car onto the road.

Finally, we're on our way.

My parents are officially old. It may be a Thursday, but clearly, we're out for a Sunday drive. After what feels like an eternity, we turn onto the gravel driveway leading to our cottage. When we pull up, I see several unfamiliar cars in the driveway.

"What's going on?"

"I have no idea," Mom says too quickly, giving away the fact that she knows something.

She beeps the horn, and seconds later, Alex opens the front door. He's dressed in khaki pants and a light blue button-down shirt. And he's wearing the sexiest smile on his face.

Making his way to the car, he opens my door and helps me out.

"Welcome home, baby girl."

"What is all this?"

"Let's go see." Alex opens the door for my dad, who's wearing a matching grin.

"You're all in on whatever this is, aren't you?"

All I get in response are smiles and laughs.

"Patience, Natalie," my dad says as he moves from the car to his chair. "You were never good at waiting for a surprise."

"That hasn't changed," Alex adds while pushing Dad's chair across the path leading to the front door.

I grab the screen door and hold it open so Alex can push the chair inside. Walking in behind them, I freeze. Tony and several sous chefs are in my kitchen. By the aromas wafting through the air, he's been busy cooking. The French doors that lead to the patio are open. There are tables surrounded by fire pillars, the flames flickering from the soft breeze coming off the lake. Milling about outside are our friends and family.

"Alex?" I ask.

"Yes?" he counters.

"Why is everyone here? What's going on?"

He turns to me and takes my hands in his. "I don't want to wait any longer to make you my wife." My hands tremble in his grasp. "Tonight, we're having dinner with our friends and family. Tomorrow, we're getting married."

I blink back tears. "You did all this?"

"I had a little help." He motions to my parents, who are watching from the other side of the room.

"You two knew about this?"

"We did," Mom says proudly. "You have an amazing man there."

My heart is bursting with love for the man next to me. "I don't know how you did this," I whisper. "But it's perfect."

"You haven't even seen it yet."

"I don't have to see it to know."

He leans in and kisses me. "Let's say hi to everyone before I change my mind and keep you all to myself tonight."

"I like the sound of that."

When Lana sees me, she runs up and squeezes me in a hug. "Can you believe he did this?"

"I'm still trying to process everything." I'm overwhelmed by everything I see.

"Before we start our meal," Alex says, getting everyone's attention. "I want to take a moment to express my gratitude. I would never have pulled this off on my own. Even with such short notice, you've all helped create something incredible. Without each one of you, none of this would be possible. From the bottom of my heart, I thank you."

When Alex finishes his speech, Tony signals to one of his staff to begin serving the meal. This evening's dinner is light and delicious. But sharing this special time with our friends and family is even more precious.

After the dishes are cleared, everyone lingers, talking and enjoying the evening.

"Natalie, can you come with me for a second?" Mom stands.

I look at Alex, and he nods in approval.

"Where are we going?"

"You'll see." Mom gives me a rare smile.

I follow her into the house, trying to figure out what she could possibly have up her sleeve. We stop outside our bedroom. Mom takes a deep breath before turning the handle and opening the door. She moves aside so I can walk in.

"Oh, Mom." I hurry over to our bed and run my hands along the antique lace. "It's Grandma's wedding dress."

Mom walks over and puts her arm around me. "Do you like it?"

"I love it." With a trembling hand, I brush away the tears cascading down my cheeks.

"Let's try it on. Mrs. Fisher will be along shortly to make any last-minute alterations."

I hug her tightly. "This is perfect, Mom. Thank you so much."

When I was a little girl, I loved sleeping at my grandma's house. She'd pull out her photo albums and tell me the stories of the pictures and the people in them. My favorite was when she took out her wedding album. Each time, I told her I wanted to wear her dress when I got married. She'd light up and tell me about the day she married my grandpa, Isaac.

The year was 1942. It was just after the Japanese attacked Pearl Harbor. Although he was only seventeen, Grandpa had his father's blessing and joined the army.

"Anne, they're planning to send me to Europe. I don't want to leave without having you as my wife."

"That was my romantic proposal." Grandma laughs. "I was only sixteen when I married your grandfather. We were married fifty years when he passed away." Her eyes fill with tears. "It was just a few months before you were born. How I wished you could've met him."

One day, when I was sixteen years old, Grandma brought me to her room. She opened her closet and took out a box. Inside the box was her wedding gown.

"I won't be here when you're getting married," Grandma says.

"Don't talk like that."

"Natalie, I'm eighty-three years old. My days on this earth are coming to an end." She takes my hand in hers. "Try the dress on. I want to have the memory of seeing you in it."

So, I did. Grandma helped me zip up the ivory gown, and together, we stood in front of her full-length mirror. Tears sprang to her eyes.

"My sweet granddaughter. You've made me very happy today. One day, you'll wear this dress when you marry the man you love. I pray you'll have many happy years together."

That was the last time I saw my grandma. Unfortunately, she passed away a few days later. It's a memory I'll treasure forever.

I didn't bother to ask my mom about the dress. After all these years, I thought it would be too fragile to wear.

"When you showed me the pictures of the dresses you liked, I immediately thought of Grandma's dress. I didn't want to say anything until I took it out of storage and found out if it was still wearable."

If I try to talk, I'll break down. Instead, I pull my dress off and prepare to try on my wedding gown while Mom retells the treasured story.

"My great-grandma, Viola, hand-made this dress for my mom, your grandma," she says as she holds the dress out for me to step into. "She used some of the lace from her wedding gown to make this one." I turn around so she can fasten the tiny pearl buttons on the back. "Natalie. What is this?" She runs her finger along the length of the scar on my shoulder.

I swallow over the lump in my throat and give her the explanation Alex and I came up. "When we were on our vacation, we went hiking. I had a run-in with a vicious tree branch. It was really sharp and cut me pretty good."

"Yes, it did. You're lucky you didn't get an infection."

"Alex would never let that happen." I need to change the subject. "How did you manage to alter the dress? The lace is so delicate."

"Lots of prayers and Dolores," Mom says and steps back. "Turn around and take a look."

As I turn slowly towards the mirror, I take in the sight of the ivory A-line gown with its empire waist, a perfect fit for my growing tummy. The lace bodice, despite its age, feels surprisingly soft to the touch, with pearls delicately sewn along the waistline.

I can only imagine the patience it took for my great-grandmother to attach each pearl by hand, a testament to the love and care that went into crafting this dress. The flowing chiffon length of the dress drapes elegantly down to kiss the floor, completing the ethereal look.

"Didn't this have long sleeves?"

"It did." As I stand before the mirror, my mom comes up behind me, and we gaze at my reflection together.

It's reminiscent of that day with my grandma. Tears fill my eyes again.

"It's summer. Long sleeves would've been too warm. I also hoped to make the dress a little more modern for you. Mrs. Fisher took a layer of fabric from underneath to make the sleeves." Loose chiffon falls perfectly on my arm, creating an off-the-shoulder design. "Turn around and look at the back," Mom instructs.

The lace on the back of the dress has a keyhole opening. The train is attached by several pearl buttons and is a mixture of layers of chiffon and the same lace from the dress's bodice.

There's a knock on the door.

"Come in," I call.

"It's just me and—" Lana gasps and hurries into the room. "Natalie, your dress is incredible."

"I know," I say, looking in the mirror again. "I can't believe I'm getting to wear my grandma's dress."

"Dolores," Mom greets her friend. "Thank you so much for coming tonight."

Mrs. Fisher is all business as she sets a bag on the bed and walks to me, appraising each inch of the dress. "It looks like I need to tighten the shoulders just a bit, but other than that, I think it fits perfectly." She reaches into her bag and takes out her pincushion. "Hold this." She pushes the little red tomato into Lana's hand as she goes about her task of adjusting the dress.

"Is there room for one more?" Leo asks from the doorway.

"There's always room for you."

"Girl, you are drop-dead gorgeous." He leans in, kissing me on the cheek.

"Thank you, Leo."

"Okay." Mrs. Fisher steps back. "Take it off so I can stitch it."

Lana begins to undo the buttons, and I allow the raglan sleeves to slide down my arms.

"Natalie," Mom screeches. "There's a man in the room."

Leo and I have changed in front of each other before, so I didn't even think about it. But I understand my mom's objections.

"I'll turn around and close my eyes, Mrs. Clarke," Leo says.

"Kids," Mom says, exasperated.

Lana, Leo, and I laugh while Mom and Mrs. Fisher look at each other and shake their heads.

"You can turn back around," I tell Leo after I've got my sundress back on. "Do you need me to stay to try the gown on again?"

"It'll be a perfect fit when I've finished." Mrs. Fisher already has a needle and thread in her hand.

"Can I get you anything to eat or drink?"

"No, thank you." She doesn't look up from her sewing. "Go enjoy your party. I'll finish this and be on my way."

"I'll stay with Dolores. You kids go have fun."

"Thank you, Mom. This is the best gift you could've ever given me."

Alex

The three amigos emerge from the house. My attention is immediately drawn to my fiancée, whose cheeks flush a rosy hue as she giggles at something Lana whispers in her ear. Just then, Natalie catches my gaze and beams at me with her radiant smile. It's hard to believe that tomorrow, this stunning woman will become my beloved wife.

Charlotte and Stanley are the first to leave. Natalie and I walk them to their car. "Thank you both for all your help. I couldn't have done this without you."

"It was our pleasure," Charlotte says and hugs me.

"Drive safe." Natalie kisses her parents goodbye.

With my arm around Natalie, we watch until their car is out of sight.

"I can't believe we're really getting married tomorrow."

"It's real, baby girl." I take her hand as we walk back into our house. "Tomorrow, you'll become Mrs. Montgomery."

"Tomorrow can't come soon enough."

We rejoin our guests, who are laughing and talking around the fire.

"What did we miss?" I ask.

"Lana's just telling us how Natalie first learned about the lifestyle," Luna says.

"I was hoping she would've forgotten that by now," Natalie groans

"How could we ever forget that?" Brandon asks. "I thought for sure I'd be calling Alex to bail me out."

We tell stories until late in the night. Eventually, Natalie rests her head on my shoulder. "Are you tired?"

"I am."

"We're going inside. My bride-to-be is ready for bed."

"We should all turn in," my father adds. "Tomorrow's going to be a big day."

"Girls in one house, boys in the other," Lana announces.

"Says who?" I ask, laughing.

She puts her hands on her hips. "You can't see the bride on her wedding day until the ceremony."

"You have a bossy little sub there, Brand."

"She can be bratty at times." Brandon swats her ass, and she yelps. "But she's right. Time to say goodnight. You can't see Natalie until the wedding."

"Some friends you are." I roll my eyes. "Come on, baby girl. I'll walk you to our bedroom door, and we'll say our goodnights."

"Viktor, maybe you should stand guard in case he tries to sneak into her room," Brandon jokes.

I throw him the finger and laugh as I lead Natalie into the house.

I reach for the handle on our bedroom door, but Natalie puts her hands on my chest. "Sorry, Sir. You heard the rules. We need to say goodnight on this side of the door," she smirks. "Besides, my dress is in there."

"I'll keep my eyes closed," I tease.

Natalie stands on tip-toes and wraps her arms around my neck. "This is going to be the longest night of my life."

"After tonight, I'm never letting you out of my sight again." I kiss her. "I'm only a phone call away if you need me."

"I love you, Alexander Montgomery."

"And I love you, Natalie Clarke."

With a final kiss, I walk away. The next time I see Natalie will be when she's walking down the aisle. When I get back outside, Tony is finishing extinguishing the fire.

"Night, everyone. Come along, kids," Luna says and motions to Lana and Leo, who are sitting, heads together, giggling like children. "Let's go find the bride."

"He gets to stay in the house?" I pretend to whine.

"He's just one of the girls," Tony jokes.

Leo and Lana link arms as they follow Luna into the house, shutting the back door behind them.

"Boss, do you want me to stay in the main house tonight?" Viktor asks.

"The security system is on. You're off the clock tonight."

Viktor nods, pretending to accept that he's not working. But if I know him, he'll have the monitors on all night, keeping an eye on the house. The four of us walk to the security cottage together.

"I hope you don't mind," Tony says. "I'm going to head straight to bed. I'll be up before the sun to start cooking."

"Thank you for everything." I shake his hand.

"It's my pleasure. Night everyone."

"I'm heading to my room, too," Viktor adds. "See you in the morning."

Dad's the last man standing. I hope he's not ready to rush off to bed. "Do you have time for one more drink?"

"Sure."

I grab two beers from the fridge and pass him one. Dad follows me to the couch. It's been a long time since we've spent any time alone. Tonight, it feels important to have this time together.

"You gave us a good scare."

"I'm not going to lie. I wasn't sure we were going to make it out of there."

"I don't know what I would've done if I lost you." Dad's voice cracks.

"I owe everything to Max and Viktor. If it weren't for them, we wouldn't be here."

A few minutes of silence pass between us.

"Your mom would be very proud of you."

"I wish Mom could've met Natalie."

"She would've loved her." Dad smiles sadly. "She's here with us, though. I can feel her."

Now feels like the perfect time to tell him we chose a name. "Natalie and I would like to name our baby Rose Anne, after mom and her grandma."

Dad sets his beer on the side table and sits back. He doesn't say anything for the longest time. I'm beginning to think he doesn't like the idea.

Finally, he turns in my direction, and I notice tears streaming down his face. "Rose Anne Montgomery, that's the most beautiful way to honor your mother's memory."

Dad has never been the type to wear his heart on his sleeve. Not even when we said goodbye to Mom did he show any signs of emotion. Watching him cry now is unbearable. The tears I've been holding back for so long now spill out.

"Mom would want you to move on," I say quietly.

Dad looks up. "What do you mean?"

"With Luna." I wipe the wetness from my face. "If you want to marry her. I know Mom would approve, and so do I."

His features soften. "Luna was only ever supposed to be my submissive. She and I discussed it at great lengths while we were vetting each other. I never intended to fall in love."

"I know all about that." I chuckle.

"Yes, son, you do." Dad smiles. "I love Luna very much. But that doesn't mean I stopped loving your mother."

"You don't have to explain it to me," I reassure him. "I know you'll always love Mom, but she's been gone for a long time. It's okay to share your heart again."

"When we met, I was an emotional mess. I hadn't healed from your mother's death and couldn't see ever falling in love again. Luna never pushed. Never forced anything. She's always accepted her position as my submissive and nothing more. But over the past few years, something changed between us."

I lean forward, recognizing the significance of this conversation.

"I realized that her submission and unwavering patience are her gifts of love. She helped heal my heart, and I fell in love with her."

"Have you told her?"

Dad laughs. "Would you believe me if I said no? I've been too scared to admit it aloud."

"After what Natalie and I went through in Mexico, I've learned not to take a single day for granted."

"I'm afraid she'll see it as a betrayal of our contract," he admits.

"I've seen the way she looks at you. She's as in love with you as you are with her."

"I don't know."

"You need to tell her, Dad. Give her the chance to openly love you back."

"Maybe you're right. It's time to let Luna know how I feel."

We finish our beers while discussing my plans for Jelena's Hope NYC. Dad already offered to become an investor, something I'm thankful for. It's going to take a village to get this project off the ground and running.

Dad looks at his watch. "It's either late or early. I'm not quite sure at this point. But this old man needs to get some sleep."

"Thank you for everything, Dad." I swallow over the lump in my throat. "I wouldn't be half the man I am today if it wasn't for you. I love you." I hug him.

"I love you too. I'm very proud of you, Alexander."

I watch Dad walk down the hall to his room and realize what a lucky man I am.

Grabbing the blankets and pillow I left on the chair, I spread them on the couch before settling in for sleep. The last night I'll do so as a single man.

Natalie

Lana, Leo, and I shared my room last night. I don't remember what time it was when our slumber party wound down, but I'm sure I was the first one asleep.

This morning, I crawl out from the middle of my best friend sandwich, careful not to wake either of the sleeping beauties at my side, and go to the bathroom for a hot shower. I take my time drying off and putting product in my hair, praying my curls will cooperate with me today.

I slide on the white silk robe Lana gave me last night with the word *Bride* embroidered on the front. She also had ones made for her and Leo embroidered with *Bride Squad*. Leave it to my bestie to think of all the little details.

I tiptoe back through my bedroom, close the door, and head straight to the kitchen. I'm hoping to score a coffee before the day gets into full swing. When I walk into the room, I see Luna beat me to it. She's already sitting at the kitchen table, cup in hand.

"Good morning. I didn't know anyone was up yet."

"I hope you don't mind. I helped myself to a coffee."

"Not at all." I open the cupboard and take out a mug. "That's what I came out for, too."

Luna jumps up. "It's your wedding day. Sit down and let me wait on you."

Luna makes me a cup of French-vanilla-flavored goodness before she sits back down.

"Thank you for being here. It means a lot to me that you came."

"It's an honor to be included. I wasn't sure, being Sam's sub, if Alex would want me here. I didn't want to overstep."

I grab her hand from across the table. "Alex and I both want you here. You're part of our family."

"Thank you, sweetheart. That means a lot to me."

Our moment alone is cut short when Tony bursts in with homemade pastries and bagels.

"Good morning, ladies." He kisses me on the cheek. "You look well-rested this morning, pixie."

"And you brought breakfast." I grab a cream cheese Danish and a chocolate chip muffin from the tray. "You're a lifesaver."

Luna and I continue chatting while we eat and finish our coffee. When we're done, I grab our empty mugs, bringing them to the sink. "I'll wash these, and we'll get out of your way."

"You'll do no such thing. It's your wedding day." He shoos me away from the sink. "Go get ready to marry that sexy man."

I give him a peck on the cheek. "Thank you, Tony." Then, turning to Luna, I ask, "Shall we go wake up Lana and Leo?"

As we're walking down the hall, my bedroom door opens. Leo stumbles out in his boxers, his robe draped over his arm. "Good morning," he mumbles.

"Good morning, sleepyhead." I laugh.

"You're awfully chipper this morning," he says as he rubs his eyes.

"I've already had my coffee."

He kisses my cheek. "I'm going to the guest room to shower, and then I'm getting myself a cup of caffeine."

Luna and I walk into my bedroom and find the bed empty. The bathroom door is open, and the shower water's running. "Looks like everyone's already up. And they made the bed."

"Seems that way."

"Good morning," Mom says, walking into the room behind us.

"Morning, Mom."

"Morning, Charlotte." Luna and Mom exchange hugs. "I'll give you two some time alone."

I grab Luna's hand. "You don't have to go."

"There's something I need to do. I'll be back in a few minutes." She closes the door softly behind her.

"I can't believe my little girl is getting married today." Mom's eyes fill with tears.

"Don't start crying already." I pass her the tissue box from the bedside table. "Where's Daddy?"

"He's in the other cottage with the men. Oh, did you know there's an army of people on their way here?"

"No. I'll be right back." I rush to the living room.

Looking out the window, I see what she's talking about. Several ladies and a few men unload cars, each pulling rolling luggage behind them.

"Looks like your hair and makeup team is here," Anthony says over my shoulder.

"My what?"

"Alex hired hair and makeup to pamper the bridal party." He opens the door, letting everyone in. "Good morning, ladies and gentlemen. This is our bride, Natalie."

We exchange hellos.

"Where can we set up?"

"How much space do you need?"

"We need one area for mani and pedis and another for hair and makeup," a beautiful dark-haired woman says.

The kitchen and living room share an open floor plan. With all the activity in the kitchen, we'd be in the way out here.

"Use the guest room for nails and the master for hair and makeup." Anthony jumps in, saving me.

"That works for us."

"Thank you, Tony."

"No problem, pixie."

"Follow me. I'll show you to the rooms."

The entourage follows behind me and begins setting up their equipment. The photographer arrives shortly after to document our afternoon of pampering. Throughout the day, Tony delivers light snacks and refreshments to our rooms.

While I'm getting my hair done, my phone pings with a text.

Alex: I'll meet you at the end of the aisle right before sunset.

Me: I'll be there.

Time seems to have flown by, and before I know it, it's time to start getting ready. My mom is donning a light blue dress that flows down to her ankles. I'm surprised she allowed the stylists to not only put her hair in a fancy updo but also to do her makeup.

"You look beautiful, Mom."

"It doesn't even look like me," she says as she examines herself in the mirror.

"I can't wait to see the look on Dad's face when he sees you."

"He won't even notice." She waves her hand, blowing me off.

"If he doesn't, I'll check his pulse."

We both laugh.

Lana comes out of the bathroom. "Can you help me with my dress, Mrs. Clarke?"

"Sure, honey. Turn around." Mom zips up her dress. "You look stunning."

Lana's wearing a deep purple chiffon dress with a sweetheart neckline accented with off-the-shoulder sleeves that mimic mine.

"Brandon's going to go crazy. You'll be walking down the aisle next," I say, imagining my bestie's wedding.

"I don't think so. Marriage is not in my plans."

"Not in your plans? What do you mean, dear?" Mom asks.

"Natalie, can you help me with my bowtie," Leo interrupts.

"Let's see what I can do. Sit down." I stand next to him by the bed and adjust his tie.

I don't know what Lana's talking about. She's told me she wished Brandon would propose to her. I'm going to have to try to get her alone so we can talk.

There's another knock on the door.

"I'll get it," Mom says. She opens it just a crack to see who it is before pulling it all the way open. "Luna, don't you look beautiful."

"And you are a gorgeous mother-of-the-bride."

"Speaking of the bride, I think it's time we get her dressed." Lana grabs my gown.

"I'll step outside while you change," Leo offers.

Lana holds out my gown so I can step into it. I open my robe, unashamed of my near-nakedness. My dress leaves no room for a bra, and my panties are barely there—white lace in the front and a string of pearls in the back.

"Those pearls are so hot. It's a good thing Alex won't know what's underneath until later."

"Svetlana," Mom scolds.

"Sorry, Mrs. C." She shrugs. "But it's the truth. He's going to go crazy when he undresses her tonight."

Mom's cheeks turn bright red. Luna slaps Lana's arm and laughs.

I step into the dress and pull it up just as Lana's phone rings.

"Saved by the bell," Lana chirps and hands her job off to my mom while she grabs her phone from the dresser.

I make a few last-minute adjustments while Mom fastens the buttons.

"You can come back in," I call to Leo.

"You're even more beautiful today. If I wasn't into men—"

Lana puts the phone on speaker, thankfully interrupting Leo.

"How is my little girl today?" Maxim asks

"I'm good, Papa."

"Turn on your camera. Mama and I want to see your dress."

"Svetlana," Irina gushes. "You look beautiful."

"Thanks, Mama." Lana turns the camera around. "Say hi to everyone."

We all say a collective hello to Maxim and Irina.

"Natalia," Maxim says. "You are a most stunning bride. I wish we could be there to celebrate with you today."

"So do I."

"I'll have them on video the whole time. They won't miss a second."

"Hi, Natalie." Amelia pops on the screen.

"Hi, sweetheart." I smile and wave. "How's everything going?"

"I'm starting to get used to it here. Miss Irina is teaching me Russian, or at least trying to."

"I hope you do better than I have." Russian is not an easy language to learn. I can manage a few words to get by, but mostly I rely on Alex to do the talking for me.

"You look like a princess, Natalie."

"Thank you."

"When will I get to see you?"

"I'm not sure," I answer honestly. "We'll talk to Max and Irina and see what they can do, okay?"

"Yep. Gotta go."

We spend a few more minutes talking with Max and Irina before Mom reminds us of the time.

"I have to finish getting ready. I don't want to be late for my own wedding."

"Pozdravlyayem vas oboikh I nadeyemsya, chto u vas budet mnogo schastlivykh let vmeste," Maxim says.

I look to Lana to translate.

"He said congratulations to both of you. And they hope you have many happy years together."

"Thank you, both."

Lana disconnects the call, promising to call back when the ceremony starts.

"I can't believe I'm about to marry Alex."

"And it's all thanks to me." Svetlana smiles proudly.

I grab Lana's hands. "I'm so grateful you asked me to go to Fire and Ice with you that night," I say quietly. Despite all my efforts to not get emotional, my eyes fill with tears.

"We just spent hours getting our makeup done. There will be no tears yet," Lana jokes.

Mom walks over, interrupting our moment. "It's time to put your veil on. Come sit down."

Carefully, she sets the delicate crown on my head. The photographer has her hold the pose for a picture.

"It's the exact veil I wanted." I bring my hands to the crown, touching it gently. "How did you know?"

"Aren't you glad I know your Pinterest password?" Lana laughs.

The crown is an intricate weave of ivory flowers, pearls, and Swarovski crystals. Attached to the crown is a luxurious tulle that pools at the back of the dress.

"It's your something new," Mom says.

"I have your something borrowed," Lana says, handing me a box. "Open it."

"It's stunning." Inside is a silver chain with a teardrop-shaped diamond.

"My mama wore it on her wedding day. She said she'd be honored if you'd borrow it for your wedding day." I touch my collar. "Don't worry." Lana reaches into her bag. "I have the key."

"How did you get it?" I ask quietly as she works to unlock it.

"Alex wasn't happy at first. But when I explained why, he gave me the key and his permission to remove it for the ceremony." She takes my collar and the key, placing them in the jewelry box. "I'll make sure this gets back to Alex. Turn around."

After she fastens the necklace, I look at it in the mirror. "It's beautiful."

"I have your something old. Well, it's actually from Sam," Luna says and hands me another smaller box. I open this one and find a pair of diamond earrings. "These were Alex's mom's earrings. She wore them on their wedding day. Rose made Sam promise to save them and give them to the woman Alex chose to marry for her something old."

Tears prick my eyes. "This means so much to me."

"We forgot your something blue," Lana says.

"I hope I'm not overstepping, but I have something blue for you," Luna says hesitantly as she hands me a small box. Lifting off the lid, I find a blue crystal angel and a locket hanging from a small silver chain.

When I open it, I see a photo of Michael on one side and a woman I don't recognize on the other. "That's Alex's mom, Rose. They're both your guardian angels."

"Luna, I don't know what to say." A teardrop slips down my cheek.

"If I have your permission, I can attach it to your bouquet. Both Michael and Rose will be with you on this special day."

I wrap my arms around her. "This is the most special gift you could give me. I'll treasure it long after today."

"Thank you for allowing me—"

"Luna, you're part of our family. Today wouldn't be complete without you here." I look around the room at my friends and family who've made today so special already. "I can't thank you enough. I love you all so much."

Now everyone is dabbing at the tears in their eyes.

"Enough of this crying, ladies," Leo says, wiping his eyes. "You'll ruin my makeup."

His comment makes us all laugh. Another knock on the door interrupts us.

"I'll get it." Leo hurries to the door.

He opens it to let Tony, whose arms are full of white boxes, into the room.

"Where can I set these?"

"On the bed. What's in them?"

"Your flowers." Tony puts the boxes down and spins around. "pixie." He stops mid-step and takes me in head to toe.

I feel a blush creep up my cheeks.

"You're breathtaking. Alex is a very lucky man."

"You've ogled the bride enough. Out you go." Lana shoos Tony out of the room, closing the door behind him.

I wish they'd leave the door open. Each time it closes, I fight the feelings of suffocation and fear. But if I asked, it would draw too many unwanted questions from my mom. Lana's watching closely and provides a much-needed distraction.

"Let's take a look at these flowers." Lana's already opening the boxes.

Inside the first two boxes are wrist corsages for Mom and Luna. A third small box holds a deep purple orchid for Leo that I pin to his jacket. The photographer moves around us as I straighten the flower, capturing every second.

"Here's my bouquet," Lana squeals. "It's gorgeous." Her flowers are orchids in various shades of purple. Not only is it beautiful, but the fragrance from the flowers is heavenly. "Open yours," Lana urges.

I open the final box and lift out my bouquet. It's exactly like the pictures I saved. This is probably the only time I'll be thankful someone else knew my password.

Luna walks over and attaches my guardian angel to the ribbon on my bouquet.

Looking around, a feeling of warmth flows through me. Generations of women, some of whom are no longer with us, have played a role in making today special. Their love surrounds me right now. The baby must feel it, too, because she starts to kick.

"It's time," Leo announces. "Are you ready to go get married?"

There's nothing I want more.

<h1 style="text-align:center">Natalie</h1>

WE MAKE OUR WAY OUT TO THE LIVING ROOM. LANA WALKS BEHIND ME, holding up my train so it doesn't catch on the floor.

"You look stunning," Dad says when he sees Mom.

"Oh, Stanley." Mom waves her hand at him.

"You're as beautiful as the day I married you."

Mom leans down and, in a rare public display of affection, kisses his cheek. "I love you, you silly man."

I'm glad the photographer was right there and got it all on film

The front door swings open, and Viktor walks in. When he sees me, he freezes. "You're the most perfect bride. Alex is a lucky man." He kisses my cheek. Clearing his throat, he says, "We're ready to start."

"We're ready, too," Lana answers.

"I'll see you out there." Viktor takes one final look at me before leaving the room.

Lana sidles up to me. "If I didn't know better—"

"Don't," I say, interrupting her. "We've been through a lot together, that's all."

"Whatever." She rolls her eyes. It's obvious she doesn't believe me.

"Time to go, ladies." Leo throws open the French doors with a flourish.

Instrumental music floats on the breeze. When I peek out, I see a string quartet off to the side. I don't know how Alex pulled this together, but he didn't miss anything.

Sam walks through the open doors, stopping to compliment Luna and then coming to me. "My son chose a wonderful young woman to become part of our family." He kisses my cheek.

"Thank you."

"Are you ready?" he asks Luna.

"Always," she responds, sliding her hand through his bent arm. Together, they walk outside and down the flower-petal-covered path to take their seats.

"May I?" Leo asks Mom, offering her his arm.

"You may," she says.

Leo leads Mom down the aisle, whispering something in her ear and making her laugh. I'm thankful my parents accepted Tony and Leo without too many questions. I wish they'd have accepted Michael and Evan the same way. I'd have my brother here with me today.

"Are you okay?" Lana interrupts my thoughts.

"I'm missing my brother, but I'll be okay."

"I'm sure he'd be very happy for you." Lana gives me one last hug before walking down the aisle to stand beside Leo.

<h1 style="text-align:center">Alex</h1>

I CHECK MY WATCH FOR THE HUNDREDTH TIME. MAYBE IT NEEDS A NEW battery or something. The hands of the clock don't seem to be moving. Returning to the mirror, I stab at tying my bowtie, which is proving impossible because of my trembling hands.

Get it together, Alex. It's not the first time you've worn a tux. But it is the first time, and the only time, I'm getting married.

There's a knock on the door a second before it opens. Viktor stands in the doorway. "Are you ready, boss?"

Spinning around to face him, my shoulders slump, and my arms hang useless at my sides.

"You're a mess. Get your ass over here."

I've never been that guy. But I guess there's a first time for everything. Reluctantly, I shuffle over to Viktor, who takes charge, tying my bowtie with practiced ease.

"Thanks for having my back," I mumble.

He gives it a tug, making sure it's straight, before stepping back. "I'm ready. You're ready. Let's get you to your girl."

I grab his shoulder. "Wait a minute."

"What's up?"

"Thank you." I stop to swallow over the lump in my throat. "We wouldn't be here today if it wasn't for you."

"It's all good, boss," Viktor smirks but then shocks me by pulling me in for an uncharacteristic hug.

"Are you two done with your love fest?" Brandon laughs from the doorway. "The ladies are ready."

Brandon's smart-ass banter lightens the mood. With my wardrobe issues fixed, I'm able to regain my composure.

"What are we standing around for? It's time for me to get married."

Natalie

I look out the doors and see Alex and Viktor, who are caught up in a private conversation. Alex looks gorgeous in his black tux, and I can't take my eyes off him. Finally, he looks up and sees me for the first time. A sexy smile lights up his face.

I never thought I'd say it, but I'm thankful Tommy cheated on me. What I thought was the worst night of my life was actually the first night of my forever.

"Are you ready to go get married?" Dad asks.

"I am."

Dad wheels himself onto the patio. I follow behind. Panic sets in when we get to the edge of the concrete. I didn't think about this part. How am I going to get his wheelchair through the grass? I look around, expecting to see someone coming to help, but no one makes a move.

"How are we going to—" I stop mid-sentence and watch as Dad locks the wheels of his chair. He places his hands on the armrests and pushes himself to a standing position.

"Daddy." My hand covers my mouth.

Taking a step forward, he extends his hand, and I place mine in his. "Did you think I wouldn't walk my little girl down the aisle?"

I'm speechless. Tears blur my vision. This is so much more than I expected.

The quartet begins to play Pachelbel's Canon in D, and we slowly walk down the aisle.

Yesterday, when Alex told me we were getting married, I didn't have time to think about any of the details. I guess I assumed someone would push Dad next to me. It wouldn't have been the original plan, but that didn't matter anymore. The most important thing is Alex and I are alive, safe, and getting married.

When we reach the end of the aisle, Alex steps forward. Dad joins our hands, placing his on top. "I'm trusting you to take good care of my daughter."

"You have my word. I'll protect her until my last breath."

Dad kisses my cheek before sitting next to Mom. Lana steps up and takes my bouquet.

Then, Alex and I take the final steps and stand before Viktor.

Alex

Canon in D plays just as Viktor and I get into place. Looking up, I catch the first glimpse of my bride. Her eyes meet mine, and I forget to breathe. She's stunning. For a few precious seconds, there's only her and I. Then panic registers on her face. Although I'm prepared for what's about to happen, she isn't. Natalie gasps when her dad stands from his wheelchair and offers his hand to walk her down the aisle.

A few days after I asked Charlotte for help, I got a phone call from Stanley. He told me about his progress in physical therapy and that he'd be walking for our wedding. He also swore me to secrecy so he and Natalie could share this special moment.

When they finally reach the end of the aisle, I step forward. Mr. Clarke puts his daughter's hand in mine. The symbolism of a father handing over the responsibility of caring for and protecting his daughter to another man. I give him my word that as long as I'm breathing, I'll protect her with all I have. When I look into Natalie's eyes, we both know the truth to my statement.

I've already killed to save her life—to keep her mine.

"Natalie, today, my life joins with yours. You are the strength I never knew I needed. The piece of my heart I didn't realize was missing. There's no one else I want to build a forever with. I promise to love you with all I am—for all eternity."

Natalie

"Alex, You love me in ways I never dreamed possible. You are my every dream come true. My light in the darkness. You taught me what being loved truly means. I promise to share my whole heart with you and to show you my love every day. I promise you, my love, my husband, to forever be by your side."

"You may kiss your bride."

Alex flashes me his sexy smile before he leans in and places a chaste kiss on my lips. He pulls back just enough so I can look up into his deep blue eyes. "Shall we give them a show?"

He doesn't need my permission, but I smile and nod anyway. Placing his hands on my waist, he pulls me tight against him. Gentle and passionate, his lips meet mine. I open, granting him access, and he dips me in his arms as the kiss turns more demanding.

Viktor clears his throat, a not-so-subtle hint for us to end our kiss. Then, Alex threads his fingers with mine, turning us to face our guests.

"Ladies and gentlemen, it's my honor to present Mr. and Mrs. Alexander Montgomery."

My gaze travels across the yard, where a small gathering of our family and closest friends now stand, applauding. Lana's holding her phone out so Maxim, Irina, and Amelia can be a part of this moment. Most of those in attendance know how close we came to not being here. It makes this moment all the more special.

Alex leans over and places one more kiss on my lips before leading us back down the aisle. Our guests toss handfuls of birdseed at us as we pass. Instead of going to the reception tent, he leads me into the house and straight to our bedroom, where he locks the door.

"You're a stunning bride, Mrs. Montgomery."

I smile when he says my new name. "You don't look so bad yourself, Mr. Montgomery."

"I wish we could skip right to the honeymoon." He backs up, appraising me with hooded eyes.

Chills cover my body, and I bite my lower lip. I want nothing better than to peel his clothes off and spend the rest of the evening celebrating our marriage—alone.

"I have a surprise for you." Alex reaches into his pocket and pulls out a small box with a silver ribbon tied in a bow.

"Another surprise?" I take the box. "Do you want me to open it now?"

"Yes."

I untie the ribbon and lift the lid. Inside are two silver rings. A pearl dangles from a small chain on each one. "They're beautiful. But how do I put them on?" I've never seen a pair of earrings like them.

"Let me help." Alex reaches behind me and opens the first few buttons of my gown. The bodice loosens enough to slide down, allowing my breasts to spill free.

"Aren't they for my ears, Sir?" Uncertainty fills my voice.

Alex laughs. "No, they aren't." He steps back and takes one of my breasts into his hand, kneading it gently. "I checked with the doctor to make sure these are safe." He lowers his head and takes my nipple in his mouth, licking and sucking, eliciting a soft moan from me.

He releases it and takes the ring from my hand, placing it around my nipple and squeezing it so it clamps tightly. Then, he lavishes the same attention on the other breast before adorning it with the jewelry.

His heated gaze travels over my body. "You are so beautiful."

I don't think I'll ever get sick of how his eyes fill with lust when he looks at me. Alex makes me feel sexy and adored. I shimmy back and forth, making the pearls sway. Their weight causes me to become even more aroused.

"baby girl, you need to stop that." He adjusts the prominent erection visible through his pants. "We have a backyard full of guests expecting us to be at our wedding reception."

Right now, I'm not caring about the people waiting for us. I'm wet from arousal and want him to continue undressing me. Batting my eyelashes, I move closer and snake my arms around his neck. "Surely, just a few more minutes wouldn't hurt." I run my tongue across the seam of his lips.

"You're quite the temptress, Mrs. Montgomery." Placing his hands on my shoulders, he pulls the bodice of my dress up and turns me around to button it. "When I rid you of this dress." He kisses my exposed neck. "I plan to bring you pleasure." He kisses my shoulder. "All night long."

His hands slide down my arms, and my head falls back onto his chest. "I don't want any interruptions while I'm making my wife scream my name." He steps away, and my body immediately misses the contact. "But right now, we have guests."

I blow out a frustrated breath. Alex's ministrations have ensured my body will remain aroused all night. "You, Sir, are a cruel man."

"I always make good on my promises." He smirks.

It takes me a few minutes to straighten my dress and remove the veil. Once I'm finished, Alex unlocks the door, and we walk down the hallway.

Lana's waiting for us in the kitchen. "I was wondering how long you two would be." She puts her hands on her hips, a cheeky smile on her face. "Do you want to take the train off now?"

"I almost forgot."

"I bet." She waggles her eyebrows.

Lana makes quick work of unbuttoning the long train. "Thank you. The dress is so much lighter now."

"I'll go hang this up. I'll be out in a minute."

"You're the best."

"I know," she calls over her shoulder as she hurries down the hallway.

Hand-in-hand, Alex and I walk across the yard. The tent for the reception is set up closer to the water. I was so caught up in the ceremony I didn't even look down here. Yet, what I see takes my breath away.

"Do you like it?"

As the sun begins to set over the lake, a gentle pink hue spreads across the sky behind the tent. The warm breeze causes the sheer ivory curtains to billow. While delicate fairy lights draped over the canopy emit a soft and romantic radiance.

A string quartet is positioned in the middle of the tent, which will later become the dance floor. Their music fills the air with sweet melodies. Surrounding the central area, each couple has their own table adorned with ivory linens and centerpieces that coordinate beautifully with the flowers in my bouquet.

For the moment, we're able to remain unnoticed and watch our loved ones as they mingle, laugh, and sip champagne, enjoying the exquisite hors d'oeuvres.

"It's perfect," I whisper.

Anthony, acting as the master of ceremonies, notices we've arrived and asks everyone to take their seats. We settle at our table as servers emerge from the house carrying silver trays overflowing with food. Dinner is a formal, plated event starting with Pacific oysters as the appetizer. Alex winks at me as he raises an oyster shell to his lips and swallows.

The movement of his mouth is sensual, and my core clenches in anticipation of what magic his mouth will do later. Over the next few hours, we're served several more courses, each dish more delicious than the previous one. When the meal is through, the servers clear away the remaining dinner plates.

Brandon stands to make a toast.

"Ten years ago, Alex showed up in New York City, a transplant from Seattle. As fate would have it, we bumped into each other at a local establishment." Brandon pauses and smiles. "We hit it off instantly. He's become more than just a friend—he's my family. Two years ago, the beautiful woman at his side also came into that same establishment. That night, when yours truly introduced you to each other, it was clear there was an instant connection—I take full credit for this marriage." Our guests share a laugh.

"On a more serious note, it's been a privilege to watch your relationship evolve into the love you share today. I speak for all of us when I say how happy we are for you both." He turns to our guests and raises his glass. "Please join me in wishing Mr. and Mrs. Montgomery many years of happiness."

A symphony of chiming champagne flutes announces the group's collective toast.

Tony calls us over to a table holding our wedding cake. Like everything else, it's an elegant design consisting of four white tiers. Dark purple orchids cascade down one side. With both of our hands on the knife, we cut a piece from the bottom layer.

"Vanilla?" Alex laughs.

"French vanilla with edible glitter," Tony chuckles.

Alex and I each take a small piece and, with arms entwined, feed each other. I moan when I taste the decadent cake. "You'll be doing a lot more of that tonight." Alex leans in close and licks a piece of frosting from my lip. "Delicious."

Before I can respond, Tony calls us to the center, where the string quartet has been replaced with a DJ. "May I have the bride and groom for their first dance?"

Ed Sheeran harmonizing with Andrea Bocelli's smooth tenor begins to play. The Italian rendition of "Perfect," a romantic tale of two lovers, fills the night. Alex places his hand on the small of my back and holds me tight against him while he quietly sings the lyrics to me, just like he did the first night I danced in his arms. Swaying to the music, our bodies move together as one.

If this is a dream, I never want to wake up.

"You are mine," Alex whispers when the song ends. "I love you, baby girl."

The next song is an upbeat tune, and our guests join us on the dance floor. I'm having the time of my life dancing with my friends. Even Alex, who's usually serious, is smiling and laughing while he's dancing with us.

When the music changes to a slower melody, it takes me a minute to recognize the song "Dance with My Father." Last year, I came very close to losing my father, the man who right now is proudly walking on his own to meet me on the dance floor. Alex steps aside as Dad takes my hand. I can't stop the tears from sliding down my cheeks.

"I can't believe my little girl is a married woman," Dad says as we move slowly to the music. "You chose a good man."

"I had a good example."

"I was far from perfect, sweetheart. I made so many mistakes." He's now shedding his own tears. "If only I could go back and do things differently, better. Maybe Michael would—"

"He's always right here." I put my hand over my father's heart. "I'm sure he's watching and knows how much you love him."

Dad's unable to speak through his tears. He nods and pulls me close as we finish our dance. When the music ends, I walk Dad back to his table.

"Thank you for the dance, Daddy."

"Thank you, my sweet daughter."

I nearly collide with Viktor when I turn around. "I was coming to ask for a dance, but you look worn out."

"I am."

"Why don't we sit this one out."

I loop my arm in his, and we walk back toward our table, grabbing water at the bar along the way.

We stop walking when I see Alex and his father standing outside the tent. I watch as Sam pulls him in for a hug. Alex's body shakes as he cries in his father's arms. There was only one other time I saw Alex this emotional. The memory nearly wrecks me, and I hold onto Viktor for support.

"He's a Dominant, Natalie, but he's also a man. Over the past two months, you and he have been through more than most people experience in a lifetime. Alex has been bottling up his feelings for too long. It's time he lets it all go."

Alex has been my rock while I've been recovering from the trauma in Mexico. But Viktor's right. He hasn't taken any time for himself. To heal from the things he experienced. It's a moving sight to see my Dominant seeking the safety and comfort of his father.

"Let's give them a few moments alone," Viktor says as he pulls out my chair for me to sit. "Do you need anything else?"

"I wouldn't mind more cake." I grin and put my hand on my belly. "We're both kinda hungry."

"Stay here. I'll go grab it."

"Enough." Alex jokingly pulls Viktor away from me. "I think I'll take my bride back now."

Viktor shakes his head and walks away.

"Has Viktor ever had a girlfriend?"

"No idea. He doesn't talk about his personal life."

"May I dance with my wife again?"

"I thought you'd never ask."

I'm dancing with Lana when Alex comes up behind me, wrapping his arms around my waist.

"Are you ready to go, baby girl?" He nuzzles my neck, reigniting my earlier arousal.

"Yes, Sir." I spin around in his arms. "I have to throw my bouquet first, though."

There are only two single ladies lined up behind me as I toss the flowers over my shoulder. Lana quickly steps out of the line of fire. Luna easily catches it, her cheeks turning red.

Then, Alex surprises me by scooping me into his arms. Our guests whistle and cheer as Alex carries me to our cottage for our first night as husband and wife.

The End

Epilogue

EVERY ONE OF THEM IS OBLIVIOUS TO MY PRESENCE ACROSS THE LAKE. But I'm here, hidden from their view, a mere spectator on the sidelines watching their lives play out. But not for long. Alex believes he's the knight in shining armor, a gallant hero who's saved the princess from the fire-breathing dragon and now gets to live happily ever after—but this isn't the average fairy tale. In this story, the dragon hasn't been defeated. He's lurking in the shadows, waiting for the perfect time to strike and exact his revenge.

While they've been living their happy little life, I've been busy putting my plan into place.

The clock is ticking.

The plan is in motion.

Alex and Natalie won't see me coming.

Everything in their perfect little world is about to come crashing down around them, and there's nothing anyone can do to stop it.

Acknowledgments

I still can't believe I'm getting to live my dream as an author, and it's all thanks to—YOU. Each of you who took a chance on a new author. Who picked up her book and fell in love with Alex and Natalie. I'm excited for you to read the last part of their story—make sure to bring your tissues with you. *Their Forever* is an emotional roller-coaster ride, but one that I believe is so worth reading. I'm going to miss spending so much time with Alex and Natalie.

George- You are my everything! You are why I fell in love with writing again. I love every second of this incredible journey we're taking together. Our walk and plots, our late nights while you listen to endless drafts of my books. Your backward editorial notes on those yellow papers. All of our trips to signings where I'm begging you to turn around, all the while, you're encouraging me to keep moving forward. I love you more than words can express, and I'm looking forward to many more books with you.

To my kids- Thank you for all your support while I'm writing. I appreciate the dinners and the extra chores you each pitch in with. I love that you come to all my signings and are my biggest cheering section. I love you all!

Dr. C- Once again, thank you for the medical consults, this time so I could kill off a character in a medically believable way. You will always be a rock star trauma surgeon in my book!

Janelle- I'm so glad we met and that you offered me a home at your store. You and your entire staff mean the world to me. I look forward to each of my visits there. Your support and friendship are very special to me.

Dana- Thank you for beta reading. I appreciate your honesty—when it's good and bad. My books are better because of your help.

PART THREE

Their Forever

To my husband, my Sir- You have been my rock throughout this entire series. When I was lost, You helped me find my way. i look forward to living our happily ever after.

To the men, women, and children affected by the horrible act of human trafficking. Know you are not forgotten. We will continue the fight to end trafficking and to bring each and every one of you home.

Xavier

My plan is genius—hide in plain sight, and New York City is the perfect place to do just that. Here I'm just another nameless face in a sea of millions. People go about their daily lives without so much as sparing me a second glance. It's taken a shit ton of patience, but my plans are finally coming together.

I pull open the glass door of the historic building and nod at the security guard.

"How are you this morning, Xavier?" the man asks.

"I'm livin' the dream." I smile and head for the staff elevator.

As the basement doors chime, I step inside and head towards the stock room to gather my supplies. I adjust my olive-green cap, giving it a snug fit, and then push the maintenance cart down the concrete hallway. The cart's wobbly wheels squeak with every step I take. After loading my cart onto the elevator, I ride to the tenth floor, where construction work is in full swing for a new business set to open its doors in January. Everyone's been tight-lipped about the specifics of the project. While the project's details have been kept under wraps, being part of the maintenance crew has perks. People tend to let their guard down around us, thinking they're speaking in private, but we're always listening. Word on the street is that Alexander Montgomery is spearheading the opening of a women's shelter. He's always trying to play the hero.

The doors open, and I step out. "Good morning." I nod to Steve, the foreman who's standing just outside the elevator.

"About time you got here, X," he jokes. "Do you mind helping my guys get this stuff out to the dumpster?" He points to a pile of drywall pieces.

"Consider it done," I say as I move my cart out of the way and head over to the clean-up crew. Without hesitation, I gather garbage and pile it into boxes to load into the elevator. As we work, we chat about the Giant's game from last week. In this environment, I feel like just one of the guys, and there are no doubts about my place here.

What's better is no one is aware of my true intentions. And they won't know.

Until I'm ready to strike.

Natalie

Our wedding was like a dream come true, a real-life fairy tale. Although it wasn't exactly what we'd originally envisioned, sometimes even the most carefully crafted plans can be improved with a little bit of change. I don't know how Alex planned a collaring ceremony and a surprise wedding a few weeks later. I'm married to the most wonderful man in the world.

After the wedding, we skipped a traditional honeymoon. Instead, Alex and I chose to spend our first few days as newlyweds nestled away in our cozy lake cottage. Now that we're back in the city, our lives have been a non-stop flurry of activity.

"Keep your eyes closed. No peeking," Alex says as he leads me to what used to be one of our guest rooms. Recently, he converted it into a shared office space. He forbade me from peeking while the room was under construction. The crew finished earlier today, and I'm finally getting the big reveal. Alex holds my hands, leading me into the room. "You can open your eyes now."

The walls have been painted a lovely shade of soft purple, my absolute favorite color. A set of stunning ebony-stained bookshelves are neatly arranged along the back wall. The real showstopper is the custom-made black two-person desk positioned in front of floor-to-ceiling windows that offer breathtaking water views. As I look closer, I notice that Alex's side of the desk features a framed photo of us on our wedding day alongside an ultrasound picture of our baby. "I love everything about this."

"And I'm going to love working side-by-side with my wife." He wraps his arms around me from behind, splaying his hands on my tummy.

Aside from overseeing the work in our home office, Alex's other focus has been on phasing himself out of the day-to-day operations at Montgomery Advertising. That process has been going smoothly. His personal clients have all agreed to stay on with Brandon at the helm. One more week, and the transition will be complete. After that, Alex can focus solely on our Jelena's Hope NYC project.

Getting that off the ground started chaotically, but it's much smoother now that the permits have finally come through. The construction crew is in place and has begun the initial stages of demolition. Earlier today, the architect sent over the digital design for the offices and residences. Signing off on the rendering is the last step before the actual construction begins.

Alex peppers my neck with kisses. "Ready to look at the design?"

"Mmm." I tilt my head, giving him more access, and rub against the erection poking my back. "I'd rather we explore this."

"That's very tempting, Mrs. Montgomery, but I told the architect we'd get back to her by this afternoon." He releases me and pulls my chair out. "Let's get to work."

I push out my bottom lip in a pout and lower myself into my black and purple desk chair. Sex with Alex has always been good, but being pregnant has made me insatiable, craving his touch at all hours and leaving me breathless with need every time he's near. The last thing I want to do right now is look at a computer screen. Alex's playful blue eyes glance my way, and he smiles. Then, he gets comfortable in his black chair and fires up the laptop.

With a click, he opens the file, bringing to life a three-dimensional mock-up of the new facility. I lean forward in my seat as Alex begins our virtual tour of the building. I'm enthralled by the images on the screen. The program affords a true-to-life view of the proposed design.

"What's this?" I point to a cluster of rooms.

"It's our education center." Alex clicks the area, and the program zooms in on one of the classrooms. "The children in our care will need to be enrolled in school. Traditional schools don't have the support system they require. Having an in-house school allows us to meet both the therapeutic and educational needs within the safety of our walls." He moves into another room. "There are additional classrooms for adults who wish to complete their education while they're with us."

I didn't stop to consider that we'll recover children, and they'll need schooling in addition to mental health treatment. Thankfully, Alex was looking at the bigger picture. "You've thought of everything."

"I'd love to take the credit, but it wasn't my idea. It's part of the startup plans Max sent us."

The next stop on our virtual tour is the medical, therapy, and job training rooms. Each will be fitted with state-of-the-art equipment to provide the best care possible to our residents. After we finish the business area, we move up a floor to the residences.

"There will be mental health and medical professionals available around the clock for the residences," Alex explains as we get our first view of the units.

Our facility will consist of three floors with a total of eighteen apartments designed to provide separate living spaces for men, women, and children. The twelve adult apartments will house three individuals per unit and boast identical layouts with a shared kitchen and living area. The designer has carefully selected calming shades of blues and greens for the walls. Each resident will have a private bedroom and bathroom with a clean, minimalist aesthetic, furnished with a full-size bed, dresser, desk, and comfortable chair.

The remaining six units are specially designed to cater to the unique needs of children. Each apartment will house four children and a set of vetted and trained house parents who specialize in working with trafficked children. These units have an open floor plan to allow the house parents to keep a watchful eye on the children at all times. In addition to the kitchen and living room, the children's units have fully stocked playrooms filled with games and toys to keep them entertained. Like the adults, each child will have a private bedroom and bathroom to provide a safe and nurturing environment for them to heal and recover.

"I wasn't sure what to expect. Part of me feared the apartments would be sterile and institutional-looking, but they aren't. They're comfortable and homey."

"We're good to sign off on these?" Alex asks.

"We are."

"I found a few houses outside of Manhattan that our realtor is in the process of closing on." Alex opens a web browser to show me the listings. "Since Dad and Maxim are funding these properties, I sent them the links the other day to get their approval."

I'm amazed at the vast amount of progress Alex has made on this project in such a short time. When he sets his mind to something, there's no stopping him. Alex's excitement is contagious as he shows me pictures of the listings. Each house is located in flourishing neighborhoods on tree-lined streets—an idyllic setting for someone transitioning back into society.

My heart aches as I look at the pictures, knowing there are people out there right now suffering. They don't know their rescues are being planned and that they'll be safe very soon. Tears trail down my cheeks.

"What's wrong, baby girl?" Alex turns me to face him.

"Knowing we'll fill up as soon as the doors open." I swallow over a sob. "That the need is so great. The reality is hard to face."

"It's a part of society most people are either unaware of or choose to turn a blind eye to." Alex wipes my tears. "But for those who've experienced it first-hand, it's something they can never forget—never pretend it doesn't exist."

"When I decided to become a therapist, I was sure my future was in North-meadow and that my purpose was helping other youth from close-minded families like mine. In my wildest dreams, I wouldn't have been able to imagine the path my life would take. That I'd meet you. And that I'd be personally affected by trafficking. But now I know everything I experienced was leading me to this moment."

Alex gently rubs his knuckles along my cheek. "I hate what happened to us—to you. But I wouldn't want to do this with anyone else. You and I, Natalie Mont-gomery, are an unstoppable team."

He kisses me, and I bask in my Dominant's affection. With only a few simple words, he makes me feel like the most treasured woman on the planet. But as cher-ished as he makes me feel, it doesn't stop the doubts and questions plaguing me.

Being a mother has always been part of my plan. Yes, I wanted to get my educa-tion and have a career, but in my head, I always saw myself being a stay-at-home mom —like my mom was when we were little. It's hard to imagine I'd want to do some-thing the same way as my mom, but it's true. We continue to butt heads, although it's been much less lately.

I always admired Mom for her dedication to raising Michael and me. I can't imagine how she must've felt watching my dad go off to work every day, knowing she'd be alone with two young children for long hours while he was at the store. I smile, remembering the antics Michael and I would get up to. We climbed trees and tore our clothes, made mud pies in the dirt, and then brought them into the house to show our Mom the delicious *snacks* we made. Michael and I were a handful, but no matter how messy or loud we were, Mom always remained patient.

She tried to give us as many experiences as possible within a small town. We spent countless afternoons at the park playing with the other children. We spent time at our neighbor's farms, helping with their animals. From the time we were little, Mom would have us at her side in the kitchen, helping her cook.

As we got older, we spent time at the store helping out where we could. And countless art projects. Mom is very artistic and tried desperately to pass that on to Michael and me. She hoped at least one of us would be artistically inclined. Instead of masterpieces, she got finger-painted floors and crayon-colored walls.

Summertime holds some of my very favorite memories. Michael and I spent hours helping Mom meticulously plant flowers and vegetables for the family garden. As we got older, she gave us a tiny patch of our own to plant. It was hard work keeping our young seedlings weed-free and watered adequately. But when fall came, Michael and I were so proud of the vegetables we'd harvested. I've always wanted to pass the love of gardening to my children one day.

It wasn't until Michael and I were both in school that Mom started working part-time at the pharmacy. She'd wake up before dawn each morning to cook breakfast and get us ready for school. After the bus picked us up, she would get a ride into town to work for a few hours. Mom always made sure to be home before we got home from school. She'd be waiting with snacks and ready to hear our endless chatter about everything that happened at school.

While we did our homework, Mom got dinner started. When Dad would come in from work, dinner would be on the table. We sat down and ate as a family every night. After the meal, Michael and I helped with chores while Dad watched the evening news. Then, she'd get us bathed and ready for bed. Each night, Mom read us a bedtime story and then tucked us in. But her night still wasn't over. She'd head back down to the kitchen to pack our lunches for the next day.

Looking back, I don't know how she had the energy to do all that day after day. That's always been the picture I had of my future life, the kind of mother I imagined myself becoming.

Opening Jelena's Hope NYC has changed what my future will look like. I'll be a mother in a few short months, but I won't have the luxury of being a full-time stay-at-home mom. I've committed to working with the women who'll no doubt be at our center. I'm finding myself torn in two directions.

Alex has mentioned possibly hiring a nanny while I work. The thought of letting someone else raise my child is disheartening. I need to share these concerns with Alex, but I'm unsure how to approach the topic. Even though I'm running out of time, I'm not ready to put my thoughts and fears into words yet.

"Earth to Natalie." Alex places his hand on mine, snapping me from my thoughts.

"I'm sorry. I guess I spaced out." I force a smile.

"Are you okay?"

"I am." I point to the screen. "The houses are very nice."

"Mhm." Alex eyes me suspiciously. "I've instructed the real estate agent to put full asking price offers on each one."

"Fingers crossed, we get them all."

"Even if we have to go above the asking price, I'll make sure we get them."

Everything's set in motion. We're one step closer to making our dream of Jelena's Hope-NYC into reality.

Alex

After sending the last email, I close the laptop and turn to my wife. "Thanksgiving's next month."

"Yes, Sir. I recall that happening every November." Natalie gives me a cheeky grin.

She's feisty today. I like seeing this side of her. "I want to invite your parents for the holiday."

"Like they'd ever come here for Thanksgiving." She raises her eyebrows, possibly questioning my sanity.

"We have plenty of room for them to stay with us. You and your mom can have Pie Day. Maybe we can even convince them to go to the parade."

I know Thanksgiving holds so many special memories for her until the disaster last year. But the holiday is only a few weeks away, and she hasn't mentioned anything about it. I'm sure she's trying to avoid the memories, but that won't help anything. My hope is that if her parents come here, we can start new traditions—make new memories.

Natalie bites her lip. "I don't know, Alex." She stands and walks to the door.

"I want this." It's not a question. Not open for argument, yet she tries anyway.

"You know my parents won't come to the city. Especially for a holiday."

"We'll see about that."

"If you say so."

"I say so."

"Don't be surprised when they say no." Her shoulders slump in defeat. "I'll be in the baby's room if you need me."

Although the relationship with her parents has improved since this time last year, there's still healing to be done. There are things about Charlotte and Stanley that'll never change. Quirks, we have to accept. But New York City is our home. That's a fact that's not going to change. They want to be part of their daughter's and soon-to-be granddaughter's lives. That means they'll have to compromise and be willing to travel to the city occasionally.

I give them a call.

"Hello?"

"Hi, Stanley. It's Alex."

"Is everything ok?"

"Everything's great. I'm calling because Natalie and I would like you and Charlotte to spend Thanksgiving with us in the city."

"I see."

"I'd like to fly you both out the week before so we can spend time together before the holiday."

"Well, we've always had Thanksgiving here," Stanley says. Charlotte and I assumed you and Natalie would come to Northmeadow."

"I understand that. However, with Natalie this far along in her pregnancy, she can't be traveling that far."

"Hang on. Let me get Charlotte."

This isn't going quite as planned. I thought Charlotte would be the hard sell. But if I can't get past Stanley, I'm not sure how well this is going to go.

"Alex, how are you?" Charlotte asks.

"I'm doing well. I'm trying to convince your husband to agree to spend the holiday with us here."

"Oh, I see," she says, echoing her husband's initial response. "This is very unexpected."

"We'd like to fly you out the week before the holiday. You can stay with us. Maybe you can help Natalie with the nursery?"

"I'd love to be able to help Natalie get the baby's room ready," Charlotte says.

Aha. I found the right angle. I can almost hear the smile on Charlotte's face.

"I suppose it wouldn't hurt to try things a little differently this year."

"Excellent. I'll purchase the tickets and email you the information. Natalie's going to be so excited. Oh. And bring that pretty apron for Pie Day."

"Of course," Charlotte chirps. "We can't have Thanksgiving without Pie Day."

What I didn't tell them was that I'd already purchased the airline tickets. I don't want to risk them changing their minds, so I email the flight information as soon as we hang up. Then, I shoot a quick text to my father to confirm his and Luna's flight arrangements. Brandon and I spoke last week. He and Lana will be here. My last call is to Maxim, who assures me they can't wait to get here. I sit back and take a deep breath. Everyone I invited has said yes. The holiday is going to be perfect.

Now I get to go tell Natalie the good news.

Natalie

I'm standing in what will eventually be Rose's nursery if I ever figure out the paint color.

"Still trying to decide?" Alex asks as he comes into the room and stands next to me. Out of the corner of my eye, I see him watching me curiously as I study the paint swatches on the wall.

"I've narrowed it down to these two, but I can't decide if I like this one," -I point to one of the samples- "Or this one."

Alex takes a step closer to the wall. "They look the same to me."

The colors are not the same at all. The one on the right is a cool gray with undertones of blue. And the one on the left is a neutral gray.

"I think this is the one." I grab the neutral gray and hand it to Alex. "It'll be perfect with the pink accents we already chose."

"Is this your final answer?" He grins as he dangles the paint swatch in his hand.

Still feeling a bit indecisive, I take a last look between the sample in Alex's hand and the one taped to the wall. "Yes. I'm certain that's the one."

Alex takes me by the hand. "Let's get it mixed."

One of the perks of living in such a big city is the accessibility of almost anything we could ever want. We have a paint store a few blocks away, and since it's a beautiful late-October afternoon, we chose to walk. The autumn air is crisp and cool. This time of the year was always my favorite in Missouri. The tree-covered mountains turn into a canvas of reds, oranges, and yellows. Part of me longs to be at our lake house, the fallen leaves crunching under our feet, but the other part is at peace, knowing we're exactly where we're meant to be.

A few blocks into our walk, Alex says, "Looks like we're hosting our first Thanksgiving."

"My parents said yes?"

"They sure did." Alex smiles proudly.

"How did you pull that off?"

"I may have mentioned that your mom could help decorate the nursery. And that she should bring her apron."

"You bribed her?" I laugh.

"It worked." He shrugs before opening the door, holding it for me to go ahead of him. "Anyway, I can't wait to see my sexy submissive in nothing but an apron."

"So, you had ulterior motives, Sir?"

"One could call it motivation. Your parents aren't the only ones coming."

"Who else did you invite?"

Alex goes down the list of everyone who's said yes.

"I can't believe it." I throw my arms around his neck and kiss him.

A salesperson clears their voice, interrupting our public display of affection.

"May I help you?"

Without missing a beat, Alex hands over the paint swatch. While the paint is being mixed, we shop for the rest of the supplies. I suggested we hire a painter, but Alex insisted on doing the work himself. I love that he wants to be hands-on with everything concerning the baby. After the paint is mixed and Alex is confident he has enough rollers and brushes, we pay for our purchases. Then, with bags in hand, we walk back to our apartment.

Alex has been painting for the past few hours. I wanted to help, too, but even though we bought no VOC paint, his answer was still a firm *no*. I've been on the phone with Lana for quite a while discussing plans for the holiday, but now it's time to get some video of Alex painting.

I tiptoe down the hall, hoping to sneak up on him and get some candid shots. I plan to document every moment of us getting ready for our little girl. Even with the door closed, I can hear his music. I hope it provides enough cover so he doesn't hear me as I slowly turn the handle and push the door open just a crack.

Peeking around with the camera, I hit record. It takes all my self-control not to drool when I lay eyes on a shirtless Alex wearing my favorite pair of jeans that fit in all the right places. His muscles flex as he rolls the paint on the walls.

"I know you're there." Alex stops painting and turns around. "Are you recording me?"

"I am. One day, I want to be able to show our daughter these videos so she knows how loved she was, even before she was born."

Alex sets the roller down on the tray. "Is that so?" His eyes are now laser-focused on me as he stalks across the room.

"It is." I bite my bottom lip. "I want her to see how much her mommy and daddy love each other and how excited we are about her."

Alex flashes me a sexy grin right before he grabs the camera from my hand. He holds it up to film us as he leans in and kisses me before looking directly into the camera.

"Rose, your mama is my world." He kisses me again. "She's the best thing that ever happened to me." Another kiss. "I'm sure you already know, but she's also going to be the best mommy in the world. We're both lucky to have her."

Then, he turns off the camera and slides my phone into his pocket before wrapping his arms around me and pulling me against him. His hand finds its way through my hair, and he tugs it, making me look up at him.

"I want you naked and waiting for me in our bedroom. I'll be in as soon as I clean up."

"Yes, Sir."

Alex releases me and strides back across the room to complete his task. My feet remain rooted while I watch my sexy Dominant bend over and pick up the paint tray.

"Now, baby girl."

His command is all the encouragement my feet need to start moving. I quickly leave the nursery and head down the hall to our bedroom. My entire body tingles with anticipation, eagerly awaiting whatever surprises Alex has in store for me.

Alex

I'M FINISHING UP THE LAST OF THE PAINTING WHEN NATALIE TRIES TO sneak up on me. I'm crazy attracted to her on a typical day. But seeing her growing my child, my sexual attraction to her is off the charts—I can't keep my hands or dick to myself. She doesn't seem to mind either. Being pregnant has only increased her already healthy sex drive. After closing the paint can, I head to the guest room for a quick shower, knowing the extended delay will only heighten my sub's anticipation.

After I've showered, I wrap a towel around my waist and stop in the kitchen to grab a glass of ice before heading to our bedroom. When I open the door, I find Natalie gloriously naked and on her knees, waiting for me. My body responds immediately, the outline of my erection prominent from under the towel. I set the glass on the dresser and go to Natalie.

"Stand up." I offer her my hand to help her from the floor.

"That's not as easy as it was a few weeks ago," she says with a slight shake of her head.

"Come sit down." I lead her to the bed and have her sit back against the pillows. "Give me your leg."

She places her foot on my lap, and I massage one leg first, then the other.

"Mm..." she groans. "That feels so good."

"No more kneeling while you're pregnant." I finish her mini massage. "Are your legs okay?"

"Yes, Sir. They're much better now."

"Good. Now get on your hands and knees." I arrange a pillow under her stomach to give her support.

She looks over her shoulder and wiggles her ass flirtatiously, earning her a playful slap before I make my way into our closet.

When I return, I set one of my surprises in the glass of ice before stopping to admire how beautiful Natalie looks with her legs spread, baring herself to me. Her breasts are full and begging to be sucked. My erection throbs between my legs as I remove my towel with one hand and let it fall to the floor. In my other hand is her favorite flogger.

Coming up behind her, I knead the globes of her ass, preparing her for what's to come. Natalie moans softly. With a flick of my wrist, the leather tails land gently across her skin. This isn't an impact scene. My plan is to experiment with different sensations. The next hit lands between her legs, and she gasps. I run my finger through her slit before sliding it inside. She rocks against my hand.

"My greedy little sub."

"I am, Sir."

"What's your color?" Checking in has become more important as her pregnancy progresses. Her body reacts differently now than it did even just a week or two ago, and she tires quickly in some positions.

"Green, Sir."

I continue alternating between light strikes with the flogger and teasing her clit. The next gentle lick of the leather tails is followed by dragging my finger through her wetness. Then, I circle her tight entrance before sliding it in. She drops her head as I pump my finger in and out, gently stretching her.

"That feels so good."

I remove my finger, eliciting a groan from her.

"We're nowhere near done yet, baby girl." I set the flogger down on the dresser before grabbing the glass butt plug from the ice and the lube. I apply a generous amount to the cold toy before teasing her, sliding the tip in and out.

"How does it feel?"

"Mmm. So good."

"Touch yourself," I order. "I want you to make yourself come for me."

She slides one hand between her legs, circling her clit while I tease her ass with the plug. The closer she gets to orgasm, the less her body resists. Her pleasure is growing more and more.

"Come for me, now."

I push the plug in all the way as her orgasm washes over her. She drops her head, breathing heavily, but we're far from done. I help Natalie off her knees and onto her back, propping her on pillows so she's not lying flat. Then, I drop to my knees and position her legs over my shoulders. Her pussy is glistening with her arousal. It's an erotic sight. I lean in and lick from one end to the other. "You taste exquisite."

Natalie's eyes flutter open as she watches me drop my head between her legs. My tongue teases her, nipping and sucking her clit before adding my fingers, pumping them in and out. Natalie moans in response, pushing herself against me, seeking more friction.

"Patience, baby girl." I grab her hips, stilling her.

She drops her head. "Please, Sir. I want you." I love hearing her beg for me.

Without wasting time, I return to my ministrations. This time fucking her with my tongue while my hand pumps the plug in and out of her ass. It only takes seconds before she's screaming my name. But my mouth doesn't stop. I intend to take everything she has to offer. Once her orgasm subsides, I stand and fist my cock. Pre-cum drips from the tip. With hooded eyes, she watches my every movement as I line myself up with her opening and enter her slowly, allowing her to adjust to the overwhelming sensations I know she's experiencing by having both holes filled. Once I'm fully sheathed, I stop, savoring how tight she feels wrapped around me. I slide my hand up her body, stopping at her breast. I alternate between palming her soft flesh and rolling her erect nipples. Then I start moving, slow and steady.

"You feel so good." Her voice is breathy. "I need more."

"You need more?" I tease.

"Yes, Sir." She moans. "Harder, please."

That request I can oblige. My hands hold her hips as I pick up the speed and strength of my thrusts.

"Is this what you want?"

"Mmm..."

Natalie's moans grow louder, her breaths quickening as she approaches another climax. I am poised to join her, eager for the plunge into bliss. Her cries of pleasure fill the room as her body shudders with the force of her orgasm. I'm also overwhelmed with sensation as my release pulses through my body, and I fill her. Though Natalie is starting to tire, my selfish desire pushes me to continue, alternating between gently pumping in and out and circling my hips, each motion grazing her overly sensitive clitoris.

"Oh my God, don't stop."

I continue teasing her until I feel myself getting close. As I approach my climax, I speed up my thrusts. Right as I let go, I pull the plug from her ass. The sensation causes her to orgasm again—her body shudders beneath mine. Sweat drips from her forehead. She's spent.

"That was mind-blowing, Sir."

"You're incredible, baby girl." I move from between her legs and immediately miss our intimate connection. "Wait here."

I go into the bathroom and wet a washcloth with warm water before returning to my sub. Parting her legs, I clean her before tossing the cloth onto the bedside table. Then, I pull the comforter back and help Natalie to the top of the bed, where I climb next to her. She lays her head on my chest, her arm thrown over my abdomen. My fingers draw lazy circles on her back. At this moment, words aren't needed. Instead, we bask in the connection we share.

I wait until Natalie's body relaxes and she's snoring softly. Then, I carefully slide my arm from under her and get out of bed. I throw on clean clothes and go to the kitchen to cook dinner. Natalie's going to be hungry when she wakes.

Natalie

"I DON'T KNOW HOW YOU HAVE THE PATIENCE FOR THIS," I SAY TO Viktor, who's driving or, should I say, sitting at a standstill in traffic.

"If we took the subway, we'd be there already." Viktor shoots Alex a frustrated glance in the rearview. But Alex doesn't seem to notice. He has his head down, engrossed with something on his phone.

"I already told you, no subway," Alex says without looking up. "We have plenty of time to get there."

Alex and Viktor have been engaged in a battle of wills, which has had Alex on a knife's edge all morning. We have to be at Jelena's Hope NYC for a walk-through. Viktor wanted us to take the subway, but Alex has been struggling with being in confined spaces since our ordeal in Mexico. So, he insisted that we drive even though it would take twice the time. The tension between the two men is unsettling. I place my hand on Alex's leg, trying to calm him. He puts his hand over mine and gives it a reassuring squeeze.

We slowly crawl through the streets while the city's iconic yellow taxis weave in and out of traffic. Each time they zoom by, I cringe at their proximity. I would've much preferred taking the subway, too, but Alex has the last word. Finally, after over an hour, Viktor pulls up outside the Jelena's Hope-NYC building.

"I'll drop you off and meet you upstairs after I park the car."

"Thanks," Alex says curtly as he steps out.

He offers me his hand, helping me to my feet. Standing up grows more difficult as my stomach grows rounder with each passing day. Once in the building, we stop at the security desk to check in.

"Good afternoon, Mr. and Mrs. Montgomery," the guard greets us.

"How's everything today, Leon?" Alex asks. "How's your wife feeling?"

Alex never ceases to amaze me with how he makes a personal connection with everyone he comes in contact with. He has a heart of gold.

"Not well. Her body's no longer responding to the treatments," Leon says, his shoulders sagging in defeat. "The doctors are scrambling to come up with another plan."

"I'm so sorry to hear that. Please let me know if there's anything I can do to help."

"I appreciate the offer, Mr. Montgomery." He looks behind us. "No Viktor today?"

"He's parking the car. He'll be along shortly. We're going upstairs to check in on the progress."

"I'll make a note of that." Leon turns to his computer screen and begins typing.

Alex and I walk hand-in-hand to the elevator, where he presses his finger against a pad on the wall. He wasn't kidding when he told me this building has state-of-the-art security. Alex explains if someone who isn't programmed into the system enters through the underground parking, the elevator will only take them to the ground floor. "It ensures no one can access any of the upper floors without going through security first. We'll program your fingerprint while we're here."

"What about the steps?"

"They're equipped with the same technology."

"That's amazing."

The elevator ride is fast and smooth as it brings us to our floor. The last time I was here, the demo had just finished, and the place was a blank slate. I'm anxious to see what

progress has been made.

Steve, the construction foreman, is waiting for us when we step out. "Good to see you, Mr. Montgomery." The men shake hands. Then he quickly glances my way. "You as well, Mrs. Montgomery."

"It looks so different in here from last time."

"We've been busy," Steve says. "Are you ready for the tour?"

We follow Steve to a sectioned-off area to our right. This will eventually be the reception area. Alex and Steve don't waste a second discussing technical things I don't care to understand.

Touching Alex's arm, I say, "I'm going to look at the design samples." I motion toward a table.

"I'll be over in a minute," he assures me and then returns to his conversation.

We've already signed off on the paint. This time, the designer has left several options for the hardwood floors. There's also a tablet with digital photos of the furniture that'll be used in the reception area. Although it's commercial-grade, the couches and chairs look plush and inviting. Several fabric swatches are laid out for us to choose from. At first glance, the light grey fabric stands out. It seems to meld with the peaceful aesthetic we're seeking to achieve.

"What do you think?" Alex asks, coming up behind me.

"I love the choices. But something's missing." I look around the room. Alex and Steve stand silently, watching me. "The colors are soothing, and I'm sure once the furniture gets here, it'll help, but it feels sterile. When the survivors step in here for the first time, they'll likely be in fight or flight mode. This area is going to be their first impression of Jelena's Hope-NYC. It needs to feel safe and comfortable—they need to see life. What would you think about adding some plants and maybe a large aquarium?"

Alex looks around as if he's trying to envision what I've described. "I think that's an excellent idea. Steve, will you contact the architect and put that into action?"

"Yes, sir," he says, although he looks unsure. "How about we continue the tour?"

Alex places his hand on the small of my back as we follow Steve to the offices. While we walk down the spacious hallway, Steve says, "There's someone I'd like you to meet." Steve checks in a few rooms but doesn't seem to find whoever he's looking for. "I was hoping to introduce you to X-man?"

"Excuse me?" Alex asks.

"That's the nickname we've given the guy. He's one of the building's maintenance men that's been helping out." Steve checks in another room. "He was just here. I guess he went on break. The guy's a hard worker. I'm thinking about offering him a permanent position on my crew."

"If you think he's a good fit, I'll trust your judgment. I'm sure we'll catch him next time."

After the tour of the business section, we come to the private elevators that service only the floors belonging to Jelena's Hope-NYC.

"Hey, Steve," one of the men calls. "There's a phone call for you."

"I've been waiting to hear from one of the product suppliers. Do you mind continuing the tour on your own?"

"We'll be fine," Alex assures him as we step into the elevator for the quick ride up to the next floor.

Stepping out into the first of our residential units, no one would ever suspect this was anything more than a high-end apartment building. The hallway has dark floors, but with the bright lighting, it balances well. I'm not sure if it's authentic hardwood or a laminate. Either way, it's beautiful. What steals the show are the hand-painted murals on the walls. We're walking through a jungle with life-like trees and animals. It's magical.

"Obviously, this is the children's floor," Alex says as he opens the door to the first apartment.

As we step into the open expanse, sunlight pours in through floor-to-ceiling windows, illuminating the entire space. To one side, a cozy living room greets us with plush couches and chairs. They're arranged to face a generously sized flat-screen TV mounted on the wall. Nearby shelves overflow with books and games. Brightly colored bean bag chairs complete the inviting atmosphere.

On the opposite side of the room, a modern kitchen and dining area beckon with gleaming white cabinets and sparkling marble countertops. Top-of-the-line stainless steel appliances add a touch of luxury the houseparents will appreciate. An expansive island with several chairs separates the eating area from the rest of the room, creating the perfect spot for a quick snack. A large dining table sits before the windows, comfortably accommodating at least seven guests for more formal meals.

"This is exactly how I pictured it." I squeeze Alex's hand in excitement. "It feels like a home."

We proceed down the hallway until we reach the first door. Alex opens it to reveal one of the children's bedrooms. At first glance, the space appears somewhat generic, eliciting feelings of disappointment. However, I remind myself that the minimal design is intentional. These rooms are designed to provide a safe haven—a peaceful and unstimulating environment. As the children settle in and become more comfortable, they'll have the opportunity to personalize and decorate the space to their liking.

Two windows fill the room with natural light, but heavy curtains can be drawn to darken the room when needed. Across from the windows sits a cozy twin bed, complete with a fluffy white comforter and an abundance of soft pillows. Much like the play area, the bedroom features a bean bag chair and a small shelf that will eventually be filled with books and toys.

The last wall holds two doors.

"Which one should we look behind first?"

"You pick."

I chose the door on the left, which opens to a bathroom complete with a tub and a walk-in shower. The last door leads to a walk-in closet just waiting to be filled with clothes.

"When the kids arrive, they'll have nothing. So how do we know what clothes to buy? What sizes we need?" I ask Alex.

"Honestly, I have no idea." He pulls his cell from his pocket. "Let's call Max and Irina for some guidance."

"Pardon me for eavesdropping," a dark-haired woman says as she walks into the room. "I can answer that for you."

"Imani, it's so good to finally meet you." We've had many online conferences with our designer, but this is the first time we're getting to meet in person.

I offer Imani my hand, but she surprises me by pulling me in for a hug instead.

"It's great to finally meet you, too," she says, shaking Alex's hand. "In answer to your question, Irina and I have spoken at length. She's instructed me to purchase wardrobe staples—pants, shirts, pajamas, everything a child needs in nearly every size. I've done the same for the adults as well. Each floor has a general closet room to pull from. Once the child or adult is settled, we can get their exact size, and if they'd like, they can help choose their clothes," she explains. "Irina stressed the importance of providing each person freedom with as many choices as possible."

"Given that so much of their freedom has been stolen, that makes perfect sense and answers my question." I smile.

"What do you think about the apartment?" she asks.

"You've done a wonderful job.

"Have you been in the parent's suite yet?"

"Not yet," Alex answers.

As we walk down the hall, Imani explains the other three children's rooms are identical to the one we were just in. At the end of the hall, we come to a set of double doors. "This is the parent's suite. I've tried very hard to make it a luxurious sanctuary."

I'm speechless as I look around the room that's set up like a loft apartment.

"I've spoken to each of the couples to get their input on the design," she explains.

"Imani, this is exquisite." Alex compliments her work.

A kitchenette and a cozy sitting area with a fireplace are on our left. Opposite that area is a sleeping area with a king-size bed. Like the kids' rooms, there's a spacious walk-in closet and a large bathroom. The walls in this room are cerulean blue, and the floor is covered in a cream-colored carpet.

"This particular couple requested a coastal design," Imani explains. "The linens and décor will arrive later this week."

"I love it." I walk toward the window and look out at the view of Central Park. "This job will be demanding. The couples will need this sanctuary to escape to at the end of the day."

"Then I've accomplished my goal." She smiles proudly.

"You've done an excellent job," Alex adds.

"Thank you, Mr. Montgomery. Shall we go up to the adult floors?"

The three of us do a walkthrough of an apartment on each floor and find them in good order. Imani took our initial vision and ran with it. She far exceeded our expectations.

"Thank you for the tour. " Don't hesitate to contact us if you need anything," Alex says.

Xavier

"Xavier, do you have a minute?"

"Sure thing." I wipe the sweat from my forehead. "What's up?"

"You've proven to be a valuable asset to my crew. I want to talk to Mr. Montgomery about hiring you to help complete this project."

"Oh?" I'm pleasantly surprised at this turn of events.

"It would be a pay raise and the chance to join us permanently if you're interested."

"Can I let you know in a few days?"

"That'll be fine. Mr. Montgomery will be here any minute, and I want to introduce you to him."

Shit. That can't happen. "No problem. I'll be here."

I go back to work and wait until Steve is out of sight. Then, I slip into the stairwell and hurry to the basement. There's no way I can be around while Montgomery's here. I've worked too hard for my plans to be ruined. My plan is complicated, especially with the buildings' tight security. But, if you watch and listen, the weak spots always show themselves.

In this building, the weak spot is Leon, the head of security. He has a wife with a terminal illness. The doctors have tried everything to get her out of pain, but it hasn't worked. Leon's desperate to see her pain-free, and I happen to have what he needs. It didn't take too much persuading. In exchange for some product that helps his wife, Leon's agreed to turn a blind eye when I need it. It was like giving candy to a child.

Once I'm in the basement, I head to the employees' locker room and open my locker to double-check that the package I brought is still hidden. There are just a few more pieces I need to get in place. Then, I'll have everything I need to move forward with my plan. I close the door and make sure it's locked securely. I can't risk being careless.

Just a few more weeks...

Alex

Me: Great. Keep me updated.

"I still can't believe you convinced them to come here."

"What can I say? I can be very persuasive."

"I seem to remember that about you." Natalie grins.

It's taken a few hours, but I'm finally tightening the last screw for my daughter's crib. I stand back and admire my handiwork. "What do you think?"

Natalie pushes herself to stand from the rocking chair and walks over to look at the white canopy crib.

"I love it." She runs her hand along the rail. "And I love you, Sir. May I show you how much?"

"Are you topping from the bottom, baby girl?"

"Maybe." She bats her eyelashes at me.

Other Doms might see that as a problem, but I don't. Natalie knows her place as my submissive, but she's also my wife, and I enjoy this playful, seductive side of her. I love that she's not afraid to initiate sex, so I play along.

"You do remember your parents are on their way?"

"I do, Sir. They haven't left the airport yet, so we have plenty of time." She begins unbuttoning her shirt and starts walking toward the door.

I watch her shirt slide down her arms and flutter to the floor. While Natalie walks, she reaches behind her to unclasp her bra, tossing it to the floor. I trail behind her like a moth attracted to a flame. When she gets to our bedroom door, she stops and looks over her shoulder. "That was all I could manage gracefully." She giggles.

"Go sit on the bed," I order and strip my shirt, tossing it to the side. Once I'm in front of her, I lean in for a long, slow kiss. My hands caress her breasts while I kiss my way down her neck, nipping her skin as I trail my mouth down to her nipples. "Lay back." The phone rings, momentarily distracting me. I don't check who it is before swiping the screen and sending the call to voicemail. Then, I toss my cell to the other side of the bed. "Now, where was I?"

I slide her leggings and panties off before spreading her legs wide. Getting down on my knees, I don't waste any time. I dive in like a starving man, my tongue going right to work. She gasps.

"Do you like that?"

"Yes, Sir. Very much." Her voice drips with need.

I go right back to work and drag my tongue down her pussy and into her wetness. She moans while I fuck her with my tongue, my fingers teasing her clit. Her body is so responsive. She's close already, so I pull back and tease her with my fingers.

Natalie lifts her head. "Please, don't stop."

"Don't stop this?" I run my finger down her wet slit. "Tell me who you belong to?"

"You, Sir. I belong to you.

"Only me," I say and slide two fingers inside her while my mouth attacks her clit. It's only seconds before she's crying out, her body squeezing my fingers. I lick and suck, extending her orgasm until she begs me to stop. Standing, I open the button and zipper on my jeans, freeing my erection. "Do you know how much I love you, baby girl?"

"I do," she says quietly.

Leaning over her, I'm careful to keep my weight on my arms as my lips meet hers. She grants my tongue entrance as I kiss her slowly and deeply, allowing her to taste herself before I roll over and position her on top of me. Using my hands for balance, she lowers herself onto my cock. Her body feels like my personal heaven as she raises and lowers herself in a slow rhythm. Her eyes never lose contact with mine.

My phone rings, and I reach over to silence it. Anyone who's trying to reach me will have to wait.

Her hands go to her breasts, kneading them and rolling her nipples between her fingers.

"Fuck, you're gorgeous."

She smiles seductively.

Seconds later, my phone rings again. Viktor must be getting close. I swipe the phone ignoring the call one last time. As much as I'd like to spend the rest of the day worshipping Natalie's body, our time alone is almost up.

"Touch yourself. I want you to come with me."

Natalie's hand goes between her legs while I grab her waist and take control.

"Don't stop." She throws her head back. "I'm so close."

A few more thrusts and I explode. Natalie follows right after, her body squeezing my cock, draining every last ounce of myself inside her. She leans forward, her elbows on my chest, leaving room for her tummy. I run my fingers through her long hair, tucking her curls behind her ears.

"Are you okay?"

"I'm better than okay." She pushes on my chest to adjust her position. "Other than your phone ringing, that was perfect."

I reach out and grab my cell. "Viktor has terrible timing." I unlock the screen and see it wasn't Viktor who's been calling. I carefully move Natalie to the bed beside me and sit up to listen to the voicemails. "Shit."

Natalie watches me, concern etching her features.

"There was a fire at the job site." I pull up Steve's contact.

"How bad was it? Did anyone get hurt?" She rapid fires questions.

"I don't know. Go get cleaned up while I figure out what's going on."

Natalie gets up, gathers her clothes, and heads into the bathroom. I call Steve while I'm getting dressed.

"What the hell happened?"

"I'm sorry to bother you, but we had an issue."

"Tell me everything," Steve explains, saying that one of his crew members was careless while welding and started a small fire. "How much damage was done?"

"Everything was contained to the immediate area." His voice shakes from nerves. "I'll cover the costs of the damage."

"And the employee?"

"He's been let go."

"How far behind schedule will this put us?"

"Not long. A week at most. We'll work overtime to fix the damage and get back on track." He pauses. "I won't let anything like this happen again. You have my word, Mr. Montgomery."

"I trust that it won't." I disconnect the call before I completely lose my cool and fire him. Sitting on the edge of the bed, I run my hands through my hair.

Natalie comes out of the bathroom dressed and freshened up.

"Did you find out what happened?"

"A careless employee is what happened." I blow out a frustrated breath before I stand and kiss her forehead. "It's handled now."

My phone chimes, and I check the text.

"It's Viktor. They're pulling into the garage now."

Together, we make our way to the elevator to greet her parents.

Natalie

"Sweetheart, you look adorable," Mom gushes as she hugs me. "How are you feeling?"

"I feel terrific." I reach out to hug my father. "I'm so glad you guys came."

"Alex offered a deal your mom couldn't resist." Dad winks at me.

"Let me give you a hand with those, Viktor." Alex reaches out and takes a suitcase from him. "Follow me. I'll show you to your room."

Mom links her arm with mine as we walk through the house.

"Natalie, your home is gorgeous. I had no idea." Mom chats about the flight and the constant traffic she hates so much until we walk by the nursery, where she stops dead in her tracks. "Is this my granddaughter's room?"

"It is. Would you like to go in and see it?"

Mom walks into the room ahead of me and looks around silently. I stand next to her and examine her face, trying to figure out what she's thinking, but I'm falling short.

"It's still pretty bare," I explain. "But what do you think so far?"

Mom cups her hands over her mouth, and tears spill down her face. "I think it's perfect."

I'm filled with pride as I tell her how Alex painted it and put the crib together himself. "I have the theme picked out. We need to finish getting everything and decorate the room."

"Let's have a baby shower while we're in town." Mom suggests.

"What?"

"Your friends and Alex's family will all be here, right?"

"Yes. But when are we supposed to find time to plan and actually have a baby shower? No one else is coming until next week, and they're only staying for the holiday." I can't imagine how this could possibly work. "I'll have to ask Alex and get his permission."

"His permission?" Mom looks taken aback.

Think fast, Natalie. "Alex, Sam, and Maxim will be tied up with business." My words come out hurried. "Things for Jelena's Hope."

"What's Jelena's Hope?"

The more I say, the worse I'm making things, so I'm glad when Alex and Dad join us in the nursery.

"It looks real good, son."

"Thank you." Alex smiles proudly.

"Alexander, I want to have a baby shower for Natalie while we're all in town, but she says she needs your permission?"

I shrug.

"We always make decisions together, Charlotte. I'm sure you understand."

"So, that's a yes?" Mom asks expectantly.

"Would you like to have a baby shower?"

"I'm not sure when we could pull it off, but yes. I think it would be fun."

"Perfect. That's settled," Mom says.

"Let's head to the kitchen and have a snack while we make plans," Alex suggests.

My parents sit at the table with Alex while I get the Charcuterie tray and drinks. I try to ignore the questioning glances from my mom when I make Alex's plate and set it on the table in front of him before taking my seat. While we enjoy the delicious meats and cheeses, Mom uses her party planning magic to devise the perfect plan. By the time we finish eating, the shower is planned, and Mom's buzzing with excitement. Armed with Lana and Irina's phone numbers, she's already texting them and giving instructions for their parts. With Mom distracted, I start clearing the table.

"Are you done, Sir?" I whisper.

"Yes, baby girl. Thank you." I take his plate.

"You should be waiting on her while pregnant," Mom quips. "Not the other way around."

"Don't be silly. I'm pregnant, not incapacitated." I laugh and shake my head as I take the dishes to the sink.

Alex and Dad move to the couch and turn on the TV. Mom joins me.

"Is everything okay between you and Alex?" she asks.

"Why would you ask that?"

"Things seem different. You're waiting on him hand and foot." She looks over her shoulder to where they're sitting in the living room. "And I heard you call him sir?"

"Oh, that." I wave my hand. "That's just a silly nickname, and I enjoy waiting on him." I put the last plate in the dishwasher. "I seem to recall you caring for Dad the same way."

"I guess so," she says, but her words lack conviction.

I dry my hands and start the dishwasher. "Alex and I are perfect, mom. I promise." I look into the living room and catch my husband's gaze. He gives me a panty-dropping smile, and I immediately wish we were still alone. "He's everything I've ever wanted and more. Come on, let's go watch the movie."

Alex

It's been a long week with Natalie's parents here. I thought our apartment was big. However, I stand corrected. Nothing is big enough when Charlotte's around. Thankfully, everyone else has arrived, and her attention is now entirely centered on Natalie's baby shower, an event that's happening after Thanksgiving dinner tomorrow.

Today is the Clarke Family's famous Pie Day. Everyone's up extra early for the occasion. Charlotte brought her treasured apron, and Natalie's wearing her matching one. Charlotte was kind enough to make aprons for Luna, Irina, and Amelia—how, I'm not sure, with such short notice. She also brought one for Lana, but she didn't come today. Brandon said she wasn't feeling well but would be here tomorrow. Something's up with those two, but neither's talking about it. That's an issue for another day.

Right now, the women are gushing over Charlotte's talent as a seamstress. All their cell phones are out taking selfies in their new baking attire. I'm watching from the edge of the kitchen, imagining Natalie wearing her apron with nothing under it and what I'd like to do to her on the granite counter.

"Are you ready to go?" Dad asks.

"Sorry, I got distracted." I push off the door frame.

He laughs. "Come on, let's let the ladies do their thing."

Viktor, along with my dad, Stanley, Brandon, and Maxim, wait at the elevator. We ride down together to the parking garage and hop into the car. Maxim insists on taking the back seat while we navigate through the congested streets. Since preparations for tomorrow's parade are in full swing, we're forced to take a longer route to reach our destination.

"We could've gotten here faster if we walked," Viktor mumbles when we finally pull into the underground parking.

"Everything's almost finished," I say as we ride up to our floors. "We're waiting on some of the medical equipment. Our goal is to open right after the New Year."

"What is this place, Alex?" Stanley asks.

"This is why I stepped away from my company." The elevator doors open, and we step out into the newly completed reception area. "Welcome to Jelena's Hope, NYC. It's a shelter for abused women and children." That's a basic explanation and should be enough for him to not ask too many more questions.

"I had no idea you were doing this."

"I know how passionate Natalie is about helping youth. And since Maxim's already involved in something similar in Russia, we decided to expand on his efforts here in the city."

As I look around the space, I realize it's the first time I'm seeing it completed. I take a few minutes to appreciate the transformation. At the end of the room, there's an exquisite teak reception desk, and behind it, sparkling letters spell out *Jelena's Hope*.

Instead of the typical waiting room vibe, there are sofas and chairs arranged in a relaxed sitting room fashion with live flowering plants placed amongst the furniture. Rather than television, the room's highlight is the acrylic saltwater aquarium installed in the center, with a colorful live reef as its centerpiece. The reef has small inscriptions worked into it, displaying positive affirmations like *strength*, *hope*, and *love*.

I spend a few minutes observing the diverse range of fish in the tank. Natalie worked closely with the designers to select the ideal fish species to represent our mission. Among the sea creatures present are clownfish, which are recognizable from a popular animated movie and believed to be spirit guides for overcoming challenges. The tank is also home to a Flame Angel, a Yellow Watchman Goby, a Hawkfish, a Blue Hippo Tang, and a Yellow Tang, among others. It feels as though we've brought a piece of the ocean into our reception area.

"Alexander, this design truly speaks to the heart of Jelena's Hope," Maxim says, clearing his throat in an attempt to hide his emotions. "It is about restoring hope to those who have endured the worst of what humanity has to offer."

"It was all Natalie's idea." I smile proudly.

"Mr. Montgomery," Steve says, rushing up to me. He skids to a stop when he sees I'm not alone. "Mr. Solonik, I wasn't expecting you today."

"I find unannounced visits tend to be the most productive."

"Yes, sir."

"I was informed there was an issue with an employee. A fire?" Maxim begins to interrogate Steve.

"One of my welders didn't follow the safety guidelines, resulting in a small fire in a medical room. It was put out immediately, though." Steve stumbles over his words. "I covered the costs for the repair, and the employee was fired. I assure you I take job safety seriously."

"Viktor. Please accompany Steve to ensure the quality of the operation. We would not want any more *accidents*, would we?" Maxim glares at Steve.

"Yes, sir. Let's go." Viktor starts walking down the hall while Steve scrambles to keep up.

I shake my head and chuckle. "Do you enjoy scaring people?"

"This project is of the utmost importance, and I expect nothing but the best from the people we have hired. Scaring people is just a bonus," Max says, cracking a smile. "Will you lead our tour, Alexander?"

Viktor is waiting for us in the reception area when we return from touring the facility.

"Everything looks good, boss," he reports. "I don't foresee any further issues."

"Excellent. Now we can concentrate on celebrating the American Thanksgiving and *moya vnuchka.*"

"This baby is one lucky little lady," Dad adds. "She has three sets of grandparents."

"Poor thing will never get a date," Viktor quips.

"Good," we answer in unison.

Viktor rolls his eyes and almost cracks a smile.

Natalie

Mom has a captive audience with Amelia. She went wild when she saw the apron my mom made for her. The fabric has Amelia's favorite boy band on it. I have no idea how Mom pulled that off, but it's perfect. Once she put it on, she even talked my mom into taking selfies with her.

Now, Amelia and Mom are rolling out the homemade pie crusts. Mom instructs Amelia on how to properly flour the surface so the dough doesn't stick. But when Amelia tries, she ends up with a face full of flour. She and Mom share a laugh. It's so nice to see Amelia smiling and carefree.

Irina, Luna, and I are sitting at the table watching the mayhem at the kitchen island. Irina's peeling apples, Luna's slicing them and passing them to me. I'm eating them—well, that and mixing the apple slices into the seasoning.

"Amelia seems like she's doing well," I say quietly.

"She's come a long way in a short time." Irina sets her peeler down and gazes at the young teenager. "When Amelia first came, she'd wake every night screaming from nightmares. It broke my heart because she would be inconsolable. We couldn't touch her or hold her. All we could do was make sure she was safe until she calmed down and fell back to sleep." She shifts her gaze to me. "Thankfully, the nightmares seem to have subsided. She still has much healing to do, but she's a tenacious young lady. I think she will be successful."

"I'm grateful she's getting a second chance."

"It's all thanks to you." Luna places her hand on mine.

"I can't take credit for it. It was Michael and his team that rescued her."

"Are you three done with those apples yet?" Mom asks. "We're ready to fill the pies."

"We are." I get up and bring my bowl of sliced apple pieces over to the counter.

Amelia picks up the bowl. "Do I just dump them in?"

"No," Mom shrieks, making me laugh.

"Mom is super particular about how the apple pieces go in the crust."

"The inside needs to look as pretty as the outside," Mom says.

"But I think it tastes yummy either way." I smile and pass Amelia a cinnamon and sugar-covered apple slice.

Amelia takes a bite. Her eyes open wide with delight. "I've never tasted anything like this. It's delicious. Can you show me how to put them in neatly, Mrs. Clarke?"

"Of course, dear." Then, Mom and Amelia set to work layering the apples.

"I'm going to get started on the spiced pecans," Luna says, grabbing the bag of nuts and bringing them to the stove.

"Irina, would you like to help me make the pumpkin pie?"

"I would love that." She joins me at the other end of the island.

This year's Pie Day is turning out to be one of the most enjoyable days we've had yet.

I don't even realize how much time has passed until I hear masculine voices approaching the kitchen.

"It smells delicious in here, ladies." Alex comes from behind and plants a kiss on my cheek. "How are you and baby Rose doing?"

"We're good. How did the inspection go?"

"Everything looks good. Should be smooth sailing from here."

I look over Alex's shoulder and see my dad and Mr. Montgomery carrying several brown paper bags.

"Oh my God, is that Chinese take-out?"

"You didn't think we'd have Pie Day without it, did you?" Dad chuckles.

Luna and Irina begin clearing the table, and Amelia joins them to help. I excuse myself to take a trip to the bathroom. When I come out, mom's waiting in the hallway.

"I'm so glad you and Daddy came out here." I hug her. "And you're doing a great job with Amelia. She seems to be enjoying herself."

"She's a sweetheart," Mom says, looking over her shoulder. "I don't understand something, though." Oh no. I know exactly where this conversation is going. "How did a young girl from Australia end up in Russia?"

"I'm not entirely sure." I shrug.

"She seems to be very attached to you." Mom cocks her head to the side. "How did you meet her?"

"She was at Max and Irina's home when Alex and I visited a few months ago. We really hit it off."

"And they're adopting her?"

"They are."

"It's all very strange." Mom crosses her arms. "There seems to be something I'm not being told."

Mom's perceptive and quite a bit nosey. I know she won't drop this, so I have to tell her what I can. The last thing I want is for her to start asking Amelia questions she's not ready to answer.

"Come in here." I lead her into my bedroom and close the door. "Have a seat."

She perches on the edge of my bed. I sit beside her while I tell her about Jelena and how she was kidnapped. I leave out the details of the trafficking ring.

"I had no idea." Mom puts her hand over her heart. "I can't imagine the heartache that's caused for Max and Irina."

"It was a challenging time for them. But they took their tragedy and decided to help others. I'm pretty sure that's how they found Amelia, but I don't know the details. Those are things they like to keep private. I'm sure you understand."

I continue to explain a bit about Jelena's Hope, saying that it was born to help women and children who needed a safe place to start their lives over.

"Does this have something to do with the secret project Alex is working on?"

I nod. "It does. We've been so moved by what Maxim is doing that we decided to open Jelena's Hope- NYC. That's where they went today. Max wanted to see how it was coming along, and Alex couldn't wait to show it off."

"So, it's a place for abused women and children?"

"Pretty much, yes." She's more correct than she knows.

"You aren't planning on working there, are you?"

"I am."

"How will you do that when you have a new baby?"

I've been asking myself those same questions, but I really don't want to get into that discussion right now. "It won't be full-time, only what I'm comfortable with. We should get back. They're going to think we got lost."

Mom stands and looks at me, concern marring her face. "You know I disapprove of you working outside the home while you have an infant. As wonderful as this place sounds, I also sense that it could be dangerous—"

"There's security at the building." My stomach grumbles loudly. "I'm starving. Can we talk about this later?"

Mom nods, and together, we walk back to the kitchen.

"I was just about to send a search party out for you two," Dad jokes.

I grab a plate and fill it with Alex's favorite foods. Mom looks on as Luna and Irina do the same for their men. I can see the questions forming in her head, but luckily, she doesn't voice them.

While we eat, the timer on the oven goes off. Mom removes perfect-looking pies from the oven and sets them on cooling racks.

"Those smell delicious," Maxim says. "Do we get to taste them tonight?"

"Absolutely not." Mom places her hands on her hips. "They're for dessert after dinner tomorrow." Maxim's deep laugh fills the room. He gets a kick out of getting under Mom's skin. "Are we ready to watch the movie now?" Mom asks, her brow furrowed.

"We're going to deviate from tradition just a bit," I say cautiously.

"Oh?" Mom asks, surprised.

"They're inflating the balloons for the parade in Central Park. We want to take Amelia and anyone else who wants to come to see it," Alex says.

"Can we go, Sir?" Luna asks Sam.

"Of course. Go get your jacket. It's going to be chilly." Luna hurries off to their room.

"Same goes for you, Amelia," Max instructs.

"Okay." She skips off to grab her jacket.

"Will you two come?" I ask my parents.

"As much as I'd love to," Dad says. "I'm feeling pretty worn out from our outing earlier. So I think we'll stay back."

"Okay." I sigh. "I'll video call when we get there so you can see it. Then, when we get back, we'll watch the movie."

"Sounds great, sweetheart."

"Don't overdo it," Mom adds.

"I won't," I call over my shoulder.

The group of us head out.

Despite his protests, Max and Sam talk Alex into taking the subway, something I'm grateful for. If he'd insisted on driving, we'd never get there before they closed off the park to visitors.

Alex

Central Park is buzzing with activity. Amelia grabs Natalie's hand, her eyes huge with delight as she takes videos and pictures of the iconic balloons being inflated.

"She's so patient." Dad comes up next to me. "She's going to be an amazing mother."

"That she is." I try to smile, but I've been distracted since we arrived. "Viktor?"

"Yes, boss."

"Keep a close eye on Natalie, please."

"What's wrong?"

"I don't know. Something feels off."

"I don't see anything out of the ordinary." Viktor looks around. "But I'll stick with her and the kid."

Logically, I know it's most likely a trauma response, but I can't shake the feeling that we're being watched—followed. Although I remain aware of the crowds around us, I keep my thoughts to myself. I don't want to say or do anything to ruin the fun.

I startle when Maxim puts his hand on my shoulder. "Are you okay?" he asks, concerned.

"I'm good. Just a lot of people."

"Thank you for giving us this wonderful experience. Amelia is having such a wonderful time," Maxims says while watching his daughter laughing at something Natalie said. "I love to see her smiling." "She's really enjoying herself." I smile, watching her.

"You are giving her experiences she'll never forget. One's I am certain she will ask to come back for again." Maxim laughs.

I look at my pregnant wife, her hand on her round tummy as she points out the Olaf balloon. Amelia may be a teenager, but she missed out on so much of her childhood. Natalie's taking her role of surrogate big sister seriously. She's been introducing her to all the Disney movies. Right now, *Frozen* is her current favorite.

"And next year, you and Natalie will have your child with us," Maxim adds.

I didn't think about that. Next year, Natalie and Amelia will be showing these balloons to our little girl. Another shiver runs down my spine, and the hairs on my neck stand on end. I'm done ignoring this. "Hey everyone, how about we head back? I'm sure Stanley and Charlotte are anxious to continue with their family traditions."

"That's a good idea," Natalie adds. "Anyway, my feet are killing me."

"Let's get you home then, baby girl." I take her hand as we all make our way to the subway station to return to the safety of our apartment.

Xavier

It takes all my free time before and after work, but I'm able to keep tabs on the movements of the Montgomerys. Most people are creatures of habit and don't pay attention to their surroundings. I'm not complaining because it works in my favor.

Right now, they're among the crowds wandering Central Park, watching these ridiculous balloons being blown up. The amount of people milling about makes for the perfect cover. I can follow them from a short distance without worrying about being spotted.

Montgomery must be feeling paranoid these days. Natalie never leaves the apartment alone. Even now, he has his lapdog sticking to her side like glue. He should be the one by Natalie, but instead, he's hanging back, talking to another man.

I'm not certain, but from what I've heard from the guys at work, he's a Russian named Maxim Solonik. I've done web searches on him and found out he's some hotshot in Russian oil. Why he hangs out with Montgomery is beyond me. I'm not sure who the other man is, but by how much they look alike, my guess is he might be Montgomery's father.

Everyone in their little group seems to be enjoying themselves right now. Everyone but Montgomery. He looks tense.

Can you feel me watching you?

Don't worry. Your time's almost up.

We'll see each other soon.

Natalie

The tantalizing scents of turkey and stuffing drift into my bedroom from the kitchen, waking me. I'm sure Mom and Dad were up at the crack of dawn and are already hard at work preparing the meal. I stretch and turn to discover that Alex's spot in the bed is vacant. He must be helping cook, too.

Recognizing that this may be my only moment of tranquility for the day, I take advantage of it. I remain in bed, enjoying being alone with the baby, who's currently performing acrobatics. It's a peaceful start to what promises to be a busy day.

"You'll be out here with us next year, Rose." I rub my belly. "Thanksgiving's your mama's favorite holiday. Last year almost ruined that, but we aren't going to talk about that. This year's a new beginning. We're going to make new memories—happy memories.

Hopefully, all our family will come here to celebrate with us every year. I want you to be surrounded by people who love you. Today's also our baby shower." I feel a strong kick in the center of my stomach as I sit up. "I guess you like that idea."

Before going out to the kitchen, I change out of my pajamas and into a casual dress that'll be comfortable to wear with my expanding waistline. Then, barefoot, I pad down the hall in search of something to eat. The sounds of happy chatter and laughter fill the room. I try to remain unnoticed and peek around the doorway, taking in the sight.

Everyone's here today, and they're all in my kitchen. Mom has clearly taken charge. She's paired off the couples and delegated many of the responsibilities. Everyone's hard at work and looks to be enjoying themselves, except for Brandon and Lana. I can feel the tension between them from here. Mom tasked them with making her sweet potato casserole. Although they're working side-by-side, they're certainly not working together. Their movements are stiff, and their conversation is non-existent. I need to get Lana alone for a few minutes to find out what's going on.

"Are you going to join us or just keep watching?" Mom asks.

My cover's been blown. "I was just watching everyone together." I walk over to Mom and put my arm around her. "You have no idea how happy this makes me."

"I think I do, sweetheart." She points to the food tray on the counter. "Alex was kind enough to buy breakfast for everyone. Grab yourself a bagel, and then get over there and help your husband set the table."

In the dining room, I spot Alex and Amelia, both of whom are engrossed in something on their cell phones. Amelia has a pile of cloth napkins and is trying to fold them into what looks to be turkeys. I'm impressed. She's doing a great job.

Alex has the table set with our Mikasa Love Story China dishes. He's standing in front of a pile of silverware, going back and forth between the different-sized utensils and whatever he's looking at on his phone. Mom's very particular when it comes to formal dinners, and Alex takes his task seriously, making sure each utensil is put in the right place.

I quickly toast a bagel and add cream cheese before taking my dish and joining them. "You two are doing a great job," I say and take a bite.

Alex looks up at me, confusion marring his gorgeous face. "Your mom issued her warning that the table must be set correctly. Thank God for YouTube because I don't have a clue as to what goes where. And then there's this horn thing," he says, holding up Mom's cornucopia and pointing to the fresh foods on the table. "She told us we had to arrange this too."

"What is that, Natalie?" Amelia asks genuine curiosity in her voice. I tell Amelia the story of the cornucopia while I finish my bagel. Her eyes widen as she listens to me tell her how that used to be Michael and my favorite thing to do.

"You have a brother?" she asks.

I swallow over the lump in my throat. "Yes."

"Is he coming today?"

"He died when I was a teenager." And I'd give anything to have him back.

"I'm sorry," she says, looking down at her hands.

"It's okay." I reach out and touch her arm.

This year, more than any other, I wish Michael was here. He and Evan would've been over the moon about becoming uncles. And having everyone together, without arguing, was all either of us ever wanted.

"He's still with me here." I put my hand by my heart. "Let's get this table set before Mom comes over and scolds us." I quickly change the subject before I get too emotional.

With the three of us working together, we get the table set perfectly in no time. Then, Mom comes over and inspects it. "Did you make these yourself, Amelia?" she asks, pointing to the little turkeys in the center of everyone's plate.

"Yes, ma'am."

"I've never seen anything like it." She picks one up to inspect it. We all hold a collective breath. "But I love them."

Amelia beams with pride.

A few hours later, we're all gathered around the table that's loaded with the food everyone's worked so hard to prepare. I snap a few pictures on my cell phone to document the occasion.

"Before we eat, we always go around the table and say something we're thankful for," Dad says. "I'll start. I'm thankful to be here, in this crazy city, celebrating with my daughter and son-in-law."

"This is the first time I'm celebrating an American Thanksgiving," Amelia says. "I'm thankful for being safe, for having food to eat." She looks at Max and Irina. "And for having a new family."

"Our family has much to be thankful for," Maxim adds. "Amelia's adoption was finalized last week. She is now legally Amelia Solonik, our daughter," he says, a proud smile lighting up his face.

I think about the first time I saw Amelia. I didn't know how long she'd been there, but it was long enough that fear of disobeying was instilled in her. The emptiness I saw in her eyes—she'd already given up.

What Alex and I went through was horrible, and I wouldn't wish it on anyone, but so much good has come from it. I hate knowing Amelia was raped before Michael's team found her. But they did find her and got her to safety. That's the most important part. And her being adopted by the Soloniks is truly the cherry on top of it all.

Alex goes last. He grabs my hand before speaking. "This amazing woman sitting beside me has made me the happiest man in the world. She's given me so much more than I ever thought I'd have. Thankful doesn't come close to expressing my feelings today." He leans over, kisses my lips sweetly, and whispers, "Thank you, baby girl."

I look into his blue eyes, forgetting anyone else is in the room—it's only us. "i love You, Sir."

"Let's hold hands and say grace," Dad interrupts our moment.

After the blessing, everyone fills their plates and enjoys the feast before us. The Thanksgiving meal is delicious, but what makes today truly special is being surrounded by my family.

This past year has been marked by so much heartache and near tragedies. It's as if today's celebration has brought us full circle. All of the bad is behind us now. Our family only has wonderful things to look forward to.

Natalie

After dinner, Mom shoos me from the apartment. "You and Viktor should go downstairs for a bit. I'll call you when we're ready." Her eyes dance with excitement.

I look to Alex for approval. He nods.

"Come on, Vik." I start walking to the elevator. "We're being kicked out."

Viktor follows me, laughing. "Your mom is—" He pauses. "A lot."

"Tell me about it."

"Natalie, wake up." Viktor shakes my shoulder gently. "It's time to go upstairs."

I stretch and yawn. "Sorry about that. I didn't realize I had fallen asleep."

He laughs. "We were only five minutes into the movie, and you were snoring."

"Snoring?"

"I had to turn up the volume because you were so noisy." He winks at me.

"You're terrible." I elbow him as I walk by. "Let's go. We have a baby shower to get to."

"This'll be a whole new experience."

To say I'm shocked at what I see when we get back upstairs is an understatement. Not only are several of our friends from Fire and Ice here, but in a matter of a few hours, Mom successfully transformed the entire dining room from a Thanksgiving celebration to a baby shower. The room is adorned with pink crepe paper that stretches from end to end. Shiny spiral streamers displaying baby bottles, booties, and pacifiers hang from the ceiling. A pink tablecloth covers the table, and several stuffed elephants sit atop a bed of baby-themed confetti. In the corner is a stack of exquisitely wrapped presents.

"How did you do all this?"

"Your mother's a very efficient party planner," Irina says.

"I've missed seeing you," Mistress Star says and squeezes me in a hug. "I was so happy when Lana called and invited me to your shower."

"Look at you, girl," Leo exclaims as his hands go straight to my tummy. "How's my little niece?"

"She's very active today."

"I feel that." He laughs.

"You look terrific, Natalie." Tony embraces me. "Pregnancy suits you."

His compliment makes me blush.

Alex comes over and takes my hand. "Let's have dessert, shall we?" He pulls out a chair for me to sit on.

Our guests take their seats while Mom and the other ladies bring over the pies and a two-tiered cake. It's covered in pale grey and pink fondant to match the colors of our nursery. On top is an elephant holding several pink balloons.

"Look at that cake," I exclaim. "It's adorable. How did you manage to get this on a holiday?"

"I told you Maxim is bossy," Mom chuckles. "He's responsible for that."

I look at Max, "Thank you so much, *dedushka*."

"Nothing will stop me from giving you and *moya vnuchka* everything."

Plenty of pictures are taken before we cut into the desserts. The cake is decadent chocolate with a chocolate ganache between the layers. When dessert is served, our guests rave over the pies.

"Mrs. Clarke," Anthony says. "You must give me your recipe for this pecan pie. My customers will love it."

"You want to use my recipe for your restaurant?" Mom sounds shocked.

"Of course, I'll compensate you for it," he adds.

"There's no need for that, Anthony," Mom says, waving him off. "I'd be honored for you to have it."

We take our time enjoying the plethora of desserts on the table. By the time we finish, there's only half a slice of pumpkin pie and one tier of cake left. I'm so stuffed I don't think I can move.

"Let's get to the presents," Lana chimes in.

"That sounds like a great idea. I can't wait to open them."

Alex moves an armchair from the living room, placing it next to the stack of presents. "Come sit over here."

"Gladly." My back's aching from sitting on the unforgiving dining chairs for so long. Alex pulls another chair from the living room so he can open gifts with me.

"Amelia," Mom calls. "Come help me with the ribbons."

Lana begins passing us presents, one at a time. Carefully, I take the ribbons off and hand them to Amelia. She and Mom are making the traditional ribbon *hat* for me to wear after opening the gifts. I have no idea how the tradition started, and although I'll look ridiculous, we'll have a laugh looking back at the pictures.

The first gift I open is from my parents. "Oh, mom. It's stunning." I hold up a handmaid patchwork baby quilt. In the center are two elephants.

"The ladies from church worked on it with me. I was hoping you'd like it."

"I don't just like it. I love it."

"It's exquisite, Charlotte," Alex says as he runs his hands over the impeccable stitching. "This was truly a labor of love, and we'll cherish it."

Mom wipes at the corner of her eyes.

Lana and Brandon's gifts are next. The first is a designer baby pram.

"I read it's all the rage with high society in the city," Lana says, waving her hand.

I don't care about keeping up with trends, but the pram is stunning. The second present is a fancy bassinet that rocks.

"The lady at the store said this thing is magic," Brandon adds, uncertain.

"It's a smart bassinet," Alex says as he reads the box. "It'll sense if the baby is fussing and gently rock her."

"I figured if it works, I'll get the award for best uncle."

We all share a laugh.

"These gifts are from us," Maxim says. "As you know, we do not have these baby showers. Most Russians believe it is bad luck. However, I am not like most Russians and do not subscribe to such superstitions. We are here and wish to participate in your traditions."

He hands me a beautifully wrapped gift. The paper is so pretty, I don't want to tear it. But Maxim encourages me to open it. I lift the lid off the box, and Alex takes out a set of wooden nesting elephants.

"We had these made special for *moya vnuchka,*" Maxim says proudly.

Alex opens them one at a time and places them on the dining table for everyone to see. Each is painted with unique designs. The detail on them is unlike anything I've ever seen.

"Max, I don't know what to say."

"There's more," Irina says, pointing to the gift in Lana's hand.

When I open it, I find a set of baby books in Russian.

"These are so Rose can learn our language from the beginning."

"Alex is going to have to read these to her. But maybe I'll finally be able to learn Russian as well." I giggle.

I've known Lana for years and have traveled to Russia several times, but other than a few simple words, I've not been able to master even basic communication.

We've been opening presents for what feels like hours. We're finally at the last of the gifts, and they're from Sam and Luna. Opening the box, we pull out a hand-painted trio of elephant pictures that read—*First, we had each other. Then we had you. Now we have everything.*

"This is perfect. We'll hang these over her crib." I look around at everyone. "Thank you all so very much. This is more than we could've asked for."

"You've made today extra special for my family." Alex places his hand on my belly. "Thank you all so much."

"We're not done yet," Mom says.

She and Amelia are heading in my direction with their ribbon hat. Alex looks at me with his eyebrows raised. Mom places the ribbon-covered paper plate on my head and ties it under my chin. Amelia giggles and grins as she snaps pictures with her cell phone. We don't have to wait for a day in the future. We're all getting a good laugh out of my new accessory right now.

After everyone's taken their fill of pictures, Alex and the other men move the gifts into the nursery. Unpacking and organizing them is a job for another day. Mom and the other ladies go to the kitchen to start the clean-up. But Lana quietly wanders off.

It's time I find out what's going on, so I follow her. She enters the guest room her parents are staying in and closes the door. I knock, but there's no answer. I open the door and ask, "Do you mind some company?"

"It's fine. Just close the door, please."

I sit on the bed next to Lana. "Are you going to tell me what's going on?"

She looks away and remains quiet for the longest time, and I'm starting to think she's not going to answer me.

"Things aren't okay between Brandon and me," she finally says.

"I know."

"Is it that obvious?"

"To me, yes. What's going on?" I ask.

She turns and sits cross-legged on the bed facing me. "He wants more."

"What's wrong with that?"

"I don't."

Sometimes Svetlana confuses me. She and Brandon have been together for a little over two years. When they moved in together, Lana was ecstatic. She always said she wanted the whole package—a husband, a few kids, and a dog.

"What do you mean you don't? I thought you loved him?" I ask, confused.

"He's a great Dominant, and I care about him."

"I sense a but coming." Nothing is making sense right now.

"He's ready to settle down. He wants what you and Alex have—the husband/wife thing," she sighs. "He wants to be a father."

"And what do you want?"

"I love the club and public scenes. I want to try adding other people," she says. "I'm not ready for marriage, and I don't want kids."

"Have you talked to him? Told him how you're feeling?"

"I told him what I want and what I don't want. He pulled out the contract and said we could renegotiate some things, but we haven't reached any agreements."

"What does that mean?" I ask, concerned.

"We're not on the same page anymore. So, we put our dynamic on hold," she replies, but her voice holds no emotion.

"Don't do anything you'll regret. Give it some more time," I encourage her. "Keep trying to work it out."

The door opens. "There you two are. Alex is looking for you, Nat," Brandon says.

"Please give what I said some thought," I say as I stand up.

Lana nods but says nothing.

As I walk by, I put my hand on Brandon's arm, and he gives it a reassuring squeeze. I hate this. My friends are hurting, and I don't know how to help them.

With a final look over my shoulder, I leave the room to find Alex.

Alex

THE MAJORITY OF OUR GUESTS LEFT, BUT WE WERE ABLE TO CONVINCE Natalie's parents to stay for an extra week. Charlotte's enjoying helping Natalie put Rose's nursery together. I think it's been a good activity for them to bond over. Stanley and Charlotte even accompanied us to a check-up the other day. The doctor did an ultrasound, which thrilled the grandparents-to-be. They were amazed at the images of their unborn grandchild and are going home with their own set of pictures. I can't believe how quickly Natalie's pregnancy has seemed to go. Rose will be here in just eight weeks.

Viktor and I have just finished our workout for the day, and I'm heading for a shower when my phone rings.

"I hope I got you at a good time," Steve says.

"What's up?"

"Good news. Construction's complete, and all the equipment's in place," he says. "I'm going to need you to come down and do a final walkthrough so you can sign off on everything."

I thought we still had a few weeks to go, but I won't complain about being ahead of schedule.

"Give me about two hours, and I'll be over."

I shower and am waiting for Natalie and Charlotte to return from their walk before I leave. I don't like letting her go out without Viktor, but she has her phone with the tracking app Dimitri's team installed, and she promised she wouldn't go far. She's fallen in love with a park down the street. There's a quiet little spot where she likes to sit and watch the water. I think it reminds her of her favorite place at Finn Lake.

Stanley stayed back to watch TV, but instead, he's fast asleep on the couch. Quietly, so I don't wake him, I make my way into the kitchen to get a bottle of water and a sandwich. While I'm eating, Natalie and Charlotte arrive back home.

"Did you enjoy your walk, ladies?"

"We did," Natalie says, her cheeks pink from the brisk November air.

"I'd much rather you use the treadmill in our gym."

"But then I wouldn't get to feel the sunshine and breathe the fresh air." She bats her beautiful green eyes at me.

"Fresh air? In the city?" I shake my head.

"You're being an overprotective father already." Mom waves him off. "Natalie needs to be outside. It's healthy for her and the baby."

Overprotective. If she only knew the things we've been through the past six months. How I almost lost Natalie and the baby, she'd understand why I don't want to let her out of my sight. But those are things I can never tell her. Instead, I'll have to accept that she thinks I'm a nervous father-to-be.

"You have a good point, Charlotte," I concede. "It's a big city, though, and you can't blame a guy for wanting to keep his family safe."

"I guess you're right. Maybe you should think about relocating to Northmeadow permanently," she says nonchalantly. "I'm going to wake Stanley and see if he's hungry." She doesn't miss a beat as she walks away.

"Gee, that was subtle." Natalie looks over her shoulder. "Sorry about that. The good news is they'll only be here for a few more days."

"It's fine." I stand and kiss her forehead. "I'm thankful they agreed to stay."

"Me too. It's been nice having Mom here to help get the nursery ready." She looks up at me wide-eyed. "Not that you aren't helping—"

"I understand. Charlotte's your mom. She can help you prepare in ways I can't." I brush a stray curl behind her ear. "On another note, I have some good news for you."

"Oh? What is it?"

"Steve called. The construction on Jelena's Hope-NYC is done. I'm going to run over and do the final walkthrough."

"Can I come?"

"You just got back from a walk, and you still need to eat."

"Yes, Sir." She looks disappointed.

"I'll bring you down tomorrow." I put my empty water bottle in the recycling bin. "I'm leaving Viktor here."

I pull her into my arms and kiss her. "I have stuff laid out in our room for a scene tonight." She walks me to the elevator.

"Are you sure you have to go? Can't you wait and go tomorrow?"

"I won't be long, I promise." The doors open, and I step inside. "Have something to eat and get some rest while I'm gone."

"Yes, Sir." The doors start to close, but she sticks her hand in, stopping them. "i love You."

"I love you too, baby girl."

Xavier

"Yeah, boss. Be there in a minute."

I finally have everything in place and am ready to strike. Montgomery was here a few days ago, and I almost pulled the trigger. The only thing that saved him was that he wasn't alone.

The plan involves him and him alone.

My patience has finally paid off.

The project is done, and I overheard Steve tell his crew that Montgomery is set to arrive any minute.

I shoot a quick text to a friend who, after a bit of bargaining, has agreed to help me.

X: It's time. Bring the car with the package.

Jinx: Got it. I'll be there in ten.

Act normal, Xavier. You don't need any unwanted attention.

I put my tools away and stride across the room where Steve is talking to one of the other guys. When he finishes, he turns my way. "You've proved yourself as a loyal and talented worker, X-man. Have you decided if you'll stay on with us?"

"It's great working with you. I'd like to take you up on your offer."

"I'm glad to hear that." He slaps my shoulder. "I don't have time to go over the specifics right now. Mr. Montgomery's on his way so that we can finish up here. How about we meet at my office on Monday to iron out the details?"

"Sure thing." I look at my watch, knowing if Montgomery's coming, I need to get out of here. "Break time. I'll see you Monday."

I make quick work of gathering my supplies and take the staff elevator to the basement. Once I'm sure I'm alone, I check my texts.

Jinx: I'm in place. Waiting on your cue.

X: Stay out of sight. He'll be here any minute.

I grab the product I promised Leon, slipping it into my pocket. Then I watch and wait.

Alex

While in the elevator, I have a silent debate over taking the subway instead of driving. If I take the subway, I can get there and back faster, but I'm still not over my issues with crowded, confined spaces—especially ones I have no control over. Control wins over speed, so I take the car.

I'm met with the usual city traffic, but I've lived here so long, it's something I'm used to. After hitting every red light possible, I finally pull into my designated spot in the underground parking garage. While I walk to the elevator, I make a mental checklist of things that still need to be done.

The majority of the staff has been hired and are in training. Maxim sent several of his most experienced employees to train my new staff, including a few recovered people who now work at Jelena's Hope. Having the shared experiences of the people who will eventually walk through our doors affords them a unique ability to connect with these individuals when they're at their lowest. And our new employees will only benefit from their experiences. I'm thankful they've been able to travel to New York City to help out.

As the elevator makes its way up to our floor, I find myself struggling with conflicting emotions. I'm thrilled that the construction is finally complete, and Jelena's Hope-NYC is almost ready to open its doors. But on the other hand, being excited feels out of place. After all, the existence of Jelena's Hope-NYC is a direct result of the unfathomable evil that exists in the world.

Centers like this and others around the world exist only because, every day, innocent individuals are ripped away from their lives and treated as nothing more than commodities to be exploited and abused.

I step into our facility and am reminded that there are ongoing efforts to rescue these victims, some of whom will soon be entering our doors to embark on their journey toward recovery and healing.

When Steve sees me, he jumps up. "Mr. Montgomery, glad you could make it on such short notice."

We shake hands. "I'm anxious to see the place."

"Then, let's not waste any time."

Steve hands me a binder that holds the specs for each room before we begin our walk-through. I review the checklists as we go and sign off on each section. When we finish the office area, we go up to the residences. The finished apartments look incredible. After the last signature, I pass the binder back to him. "I'm impressed with the quality of the workmanship."

"Thank you, Mr. Montgomery."

"I have some other properties that require remodeling, and I need them done quickly. Would you be interested?"

"I'd be happy to take a look at what you need done. I'm sure I can accommodate your schedule."

"I'd like to get the work started before the holidays. I'll email you the information."

"Sounds good. I'll be in touch."

I put my finger on the scanner to summon the elevator. While I wait, I text Natalie to let her know I'm on my way home.

The elevator stops a few floors down, and a well-dressed man wearing a business suit steps in. The doors shut, and a wave of anxiety washes over me. I attempt to regulate my breathing, reassuring myself that the individual sharing the confined space with me poses no harm. He's merely a fellow office worker from a lower floor. Maybe I do need to start seeing a therapist?

The elevator chimes, signaling our arrival at the parking garage. I reach into my pocket to retrieve my key fob.

Natalie

ALEX TEXTED ME THAT HE WAS ON HIS WAY HOME HOURS AGO. EVEN with the insane holiday traffic, he should've been here already. I try to reach him on his cellphone, but it goes straight to voicemail. A sense of panic begins to bubble within me, but I recognize that it's likely residual anxiety from our ordeal in Mexico.

The most likely explanation is he's stuck in traffic, and his phone battery has died - he has a tendency to forget his charger.

"Hey, guys." I pop my head into the living room, where my parents watch TV. "I'm going down to Viktor's to see if he wants to join us for dinner."

"Okay, sweetheart. We'll be here watching the end of this movie." Mom smiles.

My parents have turned into total couch potatoes while they've been here, watching as much TV as possible. They refuse to pay for cable at home, insisting they prefer to keep busy. They work very hard between keeping up with things at home and their store. So it's nice to see them relaxing.

I'm just about to press the elevator call button when the doors open. Viktor's standing there, his face devoid of all color. Two NYPD officers are with him. "Viktor? What's going on?"

"Let's go sit down." He takes my arm, but I shrug from his grasp.

"No. Tell me what's going on. Why are there police in my house?"

"Mrs. Montgomery?" The female officer speaks.

"Stop." Viktor puts up his hand. "I'll tell her."

My heart pounds. The last time I got a call from the police—

"What's going on?" Dad asks from behind me.

"Natalie," Viktor says softly. "There was an accident. An explosion."

"Where's Alex?"

"He was in the explosion." Viktor's voice is laced with pain. "He's gone."

"No," I scream and hit his chest. "You're lying."

"I wish I was." He grabs my hands. "His car exploded. He didn't make it, Natalie."

Everything goes fuzzy, and I feel myself falling.

When my eyes open, I'm lying in my bed. Mom is sitting beside me, wiping my forehead with a cool rag. Viktor's words slam back into my consciousness, and I shoot upright. "Tell me it's not true, Mama," I cry. "Please, tell me it's not true."

She wraps her arms around me, holding me tight. "I'm so sorry, honey." Her voice catches on a sob. "I'm so sorry."

"No." I push her away and get out of bed. "Viktor's lying. Alex is not dead. I would know it here." I put my hand over my heart. "I would feel it if he was gone." Storming out of the room, I set off, intending to find Viktor.

"Natalie," Mom calls after me, but I don't turn around.

I hear Viktor's voice coming from inside Alex's office. Pushing the door open, I storm into the room and stop in front of the desk, crossing my arms over my chest.

Viktor meets my penetrating glare. "I'll call you back." He disconnects the call and stands up.

"Don't come any closer," I warn.

"Natalie, please." He takes a step toward me.

"Why are you lying to me?" I shove his chest. "This isn't funny. Where's my husband?"

"You know I'd never lie to you." Viktor moves closer. "Alex is gone."

"No." I punch him over and over. He makes no move to block my strikes. "You're lying. He's not gone." Hot tears sear my face. My body shakes with sobs. Viktor wraps his strong arms around me, and I fall into his chest. "We're having a baby." I struggle to take a breath. "He can't be gone."

Slowly, Viktor slides us to the floor, never breaking his hold as he shifts me onto his lap. He rocks me back and forth while I continue to cry.

"I'm so sorry," he whispers. "Let it all out. I've got you."

I can't form thoughts. There are no words.

My world has just come crashing down around me.

"I don't know what the fuck happened," I growl into the phone. "Cars don't just explode. Is it possible one of Moreno's men made it out?"

"I will have Dimitri access the security system," Maxim says, trying to keep his tone even. "Natalia, how is she?"

"Not well. She fainted when I told her. Her mom's with her right now." I drop my head in my free hand. "Max, what do I do?"

"I do not have a full plan yet," Maxim replies. "But I will not rest until we find out who is behind this. They will pay."

The door to the office flies open and slams into the wall. Natalie marches into the room and stands in front of the desk. She stares at me, pure hatred in her eyes.

"I'll call you back." I hang up, needing to go to her.

"Don't come any closer," she warns.

"Natalie, please." I take a tentative step closer.

"Why are you lying to me?" She shoves my chest. "Where's my husband?"

"You know I'd never lie to you." I move a step closer, hoping to give her some comfort amid this nightmare. "Alex is gone."

"No," she yells and bunches her tiny hands into fists, punching me over and over. I don't move or try to stop her. Instead, I let her take all her anger out on my body. "You're lying. He's not gone." Her strikes slow and are replaced with a torrent of tears as she breaks down.

I wrap her in my arms, and she falls against my chest.

"We're having a baby." She struggles to take a breath. "He can't be gone."

Slowly, I lower our bodies to the floor, keeping her close. With my back against the large wood desk, I hold her on my lap and rock her gently. "I'm so sorry," I say softly. "Let it all out. I've got you."

She cries against my chest while I whisper softly to her, trying my best to console her but failing miserably. The woman in my arms is precious and doesn't deserve this.

I struggle to hold back my tears, but they betray me and escape against my will. On the inside, I'm feeling red-hot rage. The bastards who took Alex from her will wish they were never born. I plan to hunt them down. I won't stop until each and every one of them is dead. But right now, my most important job is to make sure Natalie and the baby are okay.

Looking up, I see Charlotte standing in the doorway, her face tear-stained. "I'll take her." She walks toward where we sit on the floor.

"No." I don't release my grasp on her.

"I'm her mother," Charlotte argues. "I'll be the one who takes care of her."

"Please close the door on your way out." My tone is clipped.

With a huff, Charlotte spins on her heel and leaves us. She didn't deserve my temper. I realize that, but I won't let her take Natalie from me. I hold her tight until her tears subside, and her body relaxes—she's cried herself to sleep. I rest my head back and close my eyes. The task ahead will be difficult. I'm not sure where to start, but I'm confident in my skills. I'll find whoever's responsible and make them pay.

What scares me most right now is the promise I made to Alex. Why did I say yes to that? Because I didn't think any of this was a possibility. But here we are. Sure, I know how to protect her, and yes, I have feelings for her—feelings I never intended to act on. I don't know how to love. And I know even less about how to care for a child. I sit with my thoughts in silence, allowing Natalie to sleep for as long as possible. Right now, it's her only escape from the nightmare she's been forced to live. Unfortunately, I know reality will return all too soon.

The door opens slowly, and Stanley peers around the edge. The rage I felt earlier when her mom tried to take her from me has subsided, although I retighten my protective grip on her.

"Is she asleep?" he asks quietly.

I nod.

He disappears, and I'm relieved he's left us alone. A few minutes later, the door opens wider. Stanley walks into the office, a blanket in his hand. He bends down and spreads the blanket over Natalie's sleeping body. "I don't want her to catch a chill." Stanley meets my eyes, and I see his heartache. "Her mom's making soup for when she wakes."

"I called her doctor earlier. He's agreed to come by and look over her and the baby." I keep my voice quiet.

"This isn't going to be easy for her."

"She won't be alone. I'll be by her side."

Stanley nods and turns to walk away. "Bring her out when she wakes."

"Yes, sir. I will."

Natalie

"Natalie." I hear Viktor's voice, but it's not right. I'm with Alex, and he's holding our baby girl. We're happy. "I need you to wake up."

I try to resist and stay with Alex, but it's useless. My eyes blink open, and I lift my head. I'm in Viktor's arms on the floor of Alex's office. "Dr. Young's here."

"Why?"

"I called him after you passed out. I want to make sure you and the baby are okay."

"Come on, Natalie." Mom's walking across the room toward us. She reaches out to help me, but Viktor keeps his arms around me. They exchange a heated glare before he reluctantly shifts his position to help me up.

"The doctor's in your room." Mom leads me by the hand. "I'll take you to him."

I look over my shoulder. "Are you coming?"

Viktor begins to take a step.

"He can wait with your father in the kitchen," Mom quips.

We walk down the hall to my bedroom, where Dr. Young is waiting, a sullen look on his face.

"I'd like to see the doctor alone."

"Wouldn't you rather I stay with you?"

I understand and appreciate her concern, but I need to do this without her hovering.

"I'll meet you in the kitchen when we're done." I step into my room and close the door behind me.

"Natalie." Dr. Young embraces me. "I'm so sorry for your loss."

"It doesn't feel real."

"That's understandable. It was quite a shock." His voice is soothing.

My whole body begins shaking.

Dr. Young touches my arm, "How about you lie down." He leads me to the bed and helps me recline against the pillows as tears trickle from the corners of my eyes. "I'd like to examine you and the baby if that's alright."

I nod.

The doctor takes my vitals. "Your blood pressure is a bit higher than I'm comfortable with, but that's to be expected right now. So, we'll keep a close eye on it." Next, he uses the Doppler to listen to the baby's heart.

Swoosh. Swoosh. Swoosh.

"The baby's heart rate is perfect." He smiles. "How about we take a peek at her. I brought the portable ultrasound."

My body's numb. Although I hear his words, it's as though they're floating around me, and I'm unable to form a response.

"Let's see your little girl," he says. "I'm going to pull your shirt up now."

The screen comes to life with the image of my unborn daughter moving about inside my body. She's unaware of the events that have taken place today—not knowing that she'll never get to meet her Daddy. It's too much for me, and I have to look away.

Dr. Young continues the exam, murmuring, "Baby Rose looks perfect, but I'd like her mommy to take it easy the next few days." He finishes the exam and cleans off the gel before replacing my shirt. "Would you like me to get your mom?"

"No, thank you. I could use a few minutes alone."

"Okay. Try to get some rest." He pats my hand before gathering his things and going to the door.

When he opens it, I see Viktor standing outside. Always my guardian.

"How is she, Doc?"

"Her pressure's a bit high, but that's expected after such a shock. I'd like to see her in the office in a few days to recheck it. If her pressure doesn't resolve, it can cause complications."

"I'll call in the morning and get an appointment," Viktor assures him. "What else do I need to do?"

"Make sure she's eating and drinking. It'll be hard, but it's important for the baby. I'd like her to rest as much as possible until I see her again."

"I'll see to it."

"Are you done with her exam?" I hear Mom ask.

"I am, Mrs. Clarke. I gave my instructions to Viktor," Dr. Young says patiently. "I'll see myself out."

"I'm going to get my daughter." Mom walks across the room and sits on the edge of the bed. "I made soup. How about you come to the kitchen and have a bite to eat?"

"I'm not hungry."

"You need to eat."

I really don't want to swallow anything.

"Doc said you need to eat, for the baby's sake," Viktor says as he walks into the room.

"Perhaps you should knock first," Mom says, clearly annoyed by Viktor's presence.

"Yes, ma'am. I apologize." He stands there for a minute, looking at me as if he wants to say something, but instead turns and leaves the room.

"Mom, you need to be kinder to him. He may be an employee, but he's also one of our closest friends. He's lost Alex, too."

"He's too familiar with you. I don't like it."

"We've been through a lot together. I trust him with my life." I stand up. "Can you please try? For me?"

She ignores my plea as she takes my arm. "Let's get you some warm soup."

Natalie

THE PAST FEW DAYS HAVE MELDED TOGETHER INTO A HAZY BLUR. I'VE been navigating through the routine motions of life without truly being present. Despite my mother's objections, Viktor has remained faithfully by my side. He tends to my every need, anticipating my wants and ensuring that I lack for nothing. Recognizing that I'm not up for socializing or conversation, he has taken it upon himself to screen my calls and visitors. He notes the names of those who've reached out to offer their love and support.

Most importantly, Viktor's there for me in moments of anguish, holding me tight as I sob through the nightmares that plague my sleep. Due to my high blood pressure, Dr. Young has instructed me to rest as much as possible. This hasn't been a challenge as I've found myself lost in a daze, lying on the couch and staring blankly at the television.

"You need to get dressed today," Viktor reminds me. "The detective will be here in about an hour." I shrug, not caring if I'm in my pajamas or not. "Let's go." He takes my hands, pulling me to my feet. "You're going to shower and put clean clothes on."

I roll my eyes but follow him down the hall anyway. He opens the door to the primary bedroom. "I'm not going in there," I say as I freeze in place. The memories of Alex and I are too strong. I know they'll suffocate me if I step into that room again.

Viktor's features soften. "Okay, we'll go to the guest room then." He stops outside the bathroom door. "You go shower. I'll get some clothes and leave them here for you."

When he leaves, I strip and step under the hot spray, letting the water run over me, praying it will wash away the overwhelming grief. The emotion originates in the depths of my soul, intensifying with each passing moment until it erupts uncontrollably. I'm unaware of my screams until Viktor flings open the shower door and lifts me from the floor. He envelops me in a towel before carrying me to the bed.

"You scared the shit out of me." He sits next to me on the bed. "I thought something happened."

Silent tears mixed with water droplets run down my face.

"Stay here." He locks the door. "I don't want anyone coming in while you're not dressed. Viktor helps dry my body, never letting his gaze drop from my face. Then, I dress in the leggings and T-shirt he brought in. He's caring and gentle as he combs and blow-dries my hair.

There's a knock on the door. "Natalie, are you in there?"

"Wait here." Viktor goes to answer the door.

Mom's eyes are huge as she looks between the two of us.

"There's an officer here to see you."

"Please tell them we'll be right out," Viktor says.

She looks past Viktor to me before walking away.

"Are you ready?" he asks.

"Do I have a choice?"

"No. I'm sorry, but I'll be there with you."

Viktor and I make our way to the living room, where my parents are talking with an NYPD officer. When I enter the room, their conversation abruptly stops.

"Mrs. Montgomery, please accept my deepest condolences," the officer says.

"Thank you," I murmur as I take a seat on the end of the sofa.

Viktor perches on the arm next to me, and Mom gives yet another disapproving glare.

"I'm Detective Walters. I've been assigned to your husband's case." The older man introduces himself. "We've concluded our initial investigation and have ruled your husband's death a homicide."

Although I already knew Alex was murdered, hearing the words spoken aloud by law enforcement seems to make it even more real. I grab Viktor's hand for support.

"It's still an ongoing investigation. We have forensic experts sifting through the debris looking for anything that will give us a cause and hopefully a suspect," he explains. "Do you know if your husband had any enemies?"

"Of course he didn't," Mom interrupts. "Alexander was a model citizen. A business-owner. A husband and soon-to-be-father."

"Charlotte," Dad interrupts. "As difficult as this is for us, the office doesn't deserve our anger. He's only doing his job."

"I mean no disrespect, ma'am. These are the standard questions." He tries his best to appease her.

"I'm sorry. This is all very difficult. Please excuse me." Mom hurries out of the living room.

"Excuse me." Dad stands. "I need to go to my wife."

"Certainly," Detective Walters replies before returning to us. "I'm sure this is very difficult for you, but are you aware of anyone who may have been looking to hurt your husband?"

"As Mrs. Clarke said, Alex was a respected member of the community," Viktor answers. "I worked with him every day. He had no enemies."

The detective looks at me. "There's no one I can think of."

"Here's my contact information," Detective Walters reaches out, handing me his business card. Viktor intercepts it. "Please call me if either of you thinks of anything that might help our investigation."

"We will," Viktor assures him.

"We weren't able to salvage much from the scene. But we were able to save a few of your husband's personal belongings." The detective holds out a small bag.

My hand trembles as I reach out and take the bag. "Thank you, Detective." Tears fall silently as I clutch the bag to my chest.

"If there's nothing further." Viktor stands. "Mrs. Montgomery needs to rest."

"Yes, of course. Thank you both for your willingness to meet with me. Again, if you think of anything, please call."

"I'll be right back," Viktor says before turning back to the officer. "I'll see you out." They exchange a few words I'm unable to hear before the officer steps into the elevator and the doors close.

Viktor

After the officer leaves, I return to Natalie, who's clutching the bag of Alex's belongings and silently crying. I sit next to her.

"Do you want to open it?"

"Will you do it?" She hands me the opaque bag.

The first item I take out is Alex's wallet, charred around the edges. Did he drop it before he got into the car? Opening it, I find all his cards and ID are mangled but still in their places. I rule out an attempted robbery.

Natalie leans forward and opens the pocket where his cash is. She pulls out a piece of paper from behind the ruined money—an ultrasound picture. A fresh wave of tears pours down her cheeks. I set the wallet on my lap and wipe her face with my thumbs. "He was so excited about the baby."

"The day I found out I was pregnant, I was afraid to tell him. I didn't think he'd be happy."

"Why would you ever think that?"

"We'd talked about having a baby someday—" Her voice trails off.

I reach back into the bag and pull out two more objects—his wedding band and a small key on a chain. Natalie's hand immediately goes to the collar around her neck.

"I don't want to take it off. Not yet."

"I don't expect you to." I slide the key into my pocket. I know who this needs to go to.

"May I have his ring?"

"Of course." I give her the platinum band, which she slides onto her thumb.

There's another subject I don't want to bring up, but we can't avoid it any longer. "We need to plan a memorial service for Alex."

"I don't even know where to start."

"I know where there's a private chapel." I take her shaking hand in mine. "If you want, I'll call and set a date for the service."

"I'd appreciate that. Viktor?" Her voice is full of desperation.

"What is it?"

"I need you to find out who did this. Find who took Alex away from me."

I look into her determined, pleading stare. "I won't stop until I do."

Pulling out my phone, I make a call to the chapel. At Natalie's insistence, we schedule an evening candlelight memorial service.

Natalie

My phone is propped on my make-up table, and I'm talking to Lana on video chat while I try to make myself look presentable for Alex's memorial service this evening.

"I hate that I'm not there with you today," she says.

"I wish you were here too."

After Thanksgiving, Lana returned to Russia with her family. She and Brandon are going through a very rough time and have decided to take some time apart while they consider the fate of their relationship.

I set the make-up brush down, frustrated. My attempt to hide the red, puffy spots on my face from crying failed. "I don't think I can do this, Lana."

"I know this is hard, honey." Lana gets close to the camera. "But you have to be strong. For Alex."

Two weeks.

That's how long Alex has been dead.

How long my world has been dark and lonely.

A part of me died with him in that explosion. Sometimes, it begs me to follow him.

Instead, each morning, I force myself to get out of bed. My body is going through the motions of living on autopilot. My mom places food in front of me at mealtimes, but I have no appetite. I gag it down to nourish my unborn baby—she didn't ask for any of this.

Yekaterina, my therapist from Jelena's Hope, offered to fly to New York City to help me through these first few months, but I declined her offer. Instead, we've been video-calling every day. She assures me it'll get easier with time, and although I nod in agreement, I don't believe her.

Life can never possibly be okay. If it weren't for this baby growing inside me, I'd have no reason to go on.

There's a knock on my bedroom door before it opens. Mom steps in.

"Sam and Luna just got here," she says. "He'd like to see you."

"You can send him back." I turn to the phone. "I have to go. We'll talk soon?"

"I don't care what time it is. If you need me, just call. I love you, Nat."

"Love you too, Lan."

I don't know how to face Sam. Losing his wife was hard enough, but no parent should have to lose a child.

It was a call I didn't want to make. I dreaded it with every fiber of my being. Viktor offered to do it for me, but I knew that wouldn't be right. Trembling with fear and sorrow, I mustered up the courage to speak, and my heart sank to the pit of my stomach.

The words were a crushing weight on my soul as they left my lips, informing Sam of the unfathomable loss of his beloved son. The deafening silence on the other end of the line was shattered by the sound of the phone dropping to the ground. The air was filled with the sounds of his anguished cries - sounds that were almost inhuman.

My heart broke at the sound of Sam's pain, causing the fragile semblance of composure that I had maintained to crumble. Luna had to step in to finish the phone call with Viktor as I was left wracked with grief and despair.

"May I come in?" Sam asks from the doorway.

I nod, already unable to speak.

Sam shuffles into the room, not as his usual confident self but as a weary man who looks like he hasn't slept in days. He holds his arms out, and I go to him, seeking refuge. Allowing him to envelope me in a fatherly embrace as we mourn the loss of the man we loved so much.

"I'm so sorry, Natalie." He rubs his hand in circles on my back. "I know how hard losing a spouse is. With you being pregnant, I can't even imagine how much harder it is."

This man just lost his only child, and he's apologizing to me—grieving for me. Sam leads me to the edge of the bed, and we sit. My body goes rigid.

"This is the first time I've been in here since—" I can't say the words. "I haven't been able to sleep in our bed." I look at the spot that was Alex's. "I can't bring myself to without him."

"I understand." He takes my hand. "It took me nearly a year to sleep in the room I shared with Rose. I wish I could tell you it gets easier, that the pain goes away, but it doesn't. Grief doesn't go away. We learn how to live with it." His gaze drifts off as though he's reliving the pain from losing his wife.

"It's been many years since I lost Rose. Although I eventually allowed myself to love again, sometimes, a sound or a smell pushes those memories to the surface. The pain hurts as much as it did in the beginning."

"I feel like I'm stuck in a nightmare. This can't be real." Sam puts his arm around me, and I rest my head on his shoulder. "I keep expecting Alex to walk through the door any second, but he never does. He's not coming back."

Tears stream down my face as the weight of the situation becomes even more overwhelming. "I don't know how to live without him," I confess, my voice choked with sobs. "Alex was my everything."

"You don't have to know right now. Take it one moment at a time, one breath at a time. And don't be afraid to lean on those who love you."

I cling to Sam, grateful for his presence in this moment of darkness. But the thought of facing the days ahead without Alex feels unbearable.

There's a quiet knock on the door. "I'm sorry to interrupt, but it's time to leave," Viktor says.

"I don't want to say goodbye."

"Tonight isn't going to be easy," Sam says as he steels his emotions. "But my son married a strong woman. I know you don't feel that strength right now. That's why you have all of us. We'll hold you up until you can stand on your own again." He rises from his place next to me. Gone is the weary man who entered the room, replaced by the strong and sure, dominant man I know him to be. He offers me his hand, and I reach out, placing mine in his.

The small stone chapel, lit only by the flickering glow of candles, is overflowing with Alex's business associates and friends. The air inside feels thick with sorrow, and the scent of burning candles only adds to the weight of it all. I sit there, numb and hollow, as person after person approaches me with kind words and memories of Alex. Their sentiments are like a knife, twisting in my heart and reopening the wound of his loss. Through it all, Viktor's steady presence is the only thing keeping me from collapsing in on myself.

As Brandon takes the stage to deliver Alex's eulogy, my heart feels like it's about to beat right out of my chest.

"Today, we gather to remember and honor a dear friend who left us too soon. We're all shocked and heartbroken by the suddenness of his passing. Alex was a wonderful person who impacted the lives of all those he encountered. He had a unique ability to bring joy and laughter to any situation." Somehow, Brandon found a way to tell everyone about me calling the police on him, making everyone laugh. Thankfully, he left out several key details.

"Alex's kindness knew no bounds, and although he's no longer with us, we can take comfort in knowing he's left a lasting impact on our lives." While Brandon speaks, it's like Alex is here with us, his spirit filling the room. Brandon's voice breaks with emotion as he talks about his friendship with Alex, and I can feel tears streaming down my face.

"I always admired you, Alex," Brandon murmurs as he looks upward, voice catching on a sob. "Until we meet again, brother."

He steps down from the small stage at the front of the chapel and stops where I'm seated. "You were his world, Natalie. Thank you for loving him." His words wrap around me like a warm blanket, and I break down. I can feel his arms around me, offering comfort and support, but it's like I'm a million miles away, lost in my grief. All I can think is that Alex should be here, with me, not in a coffin at the front of the room. And as the service comes to a close, I'm left with the crushing weight of the realization that I'll never see him again.

The repose is being held at Italiano Desiderio. When I called Anthony, he didn't even give me a chance to ask. He insisted on shutting down the restaurant for the night.

As our driver pulls up to the venue, Anthony and Leo are standing outside, waiting for us at the entrance. "Can we steal you away for a moment?" They guide Viktor and me through the restaurant, where our guests are starting to arrive. Upon reaching the backdoor, they hold it open. "Take all the time you need out here."

The walk down the path is hauntingly beautiful—peaceful despite the suffocating grief. Chinese lanterns sway gently in the breeze, casting a warm glow on the surroundings. But as we approach the gates, I feel a knot form in my stomach. This is the spot where Alex collared me, where our lives changed forever.

"Viktor." My hand covers my mouth. My heart aches as I take in the scene before me. The garden is aglow with lanterns and fairy lights, but what catches my eye are the framed photos of Alex and me lining the circular area.

Viktor takes a step back as I walk from picture to picture, vignettes frozen in time that tell our story. There are photos of us sitting in the restaurant from the night of our first date. Another of me sitting on the balcony of the bed and breakfast. Several selfies we took the day we got engaged. Seeing them all together is overwhelming. Memories flood my mind, and tears start to flow down my cheeks.

I continue my journey along the path and find a picture of Leo and me lying on the floor with the wax mural on us. There are pictures from our collaring and our wedding. The photo that hits me the hardest is Alex and me on the carriage ride in Central Park. Viktor must've taken it. I remember the feeling of Alex's arms around me and how it felt like we were the only two people in the world.

As the snow begins falling, Viktor's arm wraps around me, and I lean into him. We stand silently, surrounded by the memories of a love that will never fade.

Anthony prepared an extravagant meal with all of Alex's favorite foods. My plate sits on the table in front of me, my food untouched. People mill about, their voices hushed, but it's all become too much.

"Viktor, can you take me home?"

"You haven't even touched your food." He looks concerned.

"I'm not feeling well."

Without another second of hesitation, he stands and helps me from my seat.

"Where are you going, Natalie?" Mom asks.

"I'm not feeling well. I need to leave."

"You can't just leave when you still have guests."

"I'll speak to Tony on the way out. He'll handle everything," Viktor assures her. "Natalie isn't feeling well. So I'm taking her home."

Mom clearly disagrees, but thankfully, she doesn't cause a scene. We say our good-byes to a few people on the way out. Then, just as he said, Viktor speaks to Tony.

"If there is anything Leo and I can do for you," Anthony says, embracing me in a hug. "Just call."

"Thank you both so much. For everything."

Viktor must have called ahead because the valet is waiting with our car when we exit the restaurant. The ride back to the apartment is somber. The city that never sleeps is reverently silent as if it knows of my loss, and it allows us to have a smooth passage home.

We walk into a quiet apartment. I used to feel Alex's presence here, but now it feels empty.

"I'm going to go change. Will you wait here?"

"Sure." Viktor sits at the kitchen island while I return to the guest room where I've been staying.

I slip into pajama pants and a T-shirt and make my way back out to the kitchen.

"Your mom texted they're on their way. I should go to my place."

"Can you stay, please? I don't want to be alone."

We sit on the couch, and Viktor puts the TV on. But I don't think either of us watches it. It only serves to fill the silence.

Natalie

"I assumed you'd be coming back to Northmeadow with us," Mom argues as I fold clothes, helping her pack her suitcase.

"This is my home. Why would I leave?"

Mom sets down the shirt she's folding. "There's nothing left for you here. You belong home with us, where we can help you."

I had a feeling she would try to convince me to go back with them. Fortunately, I'm not the timid girl I once was. I've grown and can stand my ground.

"Mom, I love you, and I know you think you're doing what's best for me. Alex is gone, but *this* is my home. This is Rose's home. We're not going anywhere."

"You won't have anyone to help you," she says, genuinely concerned.

"I have Viktor."

"What does a single man know about raising a baby? Besides, it doesn't look proper for you to be here alone with him."

Not wanting to be disrespectful or discount her concerns, I resist the urge to roll my eyes. "I don't only have Viktor. There's also Brandon and Lana and all my other friends. Rose and I will be okay."

"Well, I disagree, and I hope you'll eventually see reason. But I don't want to argue right before we leave."

"Good. Neither do I."

After we finish packing, Viktor takes their suitcases down to the car. We follow behind him and start the drive to the airport. Viktor drops us off at the door so I can walk my parents to the security checkpoint.

"We're going to miss you." Dad hugs me. "Let us know if you change your mind and decide to come home."

"I love you, Dad."

I say a tearful goodbye to my mom and watch as they make their way through security. They may be overbearing at times, but I know they love me.

When we get back to the house, I make sandwiches for Viktor and me. There's a task I've been avoiding, but I can't put it off any longer. Today's the day.

"I think it's time I go into Alex's office." I take a bite. "Alex told me a long time ago that if anything happened to him, there would be a file on his desk with important papers. I blew him off then, but it's time I take it out and go through them."

"Do you want me to stay with you?"

"I need to do this alone. I'll call if I need you."

Viktor looks uncertain, but he doesn't argue. I've successfully managed to make the rest of our lunch awkward, and we eat in silence. "I'll be in my apartment. I have some calls to make," he says when he's done eating.

I stand outside the closed door of Alex's office, debating whether or not I really want to go inside. Before I lose my courage, I turn the handle and open the door. As soon as I step in, I smell Alex's cologne. It's both comforting and painful. "Oh, Sir, I miss you so much." A warmth envelops me, and I know it's Alex.

Pulling out his well-worn leather desk chair, I lower myself into it. Everything is where he left it as if his belongings were waiting for him to return. Although Alex was never secretive about his business or forbade me from being in his office, I never came here alone. Even now, it feels wrong to be in here without him. Unlike the other room he converted into an office for us to share, this was his space.

I sit back and take a few minutes before entering the code that will open the locked drawer. Once I input the numbers, the lock clicks, and the drawer opens. Just as Alex said, there's a large manilla file with my name on it. Inside are several legal papers listing various assets I'm the beneficiary of. There are directions for bank accounts and investments, including all the business information for Jelena's Hope-NYC. It's a lot of information, and I'm overwhelmed with it all. I'll know Viktor will help me make sense of it.

Under the stack of papers is a white envelope with my name written on it. My hands shake as I open it. Inside is a note in Alex's handwriting.

My Dearest Natalie,

My heart is heavy with sorrow and regret as I write these words to you. This is the hardest thing I've ever had to do because if you're reading this, I am no longer by your side. My beautiful baby girl, I am so sorry for leaving you.

Where do I start? That first phone call from Brandon. The one where he asked me to babysit the roommate who called the cops on him. After I got done laughing, my first thought was, there's no way I'm going to spend the night with a college girl who'll be freaking out—I came so close to not showing up.

But something pulled me toward Fire and Ice that night. Little did I know that it would be the start of something that would change my life forever. The night I met you felt like the first day of my life—it was when I decided to start living again. I'd finally found the missing piece to my puzzle, and that piece was you.

Since that day, you've challenged me, made me laugh and cry, and showed me what it meant to love unconditionally. You gave yourself to me, willingly submitting to me in every way possible. I never knew I wanted to be a father until the moment you told me you were pregnant. That first ultrasound, when our baby was no more than the size of a peanut, I fell head over heels in love. You and our daughter are everything to me. Please don't ever doubt how much I love you both.

As I write this, I realize that there are some practical things that you'll need to take care of moving forward. You are now the owner of everything I possess. You'll need help keeping Jelena's Hope-NYC running—don't be stubborn. Allow Maxim and Viktor to help you. Viktor is aware of all your assets and will arrange a meeting with my attorney to ensure everything's taken care of. You and Rose will always be safe and secure.

But now, I've come to the hardest part. I need you to listen to me very carefully, my love. This is my final request to you as your husband and Dominant.

There's another man in your life who has loved you for a long time. He's someone I trust wholeheartedly to love and protect you and Rose with his life. I cannot bear the thought of you being alone and vulnerable after I am gone. Imagining you in the arms of another man kills me, but I refuse to let you go through life alone.

I've already spoken to Viktor, and he's agreed to be that person for you. I want you to open your heart to him—accept the love he has to give you and our daughter.

Move on, be happy, and give Rose the family she deserves. My only request is that you tell Rose about me and make sure she knows how much her daddy loves her and that I'll always watch over her.

Please don't be sad, baby girl. I'm setting you free, but I will always be a part of you. I love you more than words can express, and although I won't be there with you every day, I'll always be a part of you.

With all my heart
~Alex

The tear-stained paper falls from my hand, fluttering to the floor. Everything makes more sense now. Viktor hasn't left my side since the day of the accident. He's made doctor appointments, helped plan the memorial service, and ran interference between my parents and me. He's stayed on the couch with me every night and held me when I woke from nightmares.

I drop my head in my hands and cry. Viktor's known about this, and he's said nothing. I should be furious with him for keeping it from me. And Alex. How dare he ask that I move on with another man?

"You promised you'd never leave me," I yell. "You lied." I stand and swipe my arm across the desk. Papers and pens fly in all directions. Alex's laptop crashes to the floor. "How could you do this to me? I hate you." As soon as the words leave my mouth, I want to take them back. "I'm sorry, Alex. I don't hate you. I could never hate you." I slide down the wall and sit on the floor. "But you left me. You left us."

A black box in the bottom of the drawer catches my eye. It's aged and worn, but I don't recall ever seeing it. I lean forward, lifting it out of the drawer. The top has etchings of a dagger piercing through a crown. The name *Moreno* is inscribed on it. What is this? I debate if I should open the lid. My gut tells me that whatever's inside is going to change everything.

Viktor

"Did you get the security footage?" I ask Dimitri, one of several men on the video conference.

"I did. But so far, nothing. It looks just like every other day in a mundane office building," he says dryly. "I also have the data from the fingerprint logins and a complete list of all the building's employees. There're no red flags."

"Can you email that stuff to me? It won't hurt to have another set of eyes on it." I turn my attention to Maxim. "Anything on the Moreno front?"

"I have checked with all my sources. No one from Moreno's organization made it out alive. We have eyes and ears on the usual suspects, but everything has been quiet," he reports.

"That's not possible. We have to be missing something." I slam my fist on the desk.

"Calm down, Viktor." Maxim's voice is steady. "Getting angry is not going to solve anything. It will only cloud our vision."

"I just sent the files," Dimitri interrupts.

"Someone has to pay for killing him. For leaving Natalie alone."

"How is she doing?" Maxim asks.

"Not well. She's barely eating and has nightmares every night." I hesitate to say the next part, but I have to get it off my chest. "Alex has asked something impossible of me, and I don't know how to honor his request." I drop my head in my hands.

After hearing that, Maxim asks everyone to log off the video call, leaving only him and me. "What has he asked?"

I take a few minutes to tell him about the conversation Alex and I had in his kitchen shortly after they were rescued from Mexico. That I made a promise to love Natalie. "What do I do, Max?" I plead. "Tell me how to help her."

"She is grieving. She needs you to be strong and patient. Do what you have always done for her."

What I've always done? I put a band-aid on things until Alex came back. That's what I've always done. But that's not going to work this time. Alex isn't coming back. This time, I'm the one she's going to depend on. There's no one coming to take over. Max tells me not to push Natalie, to show her love and support until she's ready to move on. He's confident that, in time, everything will work out.

After we disconnect the video call, I lean back in my chair. Maybe I should've made her go back to Missouri with her parents? It's probably best if she's with her family instead of me. "Why the fuck did you put us in this situation, Alex? I only know how to keep her safe. You're the one who knew how to love her."

I stay in the silence of my office, trying to compose myself—to get my thoughts together. But when I look at the time, I realize it's been a few hours, and I still haven't heard from Natalie. I know she's going through the files Alex left, and I know the letter she'll find.

Although Alex didn't tell me everything he wrote, I know she'll learn what he's asked me to do—what he's asked her to do. I don't expect her to accept it or to love me right now, maybe ever, but I'll do everything I can to honor my friend's wishes. I head back up to her apartment and find it silent.

"Natalie," I call out but get no response.

My senses go on high alert, and I hurry down the hall and find the door to the office cracked open. I see the mess and rush in. Papers are everywhere. A laptop lies smashed on the floor. Behind the desk, I find Natalie huddled on the floor, Moreno's box in her hands. Oh, God. I hope she hasn't opened the box yet—fear courses through me as I sit on the floor next to her and wait.

"You know what's in here, don't you?" she asks without looking at me.

"I do."

"I've been sitting here holding it, trying to imagine what's inside. But I'm not coming up with anything." She looks up at me. Her green eyes are seeking answers. "Why does Alex have this?"

"I'll be honest. What's in there has a story that won't be easy for you to hear. Hell, it's not going to be easy to tell. This was supposed to be Alex's story to tell you when he was ready."

"He's not here to tell me. So, you need to." She opens the box and comes face to face with the dagger that Alex used to cut Moreno's beating heart from his body.

Natalie listens quietly, her eyes never leaving the dagger, while I tell her everything I know about that night.

"Alex killed Moreno?" I see the fragmented pieces from that night coming together in her mind. "Why didn't he tell me?"

"He wasn't sure what you'd think of him if you knew he'd taken a life. He didn't want you to look at him any differently."

She sits quietly for several minutes, pondering what I just said. "This is the same dagger Alex used on my skin at Moreno's club. The one I wear the scar from?"

"It is."

"Why did he keep it?"

Michael told me how Alex held onto that dagger as though it was his lifeline. I suppose it was shock, but I don't know for sure. "I tried asking him, but he told me never to talk about it again. I didn't want to push him."

Natalie takes a long last look at the dagger before she replaces the lid and hands the box to me. I put it back in the drawer and close it, not wanting to be reminded of that time either.

"I told him I hate him," she whispers.

"What do you mean?"

"After I read Alex's letter. I got angry." She motions to the mess on the floor. "And I yelled that I hate him." A lone tear slides down her cheek.

"It's okay. Alex knows you don't hate him." I move to put my arm around her but pull back quickly. "You know what he asked me to do?" She nods. "I don't expect anything from you. I know you aren't ready to move on—you may never be ready. And if one day you are, you might not choose me." My words come out hurried. "I won't force anything—"

"Stop, please," she whispers. "Everything's too new, too raw. I'm not ready to make any decisions or promises." She takes my hand and holds it tightly. "Just please don't leave me. I can't get through this without you."

This time I do reach out and put my arm around her. Natalie moves closer, allowing me to hold her. "I'll always be here for you."

My phone vibrates with a text alert. I pull it out to see who's texting me, hoping it's Dimitri with new information.

Steve: I hate to bother you during this difficult time, but I have some documents Natalie needs to sign.

Me: Documents for what?

Steve: The explosion damaged the building. The city insists the repairs be made immediately. The new business license also needs to be signed by the end of the day tomorrow, or it could jeopardize the whole project.

Me: Is there a way to get an extension?

Steve: I already did. The city won't let it go past tomorrow without issuing fines and possibly shutting everything down.

I set the phone on my legs and rest my head against the wall.

"Who is it?"

"It's Steve. There are papers the city wants signed for Jelena's Hope. We have to go down there today."

Her body jerks up. "I don't want to go there."

"I know, but if we don't sign the papers today, Jelena's Hope could be shut down before we even get it open." I take her hand. "I'll be with you."

"Viktor—"

"We can't let whoever did this win. We have to show up and prove we're stronger. That we won't back down," I say with more confidence than I'm feeling.

"I don't think I *am* stronger," she admits quietly.

"Natalie," I cup her face in my hands. "You're the strongest woman I know."

"You'll stay with me?"

"I won't let you out of my sight," I promise.

"I need to take a quick shower and get dressed." She looks up at me, an odd expression on her face. "And, um, I need help getting up. I'm stuck."

"Is that why you were on the floor when I came in?"

"I sat down." She half cries and half laughs. "But then, when I wanted to get up, I couldn't."

I smile and do my best to hold back my laughter.

"Don't you even think of laughing at me, Viktor Dobrow," she warns.

"I wouldn't dare." I stand up and take her hands in mine, pulling her to her feet. "Problem solved."

Natalie

I KNEW, EVENTUALLY, I'D HAVE TO FACE GOING TO JELENA'S HOPE-NYC. This project isn't going away, and I don't want it to. I didn't think it would be this soon. Alex has only been gone a few weeks, and the repairs haven't even been made where the explosion happened. How does anyone expect me to go where my husband's life was violently taken? And be okay with it?

The problem is, if I don't go, the whole project could end up being shut down. And we've worked too hard to let that happen. But that does little to quell my nerves. My entire body trembles on the ride across town. Viktor keeps the conversation light, discussing everything except what we're about to do. He's trying so hard, but nothing he can say or do will make this any easier.

Viktor turns from Central Park West to West 73rd Street, where our building sits on the corner. I think part of Alex's reason for choosing this building is the view of Central Park Lake from the upper floors. While we're stopped at the red light, Viktor puts the turn signal on.

"Can we do street parking?"

"The street's full. We could circle for hours and still not find a spot," Viktor replies, his voice steady.

"There's a parking garage a few blocks down."

"Natalie, the closest parking garage is nearly a mile away."

"I'll walk. Please, Viktor, park anywhere other than here," I beg.

My words seem to fall on deaf ears because he turns into the building's garage anyway. My only solace is that he parks on the opposite side, in a guest spot. But I know that just a few feet away, around the corner, is the place my husband died.

Viktor shuts the car off and gets out. I don't move. I can't move.

He rounds the car and opens my door. "You can do this."

Panic rushes through my body. I'm cold—numb. Calmly, Viktor leans in and takes my hands, gently tugging me from my spot. When I get to my feet, I feel a gush of water.

"What's that?" Viktor asks.

"I think my water broke." I look at him. Fear of a different kind fills me. "My due date is still five weeks away. It's too soon."

"Fuck." He rubs his hand over his bald head. "This is my fault. I shouldn't have brought you here. I should've handled it myself."

My hands fly to my stomach as every muscle tightens until I'm in agonizing pain. "What's going on?"

"I think I'm in labor."

During my shower, I wasn't feeling well. I assumed I was having more Braxton hicks contractions. I've been having those for the past few weeks. Dr. Young told me they're perfectly normal, so I didn't think anything of it. The only thing different was the pain I was having in my back. But at this point in my pregnancy, I'm so uncomfortable that I blew them off. Now, I realize I should've paid more attention.

"I'll call Dr. Young." Viktor helps me back into the car and leans in, looking me in the eyes. "Everything's going to be okay."

The hospital's on the other side of the city. With Christmas being a little over a week away, traffic's at an all-time high. My body doesn't seem to care that we're only inching through the city. It keeps contracting. I try to hide the frequency from Viktor, doing my best to regulate my breathing. He's already noticeably shaken. I don't want to make it any worse while he's trying to drive, but a stronger contraction assaults me, and I grab his arm for support.

"They aren't stopping?"

I finish breathing through the contraction before I can speak. "It feels like they're getting stronger."

He glances at me, his grey eyes swirling with fear. "Just keep breathing. I'll get us there as fast as I can." He turns down a side street, undoubtedly trying to find a less busy route.

Nearly an hour later, we're finally pulling up to the hospital's valet parking. Viktor barks orders at a poor, unsuspecting attendant before rushing to help me out of the car. I don't know whether to laugh or cry when I stand up and realize the wet stains going down my pants. It feels like all eyes are staring at me.

"It looks like I had an accident," I say, embarrassed.

"Nobody's looking. Even if they are, I dare them to say something." Viktor takes my arm. "Come on, let's get you inside."

Walking proves challenging between the wet denim chafing my skin and the pain from the contractions. Thankfully, the wheelchairs are just inside the doors. Viktor helps me into one and pushes me to the elevator. "What floor?"

"Seven."

He pushes the button, and we wait. The hospital elevators are notoriously slow. Finally, a car arrives, and he rolls me in. Viktor's hand nervously taps on the chair as we stop at several floors on the way.

I reach back to still his hand. "You aren't helping anything."

"This is taking forever," he complains.

I'm usually the impatient one, so this is an odd turn of events. Finally, the doors open onto the labor and delivery floor. Viktor wheels me to the nurses' station, where two ladies sit, their heads down, doing paperwork.

"Excuse me," Viktor says. "Where's Dr. Young? He's expecting us."

One of the women looks up. "Name?"

"Viktor."

She laughs and points to me. "The patient's name."

"Oh." Viktor blushes, another thing I've never seen before. "Natalie Montgomery."

She studies her computer screen before standing. "Right this way, Mr. and Mrs. Montgomery."

Viktor opens his mouth to correct her, but I grab his hand and shake my head. At my last appointment, I took the opportunity to ask Dr. Young for a rather unusual request.

"May I ask for a favor?"

"Depends on what you need." Dr. Young smiles.

"When it's time to have the baby, I don't want the nurses feeling sorry for the poor widow having her baby alone." I stop to get control of my emotions. I intend to get through this conversation without tears. "Viktor will be with me. Please let them assume Viktor's my husband and Rose's father."

"Natalie—"

"This is going to be hard enough without Alex. I don't want to see the look of pity on their faces. I want Rose's entry into the world to be a happy experience. Besides, Viktor will be raising her with me. He'll be the only father she knows."

Dr. Young doesn't answer right away. He studies my face for what feels like forever.

"Because of the publicity surrounding Alex's accident, I think it'll be better for me to designate one nurse to your care for the duration of your stay."

It was a huge relief, but I thought I had more time. I haven't told Viktor what I've done yet. I'll have to fill him in as soon as we're alone.

The nurse leads us to a beautiful delivery suite. "My name's Esperanza, and I'll be your nurse while you're with us. I've let Dr. Young know you arrived." She opens a drawer and takes out a hospital gown. "As soon as we get you changed and hooked up, he'll be in."

"Hooked up?" Viktor asks.

Her smile is kind as she explains, "We'll attach a fetal monitor to Natalie's abdomen for a short time. It'll monitor the baby's heart rate and her contractions." She hands me the gown. "I'll give you a few minutes, and then I'll be back."

Once we're alone, I look at Viktor. "I'm scared."

"Everything's going to be okay. You're exactly where you need to be right now." He smiles, but the uncertain look in his eyes betrays him. "Do you want me to step out while you change?"

I double over from the pain of another contraction. Viktor hurries to my side and grabs my arms. "Look at me. Take slow, deep breaths. Like this." He emphasizes his breathing until I'm mimicking him. "Good girl. Just like that." He continues to talk me through the rest of the contraction.

When it finally passes, I ask, "Is there nothing you can't do?"

"What do you mean?" He looks confused.

"Where did you learn to coach a woman in labor?"

He shrugs. "I figure the pain is like a gunshot wound, and I'm familiar with that."

Viktor makes me laugh. That's not the answer I expected. "Can you help me change? With these contractions, I don't think I can do it myself." Viktor helps me out of my clothes and into the hospital gown. "There's something I need to tell you."

"Right now?"

"A few weeks ago, I asked Dr. Young not to tell the nurses about Alex. To let them refer to you as my husband and the baby's father." I pause, trying to gauge his reaction. "I didn't want to answer questions, and I didn't want pity."

"I see," he says stiffly.

"Are you mad?"

"I'll do whatever you need to help you get through this. It's my job."

I'm about to respond to his *it's my job* comment, but Dr. Young walks in.

"I wasn't expecting to see you kids so soon."

"Me either." I groan as another contraction grips my stomach.

Viktor sits on the edge of the bed and makes eye contact, again helping me breathe through the pain.

"I'm impressed," Dr. Young says. "How far apart are the contractions?"

"About every four or five minutes."

"I'm going to put the monitors on for a few minutes to see how your little one is handling the contractions, and then I'd like to see if you're dilated."

Dr. Young puts two stretchy bands around my stomach. The room fills with the sound of my baby's heartbeat. Viktor moves closer to the top of the bed while the doctor discreetly checks my cervix.

"Let's have a chat," he says and pulls up a chair. "You're almost seven centimeters dilated."

"I'm only thirty-five weeks. Isn't it too early?"

"You're a few weeks early, but Miss Rose is the boss here. And it seems she's ready to make her grand appearance. I have every confidence she'll be just fine." He looks at the readout from the machine. "Her heart rate is perfect at 155, and you're having some fairly significant contractions." He removes the straps. "Everything looks good here. There's no reason to keep you tethered to the bed."

"So, what do we do now?" Viktor asks.

"Now, we wait. Natalie's body knows what to do. She's opted for an all-natural delivery. Your job is to help her through her contractions. She can get up and walk around. There's a tub she can relax in if that makes her more comfortable. Whatever she needs to bring this baby into the world."

Natalie

After Dr. Young gives his instructions, he leaves a wide-eyed and terrified-looking Viktor and me alone. Another contraction hits. Viktor holds my hand and guides me through it like a pro.

"Should we call your parents?"

"I'd rather wait until she's born. This is going to be hard enough."

Viktor's phone rings. He pulls it from his pocket and looks at the screen. "It's Max, but I can take it later."

"It might be important. You should answer it."

Viktor walks to the other side of the room. He's whispering, so I only catch some of the conversation. They're saying something about documents that were sent to Viktor's email. I want to know what's going on. So, I swing my legs over the side of the bed, but as soon as I stand, a contraction hits hard, and I yell.

"Shit." Viktor races to my side, dropping the phone.

"That was a big one." I look at him.

"Why didn't you wait for me?"

"I can still walk, you know." I grin and point to the phone lying on the bed. "Is Max still on the line?"

Viktor puts the phone on speaker.

"What is going on?" Maxim's deep voice fills the room.

"Natalie's in labor."

"It is too soon for that."

"She's a few weeks early. But Dr. Young isn't worried."

"Why are you on the phone with me? Your attention must remain on Natalia," Max scolds Viktor. "Call us after the baby arrives."

"Will do, boss."

Viktor hangs up and sits on the bed next to me, a helpless expression on his face.

Alex and I only took the first two birthing classes before the accident, so I'm feeling as ill-prepared as he is right now.

"How about we take a walk?" I suggest.

"A walk?" He looks at me, confused.

"Walking is supposed to help labor progress. Gravity and all."

Relying on Viktor's strength to hold me, we slowly make our way up and down the hall of the labor and delivery unit. We frequently stop to breathe through the contractions that seem to be getting stronger and closer together.

"I think we should head back to the room. I'm starting to feel a lot of pressure like I have to push."

Viktor takes my arm and starts leading me back when I nearly double over from the force of a contraction. "Nurse! Nurse!" Viktor yells as though the building's on fire.

"Stop yelling." I squeeze his arm, not wanting him to make a scene.

"But you need help. Here—" He reaches out to lift me. "I'll carry you back."

I slap his hand away. "You'll do no such thing." I stop to take a few breaths. "As soon as the contraction is over, I'll walk."

Esperanza comes over to us. "Everything okay here?"

"She's in pain."

She chuckles. "That's usually a guarantee during childbirth."

"You need to do something to stop it. Give her some medication—"

"I'm not taking any pain meds. I want to do this naturally," I say, turning to Esperanza. "I'm feeling a lot of pressure. Different than before."

"Let's get you back to your room and see what's happening."

With the increasing pain, it's an even slower walk back. Once we reach the room, I'm helped into bed, and the nurse checks my cervix. "I have good news. You're ten centimeters." She smiles.

"What does that mean?" Viktor asks.

"It means it's time to start pushing."

Viktor's face turns a nearly see-through shade of grey.

"Let's get you a chair, big guy." She drags a seat over for my trusty bodyguard and helps him sit. "It's always the big, tough ones that go down the hardest," she chuckles. "You stay here. We need to focus on the soon-to-be-mom, not the passed-out new dad on the floor. I'm going to get the doctor so we can have this baby."

Breathing through these contractions is getting more difficult. This is by far the worst pain I've ever felt. But Viktor quickly regains his composure and returns to my side, guiding me through my breathing.

As hard as I try, I lose the battle, and tears fall. "Alex should be here."

Viktor leans in close and whispers, "Close your eyes. Do you feel him?"

With my eyes closed, I see my husband's gorgeous face. How, when I told him I was pregnant, his brown eyes lit up in a way I never saw before. The awe on his face when he saw our baby on the ultrasound for the first time. A warmth envelops my body, and I know it's Alex wrapping himself around me. "I do."

The door opens, startling me, and Dr. Young walks in. "I hear it's time to have this baby. Are you ready to start pushing?"

"I think so."

Things start moving pretty quickly now. Dr. Young scrubs up and puts on gloves and a face shield. Esperanza plugs in some sort of contraption that looks like it has a French fry warmer on it before coming over to my bedside.

"I need you to help hold her leg," she says to Viktor. "Just like this." She demonstrates on my other leg. Viktor follows along. "With the next contraction, I want you to push."

It feels like only seconds until the next contraction hits. I bear down and push with all my might. I'm surprised that it actually makes the contraction more bearable. We repeat this process for what feels like forever. Sweat pours from my face—I'm exhausted.

"I don't think I can do this anymore."

"Don't you dare give up." Viktor turns my face so I'm looking at him. "You can do this."

Another contraction.

Another push.

"I can see her head. Give me your hand." Dr. Young guides it between my legs to feel the top of my baby's head."

The magnitude of the moment overwhelms me.

Esperanza points to a mirror set up behind the doctor. "It's so you can watch your baby come into the world," she explains.

The next few contractions are difficult. The pressure becomes increasingly more painful.

"Her head's out. I don't want you to push quite as hard this time," Dr. Young instructs.

Viktor leans close to me. "You're doing so good, Natalie. She's almost here." He kisses my forehead gently.

While I push, I watch in the mirror as the doctor maneuvers the baby's shoulders out one at a time, followed by the rest of her body. A moment later, my newborn's cries fill the room. Dr. Young places her on my bare chest, and I wrap my arms around my precious daughter.

"Viktor, would you like to cut the cord?"

He looks to me for approval. "Alex would want you to."

With shaky hands, he takes the offered scissors and cuts where the doctor instructs. Esperanza brings over a blanket and, much to the dislike of Rose, helps me dry her off.

"I need to steal her for a few minutes."

She brings Rose to the warming bed, where she finishes drying her off. Then she gets a weight and measurement.

Dr. Young comes to my side, taking my hand in his. "I know how difficult today is for you. Celebrating the beginning of a new life while you're still grieving the loss of another." He squeezes my hand. "You did good. She's beautiful. Alex would be very proud."

I manage to smile through the tears pouring down my face.

Esperanza returns to us with a tiny bundle swaddled in a blanket, a pastel pink hat on her head. "She's 6lbs 3oz and 17 inches long." She places the baby in my arms. "We'll give you some time alone."

I look down and see familiar blue eyes looking back at me. "Hi, Rose," I say softly. "I'm your mama." She's tiny and absolutely perfect. I lift her hat and gently run my hands over her head, which is full of curly blonde hair.

Viktor sits on the bed beside me, his gaze fixed on the baby in my arms. "She's beautiful."

"Would you like to hold her?"

"I don't know." He freezes. "She's so tiny."

"She won't break." I adjust my position and pass my daughter to Viktor. Somehow, she looks even smaller in his large-muscled arms.

"*Printessa,*" he says softly. A lone tear slides down his face.

I reach over to the table beside the bed and grab my cell. I want to capture this tender moment. Then I send a text and the picture to Max and Irina.

Me: She's here, and she's perfect. As you can see, Viktor's already quite taken with her.

Rose begins to fuss. "What's wrong?" Viktor panics and passes the baby back to me.

"She might want to eat." I lower the hospital gown, and help Rose latch onto my breast for the first time.

"I'll leave and let you two have some time alone."

"Please don't go."

"But you're feeding her." He motions to my partially exposed breast. "I shouldn't be here."

"It's not like you haven't seen me naked before." I shake my head and laugh. "We live in the same house, and I'll have to feed her—quite often. Do you plan on going out every time?" I pause and look down at the infant suckling from my breast. "I know this isn't how it was supposed to be, but it's how it is. We both need to bond with her." I move over, making room. "Come, sit."

Watching Natalie endure such pain, and knowing I can't do a damn thing about it, makes me feel more helpless than I've ever felt. She's in agony, and I can't fix it. What was Alex thinking when he agreed to let her do this without medication? If it were up to me, I would've insisted she take something to alleviate this pain. It's torture watching her and only being able to hold her hand and guide her breathing.

When the doctor returns to the room, things move quickly. Natalie's legs are pulled back, and I'm instructed on how to hold one while I coach her through breathing and pushing.

I've never witnessed a woman giving birth and never wanted to. Despite the pain, Natalie looks more beautiful than ever. Although she's exhausted, she doesn't quit. She's incredibly strong as she pushes with all her might, bringing her baby one step closer to being born.

Leaning close, I whisper, "You're doing so good, Natalie. She's almost here." I kiss her forehead gently.

Esperanza sets up a mirror so Natalie can watch her daughter enter the world. I don't know if I should watch, but I can't tear my eyes away from the miracle I'm witnessing. Somehow, Natalie's tiny body opens, allowing the most perfect little human to come out. The doctor quickly lays her on Natalie's chest.

"Viktor, would you like to cut the cord?" Dr. Young asks.

I look to Natalie. "Alex would want you to."

This is for you, brother. I take the scissors and cut where the doctor shows me, officially severing the cord connecting mother and child.

Esperanza takes the baby from Natalie to clean her thoroughly. I watch, already guarding this precious new life, as she's weighed and measured. Then, the nurse wraps her tightly in a blanket and returns her to her mama.

We're left alone.

Just a few hours ago, being alone meant there were only two of us, but now, by some miracle, we're three.

I can't take my eyes off Natalie. She's radiant as she holds her daughter and whispers to her. Rose gazes at Natalie adoringly, as if she already knows who she is, and I guess she does. Their bodies have been connected for the past nearly nine months.

"She's beautiful."

"Would you like to hold her?"

"I don't know." Every muscle in my body tenses in fear. "She's so tiny."

"She won't break." Natalie adjusts her position and passes the tiny bundle to me.

I look down, admiring this perfect little girl in my arms, already knowing I'd give my life for her. "*Printsessa,*" I say softly. My chest aches when I see she has her daddy's brown eyes. He should be here, not me. A tear slips down my face. The baby begins to squirm and whimper.

"What's wrong?" I quickly hand her back to Natalie.

"She might want to eat." Natalie lowers her hospital gown and brings the baby to her breast. She quiets as she latches on quickly.

Rose cried in my arms because she knows I'm not her father. I understand what Alex asked, but I don't see how this will work—I don't have a place in this little family.

"I should leave. Let you two have time alone."

"Please don't go," she implores.

I can't be here right now, not with the emotions warring inside me, But I can't tell Natalie that. I don't want to ruin this time for her. "You're feeding her. I shouldn't be here."

"It's not like you haven't seen me naked before." Natalie gives me an incredulous look. "We live in the same house, and I'll have to feed her—quite often. Do you plan on going out every time? I know this isn't how it was supposed to be, but it's how it is. We both need to bond with her." She moves over, giving me room. "Come, sit."

Although I'm filled with uncertainty, I know she's right. Natalie and I have been through more together than most people. We've seen each other at our most vulnerable, but things are different now. In the past, I was nothing more than her bodyguard and friend, but now, I've been thrust into a role I never expected to find myself in.

Finding a woman and starting a family with her was never in my plans. I was happy on my own. I don't know how to be the man Alex asked me to be—the one who is to protect and love his family. I'll never measure up to the man he was. Natalie will never look at me with the same love and adoration she did him. And I certainly have no idea how to raise a child.

The promise I made to Alex is easily the most important promise I've ever made to anyone. I fear I'll never live up to the expectations he had for me.

Viktor

After Natalie finishes feeding the baby, she calls her parents to tell them their granddaughter has been born. It turns into an emotional phone call as Charlotte begs Natalie to return home. To let them help her raise her child. Natalie insists she's okay and wants to do this on her own. It's well over an hour before their phone call winds down. Charlotte is disappointed but, in the end, agrees to respect Natalie's decision.

Right now, Natalie and Rose are sleeping. She made me promise not to leave the room, but I need to call Maxim. So I find myself standing in the far corner, trying to be as quiet as possible so I don't wake either of them.

"I did not expect to hear from you so soon," Max says.

"I guess her labor went fast. At least that's what the nurse said." I look over my shoulder to check that the girls are still sleeping. "Any updates?"

"Nothing of significance. Dimitri is rewatching the video footage from the security cameras, but nothing seems out of place." Max pauses. "How is Natalia doing?"

"She's doing as good as to be expected. I think Rose coming early was the best thing that could've happened. It's given her something to smile about."

"That is all good, but what is it you are not telling me?" Maxim asks, perceptive as always.

"You know what Alex asked of me?"

"*Da.*"

"I don't think I can do it. I'm not the man Alex believed me to be." I put my forehead against the wall and close my eyes. "I know how to protect, and I know how to kill. But I don't know how to be gentle and love."

There's a long pause.

"Are you still there?"

"I am," Max responds. "Your concerns are understandable. You have been tasked with the most important job a man could have."

"It's a job I can't do. I've never been in a relationship, and I have no clue how to raise a child."

"You already know how to love her."

"Boss—"

"Do not interrupt me, Viktor," he reprimands. "Anyone who has witnessed you with Natalia knows you care about her. Alex was not blind to that. However, he knew you would never betray him. That is why he asked you to do this. Alex knew he would never have to worry because you already love her."

"Even if that's true, she doesn't love me."

"Not a romantic love, you may be right. But given your experiences together, you and she share a very special bond. She knows Alex's request, and eventually, she will be able to act on it," he pauses. "As for being a parent. You are the only father Rose will ever know. Your responsibility is to make sure she knows who Alex is, how much he loved her, and how much you love her. After that, the rest will fall into place." He says it like it's so easy. "When will she and the baby go home?"

"Tomorrow morning." Behind me, the baby begins to fuss. "I have to go. Rose is up, and I don't want her to wake Natalie."

I don't wait before ending the call and hurrying over to the baby trolley where Rose lies. "Shh, *Printessa*." I gently place my hand on her. "Go back to sleep." She pushes out her bottom lip, and I laugh softly. "Your mama does the same thing when I tell her what to do."

Rose's whimpers begin to grow louder. Natalie's been going non-stop since she gave birth. This tiny human is a non-stop eating machine. "Okay, I guess we're going to do this." I put my hands under her little body and lift her, holding her close to my chest. "This isn't so bad, is it, *Printessa?*"

I walk her to the windows and turn my body so the baby can look out. It's night, and the city lights twinkle in the distance. "See, it's nighttime. This is when we sleep." She seems to settle and eventually falls back to sleep. I'm afraid to lay her down, so I sit in the recliner with the baby in my arms. Carefully, I press the button that makes the footrest pop up, and I recline with the baby lying on my chest. "You and I will hang out here so your Mama can get some sleep.

Natalie

ESPERANZA WAKES ME WHEN SHE TURNS THE BEDSIDE LIGHT ON. EVEN though I'd rather be sleeping, it's time for another routine post-birth check.

"Look at those two over there." She points to Viktor, who's asleep, his arms holding Rose, who's sleeping on his chest. "Looks like she's going to be a daddy's girl."

"I think so." I smile and fight to hold back the tears, but they fall anyway. I quickly swipe at them.

Esperanza passes me a tissue from the table. "It's postpartum hormones," she says as I dry my eyes. "Is there anything you need?"

"I was told I could ask for a pump. I'm going to have to go back to work, and I'd like to get Rose used to a bottle, so Viktor," I hesitate. "So, her dad can feed her too."

Esperanza leaves but quickly returns with the machine. She explains how to use it, and it seems pretty straightforward. I keep the lights dim so I don't wake Viktor or Rose. While I pump, the words I spoke to the nurse repeat in my head. *So her dad can feed her, too.*

Suddenly, things I hadn't considered or didn't want to consider hit me hard. Rose will never know Alex. She'll never hear his voice. Besides what she's told, she'll never experience how much he loved her. All the dreams and plans Alex and I once shared were stolen. I've been left to pick up the pieces of my life and move on. I'm left with the knowledge that Alex's wish is for me to make new dreams and a new life with Viktor.

I look over at the man who's sleeping peacefully with my newborn daughter snuggled on his broad chest. He's a good man. A kind man. A man I trust with my life and now my daughter's life. He doesn't lack in the looks department either, but I'm still in love with my husband. There's no room in my heart for another man. I don't know how to put my love for Alex aside and make room in my heart for Viktor. I don't know how I'm supposed to honor Alex's request.

It's a chilly December afternoon. The weather turned wintery overnight, leaving a few inches of snow on the ground. I'm dressing Rose in a soft pink one-piece with little rosebuds. Alex chose it months ago for her coming home outfit.

Meanwhile, Viktor is pacing, an instruction booklet in his hand, looking between it and the alien invention, otherwise known as a car seat.

Esperanza walks into the room. "I have your discharge papers. You need to sign here." She hands me the papers and a pen. "I also have a cooler with your milk." She sets it on the bed and spots my cell phone. "How about I take a family picture before sending you off?"

Viktor stops pacing and looks at me. He knows the arrangement I made with the doctor, and he's gone along with it, but every mention of *family* makes us flinch. The wounds are too fresh.

I muster a smile and pass her my phone. "That would be great."

Viktor sets the instructions down and joins me on the bed, where I cradle Rose in my arms.

"Get closer, you two." She peeks around the phone. "Put your arm around your wife."

"Although his body remains tense, Viktor slides his arm around me. Esperanza snaps a few pictures until she gets one she's pleased with. "You are a beautiful family, and you've been a pleasure to serve," she says kindly.

"Thank you, ma'am," Viktor says.

"Let's get the baby in her car seat, and you three will be free to go."

While Esperanza and I get Rose situated, Viktor calls the valet to have our car ready. Despite my protests, I'm put in a wheelchair—standard practice, I'm told, and my lap is piled high with everything we have to bring home. Who knew one little person could accumulate so much stuff so quickly? Viktor carries the car seat, and we walk out of the hospital to our waiting car.

Viktor opens the backdoor, where the car seat's base is secured. Then, lifting the car seat, he leans in and attempts to attach it to the base. "Dammit," he mutters as he fiddles with the contraption, still not finding success.

"May I help you with that?" Esperanza asks.

Viktor glares at her over his shoulder. "I'm fine."

"They're always fine," she says and laughs.

"I guess you've seen this before?" I ask while watching Viktor and trying to back my laughter.

"Every day." She smiles. "First-time fathers are the most stubborn creatures."

I lose the battle, and we share a laugh.

"What's so funny?" Viktor asks, looking deflated by his continued failed attempts.

Esperanza walks up to Viktor. "Move over, and let me show you how it's done."

With practiced ease, she snaps the car seat into place.

"I almost had it, you know," Viktor mutters as he takes the pile of stuff from my lap and puts it into the trunk.

"You'll get it next time," I say as he helps me into the backseat with the baby.

Today, bringing Rose home from the hospital is one of those defining moments in life. Something that should be met with happiness and celebration. Instead, it's a quiet ride, both of our hearts heavy and missing Alex.

Viktor

Our first few days home are chaotic, to say the least. While we were in the hospital, I read a bunch of articles on Google about taking care of a newborn. I thought I had it all under control, but damn, was I wrong. Rose is a pleasant baby, but I've learned that even pleasant babies are surprisingly high-maintenance.

While we were in the hospital, she seemed to understand the difference between daytime and nighttime. But once we got home, something happened. Now, she sleeps all day and stays up all night. When Rose is awake, she's either eating—which she seems to do all the time—or needs her diaper changed.

Natalie's running on fumes, so I try to make sure she naps when Rose does. While the girls sleep, I try to clean up the house and have learned how to operate the washer and dryer. It's a juggling routine unlike anything imaginable. This crazy new schedule also means I've had no time to even think about opening the email from Dimitri.

Natalie's asleep in the guest room because I still can't get her to sleep in the primary bedroom, and Rose is asleep in the bassinet beside me. We agreed to keep all business related to Maxim downstairs, but I can't wait any longer to open my laptop to review the documents Dimitri sent. I only make it halfway down the first page before Rose fusses.

Leaning over the bassinet, I peer down at her perfect little face. "*Printessa,* I believe you came pre-programmed to know when I'm trying to work." I can't help but smile as I lift her into my arms. "Your mama said you'd be hungry soon. Fortunately for both of us, she left a bottle."

This is my first time feeding her without Natalie's supervision, and I hope I don't screw it up. Holding Rose with one arm, I warm up the milk in a cup of hot water and test it on my wrist like Natalie showed me. Then, I get comfortable on the couch and offer Rose the bottle. At first, she turns her head and refuses. "I know, it's not the real thing, but Mama's exhausted." I rub the nipple gently on her mouth, and eventually, my efforts pay off. She wraps her tiny pink lips around the nipple and sucks the milk greedily, finishing the bottle in record time. Then I readjust her position on my chest as I burp her.

"You two look like pros," Natalie says as she sits beside me and gently caresses Rose's head.

"We managed to figure it out." I smile proudly. "How was your nap?"

"It was well-needed. Thank you for watching her."

"So, while I was sitting here, I started thinking about something." I adjust my hold on Rose.

"What's up?"

"Christmas is only a few days away, and we don't have a tree."

"I'm not in the mood for celebrating."

"I understand, but it's Rose's first Christmas." I pass the baby to Natalie. "We have to do it for her."

"She won't know the difference."

"But we will. And Alex would expect us to give Rose the best first Christmas possible." I turn to face her. "We need a tree, decorations, and presents."

"Whatever you want."

"Let's bundle Rose up and take a walk to the tree lot down the street."

A part of me longs for her sassy mouth to argue with me, but there's nothing. She just shrugs and goes along with my plan. None of this is ideal, but something has to give. Rose shouldn't be living in a home shrouded by grief. We have to start moving forward, if not for us, for the baby.

With the three of us bundled up, I buckle Rose into her pram and tuck an extra blanket around her to keep her warm.

Outside, flurries dance in the breeze, adding to the spirit of the holidays. With Christmas less than a week away, the lot is pretty well picked over, but luckily, we still manage to find a decent tree. The lot attendant wraps the tree tight in netting, making it easier to transport. Natalie laughs when I hoist the bundled evergreen onto my shoulder. It's the first time I've heard her laugh in weeks, and it warms my heart. When we're back at the house, I set up the tree while Natalie goes to the closet to find the Christmas decorations.

"I told you this was a good idea," I say to the infant lying in her swing.

Natalie comes back into the room carrying two boxes. I hurry over and take one from her.

"This one has the lights in it." She says as she sets her box down.

Natalie nurses Rose while I string the colorful lights across the tree branches. Then, she gets Rose situated in her baby sling to have both hands free to help decorate the tree.

"I have something for you. Wait here." I rush down the hall to Alex's office to grab the gift I've been hiding and hurry back to Natalie. "It's nothing big." I shrug and hand her the little pink box.

She lifts the lid and looks inside. "Viktor, it's beautiful."

She holds up a silver tiara ornament with crystals inlaid across it. Engraved on it is *Baby's First Christmas.*

"I hoped you'd like it."

"I love it." She reaches out to hug me. Usually, I'd withdraw. Knowing I had feelings for her made any physical contact feel wrong. Things are different now, and I embrace her tightly. Holding Natalie feels incredible until Rose wriggles between us, prompting me to let go.

Natalie hangs Rose's ornament front and center on the tree. Together, we pull out the ornaments until Natalie comes upon a delicate porcelain snowflake. "It's Alex and mine's First Christmas ornament." She looks up at me. "I don't know what to do with it."

"Whatever you decide is okay."

Natalie holds it up, her gaze fixed on the object, seemingly unsure what to do next. After a moment's contemplation, she returns it to the box, but at the last second, she changes her mind and brings it to the tree. With great care, she hangs it on a branch, positioning it next to Rose's ornament. I'm not sure how it happens. Maybe the branch was damaged. But like a slow-motion movie, the snowflake slips from the tree. It crashes onto the floor, shattering into countless irreparable fragments.

Natalie is devastated when she sees the ruined ornament and collapses to her knees. She remains silent, but tears silently stream down her cheeks.

"I'm so sorry. This is my fault. If I didn't insist on getting a damn tree—"

"It's not your fault," she says quietly. "It was an accident. The universe seems to be trying to erase Alex from my life." She walks away and sits on the couch, cradling the baby against her.

"We aren't going to let that happen." I place my hands on her legs. "He'll always be a part of you—a part of us."

"I know, but I'll never be able to move forward if I keep pretending he's coming back." She lifts her left hand and looks at her wedding rings. "It's time I accept that he's gone," she says as she slides the rings off her finger.

I don't know how to respond, so I say nothing and watch as she walks out of the room.

I debate whether I should go after her or allow her some space before settling on giving her a few minutes alone. While she's gone, I put Rose to bed and clean up the broken ornament pieces. Then, I sit on the couch and wait for her to return.

Natalie walks back into the room. No words are needed. I open my arms to her, and she crawls on my lap, burying her head against my chest as she cries.

There are no words I can say to make this better for her. All I can do is give her a safe place to express her grief.

Natalie

Seeing the shattered fragments of our precious ornament scattered across the floor, a crushing wave of emotions washes over me. It feels like every piece of my life connected to Alex is being cruelly ripped away from me, and I am helpless to stop it. I'm exhausted from feeling like a mere bystander, waiting for the next disaster to strike. This time, I'm taking control and making the first move.

Without a word, I leave Viktor behind with the half-finished tree. There's something I need to do, a cathartic act that will bring some sense of closure. With a trembling hand, I slide my wedding rings off my finger, acknowledging the brutal reality that this is not a nightmare but my tragic new life. Alex is gone forever, and I can't bring him back.

I clutch my wedding rings tightly as I enter the bedroom that once belonged to Alex and me. My jewelry box beckons, and I pull out the little drawer where Alex's wedding band rests on the soft black velvet. It's time for my rings to join his, a symbolic gesture that brings both comfort and pain.

One day, I'll tell my daughter the beautiful story behind my ring. How it first belonged to her grandmother, Rose, and how her daddy redesigned it into something meaningful for us. Then, I'll pass the ring on to her, so she'll always have a special treasure from her Dad.

I heard Viktor putting Rose to bed. So, before I return to the living room, I check in on her and find her sleeping soundly.

When I return to Viktor, he's sitting on the sofa. The mess from the ornament has been cleaned up. Our eyes meet, and he opens his arms, inviting me to go to him. I crawl onto his lap and let him hold me. Tears come in vicious waves as I allow myself to grieve for what I decide is the last time. After this, it's time to start fresh. To move forward.

It takes a while to compose myself, but eventually, the tears stop, and we finish decorating. The rest of the ornaments are hung on the tree, and then, with Viktor's help, we hang the wreath above the fireplace. I watch as Viktor strings some extra lights around the room. "I hate to admit it, but decorating was a good idea."

"Can you say that again?" Viktor teases.

"You were right." Then, in a childish move, I stick my tongue out.

Viktor laughs, and I join him, knowing it's these small moments that are going to be what heal my soul.

"Let's go to bed. I'm exhausted." I try to hold back a yawn.

"That sounds like a good plan."

We go to the bedroom we've been sharing since we brought Rose home. After I change into my pajamas, I crawl into bed. Viktor grabs his pillow and blankets and starts making his bed. "Viktor," I sit up. "It's time to stop sleeping on the floor."

"I'm fine down here."

"Come sleep in the bed." There's no way he's comfortable sleeping on the hard floor, and I see no reason he shouldn't sleep in bed. "We don't have to share a blanket if that makes you feel better."

"I don't know—"

"Please."

I hear him shuffle around, and then the bed dips next to me as he gets in and lies down.

He slowly slides my satin nightgown up my body, trailing kisses along my skin in his path. Stopping at my breasts, he sucks on each one, ensuring my nipples are hard, and I moan in response. It feels so good. I'm close to an orgasm, and he hasn't even touched me yet. Once he frees me from my nightgown, he tosses it to the side.

"You're beautiful, baby girl," he says from where he's standing next to the bed. "I want to fuck your mouth."

I adjust my position so my head is at the edge of the bed and bite my bottom lip, knowing this is his favorite position. I can take him deep in my throat this way. He moves closer, and I take his cock in my hand. I drag my tongue around the head before teasing his slit. Then, I lick the beads of pre-cum that have already formed there.

I open my mouth and take him deep. He lets out a growl of appreciation before he grabs my hair and starts moving. Tears drip from my eyes from how hard he's fucking my face. I love it when he loses control like this. It's a powerful feeling. He's close, I can tell, but instead of continuing, he pulls out. "Turn over," he demands.

I get on my hands and knees and look back at him, taking in every inch of his muscular body. My husband is amazing. He wastes no time thrusting himself inside from behind me. He's not gentle as he continues to fuck me with abandon. My hands clutch the blankets. He reaches around and squeezes my clit, sending me over the edge. I call out his name right as I'm about to—

"Natalie, wake up." Viktor shakes me.

My eyes fly open.

"You were having another nightmare. You were grabbing me, and then you called out for Alex."

How can I tell him I wasn't having a nightmare, that I was dreaming about sex with my husband while I was reaching out for him? "I'm sorry I woke you."

"That's what I'm here for."

I lay back down and roll over, questioning my decision to invite Viktor into my bed.

Natalie

My heart aches each morning when I think about facing another day without Alex. The erotic dreams I have every night aren't helping. When I wake, I long to hear the sound of his voice, to feel his touch. It's a constant battle where I remind myself they're only dreams—he's gone.

Yekaterina and I have been discussing the grief process in my sessions. Where she can help me overcome the trauma from Mexico and the explosion, there's no prescribed treatment for grief. No timeline can be given for when the pain will ease. It's not easy, but each day, I'm learning a new *normal*. Learning how to exist in a world without Alex.

It started when Viktor insisted we celebrate Christmas—for Rose. I tried to convince him that she'd have no memory of it, but he's stubborn and said we were celebrating the holiday properly. He's gone over and above to make the day special.

I wake to breakfast in bed. Viktor made my favorite—French toast, bacon, and a cup of coffee. He got Rose up, changed her diaper, and dressed while I ate. Then, with a goofy grin, he videos me carrying Rose down the hall and into the living room. I'm not sure how or when he managed to pull this off, but there are stacks of presents under the tree.

"What in the world? How did you do all this?"

"Don't ask questions," he says, smiling. "Just enjoy it."

Viktor takes pictures and videos while I open the presents for Rose and me. Despite my initial resistance, I find myself smiling and enjoying the moment.

When I finish opening the gifts, I pass Rose to him. "Wait here. I'll be right back."

I hurry to my office and open the desk drawer to get my gift for Viktor. "I feel awful. I only have one present for you," I say, handing him the wrapped box.

"Seeing you smile is the only gift I need."

"Oh, so I can take this back then?" I pull the wrapped box away.

"Since you took the time to get it, I wouldn't want to be rude and not open it." He grins.

I laugh and hand him the present.

With a sleeping Rose in his lap, he tears the wrapping paper off and opens the box. Minutes tick by while he stares at it, saying nothing.

When he finally speaks, I swear I hear his voice crack. "I love it," he says without taking his eyes off the framed picture Esperanza took of us before we left the hospital. "It's perfect."

The following week we get calls from Tony and Leo begging us to come to their New Year's party. However, neither of us is in the mood to celebrate the occasion, so we politely decline. Instead, we spend the evening curled up on the couch, intending to watch the ball drop in Times Square, but we fall asleep before midnight.

"Come here, Natalie," he orders. Naked, I climb onto his lap. His erection rests between my legs, setting all my nerve endings on fire.

"Please, I need you." I rub myself against him.

"Natalie. It's me, Viktor. You need to wake up."

When I open my eyes, I'm straddling Viktor's lap, rubbing myself against his very prominent erection. Completely humiliated, I jump off. In a swift move, he grabs my waist, stopping me from having a collision with the floor.

"I'm so sorry. I didn't realize. I was dreaming about—"

"You don't need to apologize for having a dream." He tries to hide his arousal by pulling the blanket over his lap.

"Maybe I should go sleep in the other room?"

"Don't be silly." He puts his arm out for me to lay back down. "Come back to sleep."

Tentatively, I get back on the couch and lay against him.

What's going on? Why do I keep having these vivid dreams, and how do I make them stop before I do something I can't take back?

Viktor

I startle awake. Natalie's straddling my lap, rubbing herself against me, my body responding to her movements.

"Please, I need you," she begs.

Her eyes are open, and for a brief second, I allow myself to believe it's me she's talking to. But I know I can't do that. It's not fair to her to allow her to believe I'm Alex.

"Natalie, It's me, Viktor." I shake her gently. "I need you to wake up."

It takes her a minute before recognition creeps into her awareness, and she jumps off me as though I'm a flame threatening to burn her. This isn't the first time she's reached out to me while asleep. At first, I thought she was having nightmares. But now I know they're not nightmares. She's dreaming about Alex.

Natalie offers to sleep in the other room alone. But I've quickly become accustomed to being next to her, and selfishly, I don't want to give that up.

My wish is that one night, when she has that dream, it's me she sees—me she's reaching out for. Until then, I have to find a way to be content with only holding her and making sure she's okay.

Natalie

"I KEEP HAVING THESE VIVID DREAMS ABOUT ALEX."

"What kind of dreams?" Yekaterina asks.

"That we're together intimately."

"That's normal. It's part of the way you're grieving. It'll eventually pass."

She encourages me not to hyperfocus on them, which is exactly what I can't stop doing. Between the dreams and Rose's feeding schedule, I'm exhausted and not thinking clearly. I'm running on empty.

My parents have called every day for the past two weeks. They want to come for a visit to meet their granddaughter. But that would get complicated very quickly. First, they're going to ask why Viktor's living with me and what's going on between us. Both questions I'm not ready to answer. Then, they'll pressure me to go back to Northmeadow. I'm so tired and confused right now. I know I can't deal with it, and I'll end up exploding. I don't want that, so I keep making excuses and telling them they can come *soon*.

Lana and I video chat almost every day, but she immediately changes the subject when I bring up Brandon. Now I understand how they felt when Alex and I broke up, but at least they had each other. I don't have Alex to go to for advice on how to get them back together, and when I ask Viktor, he tells me they have to work it out for themselves. All I can do is sit by and watch my friends hurting.

Mistress Star and Leo also keep calling. Star keeps inviting me to the club, and Leo wants to get together for coffee. As much as I love and miss them, they're a part of my life that no longer exists. I send their calls to voicemail and don't return any of their countless messages. I keep hitting delete, hoping they'll give up soon.

Aside from Viktor, Brandon's the only person I let close to me. He comes over at least once a week. Maybe I feel safe with him because we're both hurting. Brandon lost not only his best friend but also his submissive, who's still in Russia, unsure if she'll ever return.

Brandon's spending the afternoon with me while Viktor goes downstairs to work. He doesn't like leaving me alone, but he's also desperate to find out who's behind the explosion that killed my husband. It helps him to work without worrying when Brandon's here.

Rose's soft coos come through the speaker on my phone. She's just waking up from her nap.

"I'll get her," Brandon offers.

"She's going to need a diaper change," I call after him.

"I can handle that." Then, I hear the door to the guest room open. "Wassup? Wassup, my precious little Rose?"

I laugh at the usual greeting of his niece, but part of me fears *wassup* will end up being her first word. He continues talking to her, and I turn the baby monitor app off, not wanting to eavesdrop on their time together.

"Can I give her a bottle?" Brandon asks when he comes back to the kitchen carrying Rose.

I know how much he enjoys feeding her, and am already a step ahead with a bottle ready to go.

"Thank you, Mommy." He kisses my cheek and sits on the couch to feed the baby while I catch up on dishes. "Can I ask you a question?"

"Sure. What's up?" I dry my hands on a dishtowel and turn around, leaning against the counter.

"What's going on between you and your Russian?"

"He's only half Russian and nothing. Why?" My words come out hurried.

"Nothing?" he asks, clearly not believing me. "He moved in with you, and I see how he looks at you. The man's in love with you." Brandon adjusts Rose to his shoulder to burp her while he walks into the kitchen. "It's okay to move on, you know."

"Why don't you put Rose in her swing? We need to talk."

He buckles his niece into her swing and turns it on low before joining me at the kitchen island. As hard as this will be, I owe Brandon the truth. "You have to promise you'll try to keep an open mind," I say before explaining the letter Alex left me and his conversation with Viktor. When I finish, Brandon remains quiet for a few minutes. It's clear he's trying to digest everything I've just said.

"I had no idea," he says quietly. "So, you and Viktor are a couple?"

"Yes. No. I don't know." I'm unable to give him a straight answer. "I care about him, and I know how he feels about me, but it's too soon. I'm not ready to move on yet."

Brandon takes my hand. "You have my support with whatever you choose." Then he not so smoothly attempts to change the subject. "Everyone at Fire and Ice has been asking about you. Any chance I can get you to come visit? Maybe bring your *half-Russian* with you?"

"Bring me where?" Viktor asks, walking into the kitchen.

"I didn't hear you come in."

"I was just asking Natalie if there's any chance she'd come down to the club. Of course, you can tag along, too." Brandon smirks.

"Is that something you want?" Viktor asks.

"Thanks again for the invite. But I don't think so."

"Suit yourself." Brandon shrugs. "How are things coming with Jelena's Hope-NYC?"

"Everything's a mess." I sigh. "We've had a hard time getting a contractor who's willing to fix the damage caused by the explosion. That's put everything behind with permits and licensing—I don't know all the details. Viktor's been handling it all."

"Sounds like a headache."

"It is," Viktor agrees. "Needless to say, the grand opening's been postponed indefinitely."

"I'm sorry. I know how much this project means to you." He looks at his watch. "Shit. I'm going to be late. I have a meeting in an hour." He jumps up and plants a noisy kiss on my cheek. "Hang in there. I'll see you soon."

"I'll walk you out." Viktor follows Brandon to the elevator.

When he returns, he takes the seat next to me. "That's a subject we haven't discussed."

"The club?"

"The lifestyle in general."

"I didn't know you're into that sort of thing?"

"I went to the club with Alex a few times. Long before he met you."

"And?"

"There were some interesting things."

"Makes sense. You are the bossy dominant type," I say jokingly.

"True." He smiles, and his grey eyes light up. "I do like to take charge—in the bedroom. But a Dominant I am not." The smile falls from his face. "Is that something you want again?"

"No," I say without hesitation. "What Alex and I had was special. A once-in-a-lifetime experience. Submitting to him was natural—most of the time." I grin. "But I don't want that with another man."

Viktor lets out a relieved breath. "I'm glad to hear that."

"Did you find anything new?" I ask as I return to loading the dishwasher.

"No," he growls. "And it's starting to get frustrating."

"You'll find it. Don't give up."

"There's no chance of that. I won't rest until the person who did this breathes their last breath."

Viktor

they're starting to shift. Almost like she's beginning to give us a chance. At least I hope I'm not reading more into things than is really there.

Valentine's Day is next week. I want to do something, but I don't know what. Unfortunately, relationships aren't exactly my area of expertise. Sure, I know how to please a woman in the bedroom, but I never cared about the whole romance thing until now.

I need advice, but men in my line of work don't have a long list of friends. Dimitri isn't even a consideration. He's a fuck 'em and leave 'em before the sun comes up kinda guy. Maxim always gives good advice. He and his wife have been together forever, but I feel uncomfortable calling my boss to ask for relationship advice.

"Shit." I pace back and forth in my office. Then it occurs to me—Brandon. "He spends a lot of time with Natalie. Maybe he can help."

I pull up his contact and tap the green button on the screen. The line rings several times, and I think he isn't going to pick up. I'm just about to disconnect.

"Hello?"

"Brandon. It's Viktor." I feel like a nervous schoolboy.

"Are Natalie and Rose okay?"

"They're fine."

"I got worried when I saw you come up on the caller ID." He lets out a deep breath.

"I didn't think you were going to answer."

"I was in a meeting. I had to excuse myself from the room."

I didn't stop to think about the time. It's the middle of the afternoon on a Thursday. He's at work, and I'm calling him with my dating issues.

"I'm sorry. I'll let you go."

"No. I'm good now."

There's a long and very awkward pause.

"Are you going to tell me why you called?"

"Well, Valentine's Day is next week."

"Did you forget my address to send me flowers?" Brandon asks.

He's being a smart ass, and I'm ready to hang up on him. But Natalie already told me Brandon supports us being together. I need to get over myself and just ask.

"I want to do something for Natalie—a date. But I don't know what to do."

Brandon laughs. "That's what all this is about?"

"Forget it. I'll figure it out myself."

"No. Don't hang up," Brandon says. "What are you thinking?"

I sink into the leather chair across from my desk. "I want to do something special for her—for us."

"Take her out to dinner."

"She won't leave the baby with a sitter," I explain. "I think she's scared to let Rose out of her sight."

"That's understandable. Why don't you wait until Rose is in bed for the evening and cook dinner for her? You know, flowers, romantic music, and candlelight. All the romantic stuff that girls love."

"Do you think she'd like that? Is it enough?"

"Natalie doesn't expect expensive gifts. She's not high maintenance like that."

Brandon's right. Natalie's the least high-maintenance woman I've ever met. The smallest thing, as long as it comes from the heart, makes her smile. Regardless, I still want to give her the world. She deserves nothing less.

"I think that's what I'll do. Thanks for the help."

He's still talking when I disconnect the call.

Wednesday was Valentine's Day. I didn't want Natalie to feel pressured, so I decided to wait until the weekend for our *date*. It's a lazy Saturday morning. We're still lying in bed while Natalie nurses Rose.

"I have to run a few errands today. Will you be okay here?"

This is the first time I'll be leaving her here alone. I'm apprehensive, to say the least.

"I'll get dressed quick. Rose and I can come too."

"There's a few things I need to do on my own."

"Oh, Okay." Disappointment flashes across her face, but she quickly masks it. "I have a few loads of laundry to do, so it's probably better I stay home."

"Great." Knowing I don't have time to waste, I hop out of bed, grab some clothes, and go into the bathroom for a quick shower. There's a lot I need to get done for tonight.

When I come back out, Natalie's just getting out of bed. A content Rose in her arms. I kiss Rose's forehead and then Natalie's. "I'll see you girls later."

"Don't you want breakfast before you go?"
"I'll grab something while I'm out."

<h1 style="text-align:center">Natalie</h1>

VIKTOR'S ACTING WEIRD TODAY. IT'S NOT LIKE HIM TO GO WITHOUT breakfast or leave me home alone. I wish I knew what was going on. "Well, Miss Rose. It looks like it's just you and me today." She rewards me with a smile, something new she started doing this week. Then, I buckle her into her baby seat in the kitchen so I can keep an eye on her while I make breakfast.

I'm in the middle of cooking when my phone starts ringing. Mistress Star's picture comes up on my screen. She's called every day this week. I slide my finger across the screen, sending her call to voicemail again. Hopefully, she'll get the hint and stop calling. The friends I had from Fire and Ice are reminders of what Alex and I shared. That's over now. I've moved on.

I manage to eat and shower before Rose demands to be fed again. While I'm sitting on the couch nursing her, I get a text.

Viktor: I made plans for us tonight—8 p.m.

Me: Plans?

Viktor: Yes. It's a formal event.

Me: A formal event? You know I'm not ready to leave the baby.

Viktor: We aren't leaving the house. Rose should be in bed by then. Be dressed and ready. I'll meet you in the dining room.

Me: What's going on?

Viktor: I'll see you tonight. Oh, and don't cook. I've got it covered.

He'll meet me in the dining room? And he's handling dinner? Other than him using the microwave, I don't think I've ever seen him cook.

"Looks like Viktor's planning a surprise tonight," I say to Rose, who's currently fighting to keep her eyes open. "He's a good man, and he loves us both. I need to learn how to love him back."

When Rose finishes nursing, I put her in the portable playpen for her nap. Viktor keeps telling me she'll have to sleep in her crib at some point. But that's in her nursery, and I've been unable to go there. I've been silently questioning if I should look for a new apartment—one with no memories.

My phone, which I left on the couch, starts ringing. "This better not be Star again." When I look at the screen, I see it's Yekaterina. I go to connect the call, but she's already hung up. Quickly, I call her back.

"Hello, Natalie," she says as the video call pops up on my screen.

"I'm sorry I missed your call. I just put Rose for a nap, and honestly, I forgot about our session today."

She asks how Rose is doing, and we chat briefly about the ups and downs of having a newborn. Yekaterina has a few children of her own and always has excellent advice.

"Is she sleeping through the night yet?"

"Not really, but it doesn't matter. I'm not sleeping through the night either."

"Are you still having those dreams?"

"Almost every night." I sigh. "Why is this happening?"

"Why do you think it's happening?" She always asks my opinion before offering her own. It can be frustrating, but I know that's how therapy works.

"Because I'm not ready to let go of Alex," I say honestly. "I know he's gone—"

"I hear a but there."

I hesitate before answering, "But something deep in my heart refuses to let him go. I can't explain what it is. Does that make sense?"

"It does. But I have a different take on your dreams. An angle you might not have considered."

"What is it?"

"You tell me that you're reaching out to Viktor during these dreams, correct?"

"Yes. And it's making things awkward. On my end, at least. I'm sure on his too, but Viktor and I don't talk about them once morning comes."

"Have you stopped to consider that maybe your heart is telling you it's time to move on? That it's time to accept what Viktor's offering you?"

I'm stunned by her words. How can dreams about my husband mean I'm ready to move on? "My dreams are about Alex, not Viktor," I remind her.

"I understand it's Alex you see in your dreams, but I think there's more to it than what meets the eye." She stops, allowing me time to think about her words. "Are you ready to explore what's trying to blossom between you and Viktor?"

Am I ready? "I don't know if I'll ever be ready." Do I tell her about tonight? I decide I should. "He's planning some sort of date for us tonight."

Yekaterina smiles. "Consider this the push you need to take that leap of faith. Give him a chance."

"I don't know." There's something I can't explain that's holding me back.

"Natalie, Alex has already given you permission to move on. If you can't do it for yourself, at least do it to honor his last wish. You never know what might happen."

The rest of the afternoon goes by slowly. Viktor hasn't come back yet, so it's just Rose and me. The laundry and dishes are all caught up, and now I find myself sitting in the way-too-silent house. My mind is replaying my session with Yekaterina. *Are you ready to explore what's blossoming between you and Viktor? You need to take that leap of faith. Give him a chance.*

In my head, I know she's right. I think even my heart knows it. Somehow, I have to ignore that quiet little voice in my head that's trying to hold me back. Our date tonight might be the perfect time to do just that.

I bathe Rose and get her into her soft, warm jammies before nursing her for the last time. She should sleep for a good five or six hours.

Viktor: Don't come out until exactly 8-ok?

Me: Whatever you say, boss.

Viktor: Holy shit, she does know how to follow orders. LOL

His comment makes me laugh. I set my phone down and go into the closet, searching for something appropriate for an official first date.

I've decided on a short red dress and black heels. My blonde curls hang softly down my back, and I even put some makeup on. It's the first time I feel like a put-together adult in months.

My phone says it's time. I leave the primary bedroom and am hit with incredible smells coming from the kitchen. My stomach grumbles in response, and I realize I haven't eaten since breakfast. I stop to peek in our bedroom to check on Rose, who's sleeping soundly.

Then, I take a deep breath and meet Viktor for our first date.

Viktor

"*Babusya*, can you please tell me how you make your *Shashlik?*" I beg the woman as I walk through the market to get tonight's dinner ingredients.

"I do not give that recipe to anyone."

Somehow, I have to get it from her. It's the Ukrainian part of my surf and turf plan.

"What do you need it for, *onuk*? You do not cook." Little does she know I'm quite a good cook, but I don't put any effort into it when it's just for me. "I'm cooking dinner for someone tonight." I hesitate. "Like a date."

"A woman?" my grandma asks. "I do not hear from you for months, and then you call for my secret recipe. And there is a woman now. How did you meet?"

"It's a long and complicated story, *Babusya*."

"When will I meet this woman?"

"I don't know." Natalie and I haven't talked about my family. She knows nothing about my past. "Can I please have the recipe?"

"If you promise to come to visit and bring your woman."

"As soon as we can, I promise."

She tells me all the ingredients and directions for how to cook a dish she's famous in her village for. After I've gotten everything for dinner, I stop by another small shop to get candles. My last stop is the florist on the corner for a bouquet of flowers. I decide on a mix of soft pink and ivory roses and peonies. Hopefully, she'll like it.

As much as I hate leaving her alone all day, there's no way I can cook dinner at home and still surprise her, so instead, I stay downstairs in my old apartment to do all the prep work and cooking. Once everything's done, I throw the oven on warm and take a quick shower. I told her it was a formal occasion, so I pull out a pair of black dress pants and a dark blue button-down shirt. I still have to get everything upstairs and set the table. Only a half-hour to go. I send Natalie a text making sure she doesn't come out early. I don't want to ruin the surprise.

By the clicks of her footsteps, I'm almost certain she's wearing heels. Damn. I wasn't sure she'd take me seriously, but she did. I slide my hands into my pockets so she doesn't see how much they're shaking. When she comes around the corner and sees the dining room, she lets out a small gasp. The lights are dim, and candles are placed around the room and on the table.

"These are for you." I hand her the fragrant bouquet.

"They're beautiful, thank you."

"You look stunning." She's in a red dress that shows off her incredible body.

Natalie blushes. "Thank you. I should get these in water."

"I'll take care of it. Go sit down. Dinner's ready."

I take her to the dining room and pull out her chair. "Would you like some wine?" I made sure to get her favorite, a sweet rosé.

"Yes, please."

After pouring our glasses, I go to the kitchen and get our food. Returning to the dining room, I set our plates down and sit across from her.

"I didn't know you could cook."

"I've never had a reason to until now."

She takes a bite of the Ukrainian meat dish. Her eyes close, and a quiet moan escapes. My usual self-control is not functioning tonight, and my body reacts to the sensual sound.

"This is delicious, Viktor."

We eat our meals without our usual conversation. I think we're both nervous. Trying to break the ice, I ask about her day. She tells me how boring it was by herself.

When we've finished, I clear the plates. "There's Baklava for dessert."

"You made dessert too?" She raises her eyebrow in disbelief.

"Actually, no. That I got from the bakery." I smile.

"I would love some, but maybe in a little bit. I'm full right now."

I leave the dishes in the sink—I'll get to them later. Then, pulling out my cell phone, I find my playlist and put on Eric Clapton's *Wonderful Tonight*.

"May I have this dance?"

She places her hand in mine. "You may."

We sway to the music. At first, our movements are stiff, but soon Natalie relaxes and allows me to hold her close while she rests her head on my chest. I close my eyes, savoring the feel of her body against mine. It feels like heaven.

When she lifts her head, her green eyes are full of tenderness. No longer able to resist, my lips meet hers. The elevator dings, interrupting our kiss. I grab the gun from my waistband, the doors open, and I push Natalie behind me.

"Natalie, are you here?" A female voice calls.

"Star? What are you doing here?" Natalie asks.

Star looks around the room. "I'm sorry. It looks like I've interrupted something."

"You think?" I replace my gun and shut the music off, aggravated by her intrusion. "How did you get in?"

"Alex gave me the code a long time ago," she explains. "I tried calling, but my calls keep going to voicemail. So, I got desperate and came over. But I see you're busy. I can come back."

Mental note—change the elevator code.

"It's fine." Natalie adjusts her dress. "We were just having dinner."

"It looks like you were doing more than having dinner," Star says with a smile.

"*Were* being the keyword," I grumble. Everything was perfect until Star crashed our date. "I have some work to do downstairs. I'll let you two talk."

"You don't have to leave." Natalie grabs my arm.

"I'll be back later." I smile but only give it a half-hearted effort.

I know I must look like a spoiled little boy stalking off in a tantrum. But I don't care because that's precisely what I'm doing.

Natalie

Viktor's clearly upset by our unexpected company. We were having a good time, but maybe Star's interruption is for the best. I turn the lights back up.

"You've been ignoring my calls," Star says.

"I'm sorry. I've been busy with the baby." I make up an excuse.

"Mhm." I know she sees—right through me and my excuses. "Can we talk?"

We sit on opposite ends of the couch. My nerves are on edge, and I bite my nails.

"Natalie." She motions to my hand.

"Sorry. Old habit."

Her expression softens. "I'm sorry I interrupted your evening. Brandon told me Viktor was planning a Valentine's date, but I assumed it was on Valentine's Day, not three days after."

"Brandon knew about this?"

"Viktor called him for advice on what to do."

I'm surprised to hear that Viktor called Brandon. "It's not what it looks like," I try to explain. "We were just—"

Star holds up her hand, stopping me mid-sentence. "There's no need to explain. You and Viktor are adults."

I look down at my hands in my lap. "Viktor kissed me, and I let him." Guilt is eating away at me. "I feel like I'm betraying Alex. Like I'm cheating on him."

"Oh, honey. You're doing no such thing. You know, I was once where you are now."

I don't know much about Star's past, but she begins to tell me that she had a longtime submissive named Jeremy.

"He and I met when we were way too young to be doing the things we were doing," she chuckles. "We were barely seventeen, but we both knew what we wanted." She explains they were together for fifteen years as Domme/sub. "Jeremy was my everything, and I was his."

"What happened?"

"We were returning from vacation and were hit by a drunk driver." Her eyes fill with tears. "I walked away with only some bumps and bruises, but Jeremy didn't make it."

My tears fall as I listen to the ache still present in her voice. "I had no idea. I'm so sorry."

"That was nearly twenty years ago now, but sometimes the pain hurts like it was yesterday." She dabs at the tears in the corner of her eyes. "I've wanted to talk to you because I know what it feels like to lose the love of your life."

Now I feel terrible for ignoring her. I thought she was trying to get me to go to the club, but all this time, she only wanted to share her story with me. She wanted to help me.

"I'm sorry for ignoring you. It was selfish of me."

"Trying to deal with grief does not make a person selfish."

"How did you move on? When did you know it was okay?"

"My situation was a bit different than yours." She tells me Brandon filled her in on Alex's wishes for Viktor and me. "Jeremy and I never married. He was collared, but we weren't interested in marriage and children. But it still took several years before I was ready to move on."

"I knew it. This between Viktor and me is going too fast."

"No, it isn't. Not if it's what you both want."

Star tells me that she never considered life without Jeremy. Much like Alex and me, they were young. Discussing their mortality didn't seem important at the time.

"Alex was always overprepared. He thought about and planned for things the rest of us would never have considered. But in this case, it was a good thing. Natalie, you know what Alex's wishes were for you if something happened to him. That's supposed to bring you peace."

"I wish it brought me peace." I kick off my heels and slump down on the couch. "I know what Alex asked, but I don't know how to do it. I don't know what it's supposed to look like." I turn my head to look at her. "How did you know when it was time?"

Her story explains her strength today. She joined a group for people who lost their partners and found healing there. "I also had the whole BDSM community at Fire and Ice to lean on," she says. "At first, I felt like I'd be betraying Jeremy if I played with another sub. I had to give myself permission to move on. In my case, I decided I didn't want to look for a long-term collared relationship." She looks off into the distance before returning her focus to me. "What Jeremy and I shared can never be replaced. I'm comfortable having fun playing with different subs. It's filled the void Jeremy left behind, and I'm at peace with it."

I think about what she said.

"How you choose to move forward is up to you. There's no right or wrong," she adds.

"I can't see myself playing the field," I giggle.

"And you don't have to."

"I also don't see myself in the lifestyle anymore. That was something I could only share with Alex."

"And that's okay too—no right or wrong, remember?"

"Viktor's a good man. He cares about me, and he adores Rose. I know we could be happy together."

"Yes, I agree with all that," she says. "So, where are you getting stuck?"

It's that quiet feeling I have. But how do I explain that to Star when I can't figure out how to put it into words myself. "Fear of making the wrong choice. Fear of judgment."

"Natalie." She leans forward once again. "What I'm about to say will sound harsh, but I need you to look at me and hear me out."

I raise my eyes to meet hers.

"Alex is dead. He isn't coming back." She's right—her words sting. "There's a man downstairs who loves you and your daughter. A man, your husband, gave his blessing for you to love. Forget about anyone else's opinions. The only people who matter are Viktor and you. I know you care about him. Accept the love he wants to give you and allow it to grow."

Rose's crying interrupts our conversation.

"I have to go get her. I'll be right back."

I return with the baby in my arms. It's the first time Star's seeing her.

"She looks like her daddy." Star reaches out and touches Rose's hand. "She's so tiny."

"Would you like to hold her?"

"No, thank you. Babies are nice from a distance, but that's where I draw the line." She stands. "It's late, and I've already taken enough of your time."

I walk Star to the elevator. "Please apologize to Viktor again for me and think about what I said. It's okay for you to love again."

Natalie

WITH SPRING IN FULL BLOOM, THE THREE OF US ARE SPENDING MORE time outdoors. We enjoy our daily walks to a pretty little park with a playground and a green grassy area. My favorite spot is a secluded area with a bench overlooking the water. We've just returned from our walk, and Viktor's on a call with Max. He's bouncing Rose gently on his knee while she babbles away. I think she's mimicking him talking on the phone.

"Thank you, Max. We couldn't have done it without your help."

The Jelena's Hope-NYC project has been on hold since the explosion. The city wouldn't let us move forward with anything until the damage was repaired. Our problem—no contractor wanted to touch the project, and who could blame them? Someone murdered my husband and still hasn't been arrested. I wouldn't be jumping at the chance to take a job with us either.

Viktor finally hangs up. "Maxim and Nicholai called in some favors. There'll be someone there tomorrow to do the repairs. They should be complete in about three weeks."

"That's such a relief. I didn't think we'd ever get it done." I hesitate, afraid to ask. "Have they found anything yet?"

"No, nothing. But we're not giving up. With time comes complacency. Someone will mess up, and then we'll make a move."

It's not the answer I want to hear, but it's the one I have to accept. With each passing day, I fear that instead of getting closer to finding Alex's killer, we're moving further away, and we'll never find the responsible person.

"Did you hear from the trainers?" Viktor asks.

"Yes," I turn my laptop so Viktor can see it.

He pulls his chair closer, putting the keyboard within grabbing distance of the baby. Her tiny fingers go straight for the keys.

"Here," Viktor hands her his cell phone. "You can play with this instead."

I shake my head, knowing that the phone is going to end up thrown on the floor within the next thirty seconds.

"The last set of houseparents are in their final few weeks of training. Imani has been in touch with them and is redesigning their suite."

"What about the other staff positions?"

"It looks like they've finally been filled. But we still have a few months before the staff will be fully trained."

"That's okay. We can't move forward until the repairs are made." He holds Rose in the air in front of him while he finishes talking. "The city is being difficult with giving us the permits and licenses." Rose giggles and reaches for his face. "They want a reinspection before they'll allow us to open."

"I understand why they're being extra cautious, but it doesn't make waiting any easier."

The next few weeks keep us busy. Viktor spends most of his time running back and forth between the apartment and Jelena's Hope-NYC. With whoever did this still on the loose, extra security's been hired for our floors. Viktor's doing everything in his power to ensure we don't have any further issues.

Rose and I are playing on the floor when Viktor texts he's coming home. She's so strong. She's holding onto my hands and standing.

"Did you hear that, princess? Viktor's on his way home."

"Fi," she babbles.

Viktor swears she's saying his name and brags that he is her first word.

"Mama," I say, smiling. "You need to say, mama." Rose giggles in response.

She's closing in on six months now and is full of personality. As much as I'm upset the opening of Jelena's Hope-NYC has been postponed, I'm also thankful that I've had all this time with her.

"When Viktor gets home, you get to try your first taste of baby cereal," I say in a sing-song voice.

"Did someone mention food?"

Startled, I pull Rose close to me. The abrupt action makes her cry. "I didn't hear you come in."

"I'm sorry. I didn't mean to scare you." He puts his arms out to take Rose, and she reaches up to him.

"Fi. Fi."

"*Ochen' khoroshiy, printessa,*" he says, smiling proudly.

I stand up and roll my eyes. "She's just making random noises. She's not saying your name." I walk into the kitchen to prepare her cereal.

"I think Mama's jealous. But that's okay." Viktor buckles her into her highchair. "You'll say mama soon." He kisses her forehead.

I bring the food bowl over to him. "Do you want to feed her?"

"I don't know how," he says. "Don't you want to be the first to feed her?"

"I'll take pictures while you do it." I love doing things with her, but I also love watching her and Viktor together. They share a very special bond. Besides, I have something I need to discuss with him.

Viktor

Last night I woke up with Natalie kissing me and trying to free my hard dick from my boxers. Everything in me wanted to let her continue, but I knew she wasn't aware. Didn't realize it was me she was touching. When I took her hand and removed it, she began to cry. She didn't understand why I wouldn't let her touch me.

"Don't you want me anymore?" she asked through tears.

"You have no idea how much I want you."

"Then take me, please take me."

Her eyes may have been open, but she was clearly talking in her sleep, and I didn't have the heart to wake her.

"Let's sleep for a little bit while the baby sleeps." I placed a gentle kiss on her lips. "We'll be together later."

And just like that, she curled against me and fell asleep. I lay awake, my self-control fraying. I want this woman, but I need her to be fully aware of who she's with when we're together. *I hope that day comes soon* is my last thought before I allow myself to fall back to sleep.

Alex's birthday would've been today, June eleventh. A few weeks ago, Natalie suggested we make a sizable donation to the Susan G. Komen Foundation in Alex's name to pay homage to him and his mom, who passed away from breast cancer.

Today, I have my own tribute to Alex that Natalie doesn't know about. She's in the living room on the floor with Rose. Lana's on video chat.

"Hey," I peek my head around the corner. "Can I steal you and Rose for a little bit?"

"Lana, I have to go. I'll call you tomorrow."

Svetlana says goodbye to Natalie but oddly ignores Rose before disconnecting the call.

"What's up?" Natalie asks.

"It's beautiful outside. Let's go for a walk."

"Do we have to?"

She's been quiet today. I know she's struggling.

"Yes, we do." I pick up Rose. "Tell Mama you want to go for a walk"

Rose kicks her legs and makes a bunch of happy sounds as though she's trying to talk.

"See, Rose wants to go for a walk."

With Rose buckled into her pram, we head out toward the park. The closer we get, the slower Natalie moves. "Viktor, I'm really not up for this today."

"Do you trust me?"

"Yes."

"Then come on." I continue walking past the playground full of laughing children and follow the path around the back of the building to where Natalie and I often come to sit.

"Viktor," she whispers.

I got permission from the city to have a Japanese Maple Tree planted near the bench we visit. Natalie walks closer and reads the plaque installed in front of the tree. *In loving memory of Alexander Montgomery- beloved husband and father*

"Did you do this?"

"I did. I hope it's okay."

She rests her head on my chest as tears stream down her face. "It's perfect, Viktor. Alex would've loved it."

I take Rose from the stroller and bring her to the tree, letting her touch it while I tell her stories about her daddy. Natalie sits quietly on the bench as she stares out over the water. Rose and I join Natalie. I put my arm around her, and she moves closer, resting her head on my shoulder. Rose reaches out, playing with her mama's face and giving her a baby's version of a kiss.

Together, we pay silent respect to Alex.

Natalie

Jelena's Hope-NYC's grand opening was supposed to be right after New Year's. But between Alex's death, Rose's early arrival, and all the complications with the construction, it was postponed. Actually, I doubted it would ever happen. It may be seven months late, but the grand opening is set for this weekend.

"Max and Irina will be here tomorrow," Viktor informs me

"Is Lana coming too?" I haven't talked to her in a few weeks. She's been avoiding everyone.

"Unfortunately, no. She's staying back with Amelia."

"Oh." My shoulders sag in disappointment.

"I'd like to take you to dinner before the ceremony?"

Lately, there's been a noticeable shift in our relationship. We're beginning to act like a couple. Despite my reservations about the right time to move on, I'm starting to let myself care about Viktor as more than a friend. Looking at it from the outside, our relationship probably seems unusual. We live together, sleep together, and are raising a baby together. But, except for the sexual advances I make while I'm dreaming about Alex, we haven't taken our relationship to the next level.

He's a man, and he can only take so much. I'm sure it's wearing on him. It's a topic Yekaterina and I discuss at every session. I'm working on building up the courage to take that next step.

"I think I'd like that."

"Really?" He looks surprised.

"Really. As long as you don't mind a baby tagging along?"

"If you're okay with it, Max and Irina offered to keep Rose while we go out. They'll bring her to the center and meet us there."

I've not been away from her at all since she was born. My belief, although erroneous, is as long as I'm with her, nothing bad can happen—another thing Yekaterina and I are working on.

Viktor waits for my answer, his face full of hope. Outside of Viktor and myself, if anyone will keep Rose safe, it's Max and Irina.

"Okay."

"Okay? You're saying yes?"

"I'm saying yes."

He lifts me off my feet and spins me around. "Thank you." He stops and slides me down until my feet touch the floor. His erection presses my body as he leans down to kiss me. The kiss starts tender. Viktor's hands move up my body and tangle in my hair as the kiss turns more demanding. Rose's cry interrupts us.

I step back, breathless from the kiss. Viktor's eyes don't leave mine. It's like we're frozen in time. Until Rose grabs onto his leg. He bends down to pick her up while I stay frozen, stunned by the moment we've just shared.

Viktor

MAX AND IRINA ARRIVED YESTERDAY. THEY'VE BEEN NOTHING BUT doting grandparents since the second they walked in, even insisting on moving her playpen into their guest room so they could get up with her during the night.

Rose was sleeping through the night, but she's getting a couple of new teeth, which is wreaking havoc on her sleep schedule. When they offered, I gladly took them up on it. It's the first full night's sleep we've had the past month—something Natalie and I desperately needed.

Max and I are downstairs in the office reviewing the video footage Dimitri sent. We finally got a small break. Dimitri got his hands on some brand-new technology to find an almost imperceptible anomaly in the video. Minutes before the explosion, the video goes off the live feed to a recording of Alex walking to his car and then back to a live feed just as the car explodes. I'm furious we've missed it for so long, but it explains why we've found nothing on the video. But other than that, we're still coming up empty-handed.

"Why do we keep hitting dead ends?" I slam my fists on the desk.

"Sometimes, we have to wait these things out," Max says calmly. "This is proof that, given time, mistakes will be discovered, and we will find who is responsible. Alex's murder will not go unpunished."

"It's taking too long."

"Patience, Viktor." Max checks his watch. "Do you not have dinner plans?"

I look at the time. "Shit." I'm going to be late.

Maxim laughs. "Go, get changed. Tonight is a big night."

Natalie has to feed Rose one last time before we leave, so she's running more behind than I am. I showered and dressed in my black suit. Now, I'm pacing back and forth in front of the windows in the living room, waiting for Natalie to come out.

I finally hear the click of heels from the hallway. When I turn around, it feels like I've been punched in the gut and can't take my next breath. Natalie stops across the room from me. She's wearing a knee-length black dress that sits off the shoulder.

I take a few steps toward her. "You look breathtaking."

"Thank you." She blushes.

"Are you ready to go?"

"I want to say goodbye to Rose first. Irina's in the nursery, changing her. She'll be right out." Her eyes roam my body. "You look amazing."

Irina interrupts us, and I quickly step away toward the windows to allow my arousal to subside while Natalie says goodbye to Rose.

"Mama's going to miss you, sweet baby."

"Tell Mama you'll see her in a few hours," Irina says, half to Rose and half to Natalie.

"You know where the breast milk and bottles are, right?"

"Yes."

"I already packed the diaper bag. You know how to use the car seat?"

"Yes," Irina answers patiently.

"The list of emergency numbers is hanging on the fridge."

"Natalie, breathe. Maxim and I have everything under control. Don't worry about us. Go with Viktor and have fun."

"Sorry." Natalie shrugs. "This is all new."

With my body back under control, I return to Natalie's side and kiss Rose. "Be a good girl for *Babushka, printessa.*"

Rose kicks her legs and blows bubbles.

"We have our phones if you need us," I add. "We'll see you at the grand opening."

I found a little Asian fusion restaurant for dinner. We're seated in a quiet corner, which allows us privacy to talk.

"I'm nervous about tonight," she says.

"That's to be expected. There's been a lot mixed up in this, and tonight's a huge step. One I know Alex would be proud of."

"Yes, I know he would. This project meant so much to him."

Our food is served, and it looks delicious. While we eat, we continue our conversation.

"Are you sure we have enough security?"

"Dimitri and his team have set up surveillance inside and outside the building. Misha will be accompanying Max, Irina, and the baby. The rest of the security team is already in place." I take her hand from across the table. "We'll be safe."

"Okay." She doesn't seem convinced. "But we still have no idea who's behind Alex's death. Do you think it's connected to what happened with Moreno?"

"I wish I had that answer." I wish that with everything in me, but the truth is, other than finding the security footage tampered with, we're no closer today than we were several months ago. "I promise, I won't give up until I find who's responsible and make sure they pay."

Natalie

Dinner was delicious. I don't know how Viktor found this place, but it was perfect. It was, however, the quiet before the storm.

Outside the Jelena's Hope-NYC building is a rather large press gathering. People make their way down the sidewalk while cameras flash and reporters thrust microphones at them, trying to get someone to answer their questions. It looks like a circus.

"Good thing we're not going in that way," Viktor mutters.

"They aren't all going to be upstairs, are they?" I ask, panicked.

"Several journalists have been vetted and given admittance. The rest will remain outside," he reassures me. "I'm not taking any chances. One of my men has the approved guest list and is stationed at the door. The only people getting in tonight are the ones on his list."

I know Viktor and Maxim are more than capable of keeping the event tonight safe. I'm attempting to take calming breaths, reminding myself to trust Viktor's plan.

When we pull into the underground parking, the anxious feelings return. Over the past few months, I've been here several times. Although the damage from the explosion has been repaired, it does little to erase the memories. I know where Alex's car was parked. I know the exact spot where my husband took his final breath. I don't know if I'll ever be able to come in here without feeling the suffocating sadness.

It takes all my willpower to push those feelings aside because tonight is an important night. I need to be strong—for Alex.

"Public speaking was Alex's thing, not mine," I say to Viktor while we ride up in the elevator.

"I'll be by your side every second."

He takes my hand and laces his fingers with mine. Together, we step out of the elevator into the lobby, already teeming with people. My heart begins to beat faster, and my anxiety level quickly rises. I squeeze Viktor's hand tighter as I look around, trying to find Max and Irina. I need to see my little girl.

"Do you see them?"

Viktor looks around, easily able to see over the people's heads. "Irina's behind the reception desk with the baby."

When Rose sees me coming, she reaches her arms out. I take her and snuggle her close. "Mama missed you so much," I say between kisses.

"She was a perfect angel," Irina beams. "How was dinner?

"It was very nice."

"*Printessa*." Viktor leans in to kiss Rose.

Rose's eyes meet Viktor's. "Fik," she says and rewards him with her beautiful smile.

"May I?" He reaches out to take her, holding her close to his chest. "I missed you very much. I love you, *printessa*." Viktor whispers.

Rose grabs his face.

"She loves you too."

It's time for the grand opening ceremony to begin. Viktor, Maxim, and I are standing in front of the reception desk, the Jelena's Hope-NYC logo on the wall behind us. Irina is behind the desk, holding Rose. Misha's stationed next to them. In front of us is a room full of journalists, Jelena's Hope-NYC staff members, Steve and his crew, and public figures—some I recognize, others I don't. I know mixed in with the crowd are some undercover men as well.

Maxim calls the room to order and then turns it over to me.

"First, I'd like to thank all of you for joining us tonight to celebrate the grand opening of Jelena's Hope-NYC. This mission was born out of tragedy when Maxim and Irina's daughter, Jelena, was stolen and sold by human traffickers. Sadly, they weren't able to find her in time. Since then, they've taken their tragedy and have done something incredible for those who are recovered. Their efforts ensure recovered persons have access to everything they'll need to fully recover and rejoin society."

I look over my shoulder to Viktor, who takes a step closer to me before returning my attention to the room. "As many of you know, a few months ago, I lost my husband." I pause, swallowing over the lump in my throat. Viktor places his hand on my arm for support, and I cover it with my own.

There's movement in the back of the room that catches my attention. A man with almost shoulder-length dark blond hair sidles up next to Steve. They shake hands, and then the man turns in my direction. When his eyes meet mine, he smiles. Goosebumps cover my body, and I quickly break eye contact. It takes a moment to shake off the uneasy feeling and continue speaking.

"Jelena's Hope-NYC was a project that was near to his heart. My husband wanted his part in the fight against human trafficking to be more than only words. He wanted to transform those words into action." A tear slips down my face, and I look up. "I wish he were here in person to share this moment, but I know he's watching over us."

Maxim steps forward and hugs me. "Thank you, Natalia."

I nod and take a step back. Viktor puts his arm around me for support while Maxim speaks to the crowd.

"What's wrong?" Viktor whispers.

"A man came in. He's standing by Steve. They look like they know each other. But there was something unsettling with how he looked right at me and smiled."

"What does he look like?"

"He has long blond hair. He's right—" I look in the back corner. "That's odd. He's not there anymore."

When all the speeches are through, Viktor disappears. I stay with Maxim and speak to a few government officials pledging their support to Jelena's Hope-NYC.

After what seems like forever, the evening finally begins to wind down. The last of our guests have just left. So now, only us and our intake staff are sitting in the lobby. Maxim's briefing them on a small trafficking ring raided two days ago in southern California. Our first clients are currently en route and are expected to arrive tomorrow.

I'm sitting on the couch nursing Rose when the elevator opens, and Viktor steps out. His tie hangs loose, the first few buttons of his dress shirt undone. My mouth hangs open at the sight of him before I catch myself.

"Where did you disappear to?" I ask.

"I was checking the identity of that guest. He's one of Steve's guys."

"I thought we met all of his employees. He must be new."

"Are you ready to head home?"

"Do you think we should wait for Max?"

"He'll be a while with the staff." Viktor reaches out to take Rose, who's fallen asleep. "I'd like to get you girls home. It's been a long night. And there's something we need to talk about."

"What's wrong?"

"Nothing's wrong. I don't want to discuss it here."

I can't imagine what's going on and why Viktor's being so secretive about it.

He carries Rose while we take the elevator to our car, where he buckles the sleeping baby into her car seat. I slide into the passenger seat and wait for Viktor to get in. He's tense as he pulls the car onto the still-congested Manhattan streets.

Viktor

The tension in the car is nearly suffocating. The drive home takes forever between the traffic and these damn red lights. I've been keeping something from Natalie that I was hoping to wait and discuss at home. But the longer I wait, the worse it's going to be. It's time to come clean.

"We're taking a trip. We leave in the morning." I spit the words out quickly.

Natalie's head whips around to look at me. "We're what?"

I take a deep breath and let out a long sigh. "Your mom called me last week."

"Oh?"

"She's worried about you. They both are." I glance at her before returning my eyes to the road. "Rose is almost eight months old. It's time she meets her grandparents."

"We've video chatted." Natalie's voice is clipped.

When Charlotte called last week, she was beside herself. She explained that every time she asks Natalie about coming to visit, she tells them *soon* or *no*. The past few weeks, Natalie hasn't even answered their calls. She and Stanley are worried about her, and they want to meet their granddaughter in person. After speaking with Charlotte, I felt I had no choice but to take the actions I did.

"We have a flight tomorrow afternoon. We're going to Missouri to visit your family."

Natalie crosses her arms over her chest. "Don't you think I should've been a part of this decision?"

There's the feisty girl I've grown to love. I smile, and a laugh slips past my lips.

"What's so funny?" She pouts.

"I haven't seen this side of you in a while. I missed it."

She lowers her arms. "I don't want to go. I'm not ready to see them. And how do you suggest I explain us?"

"I don't know what to tell them either," I say, resting my hand gently on her arm.

"But we'll figure it out together. They need to meet Rose. She deserves to know her grandparents."

"I guess you're right. I wish you would've talked to me first, though."

"And you would've agreed to go?"

"Well, no." She laughs softly.

I pull the car into our spot and turn off the ignition but make no move to get out. I turn in my seat to face her. "Natalie, I love you."

"Viktor—"

"Let me finish, please. I don't expect you to say those words back, and I realize Alex put us in an uncomfortable situation. Maybe he had no right to ask me to take his place, but he did, and I accepted." I reach out and take her petite hand in mine. "Someday, I hope you might be able to return my love, but even if you never do, that's okay. I'll always be here for you and Rose. You'll always come first in my life." A lone tear drips down her face, and I wipe it with my thumb. "Don't cry, please."

"You've been my rock since Alex died. I don't know how I would've survived this without you." She looks in the back at the baby asleep in her car seat. "Alex is Rose's father, but you're the dad Rose will know and love." Natalie threads her fingers through mine. "I've been struggling to move forward. I haven't even tried to honor Alex's request, but I've been giving this," –She motions between us— "a lot of thought. It's time for me to start moving forward. I want to give us an honest try."

My heart beats faster hearing her words. Did she agree to try? I reach up and cup her face in my hand. She leans into my touch and closes her eyes. "I don't know what our path forward looks like. We can take it as slowly as you need. I'll wait for you forever if I have to."

When she opens her eyes, I feel her emerald-green gaze deep in my soul. "I do care about you, Viktor. We've been through so much together already. Hopefully, the worst of it's behind us," she says with a sad smile. "When my parents ask, what do I say? It feels weird to call you my boyfriend." She scrunches her nose.

"Let's not overthink it. We don't have to put a label on it. When they ask, because we both know they will, I trust we'll find the right words."

Rose interrupts our conversation with a loud wail from the backseat.

"I think that's our cue. Someone's hungry."

"I'll get her."

We get out of the car. While Natalie grabs the diaper bag, I unbuckle, lift our precious baby girl, and hold her close to my chest.

With my line of work, being a father was never even a blip on my radar, but now that I've been thrust into this role, I couldn't imagine my life any other way. I know I have big shoes to fill. Even though she hadn't been born yet, Alex loved this little baby I'm holding. The knowledge that he would've been a better father than I ever could be is hard to swallow, but I strive to be a little better each day—for Rose. Because my *printessa* deserves no less.

Natalie

Summer in Northmeadow is beautiful. I've always loved looking at the rolling mountains covered in their vibrant greenery—the forests teeming with life and the fields flowing with wildflowers. The picture is so clear in my mind I can almost smell their fragrance. The memories of last summer and how we celebrated our engagement resurface. Alex and I were so happy. We thought the worst was behind us. We had no idea what terrible things lay ahead for us. That before the year was over, there would be no us.

Viktor and I are in a rental car driving from the airport to the lake house to drop our stuff off. We told my parents we'd meet them at their home this evening for dinner. I'm glad for the short reprieve because I'm exhausted. I didn't sleep last night. Instead, I tossed and turned, trying to come up with answers to questions not yet asked. Viktor turns onto our gravel driveway, and I shoot straight up in my seat. My parent's car is parked in front of the house.

"What are they doing here?"

"I'm not sure. But it's okay," Viktor says calmly.

"It's not okay." I raise my voice.

Viktor grabs my hand, just the way Alex used to. "Natalie, breathe. I'm sure they couldn't wait to meet Rose. It's okay. We've got this."

The front door swings open just as Viktor turns off the ignition, and my mom runs down the pathway to our car. She opens my door before I even have a chance.

"I've missed you so much," she says as she pulls me from the car and into a hug. "I hope you don't mind. Dad and I opened the cottages and freshened them up for you." She releases me. "And we couldn't wait until tonight to meet our granddaughter."

Viktor walks around the car, the baby held protectively in his arms. My heart melts a little each time I see them together. He sees Rose as his daughter, and he's head over heels in love with her. She had him wrapped around her little finger from the moment she was born.

Mom walks over and tries to take Rose from his arms, but she wriggles away and starts crying. "Fik." She clings to Viktor.

"What did she just say?" Mom asks, appalled.

"She's too little to be able to say Viktor, so she calls him Fik."

"Well, that's not what it sounds like to me." She crosses her arms.

I don't understand the hostility already pulsing from her. It's as though we're back to square one. Where we were when Alex and I had first met.

"There's my little girl," Dad says, walking down the path with his cane.

"Daddy." I rush over and wrap my arms around him. Both happy to see him and equally as happy for the distraction. "I've missed you so much."

"Me too, sweetheart." He kisses my cheek. "Did I hear my granddaughter crying?"

"You did. She gets a little nervous around strangers. Give her a few minutes, and she'll be fine."

"Let's get you inside. You look exhausted." Dad offers his free arm, and I slide mine through it.

Viktor, who's still carrying Rose, and my mom follow us. Once we get inside, Viktor passes the baby to me.

"I'll go out and get our bags," Viktor says and walks out of the house, leaving me alone with my parents.

"Why don't we sit down," I say and make my way to the couch. When I'm seated, I place Rose on my lap and turn her to face my parents. "Rose, this is your grandma and grandpa. They couldn't wait to meet you."

Mom, who's sitting next to me, reaches out and takes Rose's hand in hers as she talks sweetly to her. "I couldn't wait to meet you in person, gorgeous girl." Rose rewards her with a grin that shows off her brand-new tooth. "Do you remember me? We talk on that camera. But now I finally get to see you and hold you." Mom looks at me. The earlier hostility seems to have faded, and I nod.

Again, she reaches out, and this time, Rose willingly goes to her. Mom holds her close as tears slide down her cheeks. "I can't believe I'm finally holding my granddaughter." She peppers her with kisses while Rose babbles and blows bubbles, eating up all the love being showered on her.

Viktor's taking forever outside. I'm sure he's trying to give my parents and me some time alone. But I know the questions will start soon, and I'd rather he be here with me when that happens. Thankfully, the door opens, and Viktor walks in, rolling our suitcases behind him. I look up and smile, relieved he's back. He returns my affection with his own, and I see the love reflected in his eyes. I'm sure my parents can see it too.

"I locked up the other cabin. I'm going to put these in our room." The words come out so naturally as he heads down the hall toward the primary bedroom.

Mom's eyes nearly bulge out as she lowers Rose to her lap. "Our room?"

I knew it was a matter of time, and now the time's up. Somehow, I have to explain our relationship, which is hard because we haven't even labeled it. We're not exactly dating, at least not in the traditional sense, but we're more than just friends. He loves me, and I'm learning to love him. We live together and sleep together but aren't sexually involved. We're in some weird, unclassified relationship that my husband prearranged before he died. How in the world do I explain that?

I haven't answered her question yet. I haven't been able to find the right words. Thankfully, the sound of Viktor's footsteps cuts through the uncomfortable silence. He sits next to me, unaware of the confrontation about to happen. I lean against him for support.

"Do you two care to explain what's going on? Why are *both* of your bags in Natalie's bedroom?" Mom snaps.

Viktor slides his arm around me. It's possessive and comforting. "Natalie and I are together."

"Together?" Dad asks. "What exactly does that mean?"

I look into Viktor's comforting grey eyes before steeling myself and turning back to my parents.

"Viktor and I are in a relationship. We're living together."

"Living together?" Mom quips. "Don't you understand what people will say about you?"

Once again, I feel like that young girl fighting to live on her terms. The insecurity that used to plague me comes back with a vengeance as I once again find myself sitting under my parents' scrutiny. The ingrained response of caving to their demands calls to me, but I fight against it.

Each breath gets harder to take, and I shrink back further against Viktor's body. Tension and anger hang heavy in the air. Since she was born, Rose has always seemed to be able to sense my emotions. She begins to fuss and reaches out for me. Taking her from my mom, I walk to the windows, whispering quietly in her ear.

"Stanley, we're leaving."

"Wait," Dad interrupts. "Maybe we should give them a chance to try to explain this."

"I'm not interested in hearing any explanations."

"Please, Mom, don't leave." I walk back toward them. "Let me try to explain it better."

"I always got the feeling that something was off with the two of you." She waves her hand between Viktor and me. "And I was correct. The minute your husband is out of the picture, you jump right into a relationship with *him*."

"There was nothing off about our relationship, Mrs. Clarke. I was an employee—Natalie's bodyguard. We spent a lot of time together and became friends. It was never more."

"Nothing more than a friend. Is that what you call sharing a bed these days?" Mom hastily walks to the door.

"Dad, please." He's always been the one I could make more headway with—the one who could talk Mom down.

He shakes his head. "I'd like to understand, sweetheart, but I'm struggling with this myself."

Viktor follows them out on their heels while I clutch Rose close to me. It feels like the past is repeating itself, and I'm about to lose my family all over again.

Viktor

Charlotte and Stanley hurry down the stone path from the cottage to their parked car. I didn't think when I said where I was putting our bags. If I'd just kept my mouth shut. I feel responsible for this situation and follow them out.

"Mr. and Mrs. Clarke, may I please have a moment before you leave?" I have to try to fix this.

Stanley gets in the passenger seat. He still tires easily but leaves the door open. Charlotte turns to face me, arms crossed.

"Natalie and I understand that our relationship comes as quite a shock. We realize it's unconventional. It's not something we would've ever done on our own. Alex should be the one here with his wife and baby, but the fact is he's gone. It's not been easy for Natalie these past few months." I pause, allowing myself a minute to find the right words for the next part.

"We probably should have explained all this sooner. Before the accident, Alex approached me. He wanted to ensure that Natalie and Rose would be cared for if anything ever happened to him. He asked me to step in, to be there in his place. He gave his blessing for whatever develops between Natalie and me."

"That's ridiculous. Why would Alex do such a thing?" Charlotte asks.

I can't tell her about Alex's true association with Maxim. About what they went through in Mexico and how that scared him. Forced him to face his mortality.

"Because he lost his mom at a young age. He remembered the toll it took on his father and how long it took his father to be able to move on. He didn't want that for Natalie. He wanted her to love and be loved. To know that if she chose to move on, she'd have his blessing."

Charlotte drops her arms and stands taller. "That may be true, but *you* are not the person Natalie should be moving on with. She belongs with her family. We'll help her raise Rose, and maybe one day, she'll meet a nice man here in Northmeadow." She takes a step closer to me. "And you need to convince her of that. Then, you are to leave and never come back."

This woman is incorrigible. Dealing with her face-to-face, I see why Natalie loses her cool so quickly.

"Tomorrow's Natalie's birthday. We're only here for a few days, then we're going home—together. Hopefully, after you go home and take some time to think this through, you'll change your opinion."

Charlotte closes Stanley's door and walks around the car to the driver's side.

"We'd like to spend more time with you before we leave. We both want Rose to know her grandparents."

Whether she hears me or not, she doesn't respond. She gets in the car and slams the door. I watch them pull away, wondering if I've done the wrong thing bringing Natalie here. I take a few minutes to collect my thoughts before going back into the house. When I do, I find Natalie sitting on the couch nursing Rose. She looks up, her eyes filled with tears. I sit next to her and put my arm around her. Natalie settles in next to me, resting her head on my shoulder.

"I'm sorry. Maybe it was wrong to bring you here."

"There's nothing to be sorry for. This was going to happen sooner or later. I wasn't going to come on my own, and you knew that." She runs her fingers gently through Rose's curls. "You just wanted Rose to get to know her grandparents."

We sit, both lost in our thoughts, while Rose fills her tummy and falls asleep in Natalie's arms.

"Are you hungry?" I ask quietly.

"Very."

"We don't have any groceries, and it's still pretty early. Do you want to go into town to eat?"

"Honestly, no. I don't want to deal with any more people today." She wiggles a bit and pulls her cell from her pocket. "How about we order pizza instead?"

Natalie

"Touch yourself for me, baby girl." His hand guides mine between my legs. "You're so wet for me already. Do you know what that does to me?"

"Mmm." His erection against my back tells me everything I need to know.

My eyes fly open, and reality sets back in. The man who's asleep, his arm draped over me, and whose erection presses against me is Viktor, not Alex. Is today the day I give him access to my body? I get my answer when Rose begins rustling around in her portable playpen. Quietly, I slide out of bed and walk over to her.

"Good morning, princess." I reach down and lift my little girl, who rewards me with her babbles. "You have a lot to say this morning. How about we go to the other room so we don't wake up, Viktor?"

"Fik. Fik," Rose says.

"Yes, Viktor. Shh," I whisper. "He's sleepy."

With Rose in my arms, I bring her outside onto the patio. It's a beautiful summer morning. The birds are chirping, and the little bluebird family from last year is back in their nest, raising a new generation of babies. While Rose nurses, I tell her about the birdie family that her daddy and I loved watching every morning. She smiles, and a trail of milk drips down her chin. "I know your daddy isn't here, but he loves you very much." Those words hang in the air as I swallow over the lump in my throat—I refuse to cry. I don't know how long she and I sit alone, talking about the animals and the boats on the lake while Rose kicks her legs in glee.

"There you two are. You should've woken me," Viktor says as he comes out onto the patio, a mug of coffee in each hand. "Happy Birthday." He leans down and places a soft kiss on my lips. "*Dobroye utro, printessa.*" Viktor kisses Rose on the head and then passes me one of the cups.

Viktor speaks Russian to Rose as much as possible. We're hoping she'll be bilingual since we'll most definitely spend time here and in Russia.

"Thank you." I take a sip and set the cup down on the table, out of reach of Rose's tiny hands.

"You should've been the one sleeping in today." Viktor sits in the chair next to me. Rose reaches out her arms to him, and he scoops her up, kissing her belly and making her squeal in laughter. "Okay, birthday girl. What do you want to do today?"

"Absolutely nothing. I would love to stay here and enjoy the quiet."

"Whatever you wish, it's your day." He smiles. "I hope you don't mind pizza for breakfast?"

"Sounds good to me."

"When we're done, I'll run to the market and pick up some groceries for a few days, and then maybe we can take the baby down to the lake. It's a beautiful day, and I bet she'll love the water."

After we finish eating, Viktor runs out to the store. While he's gone, I try calling my parents, but the calls go straight to voicemail. I don't leave a message. As much as it hurts, I won't beg them to be a part of our lives.

After putting the groceries away, we walk down to the lake. It's Rose's first encounter with a large body of water. Viktor was right. She loves it. I'm videoing on my phone while Viktor stands at the water's edge, his pants rolled up almost to his knees. He's holding Rose and letting her kick her chubby little feet in the water. Each time she makes a splash, she lets out a full belly laugh, followed by Viktor's deep laugh. He may look like a big scary man, but Rose and I know the truth. Viktor has the kindest and most gentle heart. He has so much love to give. I realize how lucky I am to have had the love of one incredible man and to now have the love of another.

Since being with Rose and me, I've witnessed a transformation in him. He used to be serious and by the book. Few things could make him crack a smile. But something's changed. It's like a switch flipped, and he's come alive. Yes, he still has an air of danger—I know what he's capable of. But there's more to this complicated man.

When he's with Rose, he's protective—I know he'd give his life for her. But he's also gentle and nurturing. My baby girl has stolen his heart. I also see the tenderness in his eyes when he looks at me. I don't doubt he loves me with everything he has. He's solid and strong, my fierce protector who longs to be my lover.

It doesn't take long before Rose tires herself out. Her little legs stop kicking, and she begins yawning.

"I think that's our cue." Viktor carries Rose over, and I help him wrap a towel around her. "Naptime for Miss Rose."

As we walk back to the house, I struggle with an internal war of emotions. Days like today feel normal. We appear to be a happy family to anyone who doesn't know us. And at this moment, I am happy. It's my birthday, and I'm spending it with the two most important people I have in my life. Two people I love. While we were playing at the lake with the baby, I didn't have a care in the world. I didn't think about Alex. That's when the guilt settles heavily on my chest. How could I share a special moment with Rose and not think about Alex? Why does it still feel like I'm betraying him?

By the time we get back inside, Rose is asleep on Viktor's shoulder.

"I'm going to go lay her down. I'll be right back." When he returns to the room, I'm sitting on the couch, looking through the stack of papers. "We don't need to worry about that today. It's your birthday."

"There's no reason not to." I pass the papers to him as he sits beside me on the couch.

"Are you sure?"

I nod and pull out my cell to send Brandon the video of the baby at the lake. While we text back and forth, Viktor mumbles as he reads the names off the list. "Steve Martinez. Bill Johnson. Scott Maren." He flips to the next page. "Jonathan Orz. Brad Carlton. Xavier Moore. Paul Johnson."

"What was that last name?" I interrupt him.

"Paul Johnson?" he asks, a puzzled expression on his face.

"No, the one before that." I reach for the paper. "Can I see that?" I look at the name on the list. It can't be? Can it? How many people could have that name?

"What is it, Nat?"

"Xavier is Tommy's middle name." I pass the paper back to Viktor. "Could Xavier Moore be Tommy Moore?"

"Fuck." Viktor pulls his phone from his pocket and hits a button. "Dimitri, we might have a break." He explains everything before disconnecting. "He's going to look into it and call us back."

Viktor

I can't sit still as I clutch my phone, waiting for Dimitri to call me back. Nine months. Nine fucking months, and it was right in front of me the whole time. How the hell did I miss this?

"Viktor, please sit down. You're driving me crazy," Natalie pleads from the couch, where she's biting her nails.

The screen flashes to life just before the phone begins to ring. "What did you find?" Dimitri fills me in on how Tommy was released early last September. Some shit about good behavior. "So you're telling me he's been out for nearly a year, and we had no idea?"

Natalie jumps off the couch and comes to my side. "You'll break the phone if you don't loosen your grip," she whispers.

"Where is he?" I demand.

"We don't know."

I see red. "What do you mean you don't know?" How does one low-life punk not only get out of prison early but also manage to disappear without a trace?

"He's been off the radar since his release," Dimitri says. "Maxim's been briefed and is calling his contacts to start a search."

"Let me know the moment you hear anything." I disconnect the call and stare out the window.

Natalie wraps her arms around my waist and looks up at me. Her green eyes plead with me to give her answers. "Was it him? Where is he?"

"I don't know." I hold her tight and place a kiss on her head. "But I'm going to pay Delia Laurel a visit to find out."

"I'm coming too."

"No. You're staying right here." I know I'm in for a fight when Natalie pulls away from me and crosses her arms over her chest.

"I'm not waiting here. Rose and I are going with you."

This woman standing in front of me is a force to be reckoned with. How do I make her understand I'm trying to keep her safe? What if Tommy's there? I don't want her or the baby anywhere near Delia. But from the look on her face, I know there's no way she'll take no for an answer.

"We're safer with you rather than here by ourselves, aren't we?" She tilts her head and gives me a look that says she knows she's won.

I throw my hands up in defeat. "Fine."

Driving through Northmeadow, my nerves are on edge. It's not that I doubt my abilities. I know I'm damn good at my job. But today, the two most important people in my life are with me, and we're about to confront the aunt of a possible murderer. My mind is racing, trying to anticipate every scenario I might encounter.

How do I extract information from Delia while keeping my girls safe? What if Tommy shows up? He's already proven to be unstable. What if he goes after Natalie or, God forbid, the baby while I have my back turned?

I'm also berating myself for missing such a crucial detail. Tommy Moore has no business being anywhere near Natalie or Rose. I don't know his exact role in Alex's death, but I know he's involved somehow. And this time, when I find him, he won't be walking away.

We arrive at a pale-yellow house, and I spot Delia Laurel on the porch swing, engrossed in a book. I hate what I'm about to do. Interrogating a sweet old lady isn't my usual approach. But in this case, it can't be helped. Delia is Tommy's only family, and she might know his whereabouts. "Stay in the car," I tell Natalie.

"No."

I'm not a Dominant, and we don't have rules, but right now, I'm ready to take her over my knee and spank her ass until she can follow a simple command. "Natalie, I'm not asking. You will wait here. Doors locked." We have a stare-off for several long minutes. I'm not giving in to her this time. Finally, she breaks our eye contact.

"Whatever."

"Thank you." I lean over and kiss her cheek.

Delia looks up when I shut the car door and puts down her book before heading towards her front door. I waste no time and march straight up her sidewalk and onto her porch, warning her to stay put.

"Who are you? What do you want?" she asks, feigning ignorance. But I know she's well aware of who I am. What she doesn't realize is that I won't resort to violence. I need answers, and if instilling fear is the only way to get them, then so be it.

"Where's Tommy?" I demand.

"What do you mean?"

"Where is he?"

"He's in prison," she answers.

"Don't play games with me," I insist, my tone firm. "I know he was released last year. Where's your nephew?" Delia's gaze drifts past me towards the car where Natalie and Rose are waiting. A surge of apprehension prickles the back of my neck. I don't want anyone connected to Tommy laying eyes on either one of them. "This is the last time I'm asking. Where is Moore?"

"I don't know. I haven't heard from him in months."

"Did he come here?"

"No. He only called me," she answers.

"Where was he when he called?"

"Last I knew, he was in New York."

"New York?" What the hell? "Why was he in New York?" I yell.

"When he went to jail, he was addicted to so many drugs. They claimed that the correctional system here lacked the adequate resources to assist with his detoxification. They told me he had to be transferred to Rikers Island."

"How did he get early parole?"

"Tommy said it was because of good behavior."

"Why didn't he come back here?"

"Why are you asking all these questions?" This woman may look frail, but she's either putting on a brave face or she's as crazy as her nephew.

"Just answer them," I demand. "Why didn't he come back here?"

She lets out an exasperated sigh. "Tommy had just gotten clean. His probation officer thought it would be best for him to remain there until his sobriety was more established. He arranged for Tommy to go to a halfway house and join a support group. Tommy told me they'd allow him to complete his parole here once he proved he'd stay sober."

"When's the last time you heard from him?"

"Why do you want to know?"

"When was the last time you heard from him?" I'm beginning to lose what little patience I came with.

"A few weeks after he got out. Since then, he hasn't called, and I don't know how to contact him." Her eyes dart back and forth, avoiding eye contact. She knows more than she's telling me.

"What else do you know?"

"That's it."

I take a step forward, hoping to intimidate her.

"I got a phone call from someone who said he was his probation officer a few weeks ago wondering if I'd heard from him. That's all I know, honest."

"Did the person leave their contact information?"

"No."

I find Delia's reaction interesting. If Tommy had shown up, his probation officer would've wanted her to contact him. Delia nervously fidgets with the book in her hands. I glance back at Natalie, who's focused on Rose. I'm still uncertain if Delia is covering for Tommy or just repeating what he told her.

"Is my nephew in trouble?" she asks. Stress and old age show on her face. Her hazel eyes, wrinkled at the corners, are filled with tears.

My anger subsides a bit as I realize that this woman did her best to raise Tommy, and despite his issues, she still loves him. Tommy's actions as an adult are not a reflection of her, and she's not responsible for his current behavior.

"Yes, ma'am. He is."

"Did he—?

"Thank you for the information." I turn and start walking down the steps.

"Please tell Natalie I'm sorry for whatever Tommy's done this time. Whatever happens, will you make sure Tommy stays safe?"

As much as I feel for her, that's a guarantee I won't make.

I stop mid-step. "I can't make that promise," I reply firmly, without turning back to face Delia Laurel. Those are the last words I say to her before I head back to the car and give Natalie a brief rundown of our conversation. Despite whatever emotions she may be experiencing, Natalie maintains her composure. I start the car and merge onto the road. "Take my phone and send the information to Dimitri. My code is—"

"I know what it is." She smiles. The fact that she knows my passcode fills me with pride. I watch out of the corner of my eye as she types out the information and sends the text.

"We need to go back to the cottage and grab our things. We're taking the next available flight back home."

"So much for a calm, quiet day."

I feel awful that all this is happening on her birthday.

"I'll make it up to you. I promise."

Xavier/Tommy

As soon as I was released from parole, I ditched the halfway house and found myself an apartment. I sit on the tattered chair in this dump of a place I'm renting in Hell's Kitchen. But the rent is cheap, and the neighboring units are filled with plenty of others who are also trying to hide in plain sight. It's been the perfect place to go about my daily life and stay undetected.

How did I end up in New York City, you ask? When I was sentenced for shooting Stanley Clarke, I figured I'd get a few months in the local prison. My plan was to keep my head down, do my time, and go right back to my life. What I didn't plan on was being shipped to Rikers. Apparently, I was addicted to so many things no prison in Missouri was *medically appropriate*. As soon as I got there, I was forced to spend several weeks in detox.

Muscle cramps.

Nausea.

Shivering so hard, I swore my bones would shatter.

And the hallucinations—they were a special kind of hell.

Those first few days, I was sure I was going to die. Wished I would die.

After they deemed me cured, I was transferred to the general population. I quickly learned there was a pecking order among the inmates. Those on the bottom aren't likely to make it out, and I sure as shit wasn't going to be among that group—I had a life after prison to look forward to.

During those first few weeks, I stayed on the outskirts, watching and learning who was in charge. Slowly, I weaseled my way into the group that held power. Seems corruption knows no bounds, and I had no problem selling my soul to secure an early release.

I played by the rules, wore my ankle monitor, and showed up clean for all my parole appointments. That lasted only long enough to prove to the powers that be they could trust me. Money transferred hands, and my ankle monitor was removed.

What did I have to do in return? It was simple, really. All I had to do was agree to run drugs for one of the most powerful crime families in New York City. I'd make good money while I repaid my debts. Once we were even, I'd have a clear path to achieving my goal—getting my girl back.

What I didn't realize was how quickly things would work out for me. While I was visiting a neighbor, I noticed an article in the newspaper on his kitchen table. New York City's golden boy, Alexander Montgomery, was on the front page. Seems he was out playing the hero once again. The article said he was opening up some kind of shelter for abused women or some shit like that. As luck would have it, my neighbor happens to work maintenance in the same building. He couldn't stop going on and on about what a great guy Montgomery is and what a hot wife he has—how he wished he could get a piece of ass like hers.

My first instinct was to kill him for talking about Natalie like that, but then I had a brilliant idea.

"Do you know if your boss is looking for any more help?" I asked. "I could really use a job."

"I'm pretty sure he is. I'll tell him about you tomorrow."

And that's all it took. By the end of that week, I was on the payroll.

In preparation for this phase of the plan, I'd already grown out my hair and changed the color. I also got contact lenses to change my eyes. And that's how Xavier Moore was born. I laugh at how easy this has been.

By night, I sell drugs on street corners and in dark alleys. By day, I play the strait-laced, hard-working guy who's looking to work his way up.

First, I got in good with Steve, the foreman on the shelter project, and have been working right under Montgomery's nose. After some snooping around in the paper-work, I hit pay dirt—I found their home address. It felt like old times hiding out and watching Natalie from a distance, all while I planned my next move—getting rid of Montgomery for good, and I planned to do it right where he felt safest.

I've learned to spot weaknesses and exploit them. Leon, the head of security, has a sick wife. Cancer, he says. The doctors keep throwing treatments at her, but noth-ing's working. Bottom line—she's going to die. But Leon can't stand seeing his old lady suffer. So, I dangled a carrot in front of him, some free product guaranteed to make her forget her pain in exchange for a favor when I was ready. He didn't even bother asking. He jumped on it.

Since Alex's accident, Natalie's bodyguard hasn't left her side. That's not surprising since they spent so much time alone together in Missouri. It's obvious the guy couldn't wait to fuck her. That is if they weren't already screwing each other when Montgomery wasn't around. I probably did him a favor by taking Montgomery out of the picture.

He better have his fun with her now because soon she'll be mine.

There's only one complication I didn't anticipate. Montgomery knocked Natalie up, and now she has his spawn. There's no way in hell I'm going to raise his kid. I have to get her alone. Then I'll offer her a deal she won't be able to refuse.

It won't be too much longer before she's back in my bed where she belongs.

Natalie

We've been back home for a few weeks now. I'm sure Delia Laurel called my parents to complain about Viktor. However, my phone has been silent, and I can't help but worry that my relationship with Viktor may have caused irreparable damage with my parents. Despite my fear, I stand by my decision to honor Alex's wishes.

In the meantime, Rose has been making strides in her development and has recently mastered crawling. Today, I created an obstacle course for her in the living room with various toys. I love watching her determination as she moves from one toy to another.

I'm about ready to set one up for Viktor, too. He's been restless and agitated, pacing back and forth in front of the windows, constantly checking his phone for updates. Dimitri promised to call us this evening with the information. But each passing hour without an update is causing Viktor to become increasingly irritable.

"You know you can't make the phone ring." I try to make him laugh but fail.

"It's been hours, and he hasn't called yet."

"He'll call as soon as he knows something. Come here and watch the baby."

Viktor obliges and slides his large frame onto the floor next to me. Rose gets excited when she sees him.

"Fik," she says and tries to move to get to him faster than she can coordinate her arms and legs. She tumbles forward—her bottom lip quivers.

Viktor scoops her up before she cries, kisses her nose, and then sets her back down. Then, he picks up her favorite stuffed elephant, making it dance on the floor a short distance in front of her. *"ty mozhesh' eto sdelat."*

"What did you tell her?"

"You can do it." He continues encouraging her to try again. Finally, she gets back on her hands and knees and successfully crawls to him, getting her prize and then rolling onto her back. He praises her in Russian as she brings the toy right to her mouth.

"I think she's getting another tooth."

Before Viktor can respond, his phone rings. "It's him." He connects the call. "You're on speaker. Natalie's with me. What did you find out?"

"I hacked into the old lady's phone records. The call wasn't from any parole officer. It came from a burner phone. After some searching, I found the real parole officer. He was hesitant to talk at first, but after some *persuasion,* we got answers." According to him, Tommy got in front of a sympathetic judge who felt Tommy earned an early release. What makes the story even more questionable is that he had his ankle monitor removed and his parole requirements canceled sooner than his original release specified.

"Seems corruption runs deep even in America," Dimitri adds. Then, he continues the tale. While Maxim was reaching out to some business associates, the Scartelli family name came up. It appears Tommy made some interesting friends during his time at Rikers. "We don't have all the details yet, but we know Luciano Scartelli had something to do with his release in exchange for Tommy running drugs for them."

"Why the hell would Scartelli give a fuck about Tommy?"

"Because he agreed to do his dirty work."

"So, what happened? Where is he?" Viktor asks.

"That's where this story gets even more interesting. Once he was out of the criminal justice system, all records of a Thomas Moore went cold."

"How's that possible?"

"Because that's when he started going by Xavier Moore. That was a great catch, Natalie." Dimitri gives a rare compliment. "With that information, I was able to get pictures of Moore from the building's employee files. He changed his physical appearance, but Xavier and Tommy are one and the same."

"X-man," I whisper.

"What are you talking about?" Dimitri asks.

"Steve kept telling us about this new guy, X-man. He wanted Alex to meet him, but every time we were there, *X-man* was gone." The ground falls out from under me. I can't take my next breath and grab Viktor's arm.

"Look at me, Natalie." Viktor turns my head to face him. "You need to breathe."

"All that time, he was right there. Tommy killed my husband." The words leave my mouth in a strangled cry, and I break down.

Viktor pulls me against him and holds me tight. My crying startles Rose, and she begins to cry, too. Viktor scoops her up with his free arm and holds her close. "It's okay, *printessa*. Don't cry. I'll take care of you and Mommy," he murmurs and kisses my head. "Moore will pay for this."

"There's more," Dimitri says.

"What the hell else could there be?"

"A few months ago, one of the other lowlifes Scartelli employs put a call into the boss. He suspected Tommy was skimming from the product he was supposed to be selling. Said Tommy's high all the time." Dimitri hesitates. "He was concerned because Tommy was bragging about crazy shit like killing—"

"Enough." Viktor stops Dimitri mid-sentence.

"Please let him finish."

"Tread cautiously," Viktor warns.

"Tommy must've gotten a heads up and disappeared because Scartelli's been looking for a Tommy Moore. At least until Maxim spoke to him and told him to start looking for an Xavier Moore instead. Now that his cover's blown, he won't be able to hide for long." Before Dimitri continues, there's a long pause. "I found one more thing."

"I don't know if I can hear anymore."

"I'm sorry, Natalie, but you need to hear this. Knowing Tommy's past and his affinity for stalking you, I pulled footage from the security cameras outside your building."

"And?" Viktor says with an edge to his tone.

"Tommy's been watching your building."

"No, not again." My body trembles.

Viktor takes the phone off speaker and balances it between his cheek and shoulder. "I need to take care of things here. Send me everything. I'll call you back later."

He disconnects the call and turns all his attention to me.

"Viktor," I look into his gray eyes, which are usually calm, and see nothing but rage. "He killed Alex. He's been watching me—watching Rose." I try to stand, but Viktor doesn't let me go. "We have to get out of here." My instincts urge me to pack up and run. To take my baby somewhere far away. Somewhere Tommy will never find us.

"We aren't going anywhere," Viktor says sternly. "Moore will answer for what he's done, and this time, it'll be with his life."

I know I should cringe in disgust. My morals should be screaming that taking a life is wrong, but they aren't. Tommy stole my husband from me. He took Rose's dad away—she'll never know him. I don't want to hate, but I can't stop myself.

Rose continues to fuss on Viktor's lap. "This was a lot for our little girl, too."

Rose reaches out for me, and I hold her close. "I'm sorry I scared you, princess. Everything's okay," I say and look at Viktor.

"Everything's going to be okay," he echoes my words, giving me the reassurance I so desperately need. "It's getting late. How about we get Rose some dinner and then a nice warm bath," Viktor suggests. "Once we get her tucked in, I'll call Dimitri back.

I get Rose settled in her highchair while Viktor makes her cereal. She's starting to eat a little more solid food, and I'm not sure who loves it more, Rose or Viktor, who's feeding her, playing airplane, and making all sorts of silly noises. With each bite, she giggles, spitting food everywhere. Watching them play is exactly what I need. Their pure enjoyment makes it impossible to continue worrying, at least for now.

After Viktor bathes her, I get her into jammies and relax on the bed to nurse her. It only takes a few minutes before her little eyes close, and she's sound asleep. She's still sleeping in the portable playpen in the guest room that Viktor and I share. I feel bad that she hasn't used the beautiful nursery Alex made for her, but I can't bear to go in there. It holds too many memories. Viktor asked if I wanted to change it, but I couldn't do that either, so he moved most of Rose's day-to-day things into our bedroom to make it easier.

Viktor

With Rose in bed, Natalie and I return to the living room and sit on the couch. Although it's the early morning hours in Russia, I know Dimitri's awake. He hasn't slept since we started putting the pieces together. I hit the green button to connect the call.

"What's the plan?" I ask as soon as I hear it connect.

"Maxim's getting his plane ready. Misha, Timur, and I will be leaving in the next few hours. We've also been in contact with Michael. He and a few of his men are on a plane en route to you as we speak. The plan is to find Moore and take him out."

"How do you plan on finding him?" Natalie asks.

"According to our surveillance, we know Moore's using the coffee shop across from your building to hide and watch Natalie. Unfortunately, he has a sporadic pattern. Once he's out of range from the security camera, we lose track of him. The plan is to put someone inside the coffee shop who'll follow him once he leaves. The hope is to catch him in a less populated area, preferably before Scartelli. Either way, he's a dead man, but I want us to have the satisfaction of carrying out his sentence," Dimitri explains.

Natalie quietly listens as we discuss the finer details of the plan. Dimitri has the technical aspects covered, and Michael will provide snipers if needed, but a shoot-out on the streets is not preferable. Timur and I will be on the ground to capture Moore, and Misha will remain at the apartment to cover Natalie and Rose.

"Do you need a ride from the airport?"

"No. Maxim has arranged transportation for everyone."

"Sounds good. Have a safe flight, and we'll see you tomorrow."

I disconnect the call and turn to face Natalie. She's staring out the window, lost in her thoughts. Gently, I place my hand on her shoulder. "Are you okay?"

"Yes. No. I don't know." She looks at me. "What am I supposed to be feeling right now?"

"There's no right or wrong answer." She leans into me. I love the way her body feels curled against mine. "A lot of information has come out in the past twenty-four hours. I know how I'm feeling knowing Moore's behind this. I can't imagine what you're feeling." I stroke her hair.

"I never would've imagined Tommy was capable of murder." Her voice catches on a sob. "He shot my father, but I thought that was because of the drugs. Why did they let him out? He should've been in jail. Then Alex would still be alive."

I don't know how to answer her. We live in a corrupt world. What something looks like on the surface is rarely how it is. Greed and corruption are all around us, and whether we like it or not, money talks. It's that corruption and money that got Moore released from prison. I hate that Natalie's life has once again been tainted by evil, except this time, it's not something I can fix. We're forced to live with the consequences. Left to pick up the shattered pieces while trying to move forward.

"There's a lot of bad people out there who only look out for themselves. They don't care who gets hurt in the process."

"I hate it. I hate every part of it."

"I know." I take her face in my hands. "I'm sorry I can't bring Alex back, but I'm going to do everything in my power to fix this as best I can." I lean in and kiss her. "I'll take care of Thomas Moore."

She places her hand over mine. "I know you will."

"Come on. We need to get some sleep. We have a long day ahead of us."

"Oh. I promised the clinicians we'd stop at Jelena's Hope in the morning. The Mothers-To-Be program asked if I could bring Rose by."

"Are you sure you're up for that?"

"Yes. The last time I brought Rose in, it brightened up a lot of faces. It was the first time I've seen some of those women smile since they came to us," she says. "These women, whether they've decided to keep their babies or not, are facing a difficult road. Spending time with Rose seems to help."

"As long as you're certain, we'll be there, but that's even more reason to get to bed."

Natalie

Viktor is sound asleep with his arms protectively wrapped around me, but I'm wide awake. It's been several weeks since I last dreamed about Alex. Yekaterina's words are starting to ring true. Because as soon as I decided to let myself care for Viktor and accept the love he's giving me, the dreams stopped. However, in the hushed darkness of the night, the pain in my heart is screaming.

I yearn for Alex's embrace, how our limbs would entangle together. The fear of forgetting him looms over me. It's been ten months, and I'm struggling to recall the sound of his voice. Sometimes, when I'm alone, I listen to his last voicemail repeatedly, willing myself not to forget him.

Turning onto my side, I reach out and drape my arm across the man lying next to me. I hope that whatever this connection is between us will be enough. Alex knew what he was doing when he orchestrated our relationship. He realized that, given our shared history, it would be impossible for us not to be drawn to one another. He didn't want us to feel guilty for finding love after his death.

Since the day Alex died, Viktor's been by my side. He was my pillar of support during Rose's birth, cutting the cord and becoming the only father figure she'll ever know. On days when I couldn't muster the strength to face the world without Alex, Viktor held me up. He's kind, caring, strong, and capable. When we enter a room together, I can feel the jealousy from other women as they whisper about us. But the only woman Viktor sees is me.

I run my fingers over the chiseled muscles of his abdomen. I love Viktor, but am I truly in love with him? His body is a source of comfort and security, but my heart still longs for Alex's touch. Will that ache dissipate if I allow myself to be intimate with Viktor? I let my fingers wander lower, teasing the waistband of his pants. Even in his sleep, his body responds to my touch. He stirs, and I freeze. Viktor is waiting for me to give the green light to take our relationship to the next level. To show me with his body how much he loves me. But I'm hesitant, fearful of hurting him if I can't reciprocate his feelings. When we do take that step, I want my heart to beat only for him instead of wishing he was another.

As I contemplate this, my phone vibrates on the nightstand. I carefully slide out from under Viktor's arm to check the text. It's Lana. I haven't heard from her in weeks.

Lana: What's going on that the guys all left in such a hurry?

Me: Didn't your dad fill you in?

Lana: He and I aren't exactly on speaking terms right now.

Me: Why? What's going on?

Lana: He doesn't approve of the way I left things with Brandon. But stop changing the subject.

Me: Tommy's the one who killed Alex. They're coming to help Viktor find him.

Lana: Holy shit!! Tommy? I thought he was in prison.

Me: Yeah, me too. It's a long story. One that I'm not even sure I understand. Now, back to you and Brandon. When are you coming back?

Lana: I don't think I am. We both want very different things.

"Who are you talking to?" Viktor rolls over and pushes up on his elbow.

"I'm sorry I woke you," I whisper. "Lana texted."

Viktor takes the phone from my hand.

"What are you doing?"

"I'm telling her to let you sleep."

Me: It's Viktor. It's late, and we're in bed—sleeping, or at least we were until you texted. Natalie will call you tomorrow. Goodnight, Svetlana.

He hits send and passes the phone back to me before lying down.

"Bossy much?" I grin.

"When I need to be." He gives me a peck on the cheek.

Lana: What's Viktor doing in your bed?

Besides knowing Viktor is staying in my apartment, I haven't told her anything about our relationship. She has enough on her plate right now with whatever it is she's dealing with. I didn't want to add my problems to the mix. But after that text, I have some explaining to do.

Me: That's another long story, but not for tonight. I do need to get some sleep. Love ya.

Lana: You better call me in the morning! Love you too.

I power off my phone and set it back on the nightstand.

"Better?"

"Alex said you'd be a handful." Viktor pulls me close to him once again. "Now, close your eyes and sleep."

I slap his shoulder. "Maybe you should go back to sleeping on the floor."

"Too late for that. You can't get rid of me now," he says, a goofy grin on his face. "Good night."

And somehow, he falls right back to sleep while I continue to toss and turn.

Tonight, I dream of Alex once again. He's just out of reach. Each time I step toward him, he gets further away. When I finally get within reaching distance and stretch my hand out, he disappears. I'm left standing in a dark room, calling his name, but he doesn't answer. He's gone.

When morning comes, I'm still tired from the restless sleep and unsettling dreams. But I don't have time to analyze what they mean. I have to be at Jelena's Hope-NYC, and then by tonight, everyone will be here to start the hunt for Tommy.

Natalie

ROSE SLEPT WELL, THANKFULLY, AND IS BEAMING WITH SMILES TODAY. I was apprehensive when the therapy team first discussed bringing her in for this program. Rose is sensitive to the emotions of others, and I didn't want her to be traumatized by unforeseen problems. The staff assured me they wouldn't introduce Rose to anyone until they were confident it would be a positive environment for both Rose and the women involved. Viktor and I discussed it at length and eventually decided it would benefit everyone.

Jelena's Hope NYC has already had several women and even young girls come to us, either already aware they were pregnant or found out soon after arriving. Our goal is to provide each individual, regardless of age, with all available options and offer the counseling and support necessary to live with their decision. What they've already lived through has been pure hell. Their recovery alone is difficult. Adding an often-unwanted pregnancy only complicates things.

Our unique program offers a multifaceted and highly personalized approach. We focus on treating each woman with respect and ensuring she receives full support, regardless of her decision. Several women have requested to spend time with Rose and me to get a sense of what it's like to have a child. When Rose was taken out of the room, some voiced their desire to terminate their pregnancy. Knowing it wasn't an easy decision, I held them and cried with them.

Two women chose to carry their babies to term and give them up for adoption. I was present in the delivery room with both of them, supporting them through labor and the birth of their child. One did not wish to see her newborn, knowing it would only cause her to relive the brutal rapes she'd suffered. We ensured the adopted parents were present to begin bonding with the baby immediately.

The second woman took an active role in contacting the adoptive family and included them in her pregnancy. She requested the adoptive mother to be present in the delivery room. Together, they welcomed the child into the world surrounded by love and affection. She held her newborn for some time and made peace with her decision. Then, she lovingly placed her baby into the arms of the woman she trusted to show her child a life of love. These women often refer to themselves as weak, but I correct them each time and remind them they are some of the strongest and bravest women I have ever met.

Today, I am having a one-on-one session with Margarite, a nineteen-year-old who is seven months pregnant and has chosen to keep her baby. Over the past month, she and I have had several sessions with Rose. In today's session, I'm focusing on the importance of relaxing and having playtime on the floor. It sounds simple, but the woman sitting across from me has been conditioned to always be on guard. Allowing herself to relax takes effort.

While we chat, Rose pulls herself up and holds onto a chair. She wobbles back and forth as she concentrates intensely on reaching for a toy. She's starting to get frustrated at not being able to coordinate her movements, but her determination is admirable.

"What do I do?" Margarite asks.

"Nothing yet. If we rescue her every time she gets a little frustrated, she'll never learn." Margarite plays with her fingers nervously. "I know. It's hard not to jump in and help her."

"It makes me feel helpless," she says quietly.

"I understand," I reassure her. "But hear me out."

She nods but doesn't lift her head.

"You're watching her and making sure she's safe. You'll encourage her, which will eventually help her take that first step. And when she falls, because she will, you'll be there to pick her up. Then you can give her the hugs and kisses she needs and set her back on her feet to try again," I explain. "By being here and remaining present, you're proving you're far from helpless."

Margarite lifts her eyes to meet mine and smiles. A second later, Rose bobbles and falls over. She's not hurt, but she pushes out her bottom lip.

"What should I do?"

"What do you think you should do? Trust what you feel."

Margarite grabs Rose's stuffed elephant. "This is her favorite," she says, placing it in front of Rose, who reaches out and takes the stuffed animal. Her pouty lip that was there moments ago has now been replaced with a big smile.

"Look at that. You did great."

We sit and talk while Rose chews on the ear of her elephant.

Margarite was with the first group of women who came to us the day after we opened. She'd been recovered several months earlier and was in another treatment center we network with. Since it's not the norm for a woman to choose to keep her baby, the other center had no program to support her. They were excited to hear about our Mothers-To-Be Program.

With her consent, Margarite was transferred to us. She and I clicked right away. Margarite was recovered from a particularly violent ring of traffickers. During one of her sessions, she described how she was violently raped by different groups of men daily. She has no idea which man is the biological father of her child.

"What if I don't love my baby when he or she is born?"

Margarite's question hits me like a ton of bricks. The pain and fear in her eyes are palpable, and my heart aches for her. How can I possibly find the right words to comfort her when her situation is so vastly different from mine? Rose was conceived in love, but Margarite's baby was conceived during a cruel and abusive act. She'll never be able to tell her child about their father, and the thought of that breaks my heart. I think about the stories and pictures I have to share with Rose, and it only deepens my empathy for Margarite.

As I struggle to respond, I take a deep breath and try to convey as much emotion as possible. "What you've survived is unimaginable. No one should ever have to endure what you have. But you are so incredibly strong. Despite everything, you have so much love to give. I see it when you look at Rose. I wish I could promise you that when you look at your child for the first time, you'll see and feel unconditional love, but I can't do that."

Margarite's eyes widen, but she says nothing. "I can promise you that you're not alone. We'll all be here to support you every step of the way."

"She's easy to love." Margarite glances downward. "I'm terrified of looking at my child and recognizing the face of the man who raped me. Of knowing who her father is," she confesses. "It's something I don't want to know."

Her question makes me question my ability as a therapist to handle this situation. It's not a topic that can be found in any textbook, and I feel ill-equipped. I'm overwhelmed, and there's no one to turn to for help. "Honestly, Margarite, that's a genuine fear, and I'm not sure how to approach it," I admit, feeling unsure.

"I can promise you this—you won't have to go through this alone. No matter what happens, you'll have a support system to assist you." Hoping my words offer comfort, I examine her face closely.

"Thank you, Natalie."

"There's nothing to thank me for. I don't feel like I did anything helpful." I shrug. "Actually, if I'm being honest, I feel totally ill-equipped right now."

She moves to sit next to me. "You're always honest with me. You're not afraid to tell me that you don't have all the answers," she says. "I know you're hurting too. It's not the same hurt I feel, and it doesn't have to be, but maybe it's sharing the hurt that helps the most."

My eyes fill with tears. This young girl is wise beyond her years. "Honesty is something I can always promise you."

In a very uncharacteristic move for Margarite, she hugs me. For the moment, we're just two women who cry together over the precious things we've lost. What was supposed to be a low-key play session has become an emotional and cathartic moment for us both. A knock on the door interrupts our session.

"Come in," I call and quickly wipe my eyes.

Margarite protectively grabs Rose.

Viktor peeks his head in. "I'm sorry to interrupt, but I just got the call. We need to head out."

"I'll be there in a minute." He nods and shuts the door quietly.

"Is everything okay?"

"We have some friends coming in from out of town. Their plane must've landed." I stand, and she passes Rose to me. With my free hand, I help Margarite from the floor. "Are you okay with going back to your residence, or would you like me to call your therapist?"

"I think I'm okay right now." She leans over and kisses Rose's chubby cheek. "I'll see you soon, Miss Rose."

We exit the therapy room together. When Margarite sees Viktor standing across the room, she quickly drops her gaze. She still has a long road ahead of her, but I'm confident she'll eventually be okay.

"Ready?" Viktor pushes himself off the wall and makes his way across the room. "If we leave now, we should get back home before everyone gets there."

Viktor

We're home for about a half-hour when the elevator dings, signaling our guests' arrival. I meet them in the foyer.

"Didn't think we'd be crossing paths again," Michael says as he shakes my hand.

"Hoped we wouldn't have to."

"Where's Natalie?"

"She just went to put the baby down for a nap. She'll be out in a few minutes." I motion toward the kitchen. "I figured you'd all be hungry, so I had pizza delivered. Come on in."

The men follow me into the kitchen, where several boxes of take-out pizza are sitting on the counter. "Help yourselves."

They descend on the pizza like they haven't eaten in a week.

"I hope you guys planned on saving me a piece," Natalie says as she enters the kitchen.

"There she is." Michael puts his pizza down and wraps Natalie in a hug.

I realize I don't have a claim to her, but my muscles tighten seeing her in another man's arms. He whispers something to her that I can't hear before letting her go. She smiles and then turns to Timur.

"I sure have missed you." She reaches out and hugs him. He returns her affections with an awkward pat on her back. Maxim's men aren't used to so much emotion.

I elbow him.

"All right, that's enough of all this ooey-gooey stuff," I joke. "Let's eat, and then we'll go downstairs and get to work."

"Downstairs?" Natalie asks, shocked.

"Yes. We have to get a plan together—"

"I'm well aware of what needs to be done." She crosses her arms over her chest, her signature move. And once again, I know I'm in trouble. "And I plan on being a part of it."

"No."

"No?" The men all shift uncomfortably.

"You heard me. You'll be nowhere near any of this."

"I most certainly will." She looks between everyone—each man tries to avoid direct eye contact with her. "You want to lure Tommy out of the shadows? I'm the easiest way to do it."

"Viktor's right, Nat," Michael interrupts.

"It's too dangerous. We're not risking your safety," I say.

"I didn't ask your opinion."

"That's obvious," I mutter, earning me a disapproving glare from Natalie.

"It's me, Tommy wants. So, the most logical thing to do is to use me as bait." She hops onto a stool next to the kitchen island and grabs a piece of pizza, taking a bite.

Timur holds up his hands in defeat. Misha continues eating, pretending to ignore what's going on around him. Michael's men are smart enough to stay quiet. Dimitri snickers from where he leans in the doorway.

"You will have no part in this." I lean in close to her. "That's final."

She rolls her eyes. Actually rolls her eyes at me.

The elevator dings again.

"Who the hell is that?"

"It's Brandon." She smiles. "I invited him. We'll need someone to stay with Rose."

"You're fucking kidding me right now." I take her by the arm. "Come with me."

"My pizza," she protests.

I grab her plate off the counter and take it with us. "One of you tell Brandon to go home."

"Don't you dare," Natalie calls out over her shoulder. I drag her down the hall to the office and pull her inside before slamming the door shut. "Are you done manhandling me now?" She's pissed. But so am I.

"What the hell was that out there?" I put the plate with her pizza on the desk.

"I'm a part of this more than any of you." She pokes her finger into my chest. "You are not leaving me out of this. If you want Tommy, I'm the way to get him."

"I will not put you in danger. If anything were to happen to you." I put my hands on her arms and quiet my voice. "I wouldn't be able to live with myself."

"You'd never let anything happen to me." She looks at me. Her green eyes are still full of fight.

I can't help myself. I pull her to me and kiss her. It's not tender or sweet. It's full of all the anger I'm feeling right now. She kisses me back, her passion equaling mine, before pushing me away.

"You don't get to kiss me like that." She walks over to the window, turning her back to me. "I'm mad at you right now."

I come up behind her and tentatively put my arms around her. At first, she resists, but I don't let go. Eventually, she relaxes and rests her head against my chest. "I'm sorry you're mad at me."

"Sorry enough to let me help?" she asks.

"Absolutely not," I say, standing my ground.

"You're being a stubborn ass right now," she argues.

I spin her around to face me. She tries to escape, but I pin her against the window, caging her in with my arms. "You and I are just starting to figure things out between us. I can't risk losing you, not like this."

"What do you mean, not like this?"

"I won't allow you to risk your safety to leave me like that. It's one thing for you to decide you don't love me—"

"Don't talk like that."

"You need to hear it. I'm completely and totally in love with you, Natalie." I rest my forehead against hers. "If you decide not to love me back, if you choose someone else and leave me, that's one thing. I'll still be in your life. None of that will change. But if anything were to happen to you, I'd never forgive myself."

"Viktor, you know I care about you. You're the only man I'd ever open my heart to again." Her words fill me with hope for the future. "But we were discussing something else." She ducks under my arm and sidesteps me. The fire has returned to her eyes. "You will not be leaving me out of your little war plans."

My head is spinning. How did she manage to go from one extreme to the other in under thirty seconds?

With her hands on her hips, she's poised for a fight. But this time, I'm ready for her. I move so close to her that she's forced to look up to see me.

"I'm going to say this one last time. The answer is no. You can finish your pizza in here, or if you can control your temper, you can join us before we go downstairs." I turn and walk toward the door.

"Oh my God, you're impossible." She swipes her plate off the desk as she pushes past me and quickly hurries back to the kitchen.

"I'm impossible?" I mutter to myself as I make my way out of the office.

"Wassup. wassup." I hear Rose's sweet little voice and roll my eyes. When I poke my head into our bedroom, Brandon's standing there, a wide-awake Rose in his arms. "I guess they didn't send you home?"

"Timur tried, but it didn't work." Brandon chuckles. "I had to see my niece."

"If only you taught her to call you Uncle Brandon instead of *wassup wassup*."

"Are you jealous, *Fikr*?"

It's my turn to roll my eyes.

"Come on, get some pizza before it's gone. You can stay with Natalie while we get some work done."

"From what I just overheard, that's not going to go over well."

Natalie

Despite my protests, the men pile into the elevator and go downstairs to Viktor's office. Brandon stays back to keep Rose and me company. He feeds her bananas and cereal while I tidy up the mess they created in the kitchen.

"Have you heard from Lana?" I ask while I load the dishwasher.

"She called me two weeks ago and asked to be released."

I spin around, shocked. "She did what? You didn't say yes, did you?"

"I can't force her to stay if she wants to be let go."

"She doesn't mean that. Lana's confused right now."

Brandon twirls the spoon in circles while Rose opens her mouth wide. "We don't want the same things anymore," he says sadly. "So, I released her."

I pull out the chair next to Brandon. "This can't be the end?"

"She just needs more time."

"People grow and change, so we agreed we'd review our contract at the one-year mark."

"So, what happened?"

"Svetlana wants clubs, public scenes, and other men. I've done all that and don't want that life again." Brandon looks at me. "I fell in love with her and thought she loved me." He shrugs. "I was wrong. She made it clear that she has no intention of getting married, and she certainly doesn't want a family."

"I've been so preoccupied with my own life. Maybe if I talk to her—"

Brandon places his hand over mine. "It's over, Natalie."

My heart aches for both of my friends. I can only hope that somehow, with time, they'll find their way back to each other. Brandon gets up to put Rose's empty bowl in the dishwasher and grabs a washcloth to clean her face.

"How are things going between you and Viktor?"

"He's in love with me."

Brandon stops and turns to me. "Are you in love with him?"

"I don't know." I stand up to finish cleaning off the counters. "We're trying. We're getting closer. He kissed me in the office before. It was different than the other kiss we've shared. But I stopped him."

"Why?" he asks while he resumes washing the baby's face.

"It's too soon."

"According to whom?"

I lean against the counters. "What do you mean?"

"Who said it's too soon?" Brandon lifts Rose from her high chair and puts her on the living room floor with some toys. I join him on the couch. "Who sets the rules for this kind of thing? Alex gave you both permission to move on with each other, right?"

"Yes."

"Then what's stopping you?"

I sink into the pillows on the couch, my heart heavy with emotion. Every word feels like a stab in my chest as I confess, "It feels like I'm betraying my vows with Alex." The memory of taking off my wedding rings right before Christmas floods my mind, and the pain of it all resurfaces with a vengeance. My trembling hand moves to the lock on my collar, the one thing I haven't been able to bring myself to remove. It's my last link to Alex.

"Natalie," Brandon takes my hand. "Alex is gone."

"I know."

"It's time to take his collar off."

I shoot up from the couch. "No, I can't do that." I go to the window and look out over the water. The city lights reflect like a mirror.

Brandon follows, putting his arm around me. "I have the key."

"How did you get it?"

"Viktor gave it to me. He knew I'd be the one to know when you were ready."

"Well, I'm not ready."

"I don't know that you'll ever think you're ready. But it's time."

Tears well up in my eyes, threatening to spill over at any moment. I know deep down that he's right, that I have to let go, but the thought of admitting it out loud is too painful to bear. The collar represents the last tangible piece of Alex that I have left. The mere thought of taking it off feels like the final nail in the coffin, making everything real and irreversible.

As I struggle to hold myself together, Brandon takes my hand and leads me to the couch, where we sit down together. At that moment, his warmth and support are the only things keeping me from falling apart completely.

"You know, after he heard about the police incident, he fought me about going to the club that night. He didn't want to babysit a whiney young college girl." I attempt to force a smile despite the tears cascading down my cheeks. "To be honest, I wasn't sure he'd show up."

"That bad, huh?" I wipe my eyes.

"Once he saw you and then that whole flogger episode—"

"He told you?" I gasp.

"Yep. You didn't know?" I shake my head. "He didn't stand a chance after that. When you left that night, he told me he was going to marry you."

"I had no idea."

"You were his whole world, Natalie." Brandon's eyes fill with tears. "He loved you so much. And when he found out you were going to have a baby, he was over the moon. Then he came close to losing you both." He swipes at the tears dripping from his eyes.

"And here we are today, without him."

"We'll always have him here." He puts his hand on my heart. "But it's time for you to stop living in the past—in what might have been. There's a man downstairs who loves you just about as much as Alex did. Alex knew it, and that's why he set this up."

"Some days, I hate him for asking this of us."

"He knew exactly what he was doing." Brandon reaches out and takes my lock in his hand. My body shudders with sobs. "And now I'm giving you the permission I think you need to move forward."

The lock clicks open, and Brandon carefully removes the collar. My hand goes to my neck. I feel naked without it.

And alone, so very alone.

Brandon opens his arms, and I fall into his embrace as tears stream down my face. I'm unable to stop the grief pouring from deep within me. Rose sees our interaction and begins to cry.

"Do you need a hug from Uncle Brandon too?" I ask her as I lift her from the floor and bring her to the couch. Brandon wraps us both in his arms as I continue to cry until I'm too tired and my eyes begin to close. I feel the weight of Rose being lifted from my lap before I lose the battle and fall into a deep sleep.

Tommy

The small café across from Natalie's building has become my home away from home. They encourage people to linger by offering free internet to their customers. All I have to do is dress the part in khakis, a polo shirt, and a man bun. Pair that with a laptop, and I look like any other yuppies, all pretending they've got life figured out. The only difference between them and me is I do have it all figured out. I know just what I want—who I want.

And I'm prepared to do whatever it takes to get it.

I caught a glimpse of Natalie earlier. She and *Vlad*, my pet name for the guy she's shacked up with, pulled into the parking garage. They usually go for a walk in the evening, but not today. Reaching into my pocket, I grab a pill and swallow it with my last mouthful of coffee before I throw a few dollars on the table and walk out.

If she's not coming out tonight, I need to get moving. I've double-crossed some dangerous people, and if I'm not careful, I'll be in a shitload of trouble. Using a different name has bought me some time, but these people are smart. If they haven't figured out who I am yet, they will soon. And I don't want to be around when they do. I need to get Natalie and get out of here.

There are eyes all over this city. I keep to the shadows until I get to a subway entrance, where I put my hat on and pull it low so my face isn't caught by any security cameras. While I ride the train, my mind drifts back to last year. I might've strayed from the original plan, but with Montgomery right there, it was too good to pass up. Setting up that explosion was a lot of trouble, but it'll be worth it.

Very soon, I'll get my girl and bring her back home where she belongs. Not *Vlad* or the Scartelli family will be able to stop me.

It'll be just her and me like it was always meant to be.

Viktor

WHAT THE HELL WAS SHE THINKING? I CAN'T BELIEVE SHE CHALLENGED me like that. I know she only sees the soft side of these men, but make no mistake, each is a ruthless killer. And yet she chooses to argue with me in front of them. Her spunk is part of what I love about her, but I need to make her understand what the consequences of her behavior could mean for me.

My job is dangerous, and that won't change anytime soon. And I'll be damned if I allow her to be involved in my work, no matter how much she pouts. Natalie needs to control her temper, especially in front of the men I work with.

"Viktor, are you with us?" Timur nudges my arm.

"Yeah, sorry." I adjust my position and sit up straighter. Realizing I didn't hear a word of what's been said, I ask, "Can you repeat that, please?"

"I have to ask," Michael interrupts. "What's going on with you and Natalie? That looked like a lover's quarrel up there."

I didn't want to have this conversation. However, these men have risked their lives to save her once and are about to put their necks on the line again. They deserve to know the truth. No one makes a sound as I fill them in on Alex's request of me and the letter he left for Natalie.

"It's been hard, but we're figuring things out."

"Are you sure you want a girl who has a kid?" Dimitri chimes in.

"I'm sure," I bite out my response. His question irritates me. Just because he's remained unattached, choosing to fuck his way through St. Petersburg, doesn't mean that's what everyone strives for in life.

"Just checking." He raises his hands in mock surrender. "I mean, she's hot, but a kid too—"

I jump from my seat and grab him by his collar, my hand pulled back in a fist, ready to strike. "Don't ever talk about Natalie like that again. Do you understand?"

"Relax." Misha grabs me from behind, pulling me off Dimitri. "There will be no fighting between us. We need to stay focused on our goal." He looks between Dimitri and me. "You two good now?"

"Fine." I sit back down.

Dimitri adjusts his shirt, an arrogant smile on his face, before returning to his seat.

"Let's go back over what we know about Moore," Timur says, trying to get us back on track.

Despite poring over all the information we've collected, including the security footage from our building, we're still at a loss when it comes to identifying a pattern. I'm seething with frustration. Moore has been right under our noses this whole time, and I missed it. It only fuels my anger, knowing he's been watching Natalie and the baby from across the street.

Moore seems to be smart enough to keep his routine unpredictable. He comes and goes at different times without any predictable routine. One of our main challenges is that the security camera at our building can only capture so much. Once he's out of view, he might as well be invisible.

"How the fuck does he just disappear?" I get up and start pacing.

"He may not be very smart, but there's no doubt he's savvy," Misha says. "Not many people could manage a vanishing act in this city."

Michael leans forward. "I hate to say this, but I think Natalie might be right?"

Raising my eyebrows, I ask. "How so?"

"It's closing in on a year since Alex was killed. This guy has managed to outsmart a lot of people. I know you don't want to hear it, but she may be the only way to draw him out."

"No. Absolutely not." I retake my seat. "We'll figure out another way. We'll wait for him to make a mistake."

"Viktor," Timur says. "Michael's right. He's not slipping up anytime soon. How much longer are you willing to let this go on? Natalie needs closure." He stops talking, giving me a moment to digest his words before he continues, "Our best chance is to put her out there and see if he takes the bait."

I can't believe what I'm hearing. I'm ready to explode. "And how do you propose we do this?"

"When we know he's in the café, we have to let her go out alone," Timur explains. "Or at least make it look like she's alone. Then, we hope he follows her."

"You and Natalie take the baby for a walk to the park every day. We don't want her to change the route in case Moore is familiar with it. The only thing that'll be different is her going alone with Rose. It shouldn't raise too many red flags. My snipers will be in place, and you and I will be on the ground," Michael says. "We've been in more dangerous situations with her before. You know we won't let anything happen to her."

I know every man in this room would give their life to protect Natalie. I can't argue with that. And Michael's right. The situation we faced with them at Moreno's compound was next to impossible. But we pulled that off without any significant issues. These men are the best of the best. Compared to Mexico, this should be nothing.

I rub my hand across my forehead, trying to find a hole in their plan. Anything that could give me footing to say no, but I see no legitimate argument. "We can move forward with using Natalie." I look each man dead in the eye. "But Rose will not be part of this, or the deal is off."

"Fine," Michael agrees. "We'll get a lookalike doll instead."

"Not a hair on Natalie's head better be harmed, or I swear—"

"We know what she means to you." Timur puts his hand on my shoulder. "We'll keep her safe."

It started when we spent all those weeks together at that dump of a motel back in Missouri—bringing her to work every morning and home every night to have dinner together. Some nights, we'd play cards. Others we'd watch a movie. My head knew it was just another assignment, but somewhere inside me, I guess some would call it my heart, started to pretend it was real. It felt like we were a family—a couple. I developed feelings for her. I fell in love with her but knew it could never be. She belonged to Alex, and that was something I would never interfere with. I was grateful for our friendship. It was enough to keep everything in check.

Then Alex asked me to promise him that I'd step in should anything ever happen to him. He knew how I felt about her, and he wasn't threatened by it. He trusted me to remain professional, and I did. I would never have betrayed him.

Natalie losing her husband wasn't something I wished for. Alex's death didn't make me happy because it meant Natalie had lost the man she was in love with. Her world shattered around her. I would've preferred to live the rest of my life without having her in my arms if it meant she didn't have to experience the heartbreak she's lived through.

Alex's death shattered Natalie's world and left her drowning in a sea of grief. Watching her mourn the loss of her husband, the father of her baby, and the man she was supposed to spend the rest of her life with has been nothing short of gut-wrenching. It's a job that's tested me to my limits, and on countless occasions, I've questioned whether I'm strong enough to handle it.

I've come to accept that I'll always be her second choice, forever living in the shadow of Alex's memory. But that doesn't make it any easier. My heart aches with every reminder of him whenever she talks about him or mentions his name. I love her, and I know that in her own way, she loves me too. But it's hard not to feel like I'm competing with a ghost. A piece of her heart will always belong to Alex, and it's something I have to live with.

"So, we're a go?" Michael asks.

"I guess." I shrug, still not thrilled with this plan.

"Then let's go back upstairs and go over this with her." Michael gathers his things. "I'm sure she'll have her own thoughts on how we should handle this."

He laughs, and the other men join him.

I grab my things and roll my eyes, trying to keep a straight face, but end up laughing instead. Because Michael's right, my little firecracker is sure to have a plan of her very own.

Natalie

THE MEN HAVE BEEN DOWNSTAIRS FOR HOURS. I WISH I KNEW WHAT they were plotting and planning, but Viktor clearly stated that I was to be no part of it. Sometimes, he makes me want to scream—he can be so infuriating.

About thirty minutes ago, Brandon tucked Rose into bed and then came into the kitchen to join me for a glass of wine. That's where we are when Viktor and his posse stride out of the elevator and head directly toward us.

"Are you okay?" Viktor asks.

"I guess."

"You've been crying."

"Can we talk about it later?" I'm not ready to rehash what happened tonight, especially not in front of everyone.

He sits on the stool next to me. "We can."

Brandon drinks his last mouthful of wine and starts to stand. "I think I'll head out now."

"Sit," Viktor orders. "We need to talk."

"Alrighty, then." Brandon lowers himself back onto the stool, a curious look on his face.

Testosterone oozes from every corner of the room as the men file into the kitchen. Looking around, I get the distinct feeling something's amiss. "What's going on?"

"Were you serious when you volunteered to help?" Timur asks.

Now, he's got my attention. "Yes."

As Timur explains the proposed plan, I feel a sense of vindication, and my earlier irritation towards Viktor disappears.

Despite Viktor's hand resting on my thigh, I can sense the tension building in his body as Timur continues to speak. I shift my gaze toward the island and notice the disapproving expression written all over Brandon's face, as well.

Too bad, boys.

"Brandon, we'll need you after all," Viktor says.

"You need help from little 'ole me?" He brings his hand to his chest, feigning surprise.

I can't resist rolling my eyes as I listen to the playful banter between them.

Viktor leans in close and whispers in my ear, "That eye roll is going to get you in trouble one of these days."

A mischievous grin spreads across my face as I respond, "I'd like to see you try." I intertwine my fingers with his, feeling a thrill of excitement shoot through me. Viktor seems to be in a particularly flirty mood tonight. He brings my hand to his lips and softly kisses it, sending shivers down my spine.

"You're going to stay here with Rose. Misha will be here as security." Viktor informs Brandon.

"Would you be willing to babysit your niece?" Brandon asks mockingly. "Sure, Viktor. That shouldn't be a problem."

The room falls silent, all eyes darting back and forth between Viktor and Brandon. I can almost hear Viktor's blood boiling. Brandon doesn't realize he's pushing too far right now.

"Thank you. It'll make me feel better knowing you're here with Rose." I squeeze Viktor's hand, hoping to distract him. "When will all this happen?"

"There's a few things we need to get in place. Mostly, it depends on when Tommy's at the café," Dimitri says. "But we're hoping to be ready to go by the end of the week."

We move into the living room and talk well into the night until I lean against Viktor and yawn.

"Are you tired?" Viktor whispers.

"Mhm."

"Okay, guys." Viktor abruptly stops the conversation. "It's time to call it a night."

The men grab their things. They'll be staying downstairs while they're here. Viktor walks them to the elevator while I say goodnight to Brandon.

"Are you sure about this, Nat?" Brandon asks. "No offense, but your ex is batshit crazy. I don't like the sound of this."

"Tommy killed my husband. I want to make sure he suffers even just a fraction of what I've gone through the past ten months. What I have to live with the rest of my life." I look over his shoulder at the men standing with Viktor. "Those guys will never let anything happen to me."

"As long as you're sure you have my full support."

"Thank you." I hug him. "I'm sure we'll be in touch."

"Night." Brandon heads to the elevator and calls out, "Hold that door."

As I sit alone on the sofa in the dark, Viktor returns and sits beside me. The tension between us is palpable, and I can't stand it. "Viktor," I begin, hoping to clear the air.

But before I can say anything more, his sharp tone cuts me off. "Don't, Natalie," he snaps. "What you did in front of them is not okay. They're dangerous men, and you need to learn how to control your temper around them."

A sense of confusion washes over me at his warning. "They wouldn't hurt me."

"Of course, they'd never lay a finger on you. But when you confront me in front of them, it undermines my authority and makes me appear weak. If they sense you don't respect me or that I can't keep you in line, how can they trust me during a dangerous job?" Viktor explains, his tone serious.

I look down at my hands. I didn't consider that he had to work with those guys and how I made him look. "I'm sorry. I won't let it happen again."

Viktor's gaze lowers to my neck. "Where's your collar?"

I bring my hand to my now bare neck. "Brandon took it off."

"Is that why you were crying earlier?" I nod. "Come here." Viktor pulls me onto his lap.

I'm thankful for the warmth and safety he offers me, but I also feel what my being in this position is doing to him, and I try to pull away.

Please stay. "Viktor's voice is low and filled with need. I shift my position so I'm straddling him. His gray eyes bore into mine with such intensity it feels like he sees deep into my soul. He leans in to kiss me with such tenderness it takes my breath away. His hands slide my shirt up my body, and I raise my arms, allowing him to remove it. Then, he pulls his T-shirt over his head.

His eyes fixate on my black lace bra as he unhooks it, sliding it off my arms and freeing my breasts. Viktor inhales sharply as he lowers his head, capturing one of my nipples in his mouth. While he teases my breast with his tongue, his hands explore my body. My heart rate quickens, and desire ignites within me.

Lifting me off his lap, he lays me on the sofa. I don't break eye contact as he opens the button on his jeans, sliding them off and standing before me completely naked. Viktor's body is lean and sculpted. His muscles appear as if they've been carved out of stone. Dropping my gaze lower, I take in his visible erection, which reveals the depths of his desire.

Reverently, he grasps my leggings and slides them off. He does the same with my panties, kissing his way back up my thigh before lowering himself over my body. "You're so fucking beautiful," he says before his lips meet mine. My mouth opens, welcoming him. He kisses me deeply as his hips move, rubbing his hard cock against my bare pussy.

I shut my eyes tightly, struggling to maintain my composure and remain present. The sensation of Viktor's touch is exquisite, each movement sending shivers down my spine. His fingers are delicately exploring uncharted territory, leaving a trail of electric energy in their wake.

His touch is familiar yet foreign, and my mind starts to wander to a distant memory, a different time and place, where I was with another man. The emotions that flood my heart are almost too much to bear.

"Viktor." I place my hands on his chest. This man is so caring, so selfless. When I look at his face, it's nearly my undoing. I almost give in and let him take me. A tear escapes. "I want to be with you, and I thought I was ready. I'm so sorry."

"You don't need to apologize or explain." Viktor gently wipes the tear from my cheek. "It's been a difficult night." He hands me his shirt, and I slip it over my head. "When we're together for the first time, I want it to be perfect. I want to be able to take my time with you and know you're only thinking about me."

"Viktor—"

"Shh." He kisses me gently. "It's not time yet, and that's okay. I'm not going anywhere. I'll wait forever for you."

I wear his T-shirt to bed tonight and tell myself that once this mess with Tommy is behind us, I'll have the closure I need to focus on my relationship with Viktor. That my heart and mind will be his and his alone.

Then, like every night, he holds me while I lay on his chest and let the rhythmic beat of his heart lull me to sleep.

Viktor

Natalie's lying next to me, wearing my shirt. Though we've been sleeping together for months, tonight feels more intimate than ever before. Earlier this evening, I was able to touch her and appreciate her beauty. Her nipples hardened under my touch. The feel of her skin against mine was heaven. We came so close to taking our relationship to the next level until a shadow of memory passed over her, and she pulled away.

As difficult as it was, I was honest when I said I'd wait for her as long as she needed. I don't know what else to do. I can't compete with the ghost of her husband. I have to hope that one day, when I'm making love to her, and she closes her eyes, I'll be the only man she sees.

"Alex," she calls in her sleep. "I've missed you so much. I need you." She runs her hand up my bare chest. "Make love to me, please."

"Natalie." I take her hand in mine.

Her eyes blink open. "Viktor?"

"It's me, sweetheart, not Alex."

She drifts into a restless sleep. I hold her tight throughout the night while she cries out from nightmares but never fully wakes. Although I do my best to reassure her I'm here, it does little to calm her.

I'm woken from my light sleep when I hear Rose's sweet little voice babbling to herself in her playpen. I don't want her to wake Natalie now that she's finally resting peacefully. Carefully, I untangle myself from her body and get out of bed to get the baby.

"*Dobroye utro, printessa.*" I lift her into my arms, kissing her rosy cheeks.

Her chubby little hands reach out and grab my face. "Fikr," she says between baby kisses.

I've always believed a man in my line of work shouldn't have a wife or children—they're a liability. So, I never allowed myself to desire a family. But right now, holding this precious baby in my arms, everything's changed. I've never experienced this kind of all-consuming, unconditional love and had it returned.

Now, I can't imagine my life without this little girl who, although she doesn't share my biology, is very much my daughter. I look forward to a future where Natalie shares my name and carries a child we make together—a brother or sister for Rose. The feel of little teeth biting my nose snaps me back into the present.

"*Vy progolodalis*?" I ask if she's hungry.

"*Da,*" she responds.

For the past ten months, I've been speaking Russian to Rose, doing my best to facilitate her learning the language. I'm amazed each time she understands what I say, and she answers in my native tongue. I hope to teach her Ukrainian too. It's my second language, the language of my mama's family.

"Let's get you something to eat." I bop her little nose, and she giggles. "Mama and I have friends we want you to meet today."

After a quick diaper change, we make our way to the kitchen. I know the guys are there. I hear their deep voices murmuring and smell food cooking. But, when I step into the doorway with a baby in my arms, all conversation comes to a dead stop, and heads whip in my direction.

"Good morning," I say brightly. "I'd like you all to meet Rose."

Timur, who has several children of his own, is the first to get up. "*Dobroye utro,*" he kisses Rose's cheeks, making her giggle. "It's a pleasure to meet you, little lady."

"Rose, this is your Uncle Timur," I explain. "And that's your Uncle Michael." I point to the man sitting at the island, nursing a cup of coffee.

"Hey, kid. Nice to meet you." Michael lifts his mug in a toast-like manner.

"This ugly Russian right here is Uncle Dimitri." My comment earns a glare from my friend. "He can be a bit grumpy sometimes," I say quietly.

"Don't listen to him, Miss Rose," Dimitri smirks. "Your Uncle Viktor is the grumpy one."

"Fikr. Fikr," Rose says, grabbing my face.

The men in the room laugh when they hear Rose's interpretation of my name. "Not a word from any one of you," I issue a warning.

"I feel bad for the kid," Misha chimes in. "When she's older, she's never going to get a date with all these crazy Russian uncles." His comment elicits more laughter.

My protective instincts rise when I think of Rose dating. "That's fine with me. She won't be allowed to date until she's thirty anyway." I grin as I get Rose buckled into her highchair. While I make her breakfast, the guys keep her entertained. I never thought this group of highly trained mercenaries would turn into mush the moment a baby entered the room.

Natalie

IT'S BEEN A TENSE WEEK AS DIMITRI HAS BEEN MONITORING TOMMY'S movements at the café while the others finalize their preparations. Despite Viktor's reluctance to use me as bait and his suggestions of alternative solutions, such as hiring a body double, I'm not backing down. Using myself as bait is our best opportunity to lure Tommy out and get rid of him for good.

The mere thought of it sends chills down my spine as I wonder when I became the kind of person who's willing to take another's life. I know the exact moment - the day Tommy turned me into a widow.

I'm informed that today is the day, and everyone is in position. Apparently, Tommy has been at the café for an hour, sitting at his regular table with his laptop in front of him. As I attempt to apply my makeup, my hands tremble with a mixture of fear and rage. Suddenly, Viktor's reflection appears in the mirror. He stands behind me, leaning against the doorframe. His demeanor emits menacing energy in pulsating waves. After putting my lipstick on, I turn around but can't move. All I can do is observe the storm brewing in his eyes, turning them a deep shade of grey that I've never seen before.

"For the past few years, it's been my job to protect you." He pushes off the doorway and walks toward me. "Today, I'm willingly allowing you to walk into danger, and I hate it." He leans over me, placing his hands on my make-up table, caging me in place. "What I want to do is forbid you to go. Lock you in here and keep you safe."

"I understand, but we both know this will be the easiest way." I reach out and take his face in my hands, pulling him to me. "I'm not afraid because I know you'll be there."

"I'll do everything in my power to keep you safe."

He holds me against him. Although my body relaxes in his arms, there are other arms I still long to feel around me—even if just for the chance to say goodbye. Alex was taken from me without warning, but today is the day I finally get to take back the power and control.

"Are we ready?"

"Everyone's in place."

"Is Brandon here?"

"He's in the other room with Rose."

Standing on my tiptoes, I place a kiss on his lips. "Let's do this."

"You sure about this, Nat?" Brandon asks when he sees me come into the room.

"I'm sure." I get down on my knees. "Now, let me say goodbye to my little girl." I lift Rose from the floor. She squirms in my arms as I pepper her face with kisses. "You be a good girl for Uncle Brandon. Mommy and Viktor will be back in a little while." I squeeze her tight and then set her back down with her toys.

"Be careful," Brandon says, hugging me. "It's not too late to change your mind."

"I'll see you in a bit." I smile, trying to hide my nerves.

Viktor meets me at the elevator with the baby carriage. It's in the lying back position with a doll that looks way too much like a real baby tucked in, just like I do for Rose. From a distance, no one will be able to tell the difference.

"Is he still at the cafe?"

"Yes. Michael is on the ground and has a visual on him. When you get outside, don't look over there. Act as naturally as possible. Dimitri is monitoring the snipers, who are outfitted with cameras and are in position. Even though you won't see anyone, I'll be right behind you. I'm confident once Tommy sees you alone, he'll follow you. Once you get to the bench, Michael and I will make our presence known."

"Okay." My heart races.

"It's not too late to back out."

"I have to do this."

"I have something for you," Viktor says, reaching into his pocket and pulling out a diamond heart on a silver chain. "It's a tracking necklace," he explains. "I'm not taking any chances."

I turn around and lift my hair so Viktor can easily fasten the necklace.

"Thank you," I whisper, my voice cracking. I have to go now, or I may back out. "Let's do this." I push the carriage into the elevator. The last thing I see is Viktor's worried expression before the doors close and the elevator descends to the ground floor.

The doorman opens the door allowing me easy passage to the outdoors. Before walking, I look into the stroller and adjust the blanket on the doll-like I always do for Rose. Then, I turn right and head toward the park. The plan is to follow the path to the bench. Hopefully, Tommy thinks I'm alone and follows me. Thankfully, the park is usually quiet at this time of the day. We want the guys to apprehend him with as little threat to the public as possible.

As I walk, my cell rings right on schedule. Touching the green connect button, I answer the call. "Hello?"

"It's me," Viktor says.

"Hey, Lana. What's up?"

"That's my girl." I can hear Viktor's smile through the phone. "Tommy's on the move. He's about a half-block behind you."

"Have you decided to come back yet? Brandon's a mess without you."

"Michael's already in place at the park."

"I miss my best friend too."

"I'm behind Moore. He hasn't even looked back. He's solely focused on you."

"I really do hope you reconsider."

"Moore's picking up speed and getting closer." Stay calm. I remind myself. "He's within hearing distance of our phone call."

"Can I call you back in a bit? I snuck out with Rose," I pause and pretend to laugh. "I sent Viktor on an errand to the other side of Manhattan. He needs to learn that he can't boss me around."

"Cheeky little thing." Viktor chuckles. "I'm right behind the both of you. Just keep doing what you're doing."

"I'll talk to you later. I love you."

It takes him a second to respond. "I love you, Natalie."

With shaking hands, I disconnect the call. I didn't plan to say those words. They came out on their own. "Please forgive me, Alex," I whisper as I slide my cell into my pocket.

When I get to the park, I stop and look around. A few children run around on the playground. Their moms sit on nearby benches. "Next summer, you'll be big enough to play there," I tell the doll. "Let's go to our bench and watch the boats, okay?" I take the path around the park's edge, away from the playing children and their parents. Away from people walking their dogs. To the spot Alex and I first discovered, where a tree stands tall, its leaves just beginning to change color.

Viktor and I come here almost every day. And if our plan works, Tommy will follow me today. Then Viktor and Michael will apprehend him and get him into the car waiting on the other side of the building.

When I round the corner, I'm relieved to see no one's here. I sit on the bench and position the stroller so Tommy can't see in it when he approaches. Then, I pull my cell phone out of my pocket and send Viktor a quick text.

Me: I'm in position.

Viktor: Stay aware. He'll be rounding the corner any second.

My heart pounds, and for a moment, I second guess if this was a good idea. Quickly, I push that thought out of my head and let the pain and anger I feel every day without my husband take its place.

I pretend to scroll on my phone while pushing the stroller back and forth with my foot like I'm rocking Rose to sleep when I hear footsteps hitting the concrete path. People walking by is normal, and even though I'm sure it's not just any person heading in my direction, I don't look. I need to keep up the act of a typical afternoon. Everyone's safety depends on it.

Heavy footsteps stop a few feet from my right.

"Well, aren't you a sight for sore eyes," Tommy's voice croons.

I look up, startled, a reaction I don't have to fake. "What are you doing here? Aren't you supposed to be in prison?" I get a good look at him. He's thin and pale.

His hair is blond now and much longer than usual. It's matted and greasy, like he hasn't showered in several days.

"They let me out early." He smiles. "Good behavior and all."

"What are you doing in New York City?" I stand.

"I heard about your husband's untimely demise." He steps toward me. "So, I came to find you."

I look around nervously, wondering where Viktor and Michael are. "Well, you found me, and as you can see, I'm just fine. So, you can leave now."

"I'm not going anywhere without you."

"What do you mean?" Now it's my hands that are shaking.

"I've waited a long time for this, baby. With Montgomery gone, you're free to come back to me."

His eyes meet mine, and I know something's very wrong. His pupils are constricted, and the whites of his eyes are bloodshot. His long sleeves are pushed up a little. When I look at his arms, I see the marks. He's using drugs again, and I'm pretty sure he's high right now.

"Tommy," I say softly, not wanting to agitate him. "Even though Alex is gone, we're not getting back together."

"That's where you're wrong, sweetheart." He steps even closer.

I pull the stroller behind me, my protective instincts taking over despite the fact that it's just a doll.

"Don't take another step, Moore," Viktor says from behind Tommy.

A twisted grin splays on Tommy's face. "It seems we have company."

"Step away from Natalie," Michael instructs.

Everything happens so quickly. One second, Tommy's standing in front of me. The next, he's behind me, one arm wrapped around my waist, the other holding a gun to the side of my head.

"Let me go." I struggle to get out of his hold.

"Hold still bitch," Tommy warns. "Before you make me hurt you."

"Let her go, Moore," Viktor's baritone voice booms through the air. "Our snipers are trained in on you and won't hesitate to shoot."

A maniacal laugh erupts from deep within Tommy's chest. "Go ahead. I dare you," he spits, then leans in close and whispers in my ear, "If they kill me, you'll never find him."

My heart stops. What does Tommy mean, we'll never find *him?*

"Alex?" The words from my mouth are barely a whisper. "Is Alex alive?"

"You'll have to come with me to find out." He nips at my ear, making my stomach turn. "Call off your henchman."

"Michael. Viktor," I say looking the men dead in the eyes. "Put your weapons down. I changed my mind. I want to go with Tommy."

"You're not going anywhere with him," Viktor argues.

"Take care of Rose for me," I plead. I hear the safety click off Viktor's gun. "Please, Viktor." Tears stream down my face. "Don't shoot. I want to be with him."

"Are you sure this is what you want?" Michael calls.

"I'm positive. I want to give us another chance." The lie drips from my lips, but

Viktor doesn't budge from his stance until Michael puts his hand on top of the gun, forcing him to lower it.

"Good choice," Tommy yells to them. "Now, step out of the way. Natalie and I are leaving." He nudges my arm. "Drop your cell phone. We don't want anyone following us, do we?"

My fingers open, allowing my phone to fall to the concrete below. With the gun still held to my head, we walk past Michael and Viktor. My eyes lock with Viktor, silently pleading with him to not make a move. Tommy slides the gun lower against my back so we don't draw unnecessary attention as we walk past the people in the park. We approach a waiting car, and Tommy slides the gun into his pocket.

I look over my shoulder. Michael's physically holding Viktor back. His hands are balled in fists, his face red with fury. I know he doesn't understand why I'm doing this, but if there's a chance Alex is alive, I have to take it.

I know that no matter what happens, Viktor will find me.

Tommy

With a tight grip on Natalie's arm, I lead her to a waiting car. The other day, an old friend stopped by to let me know he's no longer working with Scartelli. He was hoping we could hook up and find some side jobs. It just so happened I was in need of a car and driver, and Jinx fit the bill perfectly.

"Get in." I open the car door and push Natalie onto the seat.

"Where are we going?"

"Home."

"Is Alex alive?"

"Shut up bitch." My hand connects with her face, hoping to silence her. Her hand flies to the red mark left behind, but at least she's stopped talking.

The ride back to my apartment is hell, as usual, but it gives me time to replay the past few months and how all my planning has finally paid off.

Setting it up was child's play. As soon as I found out the boss was asking Montgomery to come in for a final walk-through, I knew that was my cue. That night, I got myself a body. One would think acquiring a body would be a difficult task, but actually, it was quite easy.

Behind my apartment is a dumpster-lined alley where homeless people tend to linger after dark, looking for scraps left behind. I've been hanging out there for the past several weeks, pretending to be one of them. I made friends with Joe, a guy who once had it all—a good job, a house, a wife, and kids. He even had a fucking dog. But he got involved with the wrong crowd and made some bad business decisions. The schmuck lost his job and started drinking.

His wife didn't want to put up with him, so she kicked him out. Poor Joe found himself alone and in my alley. He didn't realize that he was pouring his heart out to the wrong person and became my perfect target. All I had to do was keep showing up to learn his pattern. My man Joe wasn't very street-smart, so it took no effort at all.

Like so many nights before, Joe strolled down the alley and sat next to me. What he didn't know was this night would be his last.

We often shared a bottle of vodka, so he was none the wiser when I passed him an already-open bottle.

Except this time, we weren't sharing.

The pill-laced liquor was meant only for him. After a few slugs, he passed out cold. Jinx was there to help me drag his limp body into his car. Once we got him in the trunk, I gave him a shot of heroin large enough to kill a horse. Bye-bye, Joe.

When I got to work the next morning, I stopped by to see my friend, Leon, who was now indebted to me for helping his dear wife get out of pain. His job was to cut the live security feed when Montgomery was leaving, replacing it with some older taped footage. That would give me the cover I needed for the next phase of my plan. Leon started to ask me why, but dangling some more product for his wife was all the incentive he needed to keep his mouth shut—done.

The last step was patience—something I've become very good at. I had to stay out of the way while Montgomery took his tour and wait for him to leave. That's when things really started to get fun.

The elevator stopped a few floors down, and a well-dressed businessman entered. Who was that man? It was none other than Jinx. The guy doesn't clean up half bad. Just as Alex was about to step out of the elevator to go to his car, Jinx stuck him with a syringe full of Special K. Montgomery didn't know what hit him. In less than thirty seconds, he was unconscious on the ground.

Jinx stripped Montgomery of his personal belongings. Then we made the switch. The dearly departed Joe was placed in Montgomery's car with all his personal effects, and Montgomery came with me. Then we got the hell out of there just before the vehicle exploded. And just as I suspected, no one questioned the identity of the person who perished in such an unfortunate accident.

See, I never intended to kill Montgomery, at least not right then. No, Montgomery deserved to suffer. He took something from me that was never his to take. Now, it's time for him to have a taste of his own medicine. It's his turn to see how it feels to have his girl stolen right out from under him while he watches helplessly from the sidelines. All I had to do was mention the possibility of Montgomery being alive, and Natalie was putty in my hands.

Luck has been on my side from day one. Inside the apartment I'm renting, I found a secret room, a bomb shelter that must've been a leftover from the Cold War era. It's been the ideal guestroom for Montgomery. He gets to stay chained to the wall, where he watches streaming videos of Natalie and *Vlad* playing house with the kid. I let the stream play over and over for hours at a time. He's watched his daughter's first ten months of life with another man being her daddy. The best part is the dreadful look on his face when he sees his grieving widow happy and smiling in *Vlad's* arms. I've loved every fucking second.

Finally, Jinx slows to a stop at my apartment.

"Welcome home, Natalie."

Natalie

I TRY TO RUB AWAY THE STING LEFT FROM WHERE TOMMY HIT ME. I'M terrified of being anywhere near him while he's in such a deranged state. And whoever this guy is driving doesn't seem to care either. But I had no other choice. If there's even a possibility of Alex being alive, I have to take my chances and find out—find him.

Tommy's quiet the whole ride, seemingly lost in his thoughts, and that's fine with me. While he's quiet, I look out the window, trying to keep track of where we're going. I'm good for a while until we get to a part of the city I'm unfamiliar with, and then I lose my bearings. Eventually, we turn into an alley and stop behind a dilapidated building.

"Welcome home, Natalie." Tommy grins. "Now, you're going to be a good little girl and come with me quietly so I don't have to drug you, right?"

He grabs my wrist and pulls me across the sticky leather seat. As soon as we're out of the car, the driver races away. Tommy's hand never leaves my wrist as he unlocks the door.

"Let's go," he says, and we start walking down a set of steps.

"Is Alex alive?" As soon as the words leave my mouth, I realize my mistake, but it's too late. Tommy spins around on the step, nearly causing me to fall.

He grabs my shoulders and squeezes. "I don't want to hear his name, do you understand?"

I nod in response.

At the bottom of the steps is another door. Tommy puts the key in the lock, and with a click, it opens. He steps aside, motioning for me to go ahead of him. "You're home now." Tommy flips a switch, and the lights come on. We're in a dingy apartment. The air is stagnant and musty. There are several small windows in the cracked concrete walls, but they don't look like they open. The place is sparsely furnished with only an old, torn sofa and a coffee table. No television. The kitchen is small and hasn't been cleaned in weeks. Flies circle a stack of dirty dishes, no doubt feeding on the rotting food.

"Are you hungry?" Tommy asks, his demeanor now calm.

"Not really." The stench alone is enough to make me lose my appetite.

"I know it's not much." Tommy looks around nervously. "This city is too damn expensive. We won't be here long, though."

"What do you mean? Where are we going?"

"We're going back to Northmeadow." Tommy flops on the sofa and picks up a plastic pill bottle from the table in front of him. He dumps two pills in his hand and swallows them.

"You're back on drugs?"

He appears annoyed by my comment. "Medicine. For my back pain."

I don't want to deal with an angry Tommy, so instead of being hostile, I take a different approach. "I didn't realize it still bothered you. Is there anything I can do to help?"

He ignores my question, lost in his own train of thought.

"Like I said, we're going back to Northmeadow as soon as I tie up one more loose end." He pats the sofa next to him. "Come sit with me. I've missed you."

Hesitantly, I start walking over to the couch when a cockroach crawls out from under it and crosses my path. I scream and jump back, afraid of the giant bug.

Tommy laughs. "Don't worry about them. They won't hurt you."

"I don't like it here, Tommy," I say as I sit next to him.

He puts his arm around me, pulling me close to him. "I know, sweetheart. You deserve better than this." He runs his fingers through my hair. "But it's only for tonight. Unless you'd rather leave now?" Tommy sits up suddenly. "Yes. Let's get this over with and get out of here tonight."

"What do we have to do before we leave?" As much as I don't want to be here, I have to stall him long enough for Viktor to catch up with us.

"We have to kill Montgomery."

Alex

After all this time, I still can't figure out what happened. I remember leaving Jelena's Hope and getting into the elevator. It stopped a few floors down, and another man, I assumed an employee from a lower floor, stepped in.

Then, I go blank.

The next thing I remember is waking up in this stuffy, concrete room stripped down to my boxers. My wrist is connected to the wall by a chain. Next to me was a water bottle, a bowl of rice, and a bucket—my bathroom facilities. The ceiling has old-style fluorescent lighting that's turned off and on at regular intervals.

The only other thing in the room is a TV mounted on the wall across from me— I remember thinking that was an odd addition to this space. It was days before the large door creaked open, and my captor made his identity known. Standing in the dim light was none other than Thomas Moore.

"What the hell's going on, Moore? Why aren't you in jail?"

"You thought you won when you had me locked up. But it looks like the tables have turned," he sneers.

With the click of a button, the TV came to life. On it are images of Natalie and my daughter. At first, I was concerned. It was too early for Rose to be born, but she looked healthy. And Viktor was right by Natalie's side.

"They all think you're dead." He laughs. "And your little whore didn't even wait to move on with Vlad. I bet she's been fucking him behind your back the entire time." He stoops down next to me. "You were nothing to her, Montgomery. Just someone to warm her bed until the next thing came along."

"And you think you mean something to her?"

Tommy's fist lands across my face. "Shut the fuck up."

"What's your plan now? How long do you think you can hold me hostage?"

"You're going to watch your widow with her new man until I decide it's time for me to take her. When I bring her back here, I'm going to make you watch as I fuck her sweet

little cunt. Then, she and I are going back to Northmeadow together." Tommy turns to walk out of the room. "Oh yeah, and right before we leave, I'm going to kill you."

Bile rises in the back of my throat when I think of him laying a finger on Natalie.

The monitor turns on daily and shows me videos and picture collages of Natalie, Rose, and Viktor. Rose has grown so much, and she's beautiful like her mama. Natalie is finally starting to smile again. She and Viktor look happy together. Watching my wife in another man's arms is hard, but they're both doing just as I asked. Knowing that Natalie's not alone brings me peace.

Moore thinks he's torturing me by showing me these scenes, So I show him the rage and disgust he expects while I try to figure out how I can possibly get out of here alive. And if I don't, if he kills me, I'll die knowing my girls are safe and loved.

But Thomas Moore is playing a game he can't win. He might get rid of me, but Viktor will never allow him near Natalie.

Viktor

"Why the hell didn't you let me kill the bastard?" I yell in Michael's face.

"Didn't you see the look on Natalie's face after he whispered in her ear? Her entire demeanor changed."

"Who cares?" I grab Rose's stroller with the baby doll and pull out my cell phone, hitting Dimitri's contact. "You just made our job more difficult."

"What happened?" Dimitri answers.

"Moore has her. Are you tracking her?"

"I am. They're moving south."

"Don't lose them. I'm on my way back to grab supplies." I glance over my shoulder at Michael. "Then I'm going after them."

Next, I call Maxim.

He answers on the first ring. "Do you have him?"

"No. But Moore has Natalie."

"What the hell went wrong?"

"I'm not sure." I shove the stroller out of my way. It's only slowing me down. "Moore said something to her. Then she insisted we let her go with him. Something's not right."

"Is she wearing the necklace?"

"Yes. Dimitri's tracking her. They're on the move. I'm heading back to the apartment. Then I'm going after Moore."

"I am calling Scartelli. Do not do anything until you hear back from me." The phone disconnects.

Once I'm back at our apartment, I repeatedly hit the elevator call button. It isn't moving fast enough.

"The only thing you're going to do is break it," Michael says.

"I don't want to hear your voice." I point my finger at his face. "If it weren't for you, we wouldn't be in this situation."

"There's more to this, Viktor. We need to take a minute and regroup. Try to figure out what's going on."

"If he hurts her. I'll kill you."

"I'll hold you to that," Michael replies.

The elevator ride is quiet. When the doors finally open, I rush out and head straight to the office.

"What's going on?" Brandon asks.

"Moore has Natalie." I don't stop as I bark out the words.

"What the hell happened?" Brandon yells.

Rose startles and begins crying. I freeze mid-step and then go back to pick her up. "Don't cry, *printessa*. Viktor's going to get your mama back." My cell phone rings. "What did you find out?"

"I spoke to Scartelli. He sent one of his guys, someone named Jinx, out looking for Moore last week. Moore was finally tracked down at a joint he frequents. Jinx told Moore that Scartelli cut him loose and he needed a job," Maxim explains. "Jinx called Scartelli a short time ago. Said Tommy's high as a kite. He has been carrying on all day about having to tie up loose ends after he picked up his girl."

"Loose ends?"

"Apparently, Jinx gave Moore some assistance the day of the explosion. Told Scartelli he helped Moore switch bodies, some homeless guy for his intended target. Jinx did not know who the guy was or what he did with him until today. He has been holding Alex hostage in an apartment in the city this whole time."

"What the hell?" I raise my voice, making Rose cry again. "I'm sorry, sweetheart." I pass her back to Brandon and storm off toward the office with Michael on my heels.

"Jinx informed Scartelli that he dropped off Moore and a pretty blonde about twenty minutes ago. He gave Scartelli the address. Then Scartelli doled out Jinx's punishment for his role in this mess. He will not be a problem anymore."

"That bastard. He wanted everyone to believe Alex died in the explosion. None of us even questioned the identity of the body."

"We had no reason to." Maxim's voice is strained. He's barely hanging onto control. "All this time, Alex has been alive."

"Fuck," I yell as I throw open the door to the weapons safe.

"Dimitri's sending the address now," Michael says. "They're in Hell's Kitchen."

"Viktor." Maxim's voice is serious. "Moore has a syringe containing a lethal dose of heroin. He plans to use it to kill Alexander."

"We're wasting time on the phone. I'll get them back." I disconnect the call and stick my cell back in my pocket.

Michael's on a conference call with his team, giving them the address so they can meet us there while he loads up with extra ammo. I finish getting my weapons and then grab the Narcan. I thought Alex was crazy insisting we keep some on hand, but I'm incredibly thankful right now.

"Ready?" I ask Michael.

"Let's roll."

Natalie

Whatever Tommy's taking has him wired, and he can't stop moving. I need him to trust me, so I choose my words carefully. Somehow, I have to buy myself some time. If Tommy's to be believed, Alex is not only here somewhere, he's still alive. I have to find him before it's too late.

"I think we should eat before we leave, don't you?"

"You're hungry. See, I still know you." Tommy looks proud of himself.

"Yes, you do." I run my knuckles down his face. "How about I cook us some dinner?"

"Yeah, that's a good idea. I'm starving."

"Okay. I'm going to go to the kitchen." I stand slowly, not wanting to spook him. "And I'll see what you have that I can make."

Tommy nods.

I walk over to the kitchen and open the fridge. There are several cans of beer and a bottle of ketchup. Nothing useful. In the freezer, I find a few frozen dinners. Pulling two out, I read the directions and throw them in the microwave.

"Do the dishes while you're over there," Tommy calls from the couch.

"No problem, babe."

While the food cooks, I start sorting the dishes to clean them. To think, if I married him, this would've been my life. I shiver at the thought. I need to stay focused on my goal.

Looking over my shoulder, I see Tommy's head has fallen back. His eyes are closed. He's either asleep or passed out—either way works for me. I leave the water running while I look around for something to use as a weapon. That's when I see his gun hanging out of his pants pocket. I move as slowly and quietly as possible. This is my only chance, and I don't want to know what'll happen if I fail.

Carefully, I wrap my fingers around the handle and slide the gun from his pocket.

Tommy doesn't move. Then I tuck it against my side in the waistband of my leggings. My long, loose shirt is perfect for concealing the weapon.

"Aren't you supposed to be doing dishes?" Tommy wakes up abruptly.

"I was just coming to check on you, babe." I force my lips to touch his.

"That's my girl. I knew you'd see things my way once you were away from him." He takes my hand in his. "You know we were always meant to be together."

"I'm sorry I didn't realize it sooner."

He pulls me into him. "I forgive you. That's all in the past now." Then, recognition sweeps across his face. "I almost forgot. We have something important to do. Come with me."

"I made dinner." I try to pull him toward the kitchen. "I thought we were going to eat."

"This is more important," he insists. "We'll eat after." He grabs my wrist and leads me down a narrow, dark hall and through a doorway that's missing its door. We're standing in what must be his bedroom. Tommy looks between the bed and me. "I can't wait to sink my cock inside your tight cunt." He leans in and kisses me. I try to pull away, but he holds tight.

His tongue pushes its way between my unwilling lips as his hands roam down to my ass. "And then I'm going to take you here just like I've always wanted to. I'm going to fuck you until you forget you've had anyone else but me." He pulls back, his glazed-over eyes roam up and down my body. "But first, I have a surprise for you."

He pushes a small table out of the way, revealing a door hidden in the wall. Then, he unlatches a lock and pulls a handle that opens a large door. "Come on." He motions for me to follow him.

When I step into the room, my heart stops. There, huddled in the corner, chained to the wall, is Alex. He's deathly thin, and his complexion is nearly translucent, but his chest slowly rises and falls. "Oh my God, Alex. You're alive."

Tommy cackles. "Barely." He kicks Alex in the side. "Get up, Montgomery. You have company."

"Alex, it's me. I'm here."

Alex groans as he lifts his head and slowly opens his eyes. "Natalie?" he asks, his voice hoarse. "Is that really you?"

Tommy grabs me and pulls me to his side. "It's really her, and she's here with me." He leans over and attacks my mouth. I struggle against him. "You like it rough now? That fucking turns me." He grabs my hand and puts it over his erection.

"Get away from her, you sick bastard," Alex says weakly. He attempts to stand but falls to his knees.

"Alex." I try to go to him, but Tommy grabs me.

"Where do you think you're going? You're staying right here. Montgomery's going to watch me fuck you." Tommy pulls a set of handcuffs from his pocket and, grabbing my hand, snaps it over my wrist, attaching the other side to a clip on the wall. "This will keep you right where I want you while I take care of him." Tommy pulls a syringe from his pocket. "You'll live just long enough to watch me sink my cock deep into your wife."

While Tommy's back is turned, I use my free hand to pull out the gun. "Don't move, or I'll shoot you."

"What the hell?" Tommy spins around, shocked, but quickly composes himself. "You'll never pull the trigger on me, baby." He takes another step toward Alex.

My hands shake as I click the safety off and fire. The bullet hits Tommy's leg.

"You fucking bitch," he yells.

Everything moves in slow motion.

Tommy lunges at Alex, piercing him with the needle. "No," I scream as I fire a second shot, this time hitting Tommy in the chest. He falls to the floor and turns his head to face me.

"You think you saved him by killing me, bitch." Tommy's words are gurgled as blood drips from the corner of his mouth. "But Montgomery's going to die, too."

Then, Tommy takes his final breath.

I killed him.

"Alex," I scream, but he doesn't respond. I tug my hand, but the cuff's too tight.

Alex slumps lifeless next to Tommy's dead body.

"Alex, please stay with me. You can't leave me."

Viktor

WE ARRIVE AT MOORE'S APARTMENT AT THE SAME TIME AS A BLACK Mercedes with opaque windows. Its driver steps out, opening the rear door. Luciano Scartelli emerges from the vehicle. However, before he can utter a word, gunfire erupts from inside the building.

"Fuck." I don't waste time on introductions. I immediately pull out my weapon, test the door, and discover it isn't locked. Rushing inside, I take the steps two at a time and end up stopped at another door—this one's locked. Determined to gain entry, I kick the door down.

"Natalie. Are you here?"

"Viktor?"

"Where are you?"

"Down the hall," she cries. "Please, hurry."

I race down the narrow hallway in the direction of her voice. When I finally get to her, I find her handcuffed to a wall. "Are you okay? Did he hurt you?"

"You have to help Alex." She pushes me with her free hand. "Tommy had a syringe. I think he overdosed him on something."

I spin around and see Tommy's body lying in a pool of blood. Next to him, Alex lies lifeless on the floor.

"What the hell?" Michael asks as he runs into the room behind me.

I'm already on my knees administering a dose of Narcan to Alex. "Get her out of those damn cuffs," I yell.

As soon as she's free, she rushes to Alex's side. "Is he alive?"

I've given the medication, hoping it's the right antidote, but Alex still isn't responding, so I start CPR. "Michael, call 911."

"The ambulance is already en route," Scartelli says. "Get the girl out of here."

"I'm not going anywhere." She clings to Alex's hand as tears pour down her face. "Alex, please wake up. You can't leave me."

"She needs to be gone before the cops get here," Scartelli instructs. "My men will take care of this." He motions to the bloody scene where one of his men is already cleaning the prints off the gun.

"I'm not leaving him."

I continue chest compressions while the debate goes on around me. I am torn between staying to work on Alex and ensuring Natalie's interrogated by the police or turning over Alex's care to Michael and getting her out of here as quickly as possible.

"I'll take over." Michael pushes me out of the way and continues CPR. "Go with Natalie."

As the wailing of sirens grows louder, I clasp Natalie's arm in a tight grip. "We need to leave now." She tries to resist, but I grab her around the waist and pull her away from Alex. I turn to Scartelli. "You better make sure this doesn't come back to her.

Natalie

"ALEX, PLEASE WAKE UP. YOU CAN'T LEAVE ME," I BEG, BUT ALEX remains unresponsive.

The sound of sirens grows closer with each passing second. I'm sure the ambulance, as well as the NYPD, are on their way.

"She needs to be gone before the cops get here," a well-dressed older man instructs. There will be questions about the man lying on the ground with a bullet hole through his chest, but I don't care. I feel no remorse and would do it again if it meant saving Alex.

Viktor takes my arm. "We need to leave now." I kick and scream, fighting against his hold, but it's useless. His strong arm wraps around my waist, dragging me away from Alex. He stops in the doorway and warns the man. "You better make sure this doesn't come back to her."

"You have my word. I'll be in touch with the hospital information," he assures Viktor. "Now get her out of here."

Viktor takes the steps two at a time, carrying me as if I weigh nothing. We exit through the back door, and he sets me down next. "Get in the car."

I look at the door to the apartment, considering trying to make a run for it.

"Natalie, now. We need to be gone before the cops get here," Viktor pleads, but I don't move. "Dammit, Natalie." He opens the door and pushes me into the car. Then, he rounds the front and jumps in the driver's seat. The tires squeal as he pulls away quickly.

"Is he going to make it?" I ask through my tears.

"They'll do everything they can," he reassures me.

"Who was that guy?"

Viktor's phone rings. He pulls it out and tosses it on my lap.

"Put it on speaker."

"He'll be at New York Presbyterian," an unfamiliar voice says. "Take the girl home to shower and get rid of her clothes."

"Who is this?" I ask.

"Natalie, stop," Viktor warns.

"Wait for a call." The line goes dead.

"Was that the same man that was at Tommy's? Who is he?" I've never seen him before, so I'm sure he isn't one of Maxim's men.

"Someone you don't want to cross."

"Why was he there?"

"He was looking for Tommy."

"Why?"

"Natalie, please. Not now."

I take as many side streets as I can to avoid traffic. Natalie needs to be as far away from that place as possible. And I have to trust Scartelli will keep his word. Finally, we're pulling back into the parking garage.

"We're going to my apartment, where you'll shower, and we'll wait for a call."

My heart is racing, my mind consumed by a single thought—I need to get to the hospital. I don't give a damn about taking a shower. "I want to go to Alex."

"We can't. Not yet," Viktor replies.

Desperation washes over me as we walk into Viktor's apartment. But instead of rushing to the hospital, I'm led to the primary bathroom. My nerves are shot as Viktor barks out his orders, "Take your clothes off and get into the shower." I comply, but I notice his eyes avoiding my body.

"Viktor—"

"I'll explain everything when you're done." He grabs the pile of clothes. "I'll be back in a few minutes." Every second feels like an eternity as I wash away the evidence of my crime.

After finishing my shower, I reach for one of Viktor's dark grey towels and head to his bedroom to change into fresh clothes.

I walk into the kitchen and find Viktor sitting on a bench at his kitchen island, his head buried in his hands. Walking up to him, I place my hands on his shoulders, and his muscles tense under my touch.

"Will you tell me what's going on now?"

"Have a seat." He gestures for me to sit next to him and slides a bottle of water to me. "While Dimitri was searching for Moore's whereabouts, he uncovered Tommy's involvement with the Scartelli Family."

Viktor explains that Tommy double-crossed them, and they were out for blood but arrived too late. "Scartelli will make sure none of what happened is ever traced back to you."

I take a drink of the cool liquid, trying to wrap my head around the events that occurred in the past few hours.

"I need to ask you something."

"Anything."

"What happened? Why did you go with him?"

"Tommy told me if you or Michael shot him, we'd never find *him*. I knew he had to be talking about Alex." I take Viktor's hand in mine. "I had to go. I needed to see if Alex was still alive."

My cell rings, but I don't recognize the number. I look to Viktor for direction.

"Answer it, but don't let on you know anything."

"Hello?"

"Is this Mrs. Montgomery?"

"It is."

"Ma'am, this is Detective Walters. We met shortly after your husband's accident."

I put the phone on speaker so Viktor can hear, too. "Yes, I remember."

"I'm not sure how to say this." He stumbles over his words. "Your husband was found alive tonight."

"Excuse me. Can you repeat that?" I don't have to pretend. His words are a shock because it means Alex didn't die in that room after we left. My tears fall like rain.

"Your husband is alive, ma'am." Detective Walters repeats the words I never thought I'd hear.

"How? Where is he? Is he okay?" I fire off rapid questions.

"A short time ago, Mr. Montgomery was brought to New York Presbyterian Hospital. He's in the ICU in serious condition," Detective Walters explains. "The rest is a complicated story that's best told in person."

"I understand," I reply. "But right now, my priority is getting to my husband."

I hang up the phone and look at Viktor. "Will you please take me to him?"

The car ride to the hospital is silent, the weight of fear and uncertainty heavy in the air. My mind is racing with thoughts of Alex. He's alive. How is that even possible? What does this mean for Viktor and me?

It takes entirely too long before we pull up outside the hospital. Viktor hands the keys to the valet. I hurry inside, adrenaline coursing through my veins. The elevator ride feels like it takes forever, each passing floor causing my anxiety to rise.

Finally, we reach the ICU floor and are met in the waiting room by Detective Walters. Tears well up in my eyes when I see the concern etched on his face, and I can't help but wonder what kind of news he has for us.

"Mrs. Montgomery, may I have a moment of your time?"

"I'd prefer to go to my husband."

"I just have a few quick questions."

"Can't this wait? As you can imagine, Mrs. Montgomery is shocked to learn her husband is alive after all this time and wants to go directly to him," Viktor says.

"Unfortunately, this can't wait. It'll only take a few minutes."

"Make it fast." Viktor's tone is edgy.

"Are you familiar with a Thomas Moore?"

"Yes, I am. We dated in high school back in Missouri. Last year, he shot my father in an attempted robbery for which he went to prison."

"Well, ma'am. It seems Mr. Moore was released early and had been living in the city under an assumed name."

"What does this have to do with Alex?"

"We found evidence in Mr. Moore's apartment that connects him to the explosion we thought killed your husband." The detective cracks his knuckles nervously. "It appears Mr. Moore has been holding your husband hostage ever since."

"Holding him hostage?" Although I was there and saw it for myself, it's easy to be shocked. All of this sounds like a movie plot rather than real life. "Where's Tommy now? I'm assuming you've apprehended him?"

"He was shot and killed tonight, ma'am."

"Oh, my God."

"One of his neighbors heard a gunshot in Mr. Moore's apartment and phoned the authorities. When the officers arrived, it was clear there was a break-in," he explains. "Upon further investigation, we uncovered a hidden room in Mr. Moore's apartment. That's where we found Mr. Montgomery and Mr. Moore."

A doctor enters the waiting area, interrupting the detective. "Mrs. Montgomery?"

"Yes."

"I'm Dr. Stevens. I've been caring for your husband since he was brought in earlier."

"How is he? Can I see him?"

"Let's have a seat." I don't want to *have a* seat. I want to see my husband. Viktor must sense my apprehension and guides me to a chair where he stands at my side. "Your husband's a very lucky man. He was injected with a large dose of heroin. If that good Samaritan didn't administer the Narcan when they did, Mr. Montgomery wouldn't be with us."

"Good Samaritan?" I ask.

"We don't know who it was. They were gone by the time my officers arrived," Detective Walters adds.

"Is Alex going to be okay?"

"He's malnourished and suffering from multiple injuries. None of which appear to be life-threatening. Although he's still unconscious, his vitals are strong. I expect he'll wake soon, and I'll be able to assess more then."

"Do you have any more questions for me, Detective? If not, I'd like to go to my husband now."

"That's everything, ma'am. I hope your husband has a speedy recovery." Detective Walters leaves us with the doctor.

"Can you take us to Alex, Doctor?"

My heart races as Viktor and I follow the doctor down the hall. Dread fills me as the all-too-familiar smell of antiseptic permeates the air, reminding me of the night my father was shot. I can feel the weight of the past settling on my shoulders like a heavy blanket. The constant beeping of the monitors is a stark reminder of the precariousness of life, and it sends shivers down my spine.

But this time, when we stop outside a room, it's not my father lying in the bed— it's Alex. His eyes are closed, and he looks too peaceful, too still. Tubes and wires are attached to his body. The steady rhythm of the monitor is the only sound in the room.

As I take in the scene before me, tears stream down my face uncontrollably. I try to wipe them away, but they keep coming, blurring my vision. Seeing Alex in this condition is almost unbearable. Sensing my pain, Viktor puts his arm around me, and I find comfort in his embrace.

"I know it's difficult to see a loved one in this condition. The good news is he's breathing on his own. Mr. Montgomery's body has been through a lot and needs rest. But I'm confident he'll be okay," the doctor reassures me. "Go in and talk to him."

Viktor leads me to a chair by Alex's bed. "I'll give you some time with him," he says quietly before leaving the room.

"I'm here, Alex." I take his hand in mine, relieved to feel its warmth. "Please open your eyes." Alex doesn't stir. Doesn't wake.

Alex

My body feels like it was hit by a train. Muscles I didn't know existed hurt, and my head is throbbing. I open my eyes, and the room slowly comes into focus. I'm in a hospital. But how did I get here?

Natalie. She's next to me, her head resting on my bed. She's holding my hand—she's sleeping. Is this another dream? I don't move or speak, afraid she'll disappear if I do.

Eventually, she stirs and lifts her head.

"Hi, baby girl." My throat is dry, and my voice cracks when I speak.

"You're awake." She sits up quickly. "I need to call the nurse."

"Wait." I hold her hand. "I just want to be with you for a minute."

"You're alive." She begins to cry. "All this time, I thought you were dead."

"It's okay." I wipe a tear from her cheek. "I'm here now."

She looks at my chest, covered in bruises, some old, some new. "What did he do to you?"

"It's just a few bruises. They'll heal."

"You're so thin." She gently runs her hand down my cheek.

"Feeding me wasn't Tommy's top priority."

"There's so much to tell you. You need to meet your daughter." Natalie grabs her phone.

"No, not here."

The door creaks open, and a doctor walks in, interrupting us. "Welcome back, Mr. Montgomery. I'm Dr. Stevens."

"It's good to be here, and please call me Alex."

"How are you feeling, Alex?"

"My head's throbbing."

"That's to be expected. In addition to being severely dehydrated, you had quite the concoction of heroin and Narcan. I'll make sure you get something for the pain. But first, I'd like to examine you." He takes a few minutes to study the readouts from the machines. "Your heart rate is steady, and your blood pressure has stabilized. I think we can get rid of these." He begins to remove some of the wires and the oxygen tubes before doing a physical exam. "You've lost muscle tone and will need physical therapy so we can get you walking again."

"He can't walk?" My heart sinks.

"Due to the lack of nutrition and being restrained, Alex's muscles have become too weak. But I suspect he'll be up and around in no time."

"How long do I have to stay here?"

"I'd like to keep you at least overnight for observation."

"Overnight, I can do. But I'm going home with my wife tomorrow." I squeeze Natalie's hand. "I have a private gym where I can do my physical therapy. Just let me know if there's anything special needed, and I'll make sure to get it."

"Is he always this bossy, Mrs. Montgomery?"

"You have no idea." She laughs.

Dr. Stevens chuckles. "I think that can be arranged. You've been away from your family long enough. I'll see that you're provided a list of any supplies you'll need for rehab."

Shortly after the doctor leaves, Viktor comes into the room. "Welcome back, boss."

"Good to be back."

"I'm not staying. They told me you were awake, and I wanted to see it for myself." Viktor turns to leave. "I'll be in the waiting room if you need anything."

"Can you call Brandon and have him bring Rose down?"

"No," I interrupt.

"Don't you want to see her?"

"I don't want her to see me like this. It'll scare her," I explain.

"Do you need anything else?" Viktor asks.

I shake my head and wait until he's out of the room, and I'm alone with my wife. Carefully, I slide over and make room for her next to me. "Come here. Let me hold you."

"I don't want to hurt you."

"You won't hurt me. It's been too long. I need to feel you in my arms."

Natalie slips off her shoes and slides into bed next to me. She feels like heaven in my arms. Despite my current state, my body responds to having her close.

"What did he do to you?"

I try to answer her truthfully without telling her the details she doesn't need to know.

"Mostly, he tried to play mind games with me by showing me videos of you and Viktor with the baby. He thought he was torturing me, and I let him believe that, but in reality, it gave me peace seeing that you and Rose were safe."

"We're going to need to talk about that letter you left," she says. "What you asked us to do—"

"But for once, you obeyed," I chuckle. "I thought I was going to die. But knowing you were happy and moving on with Viktor got me through."

"I feel so guilty. Like I betrayed you."

"baby girl, I don't want to hear you talk like that again."

This time, a nurse enters, interrupting our conversation. "I have some medicine for your headache. It's probably going to make you a bit drowsy." She hands me the pills and a glass of cold water. "If you need anything, just hit the red button."

As much as I don't want to let her out of my sight, Natalie's been through a lot today. She killed to save me. That's a lot to deal with. I know that firsthand.

"You should go home and get some rest. I'm sure Rose misses her mama."

"I'm not leaving you." She grabs my hand. "Brandon's with her, and we'll be home tomorrow."

I don't want my daughter to meet me while I'm useless. I can barely stand on my own, and my arms can't hold her. When I see Rose for the first time, I intend to be healthy and strong. If I know my wife, she's going to fight me on this, but that's a bridge we'll cross after I'm home.

"Have you eaten?" I ask, changing the subject.

"No, Sir."

"I need to speak to Viktor. Can you get him?"

"Sure." Natalie disappears down the hall and returns with Viktor by her side.

"What's up, boss?"

"Natalie needs to eat, and I need to speak with you."

"Michaels in the waiting room. I'll send him with Natalie if that's okay?"

"That'll work." Michael more than proved himself in Mexico. I trust him with my life, and that of my wife's as well.

"Can I bring you anything?" Natalie asks.

"No, thank you, baby girl."

Viktor escorts Natalie to Michael before returning to the room and closing the door behind him. We spend some time debriefing everything that's happened over the past twenty-four hours. I feel the drowsiness from the medication, but I fight it. I'm not ready to sleep.

While we're talking, another nurse comes in and hands me a list of the equipment I'll need for my physical therapy program. The first item on the list is a wheelchair. Knowing that I'll be leaving this place tomorrow, unable to walk on my own, is a difficult pill to swallow. Now, I understand what Stanley went through all those months he was stuck in a wheelchair.

"I'll be staying in your apartment until I'm back to myself."

"What do you mean?"

"I refuse to meet Rose like this," I explain. "I'll stay in your apartment, so I'm close, but until I can walk, I will not rejoin my family in our home."

"Rose isn't going to care if you can walk or not," Viktor argues.

"I care." I hand him the list. "Can you make sure everything on here gets delivered to the apartment?"

"Yes, boss."

"Wait," I say as he stands to leave. "Thank you for honoring my wishes and caring for my girls while I was gone."

"It's what I promised." He turns and leaves the room.

Viktor was distant, almost cold. His feelings for Natalie are very real. I'm sure my coming back from the dead isn't going to be easy for him.

What kind of mess did I create?

Viktor

WITH A HEAVY HEART, I SLOWLY MAKE MY WAY OUT OF ALEX'S ROOM. I fumble with the list, and with shaking hands, I quickly look at it before texting it to Dimitri. He can get started on ordering everything Alex will need.

My mind is racing with a million thoughts, each more painful than the last. As I step into the ICU waiting room, I'm struck by the silence surrounding me. The emptiness of the room mirrors the emptiness in my heart, and I feel myself crumbling under the weight of it all. I slump into one of the chairs, and with tears threatening to spill from my eyes, I put my head in my hands.

The world around me seems to fade away, leaving me alone with my thoughts. I can't help but think about Natalie, the love of my life, and the plans I had for our future. The ring burning a hole in my pocket serves as a painful reminder of what could have been. I was going to propose to her after Moore was taken care of. We were supposed to have forever, but now it feels like nothing but a distant dream.

But that's not all. There's Rose, the precious little girl who, like her mama, owns a piece of my heart. For the past year, I've been the father in her life. Hell, I've been there for her since the day she was born. I cut the cord that connected mother and daughter. The thought of losing Natalie and Rose is almost too much to bear.

I'm lost, confused, and heartbroken. I don't know where to go from here, but one thing is sure—everything has changed, and nothing will ever be the same again.

"You okay?" Michael's voice cuts through my thoughts.

"Where's Natalie?"

"I delivered her safely back to her husband." He sits in the chair next to me. "You look like shit. What's going on?"

Do I tell him? Do I want him to know what a selfish bastard I'm being right now? "Just trying to process all this." I give him the short, uncomplicated answer.

"You mean, you're trying to figure out how to give Natalie back to her husband?"

"Exactly. I feel like shit because I know I should be happy for her instead of wishing Alex was still gone."

"But a part of you does wish that." Michael looks me dead in the eye.

"What kind of person does that make me?"

"A man. One who's in love with a woman he thought he'd get to spend his life with. But then life threw a huge curveball and brought back the man she's supposed to be with."

"I can't do this. There's no way I can go back to just being her bodyguard. I can't just stop loving her."

"That's a lot to process." Michael puts his hand on my shoulder for support.

"I won't stand in the way of Natalie and Alex reuniting, but I also can't stand by and watch it happen. I don't know what to do."

"You don't have to have all the answers tonight," Michael reassures me. "Give yourself some time to process everything. You'll find your way."

The waiting room walls are suffocating me, crushing my chest with each passing second. I feel like I'm trapped in a box, and the mere thought of staying here for another minute makes me want to scream. I can't take it anymore. I need to get out.

I jump to my feet. "I have some calls to make," I say, my voice shaking with emotion. I hurry out of the room, my legs moving faster than my mind can process. I rush to the stairwell, my breath coming in short, sharp gasps. I don't stop until I'm outside, the cool air hitting me like a punch in the gut, and I gasp to take a deep breath.

I know I'm not a good guy. I've killed more people than I can count—all in the name of exacting justice. But just this once, I thought maybe I'd have something good in my life. Natalie was the light in my dark world, the one person who made me believe I could be more than just a killer. I thought I had something good in my life, and now it's all slipping away.

Tears prick at the corners of my eyes as I realize what I have to do. I have to let Natalie go back to her husband, the man she belongs to. It's the right thing to do, I know that. But it hurts, oh God, it hurts so much. It's like a knife in my heart, a reminder that my past sins can never be washed away. I'll never be able to atone for all the lives I've taken, all the pain I've caused. I'll never deserve anything or anyone good in my life.

Once I regain my composure, I look for a quiet place to call Maxim. My hands shake as I dial his number, my mind racing with everything I need to say. But for now, all I can manage is a simple plea.

"Help me, Max," I whisper into the phone. "Please, just help me."

Alex

"WHAT DO YOU MEAN YOU'RE MOVING INTO VIKTOR'S APARTMENT? Would you please tell him he's crazy?" Viktor, who's driving us home, shrugs his shoulders, refusing to get involved. He's barely spoken two words to either of us all day. Something's not right, and I'm sure it has to do with his feelings for Natalie. That's something we're going to have to confront. But right now, I need my wife to accept my plans.

"I won't meet my daughter until I'm healthy and able to walk," I insist.

"This is crazy." She crosses her arms, ready for a fight.

"Natalie, I need you to understand. This is important to me."

It takes a few minutes, but finally, her features soften. "Yes, Sir. I hate that more time is going to pass that Rose won't get to know her daddy."

"It won't be for long. Then we have forever together."

"Forever." She rests her head on my shoulder. "I like the sound of that."

The rest of the car ride home is in silence. I'm certain Viktor and Natalie's thoughts are as heavy as mine. So much has happened while I was gone. This transition isn't going to be easy for any of us.

We pull into the parking garage, and I'm filled with a sense of calm.

Viktor takes my wheelchair from the trunk before opening my door and helping me into it. Despite my protests, Natalie insists on pushing. When we exit the elevator, the feeling of being in familiar surroundings is surreal.

"Dimitri installed a few cameras upstairs so you can see and hear Rose." Viktor turns the TV on, and the screen comes to life. "You can watch all the feeds or choose one to see up close." He chooses a camera that's in Rose's nursery. Brandon's giving her a bottle, rocking her to sleep.

"This is perfect. Please tell him how much I appreciate it." I stare in awe at my daughter.

"I'll be upstairs if you need me." Viktor leaves quietly.

Natalie watches him. Sadness reflects in her eyes.

"He's in love with you."

"I know," she says softly.

"And I think you're in love with him too."

Natalie looks at me. "Alex, I—"

"Shh." I take her hands. "It's okay. I was dead. What happened between you two was exactly what I orchestrated."

"I don't know how to make this easier for him."

"We'll figure it out together."

"Frikr." a sweet little voice comes through the TV, stopping my heart. She holds her little arms out to him.

"There goes her nap," Brandon says with a smile as he passes Rose to Viktor. "Uncle Brandon needs a nap now."

"Can you say bye-bye to Uncle Brandon?"

"Bye-bye, wassup." She opens and closes her chubby little hand.

"Wassup?" I ask, confused.

Natalie laughs. "Ever since she was born and Brandon would visit, he says *wassup*. Now, that's what she calls him. No matter how hard we try to get her to call him Uncle Brandon."

"I bet he loves that." I chuckle.

"She can do no wrong in his eyes."

It's only a few minutes before the elevator dings, signaling someone is coming.

"And he can even rise from the dead," Brandon says as he comes into the apartment.

"Brandon." Natalie slaps his shoulder. "So not funny."

"It's all good, baby girl."

Brandon leans down and hugs me. "Seriously, I'm glad you're back."

"So am I."

A soft male voice singing plays through the speakers, and I shift my attention back to the TV. I'm transfixed by the image on the screen. Viktor's sitting in the rocking chair, snuggling Rose. Her tiny hand touches his lips as he sings softly to her.

"He loves that little girl," Brandon says.

I have no words to answer him. My heart's being shredded into pieces watching the two of them together. Viktor and Natalie are in love, and he loves my daughter as if she's his. It's clear Rose loves him just as much. In her eyes, Viktor is her father.

This mess is all my fault. No one ever imagined I'd come back from the dead, and they moved on without me. I'm left wondering if I still have a place in their lives.

"Well, I just wanted to stop and say welcome home," Brandon says. "I'm going to head out."

Natalie reaches out and embraces him. "Thank you so much for taking care of her."

"Anytime."

Natalie's phone rings, and she steps away to answer it.

Once we're alone, Brandon reaches into his pocket and hands me a box. "It's her collar. I took it off, but I've been carrying it with me, not quite sure what to do with it. Now I know why. This belongs to you."

I take the box from him. The absence of her collar and wedding rings suddenly dawns on me, hitting me hard.

After she finishes her call, Natalie walks Brandon to the elevator while I wheel myself into the living room and over to the windows. I'm trying to process what everyone has gone through all these months while they believed I was dead. The heartache my wife must've felt giving birth to our child without me by her side. The pain of waking up every day without each other. I know because I experienced those things, too.

"What's on your mind?"

"Come here," I take her hand and lead her around the chair to sit on my lap. "I'm so sorry I left you."

"Alex." She cups my cheek with her palm. "You don't have to apologize."

"I feel like I do. You've been living thinking I was dead. I can't imagine how difficult that was."

She closes her eyes. "My world was dark. I was lost." When she opens them, she looks at me with her piercing green stare. "If it wasn't for the baby, I don't know if I would've been able to continue on. Rose saved me."

The anguish in her voice cuts deep into my soul.

"I can't imagine what you endured. My psycho ex-boyfriend chained you up in an old panic room. He hurt you. Forced you to watch us live."

"I felt helpless." For the first time since being rescued, I allow myself to feel the emotions I've been holding back. Tears fill my eyes. "While we were being held with Moreno, things looked bleak, but I never gave up hope. But this, I was certain I was going to make it out of there. Every day, Tommy reminded me that he planned to kill me."

Natalie leans forward, her lips meeting mine. "You're back now and never leaving me again," she says between kisses.

Natalie

Leaving Alex behind is difficult, but I have to come upstairs to feed the baby before putting her to bed. Viktor's been transitioning Rose to her crib overnight, but this is the first time since her birth that I've been in the nursery. I know Alex is watching the camera as Rose latches onto my breast. She brings her tiny hand to my mouth, and I shower it with affectionate kisses.

"Your daddy's home, sweet girl," I tell her. "As soon as he's better, you'll meet him." She smiles as though she understands what I'm saying, and milk drips from the corner of her mouth. "He loves you so much."

I look up and see Viktor standing in the doorway. "You can come in, you know." He doesn't move. "Please, Viktor."

Silently, he makes his way into the room. "I was surprised to find you in here."

"Me too. But it feels right."

"My little *printessa*," Viktor whispers as he gently brushes his hand over Rose's brown curls. His grey eyes fill with tears.

"Nothing needs to change." I place my hand on his.

"Everything's already changed." He pulls away. "I no longer have a place in yours or Rose's life."

"Don't say that." My voice cracks. "You'll always have a place in our lives."

Viktor looks toward the camera mounted on the wall. "Not anymore," he declares with a voice thick with emotion before walking out of the room, leaving behind a trail of heartache and despair.

Tears stream down my face while Rose finishes nursing and drifts into a peaceful slumber. Trembling with emotion, I carefully lift her and lay her down. It's the first time I've placed her in her crib. She looks so tiny.

Me: I'm going to shower and put pajamas on. I'll be down soon.

Alex: Take your time.

After a hot shower, I go in search of Viktor, but he's nowhere to be found. Instead, Dimitri's sitting at the kitchen island, his laptop open.

"Where's Viktor?"

"He left a while ago."

"Left? Where did he go?"

"No idea. He didn't say."

I head back to my bedroom and grab my phone.

Me: Where are you?

Viktor: I'm out.

Me: We need to talk.

Viktor: Not tonight.

Me: Please don't shut me out.

Viktor: I need some space. Dimitri said he'll stay with Rose until I get back. Go to your husband.

I take a deep breath knowing how badly Viktor's hurting right now because I'm hurting too. No matter how wrong it may be, I'm in love with two men and don't know what to do. How do I keep them both in my life? Because I don't want to lose either of them.

I'm packing an overnight bag to bring some clean pajamas and clothes to Alex. While I'm in our bedroom, I also grab our wedding rings. As I slide mine back onto my finger, a broken piece of me mends back together. I put Alex's ring on my thumb to return it to him.

Before I leave, stop in the kitchen to talk to Dimitri. "Viktor said you'll be here until he gets back?"

"Yes."

"I have the baby monitor app on my phone. If she wakes, I'll be right up."

"No problem," he answers, not taking his eyes from his computer screen.

"Alrighty then. Good night."

"Mhm."

I roll my eyes as I walk away. It's no wonder he's single. No girl can possibly compete with his electronics.

Walking into the downstairs apartment, I hear Alex's deep voice coming from down the hall. It sounds like he's in the office. On the way, I put his clothes and wedding band on the dresser in the guestroom.

When he sees me in the doorway, his face lights up. I missed seeing his blue eyes, the same ones his daughter has. After all this time, he still gives me butterflies. Then he hits a button, putting the phone on speaker.

"She just walked in."

"How are you holding up?" Sam asks.

"I think I'm still in shock." I walk over to Alex. "It's truly a miracle."

"Yes, it is. Alex told me what happened. Are you okay?"

He's referring to the fact that I killed Tommy. Something no one's mentioned since Viktor carried me out of the apartment.

While I sat in Alex's hospital room, waiting for him to wake up, the stillness of the room allowed me to relive the moment repeatedly in my mind. I chose to end someone's life, someone I knew and once cared about.

I'm sure I should feel remorse, but no matter how deep I looked for it, I found none. If I were to face the same situation again, I'd make the same decision to pull the trigger.

"I'm okay," I say, knowing I mean the words with all my heart. "Alex is back. That's all that matters."

"Luna and I would like to come in. I want to see you, son."

"Really, Dad?" Alex rolls his eyes.

"Yes, really. I thought you were dead. I need to see for myself that this is real."

"I assure you it is."

"You and Luna are welcome to come as soon as you'd like," I interrupt. "Don't mind my husband. He's being a bit stubborn right now."

That comment earns me a stern look from Alex, but I ignore it and place a kiss on his cheek.

"I'll book a flight and let you know when we'll be arriving. Talk to you soon."

"I don't want them to see—"

I put my finger over his lips, stopping his next words. "No one cares that you're in a wheelchair. It's only temporary while you recover. Your father thought he had lost you. Let him come see you."

"I guess you're right," Alex says and looks down. "I just hate this." He motions to the chair.

Alex

Natalie helps wheel me into the bedroom. "I brought some pajamas. I thought you'd appreciate getting cleaned up and into your own clothes."

"That sounds wonderful."

Between the two of us, I'm able to transfer myself from the chair into bed.

"Wait here," Natalie says and disappears into the bathroom. A few minutes later, she comes out with a washcloth, towel, and a bowl of warm water.

Carefully, she strips my clothes off and begins washing me. It's been so long since I've felt her touch. I'm hard as a rock, desperate for more. Pulling her close, I kiss her. "I need you."

She puts her hand on my chest. "I don't think that's a good idea. The doctor said you need to rest."

"Does it look like I need rest?"

She looks at my dick, that's hard and dripping with precum. "Well, no. But I don't want to hurt you."

"baby girl, you could never hurt me." I try to pull her over my body, but with my limited strength, I'm not successful. She steps away from the bed. "Where are you going?"

"I'm going to give my husband a show," she says as she slowly pulls her night-gown up her legs. Slowly, she exposes her midsection, then her breasts, before removing it entirely and tossing it on the floor.

"You're gorgeous." I'm in awe of my wife.

"I'm afraid my body isn't quite back to where I'd like it."

"Hush. You're perfect. Now come here."

Natalie climbs onto the bed and straddles me. I pull her to me, pressing her breasts against my chest as I kiss her. She rocks against my erection, coating it in her excitement before she pushes herself up. Taking my cock in her hand, she lines it up

691

with her entrance as she slowly lowers herself. I close my eyes and moan as her body envelops mine, inch by inch.

"Don't move, baby girl."

"Am I hurting you?"

"No. But if you move, I'm going to come right now, and I don't want this to end yet."

She smiles seductively and places her palms on my chest. I reach up and take her breasts in my hands, rolling her hard nipples between my fingers. "I've missed you so much."

Natalie moves slowly, lifting and lowering herself onto my hard length. I watch with rapt attention, savoring every second. Having sex with my wife is something I didn't think I'd ever have the chance to enjoy again. She drags her hand down my chest and between her legs. I watch as she plays with her clit and groan in appreciation.

"I'm so close, baby," I growl and grab her hips, taking control of the speed.

I'm a desperate man starving for my wife, aching to climax inside her. It only takes a few thrusts before Natalie throws her head back in ecstasy, her inner muscles squeezing my cock. It's enough to send me over the edge. My orgasm is so intense I see black at the edge of my vision. I pull her against me as we ride out the waves of our climaxes together. She remains on my chest as we come down from our shared high.

I've used up every ounce of my energy but don't care. There was no way I would not be inside my wife tonight.

Gently, she pushes herself up. "Are you okay?"

"I've never been better." A yawn escapes, and Natalie slides off me. I immediately miss the warmth of her body.

"Let me finish washing you, and then you need to rest."

"I need you." I reach for her.

"I'm not going anywhere. But physical therapy starts tomorrow. You need some sleep to be ready to work."

As much as I want to take her again, she's right. I'm spent and need to sleep so I can regain my muscle strength. There's a little girl upstairs I'm dying to meet.

Natalie

I FINISH ALEX'S SPONGE BATH AND GET HIM INTO HIS PAJAMAS.

"You put your rings back on."

"I did," I say and hold up his wedding band.

"How did you get it?"

"The police brought it to me with the rest of your belongings after the explosion."

"Will you put it on for me?" He lifts his hand, and I slide it back onto his finger. Then I crawl into bed next to him. Alex wraps me in his embrace, and we fall asleep, clinging to one another.

My sleep is interrupted all night. Each time I wake up, I'm afraid to open my eyes and find this is just another dream. But it isn't. Every time I check, Alex is still next to me, sleeping soundly.

Rose babbling away on the baby monitor app wakes me. I hate leaving Alex, but I need to feed her. Carefully, I slide out of bed and leave the door cracked open.

"Good morning," Timur says, coffee cup in hand.

"I didn't know you were here."

"I knew you'd need to tend to the baby, and Alex would need help getting dressed and fed. And I'm the best cook among us." He chuckles.

"I appreciate it." I sigh deeply. "I wish Alex would just come home—to our home."

"He's a proud man."

"He's being hard-headed."

"Natalie, Alex has been through a terrible ordeal. One he didn't think he'd survive." Timur's tone is patient. "He needs time to process everything."

"I understand, but Rose needs her daddy."

"And she'll have him—forever. Right now, you need to give him a little time. Don't rush him."

"I'll try." Rose's babbles turn into whimpers. I hold up the phone. "Miss Rose is beckoning me. I have to go. Please tell Alex I'll be down at naptime."

"Will do."

When the elevator opens to our apartment, I feel like I've entered Grand Central Station. Michael and his team are in the kitchen, no doubt discussing everything that's happened the past few days.

"Good morning," Michael says. "Can I get you a coffee?"

"I'd love one, but I have to feed the baby first."

"I'll bring one down to you."

As I get close to the nursery, I hear Viktor's deep timbre as he talks to Rose. I stand just out of sight, listening to him.

"I'm not going to be here much longer, *printessa*. You and your mama don't need me anymore. Your papa's home now. There's no room for me."

"There's always room for you." I make my presence known.

"Mama," Rose squeals.

"Good morning, sweet girl." Viktor passes her to me. "Don't listen to Viktor. He's not going anywhere."

"Natalie, we need to talk." Viktor's tone is serious.

"Pull up a seat," I say as I get comfortable in the rocker to nurse Rose.

"Not here. Not now." Viktor moves toward the door. "Take your time with the baby. We'll talk later."

He disappears before I can say anything. "Men," I say and look down at Rose. "I don't understand them at all."

Rose rewards me with a smile. Now that she's eating more solid food, she's only nursing first thing in the morning and before bed. Pretty soon, she'll have outgrown this part of her infancy. I savor this time we have together, just her and me.

After she finishes eating, I get dressed for the day, and we join the guys in the kitchen. This time, Viktor's with them, and I hear Maxim's voice coming through the cell phone on speaker in the center of the table.

"Say hi to *dedushka*, Rose."

"Is that *moya vnuchka?*"

Rose squeals and kicks her legs when she hears Max's voice.

"Yes, it is."

"How are you today?"

"I feel like I'm living in a dream, Max. I'm still afraid to believe it's real."

"It is not a dream, Natalia. You and Alexander deserve your happy ending." Maxim pauses. "We were just discussing relocating Timur's family to New York City."

"I didn't realize Timur was planning to stay here," I say.

"I'll be taking Viktor's place," Timur interjects.

"Why is he taking your place? Where are you going?" I look to Viktor, who's standing off to the side, arms crossed over his chest, but he refuses to look at me. "Where's Viktor going?" No one answers me. "Would someone please tell me what's going on?"

Dimitri picks up the phone and takes it off speaker. He switches to Russian as he talks to Max.

"Viktor?" More silence. "Viktor, please say something."

"Let me take Rose while you two talk." Timur reaches out, and Rose gladly goes with him.

"Can we talk alone?" he asks.

Viktor

I LEAD NATALIE TO THE BEDROOM WE'VE SHARED FOR THE PAST TEN months. The room where I've held her every night. To the bed we shared together.

"Sit," I instruct her.

She perches on the edge of the bed, and I pull the armchair over to sit across from her. Natalie stares at me as if she's trying to read my thoughts. I don't know how to say this. How I'm supposed to walk away from her. An uncomfortable silence lingers between us—neither of us wanting to speak.

"I don't want you to leave."

"I can't stay."

"Why not? Nothing has to change." Her words are hurried. "You can't leave."

I drop my head.

Nothing has to change.

Can't she see that everything's already changed? I look up and meet her gaze.

"The day we thought Alex died was the day I started to fulfill Alex's request of me. It was the day I took all my feelings for you, the ones I kept locked away, and allowed myself to love you for the first time. But Alex isn't dead anymore, and you aren't mine to love."

"But—"

"Let me finish," I cut her off. "Your eyes sparkle again, something I haven't seen since Alex left. I can't compete with that, and I'd never ask you to choose between us. He's your forever." I reach out and wipe a tear from Natalie's face. "I can't stay because I can't stop loving you."

"I know I'm being selfish asking you to stay, but I can't help it. I love you too and don't want to lose you."

"You'll never lose me. If you ever need me, I'll be there. But I can't be here every day and watch you in Alex's arms—even if that's where you belong."

"You promised me you'd never leave. That you'd always be here," she cries. "Was that a lie?"

"No, sweetheart. It wasn't a lie." I reach into my pocket and pull out the ring I've been carrying with me. "I bought this for you. I was planning to ask you to marry me after we took care of Moore."

"It's beautiful," she says through her tears.

"I was going to promise you forever. But it wasn't meant to be." I put the ring back into my pocket. Taking Natalie's hand in mine, I stand and pull her to her feet. "For ten months, I was the luckiest man on earth. I had the honor of loving you and having your love in return. I'll never forget what we had. I love you, Natalie. I always will." I lower my face, my lips meeting hers. Tears spill from my eyes as she grants me a final kiss.

"I love you, Viktor." She holds my face in her hands. "There's a piece of my heart that will forever be yours."

Her words sear into my heart, and I have to hurry from the room while I still have some sense of composure. I close the door and hear her crying on the other side.

It takes everything I have in me to walk away from her. Maxim's jet is waiting at JFK to take me back to Russia, but I need to talk to Alex before I leave.

Natalie

"I LOVE YOU, NATALIE. I ALWAYS WILL."

Viktor's words will forever be etched in my heart. My trembling hand touches my lips where he just kissed me. The depth of his love and heartache was palpable, seeping into every fiber of my being. Viktor is an incredible man who's selfless and caring. His love was the very glue that held me together. His arms were the safety I clung to.

But now, as I stand at the crossroads of my heart, I am forced to confront a harsh reality. Each time I tried to take the next step in our relationship, something held me back—that something was Alex. Even though I love them both, I know in my heart that I can't have them both. It's a selfish thought to wish for, and the harsh truth is that I must choose between them.

My heart is heavy with the weight of this decision, and I know that whatever I choose will shatter one man's heart. Yet, despite the pain, I know I'll always choose Alex. He is my true love, my soulmate, and the one who has always held the key to my heart. It's a choice that breaks me, but I know it's the right one.

I take a shower, allowing myself to purge all these overwhelming emotions. After I've dried and dressed, I feel a bit better. When I go into the living room, I find Timur playing with Rose.

"Where did everyone go?"

"They've left for the airport." Timur looks at me, compassion in his gaze. "Are you okay?"

"I don't know." I sink onto the couch, willing the tears not to fall again.

"He'll be okay. He needs time." Timur moves from the floor to sit beside me on the sofa.

"I want them both in my life. I don't want him to leave." Rose toddles over, holding her arms out to me. "The pain in his eyes when he said goodbye physically hurt. I never meant for any of this to happen. Viktor doesn't deserve to have his heart broken. He's a good man, but Alex is my husband. I—"

"Viktor would never ask you to choose him over Alex," Timur interrupts me mid-sentence. "He loves you. Enough to set you free to return to the man you belong with. Somewhere out there is a woman who'll return all the love Viktor has to give. When the time is right, he'll meet her."

I snuggle Rose and kiss the top of her head. "Please don't misunderstand. Alex coming back to me is a miracle—something I never imagined. But Viktor leaving is a huge loss." I look to Timur. "Viktor's been an important part of my life. We've shared so much together. I love Viktor, but not in the same way I love Alex. At the same time, I don't know how to move forward without him."

"One step at a time. That's all anyone expects." Timur offers me a kind smile. "Alex is certain to have hurdles to overcome, and he's going to need you. He's been through quite an ordeal. You and he need time to get reacquainted with each other." Timur reaches out and takes Rose's tiny hand in his. "And there's this little princess. She still has to meet her daddy and form a bond with him."

"Right now, everything feels so overwhelming. What do I do first? How do I move past this?"

"I hope I'm not overstepping with my next statement," Timur says cautiously. "But have you spoken with your therapist?"

"No. Not since Alex came back," I admit. "She's tried calling, but I didn't answer."

"May I suggest you take a few minutes to connect with her before you go to Alex? I'll keep Rose this afternoon. You need to take some time to care for yourself."

"Are you sure?"

Timur scoops Rose from my lap. "I have four *mladensty* of my own. I think I can handle one little one for a day."

I lean over and give Timur a peck on the cheek. "Thank you for talking with me."

I think about his words while I go to Alex's office to call Yekaterina. First, I owe her an apology for ignoring her, and then I'm hoping she'll be able to help me sort through this crazy mess of emotions.

Viktor

After I say goodbye to Natalie, I take a few minutes to compose myself before heading downstairs to Alex. Before I leave, we need to talk. I have to be honest with him about everything that's happened between Natalie and me before I leave.

I've known Alex for many years. He's more than just my boss. He's my friend. And as brutal as this will be, it's something I must do. I hope my relationship with his wife hasn't screwed our friendship up for good.

When I get to the apartment, I find him and Misha eating a late breakfast at the kitchen table.

"Care to join us?" Alex asks. "Timur made enough for an army."

"No thanks. I only have a few minutes." I look around nervously. "I was hoping we could talk."

Misha grabs his plate. "I have some work to do. I'll be in the office if you need me."

I wait until I hear the door close before sitting across from Alex. "You look much better today." His color's coming back, and he already looks stronger.

"A good night's sleep and some food will do that." He studies me for a minute. "But I don't think you came to talk about how good I look."

"No. I didn't. I—"

"Before you say anything," Alex interrupts. "While Tommy was holding me, he tried torturing me by showing me pictures and videos of you and Natalie together." I remain quiet, not sure how to respond. Alex continues, "What he didn't realize was showing me those videos was what got me through. It meant you were both doing what I asked. Natalie and Rose were safe and loved."

"I don't know what to say." I'm never at a loss for words, but at this moment, there's nothing. How do I tell a man being allowed to love his wife has been the best time of my life?

"I know how much you love her. I see it when you look at her. And I know all this has thrown a wrench into things." Alex takes a deep breath. "Part of me wonders if my coming back into her life isn't the right thing. She loves you, and Rose is bonded with you. Maybe they're better off without me?"

"You're wrong. Natalie loves me, yes, but I'm her second choice. She'll never love me the way she does you. I don't want to leave her. I want to make her mine and keep her forever," I confess. "But I can't do that. You're her heart. Her whole world. When she thought you were dead—"

My mind drifts back to the day we got the news of the explosion. The light in her eyes went out. I genuinely believe if it wasn't for Rose, she might have tried to end it then. But once Rose came, Natalie had a purpose to get up every day.

There was still an empty place in her heart that I could never fill, no matter how much love I gave her. That place was never meant for me. Sure, she loved me, and we were good together. But I know she'll never look at me the same way she looks at Alex. He's her destiny—her forever.

"I need to tell you everything that happened between Natalie and me. The things you didn't see on Tommy's camera."

Talking to another man and telling him the intimate moments you've shared with his wife is the hardest conversation I've ever had. While I speak, I try to avoid looking Alex in the eye because the pain I see there is too much. Alex remains calm throughout everything I have to tell him. When I'm done, he says nothing for a few tense minutes.

"I know that wasn't easy for you to say, and it was equally as difficult to hear, but I am grateful for your honesty," Alex says. "That's exactly why I chose you. You're a good man, Viktor. I'll never forget what you've done for my family and me."

How do I respond to that? Do I thank him? No response feels appropriate. "I wanted to know everything before I leave."

"You're leaving?"

"I have to." I look him in the eye, willing to accept whatever punishment he might give. "Alex, I'm in love with your wife. I can't and don't want to stop loving her."

"Does Natalie know?"

"Yes."

"And?"

"She begged me to stay, but I can't. There isn't room for both of us, and she belongs with you. Timur will be staying on in my place."

"I see." Alex's eyes fill with tears. "Words can't express my gratitude for how much love you showed them both in my absence."

"There were many days I hated you for asking that of us. But I also want to thank you. I've never experienced a relationship. Never had the love of a woman. Ten months of loving her and feeling her love in return was an honor. She's an extraordinary woman, and you're one hell of a lucky man." I stand to leave.

"I'll never forget what you've done for me. For us." Alex reaches out to shake my hand. "Please keep in touch."

"Will do, boss," I say the words but have no intentions of doing it. I have to make a clean break.

The elevator takes me to the underground parking for the final time. Michael and the rest of the team are already in the black SUV when I climb into the front passenger seat.

"You good?" Michael asks.

I nod, fearing that the dam holding back my emotions will burst if I speak.

As Michael drives us to the airport, I sit in silence, gazing out the window while the men in the back talk amongst themselves. None of them make an effort to draw me into their discussion.

When we reach the tarmac, Maxim's plane is already waiting for us. Each man grabs their luggage and proceeds to board the aircraft, anxious to return home. Yet, I find myself frozen beside the SUV. I'm at a crossroads. I must choose between boarding the plane and flying to the other side of the globe, away from the woman I love and the little girl who has become my own, or returning to Natalie and begging her to choose me.

"What's going on?" Michael stands beside me.

"Just debating my options."

"You know she's meant to be with him. Your only option is to get on the plane and set her free. You need to give yourself permission to be free as well," Michael says as he walks away.

His words echo in my head. *Set her free.* She was never mine to keep. I close my eyes and take a deep breath before steeling my shoulders and walking to the jet. I climb the steps and resist the urge to turn around, fearing I won't get on the plane.

It isn't long before we're taxiing down the runway. Then, finally, the plane's wheels lift from the ground, and I'm on my way back to my home country.

Tears fall, knowing a piece of my heart will always belong to Natalie.

Natalie

"It's okay to admit you have feelings for him," Yekaterina says.

"Knowing Alex was alive all that time. Kat, I feel like I cheated on him. We slept together every night. I let myself fall in love with him," I confess. "We came very close to having sex."

"Natalie, this situation is far from what anyone would call normal. Nothing that happened between you and Viktor was wrong. Look at me," she instructs. I look up at the camera. "Be honest with Alex. He's a reasonable man."

Her comment makes me laugh through my tears. "Reasonable, usually. Possessive and dominant—always. I'm afraid of what Alex's reaction will be when I tell him everything."

"Remember, it was Alex's wish for you and Viktor to be together. No one could've envisioned the twist this situation would take."

She's right. My husband literally came back from the dead. That goes far beyond anything imaginable. What a complicated mess this is.

"Natalie," Yekaterina's tone turns serious. "Are you struggling because you want to be with Viktor?"

"I have no doubt that I want to be with my husband. I love Alex. He's my world. The fact that we have this second chance is nothing if not a miracle. And I know this is selfish, but I love Viktor, and I want him, too. I don't want him to leave."

"Because you care about him, that is why you must let him go. It's the only way you'll be able to reconnect and move forward with Alex. More importantly, it's the only way Viktor will be able to heal his broken heart and move on," she says sympathetically. "You have Alex and Rose. Viktor is alone. He'll be okay. But he needs distance and time."

"As hard as it is, I do know that. Hopefully, one day, we can continue our friendship."

"One step at a time, honey." She smiles. "Now, take a few deep breaths and go to your husband."

"Thank you for taking my call."

"We'll talk again in a day or two. But if you need me before then, don't hesitate to text."

I disconnect the video chat and take a few cleansing breaths before leaving the office.

Timur's just exiting Rose's nursery. "She's all fed and napping soundly."

"Thank you, Timur. I'm going downstairs with Alex. He should be finishing up his physical therapy session. If you need me, just text. I'll have my phone."

When I get downstairs, I hear noises from the gym. Alex must not be done with therapy yet. Not wanting to interrupt, I stand quietly in the doorway and watch. Alex is lying on a mat while his therapist rotates and stretches his leg.

"I can see you in the mirror," Alex says. "Come in."

"I didn't want to interrupt."

"Natalie, this is Craig. Craig, this is my wife, Natalie."

"Pleased to meet you," Craig says. "Alex hasn't stopped talking about you since I got here."

A blush creeps over my cheeks. "It's nice to meet you, too."

While he continues stretching Alex's legs, he explains what the recovery plan will look like.

"Alex is lucky he was in such good shape before all this. It means he hasn't lost too much muscle tone, and what was lost will come right back with exercise. The biggest issue we have to deal with is atrophy. These stretches will help with that," Craig explains. "It won't take long for him to walk independently, but he'll need to not overdo it. His muscles won't be completely back to normal for about six weeks."

"Is there anything I can do to help on the days you aren't here?"

"I'm leaving instructions with the stretches and exercises he'll need to do daily."

I take the papers Craig hands me and start flipping through them. While I'm reading, Craig helps Alex from the mat and onto a chair next to me.

"Alex is strong enough that I think we can get rid of the wheelchair. I brought a walker he can use in the house. He can use the chair if he gets tired, but I'd like to see him up and moving as much as possible."

"I won't be using the chair," Alex interjects.

"Don't push yourself too hard, or you'll just set your recovery back."

Alex waves him off, and I giggle.

"Well, that's everything for today. You did well."

Alex grabs the walker and stands, holding onto it. We take a slow walk down the hall to see Craig out.

Alex

ONCE CRAIG LEAVES AND WE'RE ALONE, I TURN TO NATALIE. "YOU'VE been crying."

"It's that obvious?"

"We need to talk," Natalie says.

As we walk to the living room, I'm awkward and uncoordinated, but I eventually settle onto the sofa independently. In the silence of the room, Natalie fidgets with her fingers, and I can sense that saying goodbye to Viktor was as hard for her as it was for him. Although we need to address the situation, I don't want to force her to speak about it. I'm hoping she'll open up to me of her own accord.

"Viktor and I shared a bed every night for months. He held me while we slept. I let him kiss me—touch me. We never had sex, but we came very close. I fell in love with him," she confesses as her tears fall.

Even though I already knew everything, hearing it from Natalie is like another punch to the gut, and I have to force myself not to react.

Since I spoke to Viktor earlier, I've been struggling to temper the jealous, possessive Dominant in me who wants to express the rage I feel knowing another man touched my wife. It's hard to hear, but I have no right to be angry. I'm the one who gave them permission to be together. They had no idea I was alive.

"When he said goodbye earlier, he kissed me. And I let him." Tears pour down her face. "I'm sorry. I feel so guilty for allowing it."

I pull her to me and hold her tight. She nestles her head on my chest. "Neither of you did anything wrong," I say quietly. "The circumstance we all found ourselves in was unimaginable."

"I feel like I cheated on you," she cries.

"I don't ever want to hear you say that. You did no such thing." Taking her by the shoulders, I pull her back to see her face. "What you and Viktor feel for one another, whatever happened between you, is okay. I understand."

"You do?"

"It was my doing that put you both in that situation. But I also have faith in us." I use my thumbs to wipe her tears. "We have a once-in-a-lifetime love that nothing and no one can come between."

"I kept dreaming about you. The dreams were so real I'd wake up expecting to find you next to me, but you weren't there. I'm so afraid this is a dream, and I'm going to wake up, and you'll be gone again."

"baby girl, this isn't a dream, and I'm not going anywhere."

The next couple of weeks are filled with intense physical therapy sessions. Each day, I work harder than I did before. I'm pushing all of my limits. Natalie's no longer allowed to help with my therapy because she gets too nervous seeing me struggle. Instead, Misha and Timur take turns working out with me. What makes me work so hard? My daughter lives one floor above me, and she doesn't even know I exist.

That's why today's a big day. I woke early and am watching the monitor. Rose just woke up Natalie. They're lying in bed while Natalie nurses her.

It's time.

The elevator doors open, and for the first time in almost a year, I'm finally home.

"Alex," Timur says when he sees me walk in.

"Shh. I want to surprise Natalie."

"It's good to see you home, boss." Timur gives me a quick hug. "I was just about to leave for the airport. My wife and kids will be here in a few hours."

"Go, spend the day with your family. I plan to do the same."

"Misha went out for an early morning run, but I expect him back any minute. I'll instruct him to stay downstairs."

As I near the bedroom, I hear Natalie talking to Rose. She's telling her what they're going to do today, including a walk to the park.

"I'd love to accompany you ladies," I say as I walk into the room.

"Alex," Natalie exclaims. "You're here, and you're walking on your own. Why didn't you tell me?"

"Because I wanted to see the look on your face."

Rose, who's still nursing, tries to look around without unlatching from Natalie's breast. I walk over to the bed and sit next to Natalie.

For the first time, I lay eyes on my daughter. She's so beautiful. She takes my breath away. Rose makes eye contact with me, and I see familiar dark blue eyes looking back. When she smiles, milk drips down her face. Natalie adjusts Rose's position, sitting her up. It's then that my world comes to a screeching halt.

"Dada," Rose says and reaches her arms out to me.

I take my daughter in my arms. Her tiny hands come to my face, and she places a wet kiss on my nose. I can't help the tears that fall down my face. When I look over at Natalie, she's also crying. "How does she know?" I ask.

"She heard your voice for months while she was inside me. Since she was born, I showed her your pictures and told her stories about you."

"Dada. Dada," Rose says again and giggles. Her laugh is perfect and fills my soul with a love I've never known.

"Yes, sweet girl. I'm your Daddy." I kiss her chubby cheeks. "And I love you very much."

Rose and I continue our Daddy/daughter time while Natalie showers. Although I've missed the first ten months of her life, right now, it doesn't feel as though I've missed a second. The magnitude of unconditional love I have for my daughter is indescribable.

"I promise Daddy will never leave you again."

Misha stays a few steps behind, allowing us the space we need to bond as a family. His watchful gaze, constantly scanning the surroundings for any sign of danger, makes me feel secure and safe. It's a different feeling than when Viktor was with us. I can't help the tinge of sadness I still feel at losing him. It'll take some time, but I trust we'll adjust to our new normal.

My heart swells with emotion as I watch Rose and Alex play together on the swing set. I'm still in complete awe of how Rose immediately knew who Alex was and how strong their connection is. It fills me with indescribable joy. Alex pushes Rose gently in the baby swing. She giggles uncontrollably each time she gets near, and he tickles her little feet. I snap picture after picture, wanting to capture this moment and hold onto it forever.

As I sit on the bench basking in the warmth of my family's love, my cell phone buzzes in my hand. It's my mom. I haven't heard from her since they walked out of the cottage months ago, and I feel torn about whether to answer. I don't want anything to ruin this perfect moment. Something in me decides to take the call, and I answer with a shaky hand, bracing myself for whatever news may come my way.

Not knowing how this conversation is going to play out, I walk away from where Alex and Rose are playing so I don't interrupt them. "Hello?"

"Natalie, it's mom." I don't speak. I have nothing to say to her. "I had to call you. I just hung up with Delia Laurel. She told me Tommy's dead."

I hear her sniffle. She's crying. How do I respond to that? Do I tell her the truth? That I'm the one who took Tommy's life, and I'm happy I did. That I'd do it all over again. I don't get a chance to respond because she continues talking.

"Oh, Natalie. I'm so sorry for how I behaved when you were here. I was out of line and had no right to judge you or Viktor."

I hear her apology, but that does little to lower my defenses. "No, you didn't."

"Dad and I have talked about it at great length. It's not up to us to tell you how to grieve your husband or how you should move forward. Or who you should move forward with."

She doesn't know Alex is alive. This is a genuine apology. But why? "I appreciate your support, but why the sudden change of heart?" I struggle to keep my icy tone under control.

"Talking to Delia brought back so many memories. So many of the emotions we experienced when your brother died. Delia loved Tommy as if he were her own child. She knows she made mistakes with him. Natalie, we made so many mistakes when Michael told us who he loved. If only we'd done things differently. Looked past our own prejudices and accepted how much Michael loved Evan. He'd still be with us." She pauses, trying to control her sobbing.

"We've been doing the same thing with you—making the same mistakes. It's taken another tragedy for us to realize that we don't want history to keep repeating itself. Dad and I know it's us who must change. We're going to do things differently from now on. We just hope it's not too late. We want to spend more time with you and Viktor."

I find the nearest bench needing to sit. I hate that it's taken another tragedy for my parents to finally see reason, but I accept it nonetheless. "Is Dad with you?"

"Yes, dear. He's right here."

"Can you put the phone on speaker and maybe sit down? I have something I need to tell you."

I hear the scuffle of her pulling out a kitchen chair and sitting down.

"You're on speaker."

I look up and see Alex walking toward me with Rose in his arms. I mouth *it's my parents* to him. Quietly, he sits next to me with Rose on his lap. She reaches for the phone.

"Fikr?"

"No, Rose, it's Grandma and Grandpa."

"Is that my little granddaughter?" Dad asks.

"It sure is. It's a beautiful day, and there won't be many more before it gets cold, so we came to the park to play."

"Gampa," Rose says, leaning into the phone.

"She said my name," Dad says proudly. "Did you hear that, Char?"

"I did. Rose, can you say Grandma?" Rose's attention has already moved on, and she's watching a group of children running by.

"I want you both to know I forgive you and that I, too, hope we can move forward and do better." I grab Alex's hand. "There's something else I need to tell you. Something that's kind of unbelievable and nothing short of a miracle."

"Go ahead," Dad says hesitantly.

I don't know how to say it, so I blurt it out. "Alex is alive."

"What did you say?" Mom asks.

"Alex is alive. He's sitting here next to me." There's no reaction from either of my parents. "Are you guys there?"

"We're here," Mom says. "But I don't understand."

"It's a complicated story, Charlotte," Alex adds.

"Alexander? Is that really you?"

"Alive and in the flesh." He laughs.

"How?"

"As Alex said, it's a complicated story. One I don't think we should discuss over the phone."

"Did Thomas Moore have something to do with this?" Dad asks.

I look to Alex, unsure how to answer Dad's question. "He did," Alex says. "Tommy got mixed up with the wrong crowd and then tried to take his revenge on me for marrying Natalie. Unfortunately, it's this situation that led to his death."

"Delia said he was shot. It was during a break-in, but she asked them not to tell her any more details," Dad explains. "Did you—"

"No, it wasn't me who shot him," Alex interrupts. "I have no idea who did it."

I look at Alex and shake my head. I don't want him to lie for me, but he puts his finger to my lips, silencing me.

"I'm sorry for whatever Tommy did, son. We're mighty glad you're still with us."

"Me too, sir."

"And Viktor?" Dad asks. "I know how much he cares for Natalie and the baby. How's he handling all this?"

"He's decided to return to Russia. I'm sure you understand," Alex explains. "We have new security in place."

"I still don't understand why you need security?" Mom questions.

"It's just a precaution. Being a successful business owner and now having the women's shelter can attract unwanted attention. Can't be too safe where Natalie and Rose are concerned."

"Well, that makes sense," Mom agrees.

"Rose is getting sleepy, so we need to head back home. We'll make plans to visit soon."

"Please do," Dad says. "And welcome home, son."

"That was unexpected," I say when we hang up.

"Everything has a way of working itself out." Alex leans over and kisses me.

Once he gets Rose buckled in her stroller, we begin walking back to our apartment.

The phone call and apology came as a complete surprise. But I'm grateful to have everything and everyone I love back in my life. This time, I hope it's for good.

Alex

Brandon buzzes me into his apartment building. Today's our final online class with Master Kiyoshi. I get to his door and knock.

"You're late," he says as he pulls the door open.

I finish my text and look up. "What the hell?" Standing in front of me is my best friend, I think.

"A little birdy told me you preferred blondes," Brandon says as he fluffs a long blond wig. He steps aside, but I don't move to go in. "What are you waiting for, handsome?"

"What's wrong with you?" I take a few tentative steps into his apartment.

Brandon's wearing gym shorts and a woman's maternity shirt with a pillow stuffed under it. He's lost his ever-loving mind.

"We're practicing Shibari for your pregnant wife. How can we do that without you having someone pregnant to practice on?"

I can't hold it back, and I double over laughing. "You are one crazy son of a bitch, you know that?"

"Just devoted to the cause, brother."

As we walk to his office, Brandon puts his hand on his back, acting as if he's heavily pregnant. What he doesn't know is I'm recording him. He pulls out his desk chair and gives his best impression of a pregnant woman sitting down. I can't wait to see Master Kiyoshi's reaction to my insane friend.

Brandon pulls up the website and logs into our video meeting room. Master Kiyoshi joins us a few minutes later. His eyes grow wide when he sees a blond-haired Brandon.

Trying to maintain his composure, he greets us. "Good afternoon. Are you ready for our last class?"

"Yes, sir. I am."

"Let's start with the first binding. I'll give you any necessary corrections as you work." Brandon stands, and Master Kiyoshi gets the full view of his body. The always quiet and serious Shibari Master breaks into hysterical laughter. "Brandon, may I ask what you're doing dressed like that?"

"You must be mistaken. My name is Natalie," he says in a high-pitched voice.

"What is going on?" Master Kiyoshi asks, clearly confused.

"Alex needs to practice on a pregnant woman, and since we don't know any," – He does a little twirl— "I've transformed into one."

Tears roll down Master Kiyoshi's face as he listens to Brandon's explanation. Brandon looks back at me and sees my cell out, taping this entire spectacle.

"Oh no, you don't." Brandon takes a swipe at the camera. "Shut that thing off."

"Natalie dear, don't get yourself all worked up. It's not good for the baby," I say, laughing. "We want to preserve these moments to show our little girl one day. Now stand still like a good girl and let your Dominant tie you up."

"Alex, stop recording right now," Brandon protests.

"Be a good little sub and stay quiet, or I'll have to gag you," I threaten my friend. "On second thought, keep talking. Gagging you will make this video even better."

Brandon pulls the pillow out from under his shirt and takes a swing at me.

Master Kiyoshi is clearly entertained by our banter. He hasn't stopped laughing.

It takes a while for Brandon and me to compose ourselves, but finally, Brandon ditches the wig and the woman's shirt, and we get to work.

In the end, the Shibari Master is pleased with my technique. This is going to be the perfect Christmas present.

It's been nearly a month, but I've finally recovered to my post-almost-death health. I've held off on collaring Natalie until I felt strong enough physically and emotionally to be the Dominant she deserves.

She's just put Rose down to sleep for the night and is on her way back to our bedroom, where I'm waiting for her with her collar laid out on the bed. She gasps when she steps across the threshold to our room.

"Close the door behind you and strip, baby girl."

"Yes, Sir."

She shuts the door quietly and begins a sexy striptease for me, starting with my favorite pair of grey leggings that hug her curves. Slowly, she slides them down her legs before she kicks them out of the way. Then she grabs the hem of her light pink T-shirt and slides it up her abdomen and over her lace-covered breasts. Her shirt soon joins her pants in a pile on the floor. She bites her lip and turns around. I'm treated to a sexy view of Natalie's ass in a black thong. My erection strains against my zipper, aching to sink into her. Then, with a quick look over her shoulder, she unhooks her bra, letting it fall to the ground.

I can't wait any longer and come behind her, wrapping my arms around her, my hands going straight for her breasts. She rests her head back on my chest as she moans quietly. I slide one hand down her taut abdomen and into her panties. Feeling impatient, I grab the side of the fabric and tug, tearing it and tossing it to the side.

"They were one of my favorites," she pouts.

"I'll buy you new ones." My mouth descends on her neck, sucking and biting my way down while I tease her clit with my finger. "Tonight's a night we've both been waiting for. I'm going to put my collar back around your neck where it belongs."

Natalie smiles. "I've waited for this moment, Sir."

"Kneel," I command. Natalie turns to face me and lowers herself to the floor, her legs slightly open and her gaze down. My beautiful submissive. I lift her collar from the bed and hold it in my hand. "Look at me."

She lifts her face. I'm in awe that this woman is mine. That against all odds, I've made it back to her once more.

With trembling hands and a heart full of emotion, I begin speaking, "Just a few weeks ago, I didn't think I'd ever see you again. I thought all hope was lost. But fate, or perhaps the universe itself, has granted me a precious gift, a chance to hold you again and feel your presence by my side." My emotions are overwhelming, and I struggle to find the right words.

"Now, I stand before you, ready to offer myself to you once again. To be your husband, your protector, and your Dominant. I'm asking for your trust and your submission. I'm offering you a symbol of our bond. With it comes my solemn promise of unwavering devotion, unconditional love, and steadfast support. And so I ask, would you do me the incredible honor of accepting my collar and gifting me with your submission?"

"I would love nothing more, Sir."

I place the collar around her neck and connect the two ends of the chain with a lock, then I kneel before her—a Dominant, a man, humbled by the love of this woman. "Everything I have, everything I am, and everything I will be, is yours."

With her collar back in place, she's never looked more radiant.

"I have a gift for you," I say as I get to my feet. "Wait here." Making my way into our closet, I grab the box Brandon brought over earlier and the bouquet of white roses I hid in here. When I return, I set the box, wrapped in Christmas paper, on the bed and lay the roses next to it before helping Natalie to her feet.

"What is it?" she asks.

"This was supposed to be your gift from me last Christmas. Brandon's been holding onto it all this time. Open it."

Natalie grabs the box and tears at the paper. Excitement sparkles in her emerald eyes. She removes the lid and begins pulling out the contents—ropes of varying shades of pink and my camera. "What's all this for?"

"I read that women in their final trimester of pregnancy often don't see their beauty. I planned a Shibari photoshoot to highlight how incredibly beautiful you were carrying our child."

"I had no idea." Sadness washes over her face. "That would've been incredible."

"You may not be pregnant now, but tonight's a special night for us. We're reconnecting as a Dominant and his submissive. Will you allow me to use you as my canvas?"

"It would be my honor, Sir."

With a couple of touches on my phone, soft music plays through the speakers in our bedroom, setting the mood. I begin by braiding Natalie's long blonde curls and weaving a rope into it. Then, I place three pieces of thin rope around her neck, like a necklace, and being careful not to catch her collar, I braid the ropes between her breasts and down over her abdomen. Had she still been carrying my child, I would have split the rope around her tummy. Tonight, I continue to her waist, bringing it around her body to create a harness.

I caress her skin, ensuring an intimate connection with my submissive as I wrap the rope around her breasts. Her nipples harden with each pass. I finish by connecting this to the harness at her waist. Because she's no longer pregnant, I'm free to alter my design. "I need you to turn around and put your arms behind your back," I instruct.

Then, with the same braiding technique, I wrap her upper arms in rope and work down to her wrists. This rope is weaved in and out of the ties going down her back, restraining her arms behind her. I pause to look over my work and check in with my submissive. "What's your color?"

"Green, Sir."

"You may stop me at any time if anything is uncomfortable," I remind her.

"Yes, Sir. I understand.

After securing her arms, I use a heavier rope as a harness around her waist, leaving a long tail. "This will be for the suspension."

"How did Master Kyoshi teach you suspension over video lessons?"

"I had a willing volunteer to practice on."

As soon as the words leave my mouth, I see the jealousy on her face. "A volunteer?"

"Well, a semi-willing volunteer." I grin. "Don't get yourself all upset. It was only Brandon."

"Brandon? There must be a story behind that."

"He put his all into it—I have the video to prove it. We'll watch it another day. But, for now, no more talking."

She nods, letting me know she understands.

I help her lie down on the floor so I can work on her legs. Taking her left leg, I bend it at the knee and use the same braided design to hold it in place. With her leg secure, I slide a rope beneath the restraint. It will also be used to connect to the suspension ropes.

"Are you ready?"

"I can't wait."

Carefully, I attach the ends of her rope harness to a pulley system attached to the heavy-duty clip that's permanently fixed on our ceiling. Then, ever so slowly, I pull the ropes, and her body rises off the floor.

"Color?"

"Yellow. Can you adjust the suspension ropes around my waist?"

I spread the ropes out, so the pressure is more even.

"That's much better, Sir. Thank you."

I lean in to kiss her. "Almost done."

The final rope is braided around her right ankle. I pull on the rope gently, drawing her foot back, and attach it to the rope that's entwined in her braid. Then, I pull her body up the rest of the way.

Hanging nearly inverted, her legs bend and spread slightly. Her back arches, so her breasts push out—she's the picture of grace and beauty.

The last thing I do is take the white roses I had dethorned and slide them through the braided rope in the middle of her breasts.

"Do you know how incredibly gorgeous you look right now?"

She rewards me with a contented smile.

Grabbing my camera, I begin snapping pictures. I plan to capture her from every angle to avoid missing anything. The longer her body remains weightless, the more she relaxes until she's floating in subspace.

After finishing my photographs, I step back to admire her for a few moments longer.

"Natalie," I whisper, pulling her from her bliss. "I'm going to bring you down now."

"Mhm," she says softly.

Once she's back on the floor, I begin untying her with the same love and care I put into the initial ties.

During my absence, I felt so far from Natalie. Our connection was broken and desperately missed. But right now, our breaths are in sync as I allow my fingers to caress her skin while I remove the ropes.

Shibari's an incredibly sensual and intimate process, which is why I chose it for our first scene. I knew it would provide the sexual connection we crave and the emotional connection that makes our relationship so very special.

I lift her from the floor and cradle her against me as I carry her to the bed. Then, gently, I set her on top of the white comforter. Her eyes never leave mine while I remove my pants and boxers.

I've been hard for her from the moment she walked into the room. It's taken every ounce of my self-control not to rush this evening. Kneeling beside her, I explore her body with my hands and mouth—reacquainting myself with every inch of her.

We've been together since I've been back. But tonight, we're no longer just husband and wife, but also Dominant and submissive—our relationship whole once again.

I lower myself over her, kissing her lips, my tongue meeting no resistance. She opens her legs, allowing me entrance into her body. Once fully sheathed, I pause, memorizing the feeling of being inside her.

"I need You, Sir," she whispers between kisses.

"You have all of me, baby girl. Every heartbeat, every breath is for you."

Slow and sensual. I make love to Natalie. Each touch, each kiss meant to erase the terror of the past, replacing it with sweet promises of our future.

From that very first time I saw her across the room at Fire and Ice, I knew we were destined for each other. We were both terrified and tried to fight it, but destiny will not be stopped.

Natalie Montgomery, my wife and submissive, is the happily-ever-after I never knew I wanted, but she's exactly what I needed."

Every beat of my heart belongs to her.

She owns every part of me.

My heart is overflowing with love and adoration for Natalie. I promise to cherish and honor her. To spend the rest of my life ensuring that this beautiful and selfless woman, who not only challenges me but also gifts me with her submission, experiences nothing but the happily ever after she deserves.

Epilogue

Two years later...

It's the early morning hours of June eleventh. A short time ago, Natalie and I arrived at the hospital, her contractions already in full force. We've decided not to find out the sex of the baby, although we both have our guesses. I think we're having another little girl. Natalie disagrees.

Once again, Natalie insisted on not using any medication to dull the pain of her contractions. After a particularly difficult one, I'm ready to beg.

"Please let them give you something." I can't stand seeing her in agony.

"No," she says, still breathless from the last contraction.

"Do it for me." I'm desperate to see her out of pain.

"If I can do it, so can you."

And she thinks I'm stubborn.

The contractions are coming in quick succession, and Natalie's face contorts in pain.

"Look at me, baby girl. You've got this." I help her breathe through the worst of it. "It's going to start going away now," I say as I watch the printout on the monitor go down.

"Call Esperanza. I need to push."

My heart rate spikes. "You can't push. No one's in here."

"That's why I asked you to call her. Now, Alex. This baby's ready to come."

Instead of pressing the red button and waiting for someone to answer, I open the door. Luckily, Dr. Young is writing in a chart at the nurses' station.

"Doc, we need you," I call down the hall. "The baby's coming." Dr. Young finishes what he's doing before he and Esperanza begin walking down the hall. "Hurry, please." They're moving far too slowly for my liking.

Finally, they get to Natalie's room just as another contraction causes my wife more agony. She scrunches her face, struggling to breathe through it. I rush over to her, grabbing her hand. "I'm here. Breathe with me."

She mimics the short, quick breaths we learned in our child birthing class. I missed the final weeks of Natalie's pregnancy and Rose's birth. This time, I made sure to be there for everything.

Dr. Young finishes checking Natalie, and Esperanza is readjusting the bed like it's a transformer toy.

"She's ten centimeters," Dr. Young informs me. "Looks like you'll be sharing your birthday with your new baby, Alex."

Esperanza instructs me on how to hold Natalie's leg right as the next contraction hits. Then, Natalie bears down and pushes with all her might. We continue this process over and over until Dr. Young tells me the baby's head is crowning. That's when I switch positions, taking my spot next to the doctor to help bring my baby into the world.

"One more push, baby girl. You can do it."

When the contraction hits, my strong, brave wife pushes, and our baby's head emerges.

"Ease up on the next push, Natalie," Dr. Young instructs.

With his hands over mine, he helps me maneuver our baby from Natalie's body into the world.

"It's a boy," I say reverently and lay our son on Natalie's chest.

Tears pour down my face. I'm overwhelmed at the sight of my child, who just moments ago was nestled inside Natalie's body.

"Are you ready to cut the cord, Alex?"

"I think so."

I take the offered scissors and cut where the doctor shows me. I've officially severed the cord between our son and his mother. Then, I return to my place next to my wife, tucking a stray curl behind her ear.

"You are amazing."

"I'm so glad you're here, Alex." She looks up at me, tears streaming down her face. "Happy Birthday."

"This is the most incredible present you could ever give me, baby girl." I lean over and kiss my wife. "I love you so very much."

"And I love you."

Esperanza takes our son from Natalie to finish cleaning him and get his measurements. I stand over her shoulder, watching like the nervous father I am.

"You're even worse than Viktor was," Esperanza jokes.

When we made our birthing plan with Dr. Young, Natalie insisted on explaining everything to Esperanza. Then she asked the older woman to be her labor and delivery nurse again. Esperanza was so moved by our story she readily agreed.

"He's tiny," she says. "Five pounds three ounces and sixteen inches."

"Is he okay?" I ask, concerned.

"He's perfect." With the ease of a practiced nurse, she swaddles our son tightly in a blanket. "Does he have a name yet?" Esperanza asks as she passes the baby back to Natalie.

Natalie looks at me, and I nod. "His name is Michael Alexander Montgomery," she says.

Our son's name is a tribute to two extraordinary men. Michael, the uncle who will always be his guardian angel, and Michael, the man who saved our lives. I'm honored for my son to carry their name.

Esperanza writes it on his crib card, and then she and the doctor leave the room.

"Would you like to hold your son?"

I sit on the bed next to my wife as she passes me the tiny bundle. Cradling him in my arms, I'm moved beyond words as I gaze at the most perfect baby I've ever seen, except for his sister.

There's a knock on our door a second before it opens. Dr. Young has Rose in his arms. "Someone wanted to meet her little brother." The doctor sets her on the bed beside me before he leaves us again.

"Rose, this is your baby brother, Michael."

Rose looks curiously at the sleeping baby before she reaches out to touch him. Natalie reminds her to use gentle touches.

"Mikel," Rose says as she touches his cheek.

Natalie and I both laugh.

"It's clear she spends a lot of time with her Russian family."

Michael starts to fuss. I hand him back to Natalie, who helps him latch onto her breast for his first meal. Rose crawls onto my lap and watches.

"Mikel hunry," she says.

"Yes, Rose. Michael is hungry." I kiss her head.

Then, I watch as my newborn son suckles from his mother's breast while I hold our toddler on my lap.

This is my family—the realization is overwhelming.

"We're finally complete," Natalie says, looking up at me.

She's right. Baby Michael was the missing link. With him in our lives, we're whole.

I pull out my cell phone and open the camera. Then, I help Rose get close to Natalie as I lean in and take the first photo of our perfect family.

It's true. We've been to hell and back. Our relationship has survived things that would make some of the strongest couples break, but not us. The love we share has grown and strengthened like metal forged in a fire.

This woman beside me is my yesterday. My today. My tomorrow.

The End

As Viktor navigates the dark waters of loss and regret, he clings to the hope of forgiveness. Can he overcome his past and find peace or will his mistakes forever define him? Find out in Victor's unforgettable story, His Melody

Find Tara's Books Here

Acknowledgments

First, I have to thank my husband, George. Alex and Natalie's story wouldn't be what it is today if it wasn't for your help. I thought it was a lot of work getting these books out the first time, but getting them out for their re-release has been a whole new experience. There's no one else I'd want to do this with. You're the brains behind the operation. You're my plot twist generator. You are the most patient man, listening to me read and re-read each book until you could recite them from memory. And then there's research—the best part of this gig. You are my yesterday, my today, and my tomorrow. i love You!

To my children (and you, too, Jonathan)- thank you for all of your patience. I know there are many days I stay locked away in the office or sit with my headphones on in the living room. I appreciate your patience and support. The five of you are my biggest cheering section. Your encouragement keeps me going on days when I want to give up. You give me ideas for what to post on social media. And you're always ready to go to all my signings. I love you all very much.

Thank you to my beta readers. You ladies are speed readers! I appreciate and value your honesty. You aren't afraid to tell me when something needs to be corrected. You've helped make these stories better and this experience much more fun.

To all my new readers. Wow! It's been quite the journey with Alex and Natalie. I've loved getting to know each of you and am so very thankful for the love and support you've shown me. I have many more adventures planned, and I hope you'll be there for all of them.

About Tara

Tara Conrad is the author behind sizzling and passionate love stories that ignite the senses. Her novels celebrate the fiery intensity of desire. They're known for having a blend of deep emotional connections, relatable characters, and captivating plots that ensnare readers from the very first page to the last.

Tara's married to her soulmate and Dominant, George. They are about to celebrate their 30th anniversary and are more in love today than yesterday. George encouraged Tara to start writing, and with each passing day, she's more thankful for his insistence that she tell her stories and his partnership on this journey. There's no one else in this world she'd ever want by her side. He is her happily ever after.